To La

The Prophecy of the Kings

Book 1

Legacy of the Eldric

By David Burrows

Best Wishes

David

Second Edition January 2010
Copyright © D Burrows 2010

The Prophecy of the Kings trilogy comprises
Book 1: Legacy of the Eldric
Book 2: Dragon Rider
Book 3: Shadow of the Demon

Cover artwork by Philip McDonnell.

ISBN 978-0-9556760-8-6

Printed and bound in Great Britain by
CPI Antony Rowe, Chippenham and Eastbourne

R.Amlurych

Elista

Hullin

Morloch

Trosgarth

Chalynth

R.R.Rallin

Turn Marsh

Thandor

Kaldor

Bay of
Leole

R.Astnor

Kinlin Castle

KinAnor

KinKassack

Allund

Tanel

Thrace

Dundalk

CarCamel

Pendrat

R.Torrid

R.Paele

West Meath

Bhutan

This book is dedicated to my wife Gail and sons Andrew and Stuart.

Thanks go to all my friends who encouraged me in this work. Special thanks to Alistair and Anup for their motivation and help. Thanks also go to Earmie, a dedicated reader who helped with the editing. A special thanks to Phil for the excellent artwork.

Prologue

"Lay the body there," Chanathan said pointing.

The three men carrying the corpse dropped their burden with a meaty thud to the forest carpet. The men looked disgusted by their task. An owl hooted and one of the men looked around, fear glinting in his eyes as he scanned the hidden recesses between the trees.

"It's an owl," one of his companions said. Chanathan could hear the tenderness in the voice. Only months ago the sight of another man's fear would have elicited sarcasm or even bullying, but after the recent horrors there was a greater bond between these men. *Battle brothers* was a common enough expression, but only men who had stood shoulder to shoulder in the darkest moments of combat truly understood what that meant, men who had felt blood splash their hands and blades and experienced the pervading stench of blood, sweat and steel in their nostrils. That was how such close bonds were forged.

Chanathan stepped up to the corpse and spat in its eyes. The body was that of a man in his thirties. He wore a robe whose colour in the dark of the forest was difficult to decide. It did nothing, though, to conceal the bloodstain that marked the deep wound that had killed him.

Chanathan turned on his heel. Coming between the trees in file were others who had fought demons only hours before. It had been close, but Drachar's death had finished the bloody conflict and even now, men of the alliance were hunting down the enemy as they sought to escape. Many of the approaching men were sorcerers and all were clearly bone tired, stumbling as they came into the clearing. Even though they were exhausted Chanathan knew that one final act was required to guarantee an end to the bloody war.

Ashona approached Chanathan. She looked close to tears, and Chanathan felt pity overwhelm him. His own tears threatened and he choked down his emotions, but could not stop himself from taking her hand.

1

Victory felt so very hollow, not at all how he had imagined it to be so many months ago — death still befouled his mind like a toxin.

"Swiftly, we must bind his spirit. It must *not* be allowed to escape or the demons will crown him their king," Chanathan said.

"Surely not," Ashona replied. "How can the demons still follow *him* after what has happened? He *failed* them. He is dead. We have killed sorcerers by the score. They cannot summon demons — not for a hundred years at least."

Chanathan shook his head. "You are wrong, I fear. *He* made a pact with the demons, a pact that even death cannot undo. He has given the demons everything they wanted. Countless souls sent screaming to their world for eternal damnation. If they get *his* soul too, they will bow to him and call *him* Lord."

Ashona sobbed. "Then we have failed!"

"No. Not if we can banish his soul."

"And how can we do that?" Ashona pleaded. Chanathan looked past the grime of battle and into her eyes. With more affection than he had ever felt before he stroked a strand of hair from her face.

Without replying he turned to the other sorcerers who by now had spread themselves around the clearing. They looked a sorry bunch, blood-soaked and covered in gore. Some distance away he could hear the army celebrating; men calling out to each other, glad to find friends and relatives alive; drinking away the cold fear instilled by demons only moments before. Abruptly singing filled the air. Only troops fresh from the horrors of war could show such emotion. By comparison the men around Chanathan were silent, begrimed with blood and barely able to stand.

"We must act swiftly. Until this night is done his shade will be confined to his earthly body. You there, Carlan, Aswall and Harecht, draw a rune of binding around the corpse. Tarlam and Herest, summon elementals at each corner of the rune. Air, fire and water will do for what we need."

The men set to their activities while the others fell back to watch. As they worked, the din from the army became background noise. Forest creatures occasionally called out, distracting Chanathan from his musing. What he planned had never been tried before and he had to think, if this went wrong he would doom his men, and himself.

Finally the others were ready. He looked down at the corpse now lying at the centre of a rune, diligently drawn in the dirt. At each of the rune's corners, tiny elementals glowed; their small voices clear even with all the other sounds around them.

The sorcerers gathered while the three soldiers hovered to one side, knowing they were witnessing a truly significant moment in history. This was a solemn time.

Chanathan raised his eyes skyward, Casting a rune in the air with his hand he called aloud, "Drachar, I summon you!"

Nothing stirred. A breeze caused the trees to sway and for a moment the rustle of leaves drowned out the distant celebration.

"Drachar!" Chanathan called more urgently. "You are summoned to pay for your crimes."

A pungent smell filled the clearing. Unable to help themselves some men stepped back, fear pounding their hearts like poison coursing through their veins. A silver shape appeared, hovering eerily above the corpse.

"Bind them, both body and soul," Chanathan ordered and others immediately spoke, casting runes to strengthen their earlier spell.

The glow took strength and the indistinct form of a man appeared. Hollow eyes stared deep into Chanathan's soul and for a moment he nearly quailed, but then, by his side, Ashona squeezed his hand. All at once he was glad of her presence.

"Foul creature! Abomination!" Chanathan roared.

The spectre laughed. "But I am one of you," a ghostly voice whispered, grinding the nerves of all present. "I, too, am one of the Eldric."

"How dare you!" Chanathan shouted, suppressing a shudder. "You forsook us the moment you looked upon the demon world. Your twisted craving for power has destroyed you. You were banished. You were unmade and unnamed; the sands of your soul stained forever by the blood of betrayal. How dare you compare yourself to us?"

"You forget," answered the now mirthless voice. "We were all banished. We left our homeland hundreds of years ago because our ancestors dared to look upon the demon world. I am more like you than you would care to admit."

Chanathan was stunned into silence. The spectre faded briefly and for a moment Chanathan thought it was gone.

"Bind it!" Prince Ellard said, stepping forward, looking up at the spectre. "You are a traitor! You killed the King!"

"He killed me first," the spectre said in a peevish tone.

"Damn you! You betrayed your people! We will not let you find your way to the demon world," said Ellard. To Chanathan it seemed that his eyes flamed with passion.

"But you cannot stop me! I am Drachar! I do as I will, and *I will* damn you all."

3

There was a silence for a moment. Even the revelry seemed to have stopped as though the world was holding its breath.

"But you are wrong," Ashona said softly. At the start of the war she had been such a gentle soul, but looking at her now Chanathan held his breath at what he saw. Her eyes bored into Drachar's and her shoulders were set in utter defiance. "We will banish you but not to where you expect to go! Prince Ellard, give me your sword. Only one of the seven will help with this spell casting."

Ellard stepped forward and handed his weapon over. Except for silver runes that danced along its length it was a dull black that seemed to absorb what little light there was.

"What are you going to do?" Fear tainted Drachar's voice, and he appeared to shrink.

Ashona chanted as she drew a rune over the blade. Chanathan realised then her intent. The sword amplified the power of the person holding it. The rune was to open a gateway to another world and for a moment Chanathan feared Ashona was opening a gateway to Hell. He did not recognise the rune at first and then comprehension dawned.

Prince Ellard must also have realised for he rushed over to take back his sword, but Chanathan laid a hand on his shoulder. "It is all right. She knows what she is doing. She is opening a gateway not to another world but between them."

Ellard frowned. "The nether regions?" he asked

Behind them Drachar wailed. His form glowed brighter and the surrounding sorcerers' voices became more urgent. At that moment an elemental expired, its scream echoing into the night air.

"Help them," Chanathan ordered and others joined the sorcerers about the rune, summoning elementals to bind Drachar in place. Furiously he struggled and then the gateway was complete, purple and green streaming from it.

"Go!" Prince Ellard commanded, laying his hand on his sword. The ghostly shape drifted towards the gaping rent in space. An icy wind gusted, a prelude to the nothingness beyond.

"You shall not stop me!" he screamed. "I will return and then I will destroy you, your children and their children." The light from his ethereal form was being slowly sliced thinner as it progressed through the gaping wound. Then abruptly it was gone. Ashona stopped casting the rune and the rent slammed shut, Drachar's final scream fading away.

Night noises about the forest returned as though the banishment had forbidden sound.

All at once Chanathan sensed that it was too much for Ashona. She sat on the ground as though her legs could no longer support her. Others were leaving but at her collapse, they paused.

Ashona cried out, "I see it! I see the future. Drachar *will* return! I see the fires! I see the death!"

Chanathan knelt by her side. "Calm yourself. That is not possible." The three soldiers came over, wanting to help but hesitating, too afraid to come too close.

Chanathan gently took her face and made her turn to look at him. "We have won. We have banished Drachar's shade. This land is safe now."

Ashona stared past Chanathan. He sensed she was seeing into another world.

Her voice was so low that he had to strain his ears to hear her. By his side one of the soldiers gasped. "It is a prophecy," he murmured in awe.

> *When Tallin's crown once more does shine,*
> *Drachar's shade will rise sublime,*
> *Three Princes Royal through time will sleep,*
> *An appointment with destiny three kings to keep,*
> *Trosgarth's arm across the land will reach,*
> *Of war and famine his army will preach,*
> *And one will stand to oppose his throne,*
> *A king resurrected from within his mountain home,*
> *Of air, fire and water he will be born,*
> *To aid the people when all else is forlorn*

"Ashona"" Chanathan wailed, shaking her shoulders, "Ashona!" he sobbed.

The light in her eyes dimmed. She was too close to her shaol, her guardian spirit, and that had always worried Chanathan.

"Ashona," he cried.

Slowly she shook herself as though waking from a dream. "Thank the Kalanth!" Chanathan sighed, grinning broadly.

Chanathan helped Ashona to her feet. By their side a soldier made a warding sign against evil, his mouth agape. Chanathan turned to him, "Forget what you just heard. Do not mention it to anyone." He doubted he would; when she had spoken Chanathan, too, had felt the compulsion in her tone. The man stared back blankly, angering Chanathan.

"All of you!" Chanathan commanded. "Forget what happened, under pain of death."

Ashona looked at him bewildered. "Why? What has happened?"

Chanathan looked at her, truly glad she was back. "Nothing. We have won a great battle and darkness has been banished from the world."

Taking her hand he guided her from the forest, towards hope and an uncertain future.

Behind them the three soldiers remained, but for a while only. Sensing the evil of the departed soul they took to their heels, seeking the company of the living, eager to tell the tale of what they had just heard.

Chapter 1

Escape

"Please, Emma," Kaplyn said, giving her his most charming smile and using his softest tones normally reserved for special occasions, and this rated very high on his list of special occasions.

Emma pouted and Kaplyn knew he had won and she would do as he wanted, but for the sake of the game he continued the flattery. "You are very special to me and when I return…"

"And what will happen when you return? I am a serving maid. That is all…," Emma flashed and Kaplyn knew he had made a mistake.

"But you are special to me, regardless of your position. You know that," Kaplyn wheedled, coming closer and putting his hands on her shoulders, looking deep into her eyes, the way he knew she liked. He smiled again, raising his eyebrows in a questioning manner.

Emma returned the smile and beneath his hands he felt her melt.

"How long will you be gone?" she asked.

"Three weeks, perhaps four at the most," he replied. In truth he had no idea. His plans were half formulated. Emma looked downcast all at once.

"I need to go, Em," he said softly, using her pet name. "I am stifling here; I hate it."

Emma looked up and he could see the confusion in her eyes. "Most people can only dream of being in your position. How can you hate it so much?" she questioned.

"I just do," he replied. "I have no freedom. I am followed everywhere I go. That's not a life."

"But you are a prince…"

"Some prince!" he interrupted. "I'm ninth in line to the throne and some of my own brothers don't even know me. Please," he continued, "I am not asking a lot. Just distract the guard so that I can leave."

"Not asking a lot? I know Sanfred. He'll have his hands all over me before I can say how the *Kalanth* are you?"

That's exactly what Kaplyn was hoping for. He too knew Sanfred and he also knew Sanfred fancied Emma. In his mind it was tonight or never and, to escape, sacrifices were needed.

"Look, here's some gold," Kaplyn said taking out a purse he had earlier put a couple of sovereigns in for just this occasion.

Emma's eyes widened as she felt the coins within. "I would help you even without a bribe," she said. "You know that."

"Of course I do," Kaplyn said taking her in his arms. The warmth of her body and scent of her hair almost made him reconsider the folly of his leaving, but then he hardened his resolve. His mind was made up.

"And when are you leaving?" Emma asked.

"Tonight," he replied, huskily.

Emma pulled back, staring at his face as though trying to commit every line to memory. "You will come back?" she asked.

"I will return with tales to make my brothers green with envy," Kaplyn grinned.

He went over to the bed and took up his sword, buckling it about his waist. A saddlebag was next, filled with provisions for the road, and then four cloth sacks with lengths of twine followed. "I'm going to get Star," he said. Go down to Sanfred shortly. Make sure he is *inside* the guardhouse. That way he'll not see me leave.

Kaplyn pulled on a woollen cloak, not particularly suited for an Allund prince, but one that he hoped would help him to blend in with a crowd. Looking at himself in a mirror, he saw a young man in his early twenties, long dark hair partly obscuring a handsome face that often won the heart of a young lady. His leather jerkin he had secretly acquired at the market a few weeks ago. Again is it was practical rather than flashy, as was his norm. His riding boots were expensive and, besides his sword, was the only item that might give away his privileged upbringing.

Kaplyn kissed Emma and, without a backward glance, left the plush rooms of his childhood, sweeping swiftly along the deserted corridors. Thick carpet covered his footfalls. The hour was late and lanterns lit the brightly decorated corridor.

Kaplyn's heart was hammering but even still he grinned broadly. He was actually doing it. He was escaping. Through silent corridors, he traced his way to an exit, and all the while fortune remained with him. After descending a tight spiral stair, he made it to the palace back door without meeting anyone. Pausing by the heavy oak door, he listened before opening it a crack. As the door swung silently inwards, the smell of the stables greeted him. He couldn't believe it was going so easily. The sounds of

8

voices came to his ears, but the speakers were a long way off judging by the muffled tones.

Kaplyn stepped out into the night. The air was cool, not surprisingly so for early spring. Quickening his pace he hurried to the stables, not pausing to step into the deep shadow of the open door. Horses fidgeted and, ignoring these, Kaplyn went to Star's stable, swinging open the wooden gate confining her. Star nodded her head in welcome. On a peg Kaplyn kept his bow and a ful quiver. He took them down for later.

He took the cloth sacks and tied one about each of Star's hooves. She nickered and, knowing her as he did, he sensed that she didn't understand what was happening.

"Don't worry," he whispered stroking her warm flank. "Just a night ride. That's all."

He went to fetch a saddle and a blanket and then set about preparing Star for their journey, talking to her softly all the while. Once he had completed his preparations, he took her rein and led her from the stable. This was going to be the difficult part, he realised, leading Star across the cobbled roads to the gate linking the palace to the town. Once through that he was confident he would escape.

As they went he was surprised how effective the sack cloths were proving in dampening the sounds of their passage and, before long, he came in sight of the gate. He blessed Emma for there was no sign of Sanfred. Hurriedly he led Star towards his goal, the pounding of his heart in his ears sounding loud enough to alert anyone in the vicinity. A few yards away, behind a door leading to the palace gardens, a dog started to bark. Kaplyn quickened his pace and then he was alongside the gate. He felt his skin prickle with excitement and, at any moment, he expected to be discovered. And then, all at once, he was through. Before him a narrow road, flanked with tall, rickety looking buildings, led to the city gates. The shops to either side were closed; although even this late there were already sounds of activity and a few lights within.

A little farther on and he encountered the first people. They were probably staff going to bakeries or other employment requiring fires to be stoked. A few cast Kaplyn enquiring looks and, for a moment, he feared that his clothes blended less well with the common folk than he thought. It then dawned on him what the problem was. Star still had the sackcloths over her hooves. He stopped to remove them before continuing, but the din of her iron shod hooves was too much to dare going much farther. Kaplyn walked her deeper into shadow in the lee of a large building. He had to wait for the

9

dawn before the town gates were opened and reasoned that this location was as good as anywhere.

Gradually, as the sky lightened, more people started to appear and with them the occasional cart pulled by tired, dispirited looking horses. Kaplyn joined one as it passed, keeping a short distance behind it. With his heart seemingly in his throat, he followed the cart and driver to the gates. They were being opened and the guards were waving traffic out. There was no attempt to stop anyone leaving, and Kaplyn simply rode through the gate as though he had every right to do so.

A short way from the city walls, he kicked Star into a trot. A smile broke out over his face and he punched the air. "Yes!" he exalted. He had escaped, but what future lay before him he did not know.

Chapter 2

Ambush

The cracking of dry branches snapped Lars from his melancholy. Daydreaming was dangerous in a wood, especially with night approaching. Lars' staff came up automatically and he turned to face the potential threat. A man crashed through the thick undergrowth, a cudgel raised in his right fist. His wild eyes screamed silent hatred as he bore down on the big man. Lars was a fighter and instinct took over. Other men might have blocked the cudgel's downward stroke, but Lars knew that, in a fight, time was crucial. Without thinking, he lashed out with a straight arm blow, aiming the staff's end at the man's throat.

The combination of the man's momentum and Lars' blow snapped his assailant's head back, jarring Lars' arm in the process. His assailant's legs buckled and he fell to the woodland floor, a scream impossible through his damaged throat. His eyes bulged and his hands went to his windpipe as he thrashed for air, grunting with the effort to breathe. Turning, Lars sought new enemies and, to his chagrin, several men advanced, forming a ring around him. Seeing their comrade disabled so quickly, they were cautious, but greed and poverty drove them on.

"Surround him," one of the men shouted. Again Lars cursed his earlier lapse of concentration. A foolish mistake he should never had made. Slowly he turned, assessing the men before him, his staff held out, ready to counter an attack. They were a mixed bunch. All were filthy and covered in months of accumulated grime. Their clothes were torn and, where they had bothered, badly repaired. Most carried knives or cudgels and only two held swords.

"Move in together," the man who had spoken earlier demanded. He seemed to be their leader. He pointed his sword towards Lars, but didn't go forward himself. Lars kept turning but no one moved. His eyes kept straying to the leader's sword, speckled with rust, the edge chipped and blunt. If the

11

blade did not kill him, blood poisoning would. *Focus; watch their shoulders and eyes, not their weapons,* he thought.

The wounded man's thrashing became wilder. Others glanced down at him. His face had turned blue and his tongue protruded as though seeking to absorb the air he so desperately needed. A few final kicks and then he was still, his body contorted in the final spasm.

"He's killed Ballan," one of the shorter men said unnecessarily. The others grumbled and then one man shouted a curse, leaping forward, his knife raised. Lars' back was to him, but hearing the shout and cracking of twigs, he span around, sweeping the staff in an arc. The man ducked back as the staff whistled by his head, his eyes instantly turning from anger to fear. Lars stabbed down at him but he was already scuttling back out of range.

"He's one man! Everyone attack him," their leader shouted.

"You've got a sword. You attack him," a man sneered.

Lars stared into the leader's eyes, daring him. He was as tall as Lars, but lean. His nose must have been broken many times and so odd was the shape that it was barely recognisable. The leader waved at Lars with the sword's tip. "After three," he said. "One, two … *three*! he shouted, lunging forward.

Lars threw the staff forward, allowing it to slip through his fingers until he judged the length right. He grabbed the staff before the end left his hand and punched at the leader's face. He felt the staff connect, but he was already turning, using all his strength to swing the staff in a wide circle. If anyone else was going to move, his action stopped them in their tracks as they rocked back on their heels to avoid the blow. Lars was strong and he put all his effort into the blow. The wood whooshed through the air, leaving no doubt as to his strength.

The leader fell back, cursing and clutching his head in his free hand. When he removed his hand to inspect it for blood, there was a neat red circle on his brow where Lars' blow had connected.

"Anyone else who moves, dies," Lars declared. He was afraid, but knew that he daren't show that. These men were bullies and, no doubt, cowards, but their numbers might overcome their fear.

He started turning again so he could see them all. "Kill him," a man wearing a fleece urged. He spat at Lars but made no move himself.

"He isn't worth it," another man said. He was fat and bald. One eye looked infected and was weeping, making it look like he was crying.

"He looks as poor as we do," the man with the fleece commented.

"We are not quitting *now*!" the leader said. "He killed Ballan!"

"What do you care? You hated him," the man with the weeping eye growled.

The leader smiled. Black gaps made his teeth seem all the more uneven. "Not until this fat pig is dead," he spat.

"We need a bow," one man said.

"Then go back to the camp and get one," the leader raged. The man didn't need further urging, and ran off between the trees, disappearing in an instant in the growing gloom.

Lars muttered a prayer, "Slathor, give me strength!"

"What did he say?" one of his tormenters asked.

"How *the Kalanth* do I know!" the leader roared.

Lars realised he had to do something before the other man returned with a bow. Turning, he tried to determine which man might break if he charged him. He assessed each man in turn, but one seemed more likely to break than the rest. He was a short man, with wild dancing eyes and an ugly, uncaring face. He held a sword awkwardly but if Lars had judged correctly, the sword would not matter. The man was also closest to the tree line, and if Lars could make it there then he could escape into the darkness.

His mind made up, Lars roared, leaping at the man and swinging his staff. He had selected his target well, but, instead of fleeing, the man stood his ground, petrified by the suddenness of the larger man's attack. Lars swung his staff, its length keeping him from the other man's sword. The staff cracked against the other man's temple sending him flying. The blow was well timed and its shock raced along Lars' arm.

Not stopping, Lars leapt over the body as two men sought to cut off his escape. Now that the action had started, adrenalin conquered the other men's fear. With shouts they were all converging in on the big man. Lars flicked the staff out at the man on his right, missing his opponent who dodged to one side. It slowed him, but already the man to Lars' left was closing the gap.

"He's killed Arland," Lars heard from behind him. "Take him alive!"

Someone threw their cudgel at Lars' back, catching him between the shoulder blades and knocking the breath from his body. Lars stumbled forward, his attack on the man to his left failing as his loss of balance threw off his aim. Lars gasped for air as the man to his left grabbed his staff but, rather than slow down, Lars let go, abandoning the weapon. The other man, not expecting to take the weapon so easily lost his balance, falling to the ground.

Someone from behind Lars tumbled into his legs, throwing him to the woodland carpet. Another man lashed out with his cudgel, striking Lars across the shoulders. He gritted his teeth and grabbed a handful of dirt in agony.

13

"I want him alive," the leader roared.

Twisting, Lars threw one man off him but the others had caught up. Fear of their leader stopped their blows. Lars lashed out with his fist, catching one man under the chin and throwing him backward. Someone grabbed his arm and a man threw himself across his legs. Roaring his defiance Lars threw out another punch. Lars yelled as his hair was grabbed from behind, forcing his head back. A knife pricked his flesh and a thin trickle of blood ran down his neck. Lars stilled.

"Don't move," the man with the knife said. His breath was foul and combined with the stink of his clothing was almost overpowering.

Cursing, the leader ran at Lars and booted him in the face. Lars rocked back on the ground while the men struggled to hold him down.

"You killed my brother," the leader screamed, kicking Lars in the ribs. "Tie his hands and feet. I will make you suffer," the leader continued, breathless with rage, his eyes bulging and spittle running down his chin.

The men did as they were asked and shortly Lars could not move. "Pick him up and carry him to the camp," the leader ordered.

It took three men to lift Lars, whilst two more picked up the body of the short man Lars had killed. Lars could see the bruise on his temple where he had crushed his skull.

Lars tried to escape and his efforts caused the men carrying him to let go. He made it to his knees before the leader stood over him, his sword aimed at Lars' heart. "Tonight you will die," he said. "Slowly. And before you die you will beg me for mercy, but do not expect to receive any."

Lars summoned all of his strength, trying to break his bonds. He must not die. He had to find his wife and son. With a roar of rage he threw every bit of his strength against his bonds. His muscles bunched and for the briefest moment he felt his bonds give.

The pommel of the leader's sword crashed against his temple, blackness engulfed him and he knew no more.

Chapter 3

A Chance Encounter

Kaplyn reined in his mount. The distant scream echoed in his mind. What sort of animal could make such a noise? Breathlessly he waited for another sound but none came. Even the woodland birds and animals fell silent at the inhuman cry.

Silently he cursed himself for being a fool. He should not have entered the wood. The path he was following had long since petered out and to make matters worse, he was lost. That was not quite true; he knew where he was, in a wood somewhere between Dundalk, his home, and Pendrat, his destination. His earlier excitement had waned. Now he was cold, hungry and afraid, the latter being a new experience for him.

Never before had he been so alone. Always, there were people close by. Now his neighbours might be outlaws, krell or worse, creatures that would rend a man limb from limb if he so much as looked at them. Judging it too dark to ride safely he dismounted before patting Star's flank.

"Good girl," he said, more to hear a voice rather than to calm her.

Wearily he took her rein and led her on, looking for somewhere safe to camp. The scream had unnerved him and more than anything he craved the company of people. He couldn't get the tales from his childhood from his mind, of krell and other fell creatures. He tried to dismiss them by reminding himself that these were fairytales and nothing more, but a fear of the unknown kept returning to haunt him. The Krell Wars were real enough but they were many years ago. Krell, if they still existed, roamed only the wildest regions such as the mountains and forests of the world. The wood he was in was far too small and too near the Allund capital to conceal krell. The king's troops regularly patrolled between the cities, the way was safe, or at least it ought to be...

At that moment Kaplyn stopped. Since the scream he had walked for quite some time, or at least felt he had. The trees were merciless, growing close together, making him force a passage. His hands and face were scratched and sweat now made these sting. What had made him stop was not the trees, but a light ahead. He squinted, trying to reassure himself that there was indeed a faint glow. He continued forward when he heard voices. Perhaps there was a clearing and charcoal workers, he thought. He smelled the air but could only scent damp and decaying wood.

Loosely looping Star's rein over a branch he unhooked his bow from the saddle and threw his quiver over his shoulder. He bent the bow to string it and once armed felt marginally better. Taking stock of his surroundings he inched forward trying to make no noise. All around was the faint rustling of branches and old leaves as the wind blew softly. Before too long he saw a line of trees and just beyond these, a small rise crowned with thick bushes. He became convinced that between the trees there was indeed a glow. Dropping to all fours he crawled towards the bushes, parting them to see.

Before him, the ground dipped into a glade where a large fire cast enough light to see by. A man was pacing around the fire and four men were astride a fallen tree trunk whilst three others slouched on the ground. They gave the impression of men used to living rough, hardened by nights spent in the wild and, now he had seen them, there was no doubting that they were outlaws. Some wore leather tunics torn and stained with wear, while others had thick woollen cloaks whose colour had long since faded. Their weapons were crude, mainly cudgels or knives, although one wore a sword tucked through his belt. Only the pacing man wore both a sword and scabbard, probably taken as plunder.

The pacing man abruptly stood still and threw an arm out, indicating beyond the circle of light to the rear of the camp.

"Bring him here," he growled ominously. His voice carried easily to Kaplyn. "It's time to deal with the man who killed my brother."

Two men arose from the log and walked away from Kaplyn, disappearing amongst the trees. Kaplyn ducked lower, thinking that he must return to Star. Just as he was about to leave, the men returned, pushing another man roughly before them. He stumbled in a manner suggesting his hands were bound behind his back.

He was a big man, broad across the chest, with powerful shoulders. His hair and beard were blond, which was a surprise to Kaplyn for Allunds were brown-haired and Thracians marginally fairer.

At that moment his captives were forcing him to his knees, kicking the back of his legs and pushing down on his shoulders. The prisoner resisted but their efforts were too much for him and he collapsed to his knees.

Striding towards the prisoner the leader raised his foot and slammed his heel into the prisoner's face. Toppling backwards, the big man managed to stop himself from falling. When he looked up his beard was flecked with blood.

"You will not have an easy death," the outlaw spat with undisguised hatred. "You killed two of *my* men. One was my brother — for that, you'll pay." He circled the prisoner before coming to a halt behind him. "The only thing is ... I haven't decided how to kill you — *yet.*"

"Let me finish him," one of the men sitting on the trunk offered, holding a long knife in his hand, his eyes shining with anticipation.

The leader shook his head. "He's mine. I want to see him squirm. Make sure that you hold him," he waved his hand in the direction of two of his men. He then crossed to the fire as his men leapt to their feet to stand either side of the kneeling prisoner, each gripping a shoulder. The leader's dagger reflected the firelight as he drew it before plunging it into the fire.

"Let's see how strong he is without his eyes," he said through gritted teeth.

In his hiding place Kaplyn tensed and he felt the colour drain from his face. Part of him wanted to leave and yet another part of him wanted to aid the prisoner — but what could he do? If the outlaws caught him, they would kill him. It was a dreadful dilemma, to stay and help or to leave, knowing that an innocent man might die because of that decision. Watching the outlaws torment the prisoner, anger blossomed in his chest and suddenly his mind was made up.

Crawling backwards he sought deeper shadows before rubbing soil on his face to mask its whiteness, spitting on his fingers to soften the soil. Rising slowly he stood braced against the trunk of a tree, hoping that he would not be silhouetted. His hunting bow was not meant for battle, but it was a stout weapon. He placed two arrows point first into the ground by his side before nocking a third. Taking aim he prayed to the Kalanth for an alternative.

The men either side of the prisoner struggled to hold him down as he fought against them. Removing the now glowing knife from the fire their leader advanced, clearly enjoying himself as he brought his knife deliberately towards the other man's eyes.

Kaplyn struggled with his conscience until he could not afford to wait any longer. Drawing his bow a fraction more, he released the arrow. A scream of agony rang through the trees as the arrow hammered into the outlaw's shoulder. With a mingled wail of pain and rage, he dropped his knife.

In quick succession Kaplyn loosed the other two arrows. He was good with a bow and could put ten arrows in flight in a count of sixty heartbeats.

His aim, after the first arrow would not be good, but the effect was what he wanted.

One arrow hit the trunk the men were sitting on and the other flashed between two men. All eyes turned towards the trees, looking in Kaplyn's general direction but not at him. He kept still and it was soon clear from their bewildered looks that the outlaws could not see him. Silently he drew another arrow from his sheath and nocked it.

As though released from a spell, the men sitting on the fallen trunk flung themselves backward, behind the improvised barricade. The two men holding the prisoner let go as they, too, dived for cover behind the trunk.

"Who's out there?" one man cried out to his companions.

"Town guard?" came a muffled reply.

"Can't be," said another. "We're too far from the town. The guard would never come this far."

"King's troops then?" came back a timid reply.

"Quiet!" snapped the leader. "Use your bloody ears, and cease wagging your tongues." He alone was standing, clutching his wound; his face twisted in pain. After a moment, he seemed satisfied. "Get up," he ordered. When no one responded, he went over to the log and delivered a hefty kick to some poor unfortunate. A grunt followed.

"There's only one man, otherwise they would have attacked by now. Get out there and find whoever shot me!"

An outlaw timidly climbed to his feet. Kaplyn aimed and loosed another arrow that thudded into the trunk sufficiently close to send him scurrying back for cover.

"He's a good shot," Kaplyn heard.

"I don't care," the outlaw chief screamed. "Get out there and bring me his head!" He delivered another kick and Kaplyn heard a further grunt of pain.

Finally, one man dared to rise, either out of bravado or because of his leader's brutality. The man sprinted for the line of trees to Kaplyn's left. Kaplyn let fly an arrow but his aim was poor and the man escaped. Time was against him now with an outlaw amongst the trees. Again he feared capture, but he could not leave the other man. Not now.

Seeing their colleague's success and fearful of their leader's anger, two more men ran after the first. Events were now so out of control that Kaplyn had to shoot more accurately. The arrow hit one of the running men in the lower back, spilling him to the ground with a cry of pain. Briefly the man struggled to crawl forward, but his strength left him and he collapsed. The other man managed to reach the tree line where he disappeared from view.

Behind the log no one dared move, even their leader dropped behind cover, still berating the others for their cowardice. Forgotten and recognising an opportunity to escape, the prisoner climbed with difficulty to his feet and started to run towards the trees in the opposite direction taken by the two outlaws.

The outlaw leader, seeing his prisoner escaping, shouted out in rage. He stood up. A well-placed arrow barely missed his head, causing him to drop back with a yelp of agony as the barb already in his arm bit deeper.

Kaplyn shot two more shafts at the tree trunk in quick succession before scooping up his quiver of dwindling arrows. He ran through the thick vegetation, aiming in the general direction the prisoner had taken. He had little difficulty in finding him, following the sound of cracking twigs and the louder snap of branches.

Before Kaplyn could reach him the large blond man stopped and turned to face him; his feet firmly planted and defiant in his eyes even though his hands were bound.

"I'm a friend," Kaplyn said, skidding to a halt.

The big man relaxed. "Untie me," he replied, turning his back and offering his bound wrists.

Kaplyn wanted to continue running and the delay made his heart hammer even faster. However, he slung his bow across his back and drew a dagger. As quickly as he could he cut the bonds.

The big man rubbed at his chafed wrists. "Thanks," he whispered.

"Go!" Kaplyn urged. "They'll be after us."

They jogged deeper into the wood, but branches lashed their flesh, forcing them to walk. In the confusion Kaplyn had no idea where Star was. He was considering whether he could find her when something caught his attention. He grabbed the other man's shoulder, forcing him to crouch. Not far away he heard someone crashing through the vegetation.

"They're over here," someone shouted.

Kaplyn kept a firm grip on the other man's shoulder.

"Stay still," Kaplyn whispered. At first, he thought the outlaws had discovered them, but the sound of their passage through the vegetation was fading. "Come on," Kaplyn whispered and led them away from the direction the outlaws had gone, taking care to keep noise to a minimum.

After a while Kaplyn said softly, "That was close. We nearly stumbled into an outlaw. Something must have distracted him."

"Probably an animal," the other man suggested softly.

Kaplyn nodded, thinking about Star. "We need to keep walking. They'll still be looking for us."

19

In silence, they continued for the better part of the night, stopping occasionally to listen for signs of pursuit. After several stops Kaplyn decided they were finally safe; he collapsed where he stood, breathing a sigh of relief.

"I'm shattered," the big man said, sitting down across from Kaplyn with his back against a trunk. Dark rings circled his eyes and he looked barely able to stand. "My name's Lars," he said, holding out his hand. Kaplyn shook it.

"Kaplyn," he returned.

"I'm grateful you came along when you did."

"What happened?" Kaplyn whispered.

Lars shook his head. "I was foolish enough to enter the wood, that's what happened! They must have seen me as an easy target, armed only with a walking staff. I put up a fight but when the second man fell, their leader went wild, ordering me to be taken alive. Their numbers overwhelmed me."

The two men fell silent for a moment, each listening to the night noises, trying to discern if they were being followed. Above, an owl hooted and then there was silence.

"I've never seen anyone with blond hair before. Where are you from?"

"Gorlanth, it's far across the sea."

"I've never heard of it."

Lars nodded. "Not many people have. Few Allunders even know land exists across the sea. A storm keeps all but the bravest captains close to the shore. Every day I pray to return home, to my wife and son."

Kaplyn saw the hurt reflected deep within his eyes. In respect for the other man's need for silence he turned his thoughts to their predicament, estimating that about half the night remained. "We need to leave," he announced at last.

"Can't we rest here, for a while at least? After all it would be safer continuing in the morning, when it's light."

Kaplyn was not so sure. The wood made him nervous and he was keen to leave. He conceded, however, that it was more dangerous travelling in the dark.

"Very well, we'll stay here, but we need to take turns on guard."

Lars nodded and Kaplyn offered to stand the first watch. For a while he sat awake, listening to Lars' snoring which seemed loud enough to attract a host of outlaws let alone whatever creatures lurked in the wood. Kaplyn though about his brothers and what they would do in this situation. The thought made him smile. Karlan, the eldest was pompous in the extreme. He would order Lars to stand watch while he slept soundly. For a moment,

Kaplyn felt a pang of jealousy towards Lars. Why should he sleep while Kaplyn was awake, but then he considered the experience Lars had just suffered? He decided to let him rest.

His thoughts turned to Emma and he felt a twinge of guilt. She and Sanfred might be in trouble by now. He would make amends upon his return he decided, but the guilt remained.

He regretted the loss of his belongings and especially Star, nevertheless he realised there was no going back. He had clothes, his purse and a few gold coins secreted into the lining of his leather jerkin so he could afford to replace his losses. Then his mind turned to the man he had shot. Even though he was an outlaw, he hoped he had not killed him. It was an uncomfortable thought and one that would prey on his mind for some time.

After a while, when Kaplyn felt that he could not stay awake any longer, he shook Lars' shoulder. The big man stirred and looked around blearily. "Your turn to keep guard," Kaplyn said.

Lars grumbled, sat up and looked out into the darkness. Kaplyn waited to make sure his companion was taking his duty seriously, then laid down and instantly was asleep.

Chapter 4

Pendrat

"Are you still angry?" Lars asked.

"You *were* meant to stand guard," Kaplyn complained After setting off, they had struggled through the wood until finally emerging from the trees at about mid-morning. Presently they were crossing an open field and their boots tugged as they tangled with the long grass.

"Nothing happened though," Lars answered. "I know it was wrong, but I was *really* tired."

Kaplyn regarded the other man. The night before he had cut an imposing figure, but the light of day told a different story. He was carrying too much weight and the colour of his nose suggested he was fond of ale. However, at the moment he looked genuinely sorry, like a chastised puppy.

Kaplyn was not happy though. Something had awoken him. Something he had not recognised. He had sat bolt upright, his arms flaying at whatever had disturbed his sleep and he could not get the image out of his mind. A face had peered down at him, green glowing flesh and almond eyes with a tongue that had flickered across small pointed teeth. Kaplyn was sure that he creature had touched his forehead. Then Kaplyn had yelled, waking Lars who had clearly been asleep the whole time.

By the time Kaplyn was on his feet with his sword in his hand, whatever had been near had gone. He had felt peculiar ever since, tainted as though touched by something evil. He rubbed at his forehead and then looked at his hand but there was nothing to see. He wiped his hand on his trousers. He did not mention his experience to Lars. He now felt foolish, having jumped at the shadows. Upon sighting the creature his immediate thought had been of krell, but now imps and demons seemed to plague his mind. Fairytales, he scolded himself angrily.

"I suppose we are both rested," Kaplyn grumbled, in answer to Lars' earlier question.

Behind them a rook cawed, causing Kaplyn to glance back. Something had disturbed it, and its flurry of wings carried easily on the still air. His face fell and he groaned.

"Don't they ever give up?" Kaplyn groaned.

Lars looked around. Kaplyn couldn't tell how many were following; they were still some distance. He broke into a run, urging Lars to keep up.

Think! What were their options? Ahead, there were a couple of copses, but hiding was a last resort. A rabbit scampered from a thicket, startling Kaplyn. It zigzagged in front of them before bolting into a gorse bush. Kaplyn kept running. Lars lolled along by his side, his face flushed.

Rounding one end of a copse Kaplyn saw a stockade wall. "A farm," he gasped. "Keep running, it's not far. We'll make it before they catch us."

Kaplyn risked glancing back; five figures were following and the gap between them had shortened. As he ran, his sword slapped against his thigh and he feared it would trip him. He held it still with one hand whilst he ran.

Returning his attention to his front, he had a better view of the farm. The palisade comprised trunks lashed together and above that, thatched roofs supported chimneys that were venting grey smoke against a blue sky.

"Ho the farm!" Kaplyn shouted, waving his arm as he ran. "Ho!" he shouted louder, catching sight of a figure silhouetted on the wall. The pungent smell of livestock mixed with wood smoke filled the air.

Within bow range Kaplyn came to a halt and, behind him, Lars staggered to his side. Kaplyn looked back but there was no sign of their pursuers. They must have hidden in one of the copses, probably waiting to see what happened next.

By now there were several figures on the wall and to Kaplyn's consternation some were armed with bows. Two men approached through a gate, both carrying pitchforks. The taller of the two was the older, grey haired and with a rugged face no doubt acquired from long days spent in the fields. The other man, probably the first man's son judging by his age, was darker but broader. Neither smiled as they came to a halt.

Kaplyn couldn't read their expressions. "I'm Kaplyn. We are lost and fleeing outlaws. Last night they captured my companion here, Lars, and I managed to free him." By his side, Lars was red faced and breathing hard.

At the mention of outlaws, the grey haired man's eyes sought the land behind them. "How many?" It was a demand rather than a question.

"Five," Kaplyn answered.

The other man snorted. "Cowards — the lot of them. They're content to waylay a lone man, but they'll never attack here, with so many."

"I may have killed one of them last night," Kaplyn answered truthfully, "and Lars killed the chieftain's brother. That makes them all the more dangerous."

The farmer's stoic look broke as he smiled. "Did you now? Killed some of them did you? Good for you."

"I want to buy a horse, and food," Kaplyn asked, sensing they had the farmer on their side.

"I have a horse, but it's not for riding," the farmer answered.

"I can pay for it," Kaplyn took out his purse, counting out fifteen silver *calder.*

The other man's eyes widened. "You'd better see the animal before offering your money." He turned to his companion. "Kroner, go and fetch bread and cheese for these men. And fetch them a skin of wine while you're about it."

The farmer then led them through the gates where six other men and a handful of children stared at them wide-eyed.

"Go on," the farmer said. "Stop gawping and get on with your chores."

"Will you be all right? I mean with the outlaws out there?" Kaplyn asked.

The farmer smiled. "As I said, outlaws are cowardly creatures. Besides, there will be more men here by nightfall when they come off the fields. Thanks for the warning though.

"Here we are," the farmer said as they arrived before a tall barn. Inside, they were presented with a very stocky plough horse. It eyed Kaplyn as he approached and gently butted his shoulder, seeking a titbit.

"You have no other?" Kaplyn asked. The farmer shook his head.

The animal had been well looked after and was clearly big enough to carry them both. Sighing, he decided it would have to do and he offered the farmer the coins. At that moment, Kroner returned with food wrapped in a large cloth and a skin of wine.

"Would you like to stay for a meal?" the farmer offered.

"Thanks for the offer, but no," Kaplyn replied. "We need to get to Pendrat."

"It's some distance. You're welcome to stay the night," the farmer offered, but Kaplyn shook his head.

"The sooner the outlaws see us leave, the safer for you and your family. Can you direct us? I have no idea where we are."

24

"Aye. You're not far from the Pendrat road." The farmer led them outside where some women had joined the men folk to see the strangers. "Go that way for a quarter mile and then you'll find the highway. Bear left and just keep riding. You'll not be there until late though. We'll watch your trail for a while and make sure that no one follows you."

Kaplyn and Lars thanked the two men. At the gate, Kaplyn mounted but Lars struggled, muttering all the while. After several attempts he finally admitted that he had not ridden before. His face flushed red with embarrassment. Kaplyn dismounted, cupping his hands to help him and then Kaplyn mounted in front of Lars. They set off, waving to the farmer and his family as they left.

As they rode, Kaplyn kept looking back but after a while became confident that any pursuit was far behind. He hoped he hadn't visited ill on the farmers.

Gradually, the land became more wooded. The trees made Kaplyn nervous; he had preferred the open countryside. Lars was gripping his waist so firmly that Kaplyn was having difficulty breathing.

"Tell me about your homeland," Kaplyn asked, seeking to set the other man at ease.

There was a short delay and gradually Lars' grip relaxed. The horse swayed as it walked but being such a broad animal their seat was secure, even without a saddle.

"It's beautiful...," the big man started wistfully, "... although the weather is more extreme than it is here. It's colder in the winter and the nights are longer. The summers are warm, though, and the spring is glorious when violets carpet the meadows. And the mountains..." His voice caught and Kaplyn glanced back. Lars' jaw was firmly set and his eyes sparkled with unshed tears. Kaplyn looked to their front, embarrassed to have seen the other man's pain.

Lars did not seem to notice and continued his tale. "My people live in villages along the coast. Our homes surround a central, long hall. In the winter nights, we tell stories and drink beer.

"I miss it," he sniffed loudly. "You'll have to forgive me; I left behind my wife and son and have no way to get back to them." After a pause he continued. "What about yourself — where are you from and what do you do?"

The question caught Kaplyn by surprise. "I'm from Dundalk," he managed after what he hoped wasn't too long a pause. "I served in the palace guard for a couple of years but didn't get on with one of the Hest

Commanders, so I decided to leave." It was a lie, but reasonably close enough to the truth to be plausible.

"What's a hest?"

Kaplyn glanced back. "It's a small unit of men in the army." At that moment, a bird took flight at the side of the path, startling the horse and Kaplyn. He hoped it wasn't a sign for the lie that he told.

"The palace guard?" Lars said, suitably impressed.

"It sounds better than it was," Kaplyn answered, dreading any further questions. Swiftly he changed the subject and for the rest of the day they chatted about Allund and its people. By early evening the scenery had changed, becoming gently undulating. The strong scent of bracken carried upon the evening breeze and soft sunlight pleasantly warmed their faces.

Kaplyn urged their mount to greater haste as the sun started to sink below the surrounding foothills, casting long shadows across the narrow path. He was fretful that they had not yet seen Pendrat. The wild, as they had already found to their cost, was a dangerous place and they had been lucky that they had encountered nothing worse than outlaws.

Just when he was about to give in and suggest stopping for the night, they crested a hill and at last below them was Pendrat. The path they were following ended at a rickety looking bridge, spanning a deep gorge. The other end of the bridge led to the main gates, which for the moment at least were open. Within the town, lamps were being lit and tiny flames sprang into being along the narrow streets as though by magic. Spurring their mount down the gentle incline they hurried towards the town and safety.

The bridge's wooden planking clattered noisily as they crossed. Some sounded loose, much to Kaplyn's alarm. He looked over the side. The ravine fell away sharply towards a narrow, turgid stream whose waters frothed white against grey boulders. A stink of rotting vegetation wafted up, causing him to turn away.

At the bridge's other end two sentries stood idly, leaning against their spears. They stared up at the men as they rode by, humour sparkling in their eyes. Kaplyn feared that they might be stopped, but then they were beneath the thick stone walls and in the town proper.

People thronged the main street but parted to let them pass, nudging partners or friends, smiling or laughing at the newcomers' misfortune to be riding double on an aged plough horse. Looking up to avoid their stares, Kaplyn saw bright banners suspended between the buildings.

A juggler was performing by the side of the street, keeping three balls spinning in the air. He shouted something to Kaplyn who could not quite hear what was said, but it caused merriment to those surrounding the performer and they laughed gaily.

Kaplyn's gaze swept the crowd seeking the distinctive uniform of the palace guard and wondering whether they had already been here. There was no sign of them and so he aimed towards a large inn, nested between tall buildings, whose weather-stained beams sagged in the most alarming manner. A squeaking sign proclaimed it to be "The Thirst and Last." Kaplyn dismounted while Lars practically fell off as his legs buckled beneath him.

A scraggly youth emerged from an alley to one side of the inn. "Can I take your horse to the stable?" he offered, holding out a grubby hand.

"Aye, thanks," Kaplyn replied. "Here's a couple of copper *tell*. Take good care of him and make sure he is well fed and watered."

"Do you have any money?" Kaplyn asked turning to Lars.

"No. They took everything. I was going to enter the wrestling, although I was hoping to lose some weight beforehand." He patted his paunch. "It appears I've developed a taste for your countrymen's ale."

Kaplyn considered for a moment. Taking out his purse he took out some silver calder. "Here. Take these," he offered.

The other man shook his head. "I cannot," he said. "It's not right."

"Pay me back when you win," Kaplyn grinned, forcing the coins on the other man. "Now let's see if there are any rooms left."

Inside, the tavern was busy; the air was thick with smoke from numerous pipes and a badly vented fire. Kaplyn paused uncertainly. He had never experienced anything like this before and turned to see what Lars made of it. The big man stood by his side, clearly at ease in the strange surroundings.

The smell was overpowering; a combined reek of spilt ale and months of accumulated cooking odours. He would have to get used to it, especially if he was claiming to be an ex-palace guard!

Kaplyn forced his way to the bar. Within moments, a sullen looking landlord appeared, wiping his hands on a greasy apron.

"What can I do for you, gents?" he shouted above the hubbub.

Kaplyn shouted a reply. "Two rooms for two nights ... and supper."

The landlord eyed Kaplyn's clothes and his eyes narrowed. "That'll be two pieces of silver. Each."

Kaplyn started to fish through his purse and the landlord's eyes nearly fell out of their sockets. Clearly, he had expected Kaplyn to barter at least.

"And three copper *tell* for the meal...each," he added.

Lars started to complain but Kaplyn mistook him. "It's all right, I'll pay."

27

"Up the top of the stairs at the back is one room and through that door is another," said the landlord, pocketing the money as swiftly as he could. "Go to the end of the corridor. It's the last one on the right."

"You paid too much," Lars advised as they started towards their rooms.

"The prices will be high because of the games," Kaplyn answered. In truth, he had no idea how much a room should cost. His purse was full but by Lars' look the landlord had cheated him. Frowning, he decided to be more careful in the future, not wanting to attract undue attention to himself. "Let's have a look at the rooms and meet up back here."

Leaving Lars, Kaplyn ducked through a door with a sign proclaiming *Duck or Grouse* above it. There was not enough room on the stair for two and he wondered what would happen if he met someone coming down. His boots thudded noisily on the steps.

At the top, a door led into a small room barely large enough for the single bed and rickety table which supported a cracked washing bowl and pitcher. The roof was only a few inches above his head and it sloped alarmingly over the bed, forcing him to crouch to reach it.

He hoped he wasn't disturbing someone below as the floor boards creaked ominously. Briefly, he wondered what was holding the place together as he sat down, testing the mattress. It was far too soft for his liking.

He went across to a small, cracked mirror hanging on the wall. He stared at his image for a while, checking his forehead. The memory of whatever had awoken him was fading but he still felt tainted. His skin looked unblemished and now, in the safety of the town, he dismissed the event as the over activity of a tired mind.

The room smelt musty. Opening the only window, he inhaled the fresh evening air. It carried a mixture of aromas — baking bread, stables and other scents of a busy town. Even with its shortcomings, at least he felt safe.

Across the street, garlands decorated many of the windows to ward against demons and other evil spirits. The townsfolk also feared the spirit world and Kaplyn, after his night of being afraid, suddenly felt less foolish knowing others feared the dark. He left the room, hoping that the meal would be better than the accommodation.

Lars grinned up at him as he sat down. Kaplyn waved to the landlord for their meal, who in turn waved to a serving girl. She disappeared briefly before returning, holding aloft a heavily laden tray with practiced ease.

Smiling broadly she set down two large wooden bowls containing a thick meaty stew and a plate piled high with large hunks of warm bread. When

Kaplyn looked down at his plate he frowned. Potatoes and meat poked through a blanket of thick, brown gravy, looking very unappetising. Using a broad wooden spoon he tasted a morsel. It was surprisingly tasty.

"It's good to have company again," Lars commented between mouthfuls, "especially with fine ale on the table."

"After last night, I'm just relieved to be within the town," Kaplyn answered. However, he had an uncomfortable feeling that his adventure was far from over.

At that moment a slurred and insolent voice at an adjacent table caught his attention.

"Aye, that's a fact!" A man hunched over a large but empty flagon of ale was saying. "Three wizards, and I spoke with them." Kaplyn's curiosity was aroused at the mention of wizards; in Allund wizards were rare.

There were five men at the table, farmers judging by their appearance. He motioned Lars to silence as he eavesdropped on the conversation.

"Don't be daft, Gillan," retorted another of the group. "There is no such thing as wizards, as we all know. If you ask me, you've been sitting here for too long and the beer has finally soaked your wits." The speaker was a small, but stout individual with a good-humoured face and smiling eyes. "Wizards are nothing more than a fairy tale and you have told enough of *those* in your time."

"How come I spoke to one then?" Gillan replied defensively, pushing himself forward to confront the other man. His face was round and fleshy and his nose was red from years of hard drinking. His eyes seemed to be having difficulty focusing and he kept blinking at his antagonist.

"Are you causing trouble again Gillan?" the serving girl asked as she collected empty tankards from the table. The others about the table grinned; Gillan was clearly known for spreading rumours — many of his own making. Gillan muttered angrily.

A hush had descended over the nearby tables as others listened in to the conversation.

"There were three of them," Gillan continued, determined not to lose face and forgetting that he had already mentioned their number. "I saw them about half a mile from the village. One of them stopped to ask me the way here. It was he that said they were wizards, "coming to entertain the good townsfolk"."

The others around the table smiled, enjoying Gillan's discomfort.

"Wizards?" Lars whispered to Kaplyn.

"Yes, I heard," Kaplyn said, slightly irritated. Then he decided he was being harsh. Leaning over he whispered to Lars, "Years ago, during the

29

Krell Wars, they were supposed to have been common, but now they are rare. At that time, some people still travelled the land claiming to be wizards, although they were more usually just clever magicians, using slight of hand to dupe their audience." Kaplyn turned his attention back to the speaker.

"And why shouldn't there be wizards?" one of Gillan's companions was saying, coming to the other man's rescue. He was a short, respectable looking fellow. The others in the group quietened to hear what he had to say. "Just because there are no wizards in Allund doesn't mean that there are none at all. And besides, look how many people are prepared to believe in other more fanciful notions such as demons; if they exist, then why not wizards?"

"Aye," a grey bearded man with large staring eyes interrupted. "That's a good point. Remember last year and old Fowler's farm!" Several nodded their agreement and, judging by their expressions, it was not a pleasant memory.

"That was never proven," replied his neighbour in a dismissive tone. "Surely you don't believe that Fowler was murdered by a demon. We're full-grown men, not daft children frightened of the dark." The man nodded towards Gillan who was too engrossed with his mug and its lack of content to take offence.

"Aye, maybe," his grey-bearded companion conceded. "But there is no denying that something strange happened that night. There are many prepared to believe that a demon took old Fowler. His wife was hysterical when we found her and her mind has since gone; she talks to no one now, save her dead husband." He sat back, balancing his mug in a casual manner on the edge of the table.

"I was one of the first to arrive at the farm," he continued softly. "That was just after his son came riding into town, crying of murder. When we arrived at the farm, *by the Kalanth*, there was the most god-awful stench." He wrinkled his nose absent-mindedly with the memory. "It was unlike anything I had ever smelt before."

"If it was unlike anything you had smelt before then how do you know it was a demon?" Gillan retorted gruffly, clearly eager to get his own back now that no one was listening to him.

The other man's face was deadly earnest and his eyes blazed angrily. "You had to be there to understand," he snapped, "and then you wouldn't be so swift to disbelieve."

"Tell them about how you found old Fowler, Bram," another member of the group prompted. He looked a nervous individual; his face was white and his eyes wide with superstitious fear.

Bram grimaced. "It's a sight that will haunt me the rest of my days," he replied sadly, shaking his head as though to rid himself of the memory. "His look — such a fearful look that I am surprised I am still a sane man for having seen it. There was blood everywhere, and someone or something had ripped his heart from his chest."

"I have heard tell," said another wisely, "that demons take the victim's heart for the heart contains the soul!"

"That would explain the fearful expression on old Fowler's face," Bram agreed. "For when the old man died his final view was that of Hell itself." His statement left his audience in an uncomfortable silence.

"Old wives tale!" a voice loudly proclaimed from behind the group. All eyes turned towards a tall, gregarious young man who gave them a mischievous lop-sided grin as he casually leant against a chair; a large mug of ale held lopsided in his fist.

"From what I hear, Fowler was an old man," the youth continued. "By all accounts he was as fat as one of his sows, and just as stupid." Taking a swallow of ale he eyed the others through narrowed slits. "His time was due — nothing more, nothing less. And, if you want my opinion, it was nothing more mysterious than a heart attack that killed him," he said gesturing about the room with his mug and wetting several people with its contents. "And," he continued loudly, having seen the filthy looks he was receiving from those that he had soaked, "if I had died from heart failure then my face would be twisted into an ugly grimace. No doubt there would be a horrible smell as well," he finished smugly.

Several laughed at this, although the laughter was somewhat forced for his story did not explain how Fowler's chest had become ripped open; nobody really believed that a wild animal had done that to him.

"Farlan, your face couldn't get any uglier!" shouted back one of the revellers. More laughter followed and this time it was heartier. It appeared that demons were for dark unlit places and not for the brightly lit "Thirst and Last."

Kaplyn shivered, remembering his night alone in the wild. That experience had left its mark on him and perhaps for that reason he was more prepared to believe the story. Others too clearly believed it for Farlan was given more space. Even if you did not believe in demons, it appeared that it was not wise to tempt providence.

"Do you believe in demons?" Lars asked.

31

Kaplyn shrugged. "No, I suppose not," he decided eventually.

Lars shook his head. "My people believe in evil giants," he said. "We believe that one-day, at the end of the world, they will attack Fallar-Ell, the home of the gods. Since coming to this land I have heard of little else other than demons."

Kaplyn nodded. "It's nothing more than folklore," he answered. "People believe in demons because our ancestors used to."

"There's logic in that," Lars replied. "But what do you think persuaded your ancestors to believe in demons?"

That was a profound question to which Kaplyn did not have an answer. In silence the two men ate, grateful at least for the company of others.

Chapter 5

The Spring Fair

The following morning, patches of light mist hugged the ground. The sky itself was cloudless and the sun felt pleasantly warm on Kaplyn's back as they made their way towards the competition arenas. By his side, Lars groaned loudly, putting his hand to his forehead.

"What's the matter?" Kaplyn asked. He could guess, but was feeling devilish.

"Too much ale," Lars moaned. He looked pale and his eyes were red rimmed. Kaplyn shook his head, grinning.

They came to a large field filled with tents whose apexes sported bright coloured pennants. Even though it was early there was a buzz of voices, occasionally interrupted by shouts of exultation from spectators.

Kaplyn was nervous, but the archery was not until later. He considered himself a good shot and fancied his chances of winning. In the meantime, he followed Lars to the wrestling arena. A long-faced official with pious eyes took Lars' entry fee, which he tossed with a loud clatter into a metal pot beneath the table by his side. Lars offered Kaplyn a brave smile as he went to join the other contestants to await their bouts.

A barrel-chested referee with wild unkempt hair and an even wilder look in his eyes bullied the men into a line.

"Stand straight," he grouched, standing before the men like a drill instructor. "When I touch your shoulder and say a number, then remember it. One's will fight two's."

He walked down the line touching each man's shoulder and saying either one or two. "Right, pair up. There are five arenas. Off you go and good luck."

The men turned, looking somewhat bemused until other referees took charge.

Kaplyn followed Lars and five other men. Their referee started the fight and, much to Kaplyn's surprise, Lars managed to win the first two bouts without any problems. He was surprisingly agile and clearly knew some clever holds. The third fight proved more difficult. Lars' opponent was about his size, but it soon became clear that he knew little about wrestling and was simply using his weight and height. Lars finished the fight with a double arm lock that, no matter how hard he squirmed, his opponent could not break. He yelped for a submission and the referee signalled that the fight was over.

There followed a short break while Lars awaited his next challenger who, as yet, had not finished his fight in one of the other arenas. Lars sat on the grass, taking time to recover. Then a tall gangly individual swaggered into the ring, oozing an air of confidence. Looking down his long nose at Lars, his lip curled in a sneer. Most contestants wore similar apparel, vests and tight trousers, so their opponents did not have anything to grip. Lars' vest did nothing to conceal his over large paunch.

The fight started and Lars circled his opponent who abruptly leapt towards the bigger man and delivered a hefty blow with his elbow to Lars' chin before stepping back. The crack from the contact was audible and a roar went up from the crowd. Someone jostled Kaplyn and he nearly lost his balance, having to grab the rope separating contestants and spectators, for support. Kaplyn glanced over his shoulder and gagged on the smell of stale breath.

"Sorry," grinned a man leaning on his shoulder and almost immediately Kaplyn was shoved again as the man became excited a second time. "Go on, Remus. Hit the lump of lard."

Lars was holding his chin and was glaring furiously at his opponent who was circling, trying to get behind him.

"Hit him again, Remus," shouted the man behind Kaplyn.

Without warning, the lighter man stepped in, delivered a blow to Lars' chin with his fist and stepped nimbly back. Lars turned to catch him but the other man kicked out against Lars' knee and again spun away.

Lars seemed to be moving very slowly against the lighter man and Kaplyn thought he could not last much longer. Already his nose was bleeding and he had a distinct limp. His opponent was clearly enjoying himself and he skipped back and forth in front of Lars.

"That's my boy," shouted the chap behind Kaplyn, and others in the crowd shouted encouragement. The jostling and the loud voice in his ear was annoying Kaplyn. Pushing back against the supporter he cast him a withering look that seemed to do the trick. The other man raised his hands apologetically and stepped back a few inches.

Twice more a fist flashed out. Lars almost looked to be standing still. Then suddenly, with no warning, Lars had caught his opponent's arm, spun and ducked under the arm, turning it harshly up the other man's back. His opponent's face dropped and he tried to stand on tiptoes but Lars forced the arm higher until Kaplyn fancied he heard the joint pop.

"Ouch," shouted the man behind Kaplyn. "That must have hurt."

Kaplyn afforded himself a smile at the other man's misfortune as the referee leapt in to stop the fight. Lars' rival dropped like a sack of potatoes and rolled on the ground clutching his arm. The referee raised Lars' arm, signalling that he had won.

Amazingly, the next bout was the final. Kaplyn pushed his way through a sizeable crowd, apologising as he went for treading on toes or having to be too forceful to gain passage. The nearest tout was a short, bad-tempered looking individual with a large hook shaped nose.

"Five silver *calder* on Lars to win," Kaplyn shouted above the din. The tout snatched the money, which swiftly disappeared into a large pocket. He scribbled something on a slip of paper and thrust it into Kaplyn's hand. He was already serving the next person and Kaplyn pushed his way from the queue while trying to decipher the unintelligible script on the discoloured paper.

If Kaplyn had known how Lars felt he might have refrained from betting. When Kaplyn arrived back at the arena Lars was standing by the ropes, doubled over with his hands on his knees. His face was pale and his knees were shaking. "Too much beer, Kaplyn." Loudly, he belched and grinned.

"He looks a bit more of a challenge," Lars said nodding to the opposite side of the arena. A broad-chested man glared disdainfully at Lars. He was of equal size, broad across the chest with upper arms almost as thick as his thighs. His nose looked liked it had been used to straighten a wall.

The referee who initially paired the fighters came into the ring. The crowd fell silent.

"In the final," the referee bellowed, "on my right hand side, needing no introduction, Darl from Pendrat,"

"Darl for champion," someone shouted.

"We're with you, big man," shouted another.

"And on my left is Lars," the referee continued above other shouts of support for Darl. "As you can see Lars is not from Allund but we don't want to hold that against him."

"Break his leg, Darl" someone shouted.

Kaplyn grimaced. By the sounds of the support, Lars was in trouble whether he won or lost.

"Let's have a clean fight. Start!" said the referee and dozens of voices shouted encouragement.

Warily Lars circled his opponent.

"Come on big man," taunted Darl. He waved a hand beckoning Lars and trying to encourage the other man to attack.

Lars shook his head. Kaplyn wondered if he was still trying to recover his breath.

A flicker in Darl's shoulders caused Lars to step aside, but the Allunder did not attack. He merely sneered at the other man's caution.

Then, with a loud bellow, Darl ran at Lars, catching his outstretched arms and forcing them back. The two men stood, toe to toe, each pushing with all of his might. Lars ducked and twisted at the same time, crossing Darl's wrists as he did so.

The Allunder also twisted, trying to prevent his elbow from locking, and at the same time, he brought his booted foot down hard on the side of Lars' knee. Lars instinctively buckled, releasing his arm lock and saving his knee from serious damage. Kaplyn grimaced, but Lars swiftly recovered as he swung his elbow up hard, catching the other man under the chin, forcing him back. As Darl retreated, blood sprang from the corner of his mouth and he scowled angrily at Lars for the affront.

"Finish him, Darl!" someone in the crowd urged. The big man took this as his cue and launched himself at Lars a second time.

The collision nearly knocked Lars from his feet. He grabbed Darl's arms, preventing him from encircling his waist.

To the crowd the fight looked like a stalemate as the two men strained. Slowly, however Lars forced Darl's arms back and the Allunder realised that he was in trouble. In desperation, he dropped to one knee and pivoted, throwing Lars' body weight over his shoulder.

He tried to catch Lars off balance, but Lars allowed himself to fall forward, maintaining a firm grip on the other man's wrist. With a fluid grace he somersaulted across the other man's shoulder, wrenching his opponent's arm as he landed.

Darl cried out in pain and nursed the injured limb. Lars rolled away from his opponent and quickly rose to a crouch, waiting for Darl's counter-attack. The other man was still recovering and seeing Lars waiting for him seemed only to infuriate him further.

Screaming with rage he ran at his opponent and kicked high, aiming at Lars' head, but Lars neatly caught his heel and ducked under the ill-timed blow. He in turn kicked out at Darl's standing leg while retaining his grip on the other, causing the big man to go down in an untidy heap with Lars on top of him.

Lars was panting from the exertion and did not look like a champion wrestler. "*Karlam*, aid me!" he bellowed.

Darl however was face down and couldn't see the look of pain the exertion cost Lars. Kaplyn grimaced; Lars was winning but marginally.

Straining, Lars forced Darl's left leg behind his right knee and then folded his right leg, trapping his left. Darl screamed.

"I submit!" he bellowed.

The referee leapt in and slapped Lars on the shoulder. "Fight's over. Let go! *Now!* Before you break his leg."

The crowd howled.

"Fix," someone shouted. "Darl, you've cost me a week's wages!" cried another.

Kaplyn did not wait to congratulate Lars but sought out the tout he had seen earlier, before the other man could escape. Kaplyn grinned, enjoying the tout's discomfort as he claimed his winnings.

"Not sure I should pay out," the tout muttered.

"Why?" Kaplyn growled.

The other man grimaced. "Well that Lars was not from these parts. He could be professional."

"You were happy to take my money, so pay up," Kaplyn countered, giving the tout an ominous look. It worked; the tout counted out a handful of silver *calder*. Counting it, Kaplyn made his way through the crowd towards Lars who was still sitting on the ground, gasping.

Kaplyn smiled down. "Well done! It was a good fight," he acknowledged, crouching down.

Lars nodded, but said nothing between loud gasps for air. Kaplyn waited patiently for the big man to recover.

"*By Slathor*! That was hell," he managed finally, groaning as he did so and gripping the grass in pain.

Kaplyn grinned at his discomfort. "Who is Slathor?" he asked.

Lars forced a smile. "He is one of my gods. We have many."

"And Karlam?"

"God of war," Lars managed.

When Lars was finally ready, Kaplyn helped him to his feet.

"If I had known that you Allunds liked to fight, I'd have found another country to be shipwrecked in. Five fights! It's too much, there has to be an easier way to earn a living."

Lars shook his head as he started slowly towards the referee who was coming towards the pair with the big man's winnings. "How much did you bet on yourself?" Kaplyn asked.

Lars paled, shaking his head. "I didn't save enough; the ale was too good. Still I'll be able to sleep content tonight as at least now I can afford a room and lodgings," he said holding the prize purse, clearly enjoying the weight of the coin.

Kaplyn led them towards the archery range. There were more people now and the pavilions created funnel points, squeezing folk together. Someone bumped into Kaplyn and inadvertently his gaze fell upon a small, grey haired old woman standing a few yards away. Claws, disfigured by arthritis, clutched a shawl yellowed with age about her throat. She glared about the crowd, looking down a long thin nose speckled in warts.

When her gaze met his, her thin lips parted, her eyes widened and to Kaplyn the world seemed to slow. He tried to look away but the damage was done.

Her arm came up and she pointed at him. He tried to step backwards but the press of bodies trapped him. At first, he assumed she had recognised him and would alert the palace guard when they came this way, but that was unlikely he realised almost as soon as the thought popped into his head. Lars stood by his side and behind them voices murmured.

"Old Kate's going to make a prediction," Kaplyn heard someone say.

As if on cue the old woman spoke in a low gravely voice, while still pointing directly at Kaplyn. "I *see* you." Her gaze seemed to penetrate Kaplyn's very soul.

People stopped to listen and Kaplyn found himself at the centre of a ring of people. A hush fell upon the crowd.

"You would destroy us all!" she muttered, shaking her head. "The prophecy haunts you; beware lest you set in motion events that cannot be stopped. The Eldric are lost, never to be found."

"I see also the ghost by your side. Oh, he is not there yet — but he will be! I know his shape and his desire, and the gleam in his eye. Death he will bring to us all. You would summon dragons: a living plague to ravage the world."

Around Kaplyn the crowd murmured and people cast him troubled looks.

"Superstition," Kaplyn said, albeit softly. He was shaking and his brain refused to function.

"Kate often sees things," a man behind Kaplyn said.

"Aye," said another. "Like the flood last year when the cattle drowned."

"*Superstition* is it!" Kate answered. "One day you will see the man I speak of. Think then upon my words. Beware the dragons, and befriend them to your cost."

Kaplyn turned his back on the woman and forced himself into the crowd. Kate had fallen silent and it was clear that there was no more entertainment, so the mob parted to let him past. Some people followed as though expecting Kate's premonition to come true immediately. Kaplyn looked over his shoulder; fortunately Kate wasn't there.

The thought of the archery competition was furthermost from Kaplyn's mind and instead he sought a quiet place behind a large tent where he sat down upon the ground. Lars joined him. Several people that had followed looked on from a distance but soon lost interest and went on their way.

"What was that about?" Lars asked.

"An old fraud, trying to enhance her reputation as a witch!" Kaplyn suggested, trembling and clearly shaken by the event.

"Dragons, though," Lars said.

"There are *no* dragons. She was deranged, probably *mad*," he complained.

Lars looked unconvinced. "Who are the Eldric?"

"Who *were* the Eldric," Kaplyn corrected. "They came over the sea several hundred years ago. For a while they brought peace and even stopped some of the wars."

"How did they accomplish that?" Lars asked.

"I can see that I need to explain our history," Kaplyn looked up to the sky. His heart was slowing and talking was helping to calm him.
"Trosgarth is a nation to the north. In the past they were constantly waging war with just about everyone. That was a time of petty kingdoms. When the Eldric arrived, they were much more advanced both culturally and militarily. They landed here in Allund," Kaplyn laughed. "That nearly started a war, but common sense prevailed and it was a good thing too. The balance of power shifted in favour of the Southern Kingdoms. Then I suppose that people became more interested in trade than fighting."

"What happened next?" Lars asked.

"Peace lasted for many years but always Trosgarth resented the Eldric. Their weapons were far superior to anyone else's; some were even supposed to have been magical. The peace ended when an Eldric Lord called Drachar sided with Trosgarth. Why he chose to do so, no one knows. The Eldric were reputedly powerful sorcerers and Drachar the most powerful of all. He was able to summon the most potent demons."

A roar from a nearby crowd interrupted Kaplyn. Overhead a few birds raced from the din, their black forms in stark contrast to the white clouds that now filled the sky.

"Do you want to find the archery?" Lars asked.

Kaplyn shook his head. "Not now. It's probably too late judging by the noise from the crowd. I'm happy to sit here for a while."

"What happened to Drachar?" Lars asked. His eyes were wide. "Did he summon demons?"

Again, Kaplyn nodded. "There was a war later called the Krell Wars."

"I've heard of krell. But what are they?"

"I don't know. I've never seen one but they are meant to be half-demon, half-human. Drachar united the krell tribes and I think that was why Trosgarth sided with him. The war was decided at the battle of DrummondCal. The Eldric, leading an army from the Southern Kingdoms, defeated Drachar, using sorcerers and summoning demons of their own. It was a devastating battle by all accounts.

"Drachar was killed but some say that his ghost was too powerful to be banished and it remained, seeking to rise again in the distant future."

"And that's the basis of the Prophecy the old woman spoke of?"

"Yes."

Lars shifted uncomfortably and his frown suggested he wanted to ask more.

"Let's find some food," Kaplyn suggested.

"My treat," Lars beamed back, patting his bulging purse. "What about the Prophecy first though?"

Kaplyn smiled. "The Prophecy is rather cryptic so don't expect to understand it." Kaplyn searched his memory before reciting it.

> *"When Tallin's Crown once more does shine,*
> *Drachar's shade will rise sublime,*
> *Three Princes Royal through time to sleep,*
> *An appointment with destiny —three Kings to keep,*
> *Trosgarth's arm across the land will reach,*
> *Of war and famine —- his army to teach,*
> *And one will stand to oppose his throne,*
> *A King resurrected in his mountain home,*
> *Of air, fire and water —he will be born,*

To aid the people —when all else is forlorn."

"I see what you mean about being cryptic. Any ideas what *Tallin's Crown* is?"

Kaplyn shook his head. "No idea."

"And the Eldric? What became of them?"

Kaplyn frowned, the other man was insatiable, but his curiosity was understandable. The Eldric had always fascinated Kaplyn. "No one knows. There's only ruins where their cities once stood. There are Eldric artefacts around, cooking utensils, the occasional sword and such, so there is no doubt they existed. But what became of them? It's said they disappeared after the Krell Wars."

"*Disappeared,*" Lars snorted. "An *entire race*! How can that be?"

"I know it sounds ludicrous," Kaplyn continued. "And there are many rumours about their disappearance. People talk about seeing Eldric ghosts on pilgrimages to this place and that."

"The old woman mentioned a ghost."

"Aye, some people believe in a Shaol, or a guardian spirit. They're supposed to watch over us, protecting and guiding us. I'm not sure if that is what she meant, but personally I still think she was deranged."

"She was certainly spooky. Her eyes were strange, I can't describe them. They seemed to stare inside you, if you know what I mean."

Kaplyn shuddered. He did know what Lars meant. "Come, let's get some food," he said rising.

Lars continued to question Kaplyn as they walked. "What do *you* think became of the Eldric?"

They crossed a relatively crowd-free area, aiming towards a tent from which came the smell of barbecued meat. Kaplyn's mouth watered. "I think they were ashamed of the destruction caused by one of their own kind. Thousands perished in the Krell Wars and to make matters worse it is said that a demon takes a person's soul when they die."

Lars grimaced. "That's horrible. But where did the Eldric go?"

"I've no idea," Kaplyn replied. They entered the tent and joined a queue of people. At the front, a diminutive plump woman was serving what looked like pork on a large slice of bread. Lars fell silent for a while. The two men arrived at the head of the queue and good to his word Lars paid.

They ate as they meandered between the tents. Kaplyn recognised a pennant flying over one particularly large tent. "Look," he said between mouthfuls, "that's where the karlot competition is being held. With any luck I may salvage something from today." Fate so far had been unkind to

41

Kaplyn, having lost his horse and nearly killed by outlaws. Things had to improve. Together the two men made their way over to the tent. Kaplyn gave the official his name and paid his entry fee.

Kaplyn played and won three games of karlot and quickly, much to his surprise, found himself in the final. In this round he was pitted against a thin faced Hullender whose eyes sparkled in anticipation.

Kaplyn guessed he was a merchant, judging by the rich cut of his clothing and numerous gold rings, which he twisted nervously. A hush descended over the watching crowd as they waited.

Kaplyn won the toss to start. Throughout the previous games, he had adopted standard openings. Now, facing his opponent in the final game, something prompted him to change tact. His opponent looked confused as Kaplyn slid the krell piece, in front of his kara-stone, forward two squares. Since there was a time limit he had to counter quickly and Kaplyn recognised his move as the dristal's gambit.

The pieces on the board represented mythical creatures and the dristal was a large bird of prey, which dwarves had ridden into battle in the final days of the Krell Wars. The move opened the opponent's defence by attacking the chanth, a demon of considerable power. Kaplyn ignored the threat and continued to build up an attack on his adversary's sorcerer. In the ensuing moves Kaplyn managed to keep one piece ahead of his rival. When an opening presented itself he confidently took his challenger's dwarf chieftain.

The Hullender, sensing victory slipping from his grasp, altered the pattern of play. Kaplyn found the sudden attack across the front of the board difficult to counter, but fortune was with him. The Hullender had left his kara-stone vulnerable and swiftly Kaplyn took the piece with a krell. He sat back in relief while a look of pain crossed the Hullender's face as he realised his fatal mistake. Finally, he smiled, admitting defeat and offering Kaplyn his hand. Kaplyn had won and his recompense was a far heavier purse than when he had arrived.

Chapter 6

Vastra

Kaplyn met with Lars later that evening in the tavern. They ordered meals and a large flagon of ale with two mugs. Lars initially looked green at the sight of the ale, but his colour soon returned after his first draft.

"Your health," he said, belching loudly and placing his mug firmly on the table.

Kaplyn looked startled. Half of its content was gone. "Your health," he replied, raising his mug and taking a cautious sip. It was a strong brew.

"At least I'm better at wrestling than sailing," Lars commented. His voice betrayed the hurt that he was obviously feeling.

"How did you become shipwrecked?" Kaplyn asked, sensing the other man wanted to talk.

Lars took another swallow of ale to wet his tongue. "Our voyage was between villages for trade," he said depositing the heavy flagon on the tabletop. "My father was the Glan-Can, which is chieftain, of our people. I was travelling with the crew to negotiate in the trade of our cargo."

"Glan-Can — is that like a prince?" Kaplyn asked.

"I'd never though of it like that, but I suppose you are correct. We don't have kingdoms and my father's land was quite extensive."

Kaplyn hid a smile behind his hand; the coincidence that both he and Lars were royalty was too much.

"Anyway, the distance was not great, barely a few miles along the coast and we had done this trip dozens of times before. It was usually safe enough and we sailed in sight of the coast so there was little chance of becoming lost." He took a deeper drink of ale and Kaplyn waited patiently for the big man to continue. Lars put his mug down and wiped his beard, signalling to the landlord for more.

43

"This time though a strong wind followed us and it soon became a storm, forcing us farther out to sea." His eyes looked distant and Kaplyn realised that the tale was painful. "The storm seemed to have a mind of its own and whichever way we turned it followed. Never before had I seen such waves. They towered over us, drenching the planking and sweeping two men overboard. Then, as suddenly as it had started, it ceased.

"It was unnatural. Behind us was a wall of black clouds, reaching high into the heavens. From within this, we could hear the loud booming of waves as they danced to the storm's frenzied tune. And yet, about us, the sea was as calm as a village pond."

The landlord appeared through the crowd and set a fresh flagon down, slopping the contents messily on the table. As swiftly as he came he went, leaving Lars to continue his story. Kaplyn topped up their mugs.

"Suddenly a shape surfaced yards from the gunwale. What manner of sea beast it was I did not know but it was a fearful sight. Its head towered over us on a long thin neck and I will never forget the fear I experienced as its eyes watched us running about the deck, like headless chickens.

"Slowly the monster dipped gently beneath the sea, as if its curiosity was satisfied and it was off to find its supper. The crew breathed a sigh of relief, hoping beyond hope that it had swum away and left us in peace. Quickly we ran to put up the sails and escape before the storm engulfed us. We were too late though; the sea erupted as the beast reared high out of the water, landing with a crash on the gunwale." Lars brought a giant hand down hard on the table top with a loud slap as if simulating the sea monster's attack. Several of the tavern's occupants jumped with shock and turned around to see what the commotion was.

Lars ignored them and continued with his story. "The wooden timbers cracked like dry twigs and the sheer weight of the creature capsized us. I dived over the rails just as the ship went down. When I surfaced I could hear the others screaming in terror, as the beast hunted them down. Then the gale hit once more.

"I grabbed on to wreckage and clung on for all I was worth, calling to Harlathan, the god of the sea, to save me. It was a fearful ride; giant waves tossed me like a leaf in a storm," Lars paused to take a drink.

"Go on. What happened next?" Kaplyn asked, enthralled.

"I don't know how long the storm lasted, but later the sea jettisoned me onto a sandy beach. For hours I lay there, trying to convince my stomach that the world was finally still.

"Since then I've been wandering around doing odd jobs, trying to get by," he looked thoughtful. "That would be nearly a year ago. I miss my wife and son, but deep down I know I'll never see them again."

Kaplyn wanted to offer him a token of comfort, but words were not enough. He needn't have worried though; Lars took a long draught of ale and grinned at the now empty glass. "Come." he said. "Our purses are full and the evening is young. Landlord!" he shouted above the noise of the crowd. "Where is that man?"

Kaplyn looked at his own ale and grimaced. He felt, rather than saw, a shadow. Swiftly he looked up and was startled to see a man standing by his side, looking down at him. The stranger must have been light-footed to get so close without Kaplyn realising.

"May I join you?" he asked, indicating the spare seat beside them.

The stranger's face was long and thin and his features fine, reminding Kaplyn of an alabaster sculpture that he had once seen. His hair was oily, raven black and cut short, accentuating a high forehead. He might have been considered handsome except for his brooding countenance. Even his clothes were sombre, although his fleece-lined doublet and short riding cloak looked expensive. Kaplyn doubted that he lacked money.

"I am Vastra," he said in a way that seemed to imply it was of some importance, "and I have a proposition for you."

Kaplyn looked to Lars, but he merely shrugged.

"Take a seat," Kaplyn finally offered, indicating the empty chair.

Vastra lowered himself as though standing was wearisome. "I'm looking for hired help. I seek an artefact and need an escort and then help in its recovery," Vastra continued.

"Recover or steal?" Lars asked.

"The work is honest. I assure you," Vastra replied tersely.

Lars looked puzzled. "Why choose us?" It was the question uppermost in Kaplyn's mind.

"I saw you both competing in the games. You both won events and I think you would be well suited to the task I have in mind," Vastra replied.

"Where are you going and what do you seek?" Kaplyn asked.

"I am travelling to Tanel," he announced boldly.

"Tanel? It's an Eldric city. It is nothing more than ruins."

Vastra nodded, "It is. I am a scholar and have been led to believe that there may be something of interest there."

Kaplyn was curious. "And what might that be?"

"Once you have decided whether to accompany me, I shall tell you more."

Kaplyn was thinking of returning home, maybe by a roundabout route to visit an old friend. Tanel was not too far out of his way though and it might prove to be an interesting diversion. Company would also be welcome on the long ride, especially after his night alone in the wild. He was uncertain, however, and did not want to commit himself until he knew more.

"You will be well paid," Vastra assured them, seeing their reluctance. "Ten *calder* to escort me to Tanel and two gold pieces if you are successful in retrieving the object."

Kaplyn was impressed; it was a considerable sum. "Tomorrow," he announced finally, having decided to be cautious. "We will decide then. Meet us first thing in the morning and we will let you know our decision."

A smile touched Vastra's lips and he bowed fractionally before rising from the table and leaving through the press of bodies.

"A strange man," Lars commented watching Vastra's retreating form.

Kaplyn shivered, surprised by the effect the stranger appeared to have on him; it was as if his soul had touched something dark and cold.

Kaplyn awoke early, cold and disorientated by his strange surroundings. The last thing he remembered was opening the window to let in the fresh night air, which had been foolhardy for his blanket had fallen off in the night, leaving him shivering. Lars was definitely a bad influence and he tried to remember how much he had drunk before retiring.

Deciding it was best not dwelling on the matter he hurriedly arose causing his head to spin. Blinking in confusion he waited for a moment for his head to clear. With a sinking heart he realised that the clothes, strewn in disarray around the room, were not how he had left them the previous night.

His brow beetled as he looked about at the mess and a sickening realisation dawned. Someone had robbed him. He grabbed his clothes, searching them. His money and all of his winnings were gone. In despair, he sat forlornly on his small bed.

His sword still rested close to his bed where he had left it and that was a blessing at least. It alone was worth a considerable sum and he would have been devastated to return home without it. He cursed under his breath and then more loudly, jumping to his feet and grabbing his shirt. Throwing it on, the threads cracked. He would find the landlord and give him a piece of his mind. Never before had he been robbed and someone had to be held to account.

Descending the tight stairs he pulled his jerkin on, noting the torn lining where he had hidden the coins in case of emergency. Again he cursed. Shouting for the landlord he stormed into the tavern. The proprietor appeared almost at once, bumping into a chair in his haste.

"I have been robbed!" Kaplyn stated bitterly. "Someone has taken my money," he continued.

The landlord looked bewildered, "Slow down, sir. Sit, and tell me what has happened."

Kaplyn ignored him. "Somebody came into my room late last night and stole my money, including my winnings."

The other man looked nonplussed; he held out his arms in a helpless manner and started to stammer a response. "Are you certain? Could you have misplaced your purse?" he asked defensively.

Kaplyn scowled. "The money has gone!"

The landlord stroked his chubby chin nervously. "How are you going to pay your bill?" he asked suspiciously.

Kaplyn was stunned. "How dare you! I have been robbed while under the protection of your roof. There is no lock on my bedroom door and you do not even employ a night watchman."

"This is a simple establishment, sir," The landlord countered. "We cannot afford such precautions. Besides, no one has ever been robbed here before."

Kaplyn realised that they were not alone; a figure was sitting in an alcove, partially hidden by the shadows. He recognised Vastra who leaned forward with an amused expression.

A sudden commotion caused Kaplyn to turn as Lars stormed into the room, wearing a look of thunder. His face was red with suppressed rage. "My money has gone," he stated bluntly. Kaplyn could see the pain reflected in his eyes; his winnings had meant a great deal to him.

Kaplyn turned to the landlord who was now pale and sweating profusely.

"You will have to pay for your rooms immediately!" he insisted. His eyes kept darting towards the door as though he was hoping for the intervention of the town guard.

"We have no money! It's all been taken!" Kaplyn hissed.

"Then you'll have to pay with something else," the landlord continued hopefully, his eyes straying to Kaplyn's sword.

Seeing the direction of his gaze Kaplyn felt his anger rising. However, Vastra interrupted before he could reply. "I might be able to help," he suggested softly, and the group's attention focused on him. "How much do these gentlemen owe?"

This was obviously much more promising and the landlord brightened visibly. "Four *calder* and twelve *tell*," he declared after a pause and much hand wringing.

Vastra opened his purse and placed coins on the table, which the landlord scooped up, muttering his thanks before darting away.

"There was no need to pay him," Kaplyn argued, turning to confront Vastra. "It's partly his fault the burglar got into my room."

"Did they take everything?" Vastra asked.

"Yes!" Kaplyn replied thinking about the hidden coins.

"It would appear that we are in your debt," Lars stated through gritted teeth.

"I'll replace your money, and add to it if you will accompany me. The offer I made last night still stands."

"I will go, if what you want is reasonable," Lars sounded defeated.

Kaplyn was in a quandary. Never before had he been penniless and he was still coming to terms with the situation. "Tell us what you want," he said, realising he had no option. His brothers would have laughed and walked away, but Kaplyn's conscience would not let him do that.

"Sit down," Vastra invited. They complied, although Kaplyn disliked being told what to do.

"I am a sorcerer," Vastra confided in them, much to their surprise. "There is an artefact in Tanel which I wish to find."

"A wizard?" Kaplyn asked uncertainly.

"A sorcerer," Vastra corrected. Something in his tone suggested that the difference was important.

"I have seen many magicians in the past," Kaplyn replied, in no mood to pander to Vastra's ego. "Can you prove that you are what you claim?"

"I do not perform tricks, if that is what you are asking," Vastra said with menace in his voice. His eyes glittered with suppressed rage. "You will be paid for your work," he reminded them. The mention of money also reminded them of their debt.

"Tanel is a ruin!" Kaplyn continued, taken aback by Vastra's anger. "There is nothing there, except stones."

"Then you will be well paid just to escort me," Vastra replied sighing. "It is little more than a few days ride, and then you will be rich."

"What is it you seek?" Kaplyn asked.

"It's a gold pendant about the size of my hand," Vastra said. "On one side is a map and on the other Eldric writing."

"How much is it worth?" Lars asked.

"It is priceless," Vastra said simply, although his eyes gleamed as he spoke. "Of course it is only of value to the right person and I am offering you a rich reward for your help," he continued, making it clear that it was worthless to anyone else but him; clearly, his trust only went so far.

"Why is it that no one else is seeking it, if it is so valuable?" Kaplyn asked suspiciously.

"Only a few people can unlock its whereabouts and, even if its location were known, its recovery would be difficult." Vastra paused as if considering how much to tell them. "There is an element of risk," he continued. "I have watched you both during the games and you seem to be capable men."

There was a moment's silence. "How do we know that you have the money?" Kaplyn asked.

Vastra unhooked a pouch from within the folds of his jacket; it was evidently full and clearly heavy. Vastra opened it and removed twenty silver *calder* and four gold coins. The purse remained bulging. Lars cast Kaplyn a glance at the sight of such wealth.

"Be warned," Vastra said suddenly, returning the coins to the purse. "I am quite capable of defending myself." The purse quickly disappeared within his jacket. "I only warn you in case you decide that you like the look of my purse rather than the work I offer."

"I'm no *thief*, if that is what you are inferring!" Kaplyn snapped irritably.

"If you are an honest man, which I believe you are, then there is no insult intended."

Vastra's apology, thin though it was, mollified Kaplyn.

"I'll meet you outside as soon as you are ready. I already have supplies and horses," Vastra said, rising.

"It looks as though our fortunes have changed once again," Lars commented.

"Aye, but perhaps not for the better," Kaplyn replied.

"Is it possible that Vastra had something to do with the theft?"

Kaplyn had not considered that possibility and frowned deeply. "No. I am assuming the thief climbed through the window. Otherwise he would have to have gone through the tavern and that is busy most the night, judging by the din. If that was the route the thief took, Vastra doesn't look capable and besides, I doubt he is *that* desperate to hire our help; there are plenty of others around." Kaplyn was seething but he was also intrigued to be going to Tanel.

"Come," he said. "We'd better not keep him waiting. I need to fetch my bow. I'll see you outside shortly."

True to his word Vastra was waiting outside. The boy, from the night they had arrived, was saddling three horses. Lars cast Kaplyn a sideways glance and grimaced at the prospect of more riding.

Vastra handed Lars a heavy double-handed sword. The big man eyed it suspiciously.

"There are many dangers on the road," Vastra explained. "I look to you two for my protection."

Lars buckled the sword about his broad waist but no matter how he tried to adjust it he looked ill suited to it. "I would have preferred an axe," he grumbled. Vastra ignored him and mounted.

Lars and Kaplyn also mounted and together the three men rode from the safety of the town. Once more the wild was calling, but as to their future...? Kaplyn was now at the mercy of someone else and he didn't like it at all.

Chapter 7

Shelter for the Night

They rode for the remainder of the day. It was a pleasant journey, at least for Kaplyn. Lars complained bitterly, sitting astride his horse as though expecting to fall off with every step.

Gradually evening claimed the land and shadows grew longer. Kaplyn felt anxious but didn't know why. There were no signs of dwellings and he certainly didn't want to spend a night outdoors. However, this was not the source of his growing discomfort.

Abruptly a lark flew overhead calling shrilly. The horses startled and crabbed across the path. Then Kaplyn understood what was worrying him. His horse was nervous and he was sensing that.

He glanced at the other two men and saw discomfort reflected on both their faces. "Do you feel it?" he asked.

"What?" Lars answered, although Kaplyn heard the strain in his voice.

"Kaplyn's correct, there is something not right this evening. We'd better hurry and hope to find shelter," Vastra answered. He spurred his mount on and they followed as best they could. Kaplyn grabbed Lars' reins and urged his own mount to canter. Glancing back, Lars was bouncing in his seat in an alarming manner, gritting his teeth in pain.

Cresting a rise, they were at last rewarded by the sight of a small settlement, although still some distance ahead. It was nothing more than several long low wooden buildings surrounded by a stout palisade, probably a farm Kaplyn realised.

By now the heavens were a mixture of fiery reds and burnished golds as the sun sank below the horizon, illuminating the underside of clouds, gathering in the darkening sky. By the time they reached the farm, apart from the skeletal silhouettes of trees, Kaplyn could barely see. He hoped the occupants would not refuse them entry for arriving so late. He halted them a respectable distance from the palisade. A thick briar bush grew in profusion

51

around its base, adding to the defences. The smell of wood smoke and cooking wafted towards them and Kaplyn's stomach growled in anticipation.

"Hello the farm," Kaplyn called, and in silence they waited for a reply.

A torch became visible between the posts, followed by voices. They watched the partially obscured flame dance as if by magic toward the wall, finally coming to a halt on top of the palisade.

In the torchlight a dark-haired man with a thick unkempt beard peered at them. His face stood out in stark contrast to the surrounding night as he raised his torch aloft. By his side several other figures joined him, many armed with longbows.

"We are seeking shelter for the night," Kaplyn called up.

The first figure raised his torch, looking at them between the posts as though having some difficulty in seeing them.

"How many are you?" he asked in a deep voice.

"Three," Kaplyn replied.

"Three?" the fellow questioned. "Come forward into the light so we can see you."

The man cursed the darkness as they walked their mounts forward until they were looking up at the farmer. His grey beard marked him older than Kaplyn had first thought.

"You're travelling late!" the farmer accused.

"We are returning from Pendrat and the games. This is the first farm we have seen this evening," Kaplyn explained.

"The games?"

Kaplyn had deliberately mentioned them, hoping their account of the games would be recompense for their food and lodgings.

"Take a torch," the farmer said, waiting for Kaplyn to come forward before dropping one to his outstretched hand. "Place it twenty paces back along the path." It was a wise precaution intended to see if anyone else lurked behind.

Kaplyn complied and returned to the other two as the gates swung inwards. Inside, a dozen men carrying an assortment of weapons and farm implements surrounded them. Behind them the gate thumped closed.

"You will have to excuse our precautions," the farmer said coming down a short flight of steps leading from the wall. "There's been talk of outlaws hereabouts."

"It's a dark night and we are only too glad to find shelter," Kaplyn said.

"You're welcome to spend the night in my house," the farmer replied. "Ralph, my youngest, will see to your horses."

A strapping man in his early twenties stepped forward and took their reins before leading the animals away.

The other farmers returned to their own homes, leaving the three travellers to follow the farmer who introduced himself as Callan; the seven men accompanying him were his sons and Callan introduced each in turn.

Callan's house was a long single storey timber building, crowned with a thick thatched roof. A tall stone chimney rose into the night sky, venting the cooking fires. The windows were small and thick; coarse materials covered the openings, keeping out the evening chill.

They ducked beneath a low door and stepped down into the room. The floor inside was lower than outside giving the room additional height, much to Lars' obvious relief.

Kaplyn entered last to discover a long table dominating the room. About it several women and numerous children were sitting, watching them with awe. The table was heavily laden with bowls of steaming food and a delicious aroma filled the room. Lars brightened at the sight of the food and his eyes widened further when he saw a large flagon of ale in prime position at the table's centre. Kaplyn felt he should nudge the bigger man to make him behave.

At that moment, extra chairs appeared followed by a round of introductions. In turn, Kaplyn introduced his group as the farmer's wife served the food. Callan asked where they were from. Kaplyn repeated the lie that he was formerly from Dundalk and he had worked in the palace guard. Questions rained down on him about the King and the royal family. As a simple soldier, he should know very little about them and he found the questions awkward.

He was glad when the focus of attention turned to Lars. The tale of his shipwreck overawed them and next, Kaplyn and Lars spoke about the games.

One of the farmer's daughters kept looking at Kaplyn and he tried to look elsewhere, only to find his attention wandering back to her good looks. To his embarrassment he found that she was still watching him. Cheeks reddening he hurriedly looked away. She was about his age and very pretty. Unfortunately, he could not remember her name amongst the rush of so many.

He suddenly realised that Callan was talking to them. Feeling foolish he listened to what he was saying.

"What about your quiet companion, did he also compete in the games?" Callan was asking.

Vastra shook his head, feigning not to reply.

Not wishing to offend their host Kaplyn spoke on his behalf. "Our companion is a wizard," he declared, hoping to lighten Vastra's mood. Instead he received a withering look and too late he realised his error.

The farmer's eyes widened. "A wizard?"

Vastra cast Kaplyn a sideways look. There followed an embarrassing silence before Vastra spoke. "Perhaps there is some task that I could help you with?" he offered, half-heartedly.

The farmer's eyes brightened considerably. "Aye, that there is. If we could be the first to get our crop to market we would get a higher price," he stated hopefully; Vastra nodded.

"I have a bull which has not yet sired an heir," he continued as though he could not believe his luck.

Vastra's nod this time was barely perceptible, his eyes locked on Kaplyn as though daring him to let the farmer continue. Under Vastra's glare, Kaplyn felt a cold shiver run down his spine.

"Well, it's getting late," Kaplyn interrupted, taking the hint. "We've been travelling since dawn and if you don't mind we had better get some sleep."

"I'm sorry," Callan replied. "I had no idea time had passed so quickly; it is rare that we have visitors. We don't have spare beds, but you are more than welcome to sleep in Ralph's room. He can move in with one of his brothers."

Kaplyn thanked Callan who stood up to escort them to their room. The family bid them goodnight and Kaplyn passed close to the girl whose good looks had attracted his eye. She smiled sweetly at him and he left the room with the imprint of her face and the scent of her hair indelibly stamped into his mind.

Ralph's room was tiny and a single pallet lay on the floor. Vastra immediately claimed it. For a moment, Kaplyn wanted to order him off the pallet, but he controlled his anger, settling instead with a dark look, but Vastra simply ignored him. Muttering Kaplyn removed his belt and sword, which he dropped on the floorboards with a thud before sitting to remove his boots. He lay down, trying to get comfortable.

Not being very tired he listened for a while to the noises of Callan's family moving about the other rooms. For a while he lay awake hoping that Callan's daughter might come to the room and together they could go somewhere private. The thought made it harder to sleep but after a while not even thinking about her could keep him awake and he drifted into a silent slumber.

Soon, the only noises about the farm were the chirruping of crickets and the occasional bleat from restless sheep housed within the stockade for the night. A lone sentry patrolled the tall stockade wall, taking measured strides along the narrow wooden walkway while waiting patiently for the rays of the sun to pronounce the dawn.

Kaplyn awoke abruptly, immediately at a loss as to where he was. He became aware of raised voices outside followed by a brief glow that danced across the ceiling. The plaster was old and crumbling and had formed odd lifelike shapes. He realised that somebody had carried a torch by the window. Now it was dark. Completely dark.

"Where am I?" he croaked, sitting up.

Lars muttered something unintelligible and sat up, knuckling sleep from his eyes.

"See to the sheep and make sure they're secure," someone said in a muffled voice.

"Right you are. You fetch my bow and I'll meet you around the front," came the reply.

Kaplyn remembered then, the farm and Callan. "Lars, something's going on. Where are my boots?" He groped round with his hands. Lars opened the door allowing a soft light, cast by the dying embers from the fire in the other room, to filter through.

"Are we getting up?" Lars asked, yawning and stretching. "It must be about midnight."

"You two can get up," said Vastra from the bed. "But don't expect me to." He turned over and pulled the blanket over his head.

Kaplyn glanced at Lars who shrugged. Kaplyn grinned, the more he knew about Vastra the less he liked him.

Outside, Kaplyn nearly bumped into a knot of people standing by the door. Other farmers surrounded Callan and his sons. Some were holding torches while others armed themselves with bows and arrows, much to Kaplyn's consternation. Somewhere beyond the stockade an eerie howl filled the air. Immediately another howl followed, but closer.

"Wolves," Callan explained looking towards the distant sound.

Kaplyn frowned. "Why are you concerned? The stockade will keep them out surely?"

"This howling has being going on for some while and the volume, suggests an uncommonly large pack. We're manning the walls as a precaution." Callan replied, stringing his longbow, placing one end against his foot and bending it using both hands. His wife handed him a quiver of arrows. "Thanks," he acknowledged.

Kaplyn thought he sounded nervous. "Where are our horses? I have a bow."

"I'll fetch it," Ralph volunteered from behind his father.

"I'll come with you and get my sword," Lars said. Both men left and returned shortly. Ralph handed Kaplyn his bow and a quiver of arrows.

"OK, if we're all ready? Let's go then," Callan said.

Kaplyn stumbled in the dark. About him the farm was a riot of different noises; sheep were bleating, dogs were barking and loud thuds came from the stables as the horses bumped against the wooden walls. Thunder crashed close by, and abruptly the noise from the animals escalated.

When they mounted the palisade steps the wolves' howling increased. Around Kaplyn, men muttered angrily.

"What are wolves doing down here this time of the year?" one fellow asked no one in particular. He held his torch over the stockade wall, trying to increase the range of its glow. All at once a grey shape slipped into view.

"Bloody animal," one man shouted above the general din. He rapidly bent his bow and nocked an arrow but the wolf was gone.

"Some of you hold the torches out," Callan suggested. "Get some boys up here," he called over his shoulder. "Give them torches."

Shortly some youths arrived. One lad passed by Kaplyn. He looked about twelve. His eyes darted about the adults and when someone handed him a torch he jumped in alarm. "Hold it out over the stockade," the man proffering the torch said. "Hold it high, so that the archers can see."

The lad nodded and stood beside Kaplyn. Kaplyn felt sorry for him. It was dark and cold and the boy had probably just left the comfort of his bed.

"A chilly night," he offered and the boy nodded, seeming incapable of speech.

"It'll be alright," Kaplyn tried to reassure him.

By now a pool of light illuminated a short distance from the stockade wall.

"Over there!" One man yelled. Immediately several arrows flew to the spot. However, the wolf had slipped back into the shadows.

"Damn, not even close," someone muttered.

"Another one!" Bows bent and arrows flew. Angry curses followed the wolf as it escaped.

Three more shapes ran from the darkness, sprinting for the palisade. From their position on top of the stockade, the farmers only caught glimpses of the wolves. Several bows sang and arrows struck the dirt about the racing forms. No wolves were hit and they were soon lost from view beneath them, hidden by the thick briar hedge.

"Blast and damn — missed." One chap cursed. "They're too fast."

The men leant over trying to see the wolves, but the palisade itself made it difficult to look down and the briar hedge concealed them. Below, they heard the frantic scratching of claws on wood.

"What the hell is going on?" Kaplyn heard. "Wolves don't attack farms."

"Tell them that," someone answered.

"They're demon lead," shouted another.

"Hold your tongue," Callan called. "I'll have no such talk, especially in front of the youngsters."

Several more shapes bolted from the darkness and scores of arrows thumped into the ground around the racing forms. Voices shouted warnings to others to prepare, but the wolves were difficult targets. With growing confidence, more ran from the darkness, racing towards the wall. Abruptly yelps filled the night air as arrows finally found targets.

"We would do better if we had something to stand on, so we could shoot down over the palisade, Callan," Kaplyn suggested.

The farmer nodded and shouted down to his wife to get as many people as she could to find boxes and stools.

"And boiling water," Kaplyn called as an after thought. "Where is Vastra?" Kaplyn muttered under his breath.

Lars shook his head. "Probably still in bed!"

Women arrived, each carrying a stool or box that the men used to step up to shoot down upon the briar. Cauldrons filled with boiling water followed and farmers tipped these over the wall and onto the briar. Several wolves broke cover and arrows swiftly brought these down.

Still more wolves came. The wolves' recklessness alarmed Kaplyn; even though bodies littered the ground, newly arriving wolves seemed undeterred. To make matters worse, the sound of splintering wood suggested some were close to breaking through.

Within the compound young children screamed hysterically. Most of their parents were busy on the wall and the few that remained within the compound struggled to keep control.

"I'm no help here," Lars said. "I'll go below."

Kaplyn barely nodded as he released another arrow, sending a shape stumbling head over heels. He glanced over his shoulder. The pandemonium below startled him; people were scurrying back and forth and smaller children were huddled together, crying.

Abruptly a scream rent the night air.

A wolf loped around the corner of a building, followed heartbeats later by a second. Both paused, teeth bared. Kaplyn saw a small boy standing alone, howling with fear. The wolves started to lope towards him, swiftly gathering speed.

"Lars!" Kaplyn screamed, pointing. "The boy!"

Lars turned and saw where Kaplyn was pointing. Bellowing, he sought to distract the animals as he sprinted towards the boy, his sword raised.

Lars arrived first. Bowling the boy out of the way his sword fell, cleaving the skull of the nearest wolf, which was in mid-leap. Even at a distance, Kaplyn heard the thud of the sword's contact. The wolf collapsed in a growing pool of blood just as the second wolf leapt at Lars who was struggling to free his sword from the downed wolf's skull.

"Look out!" Kaplyn yelled.

The wolf hit Lars, tumbling them both to the ground. For a moment neither moved; then Lars pushed the body off and stood up. An arrow protruded from the beast's side. Farther along the wall towards Kaplyn, Ralph lifted his bow and Lars acknowledged his help with a wave.

A woman ran to the boy, scooping him up and sprinting to a nearby building. Seeing this, men started to forsake the walls to protect their families.

Then a new and more terrifying howl carried on the still night air freezing Kaplyn's blood. This was different to the other howls, like that of a wolf, yet much more powerful — a portent of evil.

Callan turned to Kaplyn. "What *in the name of the Kalanth* was that?"

"*Werewolf*!" one of the men close to Kaplyn muttered. Others agreed and a murmur went around the defenders.

Kaplyn turned and found Vastra standing there. Overcoming his shock he asked, "A werewolf? Is that possible?"

Vastra shrugged. "I've never heard of werewolves except in tales."

"If you are a *wizard* then you should help!" Kaplyn said. His patience of the other man was wearing dangerously thin.

Vastra scowled. "I'm a *sorcerer*, not a wizard. Whether I help or not is my decision, not yours. However, I *have* decided to help. Look to the torches, what do you see?"

Kaplyn frowned. "I don't understand"

"What colour are the flames of the torches closest to us?"

"Blue."

"And flames burn blue in the presence of a demon," Vastra returned.

"A demon! You are kidding?"

"Not a demon fully manifested in this world, but I suspect a wolf has been possessed. It's probably trying to seek a human host."

Kaplyn couldn't believe what he was hearing. Vastra shook his head as though he knew it was a waste of time trying to explain.

"Give me one of your arrows," Vastra said.

Kaplyn complied and using the tip of a small knife, Vastra scratched a rune on the arrowhead. Kaplyn frowned and the frown deepened when Vastra spat on it.

"The rune needs a water-elemental, otherwise it is just scratches on metal," Vastra explained. "If it is a demon, then the rune will cause it greater harm than the arrow ever could. Look to your front. Don't be alarmed for I will conjure a light. It won't last long so you will have to be quick to spot the possessed wolf."

Kaplyn turned to face the night, certain that Vastra was mad.

Vastra muttered something. A bright light flared, illuminating the ground before them, causing Kaplyn to jump in shock even though he had been warned. The glare made him squint while his mind reeled with the knowledge that he had just witnessed real magic.

To his front was a sea of writhing bodies. Hundreds of wolves filled his view. Round marble eyes stared back, reflecting the light, making the animals seem hellish.

"Look! There! Near the back of the pack!" Vastra said.

Kaplyn didn't know what to look for and then all at once he did. One wolf reared up amongst the bodies. It was unnatural. It tried to stand on hind legs as though human. Kaplyn drew back his bow, sighted and let loose the arrow without pausing.

By his side Vastra muttered something unintelligible, causing the arrow to flare in its flight like a shooting star. A deep-throated cry filled the air as the wolf reared backwards, falling amongst the others.

Abruptly the light failed and night returned. Kaplyn retained an image of the wolf in his mind and the look of baleful hatred on its face horrified him. Never before had he encountered such a thing. He now had an inkling why his people were so superstitious. If Vastra was correct and this was a *possession,* then what would a full fledged demon be like?

All around Kaplyn was a stunned silence; abruptly the wolves in the briar hedge broke cover, running away from the farm. Howls filled the air, but these seemed more normal and there was even a note of fear.

Kaplyn turned to talk to Vastra but he was gone; it was almost as if he had never been there. Kaplyn shivered. Soon he was alone and there was no sense remaining. Within the stockade the people remained busy and Kaplyn

59

avoided them as he made his way back to his room. Vastra was either asleep or feigning it and Kaplyn was too stunned to seek answers, or even to wait for Lars. All at once he felt a dreadful lethargy. Throwing himself onto the floor and kicking off his boots, he was asleep in seconds.

The morning came much too quickly. Sunlight streamed through the chinks in the fabric covering the window. Kaplyn and Lars awoke to find Vastra lying on the pallet, staring at the ceiling. Together the three men rose and returned to the main hall where they found Callan and his wife waiting to serve them breakfast.

"Thank you for last night," Callan said. "We killed upwards of thirty wolves. I had my men burn the bodies in case the sheep get wind of their stench."

"Did they find anything unusual?" Kaplyn asked, sitting down.

Callan shook his head and laughed, "You mean the mutterings about a werewolf? I think we let our imagination get the better of us. Your friend's light scared them off though. That was a fine piece of magic, if I may say so."

"Is that what happened? I wondered why the wolves turned tail, if you'll pardon the pun," Lars said. "They ran off because of the light? Well I suppose that makes sense. It scared me half to death. You should warn someone before doing that, Vastra."

Kaplyn convinced himself that he was being silly; it was a wolf he had shot and nothing more. He helped himself to bread, which he buttered and smothered in honey. He caught Vastra eyeing him but the other man looked away. Kaplyn felt foolish all at once. Had Vastra been teasing him about a possession?

"It's a strange portent though, the wolves attacking last night, especially coming so soon after the krell raid on Burland farm," Callan said.

Kaplyn was shocked. "I hadn't heard about any krell raids."

"Where have you been?" Callan asked. "Krell have been raiding the borders for several years now. And they are becoming bolder. Burland was a good day's march from the mountains and their route must have taken them close to Kinlin castle. They killed or captured everyone, and only three men survived. They were in the fields and returned to find no one left, other than charred corpses."

"I'm sorry," Kaplyn said, genuinely disturbed. "The news had not reached Dundalk."

Callan nodded. "The survivors live with us now and we are stronger for it. By the time the King's troops arrived the krell were long gone, but to give

60

the Hest Commander his due, he followed them as far as he dared. The mountains are a dangerous place and I cannot say I blame him for quitting. Perhaps if we were richer then the King would choose to protect us better."

Kaplyn frowned, fighting an inner rage. He did not like to hear accusations against his father, especially ones suggesting his people were being left defenceless. He vowed to speak with him upon his return.

Callan toyed with his food. "You would be welcome to stay with us," he said. "We could use your bow arm and your friend's strength." Callan smiled at Lars and then timidly looked at Vastra. "I admit that a wizard would be more than useful. What do you say?" he asked.

The offer touched Kaplyn. "I'm sorry," he replied, not wanting to hurt Callan's feelings. "Your offer is tempting, but unfortunately we have other commitments."

Callan smiled. "Never mind. You did us a good service last night. If you are ever in the area and need a place to stay then you would be more than welcome to stay with us. Callan suddenly brightened. "Now, if the offer still holds, then we would appreciate your friend's help with the corn, and there is my bull."

At the edge of a large field a small crowd gathered, waiting to see Vastra cast his spell. Rumour had swiftly spread that Vastra was responsible for the light the night before and anyone that wasn't otherwise busy crowded around, eager to see magic performed.

Vastra glowered at Kaplyn before crouching down to study the tiny green shoots poking above the rich soil. Kaplyn smiled. That he had riled Vastra was a small victory. He grinned across at Lars but the big man was intent on Vastra who was experimentally rubbing soil between his fingers. He looked satisfied and he started to trace a rune in the dry soil, muttering a few words as he did so. The crowd edged forward, trying to hear better and many looked disappointed as though they had expected the shoots to leap from the soil to a brazen fanfare.

Vastra merely arose and the crowd reverently parted to let him pass as he started towards the stockade.

"Is that it?" Callan asked uncertainly, watching Vastra's retreating form.

Kaplyn nodded, not knowing what to say; last night was the first time he had seen magic performed and he, too, was not sure of what to expect. The farmer beamed as together they followed the reticent sorcerer back to the stockade and his prize bull where a similar spell was to be cast.

61

Afterwards the crowd dispersed happily believing that the bull would now sire many heirs.

While they returned to Callan's house, Vastra remained silent, ignoring Callan's thanks. Kaplyn couldn't understand his behaviour, after all the farmers had been more than courteous. Even though it was simple fare, it was all they had to offer. At the house Ralph, holding their horses, awaited them. Some children came to watch them go and Kaplyn noticed the girl from the previous night, standing behind the small figures. He smiled awkwardly, pleased by her attention but feeling guilty about the thoughts he had harboured towards her the night before.

Once more Callan thanked them for their help, reminding them again that they were welcome to stay. Kaplyn looked at the girl and quickly returned his attention back to Callan as he was forced once more to reject his well-meant offer. A memory of Emma declaring that she was only a maid sprang to mind. What would his father think if he knew he was eyeing up a farmer's daughter? Kaplyn thanked Callan for his hospitality and together the three men mounted. As they set off Kaplyn glanced back and the girl waved to him. Smiling broadly Kaplyn returned her wave, all thoughts of his earlier guilt banished as he grinned broadly. It was going to be a beautiful day.

Kaplyn's mood changed as they rode. He kept thinking about Vastra's ill temper when dealing with Callan. A short way later and he could contain himself no longer. "Why were you rude to the farmers, Vastra?"

"Because they are clods," Vastra sneered. "They do nothing more than dig in the dirt, hoping for better days."

The outburst surprised Kaplyn and he signalled to Lars to keep him from voicing his own anger. For a while they rode in silence. Kaplyn frowned as he considered what might have upset the sour wizard. He was losing patience with the other man and was debating whether to leave him and to head for home. Emma would be pleased to see him and his brothers' would be green with envy when he told them about his recent adventures. Initially he had felt obliged to accompany Vastra, after he had paid for his lodgings, but now he felt that debt was paid, especially after helping to defend the farm against the wolves.

Just as Kaplyn was about to say something, Vastra broke the silence and this time Kaplyn detected a note of sadness. "I used to live in such a farm with my mother. I never knew my father and, until recently, I did not know who he was. Can you imagine a small boy growing up in such a close-knit community without a father? Bastard they called me." His face flushed red and his eyebrows beetled.

"I was later told that my father was a traveller who stayed the night, requesting lodgings — as we just did. He was with a group; rich men, possibly even nobles — or so many thought. The sight of their wealth no doubt turned my mother's head. I questioned others in the village and one man claimed to have seen a crest on their saddles. He drew it in the dirt and I copied it. Later I discovered it was the royal crest, no less!"

Kaplyn's heart lurched, he had a terrible premonition of what was to come. A crow rose from the bushes to their side and cawed shrilly into the air as though voicing its own anger.

Vastra's eyes blazed with suppressed rage. His eyes flickered briefly to the crow as he composed himself before continuing. "Some years later I found out who my father was.

He seemed to be waiting for them to ask whom, but neither did.

"It was the King!" Vastra announced.

Kaplyn's breath caught and he stared at Vastra, not wanting to hear any more.

"He was in his early forties then, but there was no mistake," Vastra continued.

Kaplyn was stunned. His heart was beating furiously and he felt his face redden. "You cannot be sure it was the King," he stated firmly.

"Oh, but I *am*," Vastra sneered. "Much later my mother, amongst others, described him to me and I have since seen him with my own eyes. There is no mistake.

"Also, do not forget, I am a *wizard*," he spat the last word as if it was a rotten taste in his mouth. He glared angrily at Kaplyn. "I have ways of finding out the truth — ways that you could not imagine."

Kaplyn couldn't believe it and he wanted to protest.

"That is not a reason to hate the farmers," Lars interrupted. "They work hard. You saw their homes. They have so little and yet they were willing to share their provisions with us."

"They are happy to live their lives as slaves and have neither the intelligence nor wit to seek a better life!" Vastra snapped.

"You were lucky to be able to escape such a life, and you should not begrudge the farmers theirs. Not everyone is capable of magic!" Lars replied.

Vastra looked furious. However, he bit his lip and refrained from a retort.

Kaplyn also remained silent — his feelings in turmoil. He had kept his origins a secret from the other two men and now, more than ever, he must guard that secret. His gaze kept going to Vastra and he realised that, if he spoke the truth, then they were half-brothers. He *couldn't* believe him, nor the coincidence that had brought them together. He was perplexed, but reasoned that he had better stay with Vastra — if only to keep an eye on him.

Was Vastra a threat to his father? The venom in Vastra's voice suggested he was, and a premonition of fear sent a shudder down Kaplyn's spine.

Chapter 8

Dark Thoughts

They camped by a shallow stream that gurgled merrily over pebbles. It was a pleasant site, but Vastra chose to sit apart. Kaplyn and Lars cooked a meal and called Vastra over as soon as it was ready. Stiffly he arose as though his joints pained him and he came across to sit beside them, accepting a plateful of a thick stew without uttering a word of thanks.

Kaplyn sought to engage him in conversation, trying to keep his own feelings in check. "You mentioned a difference between sorcerers and wizards. What is it?"

Vastra searched Kaplyn's expression as though judging whether he was mocking him. Finally, he set his plate down and started to speak.

"When I was young, about six or seven years old, an old man took me under his wing. He must have seen the other boys bullying me or perhaps he was lonely and sought company. Whatever the reason, he suggested that I help him, and become his apprentice. He was the town's wizard. Wizards are the Akrane in the Eldric tongue. He was held in high regard by the farmers, but being a wizard his power was limited." Vastra looked at Kaplyn.

"Go on," Kaplyn urged.

"Well he could do magic, but it was a mean sort of magic. Simple things like telling when it would rain, encouraging seeds to germinate and such like"

"That sounds like useful magic to me," Lars interrupted.

Vastra ignored him. "He taught me to read and write. I remember being terribly excited. He had a small library and I enjoyed reading above all else. After about a year he showed me his spell book. Then, it seemed a marvel but in reality it was very shabby. He explained that anyone able to be a wizard was like a receptacle within which magic could be harnessed. All Akrane wizards were like that and the greater the wizard the deeper the capacity for magic."

Vastra paused. He toyed with a stick, drawing in the soil by his feet. "He taught me to draw the symbols from his book. Runes they were, and the more intricate the rune the more powerful the spell. I learnt swiftly, memorising each symbol, even though I did not yet understand them."

"Once I had mastered the runes he taught me their names, making me repeat them over and over. Only then did he take me to one side to try a spell. I traced the rune and spoke the name. We both waited. It was a simple spell to light a fire. However, nothing happened. I was devastated and I tried repeatedly to cast the spell. The old man knew long before I would admit defeat that I didn't have the capacity to be a wizard." The stick Vastra was toying with snapped as he pressed it into the ground.

"While I was training the other boys feared me, lest I learn some great magic. After my failure they tormented me more than ever."

Vastra looked Kaplyn in the eyes. "You asked what the difference was between a wizard and a sorcerer; then I will tell you. The old man had other books and one told of the Eldric sorcerers — Narlassar they named themselves. Sorcerers use the spirit world for their spells and that is *far* more powerful than the Akrane magic, for it is boundless."

Kaplyn wanted him to stop but the tale captivated him. The Eldric intrigued him and he hungered to know more. "What happened?" he asked.

"I hid a book about the Eldric in my bedroom. There were runes in it that seemed to speak to me and I felt that I knew some of their names. I traced one in the soil using a stylus and said the name aloud. Nothing happened so I spoke the name again, repeating it in different ways. After many attempts a flame flared into being, spinning in front of me as though in a dance. I was amazed. It was a fire elemental and it was beautiful, like a tiny figure within an orange flame. It disappeared after a while and so I cast another rune and spoke that. It was a water elemental and that too danced around my room until fading."

"I found that while an elemental was present I could cast some of the spells that the old man had taught me. I was using *his* magic, but through the spirit world."

"When the old man found out he was furious — and afraid. He refused to speak to me, but I was not bothered for I had my magic and next time the others bullied me I summoned a fire elemental. It worked a treat, burning the bully's hair and scalp, too, before disappearing. After that no one picked on me again and I was finally treated with respect."

Kaplyn was stunned. He could imagine the farmers leaving Vastra alone, but not out of respect. They would have been terrified.

Lars, too, looked taken aback.

By now it was dusk and only a few birds were singing. It had been only one night since the wolves had attacked, and Vastra was scaring them with ghost stories. Kaplyn grimaced.

As though prompted by his thoughts a lone wolf howled in the distance and Kaplyn jumped before looking over his shoulder.

Vastra sneered. "You're afraid," he laughed. "I tell you stories about elementals, and you are afraid. There are forces in the world far more terrifying."

"What do you mean?" Lars asked.

"Demons," Vastra said.

"And you know about them?" Kaplyn asked.

Vastra remained silent but held his gaze.

Kaplyn grew annoyed. "I have heard that wizards are every bit as powerful as sorcerers."

Vastra snorted. "Perhaps if a wizard had a kara-stone, but not otherwise."

"What's a kara-stone?" Lars asked.

"A kara-stone is used for storing magic," Vastra continued. "Some think that a kara-stone is what remains when a wizard dies. There are other theories, but there is no doubt that the stones are rare. With one, a wizard can increase his powers and some say become as strong as a Narlassar sorcerer, but frankly I don't believe that!"

"What do the stones look like?" Lars asked.

"I don't know. I've never seen one, although I believe they are simply stones to look at."

They fell silent and then Vastra rose. "I'm going to turn in," he said.

"What about a guard?" Kaplyn said. "You'll have to take turn at sentry."

Vastra sneered down at him. "I am not afraid of the night." He turned, seeking a comfortable spot to lay his blanket.

"I don't trust him," Lars whispered.

The other man's honesty relieved Kaplyn. "I agree. But I have reason to stay with him for a while at least."

Kaplyn didn't want to explain that Vastra was a threat to his father, not without giving away his own identity.

"We need to take turns on guard," Kaplyn said. "I'll take the first watch."

Lars nodded and laid his blanket by the fire.

Kaplyn looked out into the growing night. Vastra was becoming more and more of an enigma. Fate had brought them together and Kaplyn knew he should keep Vastra close. He was very afraid of the consequences otherwise.

Later the next morning, as they rode, the scenery changed and they found themselves on the edge of a flat plain, stretching far into the distance. Ahead, low hills interrupted the skyline and Vastra explained that Tanel lay at their base. Herds of wild deer fed upon lush grass, moving away each time the riders drew even remotely close. Finally they could see the ruins of Tanel ahead and, in anticipation, they increased their pace.

Kaplyn was very disappointed. As he had predicted it was nothing more than ruins. A few buildings partially survived, but these were husks without even roofs. At some time in the past the city walls must have collapsed and people had probably scavenged the stones for their homes, judging by how few remained.

They paused at the city's boundary. Vastra was still moody and their arrival had done little to cheer him. "Come," he said simply, turning his back to the city.

Riding a few hundred yards Vastra dismounted, bidding them do likewise. Lars tethered the horses to a nearby tree and joined them, looking back at the remains. Vastra walked forward, taking a pouch from his belt before squatting on the ground. Kaplyn was surprised to see the bag only contained sand, which Vastra used to trace an intricate design on the ground. The rune was very complex and Kaplyn and Lars watched in silence.

Once satisfied, Vastra started to speak arcane words that slipped from Kaplyn's mind immediately after hearing them. As before at the farm, nothing appeared to happen, but then the air shimmered and all at once the ruins were gone — in their place was a city; no longer the crumbling remains that had marked the site previously, but a whole city; a city of tall, bright spires and high, solid walls.

Both Kaplyn and Lars stepped back in fear.

"How is this possible?" Kaplyn asked, truly in awe of Vastra.

'This city exists in another time," he said, smiling with pride. "The Eldric did this to safeguard their home."

Kaplyn and Lars could not take their eyes from the walls. A faint circle of light shimmered between them and the city, as though they were seeing it through a giant lens.

Kaplyn had the distinct impression that the city was still a long way off, even though it appeared to be only a few hundred yards away. There were two walls encircling it, and within they could see spires and rooftops.

The inner wall towered protectively above the outer wall and together they wove an intricate pattern around the circumference. Bridges, guarded by tall watchtowers, linked the walls at intervals and a tall tower rose at the city's heart, a silver pennant flying bravely from its peak.

"Are you sure it's uninhabited?" Lars asked. Kaplyn agreed; he could easily imagine people watching them from the narrow windows.

Vastra pointed to the central tower. "That tower is where you will find the pendant. There is an element of risk and I don't know what you'll find inside. No doubt the buildings will be old and may even be unstable. Remember that the pendant has a map on one side and Eldric writing on the other."

Kaplyn felt breathless with the prospect of exploring and wanted to start immediately.

"We should rest before entering," Lars suggested, seeing Kaplyn's look of eagerness. "It would be wise to be refreshed before starting."

"Very wise," Vastra answered. "Tonight, I will keep watch."

Kaplyn looked at Vastra uncertainly, remembering his refusal to stand guard on previous occasions.

"Have no fear," Vastra said. "I will stand guard. Lars is correct; you need to be rested before entering. Tomorrow will be the greatest moment of your lives."

Kaplyn looked at the city with a mixture of fear and anticipation. *What could go wrong?* he thought. After all, the city *is* deserted.

A silver pennant flew over the central tower, a last defiant symbol of the greatest nation to populate the land; and yet all that now remained was an empty city; only a sanctuary for the ghosts of the forgotten past. By now, the sun was sinking quickly and the shadows were lengthening like giant snakes as darkness crept from the hollows in its eternal struggle to lay claim to the land.

In the distance, a wolf howled welcoming once more the coming night, causing a shiver of trepidation to flutter down Kaplyn's spine.

When morning came, Kaplyn awoke feeling greatly refreshed even though he had woken in the middle of the night. He had been gratified to find Vastra pacing the camp's perimeter. At least, on this occasion, he had kept his word.

Kaplyn rose and went over to Lars to wake him. The other man grumbled before sitting up, rubbing his eyes and blinking at the Eldric city as though he had forgotten about the previous day's events. Vastra had already prepared breakfast and together they ate in silence.

Kaplyn enjoyed the silence. He was afraid but did not want to admit it. He took in his surroundings. It was early, the sun had barely risen and only a faint glow lit the horizon. The sky was overcast but it looked like it would clear later. The air smelt wonderfully fresh, carrying with it the gentle scents of spring. In all likelihood it was going to be a beautiful day. Nonetheless he could not still the hammering of his heart and the trembling of his hands.

All too soon the moment came to leave. Taking his bow, Kaplyn stood by the camp's perimeter, looking towards the great walls. Lars joined him and glancing at the other man he saw the fear in his eyes. Kaplyn smiled to himself, recognising his own inner turmoil. At that moment a golden dawn framed the city whilst around them birds twittered, welcoming the birth of a new day. Kaplyn's smile turned into a grin at the prospect of an adventure.

"Come on," he said, slapping Lars lightly on the shoulder. The other man smiled back.

"Aye, if we leave now we can be back for lunch!"

"Is that all you think about, food?"

"Don't forget the beer," Lars replied, grinning broadly.

Vastra was ready with ropes and grappling hooks. In high spirits they walked towards the halo of light and the city beyond. The two men paused in front of the shimmering air.

"I don't suppose there is any point in waiting?" Lars asked.

Kaplyn shook his head. Together they stepped forward and immediately Kaplyn felt as though his muscles were leaden. It was almost impossible to move and he really had to struggle to make progress, as though walking through deep treacle.

Kaplyn tried to look at Lars, but even that was hard work.

"Keep going," Kaplyn urged as he struggled on, and then all at once, as quickly as the strange feeling had come, it left as though a giant invisible hand had released him.

"What *by the gods* was that?" Lars proclaimed. "Vastra could have warned us. I thought we had triggered a trap!"

Kaplyn looked back. The halo of light was behind them and they could see Vastra beyond, although he was strangely still.

"I have no idea what it was. It doesn't seem to have been a trap; after all nothing happened," Kaplyn replied.

Now they were through the halo he could see the city more clearly. Up close, signs of weathering made the stonework seem less mystical.

"Come on, let's see if we can enter," Kaplyn said.

They aimed towards a large, double gate flanked by tall watchtowers. The timbers were thick and durable; each plank was twice the height of Lars. The big man strained against the portal, but it remained shut.

"It seems the Eldric didn't want anyone to enter," Lars conceded.

Kaplyn looked around. "It would take at least a day to walk the perimeter and even then we might not find another entrance unlocked. Can you throw a rope over the outer wall?"

Lars nodded. To Kaplyn's amusement it took several tries but eventually a grappling hook sailed over the wall and a rope dangled from the battlement. Lars gave it a tug to check it was secure.

"After you," Lars offered.

Kaplyn looked up and, taking the rope in both hands, started to climb, using his feet to walk up the wall. It was a difficult climb but after a while, they were finally standing on the battlements of the outer wall.

"Now where?" Lars asked. "The towers?"

It did seem the next logical step. The towers guarded a bridge connecting the inner and outer wall.

"We can but try," Kaplyn replied, knowing it was too easy and there was bound to be a complication. Access to the bridge was through the tower and a door blocked their path. Kaplyn tried the handle.

"Thought so. It's locked."

"Another rope up to the next level," Lars suggested.

Kaplyn looked over the battlements. It was a considerable distance to the inner wall which was quite a lot higher than their present position.

"Can you do it?" Kaplyn asked.

Lars grinned and set about repeating the earlier task of throwing a grappling hook over the inner wall. Again it took several attempts, but the big man's strength was equal to the task.

"Well done," Kaplyn praised him when he finally succeeded. Lars drew in the slack and then tied their end of the rope around one of the crenulations on the outer wall. The rope was at an angle from the outer wall to the inner and Kaplyn didn't like the idea of climbing it at all.

"This climb is going to be much harder than the last one," Lars said.

Kaplyn nodded. "And I don't much like heights," he admitted.

"Neither do I," Lars said.

"I'll go first," Kaplyn offered.

The hard part was starting. Kaplyn found the trick was to hook his heels over the rope and to pull and slide his way up the rope. Half way up he made the mistake of looking down, causing his head to spin. The inner wall was much higher than the outer so they were already high up.

By mid-morning, they were finally standing on the battlements of the inner wall. Both men were breathing hard and sweating freely.

"That's some view," Lars said, looking into the city.

Kaplyn nodded. Broad streets radiated from the city's heart like the spokes of a massive wheel. Tall trees and grassy verges lined the streets, and to their amazement the trees were in blossom and a gentle fragrance filled the air.

The tower, marking their destination, drew Kaplyn's attention. It arose ominously above the surrounding buildings, a giant obelisk pointing accusingly to the heavens and the gods beyond.

"I don't like this place, I feel as though we're being watched," Lars said.

Kaplyn tore his gaze away from the city and nodded. "I agree. It's a strange place. Let's get on with this, the sooner we leave the better."

They followed the narrow walkway atop the battlements for a short way and came to a tower. Kaplyn tried the handle and, to his satisfaction, it opened. They entered the cool dark interior. Stone stairs spiralled down into the depths below and Kaplyn began to feel giddy as they descended the tight and seemingly endless spiral.

At a run he came out into the open where he found himself looking along one of the broad streets. Kaplyn was in awe as they walked down the street. The houses to either side were brick with no sagging beams in sight.

"Do you think we should look inside?" Kaplyn ventured, wanting to explore.

"No!" Lars countered, almost before Kaplyn had finished speaking. "Vastra warned us that it might be dangerous. Let's not chance our luck."

"You're right," Kaplyn agreed, albeit reluctantly. He could barely take his eyes from the buildings and felt drawn to them like a moth to the flame. "What a pity. We could be passing a fortune."

All too soon they were standing in the tower's shadow, looking up in awe at its size. Kaplyn climbed broad stone steps leading to a set of wooden doors. He tried the handles but they were locked. A circuit of the tower proved fruitless and they found themselves standing before the steps once more.

"How do we get in?" Lars asked doubtfully. "I mean, we can hardly break the doors down — can we?"

Kaplyn shook his head. His gaze kept returning to a small window set ten feet above the ground. After a moment he realised why it had caught his attention and a broad smile crossed his face.

"That window's open," he said, pointing.

Lars groaned; its shadow revealed that it was only just ajar. Grinning, he stood beneath the window with his back to the wall and cupped his hands. Kaplyn placed a booted foot in Lars' hands and the other man hoisted him up.

Kaplyn reached the sill and pulled himself up, using his toes to push himself up the wall. He sat there so that he could work the window open wider.

It took a moment for his eyes to adjust to the darkness within. The room was large but sparsely furnished. He could see a few wooden chairs and a small round table, covered in a thick layer of dust. Tapestries, bleached with age, decorated the walls.

He wanted to enter.

"Lars, wait for me. I'll open the doors to let you in," he instructed. With that he jumped through the opening to the floor, barely a few feet below. Almost as soon as he did, he felt a terrible premonition. Then the light failed, plunging him into a despairing night.

Kaplyn fell. Not the short distance he had anticipated, but an eternity. Blackness engulfed him and he knew no more.

Chapter 9

Alone

"Wake up!" demanded the voice.

Kaplyn didn't want to; the pain was too great. He remembered falling, reaching out to grab hold of anything to stop his fall — his heart lurching, his arms flailing, air rushing past his ears, complete and utter darkness and then … nothing.

This wasn't a dream. His head, legs and back all hurt. A moan escaped his lips; raising his hand, he felt a lump on his temple. His eyes were open, yet he couldn't see. Panic escalated and he fought against it, trying to remain calm, breathing deeply.

Groaning, he tried to rise but agony caused him to flop back.

"Help," he croaked. Even to his own ears his voice seemed frail. "Help," he tried again, louder. Silence, not even a bird or the sound of wind. "Is anyone there? Lars, can you hear me?"

To distract himself he went through a mantra, flexing his fingers, his wrists, his elbows, checking for damage. There were no breaks, but each twinge suggested plenty of bruises.

Something was digging into his back. Sitting up resulted in beads of sweat forming on his brow. Releasing a breath, he groaned. Momentarily his head swam and he waited for the nausea to subside. Behind him, he discovered shards of wood. One long length had twine attached; his bow was broken. He cursed, it was a good bow, a gift from a friend.

Grimacing, he arose to a crouch, tangling himself in a scabbard hanging from his belt. He sucked air into his lungs and the fresh wave of pain caused him to wince. He drew the sword, checking that the blade was whole. He drew his knife and felt it. That, too, was undamaged.

An elusive glow caught his attention and he turned, trying to find it. Gradually it grew in intensity, like the coming of the dawn. Nonetheless, it took a while for his eyes to focus. A large, grey object surrounded him;

probably a wall. Something was dreadfully wrong though; with that premonition he looked down.

Lurching to one side, a cry escaped his lips; he dropped his knife, which clanked noisily. Throwing out his hands his fingers cracked against a solid surface, causing him to yelp.

It was impossible. It did not make sense.

He was crouching apparently on thin air; beneath him was a terrifying drop. He stared into the depth in disbelief before shutting his eyes.

Refusing to look down he opened his eyes and cast around for something that *might* make sense. His vision was better. He was within a building of sorts, and a circular stone built wall was about twenty feet from him. Higher up, the wall disappeared into shadows.

"*Kalanth, save me,*" he murmured. Keeping his head held high he groped for his knife. Finding it, he sheathed it before twisting around to take stock of his situation.

Relief flooded through him; there was an open doorway framed in the wall about three times his body length from his position. Beyond the doorway was a solid looking floor and beyond that a wall. He wanted to run towards it and the safety that beckoned.

"Be calm," he murmured, slowing his breathing. He risked looking down. Giddiness threatened. He swayed and fell, slamming his hand against the invisible surface. He exhaled slowly, trying to stave off vertigo.

Lowering himself to his knees he slid his hands experimentally forward, but they slipped over an unseen edge. Air whooshed from his lungs as he slammed into the invisible barrier. He swore, but common sense made him lie still. He dare not move, not without knowing how far the platform extended. His arms were completely over the edge. Extending his reach there was no sign of anything below. If he had run to the door as he first wanted, he would have fallen and he could only guess how far that was.

Sweat trickled down his brow and stung his eyes. Blinking, he felt to his left and found a similar drop; to his right however the path continued. It was not very wide, he had been lucky not to fall off when he had first lost his balance. To his irritation the path led him away from the doorway and he had no option but to follow on his hands and knees. The path took a few more turns, but then headed once more towards the doorway.

With only a few yards to go a clang sounded from above. It was distinctly something large and metallic striking stone. An eerie shriek followed, echoing from the shadows above, causing him to jump. He concentrated hard on the door ahead, too afraid to look up. The distance was too far to jump and he struggled to recall the last few turns. Was there a pattern?

His mind blanked as a louder scream reached him.

Involuntarily, he looked up just as a black shape detached itself from the shadow. Giant wings beat the air clumsily as though the beast was unused to flight; each stroke sounding like the snap of a ship's sail in a storm.

Scrambling forward his hands searched for a path and for a moment he made progress, but once again the floor disappeared under his fingers and again he fell flat. Another scream sounded and the flapping of wings seemed right above him.

The opening was barely the length of his body away. Scuttling into a crouch he hurled himself at the doorway. His injuries flared afresh, tearing a cry from his lips. He tumbled into the wall, winding himself. A dry flapping sounded behind him. Fighting for breath he grabbed his dagger, turned and thrust it before him.

The creature flew hard at the doorway causing him to recoil, crying aloud, but the wall at his back blocked his way. It screamed in frustration. Fortunately for Kaplyn it was too large to fly through the doorway. However, it refused to leave and its wings beat frantically, keeping it near its prey.

It extended a leg, trying to land. With a shout he jabbed with his knife, causing it to retreat. Its head cocked to one side and malevolent eyes locked on his, as though willing him to come out. The head was that of a man; long, greasy hair was plastered against an emaciated skull and its oily skin barely reflected what little light there was.

"Kalanth protect me!" he screamed.

The beast's forehead wrinkled. It emitted another ear-splitting scream of rage, revealing rows of razor sharp teeth. Dropping his knife, he covered his ears.

"Come to me, human," it said thickly.

Flight seemed impossible; he daren't turn away less it attack. He remembered his knife and grabbed it.

The creature hung there for several heartbeats. It was losing height and Kaplyn realised it was tiring.

"Curse you!" it shrieked. "Damn you to hell." With a flurry of wings, it disappeared into the shadows. "*Curse you!*" it screamed finally, and a hundred voices echoed back from the distant recesses of the tower.

Choking, he cast about for a safe escape. The tunnel ended by the doorway but to his left it continued. Scrambling to his feet and keeping his back to the wall, he staggered away from the room with the beast.

76

Alternately running and stumbling he fled. The tunnel widened, turning sharply to his left and, with relief, he lost sight of the doorway behind.

Sheathing his dagger he drew his sword. He wouldn't be able to wield it in the confined space but its extra reach gave him confidence. He continued, glancing over his shoulder every few steps lest the creature followed.

Legs aching, he decided to rest and flopped down on the stone. The lump on his temple was painful to touch and he wondered whether he was concussed. Nothing seemed real. The beast and a room without a floor were unbelievable.

Was this Hell? Was he dead?

A sob escaped him. He arose too quickly and pain lanced through his legs and ribs; his vision swam, forcing him to remain motionless until the feeling of weakness passed. Determination forced him onwards.

There was no change to the surroundings for some time, then something ahead caused him to pause. It was a light, but it wasn't daylight, this was too blue. A memory triggered: flames burned blue in a demon's presence. Did demons exist?

Very slowly he continued, his sword outstretched for protection. Gradually, the light grew and with it came a rushing sound. Then the reason for the light became evident. Blue flames leapt out of the floor and into the ceiling, completely blocking the tunnel. His heart sank. He couldn't go back and now the way forward was blocked!

Throwing himself down, fresh stabs of agony made him cry out. He slammed a fist into the tunnel wall and grimaced with pain. He thought about Emma, the first time in quite some while but the face of Callan's daughter came unbidden to his mind. He dwelt on her soft features for a while before realising something was wrong.

"What the…? That doesn't make sense."

Only then did he realise there was no heat coming from the flames. Frowning, he tentatively probed the stone floor ahead, finding that it, too, was cold. With a muttered oath, he thrust himself away from the wall and walked forward, his hands outstretched. His frown deepened; there was simply no heat.

Walking to the edge of the flames he thrust a hand forward, quickly snatching it back, testing the heat.

Nothing.

No heat. No burns.

He thrust his hand into the flames more slowly and for several seconds kept it there feeling nothing but a blast of air. Knowing that a delay might weaken his resolve he stepped into the flames.

The rushing air threatened to lift him from his feet. He exulted. His skin felt alive and vibrant as though the flames were purging his body; his ribs felt mended and the bruises gone. Feeling his temple even the lump was gone.

Striding into the flame's embrace his ears rang with the rush of air. Breathing deeply his lungs tingled and he felt light headed. As he walked, the flames seemed to continue forever and the further he went, the more confused his senses became. Suddenly he was no longer sure of the right direction; was he even going in a straight line and he might even now be in a room, rather than a corridor?

A flicker of orange caused him to gasp. Orange flames he understood; they meant heat. Picking up his pace he loped through the conflagration. His skin felt hot, then smouldering. He was burning. Covering his head with his arms he screamed aloud, racing forward.

Without warning he was in a corridor, free of the surrounding flames.

Yelping in agony he continued to run, throwing his sword in front of him before struggling from his jerkin. Tearing it off he threw it after his sword. Shielding his head with his arms he kicked the jacket and sword ahead.

When the heat was more bearable he slowed and, looking back, saw that fierce orange flames barred the way. Even at this distance, the heat was intense.

He could not believe he had just come from that. Bending, he retrieved his smouldering jacket, but the sword was still too hot and so he used his jacket sleeve to pick it up.

Shaking his head, despair washed over him. Staggering, he turned to continue his nightmare journey.

He had not gone far when gradually the light faded and within a dozen more paces it became black as night. The darkness was terrifying. He held his sword out protectively, using the blade to feel his way ahead. Without warning, it struck something hard, jarring his arm.

With his free hand he felt wooden planks and traced the outline of a door. His fingers sought the handle. He pushed the door open to reveal an immense cavern, stretching across a lake. It was light enough to see, although there was no obvious source of illumination and then he realised the rock was glowing.

The size of the lake astounded him. The opposite shore was lost in the distance. Immediately to his front was a small sandy beach and at its edge, water lapped, looking cold and deep.

"Now what do I do?" he muttered angrily, sitting down and glaring into the distance. There was clearly no way around the lake; wet, glistening rock walls plunged into the water to either side of the beach.

Go back? He thought. *No, that would be suicide. The flames had been real and besides there was that creature.*

Continuing forward seemed the only option. Angrily he removed his boots and jacket, making these into a bundle. He slung his sword across his back using his belt as a baldric and stepped into the water, cursing roundly at the cold. For some way the water only came to his calves. Just as he thought he might not need to swim, the ground shelved and, in less than a pace, the water came to his chest. Gasping, he threw his bundle ahead and started to swim vigorously.

"I'm going to survive!" he hissed. His thoughts went to Lars. Suddenly he was afraid that the big man might have followed him. The thought that Lars, too, might fall into this trap spurred Kaplyn on.

As though mocking his determination a distant splash caused him to start. With his own splashing he was initially uncertain of what he had heard, but the thought was enough. The gods alone knew what lurked in the lake. He foolishly tried to swim higher, keeping as much of his body out of the water as possible. Very quickly his legs became leaden and he had to swim more evenly.

Just when he felt he could go no further, a dank moss-stained wall materialised from the gloom ahead. Glancing over his shoulder, all he could see was blackness. His teeth chattering, he increased the urgency of his stroke, praying he was going the right way.

A small beach appeared at the foot of the wall, looking very similar to the one he had left. His heart sank, but at least he would be out of the water. Putting his feet down, water closed over his head; it was deeper than he had expected. He struggled to the surface, coughing and retching and grabbing his bundle.

He forced himself on and all too slowly the beach drew closer. He risked putting his feet down and this time was rewarded with soft sand beneath his feet. Rising, he waded to the beach, throwing himself onto the dry ground.

"Thank the Kalanth," he spluttered.

Trembling, he rose to a sitting position, looking back at the still waters. The beach was definitely different to the one he had set off from; this one was wider and there were more rocks. Relief flooded through him that he had crossed, but was he any better off?

A faint sound came from somewhere across the lake and for a second his heart stopped. Holding his breath he strained to hear any further noise. A swirl of water a few feet from the shore caused him to jump. A shiny black shape broke the surface, glided along for a few yards before lunging once more into the depths. He kept his gaze fixed on that point as he scrambled away from the water's edge.

The ripples lapped the beach. Whatever he had seen had been real. He couldn't move and continued staring out into the lake with cold water dribbling from his wet hair into his eyes. Where was he? He had to know.

Rousing himself from his stupor, he turned away from the beach. A tunnel beckoned immediately behind him, but before entering, he dressed. His wet clothes clung unpleasantly to his body.

A few yards into the tunnel hope came flooding back; this passageway sloped upwards. The incline increased and heartened that he might escape this hellhole he quickened his pace. However, after a while the slope became impossible. He kept sliding back and his calves were aching. Then he nearly fell and it was all he could do to remain standing, his hands flat on to the wall to prevent himself slipping back. Somehow, the slope had become severe both before and behind him. He doubted that he could go on and yet it did not make sense that the slope could be so steep. Angrily he drew his dagger. Stabbing a crack between the stones in the floor he tried to climb, but the slope seemed to be getting worse.

At least he had a purchase but he couldn't stay there forever. He had to try to reason out the situation. Was the tower somehow feeding on his fears? He remembered the flying creature from the first room and realised he had been in a similarly bizarre situation when that had appeared. The thought spurred him on. Wedging himself tightly into the corner, between the wall and floor, he attacked the mortar between two of the stone blocks immediately to his front.

It was an act of desperation, but as he dug, the mortar became softer and fell away easily until he had cleared most of it from around one of the blocks. He had initially contemplated making handholds to help him climb, but realised that he might be able to remove one of the blocks and gain access to whatever lay beyond.

A deep groan resonated about him. The intensity and suddenness caused him to slip and he scraped his knuckles against the stone in his efforts to stop himself. From the gloom below, a figure materialized. In mounting

80

panic Kaplyn once more attacked the block, but could not get a firm grip. Pushing the tip of his dagger between the stones, he tried to lever one of them out, but his knife jammed.

The figure was close enough to see tattered clothing hanging from burned and grazed flesh. The creature, for he could not bring himself to believe this was a man, carried a sword that, either due to a trick of the light or sorcery, seemed to glow eerily, illuminating the tunnel walls.

It paused sniffing the air, then went into a crouch. Suddenly it leapt closer, emitting a deep snarl.

Kaplyn twisted the dagger but the blade snapped with a loud and sickening click. Rather than try to lever the stone out he pushed hard. To his surprise, it slid effortlessly inwards.

As though sensing his escape, the creature screamed and leapt the intervening distance, its sword raised to strike.

Kaplyn pulled with all his strength on the stone on the right hand side of the opening. It came away with a crash, smashing onto the floor. He kicked it, propelling it down the slope.

The creature collided with the stone, which slammed into its calves, shattering them. It fell and then, it and the stone accelerated down the tunnel, the creature's screams continuing until abruptly there was silence.

Kaplyn closed his eyes and finally took a breath. He peered through the hole into a room; it was an armoury judging by the assortment of weapons stacked in disorganised piles.

He scrambled through the opening, and found his way blocked as his sword caught on the rough edges. Untangling himself, his wet clothes clung uncomfortably to his flesh causing him to shiver. When he was finally through, his attention went immediately to a dais in the room's centre. Someone had placed a sword and scabbard upon it. The other weapons within the room paled into insignificance by comparison.

The pommel was a semicircle of steel inset with a clear pale blue gem, and the blade was a dull jet-black that seemed to trap the very light. Drawing nearer he became aware of fine gossamer runes inlaid into the sable metal. He recognised the script as Eldric, but could not read that language. A voice came from behind him, causing him to jump and bang his knee painfully against the dais.

"Do not touch it!" the voice said.

Kaplyn grabbed the sword and span around, the point of the weapon levelled against whatever new devilry the tower had conjured. A figure stood unmoving within the shadows like a granite statue, but there the resemblance ended for he could see by the eyes that it was a living being.

81

Why had he not noticed him earlier? The figure detached itself from the shadows and came forward.

He was an old man, leaning heavily upon a wooden staff as though bearing the weight of the world's woes on his shoulders. Every few steps his staff swept the ground before his feet. His eyes were milky white and Kaplyn realised he was blind.

"Too late, I suppose," the newcomer admonished gesturing toward the blade, a disarming smile creasing his face. "Put the sword down. I mean you no harm."

Kaplyn refused to move.

"Perhaps though you are right to take the weapon," he continued, matter-of-factly. "It's Eldric made and it served its previous master well."

Kaplyn was confused. Was he blind? His milky white eyes clearly marked him as unsighted and yet he spoke as though he could see. At the mention of the sword, Kaplyn abruptly became aware of it. Its balance was perfect but it felt odd in some way; almost as though it were alive. He recalled how quickly it had come to his hand. For a heartbeat he considered dropping it, but instead gripped the hilt more fiercely.

The old man's attention was fully upon him, stunning him with the intensity of his gaze.

"Lower the sword," the other man said softly. "As you can see, I am unarmed."

Kaplyn kept the weapon raised, taking a step backwards. "I don't trust anything here," he answered, trying to keep calm.

The other man smiled. "And very sensible too. However, I mean you no harm. Now put your sword down so that we can talk."

Kaplyn found himself lowering the weapon even though his instinct was to keep it levelled.

The other man sighed and turned away. He raised a hand and seemed to feel the air above the weapons as though sensing them.

"Where am I?" Kaplyn asked.

"Tanel. It is an Eldric city."

"I know I am in Tanel, but this tower seems so unreal," Kaplyn said.

"You are in but one tower within Tanel. The tower is real, and not a figment of your imagination. The city beyond, in its day, was the finest in the land. It is deserted now, but you will find that out, no doubt."

The old man seemed to dismiss Kaplyn and his attention turned to an untidy stack of weapons. Axes, Kaplyn realised, looking closer.

"The dwarves would be interested in these," the old man said. "Although what they truly seek is not here. I feel sorry for the dwarves, very sorry indeed. Already their ordeal has begun and I fear that they will suffer greatly in the coming years."

"Who are you?" Kaplyn asked.

The old man turned to face him, smiling absently. "Ah, I was forgetting. Old men tend to ramble, or so people tell me. Now where were we?" He paused, lost in thought. Kaplyn was about to ask him again who he was when the old man became alert all at once.

"That's right. We cannot have this." Before Kaplyn could react, the other man leant forward and his fingers gently brushed his forehead. His speed surprised Kaplyn who jumped back, raising his sword protectively between them.

"It's all right," the other man assured him. "You carried the mark of a demon upon you," he said, wiping his hand on his robes as though they were contaminated.

"D...demons don't exist," Kaplyn stuttered.

"Oh, but be assured that they do."

Kaplyn shook his head, finally convinced that the other man was mad. "Do you live here?" he asked.

The old man looked about the armoury with a trace of a smile on his lips. "No, and certainly not in an armoury. Only ghosts inhabit Tanel. Once, long ago, many lived here — but the Krell Wars put an end to that.

"Perhaps you should find the Eldric and the city will awaken to the sounds of happy voices." He stopped his pacing and looked up expectantly, but Kaplyn was at a loss for words.

The other man's look of hope faded. "It seems only fair to remind you of why you are here then. You are searching for a pendant. You will recognise it when you find it. Continue on your quest through this tower and you will succeed. Do not fail though, the tower is unforgiving and you may end up becoming part of what you see."

"What am I seeing?" Kaplyn asked glancing around the room. "Is this place real?"

"Yes, it is real, though it exists in another plane to your own world. Long ago the Eldric, in their wisdom, decided to hide their cities for they could not bring themselves to destroy that which love had built."

"Where are they now?" Kaplyn asked. He found himself distracted for the briefest moment.

"Gone," came the reply, his voice sounding incredible sad. When Kaplyn looked up the other man was no longer there. He was shocked and searched the room in confusion, but he was alone.

He went to the door to see if the old man had departed that way. The door was ajar and through the crack he could see a stout wooden table blocking the way. It looked heavy. Putting his shoulder to the door, he heaved and was rewarded with a loud rasping sound as the table moved.

Stepping through he found himself in a room, empty apart from furniture thickly coated in centuries of dust. It was much larger than the armoury and was the first room to show signs of inhabitation; old ornate tapestries hung at odd angles upon the walls.

He decided to re-enter the armoury and explore the stacked weapons, thinking that perhaps the pendant was amongst them. It was a boy's dream, masses of weapons of every kind. Most of them showed signs of rust, and that somehow made the Eldric seem less god-like. He paused by the axes, stooping to pick one up, knowing that Lars would appreciate such a weapon. The one he selected was large and double bladed with a smooth ebony shaft. Fine Eldric lettering decorated the handle, but again he could not decipher this.

Finding a stack of bows he removed the twine from one, using this to make a loop by which he could carry the axe. He took a bow to replace the one he had broken earlier. The twine was too old to use but perhaps he could replace it later. He ran a thumb along the bow, marvelling at how smooth it was. It was a laminate construction; a combination of wood and bone, shorter than other bows he was used to and much more curved. He went back to the dais and took the scabbard, having decided to keep the Eldric sword which he kept drawn as a precaution. He tucked the scabbard into his belt.

He needed arrows and a quick search found several full quivers buried beneath a pile of rotting tapestries. He selected one, which he slung across his shoulder alongside the axe before allowing the tapestries to fall back into place. Lastly, he replaced his broken knife. He spent a short while longer exploring the room, but there was no sign of a pendant and so he decided to revisit the next room.

The adjacent room, apart from the door behind him, had no other obvious exit. A stout wooden chest dominated the corner and he ransacked the drawers, but discovered only tableware. Not really knowing where else to look, he slowly made another tour of the room. One of the tapestries caught his eye. It was of a dragon flying over a grassy knoll. The dragon was exquisite. It had a graceful swan-like neck and its wings were like ship's sails in the wind, trapping as much air as possible, holding it mid-flight.

Cautiously he lifted the tapestry's edge with his blade. The ancient cloth shed dust, making him cough as he brushed it from his eyes, waiting for the air to clear. Behind the tapestry was a door and, remembering the previous traps, he checked carefully around the frame before trying the handle.

The hinges groaned as the door swung inwards, causing Kaplyn anxiety in case anything living was beyond; however, the adjoining room was devoid of life. It was similar in size to the one that he was in but the outer wall curved gradually reminding him that he was within a circular tower. Skirting a wooden table surrounded by ornately carved high-backed chairs, he crossed the room heading towards another door.

He stepped through the doorway gripping his new sword for comfort and, at last, a shaft of sunlight from a small window lifted his spirits. Dust motes floated in the air, shining like tiny angels. He guessed this was where the guests retired after dining. A display of weapons dominated one wall while tapestries covered the remainder. A glass chandelier hung from the ceiling, casting small rainbows against the walls.

A flash of gold made him look twice. In the centre of the room was a desk and upon it was the object that had caught his attention and with mounting hope he crossed the room. It was a pendant with a thick gold chain. Sweeping it up it easily filled his palm. It was heavy. On one side there was a map and on the other writing, again in a fine Eldric script.

Instantly he recognised the map as being of his homeland, Allund. He also recognised the Pen-Am-Pelleas, mountain range between Allund and Thrace. He couldn't read the Eldric writing though.

Not wanting to delay any further, he looped the chain about his neck, tucking the pendant into his shirt before turning to leave.

He had a shock as he walked through the next door. Lars was sitting on a window ledge at about chest height from the floor. It was clear that he was about to enter and now his concentration was wholly on the short drop to the floor below. What was bizarre though was that there was a hole in the floor just below the window and the other man seemed oblivious to it.

"Stop!" Kaplyn cried.

Lars visibly jumped and when he looked up a broad grin lit up his face.

"Kaplyn," he said. "Where by *Slathor* have you been?" He shifted his weight as though about to jump down from the window ledge.

"Stop," Kaplyn repeated but more gently. "Do not move. Stay where you are," he warned, quickly crossing the distance between them. The other man looked back uncertainly, but clambered back onto the ledge.

"Where have you been?" Lars repeated. "You've been ages. I thought you were lost."

"It's a long story. I will tell you later but for now I have a terrible urge to be out of the city before sunset." However, the hole beneath the window and the shadows within held his attention.

"What are you staring at?" the other man asked.

"That hole in the floor," he said waving his arm in the general direction.

"What hole?"

Kaplyn was shaken. "You mean that you can't see it?" He picked up a nearby chair and walking over to the hole he held the chair over it before letting go. As Kaplyn expected the chair fell through the hole, but he didn't hear it landing.

The other man nearly fell off the window ledge with shock. "What the…? What happened to the chair?"

"I take it that's the window I entered?" Kaplyn asked. The other man nodded.

"Come, let's get out of here," Kaplyn urged. Skirting the opening, he pulled himself onto the window ledge. He paused letting the fresh breeze caress his skin. He took in the scene before him. A cobbled street separated the tower from tall brick buildings opposite. Without waiting he jumped down and, with a thud, Lars landed by his side.

Kaplyn removed the axe he was carrying and gave it to Lars grinning. "You can get rid of that sword now."

The other man took the weapon and his eyes shone as he examined it. After a moment he slung it over his shoulder before dropping his sword with a clang. "Thanks. But did you find the pendant?"

Kaplyn nodded.

"What, *by Slathor*, took you so long? I was frantic with worry. It's really spooky being in the city on your own."

Kaplyn laughed, "You should worry. Wait until you hear what happened to me and what nearly happened to you if you had jumped through that hole back there."

Lars paled.

"Come on," Kaplyn urged and he started to jog, back the way they had come. Shortly, they arrived at the city walls and Lars ducked through an opening where stairs led up to the battlements. Climbing the stairs they soon arrived at a door leading out to the battlements. The sun was setting and the horizon was a mixture of fiery oranges and reds. Low gentle hills extended beyond the city and the landscape was dotted with copses. A warm breeze carried with it the fragrance of spring, lifting Kaplyn's sprits.

Looking back inside the city Kaplyn's gaze fell on the tower. From this view it did not look dangerous, but Kaplyn now knew its secret.

"We need to descend the rope," Lars reminded him. Kaplyn grimaced. The rope was tied around one of the battlement's crenulations and extended at an angle down to an outer city wall where it was tied around other crenulations on the lower wall. Kaplyn pulled on the rope, satisfied that it was secure.

Kaplyn went first and climbed up onto the battlement where he grasped the rope. With some difficulty he leant forward, hooked an ankle over the rope, and then swung the other leg over. Hand over hand he descended, letting the rope slide beneath his ankles. On the outer wall, another rope let them descend to the ground and they soon found themselves outside the city.

"Wait a moment," Kaplyn said.

He removed his jacket and wrapped the new sword and scabbard in it. For some reason he was reluctant to let Vastra see the weapon.

"Ok. Let's go," he said.

Lars led them away from the wall. Ahead, Kaplyn could see their horses and near to them a lone figure sitting on the ground. They were still some way in the distance, but they were surprisingly still. Kaplyn then noticed the large circle of air shimmering before them in the failing light. The campsite beyond was like looking through a telescope.

As before, as soon as Kaplyn stepped into the circle he could barely move as though his muscles were frozen. Panicking he struggled harder. Abruptly he was through and all at once Lars was by his side.

"I hate that," Kaplyn said. "It really feels as though you are stuck."

"Yes, I know what you mean," Lars answered breathlessly and eyes wide with fright.

Together they walked towards the camp. Kaplyn realised then that all around him were the sounds of life. Birds were singing and insects droning. In the barrier everything had been silent. He shivered and glanced back at the Eldric city. He had escaped, but at what cost?

Chapter 10

The Journey to Kinlin Castle

Vastra was sitting by the fire and as soon as he saw them he sprang up, coming forward to meet them.

"I don't trust him," Lars said in a whisper.

Vastra's eyes reflected his excitement as he came towards them.

"The pendant — do you have it?"

Kaplyn nodded.

"Give it to me!" Vastra demanded, extending a thin arm, his fingers shaking with excitement.

All at once Kaplyn was unwilling to give the pendant up, especially after all he had been through.

Vastra's smile vanished and his eyes blazed. "Give me the pendant!" he repeated taking a menacing step forward.

His action made Kaplyn even more reluctant to hand it over. By his side Lars cast him an anxious look.

Vastra scowled and then his frown softened. "Of course, your gold!" he reached into his robes and removed the heavy purse. "As promised, two gold pieces each and the silver *calder*," he fished out four gold coins and a veritable pile of silver. He looked up, but Kaplyn did not offer up the pendant.

"I'll double it," Vastra continued. "It's more than a fair price."

"We could have died in there!" Kaplyn accused.

Vastra's look was one of thunder. "You agreed!" he hissed. "Look!" He tipped the contents of the small bag onto the ground. Bright gold coins bounced on the soft grass before coming to rest. It was a small fortune. "Here is all the gold; now give me the pendant."

Kaplyn shook his head.

"It's worthless to you," Vastra said in disbelief. "What is wrong with you?"

Kaplyn remained defiant and after a while a smile touched Vastra's thin lips and his manner became more polite. "Perhaps I have been hasty. Your adventure has probably taxed you. Come, sit by the fire and relax. Tell us what happened. We will discuss the pendant afterwards." He bent down and recovered the fallen coins.

Vastra led them to the fire. The aroma of cooking filled the air. Kaplyn's mouth watered, he was famished. A stew simmered in a metal pot that sat in the embers at the edge of the fire. Stirring the contents with a ladle Vastra dished a portion out to each in turn, filling small bowls and handing them both a hunk of bread.

Kaplyn recounted his tale as they ate; however, he omitted telling them about the Eldric sword and the old man. For what reason, he was not sure?

Throughout the story Vastra often interrupted, seeking clarification. When Kaplyn had finished speaking, even Vastra looked pale. "I had no idea that it would be so difficult," he said. "But you did well to recover the pendant." Lost in concentration he toyed with his food with his spoon.

"I've had a thought," Lars announced.

"Don't strain yourself," Vastra muttered.

Lars frowned, but continued. "Some parts of Kaplyn's tale remind me of the Prophecy he told me about."

"Prophecy?" Kaplyn asked.

"You know, Tallin's Crown and all that...."

Kaplyn shook his head, "I don't understand?"

Lars continued. "There was a part in the Prophecy about someone being born of air, fire and water."

By their side, Vastra sucked in his breath.

"Your journey through the tower reminds me of that. You could argue that you were born from air, fire and water."

Kaplyn smiled. "That's rather fanciful," he said thoughtfully and even Lars went quiet as though the statement was rather lame.

Vastra though seemed agitated. "Who are you?" he asked looking at Kaplyn.

"Kaplyn," he shrugged."

"Are you concealing something from me?" Vastra demanded.

Kaplyn shook his head, but he was uncomfortable that Vastra was staring at him so intently. "I am not hiding anything," he insisted.

At that moment some instinct made Kaplyn draw back from Vastra but not quickly enough. Vastra's hand lashed out and grabbed his wrist. Pain shot through Kaplyn and he cried out. Vastra barked some meaningless words and abruptly blackness engulfed Kaplyn.

Kaplyn passed out but only for a few heartbeats. Vastra snatched back his hand from Kaplyn's wrist as though burnt.

"What just happened?" Lars demanded.

"I'm not sure," Kaplyn replied, but then realised he might indeed know. "I think that Vastra just cast a spell."

Vastra shook his head, but then seemed to reconsider. "I tried to read your mind."

"What? How dare you!" Kaplyn shouted. He felt his face grow hot and knew that he was turning crimson. "But your spell failed?" Kaplyn continued.

Vastra's eyes smouldered with suppressed fury.

"Why did it fail?" Kaplyn demanded.

"The pendant," Lars suggested. "The Eldric were powerful sorcerers, or so you told me."

"Is that true? Did the pendant protect me?" Kaplyn asked.

Vastra gave Lars a look of hatred. "Yes."

"How?"

Vastra massaged his hand. "It nulls magic. I should have suspected that."

"You mean that while I wear it, magic won't work against me?"

Vastra nodded. Kaplyn could see how much that admission pained him.

"Why do you want the pendant?" Kaplyn asked.

"It's a map to help find the Eldric," Vastra replied.

"That doesn't make sense," Lars interrupted. "Kaplyn told me the Eldric disappeared long ago."

"True. However, the pendant describes the last journey of one of their explorers. If I can, I intend retracing his steps."

"I want to go with you," Kaplyn said. A strong urge had suddenly come over him that this was important. Something that the old man had said had convinced him. It was a niggle he couldn't quite explain.

Vastra flashed them both an angry look. "Very well! You may accompany me, but *first* give me the pendant."

"No," Kaplyn insisted. "I will carry it. You may read it of course, but I will carry it."

"You don't know how to use it!"

"Use it?" Kaplyn asked

"You cannot read Eldric, so it's of no use to you," Vastra continued.

"As I said," Kaplyn continued. "I will let you read it but I will bear it."

Vastra's eyes rolled heavenward. "Very well," he snapped. "Keep it, if you must. But I hope, for your sake, it is not cursed," he added. With that he arose and stormed away.

At the mention of a curse Kaplyn saw fear reflected in Lars' eyes.

"*By Slathor*, you should be careful," Lars warned. "He is a bitter man and would make a terrible enemy."

Kaplyn nodded. "I agree, but I have done you a disservice; you deserve the gold."

Lars merely shrugged and shook his head, stroking his beard. "Gold is of no use to me. My heart's desire would be to return to my homeland, but money will not achieve that. There isn't a ship in the land willing to cross the sea." A wry smile crossed his face. "Perhaps it is fated that I should accompany you. My gods decide our fate — for good or ill. It would mean little to them. Besides, from what I hear about these demons and krell I think you will need a strong arm by your side."

Kaplyn grinned and offered his hand in friendship. Lars nearly crushed his fingers in a vice-like grip.

"I'd better hide this," Kaplyn said, rising and picking up his folded jacket with the sword still concealed inside. He crossed to the horses and the small pile of luggage. Vastra was not in sight so he swapped the sword from his jacket to a blanket, which he hid amongst his belongings. He took a moment to find spare twine for his new bow.

"It seems that the Eldric knew how to make weapons," Lars acknowledged, coming over to join Kaplyn. He was admiring his axe.

"May I see them?" Vastra asked.

Kaplyn jumped and wondered where Vastra had come from. By his side, Lars cast him an anxious look. Kaplyn looked at Vastra but saw no malice there. He must have calmed down, he handed him the bow. When Vastra had looked at that Lars handed him the axe.

"They are definitely Eldric made," Vastra said eventually. "You took a risk in taking them."

"Why?" Kaplyn asked.

Together they returned to the fire and sat down. Vastra picked up his bowl and toyed with the remaining food with his spoon. "Some weapons were custom made. To anyone else but their owner, and perhaps their heirs, they would be a curse."

He looked up at the other two men. "Oh, I was not joking about a curse. There are such things you know. These two weapons seem all right though; the writing on the axe is merely a good luck charm."

Lars and Kaplyn exchanged glances. Lars was probably thinking about the hidden sword.

"Now it is your turn to tell us about the pendant," Kaplyn said, trying not to sound concerned. He did not believe in curses but then again, a week ago, he had not believed in wizards either. "What is it and how will it help us to find the Eldric?"

At the "us" Vastra looked at Lars and scowled. He put his bowl down and picking up a twig he poked into the ash at the fire's edge. "The remainder of the quest will be hazardous," he said, ignoring the questions and staring instead into the heat of the flames.

Kaplyn wondered whether Vastra was deliberately trying to frighten them into giving up the pendant. He found himself inadvertently feeling the talisman beneath his shirt.

"You would do well to take the gold and leave it at that," Vastra continued.

Kaplyn smiled. "You will need our help. As you say it will be a dangerous journey, especially alone."

Vastra became sullen and looked as though he was going to argue, but he merely shrugged. "Let me see it," he asked.

Kaplyn withdrew it from within his shirt and held it for Lars and Vastra to see, making it clear that he was not going to let go.

He showed them the map first. A path led from Tanel through a forest and then to a mountain range where a spot was marked between two peaks. The shape of the land and the mountain range made it unmistakably Allund. Kaplyn turned the pendant over and Vastra's lips worked as he silently read the fine gossamer writing.

"It appears that if we are to learn what became of the Eldric then we must travel to the Pen-Am-Pelleas Mountains," Vastra said. He sat back but did not venture anything else. He looked pensive.

Kaplyn frowned for he had deduced as much himself from the map. "What does the writing say?" he asked.

"It's merely a description of the map," Vastra said. He emptied some herbs into a cup and took a pan of boiling water from the fire to fill the cup.

Kaplyn replaced the pendant in his shirt, eyeing Vastra warily as the other man blew upon his steaming cup. It was clearly pointless trying to get him to speak further, so he decided to retire for the night.

Kaplyn went to his possessions and took out a blanket, which he spread on the ground. He distrusted Vastra and, although he was tired he lay awake for some time listening to the night noises. He held the pendant beneath his shirt, half expecting trickery from the reticent wizard. Eventually he fell asleep. Soon dreams engulfed him and, for the first time in some while, he slept fitfully.

Kaplyn awoke to the light of an uncertain day and immediately his hand went to the pendant. His mind was in turmoil. Initially he was confused but then all became clear. As his palm enclosed the talisman he relaxed. Momentarily he had feared that Vastra had stolen it.

Birds called their morning chorus but Kaplyn failed to hear them. His mind was reviewing the terrible events of the previous day. A tremor ran down his body, probably due to the cold. Something Lars said about the Prophecy niggled but he could not fathom it; then the thought was gone.

Stiffly he raised himself onto his arm, relieving the ache in his back from sleeping on the hard ground and looked out across the large open expanse. The city was gone and all that remained were ruins. Part of him was relieved.

Vastra was standing at the edge of the camp, looking out across Tanel while Lars was trying to rekindle the fire. Lars grinned broadly. "You're awake at last," he said.

"How long have I slept?" Kaplyn asked. His throat felt parched and even to his own ears his voice sounded croaky.

"All night and most of the morning," Lars replied.

Vastra walked over and peered down at Kaplyn. His eyes were narrow and Kaplyn shivered, this time not because of the cold.

"We need to leave once we've eaten," Vastra announced, turning around and returning to the fire where he set about preparing breakfast.

"He's a moody one," Lars said. "We'll need to watch him," he added in a whisper.

"I intend to," Kaplyn replied, and together they went to join Vastra. Hurriedly they prepared and ate a frugal meal since they were eager to be on their way in advance of the rain that threatened.

As soon as they were mounted, the skies opened. A torrent of freezing cold rain fell, drenching the three men who sat miserably hunched over their horses as they rode across the large open plain. All abut them the rain formed a grey mist, blurring the landscape. Their horses struggled as the ground became wet and spongy.

Kaplyn was cold, wet and miserable. Just as he was about to suggest they look for shelter, the rain ceased.

Soon the clouds dispersed, leaving a clear blue sky at least as far as the horizon where clouds gathered menacingly. Their mood lifted as their clothes gradually dried in the warm sunshine. In the distance, a rainbow

93

appeared, stretching high into the sky, its summit lost from view in the blue heavens.

"My people have a story about rainbows. They say that at the end of a rainbow a dwarf sits forging jewellery fit for a princess," Kaplyn said. "The dwarf offered to marry a princess but she spurned him and, in a fit of anger, he persuaded his people to wage war against her people. Unfortunately, in the war the Princess was killed and in anguish the dwarf killed himself. His punishment in the after life is to make jewellery to please her."

Lars smiled. "In my land a rainbow is a staircase to the heavens for Sarl, the god of rain. He carries a great ash bow and silver arrows in his quiver. The arrows light up the sky when he hunts. You can hear his growl when he misses; he is a poor hunter and his aim is poor," Lars concluded with a grin.

Kaplyn laughed and he even thought he saw Vastra smile briefly, although he urged his horse ahead as though unwilling to share their mood.

"Sarl?' Kaplyn repeated the name, enjoying its sound. "That seems an appropriate name for a poor marksman. I should lend him my bow and then perhaps his aim would improve."

"You should not mock the gods lest they take you up on your offer," Lars countered, although his eyes sparkled with merriment. "Besides, if his aim improves, we would be in trouble."

They rode in silence before Kaplyn spoke. "These gods of yours, where are they now?" he asked.

Lars looked about him and he became serious as his eyes searched the heavens. "They're all around," he whispered softly. "If you listen you can hear their voices on the wind. They plot our trials to strengthen us for the future, testing us with blizzards, gales, famine and drought, amongst other hardships."

Kaplyn frowned, "Aren't gods supposed to be kind and gentle?"

Lars shook his head, rubbing his beard. "Let me tell you what my people believe and then you may judge for yourself. Fallor-Ell is their home and that is where our souls go when we die. It is said to be a beautiful and tranquil place.

"The gods treat us well, almost like gods ourselves. We laugh at our hardships, seeing the necessity of the cruelty thrust upon us, so we have strength and resolve for the coming battle. Food within Fallor-Ell is plentiful and game willingly surrenders to our knives for it is an honour to be eaten by the god's guests. Wines and beers flow freely in giant rivers where great buckets hang by the banks so we may drink our fill."

Kaplyn grinned at the image, which seemed an appropriate reward for the big man's soul.

Lars smiled back, but became serious again as he continued. "It is foretold that one day, at the end of time, the evil giants will gather the fell creatures of the world, and together they will attack Fallor-Ell, seeking to overthrow the gods. When this happens only the spirits of the bravest mortals will fight alongside the gods. That is why they test us, to strengthen our resolve."

They rode in silence for a moment before Lars asked, "What about your people? Do they believe in gods?"

Kaplyn shook his head; his long hair blew in the wind and covered his eyes for an instant. "I don't, but others do. Farmers often pray to the Kalanth, the Old Ones, for a good crop or fine weather."

"What are the Kalanth?" Lars asked. "I've heard them mentioned before."

"They are demigods who are said to have walked the earth many years ago," Kaplyn replied. "They were tasked by the Creator to prepare the world and to banish evil in preparation for the coming of man. There are still many shrines to the Kalanth; at hallowed sites such as a hollow or a dale where it is believed that an Old One once lived. Some farmers still leave gifts for the gods at these sites."

"Gifts?"

"Yes. Nothing much, just food or wine. It is not a surprise though that the offerings disappear. There are many vagabonds who dare the wild, living solitary lives away from civilisation."

"Have you ever seen one of these sites?"

Kaplyn nodded and his eyes looked momentarily distant. "Yes, there was such a place close to Dundalk where I lived. It was a small wood, on an uneven hillock, where a stream had carved its passage over the years. I have to admit it was an odd place," he reflected. Until then he had not thought about it much even though he had often gone there, seeking solitude away from the tedium of court. "It was very beautiful, and peaceful.

"I suppose that it was the Eldric who stopped us believing in the gods," he continued more thoughtfully. "They would have seemed very wise with their magic and their learning. They probably laughed at our superstitious fears. Over the years their culture mixed with ours and their understanding of science taught us to be less fearful of the dark. They explained many mysteries that for centuries had held our people in superstitious thraldom."

"They must have been a great people indeed to explain all the wonders of the world," Lars stated sadly.

Kaplyn realised he was being foolish, for there was still much that they did not know. The world was a big place and they had barely explored their own borders, let alone those beyond. "Perhaps we are not as wise as we would like to believe," he conceded.

Later that morning Kaplyn looked towards the distant mountains, crowned with wreaths of sombre clouds. Kaplyn expected their journey would take many days yet.

He was deliberately taking their route close to an old friend's home and he was anticipating the visit, remembering with fondness the hours spent with Hallar, his closest childhood friend.

He watched the landscape change around them while they rode. At first the grass was a rich, deep green and the ground soft, but later the scenery became undulating and on the top of each hillock was a crown of tall oak trees. Gorse and bracken grew in profusion around the stony trail, and rabbits often scampered across the path a few yards ahead of their plodding mounts, swiftly disappearing amongst the thick vegetation scant yards ahead.

They continued across lush countryside for two days, occasionally meeting sheepherders tending their fold or farmers tilling the fields, and these folk greeted them with open curiosity. The farm folk were eager to exchange food for a chance to discuss news from afar. They were all too glad of the company and a chance to break their lonely vigils.

Vastra hung back during these encounters, looking anxious to be on his way. He was aloof and distant, and his eyes often strayed towards their distant goal as though willing them to be upon the road again.

When they woke on the third morning from Tanel the mountains were more prominent, but still some distance away. The day started dreary and damp; the sky turned leaden and low clouds touched the treetops with soft misty fingers. The rain, when it came, was a downpour and once more the riders were very quickly soaked and miserable.

They were camped by the banks of a stream that offered little protection from the chill wind when Kaplyn suggested finding shelter. Vastra insisted on continuing, saying time was too short for delays. Kaplyn was growing impatient. They were close to his friend's home and they could reach it by mid-morning.

After arguing in the wet for some time, Kaplyn finally told Vastra that they were leaving. Vastra visibly fumed as they started to pack. He had no choice and, muttering, he put away his own belongings. As though making a point though he rode behind them and Kaplyn could almost feel his hateful glare on his back.

Feeling guilty, Kaplyn tried to draw him into their conversation; he had to look over his shoulder and shout above the noise of the rain and wind, but his only reply was a menacing silence and finally he admitted defeat. Wearily they rode into the lashing rain with heads bowed.

Kaplyn reined his horse to a stop at a fork in the road. Silhouetted against the dreary sky a small castle was perched defiantly upon a rocky hill. Kaplyn grinned at the familiar sight. The keep's copper roofs had long since turned green and they added a splash of colour to the otherwise monotonous stone.

By his side, Vastra cast him a questioning look.

"Someone who lives here owes me a favour," Kaplyn said. "I stopped a thief from taking his purse. He turned out to be a baron ... that is the man I saved was a baron, not the thief," Kaplyn continued. "He said if I was ever nearby then I was welcome to call in."

"Quite right," Lars answered. "You probably saved him a tidy sum and his dignity no doubt."

Kaplyn was relieved that Lars at least had accepted his tale and ignoring Vastra he spurred his horse towards the castle and the open gates that beckoned.

Chapter 11

An Old Friend

Two sentries armed with long pikes stopped them at the castle gates.

"What's your business?" the older of the two men asked. Both seemed surly at having to leave the comfort of the guardhouse. Rain cascaded from their helms and into their eyes, causing them to blink as they looked up at the riders. The sound of the rain, drumming on the nearby roofs, made Kaplyn eager to gain sanctuary and his temper was mounting the longer he was kept from being dry. .

"I'm an acquaintance of the Baron and would like to speak with him," he answered, trying to keep his voice calm.

For a moment, neither guard spoke. Kaplyn realised he must look like a beggar in his mud-splattered clothes.

"Give me your name and I'll ask if he will see you," the guard offered after a pause.

"My name is Kaplyn Lasthlan," he said. Lasthlan was his mother's maiden name and he hoped that Hallar would remember it. He gave Vastra a sideways glance in case he recognised the name, but he didn't seem to.

The guard nodded. "Go and tell the Baron that he has guests," he said to his companion who turned and left, giving the three men a curious backwards glance.

"In the meantime you can go to the guest quarters," the Guard Captain continued. "If you enter through the gate and go across the courtyard, you will see a low building on your right. That's where visitors stay; someone will meet you and take your horses to the stable."

"Thank you," Kaplyn replied, dismounting and waiting while the others followed suit. Leading his mount by its reins he led the way through the narrow gateway. As if upon command, the rain ceased as soon as they reached the inner courtyard. Both Kaplyn and Lars laughed but it was of little consolation for they were already soaked and, to make matters worse,

98

their feet quickly became sodden as they splashed through deep puddles that had formed on the uneven cobbled street.

A tall youth, in his early teens, came running from an open doorway within the large central building and offered to take their horses to the stables. Kaplyn was frustrated that he had no money to tip the boy and he was angered that Vastra did not offer. The boy did not seem to mind though as he led the animals away.

The lodge comprised several large rooms, each containing three or four beds, a few chairs and best of all a fireplace. It was mean lodgings compared to what Kaplyn would have expected under normal circumstances. A servant was lighting a fire in one of the rooms and gratefully they put their belongings onto the beds. Eagerly they gathered around the flames to warm themselves before unpacking their spare clothes from their packs.

A liveried servant entered. "Which one of you is Kaplyn?" he asked.

Kaplyn raised a hand. The servant eyed him suspiciously for a moment. "You are to accompany me," he said at length, a note of disdain clear in his vioice.

Kaplyn started forward and so, too, did Lars.

"Just the one," the servant snapped. "You'll get your turn, no doubt." The servant glared at Kaplyn. "If you have clean clothes then I suggest you change."

Kaplyn felt his cheeks flush. No one had ever spoken to him like that before. He dried himself on a towel that had been draped at the end of the bed and quickly changed. His last act as he left the room was to place his sword by his bed; it would have been considered bad manners to take the weapon into Hallar's house. His Eldric blade remained concealed within his belongings.

The entry hall was just as Kaplyn remembered. An imposing wooden staircase led up to the minstrels' gallery, which circled the lower room. On the walls hung several displays of antique weapons including pikes, swords and axes. Kaplyn had always admired the collection, many of which dated back to the Krell Wars. Even still, Hallar would be envious of his Eldric sword.

The servant led him through a side door to one of the many audience rooms. Numerous candles brightly lit the interior and standing by a large log fire was his friend. Neither men spoke until the servant left. A broad smile creased the Baron's broad face as soon as the door thumped shut. He strode over to Kaplyn and gave him a mighty slap across the shoulders.

"Orlastor, old friend," he said cheerfully. "I have not seen you for far too long."

Kaplyn grinned broadly, "Don't be formal," he said. "It's Kaplyn — and less of the old. By the looks of you, I see you are keeping well," he said.

The Baron patted his bulging waistline and looked sheepish. "I have a fine wife to look after me now," he said by way of explanation and the pair laughed. "But you are looking well. How are the King and Queen and the rest of the family?"

"Well … everyone is well! My father is still as stubborn as a mule though."

"Ah….that runs in the family."

Kaplyn frowned but couldn't deny it.

"But why are you here?" Hallar asked. "A palace messenger reported you were missing. Everyone is frantic. Look at you — you are more like a poacher than a prince. I'm surprised that the guards let you in. I can see that I'll have to speak to them later," he said with a mischievous grin. "And why are you using your mother's maiden name? It took me a while to think who it might be. I was about to tell you to be off until I realised it was you."

"You would have received my father's displeasure if you had," Kaplyn replied laughing. "It's a long story … if you have the time."

The Baron looked serious and offered him a seat, which Kaplyn gratefully accepted. Long days on horseback and the sudden drenching had left his muscles tired and stiff.

He told Hallar about Lars and Vastra. He spoke of the Pendrat fair and even bragged about his own win. In the relaxed atmosphere and by the warmth of the fire, Kaplyn felt more at ease. The Baron interrupted the story after a while for refreshments. Ringing a bell, they awaited the servant who returned promptly. It was the same man who had earlier escorted Kaplyn.

"Mulled wine for my guest," the Baron requested.

The servant nodded and glanced warily at Kaplyn as if he had cast a spell over the Baron. As soon as the other man had left, Kaplyn told him about his adventure in the Eldric tower. The Baron interrupted him on occasions and asked him to elaborate, clearly horrified that Kaplyn had endured such danger.

Strangely, Kaplyn found his memory of the events had already become vague and talking about them now brought back the strange feelings he had experienced. A knock at the door warned them the servant had returned and they fell silent as he entered carrying a tall flagon of steaming red wine from which came a pleasant, bitter aroma.

Kaplyn gratefully accepted a wooden flagon of hot wine from the servant who turned to serve the Baron before leaving.

"The thing that amazed me most of all," Kaplyn said, resuming the tale, "was that it all had to be an illusion. I kept telling myself that over and over. There was no way a lake that size could have been inside the tower but, like everything else, it seemed so real." He paused to take a sip of the wine, enjoying its flavour.

"The Eldric were mighty sorcerers," Hallar interrupted. "I could believe anything from the tales I've heard. You are fortunate to be alive. However, that does not excuse you for putting your life at risk," he admonished seriously. "You should take care, especially of this Vastra. He sounds dangerous. Are you sure that you know what you are doing? Wouldn't it be wise just to take the pendant and leave him? Then at least he cannot cause any mischief."

Kaplyn shook his head, warming his hands on the flagon. "No, I can't do that. Vastra might be right about the pendant; it could be a clue to where the Eldric went."

"Then let him take it and good riddance!" Hallar declared. His voice had lost its earlier humour and it was clear that he was genuinely concerned for his friend's safety. "After all, he freely admits that he hates your father. What would Vastra do if he knew you were his half-brother?"

Kaplyn again shook his head, swilling the warm wine in the flagon and enjoying the strong smell. "I admit that his suspicion may be aroused after my visit to see you. I told him I was a palace guard and that I saved you from a thief. I think he believes me but I am not sure for how much longer."

He placed his flagon on the table at his side and looked at his friend seriously. "It's an unfortunate business, but there is too much at stake. According to Vastra, the pendant will reveal the whereabouts of the Eldric. Think what that could mean," Kaplyn said, his eyes sparkling with excitement.

"It sounds like a fool's errand. The Eldric disappeared long ago and may not want to be found, but if you insist on pursuing this task then let me go in your place. I would keep an eye on this wizard for you."

Kaplyn raised his eyebrows. "And leave your lovely wife? "

Hallar looked exasperated, "What do you intend then?"

Kaplyn stretched luxuriously, "Tonight, a meal, a bath and a good night's rest."

"No tomorrow, you fool!'

Kaplyn feigned surprise at Hallar's choice of words. "We are going to the Pen-Am-Pelleas Mountains and will travel through the KinAnar forest. It's a short cut and will save us a few weeks going that way."

Hallar looked perplexed.

"I will write to my father before I leave," Kaplyn suggested as if reading his friend's mind. "I will tell him what I intend and explain that you tried to talk me out of it, offering all the help that you could."

Hallar brightened suddenly, "That's it! Take some of my men! I could easily spare a hest as an escort."

Kaplyn shook his head. "I've already taken a great risk coming here. If Vastra suspects who I am then I could be in serious danger and an armed escort might do just that. Your offer of help is generous, but I must decline."

Hallar sagged back into his chair looking very much defeated. The pair sat in silence for a moment.

The sun suddenly broke through the clouds and a bright light, marking early evening, streamed through the thick glass.

"If you insist on going then you must take care. You might not be aware, but there have been several krell raids on our eastern borders recently. Last time we met, I spoke to your father about this and he promised to send a patrol into the mountains to see if they could flush them out."

"That's the second time I've heard of krell raids. Yet there was no mention of them at the palace." Kaplyn rose, deep in thought and went across to the window to look out onto the courtyard. It was deserted and the light reflected brightly from the wet cobbles.

The Baron nodded. "Your father must be keeping the news from the people. I fear he is mistaken in this matter. He should be more honest. There are many who would use such news to discredit him."

Kaplyn frowned. "What are you saying?"

"For one — farmers are annoyed by the lack of protection," Hallar continued.

Kaplyn grinned. "Farmers always complain, you know that. Too much sun, too little sun — not enough rain, then floods. I think it's a farmer's lot to complain."

"That may be true, but I worry that your father is not in touch with his people. The fact that you did not know about the krell raids shows that there is a problem. The King is protecting some folk while ignoring others, and that is dangerous."

The pair fell silent. Kaplyn had always thought his father to be a good king and had never considered that the people might not think so. He could not consider otherwise.

"I have to admit, this talk of krell worries me," Kaplyn said as his thoughts turned away from his father.

Hallar nodded. "Do you remember when we were young we used to talk of the Krell Wars and the Prophecy; they were good times, but we never really gave thought to what might happen if the Prophecy came true. To live through a second Krell War would be terrible."

"That was a long time ago. We wished for war so we could be heroes. Now we are older we hope that war will never happen."

"What of Trosgarth? Is it possible their influence is growing and that is why the krell are becoming bolder?"

Kaplyn shook his head, but Hallar looked unconvinced as he stroked his chin thoughtfully.

"Trosgarth and Aldrace are no longer a threat," Kaplyn said. "The alliance is more than a match for them."

"But what about the Prophecy? I agree the alliance is strong enough to counter a threat from a sizeable army, but what if Drachar's shade was summoned back to the land? Ever since the Eldric left, there has been no defence against sorcery."

"Do not forget there has been peace since the Krell Wars; surely we can rest assured it will last for a while longer."

Hallar grinned at his friend's determination. "I'm sorry, I was being pessimistic. You are right; another war is unlikely."

He replenished his flagon and offered Kaplyn a refill. "It's nearly time for dinner. I insist you join us. I will have fresh clothes sent down for you and your friends. You can meet Gayle. I am sure that she will be pleased to see you again."

Kaplyn readily agreed, accepting more mulled wine.

"I'm not happy with you staying in the travellers' quarters though. You should be in the main building with the rest of us. Your father would not forgive me if he knew you were not being looked after properly."

"I still need to keep my identity secret, so I'll remain where we are, but we will attend dinner. That will keep Vastra guessing," Kaplyn replied, settling back in the comfort of the deep chair.

They spoke for a while longer, remembering less troubled times before Kaplyn returned to his room to pass on the Baron's invitation. Kaplyn felt relaxed and carefree for the first time in quite some while.

Later that evening Kaplyn escorted Lars and Vastra to the dining hall, carrying his Eldric sword wrapped in his spare clothes beneath his arm. Hallar had been true to his word and someone had brought them fresh clothes. A bath had been a real tonic and he felt very comfortable dressed in the rich garments. It was a marvellous feeling to be clean again. Lars, on the other hand, had been crestfallen when a servant had taken away his own clothes for laundering.

As Kaplyn led them up the broad flight of stairs, Lars looked about in awe of the rich surroundings. "You say that you stopped a thief from stealing the Baron's purse and that is why he invited you here?"

Kaplyn nodded and Lars whistled softly. "It's a good way of getting a free meal if you ask me."

The dining room was immense, dominated by a long table whose polished surface reflected the light from numerous candles arrayed about the room. A sizeable log fire burned at one end of the hall where a pair of large, shaggy hunting hounds lay as close as the heat would allow. One raised its massive head to watch the strangers and its tail thumped the floor half-heartedly before it lay back down to soak up the heat. Two richly dressed servants stood attentively by a door at the far end of the dining room while another escorted them to their seats.

There were three other guests already present at the table, and they looked unfavourably at Kaplyn and the others as they went by. Kaplyn felt annoyed for if anyone deserved a second look it was these men. Their heads were shaven and they wore ochre robes encrusted with grime as though they had travelled a long road. It was normal for a baron such as Hallar to allow guests to dine at his table, and Kaplyn assumed that they must have recently arrived and requested an audience.

Hallar and his wife Gayle entered, smiling broadly at their guests as they took their seats at the head of the table. To Kaplyn, Gayle looked as beautiful as ever. She was petite, much smaller than Hallar. Her dark hair cascaded over her shoulders and she wore her fringe long, almost hiding her eyes. She smiled mischievously at Kaplyn who hoped Hallar had warned her not to give his identity away.

Kaplyn and Lars were seated next to them while Vastra was adjacent to the other three guests. Hallar introduced Kaplyn who in turn introduced Lars and Vastra. Lars was clearly in awe of the pomp and ceremony of a formal dinner. Vastra treated the Baron and his wife graciously, but Kaplyn could see the resentment reflected in his eyes.

One of the strangers, a prematurely wrinkled man with heavy bags under his eyes, introduced himself as Aldor. His voice was deep and his speech slow and methodical.

Aldor indicated to the rotund, rather short man sitting next to him and introduced him as Diran. He had large, shaggy eyebrows that gave him a perpetual frown. Diran nodded to the other guests as Aldor turned to his remaining companion, a tall thin youth with a hawk-like nose who he introduced as Borrin.

Servants entered carrying trays of food which they arranged upon the table. Kaplyn and Lars relished the meal after so many days on the road. By comparison, Vastra ate sparingly, merely picking at his food.

Initially the conversation avoided the three other guests, apart from a few pleasantries. As the servants cleared the last dishes away the Baron turned to Aldor. "Now, what is it that you wish to discuss?" he asked politely.

"Sir," Aldor said, rising and looking serious. "Ours is a religious order based on new concepts, which we are bringing to the people."

It's money, Kaplyn thought. He cast the Baron a meaningful glance and his friend raised his eyebrows in reply, placing his chin on his hands.

"Our people's needs are few and we live simple lives. We believe that if the body is pure then the mind is capable of greatness. For this reason our followers must give up false comforts and easy living. Instead, we ask that they live frugal lives and in return we promise to enrich their souls."

Kaplyn looked at the priest's empty wine goblet, but refrained from comment.

"Our following increases daily and more are turning to our order to satisfy their longing for harmony, to fill their sad, dreary days with meaning, to have a purpose in life, to belong."

Aldor's voice was rising and the words flowed freely, coming faster and faster. A fleck of spittle ran down his chin and his eyes took on a glazed distant look as though he was elsewhere. "The old gods are no more," he said dangerously, looking at the others as if challenging them to contradict. "It is now time to turn to a new god!'

Kaplyn frowned. Although he did not believe in the Kalanth he knew that many folk still did. To some people, pronouncing them "no more" was like stating that the sun would not rise in the morning. These priests were toying with fire and there had to be more to them than met the eye if they were to gain credence.

"We can offer the people a better life; they can achieve much more with our teaching. Our god, Ryoch, is strong and has promised to guide us,

105

while those who do not will wallow and flounder in mire and dung of their own making. Ryoch offers immortality, while the Old Ones offer *nothing*. They have long since forsaken us, passing into oblivion and leaving *nought* but the ravage of time."

Kaplyn could stand no more. "What proof is there that there is a new god?"

"Our minds are the only proof *we* need," Aldor said, pointing to his own temple and eyeing Kaplyn darkly. "This lets us talk to our god and to our brothers. We have heard his voice, he tells us to follow and great will be our order in the days to come. We shall bask in Ryoch's glory. However, he is not a tolerant god and he tells us to choose. We have chosen," he said indicating his fellows.

"Then you have no proof?" Kaplyn asked.

Aldor's smile darkened. "Write something and do not show me," he suggested.

Kaplyn frowned, but asked one of the servants to fetch a quill and ink. An uncomfortable silence prevailed while the servant was away. Aldor and the others sat smugly, oozing confidence. Lars cast Kaplyn a warning look, but he chose to ignore him. Vastra frowned and leant forward attentively, a look of concern on his face. Kaplyn realised he had slipped out of his role as an ex-palace guard; a guard would not be expected to be able to read, but then he remembered that most palace guards he knew could.

The servant returned, handing Kaplyn a quill, parchment and a pot of ink. Kaplyn dipped the quill in the ink and scratched some letters on the paper.

Aldor spoke as Kaplyn wrote. "The Kalanth live." His eyes widened and his jaw dropped as he completed the sentence, realising what he had said. The other two priests cast him dark looks as if he had meant the blasphemy.

Kaplyn frowned; the priest had read exactly what he had written.

Aldor gave Kaplyn a baleful look. His voice became low and threatening and a humourless smile touched his lips. "You are wrong, and I fear for your soul." He held his chin high, his look of contempt plain for all to see.

The Baron reached for the parchment and read it. A frown crossed his face.

"What is it you wish from me?"

"We need money and land to build on," Aldor's voice cracked with excitement, he clearly assumed the Baron was conceding to his requests. "We will build a temple to Ryoch."

"And in return?" the Baron asked.

"You will be privileged within our ranks and the smile of Ryoch will shower you with riches."

The Baron paused. "I'm sorry, I cannot offer you anything."

Aldor stiffened. "Very well, but do not say that you were not warned." He and his companions left without saying anything further.

"He's a charlatan!" Kaplyn said when they had gone.

"And dangerous," the Baron added. "He's a fanatic and they are always dangerous. They convince good men to turn from everything that they hold dear, with their stories and magic tricks."

"There was no magic used tonight," Vastra interrupted softly. Having seen what Vastra was capable of, Kaplyn was inclined to believe him.

"Then how do you explain his trick?" Hallar asked.

"As you said, he is a dangerous man," Vastra replied simply.

"I did not like or trust him," Gayle said. "He is frightening. Did you see his eyes? Thank the Kalanth he is only staying the one night."

"Will you be all right sharing the same quarters with those men?" the Baron asked.

Kaplyn nodded, smiling.

Hallar shook his head, "I'm sorry now that I invited them to dinner. A friend asked me to speak with them. Had I known what they were like I wouldn't have offered."

"I have heard of these Priests of Ryoch before," Gayle said. "Apparently they have a considerable following. I have also heard, but it is only a rumour, that they preach against the King."

Kaplyn frowned.

"It appears they are an ambitious people then," Vastra said softly, without a trace of humour.

Kaplyn glanced at him while the others either did not hear him or chose to ignore his comment.

There was a moment's silence and then Hallar spoke, clearly trying to lighten the mood. "Now Kaplyn, where's this sword you told me about?"

Kaplyn bent, retrieving the bundle by his feet. He unwrapped the Eldric blade then withdrew it from its scabbard and was shocked to find the blade shining dully with a blue radiance, but the glow faded as he looked. He was about to hand the weapon to the Baron when Vastra interrupted.

"Don't touch it!" he warned icily, standing and knocking his chair over backwards in his haste. "It's an Eldric blade! You should have warned me that you had it! A weapon like this chooses its master. In the wrong hands it is a curse."

In the candlelight the blade's silver runes stood out against the dull metal as if in challenge to Vastra's wrath.

"What does the lettering say?" Hallar asked, pointing to the runes.

Kaplyn shrugged and turned to Vastra who merely scowled; although he leant forward, his face flushed, he was clearly ill at ease.

"It is an Eldric script with which I am not familiar," he grumbled.

Kaplyn frowned, hearing Vastra admit to not knowing every Eldric script came as a surprise after his constant boasting.

"I know," Hallar interrupted, "I'll summon Jastin, the librarian. He is a scholar of texts both ancient and modern. If anyone can translate the letters he can." The Baron requested a servant to find Jastin and he promptly left in search of the old man.

Vastra retrieved his chair and sat down heavily, clearly angered by Kaplyn's disclosure that he had the sword.

The servant returned after a few moments, closely followed by a grey-haired old man wearing long flowing robes. He almost ran to keep up with the younger man. Jastin bowed towards the Baron.

"How may I be of service, my Lord?" he asked in a voice cracked with age.

"Could you tell us what the inscription upon the blade says?" the Baron asked.

Kaplyn held the sword for the old man to see. He bent low over the weapon, peering closely at the fine lettering. His eyesight was obviously poor and he studied it before rising slowly with his hand on his back as though he was experiencing some pain.

"It's an Eldric script, but not one I know," he said. "However, with the aid of my books I should be able to translate it."

"You will have to write the runes down," Kaplyn said. "I will not let the sword out of my sight."

The old man nodded and from his pocket produced a parchment and a piece of charcoal. He copied the runes and then examined his work before declaring that it would suffice.

The Baron smiled as he left. "He is a good man, even if he can't see his own feet."

Kaplyn smiled, "I'm surprised he can find his books."

"Oh he doesn't need eyesight for that. He has each one's position firmly fixed in his mind," Hallar announced.

They spoke for a short while longer until Vastra declared he was tired and excused himself, wishing everyone a good night. Gayle soon followed leaving only Lars, Kaplyn and Hallar remaining. The dogs, seeing that dinner was finished, returned from their vigil (hoping for tidbits) at the table to the contentment of the warm fire where they flopped down, panting with the extreme heat, caring nought for the discussions of men.

Chapter 12

An Unwelcome Visitor

The servants replenished their goblets and stoked the fire before retiring to a discrete corner until Hallar, with a wave of his hand, dismissed them. Kaplyn and Hallar soon fell into a conversation about friends and family but Kaplyn quickly realised Lars would soon guess they were more than casual acquaintances. Over the brief period of time he had known him, Kaplyn had learned to trust him and he decided to take him into his confidence. He told him the truth that his father was the King.

"I deliberately kept my identity a secret, but when I realised Vastra might be my half-brother, I knew I could never trust him until I learnt more about him. You heard how much he hates my father. I daren't confide in him until I know what he intends doing."

"Don't worry, your secret is safe," Lars replied. "Vastra is a bitter man; he carries the seed of his own destruction within him."

Kaplyn smiled, relieved by Lars' co-operation and friendship.

All at once the flames within the hearth changed colour. A blue flame burned brightly, eerily illuminating the room with its pale radiance. The change was not natural and the three men looked at the fire, and then each other.

The dogs stood up, their hackles rising. They both faced the end of the hall, growling menacingly. Other dogs within the castle started to bark until the castle was alive with noise.

A cry of absolute terror pierced the night, causing even the stoutest souls within earshot to cower in dread. As abruptly as it started, it ended. The three men looked at one another, eyes wide with fear.

"What was that?" Lars asked.

Kaplyn reached for his Eldric sword and drew the weapon. It gave a chilling whine as it cleared the scabbard. The blade shone with an intense blue light, causing Hallar and Lars to step back.

Kaplyn stared at the blade but another scream distracted him. Together the three men raced to the door leading to the west tower, which Hallar threw open to reveal a white-faced servant who stared at Kaplyn's glowing sword.

"Fetch me a weapon," Hallar urged of the bewildered man who nodded and ran off. Lars called after him for an axe. Hallar led them to a small stone archway beyond which a steep winding staircase led to the upper levels of the west tower.

Two guards stood with swords drawn at the base of the stairs, looking fearfully up. Both seemed uncertain and the sight of Kaplyn's glowing blade made them step back, eyes wide with fear. At that moment, the servant returned carrying a heavy broadsword and an axe which Hallar and Lars gratefully took, feeling their balance.

"Fetch some torches," Hallar told the servant who gladly fled.

"What has happened?" Hallar asked.

The guards looked terrified. "We were patrolling when we heard a scream from upstairs. Tumarl and Narn went up to investigate a short while ago. Since then we've been calling their names, but there's been no reply."

"Where does this lead?" Kaplyn asked.

"The library," Hallar replied.

"The old man?" Kaplyn asked.

The Baron nodded. "He'll be up there."

Kaplyn started for the stairs, but the Baron held his arm. "Wait for the torches." Kaplyn nodded, taking a step back. Shortly the servant returned carrying three flaming brands, each burned with an unnatural blue flame and the sight caused the guards' eyes to widen.

"Demon," hissed one under his breath.

The other guard looked at the torch as if a demon was about to materialise from its fiery heart.

"You two follow me," Hallar said. "Kronar," he said to the servant, "fetch others. If we do not return soon then seal this doorway and await the dawn before sending anyone else up."

Kaplyn started up the stairs before Hallar could protest, using the light from his sword to illuminate the stone steps. He went cautiously, knowing that if it was a demon then it was already too late to aid the librarian and anyone else with him.

The guards came next. "Don't let the demon touch your heart," the older guard cautioned the other in a hushed whisper. He was referring to the old wives' tale that if a demon took a man's heart it would take his soul to eternal damnation. Kaplyn continued the twisting climb, feeling the wall for

111

support with the back of his sword arm. He held the pendant through his shirt in his other hand; the talisman seemed to aid his courage. It was Eldric made and, in the past, they had successfully fought and defeated demons.

The stairway was deliberately narrow to prevent an enemy from climbing or descending in force. It also prevented Kaplyn from seeing further ahead than the central stone column supporting the stairs. Suddenly he missed his footing and nearly fell, his heart beat wildly and the guard behind him cried out in fright.

Kaplyn continued more carefully; then all at once the blue light was no longer reflected from the stone wall beside him, and he saw a partially opened doorway ahead. An eerie green glow filtered through it. Kaplyn pushed the door wider and cautiously looked in. Row upon row of bookshelves, stacked with large dusty volumes, filled the room, making a clear view of the interior impossible.

Everything glowed with an unearthly green pallor and, as Kaplyn entered, a terrible numbing cold greeted him. The hilt of his sword seemed to twist in his grasp. Behind him the others followed equally as wary, each looking surreal in the odd light.

Kaplyn needed to know what was in the room. Crossing to the nearest bookcase, he tried toppling it. Lars, understanding his intent, helped and together they rocked it so that it slowly picked up momentum until finally it toppled backwards. The two men leapt back. With an almighty crash it smashed onto the one behind, causing that to fall with it. Within seconds, other bookshelves toppled, creating a fountain of dust and paper. Some did not quite fall and these ended up wedged against each other.

Mingled with the crashing a piercing shriek split the air. The onlookers jumped visibly as a dark shape erupted from within the mass of books and broken wood. The figure scrambled onto a precariously balanced bookshelf where it sat, looking down on them with undisguised hatred. It shielded its eyes from the glow of Kaplyn's blade, as though the light it cast was causing it pain. Behind the creature, in the wall, was a gaping hole, and from this spewed the green light and numbing cold.

The demon, for there could be little doubt that was what they faced, was easily about eight feet in height, although its immense limbs were curled up beneath it like a giant spider. A hideous grin split its ugly face and its long, pointed tail lashed angrily like a giant cat's. Its arms ended in long vicious looking talons and in one talon it grasped something that looked like it had come from a butcher's yard.

As if caught in a spell, neither side moved and then, emitting a fearful scream, the demon leapt across the intervening bookshelves, landing with a crash and a shower of debris in front of the group. Its cry froze the watchers. With a mighty swing of its arm, the demon cut one guard in two, catching the other guard a glancing blow across his shoulder. Its speed was impossible.

Screaming battle cries Kaplyn and the Baron leapt at the monster. The demon turned, lashing out, and the attackers suddenly became the attacked. Hallar blocked a vicious stroke with his blade, but the steel barely scratched the demon's flesh. The demon struck out wildly, its talon coming under Hallar's guard.

Kaplyn stepped in the way, blocking the blow with his sword. The blade sliced deeply into the demon's flesh at the elbow, severing the arm, which flopped limply to the floor, oozing green blood that hissed angrily in contact with the stone. The demon screamed. Kaplyn's blade twisted impatiently within his grip as though endowed with a life of its own; he brought the weapon around and thrust up, under the demon's damaged limb. The blade tore eagerly into the demon's flesh, emitting a deep sonorous keening as if sensing the demon's imminent demise. With astonishing speed, the demon leapt back, screaming in both rage and pain. Before Kaplyn could complete the thrust he slipped on a pool of blood and went down on one knee.

The demon, intent upon escape, raced for the hole. Lars intercepted it, swinging his axe in a wide arc. The blow would have decapitated it if it had connected, but once more, the demon's speed saved it as it ducked beneath the weapon, leaping to one side. Even so, the axe caught it a glancing blow and the demon screamed in rage. It continued its wild flight, scrambling awkwardly across the stricken bookshelves until it stood once more upon the top of a bookcase. From there, it turned to stare at the men and the look of malice froze Kaplyn's blood. Green blood oozed from its wounds, smoking when it came in contact with the bookcase.

Suddenly, with an ear-splitting cry it turned, disappearing into the hole, which continued to spew cold air and a pungent, sickly smell. Kaplyn shouted and made as if to follow, but Lars grabbed him by his shoulder.

With a loud clap the hole disappeared, cutting off the eerie glow. A rush of air doused their torches, plunging them into darkness. With trembling hands, they relit the smouldering brands while Hallar called down to the guards at the bottom of the stairs to come up and lend a hand. Kaplyn wiped the demon's blood from his blade on scattered paper.

The first guard to enter looked deathly pale and his eyes were wide with fear; at any other time he might have appeared comical, but now, amongst the bitter stench of death, no one noticed his gaunt expression. Others timidly followed and they, too, stared in horror at the carnage.

Hallar urged them to help and the urgency in his tone broke the spell binding them. The room was abruptly a hive of activity as men cleared the books and shelves in search for wounded.

A tall man came across the body of the guard cut in two, and he could not stop trembling. The other injured guard was trying to stem the flow of blood from a gash on his arm; his jerkin was soaked red from the shoulder down. The Baron attended him, applying a tourniquet. The man cried out when the Baron tightened the bandage. A colleague grabbed his uninjured arm and helped him to remain standing.

Hallar looked worried. It was rumoured that demons carried disease and he clearly feared the wound would fester.

"Take him to the surgeon," he said. Two men helped him from the room whilst others carried the halves of the other body to the cellar to await the dawn.

Hallar then ordered the men to burn anything even remotely contaminated by the demon's blood. A man picked up the demon's arm; his face grimacing as he carefully wrapped the limb in a sheet. Others mopped up the demon's blood, gathering the soiled cloths together in a pile.

When one of the guards let out a cry of shock, others went to investigate. From beneath one of the toppled bookcases a leg protruded. Men manhandled the bookcase out of the way, revealing the bloody remains of the missing two guards and the librarian. The demon had ripped their bodies apart. One of the corpses was missing an arm, which was the object the demon dropped earlier.

Kaplyn found the parchment the librarian was working on, but apart from the copy of the runes from his sword, there was nothing else. Whichever book he had been referencing was lost beneath the pile of other books.

Hallar and Lars joined Kaplyn as men started to remove the bodies.

"It's a bad business," Hallar said sourly, wiping his eyes. "I wouldn't have believed demons existed if not for tonight."

"I've never seen anything like that before," Lars said bewildered. The ordeal had clearly stunned him. Kaplyn realised that he, too, was shaking like a leaf. He tried to still his hands, but failed. Only then did he consider that they should have sought Vastra's help, but it was too late now for recriminations.

Many present started to demand an explanation for the carnage, looking expectantly to Hallar. "Quiet!" he shouted above the hubbub and a silence descended. "A demon has attacked, killing three guards and the librarian."

Several men shouted out in fear.

"It's been driven off and there is nothing to fear now." Hallar barked above the din.

"Was it killed?" one man asked.

Hallar shook his head, and more voices raised their concern. "But be assured that it has gone. I doubt it will be back. Now please leave and return in the morning to help clear up this mess."

Sullenly the men filed out, making their way down the narrow flight of stairs. Hallar posted a guard at the tower's entrance with instructions not to allow anyone to pass unless he gave permission.

Hallar took his leave of Kaplyn and Lars. They understood, there was a lot to do that night and people were coming from their rooms to ask what had happened.

"Come!" Kaplyn said to Lars. "We'd better get some rest; there is nothing else we can do here."

"Do you think *it* will return?" Lars quietly asked as they strode along the dim corridor.

"I hope not," Kaplyn answered, although there was no way that he could be certain. He thought about his sword and its blue light. It was evidently a powerful weapon against the demons and he was glad he had it, shuddering to think what might have happened otherwise, remembering all too clearly how Hallar's sword had barely scratched it.

When they returned, they found Vastra asleep upon his bunk with blankets piled in disarray about him.

"Some *wizard!*" Lars said looking with disdain on the sleeping form.

Kaplyn shook Vastra's shoulders, angrily calling his name.

Blearily, Vastra opened his eyes, looking up bewildered at the two men standing over him. He looked ill and groaned softly as he sat up. "What is it?" he demanded.

"A demon has attacked," Kaplyn replied, noticing Lars going into the adjacent room.

Vastra looked surprised. "A demon? Are you sure?" he asked.

"Of course I'm sure," Kaplyn stormed. "We fought it and drove it off."

At that moment, Lars returned, looking worried. "What has happened to our religious friends?" he asked.

Kaplyn frowned; the priests should have been in the guest quarters for it had been late when they had left.

115

"They were not here when I came in," Vastra stated.

"I'd better tell Hallar," Kaplyn said wearily, knowing that his friend already had a lot to occupy him. As he stepped once more into the cold night he heard Vastra asking Lars more questions about the demon attack, and if anyone had been killed. Kaplyn shook his head; it was going to be a long night.

Kaplyn returned some time later. Both Lars and Vastra were asleep. Wearily he sat down on his bed and with difficulty removed his boots, noisily throwing them to the floor before remembering that the others were sleeping. Lars snorted and turned over and Kaplyn paused. The other man started snoring, causing Kaplyn to grin. He went to a desk where he found paper and a quill. Swiftly he wrote a note to his father, explaining his absence and that he would return soon.

Once satisfied with the letter he continued to undress. The sentries at the castle's entrance had told him that the priests had left earlier that night. Kaplyn had questioned them further, but by his reckoning the priests had left before the demon had struck. He had then found and informed Hallar of his discovery. Between them, they had then spent some time reassuring people that it was safe to go to their beds. It had been a difficult task, persuading folk they were safe when a demon could literally pop out of thin air at any moment. With a shake of his head Kaplyn lay down, but sleep was a long while coming; his imagination kept conjuring demons from the room's dark recesses.

When Kaplyn finally dropped off, almost immediately dreams engulfed him. He dreamt about the eerie hole in the library wall and once again experienced the cold breeze and baleful green light. He shied away from the hole, comprehending the terrible danger and yet something compelled him to enter. He could not help himself. One part of his consciousness screamed not to, but in the way of dreams he stepped forward and the glowing void swallowed him up. A loud click announced that the exit had closed.

He seemed to float along a tunnel. In the frigid air his breath plumed into white clouds and his skin tingled. Then he was within an immense cavern, larger than anything he had seen before, reaching far above his head.

In slow motion he drifted across the cavern floor, effortlessly skirting large columns of rock that magically transformed from the gloom. A nagging fear accompanied him; he knew that he should escape rather than continue.

116

Lazily a demon arose from the shadows, grinning maliciously as it displayed a grizzly trophy. He could not decide what it held and then realised; it was an arm. A finger beckoned and with mounting horror he turned to flee.

The rock beneath his feet became slippery and he could not grip. Behind him the demon laughed, mocking his futile efforts. He could not help but look back and found himself involuntarily turning towards it. His mind screamed to flee, but his legs continued to slide. He grabbed at something to stop himself. Out of the corner of his eye he saw an object and as a last resort, reached out for that. His sleeping mind seemed to come to his aid and he realised that he held his Eldric sword; with recognition, he felt a familiar tingling sensation in his palm. Slowly the cavern and the demon dissolved into inky blackness.

With a sudden shock he awoke, trembling and bathed in sweat. The horror of the nightmare remained. Panting for breath his eyes searched the darkened room, but there was nothing apart from the silhouette of furniture.

Calming himself, he discovered he was tangled in his bed sheets and he realised he must have been running in his sleep; the sheets had restricted his movements, making the dream seem so vivid. As he moved to untangle himself, his palm closed about the hilt of his sword. The weapon's presence mystified him and he was sure that he had left it by the chair at the side of the bed. The glimmer of the runes was still visible in the half-light.

Should he have taken it from the tower? He recalled Vastra's warning about a curse. He also remembered, with some trepidation, the eerie crooning the sword had made as it bit into the demon's flesh, but it was too late now and if there was a curse then he could not avoid it. Besides, he thought grinning, any weapon that could wound or even kill a demon was worth keeping.

He found the scabbard on the floor and sheathed the weapon. Lying back on the hard but comfortable bed he soon fell asleep; this time he slept fitfully and dreams did not bother him again that night.

Kaplyn awoke with sunlight streaming through a chink in the curtains. He listened to people moving about outside before arising stiffly from his warm bed. Vastra was sitting on the edge of his own bed and he nodded by way of greeting.

Kaplyn bade him good morning and padded towards the window, pulling back the heavy curtain. In the daylight, Vastra looked pale as he coughed feebly onto the back of his thin hand. From his bed, Lars groaned and raised himself bleary-eyed onto his elbow, giving Kaplyn an accusing look for letting in the light.

"What are we doing today?" Lars asked. He sounded sullen as though hoping for a postponement of their journey.

Kaplyn, too, felt that the night's events had changed matters. He looked to Vastra for guidance. He was buttoning up his shirt, and he stopped when he realised they were awaiting a response.

"We need to continue today, towards the mountains," he said, picking up his trousers and putting them on.

Lars groaned.

Vastra flashed them an angry look. "If you don't want to accompany me, then give me the pendant and remain here."

Kaplyn smiled and started to dress. "You're not getting rid of us that easily!"

Vastra scowled but remained silent.

"We will need supplies," Lars said miserably.

"What do we need?" Kaplyn asked, looking up for an instant.

"We have some ropes, but that's about all. We are low on food and we are not prepared for bad weather."

"It's spring!" Kaplyn said somewhat surprised, "Surely the weather will be reasonable."

Lars shook his head and rose from the bed. "There could be a cold spell still, especially on the slopes. If we go high enough there may even be snow."

"He's right," Vastra acknowledged.

"Give me some money and I'll ask the Baron where to get supplies," Kaplyn suggested.

Vastra nodded and removed his purse, handing Kaplyn a handful of silver *calder* after fumbling with the small sack.

Kaplyn turned to Lars who was busy listing the supplies they would need.

"Two pack mules, thick woollen vests and jumpers, waterproof cloaks, and plenty to eat."

"You'd better get some torches as well," Vastra suggested. "Oh, and candles as well."

Kaplyn was relieved to have an excuse to talk to his friend before they left and he hurried off before they remembered anything else. He took with him the letter for his father, hidden in his jacket.

Hallar was sitting in the main dining hall, looking perplexed; however, he still managed a smile and greeted Kaplyn warmly.

"Any news of the priests?" Kaplyn asked taking a seat next to his friend. He sank back, enjoying the comfort.

Hallar shook his head. "No — and if they are stupid enough to go traipsing off into the wild in the dead of night then they deserve all they get."

Kaplyn could not agree more. The two men sat in silence. Kaplyn knew that Hallar would object to his leaving, especially after the night's events.

"You have decided to go with the wizard then?" Hallar asked as though on cue.

Kaplyn nodded and briefly their eyes met.

"It's a foolish quest which you would do best to forget," Hallar advised strongly. "Did the demon not make you realise how dangerous your journey might be?"

"I have considered that and in a way it has made my decision easier. What if there were more demon attacks? We need the Eldric and their power to defeat them. If we can find the Eldric, then we should."

Hallar looked away and Kaplyn could see his pain.

"I'll be as safe in the mountains as you are here, possibly safer. A demon is less likely to strike in the wilderness when there are large towns and cities full of people to prey on."

"You forget the other dangers though — krell and dwarves. If you think you are safe strolling into the mountains, then you had better think again!"

Kaplyn knew that he was right, but was not going to be deterred. "We need supplies."

Hallar nodded.

"Winter clothing, food, pack mules and other items on this list." Kaplyn continued, relieved that his friend was not going to say anything further.

Hallar arose stiffly from the comfort of his chair and called for one of the servants who promptly entered.

"Take Kaplyn's list to Ralnar and have him get the supplies ready within the hour."

The servant took the list and left.

"Before I forget," Kaplyn said, removing the coins from his pocket, "I will have to pay for the goods." He saw that Hallar was about to refuse. "It is Vastra's money and he will be suspicious if I return with both these and the supplies."

"See Ralnar when you leave; give him the money," Hallar conceded.

Kaplyn arose. "I will be back soon," he assured his friend. "Will you deliver this letter to my father? Could you also see that he gets this?" he said handing over his old sword.

Hallar took the note and the weapon. "Take care," he said, "and good luck."

After only a short while Ralnar arrived at the travellers' quarters accompanied by three men who carried the supplies they had requested. Ralnar was a thickset old man who had risen through the ranks to become the quartermaster and, like others of his kind, he did not take kindly to requests for supplies from his neatly stacked shelves. Initially he was surly, but when he saw the money his manner changed.

Lars checked the provisions and requested a few additional bits and pieces. Ralnar hurried away and soon returned with the missing items. By mid-morning they were finally ready to leave. Lars went to get their mounts and returned leading the horses by the reins. Mounting, Vastra led them through the small gateway and turned eastwards to the open fields and beyond.

Kaplyn looked back over his shoulder, knowing that Hallar would be watching from one of the upper windows. He raised his hand in farewell and turned to concentrate on their path. A terrible fear swept over him that he might not see his friend again. He was heading out into the wild on a quest leading to who knows where, following a man who hated his father. Kaplyn shuddered. He felt as though his world was collapsing.

Chapter 13

The KinAnar Forest

The day grew warm and the sun's heat was welcome on their backs. They rode across lush green fields, still damp from the previous day's rains. As the castle disappeared from view the path became narrower and more disused; brambles grew thickly along its edge making the journey more difficult. As the day wore on woods became more frequent, forcing them to ride in single file beneath heavily blossomed branches.

They continued to ride in silence as their mounts plodded along the narrow winding trail following the course of a quick-flowing stream. In places the stream was wide and shallow and water bubbled merrily over shingle. This close to the river, the air felt cool which was pleasant as the sun reached its zenith in a clear blue sky.

A wider track leading north intersected theirs, crossing the river over a small rickety looking bridge, disappearing from view into the distance. They decided to stop for lunch by the crossroads before continuing. Vastra told them the path was an ancient dwarf road, used long ago on their pilgrimages to Thandor, their ancestral home. Kaplyn looked in awe at the path, trying to imagine long ranks of heavily laden dwarves marching along it.

All too soon they finished their meal and, after replenishing their canteens from the river, they mounted their horses, setting off along the pinched path once more. Vegetation grew thickly about them, as high as their horses' flanks. Birds and insects flittered across their path, filling the air with vibrant sounds. Occasionally they disturbed a deer or some other wild animal drinking at the water's edge. These would scurry for cover in the nearby undergrowth, spooking the horses and more often than not their riders.

In the late afternoon they came across a vast curtain of trees towering high above them. The girth of each was astounding and they craned their necks to see the tops. Kaplyn could imagine what a mouse felt like, lost amongst a field of ripening wheat.

"These trees must have been growing for centuries," he exclaimed in awe.

"Which forest is this?" Lars asked.

"KinAnar," Kaplyn replied.

Vastra was staring into the forest, looking dreadfully afraid much to Kaplyn's surprise.

"I don't like this place," he announced, coughing into his hand; his eyes looked red and sensitive.

"It's the quickest route," Kaplyn explained.

"How long would it take to go around?" Vastra asked, fidgeting nervously with his reins.

Kaplyn thought for a moment. In truth he did not know, but remembered seeing the forest marked on one of the maps in the palace libraries and made a guess.

"I think it could take a week to travel its length and then another to backtrack the ground we would lose in the detour."

Vastra scowled, turning to stare deep into the wood, his eyes searching the dark places. He did not look well; his cheeks were sunken and his complexion was pale.

It was already late and Kaplyn came to a decision. "Let's camp here for the remainder of the day," he said dismounting. "You two prepare a camp and I'll scout ahead and investigate a little way into the forest. I'll look for game," he added as an afterthought, removing his bow and stringing it. He was keen to try it. He threw his quiver across his shoulder and while adjusting the strap he set off along the trail, quickly entering the outskirts of the forest.

Kaplyn was relieved to be on his own. The forest was beautiful, not dark like the wood he had encountered on his way to Pendrat. The trees were very tall and their lowest branches were high above his head. Soon the trail petered out, but that did not dismay him. The stream continued by his side and he knew that if they followed that, it would eventually lead them to the mountains. He paused, lying down to drink, enjoying the cool clear water.

For a while longer he continued, following the recent spoor of some wild animal. The ground became gently undulating and climbing a particularly steep slope he peered over the summit. Below, a wild fowl pecked at the ground. Slowly and quietly he nocked an arrow and took aim.

He was unaccustomed to the strength of the bow and the arrow passed clean through the fowl killing it instantly. It took him quite some time to find the arrow, which turned out to be considerably further into the forest than he expected. He decided then there was nothing to fear beneath the trees, which seemed so tranquil and peaceful.

By the time he arrived at the forest's edge, the sun was already low on the horizon. Lars was busy tending a fire, partially concealed within a natural hollow while Vastra was sitting with his back to a tree reading a book. To one side, the horses and mules were tethered to trees.

Lars looked relieved to see Kaplyn and equally pleased to see he had fresh meat. Vastra had earlier supplied some herbs and tubers, so they would eat well. As soon as the meal was ready, Lars served it to them on wooden platters while Vastra put a pan of water on the fire to boil. They ate in silence and when they finished Vastra made himself tea. He seemed to recover slightly as he sipped the strong smelling brew and colour returned to his cheeks.

"Did Lars tell you more about the demon?" Kaplyn ventured, secretly hoping to learn more about them.

Vastra nodded as he poured himself another cup of tea. Lars wrinkled his nose as the pungent aroma reached him. He grinned at Kaplyn.

"Demons strike at random," Vastra said, holding his mug in cupped hands while blowing on the hot liquid. Fortunately he had missed Lars' grin. "Last night was an unfortunate incident for the people of Kinlin, but it was probably nothing more than coincidence. You were fortunate though, from what Lars told me; it was driven away empty handed."

Kaplyn smiled at the wizard's unintended pun, having cut off the demon's arm.

"What do you mean, we were fortunate?" Lars asked.

"You disturbed it feeding, before it had time to claim a soul. I've read about the Krell Wars and, in those days, people believed that if a demon returned to hell unaccompanied then its power was decreased as punishment. I think Kaplyn's sword was more than it bargained for."

"I don't understand," Lars replied. "The demon had killed at least three men; why do you believe it returned without a soul?"

A smile touched Vastra's thin lips. "The demon was probably over confident. Normally there wouldn't have been a threat to see it off so quickly. Then it would have time to kill and feast on human flesh before returning to its own world, and only then would it seek a soul, or souls, to accompany it on its homeward journey."

"Is it true that demons can be summoned? Kaplyn asked.

Vastra's eyes narrowed. "Yes, but not without risk. A demon will oppose its summons with all its power. Being in this world causes them pain, or so I believe. It's a very risky spell and if the sorcerer makes a mistake the demon will likely kill him, and take *his* soul for his impudence."

"Is it possible that the priests summoned the demon?" Kaplyn asked.

"I don't think so. Summoning a demon requires considerable power and as far as I could tell last night, when the priest read your mind, he did not use any magic, at least none that I could detect."

Lars listened to the exchange patiently, but looked confused. "You say that demons strike at random. Is it possible then that my own people are at risk?"

Vastra's barely perceptible nod caused Lars to pale.

"Demons will strike anywhere there are people. If they haven't attacked your people, then it is simply because they haven't been discovered...yet."

"What is it?" Kaplyn asked, sensing Lars' inner turmoil.

"I dreamt last night that my village was attacked by demons."

"It was only a dream," Vastra said with undisguised contempt.

Kaplyn flashed him an icy glare and was about to rebuke him when Lars spoke. His voice was angry and it was the first time that Kaplyn had heard him speak this way. "*By Slathor*! Do not mock me! My people take dreams very seriously and consider them a portent."

"I wouldn't worry; it's unlikely that demons will ever again attack in force. It was Eldric sorcerers who summoned them and they have gone," Kaplyn said by way of comfort. "I have only ever heard of two attacks in my lifetime."

"Fool," Vastra pronounced coldly. "What do you know of demons? All you have heard is hearsay. I have read countless texts about them, texts which you, too, could read if you made an effort."

Kaplyn did not like being called a fool; he felt his face burn with anger. "I can read," he snapped.

"I do not mean the barbaric Allund language." Vastra flashed back angrily. "Eldric is the true script of a scholar."

Vastra sat back with a condescending sneer. "Demon attacks are *not* rare. At present they are less often than in the past but they are on the increase. Soon this land will be plagued by demons, and *then* you will see real fear." Vastra looked at them dangerously as if daring them to contradict.

Neither did and so Vastra continued. "In the past, there have been many periods when demons have attacked. If you read your own history books instead of idling your time away, then you would discover that only sixty years ago there were over two hundred attacks in Allund in just one year!" He fell silent, angrily holding up an index finger as though to further the point.

Kaplyn was stunned, although he realised that Vastra spoke the truth; it explained why his people were so superstitious. "Where do demons come from?"

Vastra lowered his hand. "Demons exist in another world, separated from ours by a void where nothing can live — other than elementals. There may even be other worlds as well. In certain periods in time these come close together, squeezing the void until it is thin enough for those with the power to do so to cross. Presently the worlds are far enough apart that only the most powerful demons can cross. But the time is fast approaching when demons will be able to travel more freely between the worlds, and then they will come — all too often."

"When's the next time when demons can cross to our world?" Kaplyn asked.

"That is not what you should ask," Vastra replied. "The occasional attack is fearful, but the consequences are tragic for only a few. I have studied the heavens and the stars," he continued, staring into the fire. The Prophecy predicts that one day Drachar's shade will return. Mark me, when that happens, there will be all-out war and *thousands* will perish!"

Kaplyn shrugged. "But that's not supposed to happen until five hundred years after the Krell Wars and that is still some time in the future."

Vastra looked angry. "Where does the Prophecy say that?"

Kaplyn did not know. It was clear though that Vastra was finished talking; he sat back and continued reading, ignoring the other two men.

Frustrated, Kaplyn gave up the discussion and, as the stars began to appear in the black velvety sky, he and Lars spread their blankets on the soft grass. A silvery moon sailed high in the night sky softly illuminating the ground below, casting long shadows upon the grey landscape. All about the camp, small animals sought refuge from nocturnal hunters and the occasional high-pitched shriek of a hunter or its prey replaced the more familiar daytime sounds.

Kaplyn lay awake looking up at the stars as though seeking the meaning of the Prophecy from within the complicated pattern of specks. He wondered whether the demon world was somewhere out there amongst the cloak of night and the thought made him wonder whether Drachar's shade also existed. Vastra's explanation worried him more than he cared to admit and it was a long while before sleep would come.

Kaplyn awoke early the next morning with gentle sunlight bathing his upturned face. He breathed the morning air deeply before rising to wake the others. After a hurried breakfast, for he was keen to press on, they once more endured the tedium of breaking camp. As if not to disappoint them, Vastra again refrained from helping. Kaplyn noticed how pale and gaunt he looked; his movements were slow as though he was in pain and he stooped like an old man.

"I do not like the feel of this forest," Vastra declared once they were mounted.

"Don't fret. I've travelled some way in and it's fine. There's nothing to fear," Kaplyn said, although deep down he was enjoying the other man's discomfort.

Vastra merely scowled.

Ignoring him Kaplyn urged his mount beneath the trees. The soothing cooing of wood pigeons accompanied them as they rode, and Kaplyn was at a loss as to why Vastra objected to taking this route. He glanced around. The other man's shoulders were slumped and he looked miserable. Kaplyn suddenly felt guilty at having forced him to ride through the forest. Still it was too late now and the journey seemed pleasant enough. Indeed it was difficult to imagine anything evil living here.

Through the dappled shade, bright pools of light shone on the woodland carpet, highlighting the rich greens of the forest. Kaplyn's spirits rose. It seemed that the world was timeless and he could imagine this forest as it was thousands of years ago. Engrossed in his own thoughts he failed to notice the trees thickening about them. Vastra become quieter as though his mood matched the changing nature of the forest.

They rode most of the day with little event. Towards late afternoon the stream they were following disappeared under ground. Much to their alarm, they realized, without it to guide them, they might become lost. Shortly after that the wood thinned and ahead they could see a glade. Within the clearing was a small pool of clear blue water. A rocky hill rose sharply from the water's edge, and a waterfall spilled noisily into the pool, filling the air about it with myriad specks of flashing lights. Bright coloured flowers grew in tight clusters about the pool. However, there was no sign of a stream leading away from it and Kaplyn guessed that this was the stream's source and the water must continue underground from here.

Both Kaplyn and Lars were hot and sweaty from the long day's ride. Kaplyn eyed the pool, considering a swim. "Let's camp here," he declared. The others did not object, although Vastra looked too ill to complain. He dismounted slowly before wearily sitting down in the shade of a large tree, leaving the other two to make camp. Kaplyn led the horses and mules to the pool's edge to drink.

He and Lars then stripped, ridding themselves of their sweaty clothes before plunging naked into the pool; the water was cold, forcing them to swim vigorously.

Kaplyn swam to the edge of the waterfall where he allowed the cold jet to massage his back, enjoying the force of the water. As he swam away from the cascade he decided to investigate the depths and swan dived, swimming down. The temperature quickly dropped and the light faded, leaving a murky world tinged with green. The cold and the darkness made him suddenly fearful and swiftly he retraced his way to the surface, breaking through in a fountain of water. There was no doubt that the pool was deep and Kaplyn felt compelled to rejoin Lars in the shallows.

When they clambered out of the water, Vastra was still sitting in the shade of the tree, looking pale. Kaplyn asked what the matter was, but Vastra replied tersely that it was a trifle. Seeing that there was nothing they could do, they set about preparing their evening meal. Vastra fell asleep so they decided not to disturb him. Much later, as night fell, they turned in and, feeling invigorated after their swim, soon fell into a deep dreamless sleep.

A slight ripple at the centre of the pool was the only indication of the fear to follow.

Chapter 14

The Alvalah

Prince Lomar stood by the small window, looking intently out upon the silvery forest beyond. Its beauty enchanted him and his heart soared at the myriad of colours. The barks were sublime shades of silver and their surfaces smooth as the purest silk. Sprouting from tiny vulnerable shoots, gold and vermilion leaves unfurled to trap the little light defusing into the leafy domain.

The silver, golds and reds combined to create a scene of immense beauty. Sighing deeply Lomar turned his gaze from the forest to his reflection trapped within the windowpane — a pale, stern countenance looked sadly back.

He was an albino, as were all his people, the Alvalah. Behind him, hanging in the great hall, portraits of his ancestors hung on the walls, each with the same deathly white pallor, fierce red eyes and hair the colour of fresh snow. The portraits were a remarkable collection. Few people could claim to know their lineage beyond two generations, and yet the collection in the hall spanned an incredible thousand-year period.

Often he studied the paintings, reflecting on his predecessors and wondering about their lives; his favourite, or at least the one he studied most often, was that of Dalamere II. Although he hated to admit it, there was an uncanny resemblance between them.

Regarding his own reflection, he pondered on the distant king who held such a grim fascination for him. The only difference between them was the permanent frown that Dalamere wore; he looked incapable of humour.

Lomar glanced at the other portraits — the one common aspect was that the subjects were all clean-shaven; none had a beard or moustache. This was true of all the Alvalah for they could not grow facial hair even if they wanted to. That was also supposed to have been true of the Eldric, a fact

128

that substantiated claims that the Eldric and Alvalah were once distantly related.

There were, however, no portraits of any Eldric among the collection and even though the Alvalah claimed kinship, there had been little love lost between the races.

Lomar frowned. Perhaps that had been the greatest difference between the races; the Eldric were forward thinkers whereas the Alvalah seemed to dwell on the past. Long ago, his people had secluded themselves in the forest, building their homes high in the branches of the KinAnar forest.

A sudden pang caused him to frown for he knew that the forest was fading. Perhaps that is why his people preferred the past for it was so hard to bear seeing the forest diminish.

Soft footfalls interrupted him. The intrusion annoyed him and deliberately he turned his gaze back to the forest, ignoring the newcomer.

A polite cough indicated that the person was unwilling to leave, forcing Lomar to acknowledge their presence. Garth, his retainer, at least had the decency to look sheepish for disturbing his Lord. He was old even for an Alvalan. His hair was long and gossamer thin and deep wrinkles etched his face. Like all Alvalah, his clothing was of the brightest colours and today he had surpassed himself with a scarlet tunic and vivid green breeches.

"Your highness," Garth requested timidly. "It's nearly time for dinner. It would be bad manners to keep your mother, the Queen, waiting."

Lomar frowned, but then realised that the old man did not deserve his hostility. He had served him faithfully for many years. Ashamed, Lomar turned away once more, angry with himself for his lack of tact.

"Garth," he said at last, "something has entered the forest; I feel..." the Prince paused, unsure what it actually was he felt. "I feel that something terrible is about to happen."

"The forest has its own defence," Garth offered. "If anything evil entered, then the forest would prevent it from getting very far."

Lomar shook his head and turned to face Garth. "That's not what I meant. Important events are occurring beyond our forest, and I don't think Gilfillan will be allowed to ignore them — not this time."

Without realising it his gaze inadvertently went to Dalamere's portrait.

Garth's eyes followed the direction of his look. "Dalamere was a tyrant," he said softly.

Lomar waved his hand dismissively. "He doesn't concern me. It's more the power that he is said to have possessed...."

"He was an evil man. It was not his power which corrupted him, but rather it was he who corrupted the power."

Lomar was unconvinced. "I once read he could separate his soul from his body, allowing his soul to walk the corridors. I also read that he used these powers to further his own ends, spying upon his friends and enemies alike, using this information to blackmail them."

"It's an old tale, often told by mothers to frighten their children. *Behave*, they are told; *otherwise the shade of Dalamere will get you*. It works too," Garth replied.

"Is it possible, do you think, for a man to separate his soul from his body?" Lomar asked.

Garth went to a chair and sat down, not in disrespect to the Prince, but merely the actions of a tired old man.

"Your father and I asked the same question many times," he admitted. "We knew quite early on that you were different from the other children." Garth smiled at the memories the conversation provoked. "I liked your father; he was a very strong man. Unshakeable, I often thought. Even still your mother could twist him around her little finger." He paused for a moment thoughtfully.

"You were four years old, or was it five, when we first suspected something was amiss. There wasn't a secret anyone could keep from you, which frightened many of the courtiers and your parents, too, at first. You had a knack for knowing what was going on, far beyond the ken of a small child. Your father had a theory about this."

Lomar waited patiently for Garth to continue.

"You know about Shaols?"

Lomar nodded, "Of course, a Shaol is a spirit which is supposed to watch over us."

"Some people believe a Shaol is more than that; a guardian spirit set to guide us. They also believe that when we die, they guide our spirits to the halls of the Creator, so that we are not lost to the evil that stalks the way between the worlds."

Lomar did not understand where Garth's train of thought was leading. Garth, sensing the Prince's impatience, continued.

"Your father and I believed that long ago a Shaol had a much stronger influence on our lives, steering us away from harm and warning us of danger."

Lomar had heard this before and, in a way, it seemed to make sense, explaining why some people appeared to have a sixth sense. "I've heard this. But over the years we have lost the ability to communicate with our Shaol and hence also our ability to sense danger."

"That is what your father believed. He also believed that our Shaol is the spirit of an ancestor. That is why the link with our Shaol was once stronger, because the relationship between the two was that much closer. For example, long ago, the Shaol could have been the person's father or grandfather, whereas now it is more likely to be a great, great, great grandfather."

Lomar looked horrified. "And you believe Dalamere is my Shaol and it is his evil spirit which enables me to see things?"

"No," Garth assured him, relieved that at least he could deny that terrible possibility.

Lomar waited for the older man to continue. Garth took a deep breath as though uncertain of what to say next.

"When your mother was pregnant with you, a seer predicted she would have twins," Garth said. Lomar's expression showed that he had not known this.

"However, when you were born there was no other. The seer was questioned but was adamant about her prediction."

"She was wrong then?"

"She had never been wrong before."

"She must have been wrong on this occasion then!"

"Consider that she was right and that in your mother's womb there had been twins. What might have happened to your twin do you think?"

Lomar shook his head.

"It could be possible that he or she was absorbed in the womb, not by your mother, but by yourself."

"You mean that it still lives within me?" Lomar asked, stepping down from the alcove to stand besides his friend.

"I do not think so, but what if that twin was now your Shaol?"

Comprehension dawned on Lomar's face. "So you think it is my brother or sister's spirit that sees things and relays them to me," he asked.

"That's possible. Alternatively it could be your brother or sister's spirit that allows yours access to the ethereal world — in effect, you have become your own guardian?" he ventured.

"How does this idea fit in with Dalamere?" Lomar asked.

Garth shrugged his shoulders. "That was long ago and he could have found access to the spirit world some other way. No one will ever know."

They fell silent while Lomar considered the explanation.

"How did he die?" Lomar asked.

"Dalamere? He was relatively young when he died, or so I believe. By all accounts he died in his sleep, but many believe otherwise, preferring to think that his soul became lost as it went upon some evil errand. Eventually, without a soul, his body died."

The thought bothered Lomar and he conjured the image of a ghostly apparition doomed to wander the halls of Gilfillan, searching for its mortal host. He felt as though someone had just walked over his grave.

Chapter 15

Ghostly Spectres

The gentle tinkle of the waterfall echoed softly in the dreams of the three travellers, lulling them deeper into sleep. Gradually, the pitch changed, becoming higher and more urgent until it was as if many voices were crying on the still night air. In his sleep, Kaplyn sensed the change and fought to regain consciousness.

He awoke at once, immediately clasping the Eldric pendant, his gaze sweeping the clearing for signs of danger, but nothing stirred. His eyes kept returning to the waterfall and his mind fastened on the soft cries that seemed intermingled with the gentle splashing. The moonlight reflected brightly from the water; sparks of silver light danced as if seeking to hypnotise his weary mind. In mounting fear he tried to awaken the other two, but neither stirred no matter how hard he shook them. Even the horses and mules seemed to be sleeping. Other than the plaintive cry of the waterfall, no living thing could be heard and an unnatural silence pervaded the ancient forest.

All at once his pendant felt warm against his chest. Drawing his sword he was shocked to see the blade was glowing eerily, reminding him of the recent demon attack. Fearfully he crouched, casting around for signs of danger.

The pool seemed to be the source of the unnatural sound and, to his horror, the water started to ripple then boil as though alive. Transfixed, he watched as a shape broke surface, clambering from the bubbling waters. Two more shapes surfaced, clambering from the pool to join their comrade standing by its bank.

Cold eyes locked on Kaplyn's and from dead throats came hollow laughter as the spectres raised dull blades.

As he slept, an all too familiar sensation swept over Lomar, a feeling he dreaded and which at first his subconscious mind tried to fight. It was something he had not experienced for some time and it triggered distant

133

memories, some happy, some sad. Restlessly he turned, entwining silk sheets about his pale body.

Abruptly, his subconscious lost its fight and he felt his spirit slipping away from its earthly shackles. All at once he was floating effortlessly and at first he revelled in the weightlessness, momentarily forgetting his bleak mood. Then he felt very cold; blackness engulfed him and at once he was desperately afraid.

Forcing his eyes open he willed himself to waken. To his amazement he was in a forest, not the one he was accustomed to, for there were no bright colours here. This was a very drab place, and the shades of greys and blacks seemed more akin to a nightmare than reality.

He was compelled to move in a particular direction and carefully he skirted the trees, preferring to go around rather than try to pass through them, which he was sure he could do. Nocturnal forest animals scampered out of his way, either seeing him or sensing his ghostly form. As the animals fled he realised that this was indeed his forest, but he was far from the silver trees; the magic in this part of the forest had long since faded which saddened him, and he wondered whether this was what he was supposed to see.

Abruptly he came to a glade and the sight that met him left him stunned.

Within the clearing a waterfall noisily cascaded into a pool. Its sound was peculiar and Lomar sensed magic at work. However, it was not the pool that shocked him; a lone figure crouched to one side, a blue-glowing sword in his outstretched hand. A second figure lay asleep on the ground, while horses and mules stood behind the two men; oblivious to the horror that confronted them.

Three silvery knights stood before the crouching man. Each wore ornate silver breastplates and tall conical helms reminiscent of a bygone era. In ghostly hands they held spectral swords that surely no earthly weapon could counter.

A memory from the previous night's conversation came back to Lomar and he remembered Garth saying *the forest has its own defence*. He wondered if the two men were evil, but decided that they were not, for he felt no malice from them. He decided that he had better act swiftly as the spectres were advancing upon the crouching man who was as yet unaware of Lomar.

Lomar saw the spectres' faces and at that moment he nearly failed. Grinning skulls looked out from under ancient helms and vacant sockets, glowing eerily, stared out with deadly intent.

"Stop!" Lomar commanded.

The figures came to a halt, their faces swivelling towards him. The crouching man also turned; a look of horror on his face.

The dark-haired man gave Lomar a jolt. He had the distinct impression they had met. He had no time to think about this as he returned his attention back to the dead knights.

Their sightless orbs locked on his but he could sense their uncertainty.

"Command us, Lord," said the lead knight. Its voice echoed clearly within his mind and yet he knew that the knight could not have spoken.

"Return to your resting place and leave us," he ordered. His heart was pounding with fear and he wasn't sure that the knights would obey. The spectre's reference to "Lord" was encouraging.

A groan sounded nearby and Lomar turned to look in that direction but could not see anyone. Again, uncertainty assailed him. Who were these people and what brought them to his forest?

The lead knight hesitated, but held his ground. "Master we sense a great evil here and it is our duty to destroy it," he proclaimed, pointing his sword in Kaplyn's direction.

Lomar was shocked. If there was evil here then surely it must be the knights.

"Return!" he commanded, hoping his voice carried sufficient conviction. "I shall attend to this matter."

The dead knight's sunken orbs fixed upon Lomar who could not help but shudder. Finally, and with some reluctance, the spectre lowered his blade. He motioned to his companions and together they re-entered the pool. The tone of the waterfall changed and briefly, the water within the pool boiled again. Gradually the surface became calm with only a gentle ripple marring the otherwise still surface.

At once forest noises returned. Lomar felt a familiar sensation as though someone had hooked his navel and was pulling him backward. Around him the forest became surreal, as though seen within a dream.

He turned to the man. "You must go," he urged. "The knights may yet return. Head north and I will find you."

A great weariness crept over Lomar and he knew no more.

Kaplyn sheathed his blade which whined eerily as though in anger. He couldn't believe what he had just witnessed. The thought of fighting dead knights had been terrifying and when he saw the newcomer he had been certain he was a demon, with his red eyes, white hair and face.

Kaplyn knelt by Lars and shook the big man. The other man groaned. "What's up?" he asked, sitting up and rubbing his eyes.

"We must leave," Kaplyn said, going over to Vastra and roughly shaking his shoulder.

"It's still night," Lars complained, arising and struggling into his boots. Vastra remained asleep in spite of Kaplyn's shaking.

Lars came over and felt Vastra's brow. "He's cold and clammy," he said, looking worriedly at Kaplyn.

"Gather your things," Kaplyn urged. "We'll see to Vastra once we are away from here."

The sense of urgency in Kaplyn's voice spurred Lars into action and hurriedly they packed their gear. When they returned, Vastra was still unconscious and no matter what they did, would not stir.

"We should not have camped so near to the water," Lars said, scratching under his armpit. "There is a host of biting things around here. Perhaps he has caught a fever."

Kaplyn shook his head. "I doubt it is insects. He looked ill yesterday. Help me get him onto his horse."

Together they lifted Vastra, his lightness surprising them both. "It's a wonder he's as strong as he is. Beneath these robes he's all skin and bones," Lars commented.

They deposited him unceremoniously across his mount.

"We'll have to walk. I'll lead the horses. You see to it that he doesn't fall off," Kaplyn said.

He led them in the general direction the spectre had indicated, not entirely sure whether to trust the apparition or not, but he had helped them and at least they were better off moving. As they walked, Kaplyn told Lars what had occurred.

"I was awake, I can assure you, and my sword was glowing, like in the demon's presence," Kaplyn concluded.

Lars was silent although he looked about the trees fearfully. "Perhaps you should draw it now and check if we are safe," he suggested.

Kaplyn partly drew the weapon but the blade was dull. He peered into the gloom ahead; in the daylight, the forest had seemed a friendly enough place but now, in the dead of night, it felt much more sinister. He realised that it was going to be very long night.

Chapter 16

Recognition

Lomar awoke shortly before daybreak. His head ached and it took several moments to recollect the events of the previous night. Vaguely he remembered that disorientation was usual after his spirit had travelled on the astral plain. As a child, it had been bad enough, but now, as an adult, it seemed much worse. It was also uncanny that it had happened so soon after discussing it with Garth. It had seemed dreamlike, and yet the events during the night had been real; of that much, he was certain. But never before had his mind travelled so far, and that thought alone terrified him.

The memory of the dark haired man's face came back to him and he suddenly remembered why he was familiar. He had seen him before in his dreams and the realisation came as a shock for, if the man truly existed, it added additional meaning to his terrible nightmares. He could see future events. He had to find out what was going on.

Arising from the comfort of his warm bed, he shivered as the cold night air caressed his naked flesh. Opening the curtain he discovered the dawn was still some time off but he refused to delay. Hurriedly he dressed. On the way out he took his longbow and a quiver of arrows. His people did not hunt nor did they eat the flesh of animals, but they still practised archery, using wooden targets for sport. He also found his sword; it was delicately wrought, slim and seemingly fragile, but the steel was strong and his arm swift.

Peering through the doorway he was relieved to find the corridor empty. He hurried towards the stairs, momentarily considering asking Garth to accompany him, but rejected the idea. If there was danger, he did not want to subject his friend to it as well.

In the darkness the corridor was eerie and for an instant he imagined Dalamere's shade searching for his body. The thought made him shudder as he started down the broad, winding staircase leading to the main palace halls, built within the bole of the greatest Gilfillan tree. From the lower palace level, Lomar went by way of the least frequented corridors until he reached the stairs leading to the forest floor far below. These had also been built within the massive trunk and had been exquisitely carved over long years. So not to disrupt the sap, the stair was a tight spiral and as a result he arrived in the stables breathless and his head spinning. He paused to let the giddiness pass. One of the horses nickered a soft welcome.

Swiftly he saddled his horse before leading it outside. Once in the open he leapt lightly into the saddle. Normally his rides were sedate as he took in the stunning scenery, but now he took little notice of his surroundings and instead turned his mount in the direction he sensed his spirit had travelled that night.

He ignored the forest creatures, which scampered up to the rider, seeking titbits that the Alvalah often carried. This time he hastened on his journey as the sun ascended in the morning sky. After his swift passage the animals milled around uncertainly, for they had never seen one of the Alvalah in haste before; however, the pale Prince was soon forgotten as they returned to their foraging.

When dawn broke, Kaplyn and Lars found themselves in a denser part of the forest. They had to force their way through the thick undergrowth and soon the humidity increased, causing the men and their mounts to sweat profusely. Kaplyn started to fear they were lost.

By midday, the trees thinned making their journey easier. Briefly, they paused for a meal and to check on Vastra. He was still unconscious and looked even more pale than the night before. Whatever ailed him was a complete mystery and they decided that they had to leave urgently. They ate a hurried meal and set off, riding even though the ground was uneven. Each rode either side of Vastra to support him and, for a while, they made good time.

Some time later Kaplyn halted them. Ahead, partially obscured by the maze of thick tree trunks he thought he could see a figure sitting astride a horse. There appeared to be only one person although the trunks were large enough to conceal an army.

Pausing, they debated what to do, while ahead the figure remained motionless as though content to let them see that he meant no harm. His inaction made them more confident and so they urged their mounts forward. As they approached, Kaplyn became aware that the stranger's complexion and hair was deathly white and his eyes fiery red. He knew at once that it was this man's spirit he had seen the night before and again he had a terrible

138

fear that he was a demon, but common sense prevailed for the stranger seemed to be as afraid of them as they were of him. Kaplyn had seen an albino rabbit once and the characteristics seemed to fit this man and so he assumed that he, too, must be an albino.

The stranger was dressed richly in a bright yellow doublet partially covered by a long, pale blue silk cloak. Long riding boots reached up to his knees, covering his britches that were green and as a bright a colour as his doublet. About his waist a broad leather belt supported a long, delicate sword and a small dagger, while about his shoulders he carried a long bow and quiver. His horse was equally garishly adorned with a rich looking saddle blanket and Kaplyn gazed in wonder at the reins that looked as though they were spun from fine gold threads. In all, the stranger seemed as out of place in the forest as they felt.

"Welcome," the stranger said when they were within a comfortable distance. "Welcome to Gilfillan."

Kaplyn was about to reply when the albino interrupted him, a look of concern on his face.

"I did not expect three of you," he said, suddenly looking at Kaplyn. "And your companion, he is ill." He urged his mount forward a few steps and bent over to examine Vastra.

"You helped us last night?" Kaplyn asked uncertainly.

The albino nodded as he continued his examination. Finally he sat back. "I do not know what ails him," he admitted.

"How did you help us? I mean, you were a ghost," Kaplyn said.

"I will explain as we ride. Firstly though, my name is Lomar and I am an Alvalan. Who are you and why is it that I was not aware of your companion last night?"

It was Kaplyn's turn to frown. "I'm Kaplyn and this is Lars. Our companion is Vastra. He's been ill since early last night. As to why you did not see him, I do not know. Perhaps his dark clothes concealed him?"

Lomar looked worried. "You must accompany me to my people. We have healers who will be able to help."

Lars glanced at Kaplyn who nodded. As they rode, Lomar asked them where they were going. When Kaplyn told him they were seeking a means of finding the Eldric, Lomar frowned.

"The Eldric have long since departed. How can you find them? Of course, that is assuming that they *wish* to be found."

"Vastra has read that the Eldric travelled into the mountains and we are following the route they took," Kaplyn explained.

Lomar's frown deepened. "That journey is madness; krell inhabit the mountains and besides, after all these years, the chance of finding anything even slightly connected with the Eldric is remote to say the least."

"We will try though," Kaplyn replied.

"Well I wish you luck," It was clear from Lomar's tone that he thought that their quest was folly.

"What happened last night, by the pool?" Kaplyn asked.

Lomar shook his head, "I don't really know. I have a gift I cannot control, but at times it seems that my spirit leaves my body and I travel to places, seeing things that I should not normally know. I also see glimpses of the future and I am sure that I have seen you in my dreams..."

Kaplyn could tell by his tone that the experience frightened the albino. Being told that the other man had seen him in his dreams was also scary.

"Last night was one such occasion," Lomar said, looking closely at Kaplyn. "I have no idea how or why it happened, but it was lucky for you that it did. The other oddity is no one else has ever seen my spirit before, but you could; I could tell by the way you looked at me."

"Yes, I could," Kaplyn answered. "And a shock it was too. I thought you were a demon. But what were those *things*?" Kaplyn asked referring to the ghostly knights.

"They were possibly some part of the forest's defence, but that is only a guess; possibly guardians placed there long ago, even before the Krell Wars, to secure the forest's borders."

"It was very nearly a successful defence," Lars said pointedly.

Kaplyn smiled although it was somewhat forced; Lars did not realise how close to the truth his words were.

Chapter 17

Gilfillan

By mid-afternoon Kaplyn detected small changes occurring in the forest; the leaves had started to take on autumnal shades of reds and golds, even though it was still early spring. Brightly coloured squirrels scampered lightly from branch to branch, inquisitively peering down on the group. Suddenly one ran lightly from a branch and across Kaplyn's shoulders, causing him to jump in shock. It paused on his shoulder as though studying him before hurtling off in its search for food. Kaplyn looked around at Lars who was smiling broadly at the tiny creature's impudence.

Within a few yards, a family of deer casually crossed the path in front of them; the doe even turned to watch them pass as her youngsters hurried into the surrounding bushes. Lomar seemed surprised by Kaplyn's and Lars' astonishment at her lack of fear.

Soon the forest changed even more dramatically; the surrounding bark became a delicate, translucent silver and the leaves even more beautiful shades of gold and red. Kaplyn found himself holding his breath in awe.

Shafts of sunlight stabbed through the intertwining branches, reflecting brightly from the leaves in a magnificent blaze of glory. By their side, a stream glittered as ripples in turn caught the light, its surface reflecting a myriad of colours.

"It's truly beautiful!" Kaplyn stated in wonder.

Lomar was watching his reaction and a smile touched his bloodless lips. "It does make your world seem dull."

"Why is it like this? I have never seen anything like it before in my life," Lars stated, looking up and nearly falling off his horse.

Lomar's smile broadened; to him, complimenting the forest was the same as complimenting the Alvalah. "My people believe that the entire world is like this," he said indicating the trees with a broad sweep of his arm. "I used to myself until last night when I saw what the forest was becoming. Where I saw you last night was a very dreary place."

"Lomar, how long will it take us to reach your home?" Lars asked.

"We will not get there today," he replied. "However, it's not far and we should arrive early tomorrow, if we can go a little farther while the light lasts."

Kaplyn glanced at Vastra and hoped that whatever ailed him was not too serious. The unconscious man was bouncing about uncomfortably on the horse's broad back.

They rode for a while longer, but Vastra showed no signs of recovery and started mumbling in his fevered sleep. Slowly the sun began sinking and, as the light failed, the colour of the leaves seemed to match that of the sunset. The ground started to rise steeply, causing their weary horses to stumble on the cluttered forest floor. Lomar's mount, by comparison, seemed much fresher, floating lightly over the soft turf. Slowly but surely they started to fall behind until Kaplyn knew they could go no further. He called softly to Lomar who turned and saw their weariness.

"Come, we will rest here this night," he said, looking guilty that he had not realised how tired they were.

They dismounted and Kaplyn removed Vastra's limp body from his horse, laying him on the soft ground before covering him with a blanket. Lars tended to the horses while Lomar went into the woods. He reappeared shortly, carrying several large, golden fruit. These he placed upon the ground and, using his knife, segmented them. Since it was warm there was no need for a campfire; indeed Kaplyn would have been surprised if a campfire was ever needed beneath the faintly glowing trees.

Sitting together, they ate the fruit, delighting in the succulent flavour. The only noise, apart from Vastra's occasional mumbling, was the chirping of crickets. Lomar offered them his flask to quench their thirst. It was a fiery drink and Lars coughed after he had taken a sip.

"What is this, Lomar?" he asked, holding up the flask appreciatively.

"It's a wine made from the fruit you are eating," he replied nonchalantly.

Lars' eyebrows rose appreciatively as he took another draught, this time taking time to enjoy the flavour.

Above them the moon peeked through the branches, encapsulating the trees in a silver radiance. Kaplyn looked up and could just make out the stars shining brightly in the heavens.

"Do you know anything about the Eldric, Lomar?" he asked.

"A little. There are some who believe that our peoples are distantly related."

Kaplyn frowned, "How can that be? I though the Eldric came from across the sea."

Lomar drank a little of the fiery liquid, wincing as he did so. "Long ago my people were more adventurous and it is said we used to live by the sea. I find that hard to imagine. I've never seen the sea; it must be very beautiful."

"It is," Lars said. "I loved sailing, but it's a treacherous business. You are at the mercy of the gods the moment you step aboard."

Lomar smiled and continued his tale. "Long ago my people supposedly built ships and travelled across the sea, seeking new lands and new wonders. It's a fanciful tale, one told before my people learned the art of keeping records, but there may be some truth in it. Anyway, it may be possible that my people left many thousands of years ago, returning later as the Eldric."

"What about the storms though?" Lars asked. "I was told that they rage almost continually and sailing far from Allund is very perilous."

"It was many years ago," Lomar conceded. "Perhaps then the great storms were less ferocious. Whatever the case, I believe the Alvalah and the Eldric are related. Many others also believe this — as no doubt many do not; it's a subject of great contention amongst my people."

"Do your people know what became of the Eldric?" Kaplyn asked, leaning forward and taking more interest.

Lomar shook his head. "There are many theories, but at the time of the Eldric's disappearance, my people had already turned their backs on the world. We are rather reclusive now, living in the forest. Our knowledge of the outside world has been second-hand for many years."

"If your people were related to the Eldric as you believe, then why do you know so little about them?" Kaplyn continued.

"We were never close to the Eldric," Lomar admitted. "Our history books tell mainly of our own histories and even though we think there was once kinship between us, there was no love lost.

"Even at that time we preferred our forests, never venturing far. The source of our outside news arrives via the few traders who still remember us. No doubt by the time we received tales of the Eldric's departure it was some time afterwards."

"I find it hard to imagine what life was like back then. By the way, do you know roughly when the Eldric left?" Kaplyn asked, suddenly realising that Lomar might know that.

"By our reckoning it would be close to five hundred years."

"That's not possible," Kaplyn said, truly shocked.

"My people have kept records ever since the Krell Wars and I'm certain it was about then," Lomar replied.

"Why is the time so important?" Lars asked.

"It might mean the Prophecy is closer to happening than we thought," Kaplyn said, grimacing. "My people believe it was only a few hundred years ago since Drachar was defeated, not *five*."

At Drachar's mention, Lomar shuddered.

"Surely Drachar's returning is only a fairytale," Lars said.

Lomar shook his head. "The Prophecy is of great concern to my people. We fear that one day someone will try to release his shade from its imprisonment."

"So you believe that he did not truly die then?" Lars asked.

"No — his soul was too strongly linked to the spirit world to die. A Narlassar sorcerer's power comes from the spirit world and that binds him to that. As to the time though, that is very uncertain. The Prophecy does not mention a time when he will return; the closest clue is W*hen Tallin's Crown once more does shine*."

"Kaplyn and I discussed that. What do you think it means?" Lars asked.

"We are not sure," Lomar replied. "But it is thought that Tallin's Crown is a constellation."

This was news to Kaplyn although it made sense. "Do you know which?"

Lomar shook his head. "The Alvalah were once great astronomers but since coming to the forest we tend not to look towards the heavens as much as we once did."

Kaplyn considered Lomar's words for a while. The news that the Eldric left so long ago concerned him. When his thoughts came back to the present, Lars was asking Lomar about the material of his cloak and the albino was showing it to the big man who was explaining the origin of the material. Now that Lars had mentioned it, Kaplyn marvelled at the softness of the cloth and closeness of the weave.

"It is made from spiders' silk," Lomar said.

Lars laughed. "That's impossible, it would take years to collect enough silk."

"Not at all," Lomar answered." The forest has especially large spiders, high up in the trees. They are venomous and harvesting the silk is hazardous, but it's considered a great honour to do so. As you can see, the thread is very strong and elastic; it makes an excellent cloth."

Kaplyn glanced up as though expecting to see spiders on every bough. It was Lomar's turn to laugh. His laughter was as clear as a bell.

"Do not fear! The spiders rarely come to the forest floor, only once a year and that is much later in the autumn."

The conversation continued late into the night. Eventually they turned in, lying on the soft ground with a blanket over them against the chill. That night Kaplyn and Lars slept better than they had for a while and when they awoke even Vastra seemed slightly improved; his skin colour looked healthier, although, as yet he had not recovered consciousness.

After breakfasting on the golden fruit, they departed with Lomar leading the way. He seemed eager now to press on. "My city is only a short journey. We should be there by mid-morning and then your friend will receive treatment."

The ride continued pleasantly and Kaplyn kept peering between the tall trees, expecting at any moment to see a clearing and a walled city. Some time later, Lomar saw Kaplyn's look of confusion and he briefly halted them, pointing high up into the trees ahead.

Between the thick foliage, Kaplyn could see wooden buildings constructed on broad tree limbs that were veritable giants amongst their kind. Kaplyn felt dizzy looking up at the dwellings and he feared what it must be like to look down from the Tree City.

Most of the buildings upon the broad branches were single storey. From some of these, diminutive figures looked down. Lomar waved and several waved in return.

Larger buildings were constructed around the trunks and these were many storeys high.

Lars looked up at the buildings and shuddered. "If the gods had intended for us to live in trees then surely he would have given us wings." He glanced nervously at Lomar who merely smiled.

"Come," Lomar said. "And meet my people."

Chapter 18

Where God's Dwell

Lomar escorted them to the base of a particularly large tree where several soldiers awaited them. Kaplyn was shocked to see that, like Lomar, the men's pallor was deathly white and their eyes fiery red. He realised that the entire race must be albino.

They were a strange people. Even their armour was outlandish and not very functional. Their breastplates looked to be made of silver with intricate patterns embossed upon them, regardless that the designs would trap a spear or an arrow point that might otherwise be deflected. Their skullcaps were also made of silver sporting tall, coloured feathers, which Kaplyn later found out denoted the soldier's rank. Their clothes, barely visible beneath their armour, were bright colours much like Lomar's.

A tall man strode purposefully forward from between the soldiers, coming to a halt by Lomar's side. His eyes betrayed his anxiousness and he looked disapprovingly up at Lomar who promptly dismounted. Smiling, he held out the reins for one of the soldiers to take.

"My Prince," the man said saluting smartly, eyeing Kaplyn and Lars warily. "The Queen has requested that you attend her in her audience room immediately."

It came as a shock to hear Lomar referred to as prince though he recognised by the messenger's tone that Lomar was in trouble.

"I shall attend her presently, after I have seen to my guests," Lomar replied quietly, but with authority.

The man looked uneasy and his cheeks flushed. "Sire, she said that I was to request your presence *immediately* upon your return."

"Then I shall attend her directly," Lomar conceded much to the messenger's obvious relief. "Would you take these guests to Garth and ask him to entertain them in my absence. One is ill and must be taken to the healers with all haste."

The messenger nodded, stepping back to allow his Prince to pass by, but before he did Lomar turned to speak with Kaplyn. "I apologise that I have to leave but I shall endeavour to return shortly. In the meantime my retainer Garth will attend to your needs. Please feel at home here."

Kaplyn thanked him and Lomar took his leave, entering a door in the base of the tree.

Two men carried Vastra away. The messenger then turned to Kaplyn and Lars and politely requested that they follow him. They entered the same tree as Lomar had moments earlier and behind them four soldiers followed.

The interior of the tree opened into large stables, against one side of which a flight of stairs spiralled upwards. Inside the stair, beautifully crafted silver lanterns softly illuminated the way. At intervals, narrow windows allowed them to judge how high they had climbed.

They finally came to a door leading to a corridor, cut deep into the heart of the ancient tree. If they had expected the forest dwelling to be frugal then they were pleasantly surprised; dazzling silks decorated the walls and a deep, rich carpet covered the floor. The furniture was exquisite, formed from branches that had grown into odd shapes. Deep shiny boughs formed fine reclining armchairs while knotted limbs made trestles upon which ornately decorated boards were placed to make tables, some of which were so fine as to be almost translucent. Indeed, the interior was more exquisitely decorated than Dundalk's palace, and Kaplyn was reminded of the Eldric citadel of Tanel, even though he had only seen it briefly. Lomar's claim that the Alvalah and the Eldric were related seemed increasingly plausible the more he learned.

The corridor led them inside one of the buildings built outside the trunk. Their escort led them through a door and into an audience room filled with yet more ornately carved furniture. A small man seated by the window arose, looking confused by their sudden presence. Kaplyn then realised it was probably their complexion that made him frown.

"Garth, Prince Lomar has requested that you attend to his guests while he has been summoned to speak with the Queen," the messenger said before leaving, although he remained outside with the escort.

After a brief and uncomfortable silence, Garth suddenly looked shocked, presumably because he had been staring at Kaplyn and the others.

"I am G...Garth," he stuttered uncertainly, blinking like a great owl.

"I am Kaplyn and this is Lars," Kaplyn said, indicating the big man by his side. Garth's eyes widened more, as he looked at the blond bearded giant who carried a broad axe strapped to his back. Lars smiled back warmly and his eyes shone with humour at the other man's discomfort.

"I'm afraid that the Prince is likely to be some time," Garth explained. "Perhaps in the meantime I can show you around?"

"That would be interesting," Kaplyn replied, glancing over Garth's shoulder at an open doorway, leading to a balcony. "How high are we?" he asked. A cool breeze blew through the opening, carrying with it the scents of the forest beyond.

"Come and see," Garth said stepping out onto the balcony.

Kaplyn turned, grinning at Lars' obvious discomfort. The other man was clearly not happy with heights. Kaplyn went through the door, stepped forward to a rail, and peered over. It was higher than he anticipated and to make matters worse the tree was swaying, albeit gently. However, he soon forgot his fears as he looked at the city and the golden forest. It was truly breathtaking. Many aerial pathways linked the buildings and a method of intertwining broad branches with thinner ones had been used to create the bridges. People of all ages walked between the trees as though the crossing was second nature. Some were carrying heavy packs or even pulling carts.

Lars joined them, his face pale, but after a while even he seemed impressed with the view.

"There's something else you might like to see," Garth said, eager to please the newcomers.

Kaplyn nodded. Garth, with their escort faithfully following, led them through corridors and then out onto one of the walkways. As they started to cross Kaplyn's fear vanished. From above it had looked much more dangerous, but now they were upon it the sides prevented him seeing over the edge.

Above, the branches had been knitted together to form a protective roof against the rain so that the Alvalah could go about the city without fear of getting wet. Garth pointed out how tight the weave was, explaining that it took several years and constant pruning to acquire the right shape.

He then led them down a flight of stairs, circling one of the great trunks. Excitedly he spoke about the city, pointing to each building and telling them its use or who lived there and they listened half-heartedly, concentrating instead on the winding stair. When they stood upon the forest floor once more, both Kaplyn and Lars visibly relaxed and they had to hurry to catch up with their eager guide who strode purposefully ahead. A large rocky outcrop stood like a giant tooth from the moss-covered ground. Garth led them towards this, telling them of its beauty, confusing them with the sudden rush of words.

A large gaping wound opened in the side of the rock and Kaplyn and Lars looked at each other as Garth halted before it, neither fully understanding what all the fuss was about. Garth, on seeing their puzzled looks, smiled and gestured towards the cave.

"We believe that this was once the home of a Kalanth," he declared excitedly. "The Old One's presence is why we believe the forest still retains its beauty while all else fades."

Kaplyn frowned. There was a certain tranquillity about the mound and he could not deny the beauty surrounding him, but he found it hard to believe that a god had chosen to live here.

"Have you heard of the Kalanth?" Garth asked Kaplyn, upon seeing his puzzled look.

"Yes, I have. My people still leave offerings at hallowed sites," he admitted.

"Is it not a little *small* for a god?" Lars asked.

Garth smiled. "Enter, and you will see."

The narrow entrance looked as though the rock had been torn open some time in its past. Inside, Kaplyn expected the cave to be cold and damp, but it was neither; instead, it was breathtaking. Small crystals, half the size of his fist, almost completely covered the cavern walls, making the place both bright and cheerful. However, to Kaplyn it was only a cave and he could not see what all the fuss was.

"Wait," Garth said in a hushed tone. "I hope we are not late."

They stood in silence while they could hear the escort outside conversing in low tones. Kaplyn glanced uncertainly at Garth, wondering why they were waiting and in the meantime decided to examine the cave once more. The upper part was nearly perfectly spherical and, on its walls, there were literally thousands of crystals, each fitting perfectly with its neighbour. However, there were some gaps where crystals were missing. These seemed to make the cavern incomplete, more so than Kaplyn could explain.

He was about to ask Garth about them when the old man gestured towards the entrance. At that moment, the sunlight increased as the sun aligned with it and then, quite suddenly, an intense white light flared brightly all around them as the crystals caught the sun's rays, reflecting them in a dazzling display. Kaplyn covered his eyes to reduce the glare, but stopped when the intensity quickly and dramatically dropped.

To his amazement coloured lights streaked by him as the glass-like surface of the cavern refracted the sun's rays. Hundreds of tiny rainbows were hurled across the cavern in a seemingly endless game. Kaplyn found himself constantly turning to watch the patterns and he started to feel giddy.

149

The light blazed a trail of glory and he began to understand why people believed in gods.

Lars was also clearly in awe and the colours danced gaily on his face, enhancing the movements of his muscles as he smiled. Kaplyn grinned and Lars broke into infectious laughter. The other two men joined in and their senses seemed heightened as if the light was purging their souls of all their worldly fatigues.

To their disappointment the display faded, leaving them feeling bereft of its beauty. Never before had Kaplyn seen such splendour and his mind reeled with the memory. There were no words to describe it. By his side, Garth gestured that they should leave.

Kaplyn asked Garth about the crystals as they made their way back towards the tree houses.

"The cavern was found long ago when my people first entered the forest," the older man replied.

"The crystals are beautiful," Lars commented.

"Yes. I believe that your people call them kara-stones," Garth replied.

Kaplyn was surprised. "I've never heard of so many existing in one place before."

"Vastra mentioned kara-stones. He believed they might be the remains of a magic user when they die, but that can't be true if there are so many together in one place." Lars said.

"I'm not sure if anyone really knows what they are," Kaplyn replied. "There is one in Dundalk, although I'm not sure if it's a true kara-stone. However, it's guarded very closely; the people believe the city's fortunes are linked with it and that, if it is stolen or lost, then the city will fall."

Garth nodded his agreement. "My people have studied the stones and have discovered that they can be used by healers."

"Will they use one to help our companion?" Kaplyn asked.

"I did not realise that you had a companion with you," Garth answered. His tone suggested that he was shocked that no one had mentioned this earlier.

"He was taken to the healers when we arrived," Kaplyn replied.

"Then it is more than likely that the healers will use a kara-stone. We could go and see him if you like?" Garth said.

"If it wouldn't disturb them, I would like that," Kaplyn replied.

Garth smiled, gesturing them to follow.

Chapter 19

Vastra's Demon

Garth led them into the trunk of one of the trees and, after a long climb, they entered a richly decorated building constructed on one of the broad limbs. He then led them into a large, well-aired room where Lomar and several men and women, dressed in long flowing robes, crowded around a low dais. They were in heated debate, although they quietened somewhat when the newcomers entered. Vastra was lying unmoving on the dais; his pallor was grey and his flesh looked flaccid. Lomar looked up and, recognising Kaplyn and Lars, smiled warmly, walking towards the two men.

"We, unfortunately, are having some difficulty in determining what ails your companion. We were about to try other means, but there appears to be some discussion about how best to proceed."

"Do not let him deceive you," one of the women healers said. She was strikingly beautiful with long aquiline features and a slim figure. "We were arguing, as no doubt you were well aware." She glared at Lomar as though daring him to contradict.

Tactfully Lomar remained silent and then he said, "This is Hannas," indicating the woman by his side. "She's our foremost healer and has studied your companion's illness, but as yet we do not know what the problem is. However, we have discovered something that is proving an enigma. There appears to be a spell deflecting our attempts to probe his illness. The spell may have been invoked to prevent such a probe as we are now trying."

"You can remove this spell though?" Kaplyn guessed.

Lomar nodded, glancing at Hannas as if expecting another argument. She interrupted him before he could say anything further. "It's a minor spell of no consequence which we can remove," she replied tersely.

"What is stopping you then?" Kaplyn asked curiously.

"It's a moral issue," Lomar explained, balefully eyeing Hannas. "If he has chosen to hide something then we do not have the right to interfere."

Hannas looked at Lomar, angrily folding her arms. "The spell prevents us from discovering what is wrong with your companion, and *your* stubbornness, Lomar, may well result in his death." The other healers within the room looked expectantly at Kaplyn, clearly hoping that he would solve the dilemma and end the stalemate.

"He is our companion. Would you accept our guidance?" Kaplyn suggested.

Many of the healers nodded and so Kaplyn continued. "If his illness threatens his life then I think you should investigate it, whatever the cause, including anything he has chosen to hide, be it deliberate or not."

"Thank you," Hannas said, smiling broadly. "*Finally,* some common sense."

With that, the Alvalans turned back to their work, positioning one of the kara-stones on a table by the recumbent form.

Hannas placed a hand over the crystal and started to chant in a high singsong voice. Very quickly, the crystal started to glimmer and Kaplyn felt drawn towards the stone as small bright lights started to form deep within it. As the pitch of her chant increased, the lights started to move faster and faster, compelling Kaplyn to draw nearer.

An exclamation of surprise from one of the healers brought his attention back to Vastra's body. A similar pattern of lights had appeared several feet above his chest and these danced in a frenzied pattern in time with those within the stone. A shocking cold penetrated the room accompanied by an uncomfortable silence, a premonition of the events to follow.

A sudden flash of light over Vastra's chest caused everyone to jump. Above him, a shape coalesced from within the whirling lights, which were moving so swiftly now that they became a blur. All at once hovering a few feet above Vastra was a creature about the size of a cat. Kaplyn initially thought that it was hairless, but as it turned baleful hate-filled eyes about the room he realised it had a long streak of hair, like a mane, hanging down its bony back. Its skin was a sickly shade of green and its limbs were long and skinny. It squatted in indignation, blinking its cat-like eyes at the hateful light. A thin tongue flickered from its mouth, revealing small pointed teeth. An incredible stench of decay accompanied the creature's appearance.

Nobody moved and the creature remained, hovering in mid-air as if dazed.

"Bind it, Hannas!" Lomar hissed. She remained transfixed, staring at the demon, mesmerised by its presence.

Lomar moved to her side, grabbing her arm. "Bind it!" he repeated.

As he moved, the creature screamed a thin piercing wail that penetrated their very souls and leapt towards them. Instinctively, Kaplyn drew his sword which suddenly flared brightly, casting back the gloom that had settled on the room. The blade crooned eerily as it cleared the scabbard. The creature cringed in fear, covering its eyes and cowering from the intense glow, mewling pitifully.

Hannas shouted commands of power above the melee, holding the kara-stone aloft. A sudden shaft of light sprang forth, filling every nook and cranny of the room. The creature wailed, falling back on its haunches, hovering eerily in space, rocking in agony.

The others quickly recovered. Most of them had hurled themselves away from the small form as it had attacked and one man had fallen over a chair, cracking his skull on a table. He held his wound, grimacing with pain.

Kaplyn's sword twisted in his hand, groaning as if eager to be let loose. Lomar's eyes were wide with fear as he looked at the Eldritch weapon as though the very sight of it defiled the room. Swiftly he recovered, turning back to Hannas. "Will the light hold it?"

She nodded. The creature wailed and Kaplyn lowered his sword which seemed to resist his efforts.

"What manner of creature is it?" Lomar asked in disgust, pointing to the apparition, which squirmed uncomfortably within the blue light still flooding from the crystal.

"A demon!" Hannas snapped angrily, looking accusingly at Kaplyn as though the creature's presence was his doing.

"It is an abomination, Your Highness," said another. "It should be returned from whence it came immediately; its very presence fouls the air and despoils our homes."

"Can we return it, Hannas?" Lomar asked.

"It's our incantation that keeps it here. We only have to stop the light of the kara-stone and it will disappear back to the hell that spawned it."

"Do it!" Lomar said, with a look of disgust as the creature mewled pathetically, futilely clawing the air as if seeking to erase the agony that bound it.

Hannas spoke a few words and the light within the crystal vanished. Instantly the demon disappeared and its cries ceased, suddenly leaving an empty silence in the room. Pure sunlight streamed in as if the sun had reappeared from behind a cloud, but somehow the room felt tainted as if some terrible crime had been committed.

"Open the windows," Lomar ordered. "What happened?" he asked.

"It was an imp I believe," Hannas said. "One of the lesser demons, but still deadly. We were fortunate."

"Kaplyn, did you know about this creature?" Lomar demanded.

"No! I knew that he was a wizard, but nothing more." Kaplyn was shocked and angry. He was also very confused for he thought that he had seen a creature like that somewhere before and then he remembered. The night when he had met Lars, he had seen something when he had awoken. Could that have been an imp? The memory was distant and he could not be certain but shivered nonetheless.

"Wizard!" Hannas spat, her eyes blazed with fury. "He is no such thing. He is a Narlassar *sorcerer*, a necromancer," she spat as if the very name defiled her. "That is what he was hiding – and that is why he is ill!'

"That does not necessarily mean he *is* evil," Lomar said. "After all, the Eldric were Narlassar and as far as we know, of them, only Drachar was evil."

"You are correct, but the imp is evil and if it is at this man's beck and call then he cannot be totally free from its influence," Hannas retorted.

"I do not understand," Kaplyn said. "Is Vastra ill and what does this imp have to do with it?"

"He's ill because he is close to a holy site, once inhabited by an Old One," Lomar explained. "He has an imp at his call and it is the forest's influence upon that which is causing his illness. Evil is not tolerated here. However, it does not necessarily mean that your companion is evil," he continued. "The Narlassar used demons to focus their powers, which they used for good."

"In any event, these strangers cannot be tolerated," Hannas stated bluntly. "They must leave Gilfillan immediately before any harm is done."

"Look after our guests and treat them well until I return," Lomar said softly. "I must speak with the Queen."

Kaplyn saw a change in Lomar at that moment. His shoulders sagged and he sounded dispirited. Before he could say anything, however, Lomar left and as soon as he was gone the other healers started arguing once more, leaving Kaplyn and Lars isolated and at a loss.

Lomar was convinced that he knew what he must do. His terrible dreams seemed to make sense, but he felt more afraid than ever before. He was about to make a decision that would affect the rest of his life and that of everyone he held dear. He was dreading talking to his mother and a great sadness overwhelmed him.

Within her chamber, the Queen was sitting at a table with a quill and parchment before her, but she touched neither. Lomar stopped in the doorway and for a moment he nearly failed. Never before had he seen his mother so anguished. Her scarlet eyes brimmed with unshed tears. She raised a hand, trying to hide her face.

"Lomar," she sobbed, her shoulders shaking as silently she wept.

"What's wrong?" he asked softly.

She smiled, although it seemed forced and tears slid down her pale cheek. "You are leaving?" she asked, sniffing softly. She rummaged through her purse, withdrawing a handkerchief and dabbing her eyes.

Lomar nodded, unable to lie.

"Your father knew that you would. He said that your gift would be called upon, but I have prayed every day since then that he was wrong!" She looked pleadingly up at him. "Don't go," she begged.

"I must," he answered.

"Why?"

He lowered his gaze, unable to meet hers. "Our people have avoided their responsibilities for far too long. We have been complacent while others have had to fight for the freedom that we take for granted."

Her eyes widened in sudden anger. "It was the Eldric who caused this evil, not us," she retorted bitterly.

Lomar shook his head sadly. "They did not help, certainly. But evil was present before the Eldric came. They merely precipitated an inevitable war."

The Queen bit her lip. "There is still time before the Prophecy comes to pass; by then it will not matter. Let it lie. It's not our concern."

"I cannot," he replied, hanging his head.

"One day, you will be king!" she countered. "You cannot leave and shirk that responsibility."

"And what sort of king would I be knowing that I did not try to save our race. Without the Eldric another war would be our downfall."

She arose as though everything she loved was broken and they hugged for a few heartbeats before separating.

"I shall return," he said, stepping from her embrace. Somehow, though, he knew it was unlikely. He left the room with a heavy heart, leaving his mother watching the door as though willing him to return. Her sobs came clearly to him as he turned into the corridor without a backward glance.

On his way to his room he sought one of the guards and asked that his guests should be escorted to the stables where he would join them. In his room, Garth was waiting, his eyes reflecting his uncertainty over the recent events. This was the moment Lomar had been dreading.

"Garth, I have to leave," he softly said.

"I know," Garth replied. "And I am coming with you."

Lomar couldn't help but smile, "Oh, I am so sorry, my dear friend, but I cannot take you with me."

Garth looked crestfallen and with Garth watching his every move like a hawk, Lomar changed into more practical travelling clothes and then packed a few belongings into a stout pack. When finished, he glanced about the room one final time before turning to leave.

Garth offered to take his pack, making it clear by his look that he would not let his Prince refuse this last offer of help. Lomar smiled and handed it to Garth who carried it down the long flight of stairs, muttering all the way.

Kaplyn and Lars were making final adjustments to the mules' heavy packs when Lomar and Garth entered. Lomar's people had provided a cart to carry Vastra and this was harnessed to his horse. His face was barely visible from beneath a thick blanket.

Immediately Lomar announced his intention to accompany them.

"No!" Kaplyn replied flatly. "We do not know what lies ahead. Besides, you have your people to consider."

Lomar silently saddled his own horse leaving Kaplyn looking on bemused. Garth shuffled past, glaring at Kaplyn as though he had bewitched his Prince.

Lomar mounted, looking expectantly down at the other two men. Kaplyn realised that they could not stop him from riding with them, if he so chose.

Lars grinned and Kaplyn cast him a dour look.

"Very well," Kaplyn sighed. "You are more than welcome to join us. But understand that the quest is likely to be dangerous," he continued. "Also, Vastra will object and may insist that you leave."

Lomar nodded, then smiled, raising a hand in farewell to Garth as they rode from the stables. Kaplyn glanced back to see Garth waving, a forlorn figure soon lost within the darkness of the great tree.

Chapter 20

Journey to the Turn Marsh

They rode down a gentle incline for a short way before Lomar requested a halt to look back one final time at the city. When at last Lomar turned his horse away he kept his gaze stubbornly fixed upon the path as though afraid to look back.

It was already late in the day and the light filtering into the forest was fading. However, it was obvious to Kaplyn that Lomar preferred to be as far as possible from Gilfillan by nightfall.

It was Lars who finally raised the subject that was also troubling Kaplyn. "What are we going to do about Vastra and the imp?" he asked in a hushed tone, even though Vastra was still unconscious.

"There's nothing we can do until he recovers," Kaplyn said. "When he does, we should keep quiet about the imp and see what he does."

Lars nodded. "I suppose you are right. If we admit knowing about it he will simply deny it."

They rode in darkness for several hours with only the light of the moon to guide them until at last Lomar called for a halt. They made camp and sat around a small fire eating fruit that they had picked upon the way. It was pleasant sitting by the gentle orange glow of the fire while high above, between the gently swaying branches, stars winked against the night sky.

Lomar asked them to tell him more about themselves, clearly fascinated by the outside world. Kaplyn saw no reason to lie, given how much Lomar had forsaken in accompanying them, and he told him openly that his father was the Allund Monarch. He also told Lomar that Vastra claimed to be the King's bastard son and spoke of his fears concerning the sorcerer.

Lars, in turn, briefly spoke of his own home and being shipwrecked and cast alone onto the Allund shores. The tale horrified Lomar and he marvelled at Lars' tenacity. Lars and Kaplyn then went on to describe their meeting and journey to Tanel. When Kaplyn described the Eldric citadel, Lomar was fascinated and asked them both to describe it in detail.

Kaplyn showed Lomar the pendant but unfortunately he could not read Eldric, although the writing looked frustratingly similar to that of his own people.

In silence, they drank wine and the forest seemed to close in around them as if seeking to protect them from the surrounding gloom. A large pale moon peeked through the thick vegetation and Lars looked wistfully up at the giant shining orb. Kaplyn saw the big man's pained look and guessed that he was feeling melancholy. He tried to think of something to distract the big man.

"These gods that you keep telling me about," he asked softly. "Does any one god rule over them, or are they all equal?"

Lars smiled. "Etu," he replied. "He created the world for the other gods to shape." He pointed up at the moon. "My people believe that he has set his eyes high in the sky so that he can watch over us. One eye is bright and that lights up the day and none can look at that without going blind, while at night he watches the world with the other eye from behind a thick cloth so that the world can sleep."

Kaplyn and Lomar smiled, although Kaplyn found it hard to believe that a god would pluck out his own eyes so that he could watch the goings-on of the world. Lomar was especially interested in Lars' homeland and he questioned him late into the night about his people and their beliefs. Lars brightened as he spoke and when they eventually retired to their makeshift beds, they all fell quickly asleep.

For two days they travelled through the forest. It was pleasant and the going easy. They were all disappointed when the forest changed back to drab colours; it seemed a dreary place after being in the enchanted wood.

Then the trees abruptly ended and they found themselves on the forest's edge looking out. Lomar looked shocked. A marshland stretched for miles before them, giving way in the distance to tall mountains, bleak and forlorn in majestic glory. They were still at least a day's journey away and the prospect of crossing the intervening bog was not a welcome one. The marsh looked barren and only long grass and the occasional shrub grew on the inhospitable ground.

"I never imagined the world could look so dismal," Lomar said.

"After your forest you will find most of the land bleak," Lars answered.

Kaplyn nodded. He, too, felt depressed at the sight and especially the smell coming from the bog.

They agreed to camp at the forest's edge and immediately set about making a fire, placing the unconscious Vastra as close to it as they dared. They hid the fire as best they could, using their baggage and the cart as a screen.

Kaplyn grew more concerned that Vastra had not yet woken, his flesh was pale and he had dark circles around his eyes. Lomar had packed a kara-stone and he used this to probe Vastra's illness and, once done, seemed positive that he was recovering now that they were out of the forest.

The evening passed unpleasantly with the constant reek from the marsh. As they sat miserably trying to warm themselves by the fire, tiny insects filled the air about them. Lars yelped as one bit him.

"Zelph," Kaplyn informed him, clasping his cloak more tightly about his throat to cover his flesh.

"They are eating me alive," Lars complained. It soon became unbearable and, judging it dark enough to hide the smoke, they decided to see if that would drive the flies away. They piled large handfuls of wet leaves on the fire and were immediately rewarded by copious amounts of thick, acrid smoke. To their relief the zelph disappeared, but the leaves smothered the heat and smoke irritated their throats and eyes. It was going to be an uncomfortable night.

In the grey light of the dawn, Lomar awoke with a start to find Vastra glaring down at him. Lomar gave out a short, sharp cry of shock, causing Kaplyn and Lars to leap from their blankets while Vastra turned to glare balefully at them.

Vastra kept blinking, his eyes red from the fire's smoke, making him look uncannily like one of Lomar's people.

"Where are we?" he croaked.

"You've been ill," Kaplyn explained. "We have travelled through the forest which now lies behind us." Vastra's gaze went quizzically back to Lomar and Kaplyn realised that he had better introduce the albino. "This is Lomar, his people are the Alvalah."

Vastra sat down as though his legs could no longer support him. Kaplyn sensed that an argument would follow and was already waiting with a retort, but Vastra merely sighed.

Lars glanced in frustration at Kaplyn and without a word set about preparing a fire and hot water for breakfast.

They broke their fast in silence and no one dared speak for fear of recrimination. For a change, Vastra ate with gusto and afterwards prepared a potion of herbs. As he drank, colour returned to his cheeks.

"How long have you lived in the forest," Vastra asked, looking at Lomar as he toyed with his cup.

"My people have lived in the forest for many generations. It was a shame that you missed seeing our city."

"You bring to mind the Eldric," Vastra said, putting the cup down.

"We believe our people are related."

"Has Kaplyn shown you the pendant?" Vastra asked.

"Yes."

"Could you read it?"

"No. The script is very similar to ours, but I couldn't make sense of it."

Kaplyn thought he saw Vastra relax. "Pity," he said, picking up his cup and sipping its contents.

"We should go soon," Lars muttered. A cloud of zelph hovered over the big man and he looked glum as he waved his hands, trying to fend them off.

Kaplyn grinned at the sight of him itching at his thick tangled beard, but his smile swiftly vanished when one of the insects bit him and he realised that their attention was shifting towards him.

"We have to cross the marsh," Vastra declared. "The tallest peak over there," he said pointing to the horizon, "is BanKildor. That is our destination."

Kaplyn nodded. Suddenly the wind increased and changed direction, blowing now from the mountains. It became much colder and hurriedly they packed their gear hoping that they would be warmer once they started to move.

When they were ready to leave Kaplyn looked out one final time over the marsh. It was a barren landscape with a few stunted trees trying to eke out an existence. White marsh-cotton was the only splash of colour, bouncing on long stalks in time to the gusting wind.

Kaplyn looked to either side of their position to see whether they could skirt the bog, but the forest swung around in a great arc, merging in the distance with the grey of the mountains.

"How do you propose we cross?" Kaplyn asked turning to Vastra.

The sorcerer mounted and looked at the marsh. "Marsh-cotton only grows on firm ground. I can see several paths — we will follow one and hope that it connects to others."

It was not a very satisfactory suggestion, but would have to suffice. The others mounted and with Vastra leading they set off, leaving the cart at the forest's edge.

Initially the ground was soft and spongy and their horses' hooves sank considerably as they went. However, they soon found a broad path, which rose slightly above the surrounding bog. It was sufficiently wide to allow several horses to ride abreast and the ground became firmer.

The croaking of thousands of frogs and the occasional splash from somewhere in the bog accompanied them as they rode. A large bird flapped noisily from the tall reeds close to the riders, startling their mounts as it ran across their path. It launched itself clumsily into the sky; squawking loudly as it went. The horses spooked, nearly throwing their riders and carrying Lars off the trail and almost into the swamp. The big man threw himself off the horse, which ran a short way and then stopped as its foreleg plunged into the mire. It took them a while to calm the animal while Lars sat on the ground, grimacing with pain and swearing never to ride again.

The fright forced them to dismount and Vastra complained bitterly at the delay. He seemed to be in a hurry and anxiously looked towards the distant mountains as if willing them closer.

Chapter 21

Betrayal in the Dark

The day passed slowly and, as the sky darkened, they appeared to have made little progress. To their chagrin, the mountains still seemed distant although behind them the forest no longer dominated the skyline. Bone-weary they decided to halt and Lars spotted a hollow where they could camp. Little was said as they unpacked; their spirits were at a low ebb. A quick search revealed little wood and what they found was damp, so a fire was out of the question.

As they settled down in the hollow, wrapped in blankets, their hope that it would afford some shelter from the wind was dashed. To make matters worse a large number of zelph surrounded them and Kaplyn considered asking Vastra to use magic to get rid of them. He dismissed the notion almost at once, knowing Vastra would take offence at a request to use his powers for trivia.

A sharp wind sprung up and at once the zelph disappeared leaving the group with large itching bites. Vastra plucked some leaves growing nearby and rubbed them on his bites and the others followed suit, gratefully finding that the itching became less severe.

Uncomfortably they settled down for the night, hugging their cloaks tightly about them to keep out the keen wind. Kaplyn's feet were icy cold and he debated putting on another pair of socks, but the thought of taking his boots off and exposing his feet to the wind was too much to bear. He looked with envy at Lars who seemed the only one unaffected by the cold.

After they had eaten a frugal meal from their rations, Vastra excused himself. Rising, he walked along the path and swiftly disappeared into the surrounding gloom.

"Where do you think he is going?" Lars whispered.

"Probably a call of nature," Kaplyn replied.

Lars' eyebrows rose perceptibly. "Can we trust him?"

"I could follow him," Kaplyn offered.

"It might be wise," Lomar said. "Especially with the imp to consider."

Kaplyn hurried after Vastra, trying to remain hidden, picking his route carefully. Vastra's tracks veered off the main path into the swamp, following a small trail probably used by animals. Here the ground was uneven with hillocks and deep troughs.

Close to a small rise, Kaplyn lowered himself to all fours and crawled to the summit. At the top, he looked through a shrub so that he wouldn't be seen.

By now it was dark, only a faint light from the moon penetrated the thick overhead cloud cover. It took him a while to locate Vastra amongst the long tussocks of grass. He was squatting about thirty paces from Kaplyn with his back to him.

Kaplyn felt foolish but remained where he was, patiently waiting. He became damp lying on the wet ground and wanted to return to the camp. Just as he was about to give up, movement betrayed a figure close to Vastra. Straining his eyes, he tried to make it out. A faint green glow emanated from it and he recognised the imp.

At that moment, the clouds parted and in the better light he saw the imp cavorting around Vastra who seemed to be having difficulty controlling it. In the still of the night, he could hear Vastra speaking, but couldn't hear if the imp replied. Kaplyn felt exposed where he was and, deciding that he had seen enough, crawled out of sight. Swiftly he retraced his path.

He had only gone a few yards when the clouds once more concealed the moon and darkness enveloped him. Kaplyn paused, momentarily confused as to which way was correct. He was afraid that the imp might be close and drew his blade to see if its glow would warn him. Fortunately the blade was dull, but he kept it drawn as he retreated farther.

Eager to find his way back to the others he quickened his pace, becoming more aware as he went that he was no longer on the original trail. He decided that he should be going more to the east, but before he could correct his mistake the ground beneath his feet heaved as something large reared up, emitting a fearful scream.

He leapt backward, but the creature threw him off-balance and he tumbled to one side, misplacing his footing. He took a couple of strides and agony lanced through his ankle as he twisted it. The marsh creature tried to charge through him as it sought sanctuary deeper in the swamp, knocking Kaplyn to one side.

Grabbing at the tall grass he dropped his sword and, with a sickening splash, fell into the marsh.

Fearing the creature would attack he desperately tried to reach firmer ground, but with each stride he was sinking deeper. After a few moments panic, he realised that it must have been as frightened of him as he had been of it. Listening to the silence he realised it was long gone.

He stopped struggling and the pain in his ankle slowly subsided. He tried to extract himself more carefully but to his horror he was stuck fast. To make matters worse, he was very slowly being sucked under the thick cloying mud, which was already up to his waist.

He ceased struggling and tried to see how far he was from the bank but the tall grass made it difficult to tell where the firm ground started and marsh ended. He reasoned that it couldn't be far to solid ground, but there was nothing for him to push against.

"Lars! Lomar!" he cried out.

Only the quiet of the night answered and he was just about to shout again when a figure noisily entered the hollow. Initially, the sight of a rescuer relieved him, but recognising Vastra his relief instantly soured.

"Vastra, help me," he said.

Kaplyn saw a flash of anger behind Vastra's eyes and then he looked coldly at Kaplyn. Carefully he came forward, testing the ground with one foot before edging forward.

By now Kaplyn's clothes were sodden and the additional weight was pulling him under more quickly.

"Throw me one end of your cloak," Kaplyn called out.

"Throw me the pendant first," Vastra replied, his arm outstretched in expectation.

Kaplyn knew he couldn't trust Vastra and he tried again to extract himself. The mud made great sucking noises and noxious fumes assailed him, causing him to gag. By now only his head and arms were above the surface.

Above him Vastra smiled. Kaplyn was furious; no doubt, if he sank, Vastra would find some means to recover the pendant. With a mighty bellow he again called for help.

Vastra looked over his shoulder, clearly ill at ease. As Kaplyn's voice faded into the night, with relief, Kaplyn heard Lars shout back. His eyes locked on Vastra's and again he saw hatred reflected there, and then the look was gone. Vastra hurriedly tried to remove the clasp securing his cloak. Shrugging it off he threw one end to Kaplyn who grabbed it. Vastra pulled, but lacked the strength to make a difference.

Kaplyn shouted again to Lars, fearing Vastra might yet take advantage. Perhaps he saw an inkling of Vastra's cowardice for he did nothing more than hang onto the cloak.

Lars' voice came back in answer, but closer this time. Again, Kaplyn shouted knowing how easily the marsh disorientated people. Almost immediately the big man entered the hollow, swiftly followed by Lomar. Lars grabbed Vastra's cloak and with supreme effort started to haul Kaplyn from the clinging mud. Lomar, too, took a hand while Vastra stood to one side, sullenly watching.

Finally Kaplyn felt himself moving and, with renewed hope, he kicked his feet to help propel himself from what might have been an early grave. After what seemed an eternity, they succeeded in dragging him clear. There he lay, panting and trembling with a mixture of cold and fear as the wind whistled around him.

Anger burst through his other feelings and he leapt to his feet, starting towards Vastra with fists clenched. Vastra glanced at the other two men, his eyes imploring their aid and Lars, seeing Kaplyn's murderous look, grabbed Kaplyn's arm.

"He was going to let me drown," Kaplyn hissed through clenched teeth. He was shaking from a mixture of cold and rage. Lars looked to Vastra for an explanation.

"I only asked for him t...to throw me the pendant first. It might have been lost as we pulled him out," he stuttered, taking an involuntary step backwards.

"By Slathor, but you are an evil man!" Lars said through gritted teeth.

He let go of Kaplyn who, with a cry, surged forward, throwing Vastra from his feet. Thinking his life was threatened Vastra muttered, tracing a rune in the air and instantly the imp materialised, scant yards in front of Kaplyn. Its forked tail lashed angrily from side to side and its eyes gleamed with anticipated pleasure.

Kaplyn reached for his sword but realised he had lost it in the bog. In desperation he clutched the pendant, raising it over his head for all to see.

"Vastra, stop or I'll throw this into the bog." Seeing the pendant the imp hissed but did nothing more, as though waiting Vastra's command.

Vastra's hesitation allowed Lars to draw his axe and Lomar his kara-stone. Shouting words of power a silver flame sprang forth, causing the imp to recoil.

Kaplyn sensed they had gained the upper hand. "Command the imp to return my sword," he ordered, waving his free hand in the direction of the swamp.

165

The imp howled causing Kaplyn to recoil and he wondered if Vastra did indeed hold mastery. Fortunately, Vastra failed to see his fear as he concentrated instead, muttering words of power, tracing a rune upon the cold night air.

Before Vastra could complete the spell, the imp lunged. Razor sharp talons opened a gaping wound across his face. Vastra screamed and recoiled.

Lomar shouted his own words of power; the light from his kara-stone flared, causing the imp to cower.

Vastra recovered and shouted a string of commands in haste and obvious fear. His spell was enough to stay the imp as it hissed and squirmed in front of him. It glared balefully, its eyes narrowed against the hated light; then, all at once and with a sudden wail, it disappeared in a flash.

The bright light temporarily blinded everyone. Kaplyn heard a dull thud by his feet and fearing attack he leapt back, holding the pendant aloft. For some moments, Kaplyn was disorientated but then Lomar shouted, "The imp has gone!"

Coloured lights flickered before Kaplyn's eyes and an afterglow of the flash remained each time he blinked. Gradually he made out the blurred shape of his sword, buried to the hilt by his feet. With considerable effort he drew it from the ground.

Vastra had not attempted to rise and he, too, was having difficulties with his vision. A deep scratch marred his face, from the side of his eye down to his lip.

Kaplyn stalked over, placing the point of his blade on Vastra's chest. He was tempted to end Vastra's vile existence, but Lomar interceded, laying a firm hand on his shoulder. As their eyes met, Kaplyn knew that he couldn't kill him. However, he knew of a better way to punish him.

He was still holding the pendant and he held it up for Vastra to see. "Tomorrow, I *will* return to Pendrat, but before I do I shall ask Lomar's people to melt this down." Vastra's betrayal was the final straw. To his satisfaction, he saw a look of fear in the other man's eyes. However, Vastra's fear only served to anger Kaplyn even more.

"You would have killed me! Is life so unimportant?"

Vastra glared defiantly back, but remained silent.

"How many men have you sent to their deaths in your efforts to recover this?" Kaplyn asked, realising that they were not the first to go into Tanel. He remembered the strange creatures he had encountered, and wondered if that had been the fate of the others Vastra had sent to the tower.

The defiance in Vastra's eyes disappeared and he looked truly afraid.

"The pendant is important," Vastra blurted out. "You must not destroy it. Without it there will be no hope and the Prophecy will fail."

"But you have killed," Kaplyn hissed. The sword remained at Vastra's throat, causing him to look fearfully down at the dark metal.

"The men went because they were greedy; that is not my fault."

The tip of Kaplyn's sword forced Vastra's head back. The blade seemed to moan eerily, like the wind in the trees. Vastra's breath came in short, sharp rasps.

"How many did you kill?" Kaplyn hissed.

"Ten. No twelve — I don't know!"

"You don't even care," shouted Kaplyn as he flung himself from Vastra in disgust. "You are a butcher and one day you'll pay for your actions." He stormed away, returning along the path back to the camp. Lars and Lomar followed, leaving Vastra trying to stem the flow of blood from his wounded cheek.

Chapter 22

Tallin's Crown

When they returned to camp Kaplyn and the others gathered wood for a fire. As they had feared, the wood proved too damp to light. Accepting defeat Lomar took out his kara-stone, placing it between them and, uttering words of power, a silver light sprang from its heart. They gathered round but the heat wasn't enough to warm Kaplyn who sat miserably on the ground, hugging his knees and shivering violently.

Vastra returned. Seeing the pile of wood, he muttered and waved his arm. Instantly a blaze sprang forth as he retreated to the edge of the circle of light, sitting forlornly on a rock.

The others eagerly warmed themselves, grateful for the heat. Kaplyn changed out of his wet clothes and, since they couldn't spare any water, was forced to scrape the mud off his body as best he could. He swore as he realised he would be spending an uncomfortable night covered in the evil-smelling mire. His boots were also sodden and he did not have a spare pair. With some effort he pulled them off and put on fresh socks, but the cold wind easily penetrated the wool. Grimacing, he pulled the boots back on.

By his side, Lomar spoke softly. "You cannot destroy the pendant."

Kaplyn frowned. "*By the Kalanth*! I can do what I like," he retorted.

"If there is a chance of finding the Eldric, then we must," Lomar continued. "Another war is inevitable and *sooner* than you think! That is too hard to bear. In such a war, my people will be destroyed utterly."

Kaplyn's frown deepened. "What do you mean — *sooner than I think?*"

"After our last discussion I went to the library to check. Tallin's Crown is a constellation and it will form a crown in about sixty years. That is when Drachar will rise once more to lead the enemy."

"That *cannot* be!" Kaplyn blurted, his thoughts in turmoil. "My people couldn't be that wrong! It cannot be so soon!"

"Lomar's right," Vastra said softly. Kaplyn glared at him but Vastra continued. "That is the first line of the Prophecy, W*hen Tallin's Crown once more does shine*. Tallin's Crown is a constellation of seven stars. Normally the constellation comprises only six stars, but every five hundred years another star moves slowly across the heavens to join this group, the resultant formation looks like a crown."

"How do you know that the Prophecy will happen though?" Lars asked dubiously.

"It *will* happen!" Vastra replied simply. "Demons have seen this world and as soon as they are able they will cross to claim souls. When Tallin's Crown is complete, their world and ours will be at their closest and the fabric separating them will be at its weakest. Trosgarth is bound to take advantage to wage war."

"*Why?*" Kaplyn asked. "They were defeated and Drachar killed. Why wait five hundred years to resume a war which will benefit no one?"

"The people of Trosgarth have not forgotten their defeat and over the years there have been many skirmishes along their borders. Our history has been deliberately withheld so that people will not panic," Vastra continued. "These attacks are not the actions of a defeated people. Trosgarth is biding its time. As soon as it can, its people will summon Drachar's shade."

"I agree," Lomar said. "Our records show that demon activity peaks in about five hundred-year cycles."

They fell silent. All about them frogs croaked loudly and an occasional splash heralded a fish or a marsh creature feeding. Kaplyn listened to the abundant wildlife, his thoughts too confused to warrant a decision. Vastra was dangerous and he doubted if they could ever trust him.

"A short while ago I had a dream," Lars said softly interrupting his thoughts; all eyes turned to the big man. "In it, my people were butchered by demons while I was forced to watch. Both my wife and son were killed. *By Slathor*, I *cannot* allow that to happen. If demons win here, then they will seek elsewhere for prey and my people may be next. The gods rescued me for a purpose and I think it is to prevent demons entering this world. I, too, believe the quest must continue."

Kaplyn rocked gently back and forth, clutching his knees to keep warm. He did not know what to do.

"If we continue, Vastra, what will we find?" he asked eventually. His tone suggested his anger had subsided although his eyes warned Vastra to reply truthfully.

The sorcerer came closer to the fire, warming his hands. He kept his eyes on the flames. "I believe the Eldric have left our world," he said softly.

"What makes you think that?" Kaplyn asked.

"After the war the Eldric were devastated that one of their own kind lay waste to the land, using Narlassar magic for evil. The Eldric couldn't accept that the blame was theirs, or perhaps they did — in any event the truth forced them to forsake this world and they fled, seeking alternative lands where, possibly, magic doesn't exist." Vastra hugged his cloak tightly about his bony frame.

"We are following a path the Eldric took long ago." He looked up at Kaplyn, but could not meet his eyes, so looked back into the flames. "They went to the mountains, to BanKildor where they found a cavern, inside which they discovered a power — a power so immense it will keep a passage open between the worlds indefinitely, enabling all of their people to cross from this world to another."

"How do you know all this?" Kaplyn asked.

Vastra looked up, his eyes sparkling with excitement. "I learned some of it through the imp. He obtained Eldric books and I have guessed the rest. The pendant and the description of the route confirm my views though. We will never know unless we look. We have the pendent and that's the key to finding out what happened."

"Vastra's correct," Lomar said softly. "If another war happens then, without the Eldric and their magic, we will surely fail. That fear has driven me from my homeland for, if a full scale war occurs in six years or sixty, my people will be destroyed and that would be a terrible burden upon my soul."

"How could this have happened?" Kaplyn asked, shaking his head. "Why are my people convinced that so few years have passed since the Krell Wars?"

Vastra poked the fire with a stick, it had already burned low and there was no more wood. He looked up at Kaplyn, "No one wants to know when the next war will occur. The people are too afraid it might happen in their lifetime and they gladly believe it will be somebody else's problem. What chance do we have against the forces of evil without the Eldric?" he said throwing the stick into the fire.

"I've studied the Krell Wars, and what I've read leaves me cold. Besides krell, there were grakyn, fell creatures that fly. Both krell and grakyn are born of this world and unlike demons they do not simply disappear in the middle of a fight. Then there are the demons themselves. Some are as tall as a building while others are so fast they can move in the blink of an eye."

Kaplyn shivered as he remembered the attack in the library and the demon's lightning response.

"We have witnessed increased demon activity. Think! The wolf attack at the farm was not normal and you saw, yourself, a demon at Kinlin castle. We have no defence against demons! It's imperative we find the Eldric," Vastra concluded looking at Kaplyn.

Kaplyn had heard enough. His eyes locked on Vastra's. "We will continue! But *mark me*, if you do *anything* even remotely underhand I will not hesitate to kill you."

Vastra remained silent and all Kaplyn could hear was the pounding of the blood in his ears.

In the morning Kaplyn awoke feeling both tired and weary. He had slept poorly and the cold had penetrated through to the very marrow of his being. The others were awakening and he was surprised to see that Vastra was still with them. He had expected him to leave during the night. His tenacity amazed him; if that had been Kaplyn he would have been too ashamed to carry on.

After eating a hurried breakfast, they broke camp and this time even Vastra helped, as though keen to show he was reformed.

They started early with Vastra taking the lead. The ground was firm, but dipped steeply to either side of the path. The bog stank, reminding Kaplyn of his plight the night before; slowly sinking in the mud and the feeling of utter helplessness. To lighten his mood he turned his mind to thoughts of family and friends, but failed; it was with a heavy heart that he rode across the bleak terrain.

Chapter 23

In the Mountains

By the end of the second day, the forest had become nothing more than a green smudge against the distant skyline while ahead the mountains were much more prominent. It was late in the day and they decided to camp. Vastra announced he needed to scout the path while the light held.

"I'll go with you!" Kaplyn declared coldly, making it clear he would not be dissuaded.

"The path forks ahead, I need to determine which one to take," Vastra explained. The wound on his face looked inflamed and was bleeding. Clearly, the imp had done more than just cut him.

Lars and Lomar remained to prepare a hot meal while Kaplyn and Vastra rode ahead. After the previous day's escapade, they had collected wood along the way so at least they could have a fire.

When they had gone far enough Vastra halted them and then dismounted. He rummaged through his saddlebags, finally producing a slither of metal and twine. He held one end of the twine with the metal suspended below it. The metal spun erratically before settling down to point the way ahead.

"Stand on your horse and see which direction the paths go," Vastra said.

Kaplyn did as he was asked. Ahead, their path split into two. He pointed out the direction of each to Vastra, who seemed lost in thought for a while before deciding which way they should go.

"The right path is the one we want, although I dare not risk summoning the imp today to verify it," he gestured at his face. "As you can see, yesterday I lost control."

"You are playing a dangerous game with that demon," Kaplyn warned.

"And without him I would be nothing," Vastra replied.

"The imp is evil. It will seek to destroy you."

172

Vastra laughed. "I have mastery over it, and it does what I command." His manner during the day had been pleasant for a change, his laughter was honest and he even smiled for a while. Kaplyn felt it was a pity that he couldn't be like this all the time, and he wondered whether the sudden change in his mood would last, but deep down doubted it.

"It does what it wants, I suspect," Kaplyn replied mounting his horse.

Together they rode back to rejoin the others. Lars had opened a flagon of Lomar's wine, which they were warming over a fire. Lomar had added herbs and a strong aroma greeted them. Wearily they dismounted and unsaddled the horses and unpacked the mules just as Lomar announced the wine was ready.

Kaplyn and Vastra joined them, crouching by the fire. The hot liquid warmed them and after a moment, they felt somewhat recovered. Lars started telling them humorous tales about his village and soon had them all laughing.

The evening was bearable until it started to rain. The company thought they were in for a wet night; however, retrieving his kara-stone, Lomar positioned it within the middle of the group. As he recounted arcane words of power, the rain falling on them ceased although the cold wind continued. Kaplyn looked up; it was as though the rain was bouncing off an invisible cover, running in rivulets down the sides.

"Where did you get that stone?" Vastra asked.

"There is a cave in our city with hundreds of these."

"*Hundreds!*" Vastra exclaimed.

"Yes, we saw them," Kaplyn interrupted. "It was magnificent, especially when the sun shines inside the cave."

"I've never heard of so many kara-stones occurring in one place before," Vastra said.

"My people believe it was once the site of an Old One," Lomar replied.

Vastra sniffed, as though rejecting that idea.

They soon turned in for the night, covering themselves with blankets and falling asleep to the gentle rhythm of rain pattering off the invisible barrier.

The next morning was dreary; the ground was soft and uneven, forcing them to walk. Continuous drizzle soaked them thoroughly. However, just when they were starting to think they could go no further, the ground rose perceptibly and at last they found themselves on drier, firmer footing. Eagerly they mounted and made better progress as the foothills gave way to steeper slopes.

A single pass led high between the arms of two large peaks, framed between which they could see the awe-inspiring shape of BanKildor. This peak was taller than its neighbours and snow-capped, explaining why the wind was biting cold.

It became too steep for the horses so they dismounted and set about unsaddling them. There was plenty of grass and the animals would not wander far for there was nowhere else for them to go besides the marsh. The only concern was that of wolves and possibly krell. Vastra said that he could cast a spell that would mask the horses' scent.

Soon they were ready and the pack mules were even more heavily laden with additional burdens taken from the horses. Lomar spoke to his mount, stroking its soft nose. When they left the animals, he explained to Kaplyn that he had charged his horse with looking after the others and, if danger threatened, he would lead them back to Gilfillan. Kaplyn smiled, but realised Lomar was being serious.

By their side a stream swiftly flowed through a narrow gorge, the rush of water drowned out other sounds, adding a sense of urgency to their quest. The banks were initially wide and flat, helping their progress. At times, the gorge became deep and with the start of spring, its waters were already showing signs of increased fury.

Lars informed them that the river they were following originated from a glacier, judging by its colour, which frothed a dirty white as the water tumbled over small rocky waterfalls. None of the men had heard of glaciers before and so Lars described the immense lakes of frozen water that flowed inexorably down the steep valleys of his mountain homeland.

For the remainder of that evening they ascended, taking advantage while the light of a grey dismal day lasted. The stream twisted and turned and occasionally huge rocks blocked the path, forcing them to climb around these. It would have been quicker without the mules, but then they would have had to leave most of their provisions behind. They endured the animals' frequent stubbornness and, more than once, practically dragged one animal by brute force before it would continue.

They managed to climb for some time longer before Kaplyn suggested they stop due to the failing light. They were fortunate to find their first real shelter in days, beneath an overhang of rock where a deep hollow afforded some protection from the wind. Kaplyn took advantage of the stream to wash the mud from his body. He had to grit his teeth for the water was freezing, making his skin burn. However, it was well worth it to be rid of the uncomfortable grime. He also washed his clothes, beating them on the rocks to shake loose the dirt. Wrapping himself in a blanket, feeling greatly refreshed, he rejoined the others.

Wood was more plentiful here and they built a fire, taking care to conceal the flames, using dry wood to reduce the smoke. Kaplyn laid his clothes close to the fire and sat back watching the steam rising from the wet garments as Lomar mulled some wine.

Lars sang songs from his homeland and started to teach the others the words of the sillier rhymes. They were in high spirits and Kaplyn suggested they take a day off to recover. Unfortunately, however, Vastra was adamant they should continue.

"We have little time left. There is only one day every five hundred years when it is safe to enter the cavern described on the pendant. Tonight it's important that I see the stars so I can decide when it is safe to enter."

"Why have you not mentioned this before?" Kaplyn demanded.

Vastra shrugged. "It's only important now we are getting near. We do have time to spare, I think."

"My people don't like going underground," Lars announced, squatting by the fire and holding a mug of hot wine in his fist. "We do not bury our dead as you do, but build funeral pyres."

"Why do you not bury your dead?" Kaplyn asked curiously.

"Long ago the gods captured Baldor, the cruellest and most cunning of the giants, luring him deep within the bowels of the earth. Some say he is trapped in a cavern made of gold so he cannot use his magical powers. It is he whom the gods fear most and it is said that one day man, in his folly, will release him and that day will herald the end of the world."

Lars sipped his wine before continuing. "On occasions you can hear Baldor shaking his prison walls and that is when the ground trembles. Once free he will release the other giants and together they will destroy the world. Then the giants will lead the assault on Fallor-Ell and all the fell creatures will unite with them."

"That's not a very cheerful tale," Lomar commented refilling their flagons with more hot wine. "Talking of which, will we be safe with such a large fire? Krell inhabit the mountains and we don't want them knowing we are here."

"We should be all right. The rock is grey and it's masking the smoke. We'll let the fire die down before it is dark," Kaplyn answered.

"I could cast a spell to alert us if anyone approaches," Vastra offered. The others agreed and they watched as he scribed the necessary runes in the air, muttering words of power.

"Why is it that you need to summon the imp on occasions and at other times you simply say a word or write a rune?" Kaplyn asked when he had finished.

"It depends on the complexity of the spell," Vastra replied. "Some spells are relatively simple and I only need an elemental to cast these."

Kaplyn was surprised that Vastra was being more talkative. Perhaps he was coming to accept them. He hoped that he was changing for the better. Indeed, because of their long journey he was starting to feel different himself; certainly he felt healthier. Even though it was hard work, living in the wild was actually doing him some good. Lars had lost weight and now that his muscles had hardened, Kaplyn doubted anyone in Allund could stand against him in a wrestling match.

From somewhere high in the mountain a lone wolf howled, reminding Kaplyn of the dangers, and his thoughts strayed to his home and family. He was looking forward to returning. He smiled as he thought about taking Lars with him back to the palace at Dundalk to meet his family and friends. Perhaps he might be able to persuade Lomar, and even Vastra, to come back with him as well. That would be worth seeing, he thought, especially the look on Vastra's face when he introduced him to his father.

In the middle of the night Kaplyn awoke to find Vastra watching the sky, clearly hoping for a break in the thick clouds. Kaplyn turned over, pulling his blankets tightly about his neck and quickly fell asleep. The prospect of the underground journey troubled his dreams and he heard Baldor's voice booming aloud in his rage as he sought to escape his imprisonment. After a while he realised it was not Baldor's voice he could hear, but his own. A tomb surrounded him deep within the humid depths of the earth and, with mounting fear he realised that he was trapped for all eternity.

When morning came, Vastra had not slept. His eyes were red rimmed and for all his efforts he had not even seen the stars. He urged them to hasten as they broke camp.

Later that day they arrived at the edge of the snow line. It was a spectacular view. Small ripples of wind-blown snow cast long blue shadows while, in contrast, sunlight reflected whitely from the ridge tops. To Vastra's relief the clouds finally cleared, leaving an unblemished sky as far as the horizon and promising at least that he might finally see the stars that night.

They decided to leave the mules farther back down the slope and so they piled their supplies on the ground before retracing their steps, leading the mules. They found a relatively sheltered spot in a crevice where they left the animals and their food. Then they started back up the slope to their supplies.

Once burdened, they continued and, although the snow was deep, the going was still relatively easy, but soon the pass became narrower and steeper. A short way farther and the stream they were following became frozen and only a trickle of water remained. They hacked a step in the ice to fill their canteens before it became completely frozen.

By mid-morning their path diverged from the stream and Vastra led them through a narrow defile. They struggled through the opening, slipping on the ice-coated rocks and then up a steep slope. Finally, they gained the top of a small ridge and from there they looked out over a wide, open valley set between two almost vertical ridges sweeping down from the peak of BanKildor. Stretching across the valley was a wall of ice which dominated the valley.

"That's a glacier," Lars stated, panting heavily. His breath plumed before him, hanging in small clouds until banished by the soft breeze. The group stared in wonder at the broad sheet of ice; no one had expected it to be so immense.

Vastra took off his pack and rummaged through the contents to retrieve the thin sliver of metal and twine that Kaplyn had seen before. He looked perplexed as the metal stubbornly continued to oscillate, refusing to come to rest. Frustrated, he put the device away and decided that the party should split up into two groups to search the ice wall, looking for a cave or an opening, no matter how small.

Kaplyn went with Vastra while Lars and Lomar went in the opposite direction. After several hours of searching, they had combed the entire surface without success. Clearly annoyed, Vastra sat down on a rock.

"It's here somewhere, I know it is," he stated angrily, more to himself than to the others.

"Are you sure this is the right place?" Kaplyn asked.

Vastra nodded.

With a mixture of feelings, the others sat down glaring at the stubborn ice wall. They had to find the way forward soon or they would freeze to death waiting.

Chapter 24

BanKildor

An eagle flying high in the clear sky caught Kaplyn's attention and he watched it glide; its huge wings splayed out into tiny fingers. The bird descended until, with shock, he realised that it was going to collide with the ice wall. He held his breath, willing it to rise.

At the last instant it flapped its wings and, to Kaplyn's astonishment, disappeared. He had to blink several times to convince himself that he wasn't mistaken. A gnarled tree grew close to the spot where the eagle had disappeared. Rising he proceeded to investigate, leaving the others behind.

Baffled, he stood facing the ice wall with no clear view as to where the eagle had gone. Abruptly a loud flurry of wings made him jump as the eagle materialised right in front of him. With a screech of outrage, the great bird soared skyward, forcing Kaplyn to duck beneath its flapping wings. There had been no warning and the bird's abrupt appearance unnerved him.

The noise had attracted the others' attention and Vastra was watching him with renewed hope. Kaplyn ran a hand along the ice and all at once, his hand came away from the surface. He had discovered a step that due to the white glare from the ice was difficult to see. Exploring further, he found an opening sufficiently wide enough to allow a man to squeeze through.

Vastra came over and was overjoyed. He beamed happily and even slapped Kaplyn on the back.

"Well done," he said several times.

His excitement was contagious and the others grinned back, relieved at last to find a way forward.

Was this the correct path though? Kaplyn was not certain, so he decided to explore a short way ahead.

Stepping through the opening, a narrow tunnel continued for a short way before abruptly changing direction, doubling back on itself but penetrating deeper into the ice. It continued in a similar vein for some while and the further he went, the quieter and warmer it became. Satisfied that the tunnel went some way ahead he retraced his steps to report his findings. Vastra was ecstatic with the news and again slapped Kaplyn on the back.

"This has to be the correct path," he said beaming broadly.

"We need to find shelter so we can tell when it's safe to continue," Kaplyn suggested.

They spent the remainder of that day looking for somewhere out of the wind and large enough to accommodate them all. Gradually they made their way back down the slope.

In the end they climbed up the steep sides of the narrow pass to where a few large boulders offered some shelter from the frigid wind. Huddled together for warmth they prepared their packs for the journey, taking only the essentials and leaving all the spare supplies. Amongst their equipment, they had oil for torches and they diligently set about making these, soaking strips of cloth and wrapping these about stout branches.

"I hope the sky remains clear tonight," Vastra said, looking at the blue heavens.

"How long might we have to wait?" Lars asked.

"I'm not sure," Vastra admitted. "I checked the stars before we entered the forest, but I cannot be certain if my last judgement was accurate or not."

Anxious that they might have a long stay ahead of them, they tried to improve their shelter, pushing their packs into the gaps between the boulders and stretching their oiled blankets above them forming a roof. Night came swiftly now that they were on the mountainside. Outside the shelter, Vastra watched the sky and slowly, one by one, the stars became visible.

"There it is! Tallin's Crown," Vastra said pointing to the constellation. "That star to the right is moving towards the others and in about sixty years time the crown will be whole once again." Vastra continued to look at the other constellations, silently considered their position within the sky.

"We are early," he declared at last with a smile, turning to face the others, his eyes shining. "We have three days wait and then we can proceed. That will leave two days to follow the Eldric trail and find the cavern described on the pendant."

They re-entered the shelter. The wind whistled through gaps their packs didn't quite block and Lars suggested piling snow about the outside to fill these. Almost immediately, after they had done this, the temperature in the shelter improved, making their wait seem more bearable.

As the days slipped by, they spent their time telling stories to keep themselves amused. It was too cold to go far from the shelter and a thick

179

crust of ice on the rocks made travelling dangerous anyway. Eventually the time passed uneventfully and on their last night, each of the company was lost in his own thoughts. They retired early with the rising of the moon in a cloudless sky, eager to be on their way the following day. The cold was intense and although they wrapped themselves in all their spare blankets, it was difficult to sleep. In discomfort, they lay huddled together to await the dawn.

In the middle of the night Vastra went to each of the company in turn, cautioning them to silence. Although they could only see his outline, they could tell he was anxious.

For a while they sat listening to the howl of the wind, wondering what had alarmed him and then they became aware of voices, coming from the narrow path below. The voices were guttural and harsh and Kaplyn realised they might be krell. Drawing his sword a fraction, to his chagrin, the metal glowed brightly. He re-sheathed it, hiding the telltale light.

Lomar crawled to the edge of the shelter, trying to peer between the boulders, but they had done too good a job in filling these. Carefully Lars picked up his axe and Lomar drew his own blade. Vastra remained hunched like a great owl, but Kaplyn could tell that he was ready to trace a rune and summon power if the need arose.

After a while, the voices faded until they could only hear the wind whistling through the pass.

"A krell patrol?" Vastra asked in a whisper.

It had been fortunate in that they had piled snow about their shelter. Kaplyn pulled aside one of the packs and crawled outside. Large white snowflakes filled the sky, standing out in stark contrast to the black backdrop of night. He couldn't see a thing and snow, freezing on his cheeks, forced him to retreat back inside. There was no way that he could tell if the krell were still about and it would be too dangerous to follow them. There was nothing else to do other than try to sleep. Lying down, with their weapons by their sides, they listened to the howl of the wind, trying hard to decide whether they could hear voices within the eerie banshee wail.

By morning, they had slept little and were eager to be moving; fearful that the krell patrol might still be in the area. They checked their provisions, leaving the remaining supplies beneath the lee of a boulder for their return. Kaplyn left the shelter first to search for tracks to see what he might learn. However, during the night it had snowed so that now no footprints remained.

Together they hurried towards the glacier and the tunnel. Kaplyn led them through the narrow gap. Repeatedly, the passage changed direction but at least he could see; a faint blue light filtered through the thick ice.

All at once Kaplyn emerged into a much wider corridor of ice at the end of which he could see a cave entrance leading into the mountainside. He searched the ground for signs that krell might have come this way, but it looked undisturbed. The others joined him, relieved to be free of the twisting maze.

"If the glacier is moving, as Lars suggested, then this cave will eventually be covered," Lomar said, indicating the tunnel ahead.

"Perhaps the maze of passages in the ice was deliberately made so that over the years only a narrow entrance is exposed to the outside world," Vastra suggested.

Lars was paying particular attention to the tunnel wall as if he had seen something inside it. Kaplyn joined him to see what he had found. Lars rubbed the surface, trying to get a better view.

"There's something behind the ice," he commented; his face pressed against the cold translucent surface.

"It's probably a rock or something," Vastra said.

Lars was staring open mouthed with disbelief. "*By Slathor*! It's a dragon!" he stated breathlessly.

Kaplyn glanced at Lars to see if he was joking, but he looked serious and so Kaplyn peered inside. There was something there, a large indistinct shape. As he peered from different angles he *could* make out more. He smiled when he saw what might be a head and wings. It could indeed be a dragon! The ice blurred his view, but of one thing he was certain; this was no rock!

"He's right, it has to be!" Kaplyn exclaimed. It looked as if it was in mid-flight and then he decided it looked more as though it had fallen and was trying to right itself. Perhaps it had crashed into the freezing water or ice and died trying to escape.

Even Vastra was amazed. He told them that he had read about dragons, but had never believed that he would see one. He wanted to explore further, but they did not have the time. Reluctantly they decided to continue.

The ground in the cave sloped gently downwards, aiming directly at the heart of BanKildor. As they went, the light swiftly faded. Behind them they could see the cave entrance and the ice, but ahead the darkness was complete.

Lomar took out his kara-stone and ran a hand lightly over its surface. It glowed dimly as he spoke but the light swiftly failed. He tried again with little success.

"What is it, Lomar? Why won't the stone work?" Vastra asked.

"I don't know," he answered.

Vastra muttered archaic words but nothing happened, although the others did not know what to expect.

"We'll have to use the torches," Vastra concluded. "For some reason the mountain is blocking our use of magic. I do not know how, although I had heard that it was possible."

They lit several torches. Even in the light, they could not tell from the rock walls why magic was blocked. It was a conundrum and without the kara-stone and Vastra's magic, they were severely disadvantaged.

Chapter 25

Journey in the Dark

Black smoke formed wraith-like clouds that lingered within the tunnel before being banished upon the subterranean winds. The acrid smoke accumulated around them, fouling the air.

Removing his pack, Vastra rummaged through its contents.

"I've planned for this eventuality. Since we won't know the time of day in the tunnel I've made some candles that will burn at a constant rate," he said, taking out a long white candle, marked at intervals with regular stripes. "Each stripe is half a day and I have numbered them so we will know how long we've been down here."

Using Lomar's torch he lit the candle and then looked at Kaplyn. "We need to reach our destination tomorrow, otherwise we will fail and our chance to discover what became of the Eldric will be lost."

"We could always return later?" Lars suggested nervously not liking the sounds of the deadline that Vastra had imposed.

Vastra shook his head. "As I have already said, there is only one day when it will be safe to enter the great cavern described on the pendant. If we miss that opportunity then we will have to wait another five hundred years."

Lars shrugged; he looked as though he would have been happy to wait forever rather than continue.

"Are you certain that tomorrow is the actual day when we can enter the cavern?" Lomar questioned.

Vastra glared at the albino. "I'm sure!" he declared, shouldering his pack and adjusting the straps.

"And what happens if you're wrong?" Lars asked anxiously.

Vastra frowned but remained silent, leaving their imagination to conclude on what might transpire.

"We'd better proceed," Kaplyn urged, looking ahead. He could see little other than a wall of darkness. It was eerie and every instinct told him to return to the surface. However, the possibility of finding the Eldric was too great a lure.

As they walked Lars kept casting longing looks behind him at the spot of light marking the exit until he finally announced in an uneasy tone that he could no longer see it. His voice sounded nervous and the declaration seemed final as if there was now no turning back.

Before them, the gloom peeled slowly back as though reluctant to disclose its secrets. Their torches revealed rough, craggy walls dotted with sharp rocky outcrops; shadows jumped about the tunnel eerily as their torches flickered uncertainly in the subterranean winds.

After walking for several hours, the tunnel suddenly dipped sharply down and they continued along the steep descent for a while longer before Kaplyn called for a halt. They sat down on the cold stone floor and started to eat. Momentarily, at least, their flagging spirits were revived.

"Are we likely to find anything living down here?" Lars whispered.

Vastra shook his head. "If krell discovered these passages then they might also discover what became of the Eldric, and that in itself would be a disaster."

"What about demons though?" Lars persisted.

"Demons inhabit another world, as I've already explained," Vastra snapped. "Besides, the mountain seems to block the use of magic. It would almost certainly prohibit a tunnel opening between the worlds."

Lars remained unconvinced and he chewed slowly on a piece of dried meat as he considered Vastra's words.

When they continued, they found that walking into the blackness was almost hypnotic. The torchlight illuminated a short way in front, but beyond that, the tunnel remained inky black. In a way it seemed as though they were standing still, while the tunnel slid slowly by.

After a short while they reached a slightly broader part of the tunnel where they decided to rest again. Apart from Lomar, who preferred to stand, they gratefully sat down.

Lomar was watching the darkness ahead. Something at the perimeter of the light caught his attention and he left the group to investigate. Holding his torch before him he stooped down. Softly he called back to the others to come and see.

Wearily they arose and went to join him. They found a deep recess cut into the rock wall and upon the floor lay a skeleton. A metal breastplate partially hid the bony chest while a tall conical helm rested at a jaunty angle on the grinning skull's brow. On top of the corpse someone had reverently laid a sword and bony fingers clasped the pommel. Any other garments the warrior had worn had long since crumbled to dust and had been banished by the subterranean winds.

"He is Eldric," Vastra declared.

The corpse's sword did not have any runes. Indeed Kaplyn was disappointed to see the quality was poor and he assumed the soldier must have been of a lowly rank.

"This proves that the Eldric came this way then?" Kaplyn asked.

Vastra nodded. His attention remained fixed on the body and Kaplyn feared that he was going to search the corpse. Kaplyn caught Vastra's arm and gave him a warning look. He remembered Lars' tale about his people's fear of being underground. There was no point in provoking his superstitions further.

"Let him lie," he whispered.

Vastra cast him a dangerous look. However, he conceded, backing away from the grave with a mock bow.

Lars missed the exchange; the darkness beyond the edge of the light held him captivated. The flickering flame of the torches caused the shadows to bob about and he watched as if he expected something to step from them.

Suddenly a low rumbling echoed from deep within the mountain and the ground vibrated ominously. They strained their ears, holding their breath as the disturbance continued to echo beneath their feet. It sounded distant and the volume was low, but coming so soon after they discovered the soldier's remains it seemed like an ominous portent. Gradually the rumbling faded, leaving the group in silence.

"An earth tremor?" Lomar suggested.

"More like Baldor," Lars muttered, his hand involuntarily making a warding gesture against evil.

Vastra was the only one who seemed unafraid. His dark form seemed well suited to the tunnels.

"It's just a few rocks falling deep within the earth," he declared. "It's gone now. We need to continue for we do not have much time remaining."

"A *few* rocks?" Lars questioned.

"Sound travels a long way in rock," Vastra continued in a condescending manner, much like a teacher berating a child. "Shall we go?" Vastra repeated impatiently, gesturing to Kaplyn to lead the way, almost as if daring him.

As a precaution Kaplyn drew his sword but it remained dull. "I'll lead. Vastra; you bring up the rear."

The sorcerer gave a mocking bow and a smile touched his lips. Kaplyn started to wonder at Vastra's apparent newfound confidence, or was it merely that he was contemptuous of their fear.

Once more they continued and the blackness seemed to peel back eagerly, snapping shut behind them. They had walked for only a short way when ahead, in the half-light, Kaplyn saw a change in the reflected torchlight. He slowed. They were entering a large cave and he peered cautiously into it before daring to enter.

It was immense and he could see much farther than his torch should allow. He looked closely at the rock wall to his left and saw that it was glowing with an orange light. Reassuringly the cave appeared to be empty.

"I have heard that the dwarves use a special rock to light their caverns," Lomar whispered by Kaplyn's side, glancing over his shoulder into the cave.

He entered, running a finger along the wall. "Look," he said holding up a glowing finger. "There are algae or something covering the surface. Perhaps it is feeding on the minerals carried in the water and emits light in the process."

Lars entered the cave, holding his heavy axe protectively in front of him like an icon against evil. The fierceness of his grip made his knuckles white.

Kaplyn understood his fear and felt as though they were intruding. It was as if invisible eyes were watching them.

Vastra overtook Kaplyn in his eagerness to see ahead.

"Is this cavern described on the pendant?" Kaplyn asked.

"Yes, but the main cavern is further on."

"Look there, a fissure!" Lars declared. His voice echoed from rock to rock as if unseen hands had grabbed it and were bouncing it from wall to wall. As the echoes continued, he looked fearfully at the others.

As if in response to Lars' outburst, Kaplyn's blade flickered brightly but then became dull once more.

They advanced to the chasm's edge and peered down into its depths. The darkness eagerly devoured the light from their torches, as though guarding its secrets. To either side of their position the chasm stretched into the distance, disappearing within the funeral gloom.

Kaplyn shook his head, "We have to cross. I can sense that is the direction we need to go."

"Let's follow the chasm on this side and see if the gap narrows," Vastra suggested.

To their dismay the fissure remained too wide to cross. "Over there is something," Kaplyn announced, leading the way.

"I don't see anything," Vastra grumbled.

"Nor I," said Lomar quietly, glancing after Kaplyn.

Kaplyn led them to the edge of the fissure where he paused. The others joined him.

"We can cross this bridge," Kaplyn said. However, he was unsure how to proceed; the first few feet of the span either had broken or had never existed.

"Is this some sort of joke?" Vastra snapped.

Kaplyn looked bewildered as he turned to face the others. "What do you mean?"

Vastra snorted and turned to continue on his way, "Come, we need to find a way to cross."

"Wait! There is one here!" Kaplyn insisted.

"There isn't a crossing here," Vastra said, glaring at him.

Kaplyn looked at the others, but they shook their heads. He frowned, confused by their reaction, but then he realised how to prove to them (and himself) that the bridge existed. Stooping down he picked up a pebble and rising he tossed it into the air.

The others watched as the stone sailed in an arc before clattering off an unseen obstacle. The noise reverberated about the cavern, but there was no further sound of the stone reaching the bottom.

"There! Now do you believe me?" Kaplyn asked.

Vastra stood dumbfounded and then his eyes widened. "The pendant," he said.

Kaplyn regarded him coldly.

Vastra looked as though he should have remained silent. "Remember, it nulls magic. The Eldric have been this way and must have cast a spell, making the way across invisible. The person with the pendant sees the bridge, because to them, the magic is void.

"That is why you should give me the pendant," Vastra continued, trying to take advantage. "You might not recognise a trap even if you saw it, whereas I would." He looked sincere, which left Kaplyn in a quandary. He accepted Vastra's logic, but did not trust him, remembering all too clearly his earlier betrayal.

"You fool, you would get us all killed and you would not even know it," Vastra snapped.

"And you would kill us all, knowingly," Lomar interrupted, his eyes flaring. "Your actions in the swamp prove that you do not value our lives. You are nothing more than a petty dealer in the black arts and, by the very nature of your evil magic, you consider us unimportant. I, for one, prefer Kaplyn being in charge of the pendant."

"That goes for me too," Lars said grinning, unable to hide his pleasure at seeing Vastra put in his place.

Kaplyn tried to suppress a smile. A difficult decision had been made for him.

Vastra looked like thunder. Had the others known how close he was to losing control they would have been less quick to goad him. "Let's continue. Time is short and already I fear we have delayed over-long," he declared, shouldering his pack and gesturing sarcastically for Kaplyn to lead the way.

Kaplyn shook his head, "The crossing doesn't span the full width. There's about a six foot gap in front of us and then the bridge starts. Beneath the edge of the bridge there is a solid column supporting it. It looks safe enough."

"We could try throwing something onto it so we can see where it starts," Lars suggested.

"Good idea, but I can already see several stones which you obviously cannot," Kaplyn replied.

Vastra shook his head; with a problem to solve his anger seemed to fade. "It would make sense for the spell to extend by a short distance; otherwise a layer of dust would eventually reveal the crossing."

"It seems a great deal of effort just to hide it," Lomar questioned. "But why is it incomplete do you think?"

"Perhaps to prevent anyone from finding it by accident," Kaplyn suggested.

"That makes sense," Vastra agreed. "The Eldric clearly didn't want anyone following this route unless they possessed the pendant. Their magic must have been very powerful to make the bridge invisible, for these caverns block magic as we have already discovered."

Kaplyn took off his pack and tied a rope to it. Swinging the heavy weight back and forth he threw it across the gap. It landed with a clatter. They could still see the sack, although the sight of it suspended in mid-air was bizarre.

"The spell must take time to work on a new object, or it only affects small things," Vastra said, thinking aloud.

With the pack on the bridge, the next step was for someone to cross. The natural choice was Kaplyn. They attached a rope around his waist and the others took the loose end, bracing themselves. Backing a few feet, Kaplyn ran, leaping into the air at the chasm's edge. To the others the attempt looked suicidal, but to their relief he landed close to his pack where he remained upright, eerily hovering in the air. Lars grimaced, turning away, clearly unable to watch.

Kaplyn took up his pack and placed this closer to the edge as a marker.

"You must jump over this to be safe. Lars, it would be best if you were to go first."

Lars grimaced. It was no great distance but the sight of the blackness below was too much. His face went pale and he looked as though he was having problems swallowing.

Lomar tied the rope about his waist. Then he and Vastra braced themselves. Lars took a couple of steps back where he paused, judging the distance. Then he ran and jumped, easily clearing the marker, but he landed badly and toppled to one side. Kaplyn grabbed his shirt and pulled him down onto the bridge.

"Close your eyes."

Lars did not need telling twice. Beneath Kaplyn's hand he was rigid with fear.

"Now stand slowly and let me guide you across," Kaplyn said.

By the time they had crossed, Lars was shaking. Away from the edge, he sat down as if his legs would no longer support him and he simply sat there, sucking in lungfuls of air, trying to calm himself.

Once Kaplyn was sure that Lars was all right, he returned for the others. First, they threw their equipment across. Kaplyn ferried these to Lars and then gave him one end of the safety rope to help the others to cross. Both Lomar and Vastra crossed without incident, although the experience clearly shook them.

As soon as Vastra's nerves settled he re-lit the candle that he had been forced to extinguish before the crossing. He judged that they had been walking now for half a day.

Nobody wanted to stop for a rest; their fear of the dark pit was too great. Setting off, Lars glanced back, hoping there would be an easier exit upon their return.

Chapter 26

Onward and Downward

It took only a short while to reach the opposite cavern wall where they discovered another tunnel leading down. They continued, letting the slope carry them forwards.

Once more they found themselves mesmerised by the constant drudgery of walking within the confined space and there seemed to be no end to the tunnel. Walking became mechanical; tiredness dogged their every step until they longed for a change in their surroundings. The farther they went the greater became their fear. However, just when they felt that they could go no further, the tunnel opened into a small cavern with several tunnels branching from it.

"Which is it?" Lomar groaned. He looked weary and constantly adjusted the weight of his pack on his back, trying to find a more comfortable position.

Kaplyn looked uncertainly at each tunnel in turn, but none of the five tunnels that the others could see caught his attention. Above them was a sixth passageway, considerably smaller than the others and, like the bridge, the chances of stumbling upon this one was remote. It was at least eight feet above the ground. However, something about this passageway held his attention; it looked darker than the others did.

"That one up there," he said finally. "I feel strongly that's the one, but..." he did not complete the sentence.

"It must be the right one," Vastra interrupted. "There is no tunnel there — I mean we can't see one," he corrected.

Lars and Lomar confirmed that they too could not see it, and once again it seemed as if the true path had been deliberately hidden from anyone without the pendant.

Lars saw Kaplyn's look of concern. "Is something wrong?" he asked.

"Something's not quite right," Kaplyn told them truthfully. "But I'm not sure what."

"Give me the pendant," Vastra insisted once more. "I will recognise if there is a trap."

Vastra's persistence annoyed Kaplyn, but a nagging doubt remained.

"If there was a spell I would see it, wouldn't I?" he asked.

Vastra's reluctance to speak was answer enough.

"No — there isn't a trap," Kaplyn stated flatly. He sensed that the danger was down the tunnel rather than at the entrance. In the quiet that followed, the torches hissed and crackled.

"There's only one thing for it," he decided, removing his pack. "I'll explore a short way." He discarded his pack and climbed to the tunnel's entrance, using protruding rocks for handholds. At the entrance he paused, searching its depths. He held a torch aloft and looked inside. The tunnel walls were bare but he was certain that this was the correct passageway for he was experiencing a faint pull that urged him to enter.

With a firm resolve he thrust the flaming brand into the hole, causing shadows to leap back as if scorched. The tunnel was empty as far as he could see, but in the distance, the darkness waited as if daring him to enter. Cautiously he pulled himself in and it was so small he had to crawl. After only a short distance, he felt his muscles stiffen as though he were crawling through thick treacle. He could not easily go back for he could not turn; he was irrevocably committed to going on. Pushing harder he continued, fearing all the while that he had triggered a trap. He was about to give up and call for help when all at once he felt as though a great weight had been removed from his shoulders and he was through whatever had constrained him.

He paused, panting hard. His eyes were wide as he stared expectantly into the gloom, but nothing happened and he collected his wits. It had been a barrier and nothing more and, upon reflection, it had felt similar to the one he had encountered outside Tanel, the Eldric city.

He could no longer hear the others, even though they were only a short distance away. He suddenly felt afraid. The tunnel was very narrow and he had to continue to find a place to turn around. As he went, the foul reeking smoke from his torch billowed about him.

Soon the tunnel abruptly widened, allowing him to stand. He could see little ahead and it appeared that this tunnel went on for some distance. Being alone was eerie and he dreaded the return, knowing that as he crawled back he would not be able to see anything behind him. Shuddering, he quickly re-entered the tunnel knowing that if he delayed, his courage might fail.

As swiftly as he could he retraced his way until he could see the others once more. They appeared to be standing still, as if frozen in comic pantomime. He crawled the final few feet, experiencing once more the resistance and the sudden snap as he reached the larger chamber.

To his relief, as soon as he left the invisible barrier, he could hear the others speaking clearly. "There is nothing up here, Vastra," he said climbing down. "However, there is a barrier of some sort ahead. Like the one we experienced, Lars, entering Tanel."

"We must be close," Vastra decided. His candle showed that about one quarter of the day remained of their first day underground. "We need to remain here for a while."

The others were none too pleased with the prospect and with reluctance they removed their packs and sat down. Vastra informed them that they had to remain there for approximately half a day to be certain they were safe. They decided to use the time to rest while taking turns to stand guard.

They were too afraid to sleep and wearily they waited for the allotted time to pass, speaking in low tones and keeping a watchful eye on the candle that seemed to take an age to burn down to Vastra's mark. When it was finally time to go it suddenly seemed too soon. With a mixture of feelings they arose, tired and stiff. Shouldering their packs, they looked to Kaplyn to lead the way.

He climbed the short way to the tunnel and pushed his pack into the opening. To the others it looked strange to see the pack then Kaplyn disappear into solid rock. As Kaplyn crawled along the tunnel, something again restrained him, but this time he was ready and he made quick progress to the wider part of the tunnel. Soon the others joined him, relief that they were through evident upon their weary faces.

"I'll be glad when we are out of this place," Lars said, brushing himself down. A fine layer of grey dust covered them all.

"What was the significance of the barrier?" Lomar asked.

"Possibly this part of the tunnel exists within other worlds as well as our own," Vastra replied quietly. Impatient to be off he hoisted his pack onto his skinny frame as he spoke. "This is a place of great peril and now more than ever we must hurry. There is not much time left and we must be back through the barrier before this day is over."

A resonant booming echoed once more from deep within the mountain. The suddenness of the sound caused them to jump and they looked about fearfully, drawing their weapons. It was much louder than before, as if the barrier had somehow muffled it. An echo rolled like thunder beneath their feet.

"And what does the barrier keep in?" Lars questioned.

Lars' tale of Baldor, the giant imprisoned by the gods, came unbidden to Kaplyn's mind. Silence returned, but this was an uncomfortable quiet, which seemed to be waiting to be broken.

Lacking enthusiasm they collected their belongings and proceeded down the tunnel, plunging steeply into the mountain's heart. The dark within this passageway somehow seemed more sinister as it hungrily devoured the light from their torches, withdrawing only slowly as they approached, as if toying with them.

For some time they walked until Kaplyn halted them. Ahead he could see another opening and he wanted to check it out, knowing that he was in some way protected by the pendant. He glanced at his sword; it was shining with an intense blue hue. Somewhere ahead danger threatened.

Warily he advanced to stand before the entrance, peering within without allowing too much light through, but he could not see anything. Slowly he brought the torch forward and the view that met him was overpowering. He was standing on a ledge, running across their path and below his feet the ground simply disappeared into gloom, marking the edge of a vast cavern; the like of which he doubted any man had seen or dreamt of before. The floor was a long way below him.

Gigantic multi-coloured stalactites, as large as the tallest building, dominated his view. Many of these joined with equally large stalagmites, creating uneven warped columns as if this was truly a temple in the dreams of a forgotten god. Crystals trapped within these ancient rocks glittered in his torchlight hinting at a vast wealth in gems, hidden since the dawn of time.

Summoning courage, he leant forward trying to see the ground far below. Shadows raced across his view and he slowed his arm to see any sudden movements.

When he raised the flaming torch further aloft he gasped in awe. The others had become impatient and, one by one, they joined him on the ledge.

"What is it?" Lars hissed uncertainly. He held his axe in readiness before him.

Kaplyn did not reply. Instead, he moved the torch once more. As if by command the shadows retreated, scolded by the encroaching light. Before them, phantoms leapt about the cave like long lost creatures from the distant past. It seemed that a prehistoric battle was being re-enacted as shadows and light competed for dominance. Huge shambling shapes formed, while smaller shadows darted from column to column. Larger shadows fell on smaller ones, devouring them, only to flicker and disappear as the torchlight

193

trapped them into oblivion and, as the light marched triumphantly onwards, the darkness slowly reappeared in patches, growing into huge dark masses once more. Every so often they half-fancied that they recognised a shape, but when they looked back it seemed to dissolve in front of their eyes.

Vastra snorted derisively, "We must press on; there is no time for games."

As though in response to the sorcerer's outburst a rumbling again resounded through the giant cave and the ground beneath their feet shook. In the distance, a white flash lit the cave, causing the shadows to retreat. The light lingered before dimming, releasing the shadows that quickly became master of their domain once more.

They stood before the immense hall in silence, too afraid to speak. Eventually in a low tone, Kaplyn broke the spell binding them. "What in Allund was that, Vastra?" he asked.

Vastra shook his head, continuing to stare.

"There's only one way we will find out," Lomar announced, gesturing that they should proceed and they followed the narrow ledge, which led to a steep stair.

As they descended the light erupted twice more, each time followed by a sonorous boom. It was difficult to see anything and the sudden light made their vision poor. Each time they waited until their eyes became accustomed to the gloom, severely hindering their progress.

It took them quite some time to reach the cavern floor where Kaplyn paused, uncertain which way to continue. At that moment another tremor started, deep within the bowels of the earth and again the men froze in fear.

Chapter 27

Nemesis in the Dark

The tremor built in intensity and Kaplyn glanced at the others. He caught Lars' gaze and saw fear flash across his face. Before Kaplyn could say anything to put the other man at ease, a subterranean breeze gusted, causing their torches to flicker. An eerie moan followed on its heels, causing a shiver to run down his spine.

"That tremor felt stronger," Lars declared, gripping the brand so tightly that his knuckles showed white.

Kaplyn shook his head. "It just felt stronger now we are on the cavern floor," though he couldn't help but glance over his shoulder at the steep stairs.

As before, a light erupted from the cave's heart, causing him to squint against the sudden glare.

By his side, Lomar raised an arm, shielding his eyes.

"Are you all right?" Kaplyn asked softly.

Lomar nodded, lowering his arm as darkness returned.

Vastra strode up, his mere presence demanding as always. "Which way is it?"

A shiver ran down Kaplyn's spine and a memory of a half-forgotten dream surfaced, but then was gone.

Kaplyn recovered. "We must be close," he answered.

"You fool. You have no idea what lies ahead. Give me the pendant before you kill us all," Vastra snapped, thrusting out a hand.

At the venom in Vastra's voice Kaplyn's heart raced but, remaining calm, he regarded the outstretched hand with contempt.

"We've said Kaplyn will keep the pendant, Vastra, so don't push us on this matter," Lars interrupted through gritted teeth.

Vastra muttered and walked to the rear of the group.

"Thanks," Kaplyn smiled at the other man, truly appreciative of his support. Lars nodded by way of return.

Kaplyn turned his attention to finding the path. The light from their torches was feeble and ahead he could barely make out the outline of a few scattered boulders and a tall column of rock. The air smelt damp and oppressive, as though being deep within the mountain's heart the very weight of the rock above was forcing the darkness upon them.

"We need to go that way," Kaplyn decided.

Lomar squinted, looking in the direction Kaplyn was pointing. "How do you know?"

"The pendant's guiding me," Kaplyn replied.

"You could be mistaken," Vastra responded sourly. Kaplyn held back a retort, as the other man continued. "The pendant's no trifle. Only a sorcerer would know its true intent."

"And that would be you of course?" Lars said, a dangerous glint in his eye.

Vastra snorted, raising his hands in mock submission, stepping back from the big man, a lopsided smile on his thin face. "So be it, but when things go wrong, you remember my council." At that moment, the ground rocked again, closely followed by an ominous rumbling.

The men glanced at each other and Vastra's mouth opened but closed again when Kaplyn glared at him. The tremor seemed threatening so soon after Vastra's warning.

Kaplyn led the way. After only a short while he stumbled on a rock and had to take a couple of extra steps to regain his balance. Raising his torch, he saw a jagged channel, intercepting their path from his right. Almost in front of him it changed course, pointing roughly the way they were going.

Kaplyn followed this, picking his way amongst the clutter of rock and pebbles. Vastra kicked a pebble and a loud clatter reverberated around the cave.

"Don't do that," Lars cautioned.

Vastra flashed him an icy look.

Kaplyn sighed. Looking across the channel, his eyes sought anything that might help him decide where to go, but the light failed to reach the other side. The channel was not deep, but he could have injured himself if he had stumbled into it in the dark.

A short while later something else appeared ahead, slowly materialising from the gloom. Kaplyn slowed, allowing his eyes time to decipher its shape.

Lomar was the first to realise what it was. "A *tree? Here*, but that's impossible?"

Kaplyn closed the distance, reaching out his hand.

"Don't touch it," Lars cautioned, grabbing Kaplyn's shoulder.

"Don't worry," Kaplyn said, shrugging his arm away. "It's a fossil, that's all."

His fingers caressed the bark. It felt smooth as glass and it shone like ebony.

"A tree couldn't grow so deep underground — could it?" Lars asked.

"Perhaps, at one time, there was an opening in the mountain above." Kaplyn looked up but could see nothing. "Also, this channel we've been following could have been a river."

"My people have a legend concerning the origins of life," Lars said. "In the beginning of time the world was bare, except for a single tree. Its roots grew deep, feeding on the earth's life force so the tree became endowed with power and its fruit blessed with life."

Stepping forward he touched the old bark, his fingers trembling. "From the first fruit came the gods. They looked upon the world and to them it must have been like a blank page, waiting to be written upon. They marvelled at the tree, wishing to make life of their own. As the fruit grew, they moulded plants and animals, making all the living creatures we see today. If this is that tree then we are blessed this day," He trailed off into silence.

"Look at the ends of the branches," Lomar said.

Kaplyn looked where he was pointing. Several gnarled shapes, hung from slender twigs. At one time, they could have been fruit, but now they were shrivelled and petrified like the rest of the tree. Lomar reached up, trying to pull one away, but it defied him, clinging stubbornly to the branch.

All at once he leapt back as though scalded. A cry tore from his lips as a light erupted from deep within the trunk, swiftly spreading through the tree.

They shielded their eyes, falling back. Then the light dimmed as a darkness spread from the trunk's centre, devouring the light until they were plunged into night.

They looked at each other dumbfounded; none dared to venture an explanation. Deep within the ground, Kaplyn felt rumbling that swiftly built to a terrifying crescendo. Then the rumbling faded, leaving a deathly silence.

All at once whispering started and its suddenness made Kaplyn jump. He span around, seeking its source, but it was all around them. It grew in volume, becoming more terrifying until all around him voices shrieked and wailed. He half fancied he felt warm breath on his face and neck and he cringed in terror.

"What is it?" Lars wailed by his side. He stumbled and almost fell as another tremor shook the ground. Kaplyn reached out to steady the other man.

"Hush," Vastra said, holding up a hand.

As though upon his command, the voices subsided to a gentle whisper.

"What's happening?" Lars snapped. "This place is not meant for mortals."

Kaplyn felt frozen to the spot with the memory of the voices continuing to haunt him.

"We should go," Lomar agreed, looking about for the quickest way out. "This place is guarded by the dead!"

"Nonsense," Vastra hissed. "We must wait. The time is nearly right and the dead, if it is the dead we hear, cannot harm us."

Kaplyn was just about to agree that they should leave when a glow drew his eyes back to the tree. Within the trunk light blossomed, slowly unfurling along its length. The intensity was less than before and he stood transfixed, spellbound by its beauty.

With night as its backdrop, the tree stood out alone, as if cast from silver and ablaze in glory. By comparison, everything else that he had ever seen paled to insignificance.

"Look!" Lars declared, drawing Kaplyn's gaze to where he pointed. Above Lomar's head a delicate bud appeared, glowing in its own light. Slowly it unfurled, revealing a myriad of tiny petals and the scent of spring filled the air.

Kaplyn stepped closer. Within the blossom a fruit was developing, swiftly swelling to maturity, holding captive in its heart the silver radiance from the tree. Glancing over his shoulder Kaplyn saw a similar bud growing further away. His curiosity aroused he went to investigate. It, too, radiated a silver glow.

Gradually, the light in the tree began to fade, leaving the fruit shining brightly upon slender branches, like tiny lanterns.

With trepidation, Kaplyn reached out to pluck the fruit, which fell easily into his outstretched palms. It was light and warmed his hand. About him, the light dimmed further and he looked to see the black patch appear at the tree's heart, slowly spreading outwards, tracing the white light's route until the tree was plunged into night. Within the blackness, Kaplyn's fruit continued to glow softly.

Eager to show his prize, Kaplyn returned to the others, only to find that Vastra also held a fruit, which he quickly put out of sight within his jerkin, blotting out its radiance. To Kaplyn's mind, Vastra's eyes smouldered but then abruptly the look was gone.

Kaplyn sensed a change occurring and instinctively knew it was too late to return the way they had come. He searched for another exit but all he could see, beyond the faint pool of light from their torches, was a wall of shadow.

Just then the whispering started again. Its suddenness made him jump and his heart lurched.

Crying, "Follow me," he leapt away from the tree. Glancing over his shoulder he confirmed that the others were indeed following. The faint pull from the pendant guided him and he hoped beyond hope that he was right to trust it. They were running in the opposite direction to the way they had come and he didn't know where the pendant was leading them.

His fear drove him on, adding impetus to his weary limbs, whilst all about him the whispering grew in volume until he could hear tormented souls gibbering and shrieking, as though the world was ending. Unlike before the voices did not fade and instead the clamour increased, swiftly becoming unbearable — so much so that Kaplyn feared invisible demons might set upon them. Cries of anguish sounded to his right and he flinched, yelping in terror as the echoes disorientated him.

To his relief, the cavern wall materialised from the dark and he could make out the silhouette of a tunnel. Instinctively he headed towards it, hoping they would make it in time.

Glancing back he saw Lars labouring at the rear of the group. He suddenly yelped, flinging his torch away.

"Karlam! *Aid me*," he yelled. His legs and arms pounded as he sprinted to catch up. Drawing his axe from its harness across his back, he desperately flayed the air as though fighting an invisible foe.

Kaplyn, not looking where he was going, stumbled on a rock and nearly fell. His ankle screamed in pain but it recovered as he hobbled on. Abruptly he was within the tunnel and he turned to await the others.

"Keep going," came Lars' scream. "Keep going!"

Kaplyn turned and fled. Almost immediately he thumped into something invisible and was held trapped like a fly in a web. He forced himself on, driving his arms and pumping his legs; ever so slowly, his limbs responded.

Then he was free and he staggered forward. Someone tumbled into him and together they fell, landing in a sprawl, driving the air from Kaplyn's

199

lungs and cracking his knees on the stone. Wincing, he hurried to his feet. Lomar had fallen over him and he helped the albino up just as Vastra appeared by their side, panting heavily, closely followed by Lars.

Kaplyn looked back the way they had come. Lars' torch lay spluttering on the ground, the flame refusing to die. All at once, it rose uncannily and danced about the cavern, as if held aloft by ghostly hands. Abruptly, it was flung at them and with a loud resounding crack, it struck the sidewall of the cavern, causing them to recoil, crying aloud in terror.

"We are safe!" Kaplyn shouted. "We are through the barrier."

"Something cut me," Lars complained. "Look!" He showed them the back of his leg. Through a tear in his trousers, blood welled up and trickled down his calf. Lomar knelt and, using a cloth from his pouch, dabbed the wound. It was deep but clean and Lomar tied the cloth in a makeshift bandage.

"We should continue," Kaplyn said. Although he had told them they were safe he didn't yet feel it. Behind him the tunnel continued, but to where he did not know.

He led them on with Lars hobbling to keep up. Finally, he could go no further. He sat upon the ground and the others flopped down beside him.

Lars was trying to retie his bandage which had partly unravelled. Lomar brushed his hand away and set to helping. The big man kept looking nervously at Vastra's face and the livid red scar across his cheek. Kaplyn remembered all too clearly the imp inflicting the wound several days ago. It looked infected and still painful.

"You needn't worry," Vastra sneered. "Your wound is clean and will heal in time."

Lars looked away and Kaplyn sensed that he felt ashamed at having revealed his fear.

"Where are we?" Lomar asked, looking about. Kaplyn was relieved that he had spoken for it broke the tension. "I thought we would be leaving the same way we came."

Kaplyn shook his head. "We didn't have time to escape that way. The climb up the stair would have taken ages. I sensed though this was the right direction, and at least there was a barrier."

"I hope this tunnel leads to a way out," Lomar replied, sounding glum.

It was a point that was also worrying Kaplyn, but there was no going back.

"We were lucky!" Vastra exclaimed.

"If this is your idea of luck, I think it is time we parted company," Lars growled.

Vastra ignored him. "The candle must have burned more slowly than I'd expected. We probably entered the great cavern later than anticipated."

"You mean we've been walking for two days!" Lars exclaimed.

Kaplyn was still holding his fruit that had crystallised and was now firm to the touch.

"Can I see it?" Lomar asked.

"Of course you can. We all helped to get it," Kaplyn answered.

"It's warm," Lomar said, cupping it in his hand.

"Can I see it?" Lars asked, holding out his hand.

Lomar handed it to him and Lars held it up. Its radiance softly illuminated his face.

He gave it back to Kaplyn who placed it in his breast tunic pocket. If Vastra still had his crystal he could not tell, but it was unlikely he had lost it after all their efforts.

"What's the significance of the crystal, and how will it help to find the Eldric?" Lomar asked.

Kaplyn expected Vastra to remain silent and was surprised when he spoke.

"Lars' legend may contain an element of truth," he conceded. "The tree's roots had grown deep into the ground, tapping the earth's lifeblood. The crystal contains magic in its purest form. In a way it is like a kara-stone, but instead of being an empty vessel for magic, it is full."

"Can the magic be used?" Lars asked, massaging his leg.

Vastra shook his head. "I don't think so, not at least in any way that I know."

"Then how will it help to find the Eldric?" Kaplyn asked.

"I can open a gateway between the worlds," Vastra admitted. "But I cannot hold it open for long, and certainly not long enough to search that world for the Eldric. The crystal contains pure magic. If it is placed in a gateway it would not be able to collapse, for if it did it would destroy the magic in the crystal and that is not possible."

"Searching worlds could take years," Kaplyn said, feeling disappointed. After all their effort he had hoped finding the Eldric would be easier.

"And we may *never* find them," Lomar stated.

Vastra merely shrugged.

After a brief rest, Kaplyn decided it was time to press on. Wearily they rose and set off. Almost immediately, the tunnel started to slope gently upwards.

"At last," Kaplyn grinned. "If it's going up then it must be the way out."

For hours they continued. The passageway became a maze of tunnels and without Kaplyn's guidance, they would have very quickly become hopelessly lost. If they had tried to remember the way back it would have been impossible, for each twist and turn looked like the last and the farther they went, the more frequently the tunnels branched.

Their earlier hope that the tunnel was going up was soon dashed though as it dipped down. This trend continued so that the tunnel in one instance led hopefully up while at the next it plunged alarmingly down. Eventually they could go no further and sat or lay exhausted, very quickly falling asleep, too tired to eat or set a watch.

Some short while later Kaplyn partly awoke. His mind was fog-filled and he thought he saw Vastra tracing a rune in the air as though in practice. Abruptly, there was a faint light but it swiftly faded. Kaplyn was far too tired to question Vastra and promptly fell asleep, but a nagging fear haunted his dreams. He did not trust Vastra.

Chapter 28

Escape

Footfalls caused Kaplyn to awaken. He felt exhausted. Vastra knelt by his side, a torch held aloft.

"We should be going," he said.

Kaplyn had a headache and could barely think. Putting his hands beneath him he climbed to his feet.

"Get the others up," he said. He couldn't fathom why Vastra seemed so awake and refreshed when he felt so groggy. He listened for a moment to Lars' complaining as he, too, was awakened.

Kaplyn rummaged in his bag and found some hardtack biscuits and dried meat. His canteen was about a third full; the water was cool on his palate and helped him to swallow the rations. The others ate in silence while Vastra paced about them, eager to leave.

"Which way is it?" Lars asked. Kaplyn looked around, uncertain. He had never thought to mark the tunnel before sleeping and one end looked the same as the other. He felt a faint pull from the pendant.

"That way," he said.

Lars looked to where he was pointing. "Are you sure?"

Kaplyn nodded.

Once they had eaten, Kaplyn led the way. They came across a sequence of forks in the path and at each one Kaplyn felt the guidance from the pendant grow less and it was becoming increasingly harder to decide which way to go.

After walking for some time, Lomar announced he could hear something ahead. Kaplyn listened and became aware of a distant roaring.

"It sounds like water," Lars offered.

"Probably a subterranean river," Vastra agreed.

As they continued, the sound became louder. Ahead, Kaplyn could see a change in the tunnel and then it opened into a cavern. Before him was a small pool and a waterfall cascaded noisily into this. What worried him most though, was that apart from the way in, there was no other obvious exit.

They had come to a dead end.

"Which way do we go now?" Vastra demanded.

Kaplyn ignored him; instead, his gaze kept going back to the waterfall. He was afraid to admit it to the others, but he was no longer sure of the direction. For some time now he had felt nothing from the pendant, and to add to his frustration the waterfall's constant thunder was making his headache worse. Uncertainly, he approached the pool to study the area better and as he came alongside it, to his relief, he discovered the way.

"The path is here," he exclaimed, excitedly pointing at the side of the waterfall. The others crowded around to get a better view, relief evident upon their faces. On the other side of the pool, by the side of the waterfall and cut into the rock face, were stone steps, worn smooth by years of constant erosion. The steps led upwards, but disappeared into the waterfall.

"How do we get up there?" Lars asked eyeing the curtain of water.

"You could always go back," Vastra snapped. Kaplyn knew that to do so would mean death. "We will wait here for you," Vastra continued, glaring at the other man.

Lars shuddered and looked toward Kaplyn for guidance.

"Pass me a rope," Kaplyn said. "I'll climb the steps. If I can get up there then I can help to pull the rest of you up."

Lomar took a coil of rope from a bag but slung it over his shoulder rather than offering it to Kaplyn. "Let me try," he offered. "I frequently climbed in the forest so I should be able to master this."

Lomar undressed while Kaplyn helped the others to pile their packs against the rock wall. Without further ado he sat on the edge of the pool and lowered himself into the water.

"That's unbelievably cold," he gasped.

The pool was evidently deep and as soon as he entered he was forced to swim. Kaplyn watched as he hauled himself out on the other side, flopping wetly onto the first step.

Almost as soon as he stepped within the full force of the water he lost his grip. His feet were washed out from under him and he fell into the water, nearly cracking his head on the lower steps as he fell.

Surfacing seconds later, coughing and spluttering, he pulled himself out. He was game to try again but after several similar attempts he sat on the side of the pool shivering badly, his chest heaving. "It's impossible," he gasped, wiping his eyes with the palm of his hand.

"There's a rock sticking out higher up," Lars declared, pointing. Above the waterfall, Kaplyn could see the rock, mainly by the shadow it cast. There was a deep V in its front face where it had cracked sometime in the past.

"If we can get a rope over it, we would at least have something to help us climb," Lars continued.

Kaplyn fetched the rope while Lomar dried himself before putting on his clothes. He was shivering almost uncontrollably.

"Light a fire," Kaplyn suggested. "Use some of the torches; we should have enough."

"I'll do that," Vastra offered and borrowing Lars' axe he splintered one of the brands for kindling.

While Vastra was occupied, Lars took the rope and tied a rock to one end. Once finished he stood by the pool's edge and started to swing the rope in an arc. He let it swing a couple of times before heaving it into the air. Almost immediately the rock fell out of the makeshift knot, clattering noisily against the far cavern wall while the rope simply fell into the pool.

Shivering, Lomar asked for the rope. He took one end and started tying a large knot.

"This would be easier if my fingers weren't frozen," he complained. As he wound the knot he tested it for weight and once satisfied handed it back to Lars.

Kaplyn watched as the big man threw the rope several times and each time it came a little closer to hitting its mark, but annoyingly it missed and dropped into the pool below. Being wet helped and, all at once, Lars managed to cast it over the protrusion. Carefully he drew in the slack; fortune was with them and the knot held fast.

"I'll try this time," Kaplyn offered.

"Keep it taut or it might come away," Lars cautioned, handing the rope to Kaplyn.

Kaplyn nodded. He stripped and, taking the rope in one hand, entered the pool. The cold took his breath away and he gasped out loud. Quickly he swam to the other side where he clambered out, grazing his knee on the rock. He didn't want to stop and think about it so immediately started to climb. To his embarrassment, his foot slipped off the very first step and he banged his already sore knee. Swearing profusely, he swayed on the spot, but the tension of the rope held him.

Climbing, he soon had to move directly into the waterfall and the torrent hit him like a sledgehammer. Desperately he clung on to the rope with water buffeting him mercilessly and for grim moments he could not move and his fingers started to slip. Summoning all his strength he reached up and, slowly, hand over hand, started to climb.

Just when he felt that he could endure no more, the force of water slackened and he looked up to see that he was beneath a slight overhang. Above him was the lip of a tunnel and gratefully he pulled himself in.

He was alone, but did not feel afraid. The air felt fresh and with mounting hope he realised they must be nearly out of the terrible tunnels and his spirit immediately soared. He called excitedly down for one of the others to come up before sitting down with the rope looped across his shoulders, bracing his heels as best he could on the rough floor.

A mumbled reply, barely audible above the constant roar of the waterfall, was the signal that someone was ready. The rope became taut as whoever it was entered the pool and then briefly went slack. Kaplyn felt the rope tighten and he helped the climber, pulling up on the rope. Its coarseness stung his hands, but he ignored it.

Eventually Lars' drenched head and shoulders appeared in the tunnel entrance. With eyes screwed shut he spat out water, spluttering for breath. Kaplyn helped him into the tunnel where the other man sat shivering, hugging his chest for warmth. Next they hoisted the packs, and then it was Lomar and then Vastra's turn to climb.

By the time they were all together, they were exhausted. Hurriedly they dressed and then Kaplyn lay panting on the ground, using his pack as a pillow. His belly growled angrily.

"I'm famished," he declared.

"Me too," Lars answered.

"Let's see what food is left," Kaplyn suggested, sitting up and looking into his pack. The others emptied their sacks but the pile of food was pitiful.

"We should share what's left," Kaplyn suggested. "It will do for one final meal."

When they had dished it out, each looked despondently at their allotted potion.

"I think we are nearly out of the caves," Kaplyn announced, trying to lift their spirits. "Smell the air; it's fresher."

Lomar breathed deeply. "I think he's right." He immediately dug deep into his pack, retrieving his kara-stone. Passing a hand over it, he spoke words of power. It flared brightly and they laughed with pleasure as warmth engulfed them. The heat helped to partially dry them while they ate.

"Where does this tunnel come out?" Lomar asked.

206

"Thrace, I think," Kaplyn replied excitedly. "That's assuming we've travelled right through the mountain and come out the other side." It was difficult to believe but no one expressed any doubts.

"Will we be welcome in Thrace?" Lars asked.

"Of course we should be. There is trade between Allund and Thrace so we should be welcome," Kaplyn offered. However, he failed to mention his own concerns; his father had often threatened his marriage to one of Thrace's princesses.

"A clean, warm bed, that's all I want — and perhaps a flagon of beer!" Lars replied, grinning broadly.

Kaplyn smiled back. They were lucky to escape with their lives and for that he was more than thankful. He removed the crystal from his breast pocket and looked at it, still glowing with a pale, silver light.

"We've done it," he declared triumphantly, looking at the others in turn. They smiled back at him, their eyes shining with pleasure. "Let's press on and get out of here."

They soon left the sounds of the waterfall behind them and the comparative silence, apart from their footfalls, was a relief. After a while Lomar extinguished the kara-stone to conserve his energy while they still had some torches.

With the prospect of leaving, Kaplyn quickened their pace. However, to his frustration, Vastra hung back, forcing them to stop for him. Calling ahead to Lars and Lomar to wait, he turned to retrace his steps to look for him. All at once he saw the light from Vastra's torch bobbing up and down, coming towards them.

Kaplyn felt a premonition of fear as Vastra appeared around a corner; he seemed to ooze confidence with every step. All at once, the imp was beside him, floating eerily in the air. Their torches flared blue, warning him too late of the demon's presence. Kaplyn drew his sword, which glowed brightly, and behind him he heard Lars and Lomar drawing their weapons as they started to return towards him. He waved them away.

"Go! Run down the tunnel, the exit must be near by now," he said backing slowly away from Vastra and the imp.

Lars paused uncertainly, "I will not leave."

Vastra and the imp halted a few yards from Kaplyn. The imp's tongue flickered in and out, its eyes fixed on Kaplyn's blade.

"Go!" Kaplyn said. "They cannot harm me. I have the pendant and that negates his magic."

Vastra smiled maliciously and started to chant a spell. Kaplyn heard Lars and Lomar turn to leave.

"We will wait for you at the exit," Lars called back.

Kaplyn needed to distract Vastra; he lunged at the imp, which leapt back shrieking angrily. To Kaplyn's surprise, the sorcerer stopped chanting and started to laugh, "You fool," he said. "You have walked right into my trap."

Suddenly, from behind Kaplyn, a scream rent the air. He recognised Lomar's cry followed by terrified shouts from Lars.

Kaplyn turned, leaping down the tunnel, silently cursing himself for trusting Vastra. As he ran, his torch spluttered and the flame threatened to expire, making it difficult to see. Turning a corner, the first thing he saw were his friends' torches. The tunnel had opened into a small cavern. Framed within it were the two men. He risked glancing back over his shoulder, but Vastra was some way back, walking towards them as though he had no need to hurry.

As Kaplyn approached he realised that they were struggling to escape, as though unseen hands held them fast.

"Stay back," Lomar screamed.

Kaplyn paused, scant yards away, uncertain what to do. Agony contorted their faces and their eyes blazed. Kaplyn looked on helplessly. Lars was clearly terrified and Lomar cried out in anguish. Kaplyn turned — at last determined to kill Vastra, who had quietly come up behind him and was watching his friends' agony as if it did not concern him.

Seeing Kaplyn's expression the sorcerer guessed his intent. "Killing me would do no good," he said raising his hands in a gesture of submission. "The spell is his, not mine."

Kaplyn was desperate to do something, but felt completely powerless. He shrugged off his pack, throwing it down. "Let them go!" he screamed, raising his sword.

Vastra did not reply and Kaplyn advanced, realising with mounting frustration the futility of the situation. If it was the imp's spell and he attacked, then it would simply retreat down the tunnel. On the other hand, if he threatened Vastra, then he would simply make the imp vanish.

Without warning he lunged at the sorcerer choosing that as the lesser of the two evils. The imp intervened, appearing many times larger than it actually was. Sharp talons raked the air scant inches before Kaplyn's face, forcing him to duck while, behind the imp, Vastra backed cautiously away.

Kaplyn attacked the imp, but as he had suspected it simply retreated, hissing as it went.

A cry from behind reminded him of his friends' plight. He risked glancing around. To his horror, they had stopped moving and their exposed flesh was turning grey.

A desperate thought came to him; the pendent stopped magic from working. Perhaps he could use it to save them.

With an exasperated cry, he threw his torch at Vastra and leapt back towards Lars and Lomar. Still holding his sword he placed a hand on each of their shoulders, realising that his back was now vulnerable.

The instant his hands touched them Kaplyn felt a cold chill run through his body and the icy touch of fear stopped his heart.

In anguish, he screamed.

Agony lanced through the very fibre of his being. The pendant's chain seared his skin. He couldn't move. Gritting his teeth, his feet felt as though they were being crushed. He was being turned to stone and the pendant was not preventing it.

The crystal in his pocket flared and he felt a brief respite but then that was gone. Already his legs had been transformed. His mind retreated to its farthest corner and then Kaplyn knew no more.

Chapter 29

A Sour Victory

Vastra walked around the three men, looking into Kaplyn's eyes. He was struggling against the spell's effect, but Vastra knew that it was pointless. The spell was very powerful and not easily defeated. Looking at the other two men, their skin was already grey and even at a distance he knew their flesh would be cold to touch; gradually they were being transformed into stone. A spell blocked the exit and this was the secret he had kept ever since Kaplyn had returned with the pendant.

He had won, but it had been close. For a long time he had feared Kaplyn would somehow read the script on the pendant, revealing the final trap laid by the Eldric so long ago. The pendant would destroy the spell after it had run its course. Sadly it, too, would be destroyed in the process. The spell was to trap anyone who accidentally came this way and the pendant was the key to unlocking it.

Vastra walked around the tableau and then a scream from Kaplyn rent the air. The sound was inhuman and Vastra covered his ears. Abruptly the crystal in Kaplyn's breast pocket flared. Vastra cried out, shielding his eyes. By his side, the imp also screamed as the light engulfed it. With a terrifying wail, it disappeared into nothingness, its screech echoing back and forth along the tunnel.

Vastra cried out in terror. Blinded by the light he had no way of knowing what was happening. *Not again! Was he to be robbed of his victory when he could almost taste it?*

He fell to the floor, too afraid to breathe while power raged all around him like a torrent. Desperately he tried to press his body into the ground. At any moment he expected to feel Kaplyn's blade pierce his flesh. He cried out for mercy; knowing that he did not deserve it.

Long moments passed as he lay whimpering on the cold floor. Gradually realisation dawned that the clash of powers had subsided. When he dared to look, his sobs turned to whimpers of relief. The transformation was complete and only statues, carved as if from the very granite of the mountain, remained.

Rising, his victory suddenly seemed sour. The clash of powers had been fearful and he wondered what had happened. Perhaps Kaplyn's crystal had fought the Eldric spell, but what then had become of it?

Removing his dagger he tried to dislodge enough stone from what had become of Kaplyn's breast pocket to see the crystal. The knife slipped and to his shock, pierced the statue by a thumb's depth. Snatching back the blade, silver sap from the crystal and deep red blood oozed from the wound, dripping down the statue and onto the floor. Vastra stepped back. The dripping slowed as the mixture congealed, leaving a pink scar upon Kaplyn's chest.

All at once he felt as though ghostly eyes were watching him and with a cry of terror he turned and fled, seeking the sanctuary of an open sky and the company of the living. For some while the slap of his feet upon the rock persisted, and the flickering light cast by his torch marked his erratic flight. Then, with finality, the light disappeared and the noise faded, leaving only silence.

A cold wind gusted, helping to congeal the pool of blood as a single, final droplet fell like a teardrop to the floor. In the darkness, the statues continued to stare into the night, their faces reflecting their final moments of fear and pain. All except Kaplyn who looked strangely resolute, as though in the transformation's final moments, he had accepted his fate.

Epilogue

As the cold light from the crystal in Kaplyn's pocket filled the chamber, the power from the Eldric spell, protecting the tunnel's exit, collided with that of the crystal. For a moment the two forces opposed each other in a titanic clash.

The sudden surge of power sent shock waves racing through the very foundations of the universe, the repercussions of which could be felt within many worlds. At that instant, the very fabric of space and time was rent; dark tears appeared suddenly within the already weakened interval between the worlds.

In one such world, a lone spirit watched over a dying land that had once been his home. He still felt, and would always feel, the blast of dragon breath that had killed him, and knew that the memory would haunt him throughout all eternity.

Shastlan. Murderer of your people!

Forbidden the full release death should bring, he was forever doomed to walk the burnt lands of his homeland; a sad ghostly spectre whom none could ever hear, if any remained alive that is.

High overhead, in a clear blue sky, a dragon flew by. Its shadow sent a thrill of fear coursing through Shastlan's ghostly veins, prompting a thousand dreadful memories; he wailed aloud in anguish. Briefly, he wondered whether the dragons knew he was there and he looked up to see a speck disappearing over the horizon. The mere sight caused him absolute terror.

Suddenly a strange sensation swept through him. He looked about in fear, suspecting at first that the dragon had returned. Behind him, he saw a gaping void from which a cold wind blew, chilling even his spectral form. Slowly the tear opened and in a fit of self-pity, he felt the urge to step within it — to throw himself upon whatever providence awaited. He glanced back on the hell that was his home, the lush green fields and the clean blue sky. Angrily he looked back at the jagged tear and carelessly he stepped into the darkness, disappearing inside.

Then the void was gone.

The shadow of a dragon streaked over the grass where the tear had been. The dragon continued to search for the power that it had felt. Its cry of rage and despair split the air.

Beyond the hole a world waited for its destiny to unfold; a destiny which fate had already set in motion.

In complete darkness, a being awoke.

For long moments, he pondered the darkness trying to recall distant memories. Nothing came. Only vagueness, a nagging doubt — and fear.

All at once, strange thoughts tumbled through his mind and he grabbed at the half-formed images, weeping at scenes of long-lost glory. Then came a complete memory. One that he held onto, feeding his hatred. It was the memory of being cast out from his own world, banished to this realm; a realm of hopelessness and stagnant death.

A name came to mind and with the name came more hatred.

Eldric!

All at once, he remembered. Long ago, the Eldric had exiled him to this place. For eons his tormented soul had patiently waited for a sign that he had not been forgotten. Abruptly memories coalesced and he knew who and where he was.

He was Drachar, and this was hell.

Angrily he glanced around, expecting only to see the hated and blessed night. Yet, in the distance, a tiny star blazed in glory. The lure of the star was strong and he felt an urgency to reach it. Slowly, on unseen limbs, he felt himself moving, but to his frustration, the light failed to come closer. He continued with more haste and greater speed, willing himself towards his salvation.

Panicking, he urged himself on, knowing that here at last was a chance to escape, a scream of glee erupting from unseen lips as he raced onwards.

Then the star was gone.

He wailed aloud in abject misery, spinning around, searching for the light in vain, but only a terrible blackness remained. A forlorn feeling of loneliness stole over him and he cursed whatever gods there were for his fate and prayed to them for release.

Sleepiness overcame him — sleep, yes sleep. Wait, his turn would come again. Then, he would be ready.

Sleep.

Drachar.

He would wait.

His time was not yet ripe but when it was he would be ready and once more the world would know evil.

Thus ends Legacy of the Eldric. The story continues in Dragon Rider.

The Prophecy of the Kings

Book 2

Dragon Rider

By David Burrows

Prologue

A cloaked figure, garbed in black with a hood drawn across its eyes, stared around at the cave. It was warm and dry, ideal for the Ritual. Black boots crushed the dry leaves that carpeted the cavern floor. The torrent outside continued as though even the Gods wept. His yellow eyes glinting feverishly; he beckoned to his companion, his hands almost claw-like with long dirt-brown nails. Another cloaked figure entered the cave, taller and broader than the first man. Behind him came a third figure, shorter, more youthful, eyes flickering about the cave in mistrust.

"Come, come," said the first man, waving his arm impatiently. His frown suggested he was not a patient man. "We must hurry if we are to perform the Ritual before dawn. Darren, do not be a slouch and hurry up."

The youth paused, anger flashing in his eyes. "Kryan, do not take that tone with me. I volunteered for this, remember."

Kryan tried to conceal his smile. Since when did a four year old boy volunteer? That was Darren's age when he was snatched from his village ten years ago and, since then, the boy's training had been intense. But whatever was certain, he was no volunteer.

Gallan was reverently placing candles about the cave. The big man's frown was one of intense concentration. Soon a gentle light illuminated the interior revealing scar-ravaged walls, boulders strewn about the cavern floor and dark, sinister looking recesses where even the light seemed afraid to penetrate.

Kryan liked Gallan; he was the silent type who just got on with jobs. He hated people who blathered, especially those with nothing much to say. Kryan breathed in the dry air, scenting the years of accumulated dust. The cave was ancient, just what they needed to summon the spirits of the dead. Kryan turned just as Gallan was handing him a knife. The weapon was silver and the hilt inlaid with gold wire. An expensive item, but Ryoch demanded no less. Kryan took the weapon and turned to Darrell.

Darrell was shaking and his brown eyes looked uncertain. His earlier bravado was gone and he now looked his fourteen years.

"Your shaol is strong, Darrell. You do not need to be afraid," Kryan said with just a hint of condemnation in his voice, deliberately bridling the younger man.

Darrell's fear vanished and anger blossomed behind his eyes. "I told you, old man," he sneered. "Watch your tone or it will be you lying on the ground and not I."

Inside Kryan laughed. He cast Gallan a look and saw that the other man understood. Darrell's training had been superb; arrogance would force him to do what they wanted. Arrogance and the belief in Ryoch, his god.

"My apologies, Darrell. You are correct, and I have overstepped myself. Now come here and kneel," Kryan said, bowing ever so slightly in mock respect.

Darrell's eyes hardened and Kryan sensed his growing rebellion.

"Oh, do not fear. You are not kneeling to me. Do you not feel *his* presence, here in the cave?"

For the first time, Darrell's eyes swept the cave interior. He, too, must have sensed the antiquity and a look of reverence crossed his face.

"He is here?" he asked in child-like innocence. "Here, with us now?"

"Communicate with your shaol, and ask him what he sees. You will have a better answer from the spirit world than from me."

Darrell did not close his eyes. He had no need. In truth, Kryan was growing afraid of the younger man and the strength of his bond with his shaol. Given time he would be powerful indeed, but the experiments must go on. If Drachar was to be served, he needed an army. An army of invincible warriors, even stronger than the growing number of warrior Priests of Ryoch, a god created in name only to serve a greater god – Drachar. Until the time was ripe for the people to believe in his return, Drachar's name must remain a preserve of the trusted. Ryoch would do, but Ryoch was a sham, nothing more, nothing less.

Darrell's eyes grew hard as though he had focussed on something upon another plane. Kryan felt a shiver run down his spine; something was wrong. He summoned his own shaol and, as always, the link was there but tenuous. His shaol was warning him, but of what he could not say. Fear cascaded down his spine and he glanced uncertainly around the cave, trying to see into the hidden depths where evil might lurk like a plague about to be released upon the world.

Kryan was playing with proverbial fire; imps, demons and devils were not to be toyed with. One mistake and his soul could be rotting in hell for an eternity of damnation.

All at once Kryan felt his age and his own arrogance died. His wrinkled flesh on the back of the hand gripping the ornate knife suddenly reminded him of his own mortality. He was so afraid to die. The aches and pains of age were suddenly forgotten and he felt an overpowering love of life. Why did he feel so threatened?

Darrell fell to his knees and turned his eyes up to look upon Kryan with a look of reverence that Kryan had never seen before. For a moment he feared that Darrell was seeing his fear as a smile spread upon the youth's face. Kryan tried to straighten his shoulders. He looked across at Gallan to see whether the other man had felt a similar premonition, but he might well have been looking at rock for all that Gallan's expression betrayed. The other man's broad features were impassive. His dark, shaggy eyebrows and long fringe all but hid his eyes. Kryan felt afraid, but knew he must continue, if not just to keep face amongst his peers.

Darrell was now smiling in almost feral glee. Kryan fell back on his last resort when cornered by something he did not understand — bullying and tyranny.

"Here, take the knife," he commanded proffering the weapon to the youth. Darrell grasped the blade and, for a moment, the two men held the weapon as Kryan turned to Gallan. "Do you have the cloak, belt and scabbard?"

Gallan nodded and for once Kryan wished that he would say something.

Turning his attention back to Darrell, he said, "You know what to do. Ryoch demands your soul."

Kryan was shocked; always when he said these words there was horror in the eyes of the person he spoke to. Never had he witnessed the calm acceptance that he now saw. It was his hand that shook, and not Darrell's, as he passed the knife over. Once more he glanced at Gallan but again it was like looking at stone.

"Ryoch," Kryan shouted and, to his own ears, his voice trembled. "Ryoch, your servant kneels before you and offers you his life." As required he felt his own shaol scream the name Drachar over and over. This time, though, he heard it clearly, rather than as though across a vast expanse of time. He again realised that something was wrong. This was going too well. Whereas they had always failed before, now doubt crept into his mind. He looked about the cavern as though expecting to see Drachar's shade smiling down on him, an evil smile of the damned.

Darrell had taken the weapon. He exposed his chest, unbuttoning the jerkin he wore and then the shirt beneath it. Still wearing the feral grin, he placed the point of the blade against his chest and then his eyes met Kryan's in silent challenge. A brief instance of pain, a grimace, a low moan escaping dying lips and Darrell sank slowly to the cavern floor before Kryan even saw the blade move. It was over and Kryan was suddenly enamoured by the power of his false god.

Shocked, Kryan watched the flow of crimson as Gallan came over with the cloak. "There is no need for that," Kryan sneered, his bravado returning as adrenalin coursed through his veins. But Gallan did not stop. He placed the cloak about the air above the corpse, and, when he removed his hands, the cloak remained, suspended in mid air. Unseen hands adjusted the cloak, tying it about an invisible throat. The hood came up and it took all Kryan's strength of will to remain standing.

Gallan looked at Kryan, his eyes dark and brooding. "You did not believe," he accused. "You have never believed. It is your failure that this moment has taken so long to achieve."

Gallan strapped the belt and scabbard about the ethereal form. The figure stooped, drawing the knife from the dead boy's body. Kryan heard his shaol screaming repeated warnings and, too late, he turned, seeking an escape. Intense pain blossomed in his back, a pain like no other. It felt as though he had been kicked by a horse and, all at once, he could not breathe. He fell to his knees, his head turning and his eyes seeking the reason for his demise.

"I told you not to use that tone of voice with me," a hollow voice said.

Kryan fell forward, his eyes darkening. He panted for breath but none came. He felt life leaving him. Behind him he heard Gallan issuing instructions to the abomination. What had he done? In his mind's eye, a phantom took shape and, with the recognition, came terror. His master was calling and behind him was his creatures; all the demon's of hell. His master opened his arms, welcoming Kryan to his domain. His failure was to be punished; a punishment lasting all eternity. Even long after he had died, his wail of remorse filled the cave.

Chapter 1

Flight of Fear

Tumarl crashed through the thick undergrowth, half running, half stumbling in his haste to escape. He ran with the unsteady gait of a man close to both his physical and mental limits. He had long since given up trying to reason, and madness threatened his fragile hold on reality. Even the trees seemed threatening. Claw-like branches snagged his clothes as though deliberately seeking to hinder his escape.

KinKassack.

A forest of such dread that no sane man would volunteer to walk beneath its shadow. A place heard of only in tales, best told sitting in the comfort of home, the storyteller murmuring in whispers, lest the evil in the world hear and curse the teller.

He was a sad reflection of a man. At one time, his face had been broad and strong, but now grey flesh hung from his bones, and he looked far older than his thirty years. He wore a permanent scowl, born from years of hardship.

Slow down, fool, a voice nagged.

Eyes wide with fright, he stopped, looking about for the speaker.

Idiot, continued the voice. *It's you. You're talking to yourself.*

Gleefully he hooted. Wonderful! He had a friend.

"Shut up!" he screamed back. A bird took flight close to his legs, causing him to yelp in fear. Staggering like a drunkard, he ran, cackling dementedly. In two more strides he misplaced his footing, stumbling headfirst into thick undergrowth. He struck his head on a root. Blackness engulfed him, and mercifully he knew no more.

Some time later, he awoke, cold and confused. Rain lashed down, running in rivulets along the length of his upturned face. Overhead, a rook cawed, the only sound of life in the dismal forest.

The shock of the fall had partially helped him to regain his sanity.

"Where am I?" he croaked. The memory of a narrow smelly mine, men working with picks until their hands bled, sweating bodies, and cries of terror descended on him. Then he remembered his escape.

They would be after him. He had to flee.

Muttering, he willed his madness to remain at bay. Picking himself up, he continued to lope along the narrow trail. The night was nearly done, and he needed to be much farther by dawn.

All too soon his hopes were dashed. Dodging between low branches, he almost collided with a rock face that seemed to appear from nowhere. His mind wailed in frustration. Would he never escape this accursed forest?

Looking up, the rock towered high into the night sky, its surface bleak and forbidding in the difficult light. To his frustration, the wall continued as far as he could see on either side of his position.

"Now what do I do?" he sobbed.

How many friends had he seen die while he stubbornly sought to escape his fate?

No! He refused to give up.

Knowing it was folly, he started to climb. It was easy at first, and he felt elated that he was finally escaping. Level with the treetops, he paused. Looking up, he still could not tell how high the cliff was. It disappeared in the dark of a dismal night.

A scream from below froze his blood, causing his heart to lurch and his fingers to slip on the surface. Scrabbling, he prevented himself from falling but at the cost of bruised and bloodied fingers. The sound was inhuman and an image of a grakyn sprang to mind. That they could fly made his predicament all the worse.

In his haste to climb he tore his already bloody fingers on sharp outcrops of rock as he hauled himself higher. It was a desperate ascent. The rock face was slippery with wet moss, and the handholds few and shallow. Panting with exertion, he pulled himself onto a ledge. It was not very wide and on it a scraggly bush clung tenaciously to life.

At that moment the moon chose to peek between the clouds, bathing the land in a silvery glow. Foolishly, he looked over the edge and his mind reeled with vertigo as he scrambled back. It was a long drop to the ground. A cold wind gusted, causing him to shiver. He realised at some time during his ascent, the rain had stopped, but that was no longer a blessing. He could see every leaf and twig far below which also meant anyone following could now see him.

Another scream sounded, stretching further his over-taut nerves. Taking advantage of the light, he looked up to the next stage of the climb. It was smooth and slick with water, with few, if any, handholds.

He cursed bitterly. He was trapped.

The bush he shared the ledge with prevented him from leaning back and turning around. He angrily pushed against it, seeking to make more room. His hand met with little resistance and, shocked, he tumbled forward, throwing up his hands to protect his head from the inevitable collision. But it never came and instead he fell flat onto his chest.

Untangling himself, he realised he had unexpectedly found a cavern. Gratefully, he scrambled forward and to his surprise, instead of narrowing, it widened and there was even sufficient room to kneel. Inside it was completely dark and he was forced to explore with his hands. His fingers traced a rough stone surface that stretched as far as he could reach to either side. The darkness was threatening, and he glanced back towards the entrance and the faint outline of light.

An assortment of rocks and nesting material littered the floor. Taking up two rocks, he experimentally struck them together. Nothing happened so he discarded one rock and tried another, repeating the process until a spark rewarded his perseverance.

Next he groped about the nesting material, seeking soft down. Striking the rocks he nurtured a tiny flame, feeding it with more down and twigs as the flame grew. Grateful for the light, he looked about. A long tunnel stretched away into the distance to either side, but he dared not explore without a torch.

By his foot, roots protruded from the rock and, by continuously twisting one, he managed to break it off. Eagerly, he tore strips from his shirt, wrapping these about the wood before holding them in the fire. Once lit, he scattered the fire, pocketing the stones he had used to light it. As he rose, his joints creaked in protest. Trusting his instincts, he chose the right hand tunnel, hoping it would lead to safety. After a while, it forked and, without hesitating, he took the left hand entrance, almost as if guided by an invisible presence.

Exhaustion started to make his mind wander and, then, abruptly, he was standing in front of a large cavern, swaying on unsteady legs. His torch spluttered, threatening to expire.

Someone was in the cave. He stepped back into the shadows, pressing himself against the wall, already knowing it was too late to hide. Nothing happened though and, upon reflection, something about the scene seemed unnatural. A shiver ran down his spine; a compulsion seemed to be driving him on, even though he was nearly dead on his feet.

If there was somebody in the cave, they would have seen your torchlight, a voice reasoned. He looked about for the speaker. This time it was not his own mad ramblings, and he could almost feel warm breath on his cheek.

Timidly he looked into the cavern. The figure had not moved and he realised there were actually three figures huddled together as though deep in conversation. He went over to them, stepping over objects cluttering the floor. The assortment of shapes caught his attention, and he recognised a long knife and more importantly several torches. Gratefully, he bent to retrieve one, nearly fainting as his vision swam.

With trembling hands, he lit it using his own makeshift torch which was already threatening to expire. Dropping that, he bent to pick up the knife and, armed, felt more confident.

His attention went back to the figures and, to his pain-racked mind finely balanced between sanity and madness, they seemed a mixture of reality and imagination.

"Statues?" he croaked uncertainly.

Silence! the voice warned.

He touched the nearest shape, feeling a cold, hard surface. The figure was that of a large man whose bearded face was contorted in a look of abject horror. In one hand he grasped a double-edged axe while the other rested on the shoulder of his companion.

Why would anyone make a statue and then hide it away in the depths of a cave? he thought.

Swaying, his attention went to the next statue. This man was smaller and conveyed an air of nobility. His features were fine and delicate although he, too, looked dreadfully afraid.

Whereas the first two men looked terrified, the third looked strangely resolute. One hand rested on the shoulder of the smaller man while his other clenched a sword held on the big man's shoulder. Something about his look suggested inner strength, a power beyond that of the cavern, and his eyes seemed distant as though he were looking into another world.

Tumarl touched the statues gently, as though sharing their pain.

There was a flaw in the last figure,; a large chip of rock had been broken off below the breast. The wound was deep and around it the stone was discoloured.

A feeling of unease suddenly overtook Tumarl, and he felt a thrill of alarm.

224

Hide! urged the voice.

Without thinking, he cradled his torch in the arm of one of the figures and retreated into the shadows. Briefly he giggled reminded of his youth, believing he was back with friends, playing hide and seek as his madness sought dominance once more.

Entering the tunnel leading away from the one he had entered, he waited and watched for his brother to come and find him, intending to jump out and frighten him with his knife. He looked down at the blade, wondering where he had found it, and a frown creased his brow.

Gradually, his racing heart slowed. He pressed himself against the cold rock. Feeling very tired his eyes started to closed.

Wake up! demanded the voice.

The voice was annoying him now and, angrily, he clutched the dagger. Glancing into the cavern, nothing had changed and he was getting bored. He yawned as once again sleep threatened.

Stay awake. Just for a few moments, the voice whined but, instead, warmth stole over him and his heavy lids seemed to fall of their own volition. Movement jolted him to wakefulness. A creature stood at the light's periphery. Immediately came recognition.

A grakyn.

Demon spawn.

It pointed its arm and barked guttural words, and a ball of flame leapt from its outstretched talon, illuminating the cavern and blinding Tumarl. An explosion followed, causing him to duck instinctively as a hurricane tore at him, trying to dislodge him from his hiding place. An ear-splitting bang followed, penetrating the very depths of his soul and causing the ground to shake.

When the blast died down Tumarl risked looking back into the cave where he saw the grakyn approaching the statues, lifting its feet to step over small fires. The grakyn's wings were tucked behind its back as it stole across the cavern floor like a cat hunting its prey.

Tumarl stifled a sudden urge to giggle, gripping harder the hilt of his dagger.

Silence, said the voice and he quietened, trusting the voice. Suddenly, he frowned as the smoke from the explosion drifted away.

The statues were gone and instead three men lay where the statues should have been. Not broken remnants of stone but people of flesh and blood.

Instantly Tumarl's madness fled. Too often he had witnessed friends butchered by creatures such as this. A red haze descended as, with a strength borne from despair, he leapt from his hiding place, raising his blade, which gleamed in the light from the burning wreckage. He covered the short distance as an eerie howl rent the air, not even aware that he had screamed.

Too late the grakyn turned as he drove the blade deep between its shoulders. With a cry of triumph he forced the blade deeper, clinging desperately to the hilt while trying to sever the grakyn's life force.

The creature reared as a scream escaped its lip-less mouth. Wildly it thrashed, seeking to dislodge its assailant. In desperation it smashed Tumarl against the cavern wall, inadvertently driving the blade deeper.

The impact forced air from Tumarl's lungs, and waves of agony lanced through his body. Gritting his teeth, he twisted the blade screaming his defiance, and then his strength failed as he collapsed, trying desperately to breathe.

The grakyn stood with its back to him, the hilt of the knife protruding starkly from its back. Then, with a thud it, too, collapsed.

Tumarl sucked air into his lungs and on wobbling legs, he stood. The fires within the cavern were dying and darkness was swiftly returning. Tumarl hung on to consciousness not needing the voice now to urge him on.

Reaching out for the double-headed axe lying on the ground, he took it up, but its weight threatened to topple him. Bracing himself, he lifted the weapon over his head and, with the practised ease of one used to chopping wood, he swung the blade. The weapon clove through flesh and bone as though they were nothing more than brittle twigs, and the blade rang from the rock, sending a shower of sparks flying across the floor.

The sparks were the last things Tumarl saw before falling unconscious to the floor.

Chapter 2

Awakening

The doe paused, one foot raised, its nose twitching as it scented the cave. Large liquid eyes searched the gloomy interior, but it was too dark to see. By the doe's side, a voice urged it forward but the timid animal hesitated, fighting its instinct to flee. Eventually, reassured by the soft whispers, it walked forward into the yawning hole.

With a final look at the tree-covered slope behind, the doe disappeared within the cold embrace of the cave.

Kaplyn.

The name seemed familiar but its very sound rang hollow, as if across a vast void.

Pain.

His body was racked with sharp needles of agony. He arched as he inhaled, and the breath felt sweet within his lungs. He held it, savouring it, too afraid to expel the fragile elixir of life. A terrible pain erupted within his chest. A scream was wrenched from parched lips, and then the pain faded, leaving behind a dull aching throb.

His eyes opened; blackness greeted him. More pain lanced through his body, and he retched dryly but nothing came. Instead an intense throbbing started behind his eyes. He groaned, letting agony wash over him until it receded into memory.

His hand snaked to his chest which burned ferociously, his fingers tracing a deep scar which had not been there before.

Or had it?

His bones creaked in protest as he tried to rise. He was starving and the pain in his belly immediately increased a thousand fold.

Groping about the ground, his fingers found his bow. The twine was attached and it took several attempts to string it. Each attempt was torture. When he succeeded, he located his quiver and, trembling, took out an arrow.

Unsteadily he started walking, his bow outstretched before him. Then, there was a light ahead, and he had to screw his eyes tightly against the glare as he hastened forward. Something was there and he paused uncertainly.

A deer stood in the entrance and surrounding it like a halo, sunlight beckoned. Kaplyn was immediately tempted to rush to the exit and the freedom beyond, but the deer was too good an opportunity, and he knew he mustn't frighten it away.

Ignoring the brightness, he nocked his arrow, leaning against the cold wall for support. He could barely draw the bow and his arms trembled.

With a twang, the arrow flew with terrible accuracy towards the deer, striking it in its side and spilling it to the ground. Kaplyn fell exhausted to his knees, dropping his bow from numb fingers. He crawled forward, coming to a halt before the body.

Pain etched his features as he tried to drag the corpse back along the tunnel. In exasperation he dropped the leg and, frustrated, sat down.

He had to get back to the others and the thought caused him to frown. He had not considered there had been anyone else with him, but now it seemed natural he was not alone.

Drawing a long, slim-handled knife, he hacked off a lump of warm flesh and, as he butchered the animal, his fingers became slick and greasy. Once he had sufficient meat, he arose, retracing his steps back into the waiting darkness, walking until abruptly the cloak of darkness fell away as a light flared in front of him.

Shielding his eyes, he tried to see. He was standing in a cavern littered with an assortment of shapes that seemed to take an age to come into focus.

A man sat before Kaplyn, blinking furiously. A stone rested on the floor before him, white light streaming from it. Kaplyn's gaze went from the orb to the man and involuntarily he took a step back. The other man's face and hair were as white as fresh snow and from beneath frosty eyebrows, crimson eyes regarded him.

The two men simply stared. Kaplyn had a strong feeling they knew each other, and then he realised the other man was an albino but could not put a name to the face.

Stepping over the debris, Kaplyn walked towards him, the meat from his recent kill held in an outstretched hand. Instantly a look of hunger swept over the albino's features, but a groan from the shadows alerted him to another person's presence. A large, powerfully-built man with long blond hair pushed himself off the floor, shaking his head as if banishing the remnants of a hangover. Broad fingers rubbed at his bearded chin, an act that stirred a memory from deep within Kaplyn's weary mind. The big man pulled himself up into a sitting position, pain reflected within his eyes.

Kaplyn handed them each a strip of meat. Gratefully, they accepted, although for a moment the albino simply stared at the offering as though it offended him.

In silence they ate and gradually, one by one, they fell asleep.

Kaplyn dreamt and a stench of terrible evil filled every recess of his being. A power, sublime in its terror, seemed to hover about his subconscious form, casting shadows that overwhelmed even the night.

Fearfully he cried out.

He put a name to the fear — dragons.

Their scent became more powerful and he felt sick, gagging with the stench, trying to cower within the dark recesses of his dream, praying that they would not find him.

"Shastlan!" he heard one of the beasts calling. "Shastlan! Where are you?" The name was meaningless.

In his sleep, he lay trembling while his fevered mind prayed for the coming dawn.

Chapter 3

Remembrance

"Kaplyn!"

The name penetrated his clouded dreams, and he struggled back to consciousness. He awoke suddenly and, yet, the memory and the stench of dragons lingered.

Lars looked down on him, wearing a look of concern. Behind Lars, Kaplyn could see a craggy cavern ceiling, scarred by the ravages of time. Shaking his head, he sat up, momentarily confused as he dropped a cold, half-eaten hunk of flesh which he had no memory of acquiring.

"Vastra?" he asked, remembering all at once the man who had betrayed them. In his mind's eye, he once again saw Vastra walking along a dank tunnel. In the image, an imp floated eerily by his side while Lomar and Lars fought against the spell turning them gradually to stone. Kaplyn shuddered.

"He has gone," a voice replied from beyond the big man.

Kaplyn turned to face Lomar who peered intently into his face for a few moments before relaxing. In his hand, he held a kara-stone, and light from this gently illuminated the cavern.

"What happened?" Kaplyn asked. His last memory was of trying to protect Lars and Lomar.

"We were betrayed," Lomar replied, his voice filled with sadness. "He trapped us with a spell that turned us to stone. By rights, we should have died. I have no idea how, but it seems that somehow the spell failed."

Lars visibly shuddered. *"By Slathor,* if we ever meet Vastra again I will *kill* him!"

"You will have to join the queue," Kaplyn replied solemnly.

"How was Vastra's spell defeated, do you think?" Lomar asked.

"The pendant!" Kaplyn exclaimed reaching into his tunic for the golden talisman. It was gone; his fingers traced instead a deep scar on his chest. He frowned. Unlacing his shirt, he looked down at his tunic, feeling once more

230

the pain in his chest. Only then did he notice the ragged tear in the thick leather and the dried blood.

His frown deepened when he opened his shirt and saw the scar. The other two men also saw it and Lars inhaled audibly.

This was no ordinary scar. The tissue was solid, almost crystalline, but it was the colour which had made Lars gasp. It was translucent like poor quality glass and seemed to glow with a light of its own.

The sight triggered a memory of the crystal Kaplyn had recovered from the fossilised tree, deep within the heart of the mountain. It, too, had glowed with a similar light and now appeared to be missing from his tunic.

"What is it?" Lars asked with a look of revulsion.

Lomar held up the kara-stone to see better. "A scar," he replied matter of factly.

Kaplyn fastened his tunic, both embarrassed and shocked. He had a spare shirt in his pack and he decided he would change into that later. His brow knotted as he remembered the events leading up to their transformation. "I thought the pendant would protect us from Vastra's spell. It was supposed to nullify magic. I remember holding on to both of you but the pendant failed. Vastra gloated; he must have known it would..." he said, trailing off into a moment's silence.

"There's something you should see," Lomar said, pointing behind Kaplyn.

Two figures lay in the shadows. One was undoubtedly a man, although his flesh was grey and his skin gaunt. He was either dead or very close to it. However, it was the other body that caught Kaplyn's attention. Rising, he walked over to it.

Ebony wings extended about the creature, partially obscuring the body beneath. Its skin was as black as coal, reflecting the light from Lomar's kara-stone like polished glass.

"This one lives," Lomar said, kneeling by the man. He had already covered him with a blanket and had made a pillow from some of their store of clothing. "Although I am not sure how much longer. By the looks of him he is half famished."

The man's flesh hung from his cheeks and his pallor matched Lomar's. His hair was streaked with grey even though he looked to be in his mid-thirties, and his eyebrows formed a rigid V as though the frown had been deeply etched into the very fibre of his being.

Lars' double-headed axe lay by the man's side and Lars stooped, easily lifting the cumbersome weapon in one massive fist. He turned the axe head, seeing the dried blood congealed along the metal. Kaplyn returned his attention to the other, more sinister shape which he tentatively prodded with the toe of his boot.

"It's dead," Lomar assured him, indicating the creature's head several feet away hidden amongst the scattered rocks.

Kaplyn grimaced. It scowled angrily back. Long, gleaming fangs reflected the white light from the kara-stone, making the creature seem alive. A single white horn sprouted from the creature's forehead, dividing into two that grew around the creature's skull like a bone helmet. Crooked talons clutched the rock either side of the body, as though in death it had tried to tear open the very fabric of the earth.

Kaplyn had never before seen such a creature. He parted its wings, revealing the handle of a knife protruding from its dead flesh.

"A grakyn!" Lomar said, raising the kara-stone so that they could see the grinning face more clearly.

Kaplyn did not question his knowledge. His people, the Alvalah, kept records spanning countless generations. He wondered briefly what had brought the man and this devil-spawn together.

"Will he live?" Kaplyn asked, turning his attention back to the man.

"Yes, but he's in need of food and rest."

"And water," Kaplyn added, realising how thirsty he was. He looked about at their supplies. "What a mess," he said, seeing most of the objects either broken or rotten. His gaze fell on his sword lying on the tunnel floor; the black metal seemed to absorb even the light of Lomar's kara-stone making it look momentarily as evil as the grakyn.

He bent to retrieve the weapon, which seemed to come eagerly to his grasp. For a moment, he could almost swear that it moved within his grip. He felt disgusted and almost dropped it. He had his doubts about the sword, but at least it was potent against evil, having used it to defeat a demon. It was Eldric-made and he had found it within one of their cities Vastra had magically summoned.

He returned the weapon to its scabbard, noticing as he did so a flask upon the floor; eagerly he bent to retrieve it. He shook it and was rewarded by a swishing sound but, taking a swallow, discovered the water was rank. Spitting and coughing, the others laughed at him as, with a look of distaste, he emptied the contents upon the ground.

"I'll go and look for water," he said and, taking the canteen, he set off down the tunnel, sensing the way by the flow of fresh air.

It did not take long to find the entrance. He welcomed the light ahead with a broad smile, but his smile vanished when he saw the body of a deer. His look turned to puzzlement when he recognised one of his arrows in its side and his hunting bow alongside it. He squatted, recovering the weapon as he looked down with sadness at the deer. He could not remember killing it and, although he often hunted, this somehow felt wrong.

"I'm sorry," he whispered, as though seeking to make amends.

Rising, he went to the entrance but trees obscured his view. In the distance, he became aware of the burbling of a stream, mixed with the gentle rustling of leaves. He made his way down the slope through thick overgrowth, following the sound of the stream. It led him to a deep bank, and he had to use the branches of overhanging trees to climb down to it. Balancing upon a large rock at the water's edge, he filled the canteen before drinking deeply. The water tasted delicious, and he couldn't remember having tasted anything as good before.

It was then he noticed the colour of the leaves. Judging by the multitude of burnished reds, golden browns and a keen wind, he realised it must be late autumn. The discovery came as a shock for they had entered the tunnels in spring — a spring that now seemed so impossibly distant. Could they have been held within Vastra's spell for that long? His thoughts immediately turned to home, prompting memories of his parents, the King and Queen, who would be worried sick by his absence.

Back in the tunnel, Lomar was still attending to the unconscious man whilst Lars was rummaging through their packs to see what could be salvaged. Kaplyn offered them the canteen.

"We should go to the entrance. At least it is light there," he suggested.

Together they carried the unconscious man and, when they arrived, both Lars and Lomar frowned when they saw the deer's body.

"How long has that been there?" Lars asked, eyeing the corpse suspiciously.

Kaplyn shrugged as they laid the stranger down, placing the remains of a cloak they had found in the cavern beneath his head.

"The meat is fresh and I found my bow by its side," Kaplyn replied. "At least we will not go hungry." He glanced at Lomar and remembered then that his people did not eat meat.

"It's all right," the albino reassured him. "I'll find something outside. There is bound to be something edible in the forest."

"We had better salvage our supplies," Lars suggested.

Together, he and Kaplyn returned along the tunnel with Kaplyn carrying a torch that did little to light the way. When they reached their destination, they stuffed as much as they were able into three packs and what they couldn't use they left behind with the grakyn's corpse. Kaplyn and Lars were only too pleased to leave the dank tunnel for the last time as they swiftly returned to Lomar and the stranger.

"We must have been in the tunnels for a while," Kaplyn said, laying his burden down. "It's autumn and the trees have turned."

"It can't be," Lars complained. "That means we were in the tunnels for six months or more."

"It's autumn now," Lomar agreed, shaking his head.

"And cold," Kaplyn added. "We'd better collect some kindling."

When he and Lars returned, carrying bundles of dead wood and cones, the stranger finally aroused. He looked befuddled by his surroundings, and his eyes searched the cavern roof as though seeking to recall where he was. Lomar went over to him and knelt by his side. Seeing Lomar, a look of abject fear crossed his face and he struggled to rise.

"Stay still!" Kaplyn urged, dropping the wood with a clatter. Both he and Lomar tried to hold the stranger down, and, although he looked half starved, he was still strong. He mewled pitifully when it was clear that he couldn't escape.

"We mean you no harm," Kaplyn said.

All the while the stranger's eyes never left Lomar's face, and suddenly Kaplyn understood.

"He's a friend!" he called, trying to turn the stranger's face towards his own. The man was panting, clearly exhausted by his feeble struggles. Slowly, however, his eyes turned to Kaplyn and then his gaze went back to Lomar. Gradually, he relaxed as Kaplyn's words sank in.

"We are friends," Kaplyn repeated now that he had the man's attention. "This is Lomar. He is an albino, not a demon. He is a man, like you or me. Now who are you?"

"Tumarl," came the reply. His voice was cracked as though from disuse.

Kaplyn smiled back reassuringly. He gestured to Lomar for the canteen.

"I am Kaplyn," he explained.

Lomar offered him the canteen, which the other man took in shaking hands.

"This is Lomar and he is an Alvalan," Kaplyn explained. "His people live in the KinAnar forest. I am an Allund and Lars is from a land across the sea."

Tumarl drank and then started to choke.

"Be careful, you'd better not drink too much all at once," Kaplyn said, slapping his back.

Tumarl finally stopped spluttering and wiped water from his mouth. His eyes strayed hungrily to the body of the deer. Kaplyn grinned and went to the carcass where he began the job of butchering it while Lars started to build a fire.

"I'll see if I can find some other food outside," Lomar said, rising and taking his leave.

Within a few moments, Lars had the fire lit and a large joint of venison was roasting over the flames, swiftly filling the cave with a delicious aroma. Soon after Lomar returned, laden down with nuts and tubers which he placed on the embers to cook.

When the meal was ready, Kaplyn shared it out. They ate seated about the fire, putting up with the copious quantities of smoke blown back into the cave.

After a while Kaplyn waved towards the rear of the cave. "That creature back there, did you kill it?"

Tumarl nodded. It was clear by his looks that he did not trust them.

Kaplyn saw his mistrust and guessed its source. "You saw us, before — didn't you?"

Tumarl's eyes widened. "You were not real," he accused. "You were stone." He pushed himself back against the cavern wall, as though seeking reassurance in its solidity.

"Are you men or *demons*?" he ventured, staring once more at Lomar. His strength was spent and he must have known he was at their mercy.

Kaplyn grinned. "We are men," he reassured him.

"It's a kara-stone," Lomar said, seeing Tumarl frowning at the stone glowing eerily upon a rock.

"I've heard of such a thing," Tumarl answered, albeit somewhat uncertainly. "Wizards use them. Are you a wizard?"

Lomar shook his head. "No but my people use these stones for healing," he replied.

Tumarl looked unconvinced and his eyes returned to the stone.

"Do you know where we are?" Kaplyn asked, changing the subject.

"Thrace," Tumarl said his face clouding as he spoke. "I was in KinKassack and I climbed a cliff to escape the forest."

"Thrace? Then we have a long walk home," Kaplyn said, grinning broadly.

Chapter 4

Tumarl's Tale

After their meal, they checked their packs to see what, if anything, could be salvaged. Some of their belongings were rotten. Lars held up a coarse shirt that had gaping holes in it, and a rope Lomar held parted easily, leaving long frayed ends and a cloud of dust. They guessed rats had scavenged material for their nests. Some of the clothes had survived and, after taking a new shirt for himself, Kaplyn offered some of these to Tumarl who gratefully accepted them, glad to replace the rags that he wore.

Before long, they lay down to sleep. They must have slept for a long time for when they awoke, the fire had nearly died. Outside it was still light and they realised they had slept through an entire day. Once more they were famished. They quickly prepared another meal, which they hungrily devoured.

Afterwards they left the cavern, intending to wash in the stream. The sight of the grakyn's corpse had cautioned them that krell were also likely to inhabit the mountains, and they did not relish an encounter with any potential enemies in their present state. Even after food and rest, they were still bone-weary. Upon leaving the cave Tumarl was initially bewildered and he kept looking around.

"I climbed a cliff to get to the cave," he said, his voice was uncertain as though he doubted his own sanity.

"There may be other entrances," Kaplyn explained. "The tunnels go for miles, believe me, we know."

"I walked that way for a while," Lomar said pointing. "There's a sheer cliff and beyond that a forest."

"KinKassack," Tumarl whispered. "That is a truly evil place."

Kaplyn saw the other man's fear and realised how dark the forest must have become to scare a grown man so much.

Together they made their way to the stream. The water was freezing cold, but invigorating, and they splashed themselves, rubbing their skin vigorously.

Kaplyn felt uncomfortable with his scar so he washed apart from the others, choosing a spot slightly downstream. In the light of day, he examined it again. He had hoped that it had been a trick of the light in the cavern, but it still glowed with an eerie silver light. Frustrated, he clambered from the water, drying himself and quickly replacing his shirt before the others saw the scar again.

Lacing his shirt, he made his way to Lomar who was standing guard with Kaplyn's bow whilst the others washed. Lomar was watching Kaplyn with a look of understanding in his scarlet eyes. No one could endure the icy water for long and, with teeth chattering, each hurriedly left the stream, clambering up the steep bank where they dried themselves on one of the few spare blankets that remained.

While they dried themselves, Kaplyn returned to the cave and placed a large log on the fire, coaxing it onto the embers with his boot. The others joined him and, for a while, they enjoyed the fire's warmth before Kaplyn broke the silence.

"Tumarl, how did you and the grakyn come to be in the tunnels?"

Tumarl looked pale. "It's a long story," he replied. The others looked on expectantly.

Hesitantly at first and then with mounting anger, he spoke. "For two years I was held prisoner; a slave of the krell, working in one of their mines, deep in the mountains to the north. We were forced to work in darkness, digging for long shifts until the sores on our hands wept and our backs felt broken."

"How were you captured?" Lomar asked.

"I was a farmer, as were most of my people. We lived on the northern most borders of Thrace. Because of our isolation we were used to krell raids, but nothing of this magnitude. I was taken prisoner in a raid on my village, one night while we slept. Grakyn led the attack, destroying the stockade wall with bolts of fire. Next came wave after wave of krell. Most of us were in our beds when the alarm was raised and by then it was too late." He looked at Kaplyn with tears in his eyes. "Many were slain, women, children — it did not matter. My wife was dragged from our house and butchered before I could even reach for a weapon."

Angrily, he threw wood onto the fire and a cloud of burning embers flew into the air. "We were not warriors," he spat, clearly angered by his own failings, "and I lost her because of that. She must have gone downstairs

237

at some point before I awoke and, by the time I did, it was too late. I was trapped upstairs. I killed several krell as they came looking for me, but their sheer number overwhelmed me and I went down beneath a press of foul-smelling bodies. They did not kill me and later I often wished they had, but they were angry that I'd killed some of them and they taunted me, saying that I should have accepted death…"

Tumarl's voice betrayed his emotions; his brow furrowed with deep ridges.

"I watched others as they were dragged from their houses and herded through the narrow streets to the village centre. They took mainly men and boys, not being interested in women, children or the old. We watched as they set fire to the buildings, many of which were still occupied."

Tumarl covered his eyes and shuddered. "In some, there were children, hidden by their parents who pleaded with the krell to let them save them, but they merely laughed. One man, Hildran, went berserk and attacked a krell close to him, knocking it to the ground. Another krell ran him through with its spear. In a way it was better that Hildran died, for his wife and two children burned that night."

Tumarl picked up another piece of wood, absently playing with it.

Kaplyn wanted to tell him to stop talking, but could tell that Tumarl wanted to continue. A tear welled in the corner of Tumarl's eye and slid down his cheek. He cuffed it away with his sleeve.

"They marched us away in one long line, and, when I looked back, I thought the sky was alight, so fierce was the blaze from our burning homes. Our ordeal had only just begun though. One or two of the wounded fell and could not rise. They were murdered where they lay and left for the crows. On the third day, a large force of krell peeled away from our column, heading towards foothills we were approaching. I guessed they were an ambush for those who might follow, if any did."

Kaplyn shivered as a cold wind blew into the cave, causing the fire to flicker. Lomar glanced at it but no one moved. It was as if they were spellbound.

"We were forced to march day and night with only short rests. Our legs ached with the strain of climbing and soon we were deep within the mountains. Some of the injured fell and we tried to carry them, but our captors took them from us, hurling them from narrow paths to their deaths on the rocks below. Then, one night, we were led into a dark tunnel which went deep into the mountain. We became afraid of every turn, thinking that we must surely meet Drachar himself so deep did we go. We were chained to one another and forced to work in shifts until our arms ached, and our minds reeled with the drudgery that our lives had become. Large wagons pulled by mules took the ore away. Where I do not know, but the mules fared almost as badly as ourselves."

Tumarl paused before continuing angrily. "They kept us barely alive; we were too weak to escape. I despaired. Never once were we taken from our chains," he said with the light of madness in his eyes. "Then, during one of the shifts, I passed out. I remember waking in the darkness to find myself alone. I had been unchained and left to rot where I lay. By then I was delirious and could do nothing. After a while I tried to crawl, but lacked the energy. At one stage I must have passed out. When I came to I was being dragged through tunnels by a pair of krell.

"I next awoke to find myself balanced on the edge of a cliff with strong hands holding me upright and the sound of laughter filling the tunnel behind me, he continued. "The moon was high and I could see the drop below me. The krell tormented me, but they did not get the fun they hoped for. I was beyond caring and when they realised this they simply let go and I fell. I was glad and welcomed death," he said looking grim. "That may be what saved me for I relaxed and may even have passed out. I awoke on a pile of flesh and bones upon which crows feasted. I howled in anger and even the birds took flight, fearing the mound of dead was awakening.

"I do not remember much after that except wandering deliriously through the forest which seemed to pulsate with evil. At first I did not care, and then, in my madness, I seemed to find strength from a reserve deep within my soul. I started to run, trying to kill myself by burning up the last of my energy but somehow I kept going." He frowned as he tried to recall his flight through KinKassack.

"I remember climbing and thinking that something was following. A tunnel — I do not remember and then I saw you three." As he looked up at the others his eyes were clouded with doubt and he shook his head. "You were *statues*, carved from stone — not *flesh and blood*!

"And then the grakyn came," Tumarl continued. "It attacked me — or was it you? I do not remember," he added, burying his head in his hands.

The others remained silent, not knowing what to say. Kaplyn was afraid that Tumarl was going to ask them what they were doing in the tunnel. He didn't think that Tumarl would trust them if he told him that they had been trapped in a spell and had, indeed, been transformed into living rock. Fortunately he did not ask. Perhaps he was afraid to do so, knowing full well how close to madness he had come.

Silently they left him to his grief, each troubled by their own thoughts.

Chapter 5

Departure

They spent several days within the cave, slowly nurturing their bodies back to health. When Lomar and Kaplyn were alone, the albino explained to Kaplyn why they felt so physically tired.

"If you are right and it is autumn, then our bodies have been held in Vastra's spell for many months. It's no wonder we are so weak for, even though magic was at work, our bodies still needed nourishment."

Kaplyn nodded, patting his friend on the shoulder. However, he failed to see the look of sadness that briefly crossed the albino's face.

"You're right of course; I hate feeling this tired. Your explanation helps. With more food and rest we should soon be fit enough to travel, but what about Tumarl? Will he be strong enough?"

"He recovers more swiftly than we do. A fire burns within his soul, a fire which has carried him through hell. I am worried about him though. Vengeance drives him, but to what end?"

Kaplyn didn't know what to say and a shiver ran through his soul.

It took three more days before they felt strong enough to leave the sanctuary of the cave, and, several times during the dark nights, Kaplyn's nightmares recurred. Each time the fear of dragons wrenched him from his sleep. He dared not tell the others about his dreams, but they guessed something was amiss since he cried out often in the night.

Dragons do not exist, Kaplyn kept telling himself, but the memory of the dark shape bound within the crystal whiteness of the glacier at the start of their underground journey came back to his mind. He tried to dismiss it, convincing himself that it had been too dark and the ice too fogged to be certain.

Why was he dreaming of mythical creatures, and why were the dreams so vivid and frightening?

Leaving the cavern Kaplyn couldn't help glancing back. He felt as though part of him remained. However, as they made their way down the steep tree-lined slope, his spirits rose. They were finally going home, and he was looking forward to seeing his family and friends. The others, too, seemed to brighten even though the day was cloudy and a cold wind persisted. The fresh mountain air felt good on their faces and they breathed it deeply, purging the last vestiges of the cave's staleness from their lungs.

For most of the day, they descended the steep slope. The trees remained dense around them, partially sheltering them from the wind that increased in strength, causing the branches to whip back and forth in a frenzy.

Later that day, it started to rain; great sheets of water fell and the descent suddenly became treacherous. They kept slipping on mud, and soon their legs felt like jelly. Lomar complained how cold his feet were, which was hardly surprising since the ground was sodden.

After a particularly nasty fall, Lars refused to get up. Luckily, a tree had stopped his slide but he was badly shaken. They decided to camp for the night and, as they sat huddled miserably beneath the tree, the rain finally stopped.

They were bone tired; sitting helped to ease the pain. Kaplyn's chest ached and he continually fingered the scar beneath his shirt. He felt strangely alone as he removed his pack, dumping it unceremoniously on the wet grass beside him. The others looked equally miserable, fatigue etched on their faces.

Lomar suggested they light a fire. Lars and Lomar set about finding kindling and, with some effort, they eventually managed to light one. Uncomfortable though they were, they tried to sleep.

Tumarl's mind was too restless to sleep, and he watched the others with mixed emotions. It was good to be in company and he was certainly glad to be free of the evil forest.

Not able to help himself, his thoughts drifted once more to his incarceration, and his anger mounted as he remembered the friends he had watched die. They had been mere shells compared to their days in the village. A tear threatened and he wiped it absently away with the back of his hand, feeling coldness as the wind dried his cheek.

After a while Tumarl's thoughts came back to the present. By his side, Kaplyn was stirring.

241

"How long have I slept?" Kaplyn asked, stretching.

"It's early evening," Tumarl replied looking about at the gradually diminishing daylight.

"I think I'll go hunting while I can still see," Kaplyn suggested, looking haunted as though he had found little solace in sleep. Arising he gathered up his bow and quiver before setting off into the wood.

Tumarl decided he needed sleep and laid his head down. Soon, not even the ghosts of his past could prevent sleep from claiming him.

Some time later, a sudden noise jerked Tumarl awake. Something crashed heavily through the treetops, and a shadow landed close to their camp. Tumarl jumped and his eyes opened wide with fear. All was darkness and he had to concentrate hard on the shape to see it. His breathing slowed as fear assailed him. Silently it approached and with each step Tumarl wanted to cry out in terror.

A grakyn. Its wings were folded back and its ebony skin reflected the firelight as catlike the lithe creature advanced. Tumarl gave out a short cry as he tried to spring to his feet, but it was already aware of him. With a simple gesture, it ensnared him in a spell of binding.

With all of his willpower, Tumarl fought the magical bonds but could not escape. Despair washed over him as he watched the creature similarly ensnare the other two sleeping men. Frantically he tried to turn to see whether Kaplyn was back, but he couldn't move.

Slowly, enjoying the sport, the creature advanced, its features twisted in an evil grin. Tumarl summoned up every ounce of strength and, with every fibre of his being, tried desperately to scream.

Kaplyn left the warmth of the campfire and ventured into the trees. He enjoyed hunting and, stealthily, he moved through the undergrowth, shadowlike as he flitted between the trees. Only occasionally did he stop to mark a tree so he could find his way back.

He had been walking for a while when he felt an intense urge to hide. The feeling was too strong to ignore and, without pausing, he fell to the ground and crawled to a nearby bush, pushing himself beneath its branches. He lay within the protection of the foliage, too afraid to even breathe — and yet, for the moment, he had no idea what he was hiding from, or why.

He became aware of voices. Knowing that he faced a tangible foe helped and the fear of the unknown diminished. With that he became curious. He inched forward, gently parting the branches. The voices sounded harsh and guttural, causing the hairs on the nape of his neck to rise.

By now it had become quite dark, and yet in front of him was a glow, seeming to come from the forest itself. He realised he was looking into a valley.

The voices were close, somewhere to his front. He edged forward using a depression in the ground for cover. Once more a feeling of danger stole over him, but he ignored it. He had to know what was ahead and his curiosity drove him on. Raising himself onto his elbows he peered between the leaves and, not more than twenty yards in front of him, he saw the outline of two dark shapes.

Krell.

At this distance, they were unmistakable. Fortunately though, they were facing away into a valley as they conversed in low tones. Kaplyn followed their gaze and, to his horror, saw hundreds of tiny campfires burning below. He guessed he had stumbled across two sentries of a sizeable army. Straining, he tried to hear what they were saying but quickly gave up, unable to understand their language.

Just when he was about to crawl back into thicker cover, a deep voice sounded, causing him to jump in alarm. His heart beat wildly and he feared that he had been seen. Terror kept him rooted to the spot as a dark shape appeared over the valley's lip.

The two krell jumped nearly as much as he did before springing to their feet and grabbing their swords, nearly bowling each over in their haste. Even in the strange tongue, Kaplyn could tell that the newcomer was berating his fellows.

Kaplyn considered retreat, but decided any movement would be folly. The sentries lowered their blades, looking sheepishly at the newcomer. The latter finished his tirade and stood in front of them, fists clenched on his hips in challenge. With another outburst he dismissed them, sending them scurrying back to their posts. Kaplyn watched as they lay down, facing him.

The newcomer left, clearly satisfied that he had frightened the pair sufficiently. Kaplyn could hear him moving away, carelessly brushing aside the vegetation on his way to inspect other sentries. Inwardly, he cursed himself for getting too close.

There was no doubt in his mind that the beings in front of him were krell, even though he had never seen the "mythical" creatures before. They were tall, gangly creatures, lithe and well muscled. Large eyes glimmered beneath broad foreheads and long, ivory fangs stood out starkly against their sallow skin. Their hands were huge, more like clubs. Their armour looked bulky and crude. Their helmets were nothing more than metal skullcaps, and both clenched swords with wicked-looking spurs along their edges

His biggest fear was that the sentries would be changed and fresh eyes might more easily spot him. Several times his heart missed a beat as he heard them change position. For ages he lay there, hoping they would leave or at least turn away.

To distract himself, he estimated how many krell there were in the valley, concluding that if there were only two or three by each campfire, then there must be tens of thousands. He had to warn the people of Thrace. As he waited, the cold bit deeper into his flesh until he felt numb and his joints ached. His scar throbbed as though reminding him of its presence.

The cracking of branches alerted Kaplyn the sentries were moving, and he held his breath. At first he thought he was discovered and nearly bolted but realised they had become bored and had turned to face into the valley again.

This was his chance. Slowly he crawled back into the deeper cover. As soon as he dared, he turned and crawled away more quickly, trying to find his original route. His jerkin was sodden and the cold wind caused him to shiver.

Thankfully he found one of his marks on a trunk and he was relieved to have taken this precaution. He smeared moss onto the whiteness, hiding the evidence of his passage before moving on.

Soon he saw the soft glow from their campfire, barely visible between the trees to his front. He paused for a few seconds to check that all was as he had left it. The camp looked unchanged, but as his eyes alighted on the fire he noticed the flames burned blue.

A *demon*.

Suddenly the flapping of wings and rustling of leaves shattered the silence as a dark figure dropped into the centre of the camp, huge wings spread wide to catch the thin mountain air. The creature landed with a gentle thump upon the soft wet grass. Kaplyn recognised it was a grakyn from the body in the cave.

Before Kaplyn could decide what to do, Tumarl awoke and with a cry tried to scramble to his feet, but the creature made a gesture, immediately freezing him. The grakyn advanced towards the hapless man, ensnaring Lars and Lomar as it went.

Kaplyn reached for an arrow and nocked it. Without pausing, he took aim. Small branches and leaves partially obscured his view, but he decided he did not have time to waste. Loosing the shaft, he leapt forward, drawing his sword and casting aside his bow. The onyx blade glowed brightly and whined eerily.

The creature arched backward with Kaplyn's arrow embedded in its side. Crashing though the undergrowth, Kaplyn leapt from the bushes, screaming his defiance as the grakyn struggled with the shaft, trying at the same time to draw its own weapon. The grakyn partly turned, shouting words of power as Kaplyn, half stumbling on the uneven ground, swung his blade around in a wide arc, bringing the blade down on the grakyn's neck.

It died mid-syllable. The enchanted blade sent the head crashing into the fire, throwing up a shower of sparks into the night sky. For several seconds the body remained standing, defying death; then all at once it collapsed, falling in an untidy heap at Kaplyn's feet.

Tumarl rose like a man possessed, his eyes wide with fear. The great cry he had summoned welled up from deep within his soul and, with every ounce of his strength, leapt from his lips to echo loudly through the night air. It was a wail of utter terror and anguish, instantly waking Lars and Lomar. They stared up at him as he continued to scream while Kaplyn stood over the grakyn's body, a strange gleam in his eye and a glowing sword crooning softly in his hand.

The cry resounded about the hills until Kaplyn could no longer be sure whether or not there were other voices mixed with the echoes.

"Grab your things!" he snapped, sweeping up his own pack and scattering the dying embers over the wet ground. Swiftly, he returned to find his bow.

Tumarl remained motionless, panting with fear.

"Come," Lomar urged, gripping Tumarl's arm.

As soon as they were ready, Kaplyn led the way down the steep slope and for some time they kept up their dangerous flight, gasping for breath and sweating profusely until all at once the tree line ended and they found themselves on open ground. The slope was no longer as steep, and running was much easier now that they could see a short distance ahead.

They raced towards a long line of trees, pausing once they entered the partial cover.

"Hush," Kaplyn said, trying to listen in case anyone followed, but it was hard to hear over their ragged breathing. He hoped the enemy sentries might assume Tumarl's cry was that of a night predator making a kill; it had sounded inhuman enough.

"Let's go," Kaplyn whispered when he was sure there was no sign of pursuit. He urged them along the tree line and as they ran told them what he had seen, his words ragged as he panted for breath.

The others glanced fearfully back as they continued their flight. Soon the ground became undulating, making the going more difficult. Then all at once the tree line ended, and they were forced to cross open ground, running as fast as they were able.

They were bone weary, yet Kaplyn drove them on. The memory of the grakyn was too fresh in his mind, and that they could fly meant the enemy could scout miles ahead with little difficulty.

Kaplyn groaned as the moon peeked through the clouds, illuminating the grassy plain before them. Its silvery light reflected from a wide river to their front. Lars stumbled and cursed roundly as he recovered his balance, arms flailing the air.

In the still night air Kaplyn could hear the constant roar of water splashing over rocks, suggesting the river was in flood.

"Where now?" Lomar asked.

"Tumarl, do you recognise where we are?" Kaplyn asked.

"This must be the Torrid," Tumarl exclaimed breathlessly. "We must be on the Plains of Rhye. That's good news; the river leads to CarCamel, the capital."

"That could be miles," Kaplyn replied in frustration. Looking back, the mountains dominated the skyline and, although they had been travelling for several hours, they had only covered a short distance. Silently he cursed, knowing their news could not wait. Without further ado, he set off with the others following.

Before they had gone far, a large shape by the riverbank materialised from the gloom. The sound of racing water intensified and as they drew closer, they realised an entire tree had been jettisoned upon the bank by the storm waters.

Lomar came alongside Kaplyn, pointing to the dark silhouette. "We could push that out into the river and use it as a raft."

No one objected although if they had been less tired, they might have, but they did not have the energy to go much farther on foot. Leaning against the trunk, they pushed the tree into the turgid water. Without Lars to help them, the task would have been daunting but, even tired as he was, the big man's strength was phenomenal.

Shortly they had the tree in the water and a raging torrent foamed and bubbled around them. It was only then they realised the foolhardiness of the plan. The force of the water was greater than they had expected and, without warning, the tree was soon racing along, dragging them in its wake.

Kaplyn needed all of his strength to pull himself along the branch he was clinging to, fighting against the dead weight of his wet clothes and boots. Each time he came close to the trunk, the tree bobbed erratically, submerging him for long seconds before he could re-surface. He jettisoned his pack knowing its weight might pull him under.

Then the water slowed and, in the brief respite, he managed to climb up onto the trunk, scrabbling to find a purchase. In front of him, Tumarl also succeeded in clambering aboard.

Kaplyn turned about looking for the others. Lomar was clinging precariously to the tree with one leg hooked over the trunk. Together they hoisted the albino onto the unstable platform.

Lars was missing and frantically they called his name as the tree raced along. A cry sounded behind them and Kaplyn and Tumarl crawled back to help. Lars' head and shoulders were all that showed above the water line, and it was clear that it was as much as he could do to hold on. Kaplyn leant out, trying desperately to reach the big man with Tumarl holding onto his belt. His efforts were sufficient to enable Lars to change his grip, and he managed to haul himself onto the trunk. Gripping the rough bark with their thighs the four men clung desperately on. They could not guess the speed with which they were travelling but the noise alone suggested the river was rushing along at a fast pace. By now they were frozen and their teeth chattered uncontrollably.

Many hours later, birds sang, greeting the dawn and, in the half-light, they could see the riverbank rushing by. Then abruptly, the tree ran aground, throwing Lomar from its relative safety into the water. He had been dozing and the sudden stop jarred him awake, but too late to stop himself falling into the tangled mass of branches.

He would have drowned if the others had not been able to rescue him. None too gently, Lars lifted his head from the water, holding his white hair in his fist as the others grabbed his arms and pulled with all of their failing strength. Coughing, he lay on the bank, shivering uncontrollably. The others were no better for the experience, and they collapsed where they stood, staring balefully at the stranded tree.

Tumarl finally arose. Clambering up the steep bank, he peered cautiously over the top to see where they were and one by one the others joined him.

"I think I recognise this place," Tumarl said above the noise of the river. "We are about two miles north of Amfarl, a small town on the northern borders of Thrace."

"Hopefully we can persuade someone to loan us horses," Kaplyn said. The others clearly did not share his optimism as they set off, limping across the soft turf.

"It doesn't make sense," Lomar stated, more to himself than to the others. "Krell are nocturnal creatures. Why then were they camped at night? I mean, wouldn't they march at night and camp during the day?"

"Perhaps they were waiting for something?" Lars suggested.

"I didn't see the encampment clearly," Kaplyn said, "but it was sizeable judging by the number of fires. That is another thing that is odd," he added, slightly puzzled. "Why do they need campfires if they are nocturnal?"

"Perhaps there were men there as well," Lomar suggested.

"Is it possible the army is from Trosgarth?" Tumarl asked.

It was a depressing thought; Trosgarth was a bitter enemy of the other nations. With heavy hearts, they continued walking across the open ground and Kaplyn looked grim as, unconsciously, he fingered the scar beneath his shirt.

They fell silent, concentrating on their journey through open fields, passing only one farm that looked deserted.

"Perhaps a war has already started," Lars suggested, seeing the desolation. None replied, but their thoughts were troubled.

At the top of a rise, they came across a cart track and their progress became easier, although the direction took them away from the river.

"This should take us straight to Amfarl," Tumarl declared, striding along the hard packed earth, rutted with the passage of countless farm carts. He seemed to be a lot more cheerful now they were on familiar ground; his stride had become more purposeful as though the very earth was nourishing his limbs.

They soon saw the protective walls encircling a small town, but, even though it was still early in the morning, there was little sign of life. Kaplyn's foreboding grew as they approached.

The gates were wide open and there were no guards. With mounting trepidation, they entered the empty street. A goat bleated loudly from within the shadows to their left and darted for the gateway and the countryside beyond, narrowly missing Lars and causing the big man to skip to one side.

A figure carrying a heavy load emerged from a doorway, a look of surprise on his face. He was middle-aged, shabbily dressed, with a crop of wild unkempt hair and several days' growth upon his sun-reddened face. For a moment he looked as though he were about to run, but his burden prevented him. He smiled as they approached.

"There's plenty for everyone, so help yourselves," he said, indicating the open door from which he had emerged. Kaplyn noticed the hinges were broken.

"Just look under the beds," the fellow added. "That's where they keep their valuables."

"Where is everyone?" Tumarl asked.

The man grinned. "Where've you been ... asleep?" he started to guffaw nervously while looking for indications of whether they were friend or foe. Kaplyn could see the contents of the box the man carried; it was full of odds and ends, some clearly valuable and others not so.

"He's a looter," Kaplyn muttered. He placed a hand on the hilt of his sword, a move which did not go unnoticed by the wild-looking man who immediately became agitated.

"Take it, if that's what you want," he held his load out to Lars; "I don't mean no harm."

Seeing that Lars was not going to take his burden, he started to place it on the ground, then paused reluctant to lose his new found wealth. His eyes darted nervously from side to side, seeking an escape. Kaplyn moved closer.

"What's going on?" Kaplyn growled. "Where are the people?"

The man backed away, stopping when he found himself against the wall of the house.

"They've gone," he whined. "To CarCamel. The king's soldiers came and told them to pack what they could carry and leave the rest."

"When?" asked Tumarl in disbelief.

"Two days since!" the man exclaimed nervously.

"What about the farms nearby?"

"They've all gone. The soldiers took them as well. No one stayed except me; I hid until all the fuss died down."

"They must be aware of the krell army then," Lars stated, looking at Kaplyn who nodded, annoyed by the looter, not liking thieves.

Suddenly, with surprising speed the stranger threw his load at Lars and, as Lars crashed backwards, he ran along the long row of houses, heading for the town gates.

Lars was about to follow, but Kaplyn restrained him.

"Let him go. He's of no use to us," he said.

Briefly they searched the town. To their dismay, there were no horses, so there was nothing else left to do but to walk, and they set off, hoping to keep ahead of any pursuit. The road from Amfarl was well made and they made steady progress. After a short way, they came across a few abandoned possessions, strewn in disarray across the road, as the town's refugees had fled in obvious haste.

For two days, they walked and at night took shelter within desolate farm buildings. There was no food and little or no sign of game. Their bellies growled and even Lars had to take his belt in another notch.

Kaplyn had not mentioned his nightmares to the others for fear that they might question his sanity. At night he became too afraid to sleep and, when he did, the evil stench of dragons seemed to surround him. His every sleeping moment was a nightmare; he felt as though dragons were searching for him. A name, Shastlan, kept recurring, but he did not know what it signified. It was with relief that he awoke in the mornings to continue their journey so he could forget his dreams for a while.

On the third day since leaving Amfarl, the river converged with their path and, on the next day, they finally saw the tall walls of the city in the distance. It was an awe-inspiring sight, with dark clouds massing behind the city. CarCamel was located on a vast plain which was only interrupted by a small hill and a few copses. At this point, the river snaked around the city, forming a protective moat on the city's western side.

As they approached, they saw jetties and, to their relief, small boats unloading their wares whilst others were furling their sails. Bright pennants flew from tall turrets, a splash of colour against the grey stone. To Kaplyn and the others, the city was a glorious sight and its stout walls looked more than welcome after their long nights of fear. Quickening their pace, they hurried towards the city and safety. They had made it.

Chapter 6

Traitors All!

The road ran down from their present position to the main gates which were open wide. A queue of people, carts and farm animals were waiting to gain access and at that moment a shaft of sunlight fell on the gate as though pointing the way.

As Kaplyn's group joined the queue the sunlight failed and it started to rain. The people groaned as they huddled against the wall for shelter. One man kept glancing at Lomar, and Kaplyn realised why; the albino's white skin and hair were unusual, to say the least. Kaplyn motioned to Lomar to draw his hood up.

The delay was frustrating but Kaplyn realised that their news of a krell army could wait a while longer and tried to relax, going over in his mind what he would say. He had not met any of the Thracian royal family at Allund functions of state before and now wished he had.

The King was Arlan, he remembered — a bear of a man with a temper to match, or at least so his father had said. Then there had been Prince Tharrad and Princess Gwen. Both were about Kaplyn's age and his father had often threatened Kaplyn with marriage to Gwen By all accounts she was not a beauty. No matter how hard he thought, he couldn't remember the names of any other royals.

Growing restless Kaplyn looked ahead to see what was causing the delay. Three sentries and a Guard Commander were seated at a table by the main gate. The Commander wore a long grey cloak embroidered with silver thread and was questioning each person before allowing them access.

Gradually the queue lessened and soon they found themselves at the front. The Commander looked up at them with curiosity but frowned when he saw Lomar's hood was up.

"Remove your hood," he said with a wave of his hand.

Kaplyn's heart sank. As Lomar swept the hood back the Commander leapt to his feet, drawing his sword.

"*By the Kalanth*, a demon!" he hissed. His men levelled their weapons at the albino.

"Wait," Kaplyn urged. "He's *not* a demon. Look to your fires."

The men glanced behind them; within the guard room, a brazier burned brightly. The flames were orange, not blue which would have been the case if a demon were present.

"Who are you and where are you from?" the Commander demanded, keeping his sword aimed at Lomar's chest. By now others were crowding about the gate to see what the commotion was all about.

"I am Lomar, an Alvalan from Gilfillan," he replied.

The Commander continued to stare uncertainly at the albino, looking deeply into his scarlet eyes as if trying to read his mind. Finally he looked at Lars. "And you?" he asked.

"Lars from Gorlanth," the big man said, clearly not liking being interrogated. Lars, too, was an enigma. Thracians and Allunds were dark-haired and dark-eyed, but Lars was fair.

The Guard Commander turned to look at Kaplyn.

"Kaplyn—from Dundalk."

"Dundalk!" the Commander snapped, backing away and toppling his chair with a crash. His weapon wavered uncertainly between Lomar and Kaplyn.

"An Allund spy," the Commander blurted, barely able to suppress a smile. "Drop your weapons."

"What! I'm *not* a spy," Kaplyn said, but he could see that the other man was in no mood to listen. Angrily, he unbuckled his sword belt, letting it drop to the ground along with his bow and arrows.

"Call out the guard," the Commander ordered. One of the soldiers left to comply.

"We're not spies! I'm from Allund," Kaplyn insisted.

"Then you admit your guilt," the Commander replied.

Kaplyn looked perplexed. "What guilt?" he asked.

"We are at war!" the Commander replied angrily.

"With Trosgarth?" Kaplyn said.

The Guard Commander, clearly put out by his stupidity, moved closer to Kaplyn and said with a glower, "With Allund!"

The news stunned Kaplyn. Just then the soldier returned, accompanied by a squad of men still donning their uniforms as they ran to the gate, trailing spears.

"I'm Thracian!" Tumarl declared. "I barely know these men."

"Then you should choose your friends more carefully," the Commander returned.

"I've been a prisoner of the krell for the last two years. I know nothing about a war," Tumarl answered.

The Commander was not sympathetic, "You'll get a chance to defend yourself. At your trial." He was smiling confidently as his men drew up in file.

"Take over, Thackary," he said to one of the men who saluted in response. "Pick up their weapons," he ordered two others. "Kaldran, take the rest of the guard and march the prisoners to the dungeons and assign two men to stand watch until I can get them relieved."

Kaldran saluted smartly before issuing orders to the men. The prisoners were formed up in single file and then marched towards the gates.

"We are *not* spies," Kaplyn insisted between clenched teeth, stopping suddenly and turning to confront the Guard Commander whose eyes blazed angrily.

A soldier rammed the butt of a spear into his back forcing him forward. He stood his ground, looking into the surly Commander's eyes.

Kaplyn tried once more. "Look, you have to listen. There's an army from Trosgarth on your northern borders. You *must* warn your superiors!"

The butt of the spear caught him once again, but more firmly and he was forced to continue. He was angry and could not believe what was happening. They had made it to CarCamel, but not to the welcome he had anticipated.

Chapter 7

The King's Dilemma

Sharroch, the Thracian monarch, sat on his high-backed throne, drumming his fingers on the wooden armrest, irritated by his advisors' counsel and angry with his Tharn Commanders. He was a small, portly man, and yet he carried an air of dignity that belied his shape and size. He considered himself a young man, having just reached fifty, no great age for a monarch, but he had the uneasy feeling that, under the present circumstances, he might not live to see his next birthday.

Why could he have not been a king during more pleasant times? he thought sourly, casting a withering glance at the assembled men. *Dullards!*

He ran a hand through his greying hair. His beard had long since lost its battle with time and was completely white. A headache was threatening and with every passing moment his temper was rising.

Let anyone step out of line now and by damn he would have his head!

He looked around the table at the assembled men. Two Tharn Commanders looked uncertainly back while the third regarded the deep shine of the counsel room table as though occupied by the reflection. It was these Tharn Commanders who were presently bearing the brunt of his anger.

The only man whose counsel he truly trusted was Astalus, the Court Wizard, who sat with two of his colleagues by his side. Astalus deserved respect, being the youngest man in the history to gain the Master Wizard's Staff; an achievement that no doubt the two old greybeards with him envied.

Much to the relief of all within the room, the King stopped drumming. "Explain to me once more," he exploded, his face turning red, "why we are on the brink of war with an ancient ally? Your advice has led me to this present course and now an army marches against us!" The men around the table remained mute.

"Astalus!" the King addressed the young magician. "What is the size of their army?"

The young wizard turned his steady gaze to meet the King's, which was more than could be said for two of the Tharn Commanders who were having difficulty finding something inanimate to look at. The third, Ballan, sat like a rock amongst sheep.

"Sire, a power conceals it. But it's poorly done," Astalus said swiftly, seeing his monarch's look of displeasure. "I have estimated their strength at between fifty and sixty thousand foot and possibly ten thousand cavalry. There is another, smaller force with them whose nature we have not been able to divine."

The King smiled; Astalus had said the army was concealed, and yet he had still found the necessary information. At least he could be trusted. He glanced at the staff that Astalus carried. It reputedly contained, bound by an eagle's claw, the oldest and most powerful kara-stone in existence. A hideous head had been shaped into the wood beneath the claw reminding the King of the supposed curse. Anyone not ordained to touch it would die a slow and agonizing death. He looked back into Astalus' cool dark eyes, seeing in them a reflection of the courage it must have taken to take charge of it.

"And where are they now?" the King asked more quietly.

"No more than two days march, Sire," the magician answered.

The King glanced at his son, Prince Alyn, who was watching the magician through hooded eyes. The King cursed silently, hating the fact that his kingdom was on the verge of war during his reign and fearful that his family might come to harm. Alyn was not a warrior, nor was he a leader of men. It had taken all of the King's anger to make him attend the meeting and, even now, he looked bored.

If anything should happen to me? the King wondered. He was glad at least that he had persuaded his daughter, the Princess Catriona, not to attend, although he had done so by locking her in her room. He did not relish the confrontation when he released her.

"Sire!" interrupted one of the Tharn Commanders. The King looked up angrily. Ballan shifted uneasily beneath the King's stern look. He was a well-built man, as strong as a grall with many years of loyal service. The King trusted him more than the other two tharns. Their immaculately tailored uniforms with gold embroidery and silver buttons bespoke their wealth which was the main reason they had risen to the ranks they now held.

Ballan carried himself with dignity and, even though he was older than the King, his hair was still dark.

"Sire, it is not too late to ambush the Allund force tonight while they sleep. We could hit them hard and then retreat to CarCamel before they reorganise."

The King shook his head. "I will not be the instigator of this war. Later, I may regret that decision, but I will not have history remembering us as butchers!"

"But Sire," interrupted Tharn Shelder, a thin faced man with a long bushy moustache, a style favoured by the senior ranks, "the last emissary sent to the Allunds did not return. We have done everything possible to obtain peace from these stiff-necked Allunds; if it must come to war then we are ready!"

"We do not *know* what became of the emissary," the King answered. "They may never have reached Dundalk! We must reason with Allund before this mess gets any worse." He glanced at Tharn Alder. Of the three he was by far the worst. He was a peacock of a man and several times during his meteoric rise to power, the King had thought to intervene but had refrained from doing so for the simple reason that he had never thought it would come to this. It had never occurred to him his tharns would be required to lead his people to war. Alder simply smiled as though the proceedings were an unnecessary interruption to his day.

At that moment, a commotion at the door interrupted the King's thoughts. A Hest Commander entered, saluting smartly. "Sire, I have an urgent message for Tharn Alder."

The King gestured for the newcomer to continue.

"Tharn, we have captured an Allund spy."

The news prompted excited murmurs and even the King sat up.

"Indeed, this is good news," the King stated, hoping it might either prove or disprove Allund's hostile intent. Alder sat back, basking in the momentary glory.

"Where was this man apprehended?" the King asked.

"Sire. He was captured with three of his comrades at the main gate trying to gain entry to the city."

"And how did our men discover they were spies?" The King asked.

"When questioned, he said he was from Dundalk."

Tharn Alder put his head in his hands, knowing full well what was to follow. The King's face turned from its earlier red to purple as his brow beetled with suppressed fury.

"Surely this *cannot* be true!" he demanded. "Allund spies simply turn up at our gate and openly declare their intent. Are they so *confident* then, these men of Allund?"

The King's sarcasm was not lost on the unfortunate Hest Commander who now realised the news had been too good to be true.

"Bring me these spies, I would speak with them," the King roared, pushing himself back onto his throne, waiting for the cries of protest.

Tharn Shelder looked thunderstruck. "Sire, this might be what they are hoping for. To gain audience with Your Majesty and then use a spell to assassinate Your Highness."

The King grimaced. "Search them thoroughly and then bring them here!" he ordered. "If I am not safe amongst my tharns and Court Wizard, then where am I safe?"

The King started drumming the armchair, much to the annoyance of those present, and a nervous silence descended. Prince Alyn shifted uncomfortably on his chair; his look suggested that he, too, was afraid of his father's anger.

It took some time before the Hest Commander returned with an escort of twelve armed men and the prisoners. The King leant forward for a better look as they were herded into his presence. They were a motley group, tired and dispirited. Two of the men, an albino and a dark-haired man, bowed, suggesting they at least understood court etiquette. The third prisoner, a big man with fair hair and a beard tinged with ginger, followed their lead although somewhat uncertainly. The King looked at the fourth prisoner who stood defiantly, refusing to bow. His eyes blazed angrily.

The King sensed his ire and addressed him first.

"Who are you and where are you from?"

"Tumarl, from what was once the village of Neath," he said through clenched teeth.

"Neath was destroyed nearly a year ago," the King replied.

Tumarl nodded. "No thanks to Your Highness and the protection of your Tharns."

Ballan rose angrily to his feet and faced Tumarl. "Remember you are in the presence of your Monarch!"

The King raised a hand to silence his tharn. "And where have you been since Neath was destroyed?"

"I was a captive of the krell, forced to work as a slave with the others of my village. Until they died within their shackles, that is!"

Things were getting too far out of hand and so stepping forward Kaplyn sought to interrupt. "Sire, I have important news," he declared abruptly,

257

glancing at Tumarl with a stern look, hoping to silence the other man before he damned them all.

Grateful for the interruption, the King turned to face Kaplyn. "Speak!" he commanded.

"There's an army of krell in the mountains to your north," Kaplyn declared. "We have travelled swiftly to bring you this news."

The King frowned while the others about the room muttered angrily.

"Be warned! It's an Allund trick!" Shelder said rising to his feet.

"If it is, it is a devious ploy," the King replied sitting back, "for I cannot make sense of it."

"We were in the PanAmPelleas mountains when we met Tumarl. He had escaped from a krell slave mine," Kaplyn continued. "I was out hunting when I saw the army. Sire, it is immense and can only be from Trosgarth."

"Trosgarth!" hissed the King. "What has that vile name to do with this?"

"This could be a ploy just to turn our attention north, my Liege," Shelder insisted. By his side Alder nodded.

Prince Alyn, who had so far remained silent, now leant forward to address the group. "Could Astalus verify this news?"

Stroking his beard the King said, "An excellent idea. Astalus, can you do this?"

"Surely, Sire," replied the young magician. "If an army exists, we should be able to locate it."

"So be it," Sharroch commanded.

Astalus arose and excused himself so that he could make the necessary preparations.

"Sire," Kaplyn tried once more. "I am Prince Orlastor," he said using his Court name. "And my father is the King of Allund." Kaplyn had expected his news to be a shock, but their reaction startled him.

"What is this? Are you mocking us? There is no king in Allund!" Sharroch countered.

"Of course there is," Kaplyn insisted angrily. "You of all people should remember, Sire, for were you not at my father's wedding?"

"This deception has gone too far, Sire," Tharn Shelder interrupted angrily.

By his side Alder nodded vigorously. "This man's obviously deranged and I cannot see the point in continuing to waste time while an Allund army threatens."

Several others around the table nodded their agreement, but something stopped the King from denouncing the stranger immediately.

"Who do you think I am?" he demanded.

Kaplyn frowned. "King Arlan," he replied, sensing a trap.

The others muttered angrily as Lomar looked at Kaplyn. Kaplyn's eyes clouded and he turned towards Lomar; as their eyes met, realisation dawned, "You knew!" Kaplyn accused.

Lomar shook his head. "I guessed, but I was not certain."

"Leave us!" The King stated flatly of his courtiers. His son looked at him questioningly, and the King nodded that he should remain. The Tharns started to protest, but the King repeated the command to leave. At that moment Astalus entered accompanied by two men carrying a brazier and kindling. The King gestured to Astalus to remain while the others filed sullenly out of the room until only Kaplyn and his companions remained.

A silence descended. "Repeat what you have just told me, about who you think I am."

"King Arlan?" Kaplyn replied. His eyes looked haunted.

"Your grandfather?" Astalus asked, turning to the King.

"Sit down," the King suggested sternly to Kaplyn and the others.

The four men sat, each looking pale.

"And who are you?" the King asked addressing Lomar.

"I am Prince Lomar and my people are the Alvalah from the forest of KinAnar."

"And you?" the King asked of Lars.

"I am Lars Asthandor from Gorlanth," the big man replied. The King looked puzzled as his attention went back to Kaplyn.

"You have something to say, I think?" he said simply.

Shocked, Kaplyn could not speak. Lomar answered on his behalf.

"Kaplyn, for that is how we have come to know him, has I think guessed what has happened. I had some inkling, but I was not certain." He, too, looked dejected.

"We were travelling companions of a sorcerer, one of the Narlassar, I believe. He betrayed us and we fell foul of a spell which ensnared us, turning us to stone."

Lomar glanced at Tumarl who looked horrified with the confirmation he had been correct and they were stone when he found them. "Tumarl found us. He was followed by a grakyn and, from his account, it appears the grakyn, thinking that we were alive, attacked us and somehow its magic shattered the spell, releasing us.

"When we came round we assumed that it was autumn of the same year since the trees were turning colour and the weather was so cold. Now I realise our error — it was not the same year, but much later."

259

Lomar fell silent, too afraid to say what he feared.

"It would be about sixty years later," Astalus said quietly.

"Sixty years!" Lars repeated incredulously. *"By Slathor*! That *cannot* be!"* He looked up at the others who were watching his expression with a mixture of disbelief and sorrow as unshed tears filled his eyes. "My wife, my son!" he groaned, shaking his head. He sat down heavily and buried his head in his hands.

Kaplyn nodded, "My parents, my family?"

"Astalus, is this possible, or is it part of an elaborate hoax?" The King asked, looking at Lars whose face was ashen.

"I could not weave such a spell, Sire, nor could any of the Akrane. But," Astalus continued slowly, "a Narlassar sorcerer could."

"If true, it's a dreadful tale," the King stated bluntly, looking at Kaplyn. "If you are lying, I for one do not know what you hope to achieve."

"There's still the question of the krell army, Sire," Astalus reminded the King.

"Bring in the others," the King said. "Do not repeat anything you have said here," he said, looking at Kaplyn darkly. "In our presence, you are Kaplyn!"

Kaplyn nodded. "One last thing, Sire. You said that there was no king in Allund. What became of my family?"

The King paused for a moment as though judging Kaplyn's strength. He was not sure whether he was lying or not. Sorcery was a dark art, and the King could only guess at what might be possible. He remembered the first time he had seen a wizard perform a spell. It had been a simple spell to provide light for a banquet, but at the time it had been a marvel.

"There was a revolution many years ago. It started when the King was assassinated. The members of the royal household were reported to have been taken prisoner and were never heard of again. A Council of twelve men now rule, but many believe that the Priests of Ryoch hold the real power."

The name seemed familiar to Kaplyn, but, for the moment, he could not remember. Suddenly he did and it left a sour taste in his mouth. The priests he had encountered at Hallar's castle were supporters of a new god, Ryoch, and their words now came back to haunt him like a curse as the others re-entered the room.

"Sire, we are ready to proceed," Astalus interrupted. The brazier was lit and by his side he held a pouch of herbs.

"Come," the King said. He and his advisers gathered around the fire. Kaplyn stood by Astalus' side, staring into the orange coals.

"I can use any flame for seeing, but the wood from the Yarra tree works best," Astalus explained as he took a pinch of herbs from the pouch, scattering these on the flames which hissed, momentarily burning a dark green. Astalus muttered words of power while his fingers traced a rune in the air above the coals, just as Kaplyn had seen Vastra doing so long ago. The memory prompted a sudden anger. He glanced at Tumarl with a clearer understanding of his hatred and his desire for revenge.

Gradually the flame grew quieter but brighter, and Kaplyn's eyes were drawn into the embers until he suddenly felt as though he were looking beyond the coals; an image formed before his eyes. He gasped audibly and tried to draw back, but was held by his own curiosity and his desire to be vindicated of the current charges.

"Look into the flame," Astalus was saying. Slowly a scene appeared which caused the onlookers to reel with vertigo. They had a bird's eye view of the countryside far below.

"That is the river Torrid several miles north of here," Tharn Ballan explained, standing by Kaplyn's side.

"Can you follow the river up stream?" Kaplyn asked.

Instantly the scene shifted, the ground scrolling eerily beneath their gaze and they watched as the river swept by.

"Stop!" Tumarl yelled as he peered over Tharn Shelder's shoulder. Astalus visibly jumped and the scene failed momentarily before reappearing. "I think that's where we joined the river," Tumarl said to Kaplyn. "You can see the broken branches left by the tree and the scar where we dragged it into the water."

Kaplyn nodded. "We need to go uphill to that tree line there," he confirmed. "There's a valley about a mile northwest from that point."

The view moved onwards and a forest appeared on a mountain slope. Moments went by and it was Kaplyn's turn to halt the proceedings. "That's the place where I saw the army," he confirmed, although there was nothing to see other than trees and grass and a small stream. There was, however, no sign of an army; Kaplyn could sense the King's eyes on him.

Tharn Shelder smiled knowingly at Tharn Alder.

"They *were* there," Kaplyn exclaimed in bewilderment. "I swear it!"

"And yet there is nothing there now," interrupted Tharn Shelder; "No campfires, or the rubbish that a large army could hardly avoid leaving in its wake."

"Wait!" Astalus stated softly, still concentrating hard. "If you look carefully, there is something not quite right." He pointed into the fire. The King leant closer. "See the trees in the valley," Astalus continued.

"Well?" the King asked irritably.

"They are not moving with the wind in the same way as those on the valley's edge." At the location Astalus pointed to, the trees thinned and their tops swayed gently in the breeze, but around them other trees swayed more violently. The difference was small, but noticeable.

Kaplyn frowned, "Could it be a freak down-draught?" he asked.

"The difference is too marked," Astalus said.

"What does it matter if a few trees are moving differently?" the King asked.

"When we tried to spy on the Allund army, there was a dark cloud surrounding them, impenetrable to our magic. That is a simple way of preventing us from spying, but we knew there was an army because of the cloud."

He paused for a moment as the others considered what he had said.

"If you do not want someone to know that an army is in hiding, then the problem is more difficult. A sorcerer can make an area appear as it was, say, two or three days ago, before an army was in position. The difficulty is in keeping the sorcerer's concentration upon the task which becomes very wearisome, and, after a while, lapses in detail may occur."

"Such as the wind in the trees?" Kaplyn asked.

"We have no way of knowing if an army is there though?" the King asked.

Astalus shook his head.

"Could you make the wind strength increase and watch the effect on the trees within the valley?" Lomar asked.

Astalus smiled. "It's a good suggestion, but I lack the power to do so especially at a distance Besides it would alert an enemy that we are aware of them, if one exists, that is."

"Could you look for where we camped and see if the grakyn's body is still there?" Lars suggested.

Astalus agreed and, with Kaplyn's help, they located their camp, although it took several searches among the thick mass of trees. Eventually, they found the spot. The signs of a scattered fire were visible, and they could just make out a dark body lying close to the remains of the fire. The King's eyebrows arched in surprise at the sight of the grakyn, but it was still far from the proof he needed.

"I want to know what is in that valley," he said at length, "And quickly. Tharn Ballan, send riders to investigate."

"That might not be wise, Sire," Astalus suggested. "If someone is trying to hide an army then they are going to great lengths to do so. Surely they

262

will have scouts who will spot riders coming up the valley in broad daylight."

The King nodded. "Have you another suggestion?" he asked.

Astalus smiled, "I have an idea which might work."

"See to it then," the King commanded.

Astalus packed his equipment and took his leave, bowing respectfully as he left.

"Take these men to the prison," the King said to the Hest Commander who, after his recent blunder, was all too eager to please his majesty. He quickly complied, leaving the room with Kaplyn, his companions and an escort. "See to it that they are treated well," the King called after them as they left.

As the door closed behind them, the Tharns started to protest.

"Sire, this is pointless. These men may have been sent to deliberately disrupt our preparations," insisted Tharn Shelder. "Besides, even if there is a krell army, who is to say it is not in league with Allund?"

It was a good point, but the King was not convinced.

"If there is an army from Trosgarth, then it is not too late to gain the aid of the Southern Kingdoms, but I need proof."

The King returned to his throne and sat down wearily.

"It may be prudent to send another emissary to talk to the Allunds," Prince Alyn suggested.

The King nodded. "We will wait first to see what Astalus can find out, and then, perhaps, this news will help to sway the Allund Commander, one way or the other."

The King dismissed his tharns. All in all, they were as ready as they could be, but the King's heart was heavy as he brooded in the silence of the large hall. They were in good strength since their forces were concentrated at CarCamel. They had a plentiful supply of food and the city had three deep wells plus there was always the river.

So far, the Southern Kingdoms had refused his repeated requests for aid. It was judged a squabble between two neighbouring kingdoms, and none of the old treaties encompassed such an event. Inwardly he cursed, frustrated that he reigned in troubled times. Not for the last time he wished for better times.

Chapter 8

Wizard's Gambit

Astalus and his two companions crowded around the narrow window set high in one of the city's many inner towers, peering out at a black crow which squawked loudly and flapped its wings in indignation. The sleek bird peered back at them as it settled once more on its perch, hugging the window ledge of the facing tower. It looked uncomfortable but remained steadfast as if to spite them.

Although the crow did not know it, the wizard's tower was a place to be feared and few dared venture there. Like the wizard's ancient staff, it was believed to be protected by charms and curses and each night bright flashes confirmed this, lighting the dark building and silhouetting the tower in stark contrast to its slumbering neighbours. Not that the crow understood anything about curses, however ….

In reality, most of the wizards' work was mundane. Often the inhabitants only performed simple spells in their laboratory, a place cluttered with many strange utensils and stacks of drying herbs and plants.

The rumour about the tower being cursed was (most likely) unfounded, but the wizards were too prudent to allow the truth to be generally known. And besides, it kept the inquisitive at bay — the only disadvantage being that it was impossible to find a cleaner. Such, however, was the life of a wizard.

Meanwhile, by the window, Astalus was busy trying to summon the sullen crow which was still eyeing the wizard as though he were a maggot crawling from a half-eaten apple. One of the other two wizards, enjoying the spectacle when he could see over Astalus' shoulder, was mumbling that the spell could not be done. This, along with the crow's stubbornness, was starting to irritate the Master Wizard. After all he had promised the King he would find out what was in the valley, and he was a very determined man.

Suddenly, with a flurry of wings, the crow abruptly appeared at the window. Astalus, who had momentarily lost concentration, jumped back startled. The other two men also leapt backward so that all three men stood huddled together, watching the black apparition as if they expected to be attacked at any moment. The crow squawked loudly as if warning them anything was possible.

"See!" Astalus declared triumphantly, recovering swiftly from his shock and trying to claim that the bird's actions were due to his own influence. "Those who doubt, fail." It was his favourite saying and it annoyed Gant terribly, as well he knew.

Gant scowled. "Be that as it may, you should not *crow* about your achievement" he said, smiling whilst Corrin scowled at the pun. "Besides," he added with a sly glint in his eye, "how do we know that the crow came because of your bidding and not the bread you are holding?"

Astalus suddenly remembered the bread in his hand and the crow screeched raucously as though in agreement. Astalus flung the bread onto the floor and straightaway the bird hopped down from the windowsill, pecking at the morsel and chasing it around the room.

Corrin tried to suppress a smile, but failed miserably and was rewarded by a withering look from Astalus who then returned his attention to the feeding crow, concentrating once more and extending his arm. Gant and his companion watched in silence; both had seen remarkable feats accomplished by the younger man, and although they goaded him, they respected him highly.

The crow seemed to sense Astalus, and it stopped eating, fixing its beady eyes on him and hopping from foot to foot in agitation. With a final squawk it flapped its wings, launching itself across the intervening space to alight upon his arm. Astalus reached around with his free arm and stroked the bird's head, smiling broadly.

"He will do as I bid!" he declared confidently, causing both Gant and Corrin to raise their eyebrows, knowing full well that they had not heard the last of this.

"We need to prepare a spell to accompany him on his journey," Astalus continued, stroking the bird's head. "A spell of seeing will enable us to penetrate a magic shield."

He threw the bird forward, allowing it to fly back to the food with another raucous cry. As it ate, the three magicians set about preparing the spell. In a mortise bowl they mixed herbs, pummelling them into a powder then adding liquid from a bottle taken from one of the many overcrowded shelves. When the work was complete, Astalus once more summoned the crow which hopped across the floor and with a flurry of wings alighted on the table.

Astalus dipped a finger in the liquid and traced invisible symbols on the creature's back. It let out a loud squawk but suffered the indignity of the wizard's touch.

Seeing the creature so docile, Gant reached out to touch it. A vicious beak stabbed at his outstretched hand and the wizard leapt backwards with a startled cry, cursing the monster. Astalus grinned at the older man as he traced the final rune over the bird's feathers.

At last the crow was prepared, and again Astalus offered it his arm, allowing it to jump up like a docile pet. The bird sat there glaring darkly at Gant who continued to curse the creature, while holding his injured finger.

Astalus ignored the other man, walking instead to the window, speaking softly to the crow before launching it towards the opening. The three men leaned out to watch the bird swiftly climbing. With a final cry, it started to fly toward the distant mountains.

Astalus smiled. He had not wanted to fail in front of the other two men. With relief he went back to the bench where he pushed aside bowls and bottles cluttering its surface, placing his staff upon the freshly cleared space with the orb facing towards him. Confidently he sat down, closing his eyes, each breath deep and even as he concentrated on the growing power within the milky white stone. The other two wizards huddled over the orb which, for the moment, only reflected the grey of their beards.

Opening his eyes, Astalus peered into the crystal. All at once the whiteness was replaced by patterns of light which danced before coalescing into a faint yet distant image. An aerial view of the city sprang into the orb's milky whiteness; tall spires crowded together, interspersed with tiny cobbled streets full of antlike people scurrying about, unaware of the observers in their high tower. Slowly the palace scrolled into view as the crow flew over the gleaming white building and the ornate gardens.

As the bird continued its journey over the high city walls, the scene was replaced by lush open countryside and a view of the fast flowing Torrid. Astalus allowed himself a smile, having been truly vindicated now that the crow was doing his bidding.

Chapter 9

Confinement

Kaplyn shifted his weight upon the hard bench, staring into the dark. Their prison stank of decay. He was pondering their misfortune and his thoughts turned to his family and friends. Grief threatened to overwhelm him.

Memories of the evening spent in Kinlin castle returned and the three men claiming to be Priests of Ryoch. All too clearly, he remembered their veiled threats against his father. Now, surrounded by gloom and held prisoner in a foreign dungeon, he realised how serious these threats had been. Was it possible the priests had been the catalyst for turning his people against his father?

Angrily, he cursed, holding his head in his hands. He should have warned his father about the priests instead of coming on this wild errand. Again he cursed, frustrated with his incarceration while his people marched to war. It made no sense, especially with an army of krell poised on the northern borders. What did it mean? His mind continued to chew upon the gristle of his fears whilst his family's ghosts haunted his thoughts.

Tumarl fared no better. Crouching in a corner of the room hugging his knees to his chest, he was clearly ill at ease with the prospect of further incarceration after so many months as a slave in the krell mines. He sat apart from the others as though the blame for his plight were theirs.

He swallowed his anger, trying to control instead the growing feeling of panic. Images of long-lost friends drifted like ghostly shades before his tear-filled eyes. Fate had dealt a cruel blow in allowing him to escape certain death only to be imprisoned within the confines of his own homeland. He prayed for release and a chance to prove his innocence to his Monarch. As though in answer to his prayers, a soft radiance filled the room, bringing relief as the darkness was temporarily banished. His eyes quickly adjusted to the light before searching for its source. On the bench, Lomar held his kara-stone, partially shielding the glow with his body as he summoned the power from within it. Tumarl looked up at the others with a faint sob as the darkness and the ghosts were banished — for the moment at least.

Lomar smiled, looking sadly at the three men. "They did not search me very well," he explained softly.

Kaplyn looked away, not wanting the others to see his grief.

The light at least allowed them to see their prison. It was a cold, stark place with not even a window from which to look out. The walls were stained with damp, a clear sign that they were deep underground.

"What do you think will happen to us?" Lars asked, his voice choked with suppressed emotions.

"If there is an Allund army marching against Thrace, then we will be held as traitors whether our story is believed or not," Kaplyn said bitterly.

Lars hung his head. "Is it possible the spell held us for sixty years?"

"Yes," Lomar replied, looking into his eyes, watching the sadness reflected there.

For a long moment they remained silent, each lost within their own grief.

"Lomar, you have implied you can see the future?" Kaplyn asked. "What do you see?"

Lomar's crimson eyes looked into Kaplyn's as though wondering whether he was strong enough to know.

"The dreams are jumbled," he said. "I have seen a great many futures and in some I see both you and Lars. I was aware of your scar before we even met, but for some reason I never saw Vastra. Of the future...? I do not know what will happen because the images are confused. Some dreams are vivid while others are less so but more frequent."

"Tell us of one that concerns you most," Kaplyn asked.

Lomar nodded. "In one dream I saw Drachar's shade leading a host of demons against our armies on a great plain. Our forces withered under the onslaught, crumbling forever into the dust."

That was not what Kaplyn had wanted to hear. "What of the Eldric?" he asked. "Have you ever seen them? Can we expect their aid?" The Eldric were a race of people who disappeared mysteriously, many years ago, shortly after the Krell Wars. Many of the Eldric were sorcerers and in a future conflict their aid would be sorely missed.

Lomar shook his head and Kaplyn sat back dejected.

"If we ever needed the Eldric, it is now," Lomar admitted. "Without them we will have little hope against the dark forces of Trosgarth. It is made worse if Allund is their ally."

"That cannot be!" Kaplyn answered, although in his heart he was uncertain.

They fell silent once more and Lomar debated what else he could tell the others. Only in his dreams did the images seem to make sense. The more he tried to analyze them, the less he understood. Perhaps it was his spirit's ability to travel on the astral plain that enabled his uncanny visions of the future. In any event, it was a curse and he wished that he was like other men.

An image of Kaplyn in one such dream sprang to mind and he quickly dispelled it, not wishing to believe that Kaplyn could become the evil he had seen. Nervously he looked at Kaplyn and, for the moment, he feared him and the power that he bore more than he feared the shade of Drachar.

Chapter 10

Revelation

Princess Catriona paced the floor of her apartments, greatly annoyed with her father for locking her in her room. Briefly a smile replaced her scowl as she considered how long it had been since she had last been sent to her room. Instantly the smile vanished and she quickened her pace.

How could he, especially when their fate hung in the balance? She stopped her pacing and looked for something to throw. Moments later a vase smashed against the door, just seconds after a timid knock suggested that someone wanted to enter.

"Enter!" she yelled, hoping that it was her father come to apologise. For a moment her pacing was forgotten as she faced the door, the set of her shoulders suggesting she was not going to be pacified easily. A silence filled the room as though whoever had knocked had decided to beat a hasty retreat instead of facing her ire.

Catriona growled as she pulled on the handle, expecting it to be locked, but to her surprise it swung inwards. Before her stood her brother, Prince Alyn, a look of uncertainty on his youthful face. For a moment, brother and sister could only stare at each other in mutual surprise before the Princess started to laugh.

"I thought it was father," she explained, hiding her smile behind her hand and trying to be serious.

Her brother smiled, shaking his head. "I'm glad it wasn't. You should have seen the look on your face," he said, entering the room. He surveyed the mess with a look of mock disdain. "You know I once tried to make my own rooms untidy. Each time I did, the servants came in to clean."

Catriona sympathised. She liked her rooms untidy, in a way it was her way of rebelling. Now she was embarrassed by the clothes littering the furniture. Tables and chairs that had graced the palace for years now served only to keep clothing from falling to the floor.

Prince Alyn smiled as he cleared away garments to find a seat. Sitting as though exhausted he turned his attention to his sister. Catriona tried to suppress her look of eagerness for news, growing frustrated when he ignored her. Always, she had been more interested in the goings on of the court while Alyn preferred the company of friends; their time spent reading and talking.

"Well?" she asked, no longer able to conceal her impatience.

"It was, I suppose, less dull than usual," he said.

She sat down on the bed, kicking off her shoes. "What of Allund? Will it be war?"

"Allund! That's not the main news. Today the guard captured a spy and what is more he was accompanied by a remarkable man. His face and hair were both white, and his eyes scarlet. The people thought he was a demon, but they were wrong."

"A spy? Then it's true and Allund has chosen war."

The Prince laughed. "Do not be too keen for war. If we lose, you will have to marry an Allund!"

Catriona shook her head, smiling. "Don't be absurd. This city will never be defeated. The walls are twenty feet thick at least and I've seen Ballan training his men. He will not let the Allunds within bow-shot of the walls. No, they will turn tail and flee at the first sight of the gates. But what of the spy? Tell me about him."

The Prince shifted uncomfortably. "Father doesn't believe he is a spy," he confided. "Apparently he and his companions came up to the front gate as bold as brass and openly declared he was from Allund. When father questioned him he seemed to think father was great grandfather . . . I think."

The Princess scowled, not enjoying being made to look a fool.

"No, honestly. You should have been there. This man, the spy, said he had been held in a spell for at least sixty years."

His sister's face suddenly became serious and she stared at her brother, trying to divine whether he was telling the truth. "You are teasing me."

"No. And what is more, the man claimed to be an Allund prince."

Catriona shook her head in disbelief. "Don't be absurd. You are making this up." She was not sure though. Rarely did her brother tell lies.

"He seemed serious enough and I think he, at least, believed this."

Catriona's smile vanished. "What did Astalus say?" she asked, half afraid to hear the reply.

"Oh, he admitted that he could not perform such a spell, but he thought that a Narlassar sorcerer might be able to."

"What else did this man say?"

"Nothing much, just that there's a krell army on our northern borders," Alyn replied.

This time the Princess did not smile; instead her look became distant and a shiver made her wrap her arms about herself for warmth.

Astalus sat by the orb, a frown of concentration upon his brow as with every fibre of his being he directed the crow north.

Treetops flashed by, but he could still see the bright reflection from the river Torrid so knew, at least, that the crow was flying in the right direction. *Fly lower* he urged, but it stubbornly kept to the same elevation as though in this matter, at least, it would not concede.

As the distance between the crow and CarCamel grew, Astalus' hold over it diminished and he feared it would break free of his spell. At last, with evident relief, Astalus recognised the forest looming up ahead and once more willed the crow to descend. This time luck was with him, and he was rewarded by the sight of the trees coming closer.

Both Gant and Corrin watched their master in fascination though neither realised how tenuous the link truly was as the bird glided over the forest below.

The crow flew yards above the treetops, gliding on a thermal uplift until it spied a valley ahead. With a snap of its wings, it veered in that direction, aiming for a tall tree. At the last moment, it slowed, landing nimbly on a broad branch which swayed alarmingly.

The crow gave out a loud squawk as conflicting emotions raged inside it. Its every instinct was to fly away, but a stronger will held it in its sway and the result was that the crow remained perched stubbornly in the treetop, angrily glaring at the scene below.

An army was encamped all around it and the noise and smells sent a chill through the black bird. It sensed all too clearly that it should be elsewhere. It hopped on alternate feet as the two powers struggled for dominance. In mounting agitation the crow squawked loudly.

T'chark kicked the rotting branch, berating the long-limbed Lang for a fool. The branch shattered scattering fragments across the soft turf of the forest. An image of his superior came to mind and he bared his fangs in anger. He had been ordered from the shelter to fetch water, and he was not happy at having to go, no matter how diffuse the light of the grey day.

He glanced at the thick clouds but the light hurt his eyes. Turning his attention to the rest of the camp he saw figures moving about. Squinting he recognised men of Aldrace. He cursed them hoping the southerners would butcher them all. His eyes went back to the encircling forest, craving the security of the shadows.

T'chark was small for a krell; the runt of the litter; always given the most onerous duties because of his height, or lack of it, while his larger cousins lounged idly about their dark shelters, thinking of new torments. He was smarter than they were though, and that would be useful in the coming days. When the war started, and they were promised it would be soon, he would show Lang and the rest of those big fools.

A noise from a tree caught his attention. Glancing up into the hated light he saw a crow hopping from foot to foot, screaming at itself. A wicked grin spread across his face as he looked about for a missile. Vindictively he picked up a stone which he hefted, feeling its weight as he eyed the bird.

With all of his strength he hurled the stone, but at that moment the bird took flight with an angry scream. The stone clattered harmlessly from the branches, falling to the ground with a thud.

T'chark watched the bird disappear into the distance and cursed it. One day he would be a powerful chieftain and then he would eat only crow and not the unpleasant offal they were presently fed.

No! he thought suddenly. *By Drachar! No — think big!*"

He wondered what boiled Lang would taste like? His yellow fangs glistened against his sallow skin as he smiled maliciously.

Astalus was flung back into his chair as the crow's will fought his and abruptly the call of the wild won. The shock of seeing the huge camp sent his senses reeling, and he was thankful that the other two wizards had also seen it. He doubted the King would believe him without corroboration. He looked at his companions' bewildered faces.

"Krell!" Gant hissed. "Then it's true?"

"Aye, and a sizeable army as well," Corrin confirmed. The colour had drained from his face which was now the shade of Astalus' orb.

Astalus was trying to recall all that he had seen about the camp, "There were men as well. Aldrace, by their dress, but I could not tell which tribe."

"*Tribe*?" Gant exclaimed. "It was the entire nation, judging by the size of the camp!"

The three men looked at each other knowing full well that the King must be told. However, none were looking forward to the prospect.

The King had not solved his present dilemma, and Astalus' sudden reappearance seemed a dark portent. His face as he entered, with his dark robes billowing about his slender youthful frame, was sufficient to warn Sharroch that the news was not good. The magician strode purposefully down the long aisle to the King's throne.

"Well?" the King asked as Astalus stopped before him, closely followed by his two old cronies scurrying in after him to stand panting by his shoulder.

"It is true, Sire. I have no doubt now. There is indeed a sizeable army as the strangers foretold, comprising both krell and men of Aldrace."

"What of Trosgarth?" the King asked.

"There was no sign of any men from Trosgarth, Sire, although we only saw a small part of the camp."

"Can you estimate the size of the army?"

"It is hard to say. Perhaps a hundred thousand, perhaps more."

"You are certain?"

Astalus nodded, "We all saw it, Your Highness. I used a crow to focus a spell of seeing which penetrated whatever power surrounded the camp. I am certain of what I saw."

"What does this mean?" the King asked fearfully. "Is it possible that this army and Allund are in league?"

Astalus did not reply.

"Summon the Tharns once more," the King commanded of one of the soldiers standing guard. The man saluted smartly and left at once.

"Where is Prince Alyn? Why is he never around?" the King asked in frustration. Astalus did not meet his gaze. On this issue, at least, he wanted to remain neutral. The King turned instead to one of the courtiers standing at the rear of the room. "Find my son and bring him here," he demanded bluntly.

The weak sunlight filtering through the high narrow windows seemed somehow to confirm the King's dark premonition as he watched the man go. It was summer and yet a chill that even a roaring blaze could not dispel, lingered in the air. The King pulled his cloak about his round shoulders as he turned his attention back to Astalus.

"What are we to do?" the King muttered.

Chapter 11

Choice

Feeling bone weary, Kaplyn stood before the King. It was the first time in a while he had not had his friends by his side and he missed them.

The King was angry. Patiently Kaplyn waited for whatever fate he might bestow, and, as he waited, he glanced around at the Tharns who glared back at him with open hostility. When the news was finally delivered he did not know whether to be relieved or not.

At a signal from the King the young Court Wizard rose to his feet.

"Your sighting of a krell army has been confirmed," Astalus told Kaplyn.

Instantly the Tharns were in uproar and the King raised his hand for silence.

"Allund and this army may be in league?" Tharn Shelder said above the din. The others fell silent as the King nodded in agreement, having considered this possibility.

"Sire, it may also be possible they do not know that the army of krell is there!" Kaplyn pleaded.

"Then why does Allund chose to march against us?" the King demanded.

Kaplyn's silence was his only reply. The King continued to look at him, weighing his options.

At last, he said, "I am going to send one final envoy to the Allund army to demand why they march against us! You," he continued, allowing his anger to show, "are an enigma! Who you claim to be is very much in doubt, but I have decided to send you with the envoy. If you can persuade your people against war, then *I* implore you to do so!"

Kaplyn felt as though he had suddenly been thrown a lifeline in a dark and stormy sea, but realised how thin and fragile that line truly was. The King's look became darker as he leant forward angrily.

"Think carefully, lest you decide not to return for I will keep your friends hostage to your goodwill. If you betray me," he said pointing a finger accusingly at him. "I will have them executed and their heads placed on the battlements to feed the crows!"

Even the Tharns remained silent, shocked by the King's ferocity.

"Tharn Ballan," the King continued. "Arrange for an envoy to take a message to the commander of this rabble. They are to take Kaplyn with them. Before they leave, you are to make sure that he is dressed properly in a manner befitting his rank as an heir of Prince Orlastor, for it is our belief that Orlastor did not die, and before you stands his grandson."

If the Tharns had intended to object, this news stopped them. Kaplyn appreciated the subtlety of the explanation which was more plausible than a story of being imprisoned within a spell for numerous years; it also had a ring of truth to it. Suddenly the fibres of his lifeline looked stronger. With renewed hope Kaplyn was led away while, behind him, the King watched in desperation.

With more than idle curiosity, Ariome watched the goings on below. A troop of cavalry bearing the king's crest and a man dressed finely but with his hands tied like a criminal were enough to attract anyone's attention. Then again, she was not just anyone.

Biting her nails she withdrew from the window as she considered the importance of what she had seen. Abruptly she dismissed it, having heard the rumours that a spy and a *demon* had been captured. She could not believe the stupidity of the Thracians; they were the most foolish people she had ever met. It was unlikely that this man was a spy. For one thing, she would have been informed if anyone working for Trosgarth had been captured, and as for a demon — that was lamentable.

More important thoughts crowded her mind; she did not have time for trivia. Events of much greater importance would occur that night.

She caught sight of herself in the mirror and she paused to consider her reflection. Her skin was almost translucent, so pale and delicate, and yet her eyes harboured a depth of power which contradicted her apparent innocence. Power and beauty went hand in hand and her master rewarded her well for her treachery. She smiled to herself, remembering the admiring looks of the men at court and their wives' hate-filled glares.

Witch, some had dared to call her; behind her back of course. She could almost imagine the men defending her, assuring their women folk that they were wrong while secretly enjoying her coy looks.

Her raven-dark hair was swept back over her forehead and her coal-black eyes smouldered beneath arched brows as she scowled at the mirror before continuing to her meeting. The only part of her body she detested was her hands, which she kept covered with silken gloves. For some reason her spells kept her face and body young, but did nothing for her hands. Beneath the silk the flesh was old and wrinkled, a permanent reminder of her mortality.

Witch.

She smiled as she considered what these women would say if they knew the true depth of her powers. She re-entered the conference room where two men, seated on a long divan, awaited her. They stared unashamedly as she swept gracefully into the room, although their looks were of respect rather than admiration.

She in turn regarded them. They had been carefully selected for their mission. Although they were currently dressed as Thracian citizens, both were Priests of Ryoch and, as part of their disguise, they had allowed their hair to grow, for Thrace had not as yet embraced the priesthood as Allund had. Both were young, confident men prepared to sacrifice their lives if necessary, and Ariome knew that that *would* be very necessary.

"It was nothing," Ariome said as she sat down, taking exaggerated care to layer the folds of her long dress. "You will of course be changing before you leave tonight?"

The two men nodded. "And you are to help us gain access to the King's quarters," one of them replied.

"Yes, there is a door to the palace which is shown on the map I have drawn for you." She passed the map across to the priest who took it and looked at it briefly before tearing it into small pieces and passing them back.

"That door will be where you will enter the palace, but from there you will be on your own for I cannot aid you once you are inside. *I* am not expendable." If the last comment was designed to elicit a response, she was sadly disappointed.

"And why can't you aid us in the palace, my Lady?" the other priest asked softly, looking deliberately at her gloved hands.

Ariome sought to hide her hands by covering them with the folds of her dress. It was a simple question which hurt her more than she liked to admit. Her powers were redundant inside the palace which had long since been protected with spells of warding. Her admiration for the priest increased; he had astutely found her one weakness, the fear of being powerless. By way of an answer she simply shrugged her slim shoulders.

The problem still remained as to how to gain entry to the palace. The door she had chosen was a good choice as it was seldom, if ever, used. Nearby there was a small garden full of trees and shrubs that would provide adequate cover. How was she to deal with the door though? Suddenly the solution occurred to her and the simplicity of the plan left her breathless.

"There's a room through the door behind you," Ariome said, smiling sweetly. "Inside, you will find two razors and towels for you to prepare yourselves. You have your own robes, I assume?"

Both men nodded.

Ariome took her leave and hurried to a door concealed behind a thick tapestry; a smell of herbs greeted her as she entered her private laboratory. It was very unlike Astalus' laboratories, far less cluttered with everything in its place. She prided herself that she needed very few aids to work magic. As a Narlassar sorcerer she considered Astalus and his kind, the Akrane, beneath her.

Closing the door softly behind her, she made her way to a long, low oak table. She needed a scanth for her plan to succeed, a small insect which laid an egg of a voracious wood eating grub. Smiling to herself she spread chalk dust over the shiny tabletop, tracing a rune in the white surface and speaking words of power to summon a fire elemental. As she completed the rune, a small flame blossomed into being, immediately tracing an erratic path but never, as though confined by the symbol, crossing the fine lines traced on the wooden surface. A faint eerie wail pierced the room as the elemental realised it was trapped; the pitch of the wail increased as Ariome started to chant in the forgotten tongue of the Eldric.

The elemental danced in agony as its life force expired. With a look of satisfaction, Ariome watched it fade into oblivion. Upon the table was a small insect that crawled across the chalk, leaving small prints in the white dust. She watched it unfurl gossamer-thin wings, revealing red and orange markings designed to frighten off predators. The insect did not fly, however, choosing instead to remain on the table as though allowing Ariome to admire its beauty.

Carefully the sorceress gathered the insect into a box. The insect was female and heavy with eggs.

Kaplyn was escorted to a courtyard where twenty soldiers of the king's troop were assembled, preparing their mounts. Over their orange tunics the men wore grey winter cloaks to dispel the chill and on their heads tall helms polished to a high sheen, decorated with a tall oncara plume. Each soldier stood by his mount's side. Their lance-tips, decorated with bright coloured pennants, were held in readiness for the order to mount.

Tharn Ballan appeared from a doorway at the end of the courtyard, striding nonchalantly across the cobbled street towards the waiting men. One of the soldiers, slightly apart from the others, saluted and together they conversed in low tones.

Kaplyn was forced to wait at the edge of the assembled men, watching the proceedings, eager to be on his way. Occasionally the two men glanced across at him. The man speaking with Ballan was in his early thirties and Kaplyn recognised he held the rank of a Second Haft Commander by the red stripe on his cloak. He was a handsome man who bore himself proudly. His jaw-line was strong as though his resolution alone was sufficient to merit command, and his dark hair was swept back over a broad forehead.

The Haft Commander signalled for a mount to be taken to Kaplyn. Swiftly a saddled horse was led towards the prisoner by a young soldier who eyed Kaplyn warily. The youth held the animal's reins, facing the bewildered prisoner expectantly. Kaplyn could only stare at the large animal in disbelief. He could not be expected to mount with his hands tied behind him. This seemed to be another in a long line of insults designed to wear him down. *Dress him finely*, the King had ordered. And that is exactly what they had done, except that he had not even been provided with a coat. The chill wind whistled through the silk shirt, causing him to shiver.

The Tharn Commander ignored Kaplyn and continued to talk with the Haft Commander. Kaplyn remained where he was, patiently waiting and ignoring the young soldier's stares. Eventually the two officers came across.

"This is Haft Tallin and he will be leading the peace envoy," Ballan stated. "I thought I had better set a few matters straight before you depart. If Tallin or yourself fail to return, your friends will be executed. Is that understood?"

"Yes," Kaplyn nodded as the Tharn continued.

"You are our prisoner and you will be treated accordingly while an Allund army threatens this city. If you betray us, Tallin has been ordered to *kill* you."

Kaplyn glanced at Tallin who continued to look at him with a steady gaze, as if the thought of killing him was simply another every day occurrence.

"Turn around," Tallin ordered, and Kaplyn complied as his bindings were expertly checked. The rope was cutting into his wrists and his hands were already growing numb; he hoped it was the cold causing the numbness and not the loss of circulation.

"Get him on his horse," Tallin ordered, turning away to mount his own animal. Two soldiers grabbed him and lifted him bodily onto his horse. He sat on the animal, gripping firmly with his knees.

Tallin mounted and took a flag of truce from a foot soldier. He urged his mount to the head of the column, giving Kaplyn an unfriendly look. The horses skittered restlessly on the cobbled courtyard, sensing they would soon be free of the confining city.

Kaplyn's horse was tethered to another soldier's mount, a burly veteran who grinned at him, causing the younger man to look away. Only then did he notice a lone figure standing close to a doorway to the rider's right. A cloak obscured the stranger's slight frame, and a hood was pulled over the head. Tallin saluted the figure, causing Kaplyn to wonder who it might be. The stranger stepped away from the doorway and approached the riders, moving towards Kaplyn. He sensed eyes fixed intently upon him from within the hood.

Tallin rode from the head of the group to intercept the figure.

"Why has the prisoner no cloak?" a female voice questioned. A slender hand bearing ornate rings swept back the hood to reveal a youthful face beneath a crown of dark, unruly hair. Her eyes, normally filled with amusement and life, now looked accusingly at Tallin as though holding him personally responsible.

"Princess Catriona, I have orders to take the prisoner to meet with the Allund army. I was not instructed to nursemaid him." Tallin's tone was respectful, although it was not without a hint of sarcasm. The Princess glanced at Kaplyn who stared back in amazement, unable to take his eyes from her face. She frowned, made uncertain by the intensity of his look. It was almost as though he recognised her. Quickly she searched her memory, feeling abashed that she did not recognise him, but growing more certain with every moment that she had never seen him before.

"There is no need to let him freeze to death in the process," she continued. She undid her cloak, revealing a long colourful dress beneath and held it out to Tallin who looked for a moment as though he was about to refuse. Instead he took the cloak and rode alongside Kaplyn, roughly pinning it about his shoulders and then, with a sidelong look at the Princess and a curt nod, rode to the head of the column.

Kaplyn continued to stare at the young woman as his horse was led away. She, too, continued to watch him, a frown of confusion on her face. Kaplyn twisted in the saddle to look over his shoulder. The Princess remained where she was, an isolated figure, a splash of colour against the grey of the barracks. *He had not thanked her for the cloak.* He cursed this oversight. Already he felt a benefit from the warm material.

Seeing her now watching him riding away brought back other distant memories, and he continued to watch until they rounded a corner and she was lost from view. Pain, mixed with other emotions, flooded through his body. Emptiness seemed to grow inside him, a pang at the loss of so many family and friends. He shook his head, confused and alone, the memory of the Princess held preciously within his mind's eye a faint hope that all was not lost.

He remembered Callin's farm, so many miles away and so long ago, where he and Lars had sought sanctuary for the night and had helped to fight off an unexpected attack from a large pack of wolves. He remembered, too, Callin's daughter, whose face he had never been able to forget during their long journey into the mountains.

Now her memory merged with the fresh image of the Princess, and he frowned in confusion. The resemblance to the Princess was uncanny. He drank in the fragrance of her perfume from her cloak. His heart lifted for the first time since they had awakened in the cavern, and hope surged through his veins.

Chapter 12

Ride into Uncertainty

The column rode across a wide, wooden bridge, spanning the flood waters of the river Torrid which had burst its banks a short way upriver. The fields to either side were swamped with brown murky water. Small shrubs peeked above the water whose swirling depths reminded Kaplyn of their recent flight from the krell army.

He wondered what the enemy was doing now and glanced nervously at the distant horizon, watching for movement and half-expecting to see a long line of dark shapes appear. To his relief, apart from a few lone trees, the wide-open fields were empty for as far as he could see. Nearby a few carts rumbled across uneven tracks, heading towards the safety of the city.

For a while longer the troop continued in double file. Occasionally riders were sent ahead to scout the land, and Kaplyn watched these dwindle into small specks on the horizon. Momentarily he fought against his bonds, not with the intention of escaping so much as getting the circulation back into his hands.

"Tallin!" he eventually called to the Haft Commander in mounting frustration.

Tallin turned to see what he wanted, and Kaplyn gestured with his head that he would speak with him. Tallin broke file to ride back to the prisoner, wheeling his horse in a tight arc to trot alongside Kaplyn.

"I cannot feel my fingers!" Kaplyn said as soon as the other man's mount had settled into a walk alongside his.

Tallin regarded Kaplyn stonily. Unlike most officers, his uniform was exactly the same as that of the troops he commanded. All too often other high-ranking officers altered their uniforms, adding gold and silver braid and more expensive materials to glorify their rank.

"Look, I've every reason to talk to the Allunds," Kaplyn continued, trying to undermine the other man's resolve. "I want to know what is going on as well as you do. I give you my word that I will not try to escape."

"You will *not* escape!" Tallin warned him. "And you are tied for your own safety. My men have little love for Allunders these days. They are probably looking for an excuse to slit your throat if you try anything foolish."

Kaplyn glanced around. The men looked back icily with no hint of mercy in their eyes. He did not doubt Tallin's words. "My people will be angered if you bring me back with my hands ruined," he stated flatly, changing tack.

Tallin considered this for a moment as their horses carried them forward in a gentle rocking motion. At last he reluctantly drew his dagger from the sheath at his belt, and the slim weapon glinted against the greyness of the day. With a deft motion Tallin leaned behind Kaplyn to sever his bonds.

Blood rushed instantly into Kaplyn's fingers, causing him to grimace. His hands throbbed wickedly, and all he could do was hold them level to try to prevent the circulation returning too swiftly. Gradually, the pain subsided into memory.

"Thanks!" Kaplyn said at last, clenching and unclenching his fingers.

Tallin nodded. "The Tharn said you are a spy," he said coldly.

"Hardly," Kaplyn replied. "I came to the city with friends. We knew nothing of a supposed war with Allund. We did see your preparations for war," he continued, noticing Tallin's look of doubt, "but thought they were due to the krell army we had sighted in the mountains."

"Ah, yes!" Tallin replied sarcastically. "Your tale of an army from Trosgarth."

Kaplyn nodded, knowing the tale seemed bizarre.

Tallin looked unconvinced. Issuing instructions to the troopers behind Kaplyn to watch his every move, he wheeled his mount away from the column and rode to its head, leaving Kaplyn still massaging his hands. He felt slightly better with his hands free, but the lack of a sword made him feel vulnerable, especially since they were riding into wilderness with the threat of enemy armies surrounding them.

The remainder of the day passed without incident and, after a brief pause for a light meal, Tallin sent fresh scouts ahead. Wearily Kaplyn was forced to mount once more, and he pulled Catriona's cloak tighter about his shoulders. The material was too light for a prolonged ride, but at least it was better than nothing, and he was grateful for its warmth, no matter how slight.

Later that afternoon, he started to notice distinct changes in their surroundings; woods became more frequent and the empty plains became wilder. Large bracken shrubs, gorse and fern replaced the grass they had grown accustomed to, making the ride more difficult.

A swarm of insects filled the air with vibrant sounds. Birds nervously took flight calling loudly as the riders passed by, and more than once a rabbit raced across their path taken by surprise by the proximity of the riders.

Against the grey leaden sky, hillocks denoted the start of the Pen-am-Pelleas mountain range. The cloud cover was too low to enable them to see the larger cousins that Kaplyn knew must be behind these, but he could almost feel their presence as the wind grew ever colder. He judged that they would reach the foothills later that afternoon. Kaplyn remembered the lay of the land from maps he had seen. The long mountain range which divided Thrace and Allund was accessible by a mountain pass which allowed caravans to travel between the countries, although the route was quite treacherous in parts.

He wondered what could have happened to cause such a rift between the two nations. Allund and Thrace had always been close allies, and once more he wondered at the part that the Priest of Ryoch had played in his father's downfall.

A few hours later, they were amongst the foothills and their mounts laboured up the steep incline. The change in scenery helped to break the monotony of the ride, but the cold was more severe. Kaplyn shivered uncontrollably and his scar ached with the constant frigidity.

One of their scouts was abruptly silhouetted on the brow of a hill ahead, racing his mount back to the column.

"An army, Sir," the soldier said, panting heavily as he reported to Tallin. Kaplyn could barely hear his words above the wind and the creaking of leather straps. "It's fewer than three hundred yards over the next rise."

Tallin was taken aback by the tidings. He had not expected to sight the army until the following day The Allunds, then, were nearer than they had thought. He had also expected to encounter the army's scouts or guards first. He twisted in his saddle to look behind, and Kaplyn did likewise.

To their rear several figures were observing them from a small ridge, signalling to another group of soldiers on a rise opposite. It seemed that the Allund army already knew of their presence.

Tallin called for the flag of truce to be raised and all eyes were set rigidly to their front, ignoring the Allund sentries.

Cresting the hill, Kaplyn was taken aback by the size of the encampment which looked like an ant's nest poked with a stick. Riders were hurrying back and forth carrying messages while men worked hard checking the disassembled parts of wooden siege engines. Kaplyn glanced across at Tallin who was watching the work with fear evident in his expression.

"They'll be at CarCamel tomorrow!" Kaplyn heard one of the soldiers saying.

"Let them come and they will get their heads cracked!" another soldier replied. Others murmured agreement.

Kaplyn was not convinced by the soldier's show of bravado. The siege engines looked formidable. These massive weapons of war must have slowed the army considerably, even when transported in parts. Soldiers were now working on the wooden frames. Animal hides were being stretched and tacked to their sides. These would later be soaked in water to prevent fires from catching as they were hauled towards the city walls. A herd of grall was enclosed within a temporary pen and their angry bellowing sounded clearly across the distance.

From within the camp a detachment of riders broke free from the main body, and the ground rumbled with the sounds of the approaching horses. Tallin called back to his men to hold and within moments they were surrounded by Allund cavalry.

"I am an envoy of Thrace and I wish to speak with your commander," Tallin shouted above the sounds of the horses' laboured breathing.

An Allund officer aimed his horse towards Tallin. "You will have to give up your weapons," the officer said coldly.

Tallin hesitated. The Allunds already had steel drawn and their weapons gleamed as though in anticipation. Tallin shrugged his shoulders in resignation, drew his sabre and handed it over.

"Give them your arms!" he commanded.

Sullenly, weapons were handed over. Kaplyn was rudely pushed by one of the Allund troops, and he drew back his cloak, showing he was unarmed.

The detail was escorted into the camp, and a crowd of Allund foot soldiers assembled to catch their first glimpse of a Thracian. Initially the familiar sight of the Allund uniforms warmed Kaplyn; then, however, grief threatened as memories welled up inside him. The uniform had changed little since the overthrow of the monarchy. The soldiers had retained the blue surcoat and dark blue cloak with a silver dagger emblazoned on the shoulder. The small conical helms that the men wore were simpler in design and more functional then those of their Thracian counterparts.

Kaplyn now appreciated why the Thracians wore ceremonial dress for, even after nearly a day's ride, they looked immaculate, sitting ramrod straight, their polished metal breastplates gleaming brightly. The Allund troops had probably hoped to find the Thracians easy prey to their swords; instead, they looked at them with a wary eye, seeing men ready and willing to fight for their land.

Kaplyn glanced around, hoping to catch sight of a familiar face, hoping to prove that the recent events were somehow untrue, but all around him strangers peered curiously back.

When they arrived at the heart of the camp, the troop was forced to dismount and the Allund officer turned to speak with Tallin. "You! Come with me and deliver your message."

Tallin's eyes blazed angrily with the insult of not even being addressed by his rank and, for a moment, he stubbornly remained where he was.

"This man," he said, indicating to Kaplyn, "is an Allund spy. I return him unharmed as a token of our good will. I have been ordered to escort him personally to your commander."

The Officer looked at Kaplyn and then shrugged his shoulders. "Very well. Bring him," he acknowledged, turning to lead the way. Four soldiers accompanied them as they passed between tents.

Overhead, the sky was starting to darken as night fell. All about the encampment, campfires were being lit as evening meals were prepared. Kaplyn inhaled the scent of cooking and his stomach growled; he had eaten little in the last few days. They hurried through the camp, heading towards a dark marquee above which flew the Allund flag, a blue boar on a white field.

Two sentries stood at ease by the marquee's entrance, spears sloped in front of them. Neither man moved as they drew alongside. One of their escorts hurried forward to hold open the heavy canvas flap which smelled strongly of age as they ducked beneath it.

Their escort led them inside where a broad-shouldered man sat at the tent's centre, facing the newcomers across a wide wooden table littered with scrolls and maps. His face seemed carved from granite; his strong, craggy jaw was set with fierce determination and his eyes glittered in the diffuse light. His mere presence seemed to command respect. As soon as they entered, his gaze fixed on the two men as though he were reading their every thought. They stopped before him, waiting for him to speak. He was dressed richly beneath the trappings of war and his thick leather surcoat creaked as he leant forward. His nose had been broken on numerous occasions, and a white scar ran diagonally across his face, suggesting that he was a lucky man not to have been blinded. The smell of hot wax filled the room from several candles that barely illuminated the gloomy interior.

Kaplyn sensed that somebody else was present, hiding in the shadows. He squinted into the darkness, but an inner canvas screen restricted his view.

"Tharn Orrin, an envoy from CarCamel," the Allund officer proclaimed, saluting smartly. Orrin casually returned the salute, not taking his eyes off the two men. His deputy stepped back, leaving Tallin and Kaplyn standing alone before him.

"Speak," Orrin growled at Tallin, seeing by his rank that he was the envoy.

Tallin saluted smartly, hiding his weariness from their long ride. "Sir, I have been sent by my Liege, King Sharroch of Thrace, to ask why an Allund army has crossed onto Thracian soil."

"Come, come," replied the Tharn with a trace of humour in his voice. "You have seen the army. Have you not guessed our intent?"

"Sir, Thrace has no grievance with Allund. Why are you here?"

"You speak of no grievances," Orrin replied somewhat bewildered. "Why, then, has Thrace ceased trading with us?"

Tallin appeared genuinely surprised by the remark. "Ceased! It is Allund that has stopped trading, slaughtering our envoys and caravans."

"*Slaughtered!*" the Tharn roared. When he was angry his scar turned purple, a sign most of his men understood to their cost. "My people go hungry whilst yours sit fat and content, refusing to share their bountiful crops while famine grips my lands."

Kaplyn doubted the Tharn's sincerity for the troops looked well fed and he himself was a large man.

"Our crops are less than bountiful; long periods of rain have ruined several years' harvest," Tallin replied defensively.

The two men stared at each other, neither willing to give ground, each considering the other an enemy. Kaplyn realised that little would be gained by this meeting. For some reason, a dark and insatiable hatred had grown between the two nations.

"Tharn," Kaplyn interrupted softly, seeking to gain the broad commander's attention. "May I speak?"

"And who, *by the Kalanth*, are you?" Orrin snapped irritably, his attention switching to Kaplyn, who almost faltered beneath his piercing stare. Before he could speak Tallin interrupted.

287

"He is an Allund spy," Tallin declared, hoping that the disclosure would anger Orrin. "We return him as he is of no further value to us."

The Tharn flashed Tallin an icy glare. "Do you mock me? This is not one of our spies!" he declared abruptly.

Tallin was clearly taken aback and an uneasy silence descended.

"Tharn!" Kaplyn repeated.

The Tharn appeared to be hardly listening as Kaplyn continued stubbornly, "I bring important news. There is an army from Trosgarth on Thrace's northern borders. Whilst we stand here bickering, that army may well be on the move."

The Tharn's brow creased. "Trosgarth? You jest. Is this some kind of trick?" He looked at Tallin.

"Our Court Wizard has confirmed it," Tallin grumbled, watching the Tharn's response carefully.

Tharn Orrin stared at Tallin in disbelief.

"Lies!" hissed a voice suddenly from the recesses of the tent. A dark figure emerged from behind the screen. The newcomer was a tall thin man who stepped confidently into the pool of light cast by the candle. His eyes were obscured by large bushy eyebrows; his cheeks were high; his jowls hung loosely in large rolls of flesh and his head was shaven. In contrast to the Tharn's great bulk, the newcomer was thin and bird-like. Kaplyn recognised the ochre robes and tried hard to remember where he had seen similar garb before.

Kaplyn felt immediately threatened by the strange man whose slit-like eyes seemed to bore into him as though seeking the darkest recesses of his soul.

"They have been sent to betray us," he declared in a low menacing tone, advancing slowly. "I demand they are handed over to the priesthood for interrogation."

That this man belonged to a priesthood was alarming; he looked fanatical and his dress macabre. Abruptly, Kaplyn's memory returned to his visit to Kinlin castle where he had been introduced to another priest wearing similar garb. That priest had tried to persuade Hallar, the local Baron, to part with cash in return for riches from a new god, Ryoch. Kaplyn remembered the name clearly as though it had only been yesterday, and a tremor ran down his spine. The priests may have been responsible for his father's death.

"That is untrue, Tharn!" Kaplyn snapped back. "I am an Allunder and I would never betray my people."

The priest hissed, his robes rustling as he strode angrily about the small tent, his attention never wavering from Kaplyn and Tallin.

Kaplyn did not relish the thought of being turned over to the "priesthood"; he had only encountered a few of their number, but did not think that they would be treated well.

"I am by rights your King and I will be heard!" Kaplyn blurted abruptly, momentarily silencing the other two men. The priest stopped pacing, a look of shock on his face.

"*King?*" the Tharn thundered, turning to look at Kaplyn. "Allund has no king. By what right do you presume to that title?"

"I am a descendent of King Garrin. My grandfather was Orlastor, his son," Kaplyn proclaimed, trying not to flinch under Orrin's stern look. Behind him he heard one of the guards speaking to the other in disbelief. A glare from Orrin silenced them.

"That's impossible!" the priest declared in disbelief, coming around Orrin's shoulder to lean heavily upon the table, knuckles white with the fierceness of his grip. "Garrin, the last Allund king, and his sons died years ago. None survived!"

"All died," Kaplyn admitted savagely, relying on his knowledge of the truth to make his story plausible, "save Orlastor, who went missing several years before the King's assassination." The priest's expression reflected his confusion. Kaplyn had guessed correctly; the news of his own disappearance so long ago had probably resulted in many wild rumours as to his fate.

"Lies, all lies," the priest snapped. His shoulders shook with fury and his eyes blazed. "Still, it matters not!" he declared, becoming surly and moving away from the desk as though preferring the shadows. "Allund has no king and the Council rules over her people. There have been many pretenders to the Throne and you will likely share their fate." He turned his back on Kaplyn, making it clear he was no longer of importance. "Guards!" he commanded, trying to remain in charge of the situation. "Remove the prisoners."

"Wait!" Orrin ordered. "If this man is even distantly related to Garrin, then the Council must be informed. It is their decision, not yours."

The priest turned, glaring at the Tharn who stared resolutely back, defying him to contradict. Clearly there was little love lost between them.

"There is still the matter of an army of krell to the north," Kaplyn reminded the Tharn.

Grateful for the interruption, the priest rounded on Kaplyn. "Trosgarth has long since faded into obscurity! There is no krell army! Your story only serves to betray you. Orrin, he would have you jump at shadows while Thrace stabs us in the back."

"I command here," the Tharn reminded the priest. "And I will not jeopardise my army while there is uncertainty. I will not leave our flank unsecured."

Two guards had entered the tent at the priest's call and were awaiting further instruction.

"As to your claim to kingship," Tharn Orrin continued, ignoring his men and addressing Kaplyn, "that is a matter for the Council to judge." The priest scowled, but Orrin ignored him as he continued. "You shall remain a prisoner until such time as you can be escorted back to Dundalk to prove your claim." Orrin turned to address his guards, making it clear that the meeting was ended.

"Return the prisoners to their comrades and make sure they are secure for the night," he instructed. Their escort saluted before stepping forward to take them from the tent.

Tallin immediately objected. "We came under a flag of truce! You cannot confine us."

"You are prisoners. I will not let you ride back to CarCamel with information about our disposition. You will be free to go when we arrive before the gates of the city, and not before."

Tallin could not argue further. One of the guards grabbed his arm, ushering him from the tent, and Kaplyn followed silently. His face was set, masking his turmoil. Arguing with the Tharn would only rouse his anger, and, as far as he was concerned, Kaplyn was simply another in a long line of pretenders. To make matters worse, if he failed to return, then his friends faced execution. It was with a downcast heart that Kaplyn followed.

For several moments after their departure, silence reigned within the tent. Orrin could feel the priest's gaze on his back as he concentrated on the maps before him, trying his best to ignore the other man. Brama Halace was infuriating; he always seemed to be on hand to question his every decision. Orrin was beginning to lose patience. Why the Council had burdened him with so many priests, he had no idea.

"That man is dangerous," Brama declared as though on cue.

Orrin's shoulders bunched in anger and he tried to suppress a retort. He calmed himself, knowing that the priests had influence with the Council and it would be foolish to jeopardise his career for the sake of caution.

Breathing deeply he said, "He will be dealt with, once he is taken before the Council — and not before."

Brama shook his head and turned away from Orrin as though afraid to meet his gaze. "A man claiming to be an heir to the throne is dangerous at normal times," he blurted out, striding once more across the floor of the tent before turning to face Orrin. "We cannot allow such a man to distract others from our cause; his presence is enough to encourage rebellion. The army is under your command, as you so rightly reminded me, but if you fail in this mission, you will answer to the priesthood as well as the Council."

The priest's threat hung in the air between the two men, leaving an icy silence.

"What are you suggesting?" Orrin asked.

"Kaplyn should be removed before rumours spread! Can you not see what Thrace hopes to achieve? By placing him here, they cause doubt."

"You mean killed, rather than removed. Don't you?" Orrin demanded.

Brama gave the Tharn a shallow smile.

"I am in command of this army," Orrin declared, slamming his palm down hard on the tabletop, causing Brama to jump. "I will not execute a man for no reason. As I have already said, he will be escorted to Dundalk in due course where the Council will decide his fate."

Brama bowed fractionally, smiling as though trying to retain his composure and then, gathering up his robes, strode from the tent leaving the flap billowing in a sudden gust of cold air.

Orrin sat back. *Why tonight of all nights*, he thought? They were one hard day's march from CarCamel. He did not relish going to war, but he had been given and had accepted the command of the army. For too long Thrace had refused Allund's request for aid. However, the seeds of doubt had already been sown. What if Thrace was suffering as much as Allund? He doubted it, but the Thracian Haft Commander sounded sincere. And this Kaplyn; was he truly an heir to the Allund throne?

Orrin suddenly felt very exposed with the Allund Council and the priests on one side, Thrace on the other and a possible army of krell to boot! He sighed, sitting upright once more. It was going to be a very long night.

As they were led through the camp, Kaplyn noticed groups of priests, armed with broadswords. Tallin noticed the direction of Kaplyn's gaze and frowned. The priests returned their stares, their interest clearly mutual.

"Priests of Ryoch," Tallin spat. "Although why so many and why armed I have no idea. In Thrace priests preach, not fight!"

"What do you know about them?" Kaplyn whispered.

"Mostly rumours," Tallin admitted softly. "I have heard that children, many as young as ten or eleven, are selected for the priesthood. Apparently they have no choice in the matter."

Kaplyn frowned. He wanted to ask more, but one of their escorts, a tall, broad-shouldered fellow, growled menacingly.

They were led to a stockade where they found the other soldiers of Tallin's command. As they were roughly jostled inside, the other prisoners rose to meet them.

Kaplyn turned to their captors. "Could I have a cloak?" he asked, hugging his chest to ward off the chill. The Guard Commander nodded, eyeing Kaplyn's thin cloak suspiciously before leaving.

To Kaplyn's relief, he returned moments later, carrying a cloak that looked as though it had seen better days. Nonetheless, Kaplyn gratefully accepted it.

Kaplyn and Tallin sat down with the others. When the guards left, Tallin grinned.

"You spoke well," he acknowledged. "It was a good thing you didn't betray us though."

Kaplyn frowned as Tallin tapped his own boot. He noticed the hilt of what he assumed to be a knife peeking above the top of his boot.

Kaplyn said nothing but inwardly grimaced. "What else do you know about those priests?" he asked.

"They are evil!" one of the Thracians by Kaplyn's side interjected. Seeing Kaplyn as a fellow prisoner had clearly reduced their distrust.

"Aye," agreed another man. "I have a friend who knows a man who spoke with an Allund who knew someone who entered the priesthood," he said conspiratorially. Tallin could barely suppress a smile and tried to hide it behind his hand.

"Apparently the priests scour the land looking for boys with an evil Shaol."

"Don't be a *fool*, Palam!" Tallin interrupted, his expression deadly earnest. "You listen to too many fairy stories. Nobody believes in Shaols."

Kaplyn objected. "Do not be too quick to assume that. I didn't believe in krell or demons, for that matter, until I saw them."

"You saw a demon?" Palam asked, wide-eyed. The others crowded around closer to better hear the story.

By Kaplyn's side Tallin shook his head sadly.

"Yes. I fought one and cut off its arm!"

Palam's eyes gleamed in the darkness and his look convinced Kaplyn that he at least believed him. "This man I spoke to," Palam continued, "he said that the priests search for boys with an evil Shaol. He knew a lad who had been forced to join the priesthood, but one day he escaped. When the boy met my friend he was convinced that the priests were searching for him. He stayed for a few days and then, in the middle of the night, he disappeared. My friend said that the lad was afraid of his own shadow, but he told him all he knew of the priests and their evil ways."

Kaplyn was shocked. A Shaol was meant to be a guardian spirit. He had never considered that they could be evil. But then why *should* a guardian spirit be pure? Lomar believed the Shaol was an ancestor of the person it watched over, and a fair number of anyone's ancestors might be evil.

"Palam, do you think that the priests were responsible for the death of King Garrin?" Kaplyn asked.

Palam frowned and his eyes searched the surroundings as though fearing one of the priests might be listening.

"Aye. It's possible," Tallin interrupted. "At about the time the Allund monarchy was overthrown the so-called *Priests of Ryoch* appeared, preaching against the Kalanth, the Old Ones. I heard tell that they even tried to infiltrate Thrace, but failed."

The Kalanth were demi-gods who were supposed to have existed at the dawn of time, preparing the world for the coming of man. What became of the Kalanth nobody knew. Some believed that kara-stones were the fossilised remains of part of a Kalanth, while others that these were the concentrated essence of magic, left behind when a wizard died.

Kaplyn shook his head sadly. If only he had left Kinlin castle and returned to the palace, then his family might still be alive.

A commotion interrupted them. Mounted men rode by their stockade, the men looking down on the prisoners with dark looks. They were heading for the camp's perimeter and the darkness beyond.

"Where do you think they are going?" Kaplyn asked.

"No doubt to investigate your claims about a krell army," Tallin said, his eyes fixed upon the departing riders.

Kaplyn cursed. "That's madness. They'll be seen coming from miles away."

Tallin looked at Kaplyn quizzically, but refrained from speaking.

Another noise nearby startled Kaplyn and he looked around. A boy of about ten years of age was peering at him through the bars of their cage. He was a skinny youth with dark smears begriming both his face and hands, probably a son of one of the camp followers. His hair was long and lank and his clothes grimy, and yet the youth had about him a look of intelligence which belied his appearance.

At the moment, his large oval eyes were fixed on Kaplyn. Within his grasp, he held a small loaf which he offered through the bars. He seemed strangely eager to speak, but something prevented him. Kaplyn smiled warmly, accepting the bread and thanking him. The youth seemed to be put at ease by Kaplyn's acceptance of his gift.

"Are you our King?" he asked in a small piping voice.

Kaplyn felt a pang. Memories flooded through his mind and grief threatened to overcome him as the ghosts of his past rose to confront him. Beyond the bars, the youth watched patiently waiting a reply.

At last Kaplyn looked up, a tear in the corner of his eye. Somehow, across the distance of time, he felt his father and brothers would understand.

"Yes," he said finally. "I am your King."

The youth smiled back broadly, his teeth flashing whitely against the darkness of the growing night and, in an instant he was gone.

Brama unfolded the kara-stone from within the soft folds of cloth. If the Allunds suspected he carried the relic, or worse, that he was a Narlassar sorcerer, he would be in serious trouble. Whatever the risks, he had to communicate with his superiors.

He shuddered that Kaplyn might be an heir of Garrick. How could such a thing be possible? Trosgarth had been involved in the overthrow of the Allund monarchy. The Prophecy spoke of a king who would play a part in the downfall of Drachar a second time, and that possibility was taken very seriously by the Trosgarth High Command. So much so that, over the years, as many monarchs had been killed as possible.

Allund had not been the first. That honour had fallen to Hullin whose lands even now were in turmoil, divided by a civil war that few of the other nations knew about thanks to its inhospitable forest and mountain borders.

Allund had been next.

West Meath was not yet considered a threat because its king was old and infirm, an unlikely candidate for a hero but his son, Prince Fiad, was another matter. Brama paused in the act of laying the kara-stone upon the narrow wooden cot, looking over his shoulder to ensure that the tent flap was down. It would not do to have someone walk in now.

Prince Fiad.

Brama frowned, remembering once more what he knew. Born in late winter, his star sign was Allalayin, an earth/air sign. On the night of his birth a meteor had apparently lit the entire sky in a brief blaze of glory.

Brama shuddered. Many spoke of the Prince as being a major player in the Prophecy. *Born of Air, Fire and Water*, the litany went.

Few had accounted for the reference to water, but that was the very nature of prophecy — unclear at the best. Still, Fiad had to be dealt with, but so long as he was a prince it mattered little. And with Bhutan ruled by a Queen, that only left Thrace. But now … Kaplyn?

He passed a hand over the kara-stone and a faint glow sprang to life at its heart. Tracing a rune over the stone, he chanted, staring deeply into the misty orb. Images formed within his mind only to fade into oblivion. He constructed a picture of Kaplyn and concentrated hard on its meaning.

Within moments, he had his reply and, waving a hand over the crystal, he wrapped it within the long folds of cloth, bundling it into the bottom of one of the many packs. Sitting upon the ground, he meditated for a while, giving thanks to Ryoch for the sign.

Kaplyn must die. At all costs.

Chapter 13

Dark Deeds in the Night

Lomar drifted into a restless doze, hovering on the edge of the deep sleep his body craved. A strange but familiar sensation coursed through his weary mind and, with a feeling of unease, he tried to fight the change. His spirit was about to break free of its earthly shackles, to escape into the shapeless shadows of the spirit world.

Desperately he tried to fight the transition, but the feeling grew until he could ignore it no more. Suddenly, he soared higher than the tallest mountain.

In a semi-dream state, Lomar cried out, cursing his ability to travel the astral plain. Garth had told him his link with his Shaol was uncommonly strong because his guardian spirit was the shade of his own twin who had died before being born. It was this link that helped him to travel the astral plane.

Gradually his mind cleared, and he awoke with the full realisation that his body was still incarcerated in the cell, but his spirit was now elsewhere. Where his Shaol had taken him he did not know, nor did he relish finding out.

He was still moving and to his horror the land seemed to be hurtling past at speed, increasing the distance between his spirit and his body. The surroundings were indistinct.

Then he was slowing and a faint radiance glowed all about. Realisation dawned; it was a mountainside and light was reflecting from deep snow. He was standing on a rock above a mountain path, and swirls of snow alternately exposed and blocked his view. For a moment, he truly feared he had died and then the sound of guttural voices distracted him.

As the wind calmed and the snow settled, his view improved. Figures were moving down the path. Krell soldiers, laden with cumbersome iron armour and large packs, laboured down the slope slipping and sliding on the uncertain footing. He heard their voices clearly now, cursing the treacherous slope and their commanders. Looking back along their line, a long column disappeared into the distance. This was not a raiding party, but a sizeable army.

Desperately, he sought a hiding place before realising the futility of the act. He was in plain view of those passing below, but the krell marched by ignoring him and he realised they could not see him.

A distinct feeling of unease made him look more closely at the mountain pass. He *knew* this place. This was where he and the others had travelled from the Turn marsh on their way to the mountains. That meant this army was heading towards Gilfillan, his home.

It was a devastating blow. He turned his gaze down the slope seeking his homeland, knowing that it was too far away for him to help, but he could see little. The cloud was low, clinging to the mountainside and obscuring the forest he knew should be there.

Thinking of his home served to make his surroundings indistinct and then, abruptly, he was standing in a long corridor. He blinked in confusion. The snow and icy gusts of wind were gone. Instead, ornate, bright-coloured tapestries and wooden walls, carved with delicate patterns, surrounded him.

His heart lifted with joy.

Gilfillan! He was home. His thoughts turned to his mother

Once again the scene shifted and he found himself standing in a darkened room. Startled, he looked about. As his eyes adjusted to the low light, he saw a broad bed covered by a thick talla-feather cover, beneath which a tassel of white hair peeked from beneath the cover.

The figure stirred and sat up, brushing his hair from his face and peering cautiously at Lomar as if seeing him as the remnant of a dream. Lomar found himself looking into the scarlet eyes of a young Alvalan who peered curiously back. It took Lomar a few moments to register that the person could actually see him.

"Dalamere?" the figure questioned, a trace of fear in his voice.

"What?" Lomar asked, frowning that the person could see him when others couldn't. "No, I'm not Dalamere," he said, recovering from his initial shock. "I do not have time to explain. A krell army is coming from the mountains. I think they will pass through KinAnar. You must warn our people. They will be on the Turn marsh within a day."

The figure on the bed frowned and started to rise. Lomar felt a distant and familiar pull. For once he desperately fought against the summons back to his body.

"Warn our people!" he cried out in frustration as the room dissolved into foggy greys and indistinct patterns. Before him, the Alvalan youth looked up with fear dawning on his handsome face as he realised that he was not sleeping.

Lomar was panicking. Never before had his spirit travelled so far and a dreadful fear assailed him. The name that the figure on the bed had uttered upon his appearance returned to his mind.

Dalamere.

He cried out in anguish. The thought of Dalamere and what Dalamere had been haunted Lomar's dreams. He was an evil Alvalan who could also travel the spirit world. But Dalamere had used his powers for his own ends, and what he learned, he had used to blackmail his way to the throne. Dark tales insisted that Dalamere had died when his spirit failed to return to his body after an evil night of spying, becoming lost for eternity.

Lomar cried out again, hoping that someone would aid him. A grey indistinct world hovered at the periphery of his vision. Scenes appeared; some vaguely familiar and others grossly unreal. His fear escalated. Usually he could feel a link with his body, not a tangible force but more like knowing which way was north, but to his horror he could feel nothing at all. He closed his mind to the terrible jumble of thoughts, trying instead to concentrate upon the cold, dank cell.

With mixed feelings he opened his eyes. The ghostly grey shapes had gone and in their place was a sharp image. He was in a long corridor, richly decorated, suggesting enormous wealth and for a moment he feared he was still in Gilfillan, but this was much wider than the corridors of his homeland. The wooden furniture also lacked the loving finish that an Alvalan carpenter would have added.

Spinning around, he sought something that would reveal his whereabouts. Just then a soldier stepped into the corridor and, with relief, he recognised his orange tunic. The Thracian sentry gave no sign that he had seen Lomar as he continued his vigil. Then a dark shape stepped out from the shadows, closing rapidly with the pacing man.

Lomar could do nothing but watch as an arm encircled the sentry's throat and a blade disappeared into his neck, stifling any cry. Lomar looked on in horror as the assassin was joined by another and together they carried the corpse out of sight.

Before Lomar could move, the assassins returned. Both wore ochre robes and their heads were shaven. Lomar had never seen men like this before and he watched in fascination as silently they crept along the corridor, daggers drawn.

By their sides, Lomar could see ghostly shapes and the men paused as though listening to silent instructions from these spectres. Lomar frowned, trying to see the shapes more clearly. It was like looking at sunlight reflected in the rippling waters of a fast-flowing stream. For a moment, he wondered if they were truly there or whether it was his imagination.

The two men looked about the corridor as if searching for something. One of them looked directly at Lomar, and all at once they were moving towards him.

He willed himself to return to his cell, but stubbornly remained where he was. The link to his body was gone. He spun around searching for even the slightest trace of the delicate thread. He wailed in fear. The sound of his cry echoed about the corridor around him.

Chapter 14

Silent Night

In the Allund camp, the young priest paused to listen while all around him men turned in for the night. He continued for another few paces before taking cover behind a large wagon. Through narrowed eyes, he studied the ground between him and the prison compound, expertly searching for cover that would take him to his goal.

It was virtually bare. Only one small shrub and a slight hollow cast sufficient shadow to conceal him. He cocked his head, searching the darkness for sentries. Two he located easily, sitting huddled together by a small campfire, their backs to him conversing in low tones as they watched their prisoners. A third sentry paced the perimeter more from boredom than duty. His clumsy gait made him easy to find.

The priest shifted nervously. He had volunteered to join the priesthood at a young age, eager to escape the demands of his father's farm. His eagerness had set him apart from the others with the result he had few friends, but, to compensate, he had often been told he had a promising future.

Now, in the dark of night, he did not want to let his superiors down. Moving away from the safety of the wagon he aimed towards the bush, clearing his mind, allowing contact with his Shaol. A strange thrill suggested a warning and, in response, he crouched lowering himself flat, hugging the cold earth.

To his left, a sentry paced across the open ground. His silhouette came between the priest and his comrades' campfire, and the priest waited for him to move on before continuing. Swiftly he reached the bush, throwing himself beneath its branches. The last stretch was more open with only the hollow in the ground for cover. It would require all of his concentration to cross without being observed, and he allowed himself a few moments to calm the swift beating of his heart.

While he waited, he counted the paces of the sentry, watching the man until certain of his routine. When the soldier turned, he crawled from hiding, counting off the seconds. When the sentry was again about to turn, he lay still, hugging the ground. He didn't move until his Shaol told him the way was safe.

Finally he reached the stockade. His greatest danger now was from the men within. Fortunately the prisoners appeared to be asleep, cloaks pulled up tightly against the chill.

The priest searched for his prey. Earlier that evening, Brama had pointed him out. They had gone openly to the stockade which had attracted quite a crowd; few of the Allund soldiers had seen a Thracian before. Brama had nodded towards a young man with long brown hair. He had no compunction against killing, but, for a moment, he wondered who the man was and why he had to be killed. Then again, he shouldn't question his orders even though once the deed was done, there was little likelihood of escape.

His Shaol located his victim. Only a few bodies separated them so the task should be easy. From within his robes, he withdrew his soot blackened blade, swiftly sawing through a rope securing one of the posts. He repeated this with two others and soon had a gap wide enough to crawl through. Once inside, he lay on the ground for a moment making certain that those around him still slept.

Blending in with the shadows, he edged away from the fence, crawling around intervening bodies until only two sleeping forms lay between him and his target.

Raising himself into a crouch, he prepared to leap. Just then his Shaol sent a thrill of alarm. So intent was he on the task, he was distracted by the urgent call. By his side a figure stirred and dark eyes fastened on his.

Too late he saw the glint of metal as the figure lashed out. A deep, biting pain lanced through his ribs, causing him to miss his footing. Instead of leaping, he fell in a sprawl onto the sleeping men. More pain erupted in his side as his own weight bore down on the knife. His mind screamed out against his failure. His sacrifice would have been worth it, but now he died knowing that he had failed. With a scream that ended in a frothy gurgle, he passed into whatever fate awaited one of the Priests of Ryoch.

Kaplyn awoke with a start, the memory of a dragon's scream ringing in his ears. A cry leapt from his own lips. He was pinned beneath a crushing weight and he struggled to free himself, but failed.

The priest's death scream awoke the other prisoners. Thinking they were under attack, they leapt from their blankets with shouts of fear.

Hearing their cries, Kaplyn's struggling increased and then, all at once, the weight was gone. Leaping to his feet, he looked about, trying to make sense of the milling shapes and pale faces.

Tallin confronted him, a wry smile on his lips.

"It seems that you have an enemy within the priesthood," he said, indicating the corpse with the toe of his boot. A dagger protruded from the figure's side, the blade buried to the hilt. Kaplyn also noticed the knife held in the priest's outstretched fist.

One of Tallin's men bent to retrieve the dagger, but Tallin stopped him just as a detachment of Allund soldiers appeared by the fence, torches held aloft.

"What's going on?" sounded a deep voice. "Stand back from the fence," the officer commanded.

Grudgingly, the prisoners gave ground, revealing the priest's corpse.

"Your assassin has failed," Tallin taunted.

The officer looked genuinely shocked. One of his men, crouching by the fence where the priest had gained access, called over. "Over here! A hole has been cut in the stockade."

Tharn Orrin appeared, buttoning his jacket and adjusting his sword. The officer of the watch moved to intercept him, and the two men spoke before Orrin approached.

"Bring the body out," he commanded. "What happened?" he asked. The question wasn't aimed at anyone in particular, but Tallin replied.

"This assassin was trying to kill Kaplyn and I prevented it."

"Where did you get the knife?" the Tharn asked.

"It's a trinket I would not be without," Tallin answered coldly.

"Tharn," Kaplyn interrupted. "What just happened proves you are making a mistake attacking CarCamel. Thrace is not your enemy."

Orrin considered Kaplyn darkly. "We shall see," he said, "Bring these two to my tent," he said, addressing the officer of the watch.

However, the guards had no chance to carry out the order. A cry from many throats rent the air followed by the clash of steel. Orrin looked alarmed and turned to see where the noise was coming from. Moments later, a man came running though the milling soldiers, his breathing laboured.

"Sir, from Haft Sefton. The priests are attacking the camp. His men are holding, but he requests reinforcements."

The Tharn glanced at Kaplyn and the others as though suspecting trickery. "Guard these men!" he ordered before hurrying away towards the sounds of the fighting, calling to the runner to summon his commanders.

One of Tallin's men scaled the stockade wall to view the battle. Below, the sentries called for him to come down, but he ignored them, peering instead to where the fighting was at its thickest. Eventually the officer of the watch called up to ask what he could see.

"There's fighting," the man answered. "I can see the priests in one group surrounded by Allund soldiers. I think that the priests are trying to come this way, but the soldiers are preventing them."

Kaplyn climbed up by the Thracian's side in time to see the two sides parting as the soldiers reformed their lines. The priests were in a wedge formation, the apex pointing towards the prisoners. Kaplyn was shocked to see how many soldiers lay either injured or dead between the two forces, and yet he could see very few injured priests.

With a cry, the wedge started forward and the Allund line collapsed before them.

"We need to get out of here!" Kaplyn shouted above the din, jumping down. The officer of the watch looked undecided as though doubting his own authority to move the prisoners, or perhaps suspecting a trick.

"We are emissaries of Thrace," Kaplyn continued, seeing the other man's doubt. "If we are harmed, then war between Allund and Thrace will be unavoidable."

That convinced the officer. Using his sword, he hacked the ropes holding the gate, calling to his soldiers to help. Very soon, Kaplyn and the others were free of the compound but ringed by sentries with weapons drawn.

"That way!" the officer ordered, pointing away from the battle with his blade.

The clamour of battle grew in ferocity and Kaplyn risked glancing back. Some of the priests had broken through and were racing after them. He called out to the others to run.

From the gloom to their front, men appeared, carrying long bows. Kaplyn feared that the archers might mistake them for an enemy, but the cries of their officer alerted the newcomers in time. Kaplyn and the others were herded through their ranks as they loosed their first volley. Behind them several shapes went down, but many more surged forward.

Another volley followed, slowing the priests' advance. Allund troops arrived behind the priests, encircling them. Torches, illuminating the scene, revealed perhaps fifty priests standing in a tight circle, surrounded by men with blades at the ready and shields raised. There was an unwillingness to attack; too many had already died at the hands of the priests.

Archers held their bows ready, awaiting the command to loose. Kaplyn did not hear the command given, but all at once arrows filled the air. He watched partly in relief and partly in horror as the priests were cut down. As one, their ranks fell, pierced with many arrows as volley after volley was poured into the tight circle. Nobody cried out, nor did they attempt to avoid their fate. Finally, no one stood within the circle that had once been men.

Silence reigned as the onlookers looked at the pile of corpses. A lone voice ordered the men back to their posts. The command spread and gradually the field cleared, leaving Kaplyn and the prisoners with their escort.

Kaplyn looked back towards their prison in horror, seeing a long trail of dead along the way. If they had remained where they were, they would have perished. Amongst the fallen, the living searched for survivors and, occasionally, a voice called out for a stretcher.

"How can so few priests inflict so much damage?" Tallin asked, looking at Kaplyn.

The Allund officer with them shook his head, equally mystified, while no doubt congratulating himself for having made the right decision to free them.

A runner approached the group and saluted the officer. "Sir, you are to escort Haft Tallin and Kaplyn to the Tharn's tent."

Once inside, they found it filled with anxious-looking officers. Orrin was issuing orders, and, as the tent emptied, he turned to Kaplyn and Tallin. Both his face and uniform were splattered with blood.

"What happened?" Kaplyn asked.

"I'm not certain," came the honest reply. "The priests betrayed us. I have no doubt you, Kaplyn, were the intended victim. Perhaps I should have taken your earlier claim more seriously?"

"Do you believe Kaplyn's claim?" Tallin asked. His eyes were wide, and his tone suggested disbelief.

"The priests did. I can think of no other reason for their actions this night."

"Where is the head priest?" Kaplyn asked, looking about the tent.

"Brama? He has disappeared and no one saw him leave." The Tharn sat down behind his table, looking troubled.

"What now?" Tallin asked.

"We have wounded to attend to, and dead to bury," the Tharn replied tersely. "I do not know how the priests managed it, but we have close to three hundred dead and over four hundred wounded."

Kaplyn was astonished. "There were less than two hundred priests! How could they inflict such losses?"

"You saw them!" Orrin stated bluntly. "It was as though Drachar guided them. Never before have I seen men fight like that, and I hope I never do again. If it was not for our archers, then our losses would have been higher."

"What do you plan to do after the wounded are tended?" Tallin asked, knowing his country's fate still lay in the balance.

"How should I know?" the Tharn answered. "I was under orders to either seek supplies or to take CarCamel by force. I am a soldier, *not* a politician. I have sent a messenger to Dundalk informing the Council about the priests' betrayal and your claim to the throne, Kaplyn."

"CarCamel is in danger," Kaplyn countered, "and so might your troops be if they remain here. You cannot defend your current position. If, however, you supported Thrace, your army could make a difference."

"Is it possible that the priests were in league with Trosgarth?" Tallin asked.

Orrin shrugged. "I cannot say for certain," he replied, his brow creased with concentration. "Have your men ready to ride at first light," Orrin said to Tallin after a moment's pause.

Tallin nodded. "And where do we ride?"

"The army marches to CarCamel!" Orrin declared, looking Tallin firmly in the eyes. For a moment Tallin scowled, but the Tharn held up a hand. "We are not fools, nor has the Prophecy been forgotten. If there is an army from Trosgarth, then my duty is clear. We shall aid Thrace in the protection of their city. Afterwards, I shall march the army back to Dundalk where I hope that the Council has a very good answer for what has happened this night."

Chapter 15

Sick Prisoner

"Lomar!" Lars repeated, cradling the albino's head in his massive hands. Lomar's deathly pallor had always worried the big man, and now his paleness seemed much more pronounced, even for an albino.

In the corner of the room, Tumarl sat with his knees pulled up to his chest, offering no help, gripped by a deep despair as he relived his imprisonment in the deep mines. Hugging his knees, he focused on the pain as Lars called out to Lomar once more. Tumarl used the big man's voice to still those crying out within his mind. He crawled towards Lars and, looking over his shoulder, saw Lomar's pale face, barely visible against the inky blackness. By his side, Tumarl could sense the big man's panic. By Lars' tone, Tumarl realised Lomar was seriously ill and might even be dying.

Faces sprang to mind of others who had died. Names tumbled through his thoughts, and tears blurred his vision. In frustration, he threw himself at the door. His fists hammered on the wood as he screamed for the guards.

Lars jumped with the unexpected commotion. He called none too gently for Tumarl to calm himself. It was one thing to have Tumarl as silent as the grave, but he almost preferred that to his sudden outburst. At that moment though, the door's wooden viewing port was flung opened and a pale light flooded into their cell, half blinding the two men.

"What's going on?" a gruff voice demanded.

Tumarl was shaking, but the light seemed to calm him.

"Our companion's ill. We cannot rouse him," Lars explained, trying to see a face beyond the light.

The guard tried to peer through the small opening, cursing that he could not see. Clearly he had heard the rumour that the man with the deathly white skin was a demon and he was afraid to enter.

Lars listened as the guard ordered a colleague to fetch Astalus or one of his wizard cronies.

Astalus entered a short while later accompanied by guards, their weapons drawn, as they fanned out around the cell, eying Lomar uncertainly. The wizard looked tired and not particularly pleased at having been roused from his bed.

He knelt beside Lomar, muttering that a physician should have been called. He shook Lomar none too gently, calling his name — to no effect. Frowning, he traced a rune upon Lomar's forehead, scattering herbs about his body. Still nothing happened.

"Fetch a brazier," Astalus commanded. One of the guards hastily retreated from the cell.

"Has this happened before?" Astalus asked.

Lars frowned. "I do not know."

"Think man! Is there anything unusual about him that you can tell me?"

"Lomar told us that his spirit sometimes travels from his body. Kaplyn told me this is how Lomar first met us; something about his Shaol," Lars offered.

"You mean his soul can be separated from his body?" Astalus asked, as the guard re-entered the room carrying the brazier. The soldier started to light it, but Astalus intervened. He spoke a single word of power and a flame leapt from the coals. The guard retreated to the corner of the cell, while his companions watched the magical flames with distrust.

Astalus sprinkled herbs on the flames, drawing runes over the burning coals before tracing another upon Lomar's forehead, calling his name softly. At first Lomar did not stir and his pallor seemed even more deathly. Tumarl and Lars were starting to fear the worse when Astalus called his name again, more urgently, the strain of his magic clearly showing in his voice.

Lomar stirred and, through parted lips, gave out a soft cry. Arching his spine, he convulsed before falling back onto the floor. This time, though, there were clear signs he was breathing.

Astalus traced another rune and called Lomar's name again. His eyelids fluttered open and he looked up, puzzled.

"Assassins!" he mumbled, trying to sit up. Astalus caught his shoulders, gently pushing the albino back down.

"What did you say?" Astalus asked softly.

"Assassins!" Lomar repeated louder. "Here, somewhere — I do not know."

"What did you see?" Astalus tried, speaking slowly and clearly, trying to calm the agitated albino.

"I saw a long corridor, richly decorated. There were paintings of people decorating the walls and a sentry. A man came up behind him and killed him; There were two of them. Both wore robes and had shaven heads."

"Priests of Ryoch," Astalus hissed. "The King!" He leapt to his feet, gathering his robes as he raced from the cell, shouting the alarm as he ran, leaving the prisoners alone in their cell with the bemused guards, who looked on as though the wizard had gone mad.

Just as Lomar wakened, Kryan, one of the priests, was laying yet another corpse upon the floor of an empty chamber. Ragil, his companion, stood guard by the partially open door. Without a word the pair ventured out into the corridor, their footsteps cushioned by the thick carpet.

As Ariome predicted, they had easily gained access to the palace. Earlier that morning, she had released the enchanted scanth as close to the door as possible. Her spell had accelerated the insect's metabolism, and, when the eggs hatched, the hungry larvae had swiftly set about the wood eating their fill. As the day wore on, more grubs hatched, and each generation completed in moments a life-cycle that would normally take months. Had Ariome been able to watch, even she would have been impressed as one generation was replaced by another — and another...

By the time the priests reached the door, it was rotten and they had wedged it shut behind them as best they could.

From there, they made their way along long corridors, instinctively using their Shaols to guide them. They had ample warning when a sentry approached, but, still, they were forced to kill twice, each murder increasing the risk of detection. Time was running out, and they still hadn't found their intended targets, the King and the Prince.

At the foot of a broad flight of stairs, they paused. The time had come to split up. Kryan signalled to Ragil to continue upstairs. Ragil nodded and started to climb.

Kryan's heart was beating swiftly as he approached the first door in his search alone. The link with his Shaol was strong, but, even still, the image of the room in his mind's eye was grey and indistinct. He could barely make out the occupant. Stealthily, he entered, shutting the door behind him and cutting off the light that filtered through.

With his poisoned knife held at the ready, he glided towards the bed. He thrust the blade into the sleeping person's throat, holding it there as the figure convulsed. He waited before withdrawing the blade. Walking confidently to the window he drew back the curtain. Softly he cursed. It was not the King. Retracing his steps he sensed that the corridor was still empty.

Shouts sounded in the distance, and he now knew it was now a race against time. Swiftly he continued along the corridor, desperately seeking the correct door, at each feeling for a presence within. The distant voices became clearer, and realisation dawned that he was too late. Selecting a door at random he stepped inside.

"Who's there?" came a woman's voice.

Kryan turned. A young girl lay on the bed her eyes heavy with sleep. She was pretty, not that it mattered. Her eyes widened as he leapt towards her. As she tried to escape, the sheets tangled her legs, and she fell to the floor with a thud. Kryan struck once. With a low moan she fell back, her lifeblood flowing from her body.

Kryan returned to stand by the door, pressing an ear against the stout wood. In the corridor, doors were opening. He cleared his mind to his Shaol. Vague images of people milling around came to his mind's eye. He heard a voice of authority that could only be the King. Kryan placed his hand on the door handle in readiness to spring out...

"Astalus! What is the meaning of this intrusion?" the King asked, stepping from his room, tying his robes about his portly frame. By Astalus' side, five guards stood panting, their eyes searching the corridor for signs of an intruder.

"There are assassins in the palace, Sire," Astalus proclaimed between gasps for air.

A thump sounded from upstairs and the King looked momentarily stunned. "The Prince!" he bellowed and started racing along the corridor.

The priest timed his moment perfectly. Flinging open the door it slammed into a guard following behind the King, throwing him off his feet into the man behind. As the assassin struck, the King threw up his arm instinctively. The blade bit deep before being deflected from bone.

The King cried out as the assassin tried to strike again, but one of the guards threw himself bodily at him causing the priest to stagger back against the wall. His Shaol screamed a warning as two guards attacked from either side.

Astalus shouted out a spell of binding, but before the first syllables left his lips, the guards closed with the assassin. Not even his Shaol could save him, trapped between two men and pinned by a third. He was impaled upon their swords; a scream rent the air as he collapsed lifeless onto the floor. Astalus cursed, as he had wanted to capture the man alive for interrogation.

The King remained standing, holding his arm and staring at the corpse lying at his feet. Another thump from upstairs reminded him why they had been racing along the corridor.

"Protect my son!" he yelled at the guards about him. "You, too, Astalus!"

As one, they ran up the stairs and then raced along the corridor to the Prince's room. Astalus threw himself at the door, tumbling headlong into the darkened interior. Urgently he summoned a light from his staff.

Furniture and broken ornaments were strewn in disarray about the floor. Prince Alyn was trapped in a corner, crouching defensively before another priest who held a slim dagger in his hand. The Prince's broad sword gave him an advantage, but, even with it, he was trapped.

The sudden appearance of Astalus distracted Prince Alyn, who looked across at his rescuer, and this was the opening the priest had been waiting for. He leapt at the younger man, screaming his victory.

In a blur Astalus traced a rune, barking words of binding. The guards behind him, heedless of the wizard's spell, launched themselves across the intervening space.

In mid-stride, the priest froze as Astalus' spell ensnared him. That should have been the end of the matter but, by sheer willpower, the priest slowly continued his advance, fighting against the spell. The Prince remained immobile, transfixed by the look of hatred upon the assassin's face, unable even to raise his own sword to protect himself.

One of the guards leapt at the assassin, hacking at the priest's exposed back. The metal bit deep, severing tendons and muscle before lodging in bone. As though released from a spell Alyn raised his own weapon and brought it down hard upon the priest's brow. The assassin dropped like a brick, his dagger falling from dead fingers.

For a while the men stared at the corpse as a large crimson pool formed about the man's shaven head. Then a cry from downstairs alerted them that something was still amiss. Astalus raced from the room to find several figures crouching upon the stairs.

Astalus ran down to find the King lying on the steps. He crouched down beside him, cradling his broad head in his arms. The King's eyes fluttered open, although the effort clearly cost him dearly. "My son?" he asked between gasps for air.

"He is unharmed," Astalus replied, his brow creased by a deep frown of concern. The wound did not look fatal, and, yet, it was clear that the King was dying. Alyn joined Astalus as others appeared from their rooms.

The King looked up at his son, smiling bravely as he felt his life seeping from him.

"Poison!" Astalus realised, speaking out loud. He racked his mind for a spell to counteract it, reaching for his herbs. However, he was too late; the King's body sagged in his arms, and a low moan escaped his lips.

"Father!" Alyn cried out. "Father!" Tears filled his eyes.

At the top of the stairs, Princess Catriona ran to the balcony; a look of foreboding upon her face. A great cry of anguish escaped her lips when she saw her father's body and her brother's tears. Collapsing, she sobbed uncontrollably.

Chapter 16

Race to Salvation

For the remainder of the night, the Allund camp was busy. The wounded were tended, the dead buried and it was well into mid-morning before the army was finally ready to move.

As a final act, the siege engine parts were torched. Soldiers rode or marched by the blaze as dark columns of smoke rose into a dismal sky where carrion crows circled the scene of slaughter, waiting their turn to investigate.

Soldiers grumbled as they marched. Rumours were rife. Some said a king had returned while others said Drachar had arisen and was marching on Thrace. There was plenty of time to reflect. That day's progress was slow, and they travelled late into the day when Orrin finally ordered that they camp for the night.

Kaplyn and the Thracian soldiers were kept together ringed by sentries, huddled about campfires for warmth. Many spent a restless night, tossing and turning in their blankets, the events of the previous night too fresh in their minds and the shadow of forthcoming events too close.

Kaplyn fared little better. His sleep was again haunted by dragons. Winged shapes flitted silently across his dreams, coming ever closer. He wanted to cry out in fear, and yet dared not in case they find him. It was as if an invisible barrier held them at bay. He awoke several times in the night, drenched in sweat, his heart racing.

At last weak, watery sunlight proclaimed the dawn. Cooks rattled metal pans, not caring that others slept, perhaps begrudging them their few moments longer in warm blankets. Then a shrill trumpet sounded reveille. Men groaned that it was too early, but arose to start their morning duties. Tharn Orrin insisted that they be given a warm meal before continuing, and that partially revived their flagging spirits. As soon as the meal was done, the wagons were packed and the lead scouts were sent out on patrol, while the night sentries were recalled for their turn to eat.

Finally, a long line of troops and cavalry waited in readiness to begin the day's march. Bright banners were unfurled to greet the day. Then the order was given, and men began their march towards the Thracian capital.

By mid-afternoon, the city came into sight. Tallin gazed upon his home whilst others in his troop muttered darkly, uncertain whether they returned as allies or prisoners. Soon, the city became more distinct, revealing tall turrets and bright pennants.

Tharn Orrin set up his command centre on a grassy knoll before summoning Kaplyn and Tallin. When they arrived, Orrin rose to greet them as they ducked into the tent. He asked Tallin to accompany him to seek an audience with their King. Tallin was to confirm to the King the priests' betrayal. Escorted by an officer and twenty Allund soldiers, carrying a flag of truce, they rode towards the city. Kaplyn watched them depart, silently wishing them luck.

"I cannot be King!" Alyn declared between clenched teeth, turning abruptly upon the other two people sitting in his private audience chamber. Through the open window, the city's bells rang out as her people mourned the death of their King.

Although deep down she had expected it, Catriona was horrified by his refusal. Her eyes were red-rimmed from crying, and she had no sympathy with her brother's wants. His anger seemed to burn deep into her soul, and she had to calm herself before replying.

"You have no option," she stated flatly. "Father is dead. Even as we speak, an army marches against us. The people need a strong king now more than ever: You are father's *heir*."

Astalus looked at Catriona with respect. All of her life she had taken an interest in the running of court, and she knew more about Thrace's people than anyone else. She also had all the qualities of leadership that her brother lacked. And yet, rather than take the crown, for it was clearly offered, she refused, preferring instead to aid him.

Her calm reaction to Alyn's outburst had the desired effect. His shoulders slumped and a look of pain filled his eyes. "I *cannot* be King, Cat," he implored, a look of pleading in his eyes. "I know nothing about court or of ruling people."

"We will both help you. You will not be alone," Astalus said, speaking softly. "Princess Catriona is right; your people need you. The assassination shows how strong our enemies are."

313

"I do not understand how this has happened," Alyn complained, slumping into one of the many ornate chairs, stretching his long legs before him and staring up at the ceiling as though seeking guidance from above. "*By the Kalanth*, what has happened? Allund used to be our ally!"

Astalus cast Catriona a sidelong glance; she looked troubled.

"Astalus, how did you know about the assassins?" she asked. "It was you who roused the palace guards, but how did you know?"

Astalus leant forward to speak more privately with the pair; his chair creaked as he moved. "I was summoned to the prison in the middle of the night. The albino was in a coma and there was little sign of life."

"Were the others with him?" Catriona interrupted.

Astalus nodded. "All save Kaplyn. He was sent with the peace envoy to speak with the Allund Commander. Lars, the big man, seemed calm enough when I entered. The other, the Thracian farmer...." Astalus frowned, trying to remember the name.

"Tumarl," Catriona jogged his memory.

"Yes, Tumarl. He had been wailing like a banshee. He seems to have a real fear of confinement since his imprisonment in the krell mines."

"He was a prisoner of the krell?" Catriona asked, somewhat annoyed that her brother had failed to tell her this. Alyn managed a feeble smile as though he considered the matter of little importance.

"Yes, and for many years by his account."

Astalus frowned as he tried to remember where he was in his narrative.

"I was in the cell," he reminded himself. "I remember shaking Lomar by the shoulders, but could not rouse him. It was clear that something was very much amiss. Casting a spell, I sought to find out what ailed him. Never before have I felt such a thing. For all the good my spell did, I might as well have been looking at wood or some other inanimate object. I cast the most powerful spell of healing I know, one that aligns the spirit with the four healing worlds of the Kalanth: air, fire, water and heaven. Lomar responded, crying out there was an assassin in the city. I immediately thought of the King and came to warn him although, because of the poison, too late."

"Have you since questioned the albino how he knew this?" Catriona asked.

Astalus nodded. Alyn grimaced, realising he should have thought to ask that.

"He was reluctant to tell me at first. Oh, I do not blame him," Astalus stated, seeing the other two frown. "His tale is incredible, to say the least, but it appears that we live in changing times. He claims that he can separate his soul from his body. How he does not know although he seems to think that it has something to do with Shaol."

"Is that possible?" Alyn interrupted sceptically. "I mean, for a man to separate his body and soul?"

Astalus shrugged his slim shoulders. "I work with magic and it always amazes me how little I know. It seems his vision was not just about us, and, even now, he is tormented with grief, claiming he saw an army marching from the mountains towards the KinAnar forest, where his people live. His fears seem real enough. If true, it is a terrible portent."

"Another army?" Catriona questioned.

Astalus nodded. "Krell, he claims. A considerable force marching from the mountains."

"And you believe him?" Alyn asked again.

"He did warn us about the assassins," Astalus reminded him.

"But nearly too late," Catriona replied thoughtfully. "He could have been planted amongst us to spread confusion."

"That would also mean that Kaplyn will betray us!" Alyn announced abruptly as though coming to a decision. He was not sure what to think of the Allunder; his claims seemed more than preposterous.

"But if there is an enemy army marching through the Pen-am-Pelleas Mountains, and Kaplyn is right about another army on our border, then that means only one thing," Catriona stated as though simply thinking aloud. The other two looked blank; it was clear they did not understand what she was implying.

"The Prophecy is coming to pass," she answered, her eyes locked upon the carpet as though she was unable to meet their eyes. "The krell tribes are united and Drachar's shade will lead them."

Alyn turned pale. "No. It's not possible!" he declared, rising and pacing across the room. "Drachar was killed centuries ago. There is no way he could return. These tales are preposterous. Men whose *souls* can be separated from their bodies, and armies of krell! I will not believe it! It is clear to me what is happening. Allund is marching against us — her priests have infiltrated the palace and killed our father. *That* is the reality!"

"We cannot be hasty," Catriona reminded him. "Allund may not have sanctioned father's assassination." The memory prompted the return of her grief so that she had to bite her lip to prevent the tears from flowing.

"Then how do we know whether Allund is an enemy or not? Even if there is a krell army, we cannot be sure that Allund is not in league with it."

The other two simply looked at Alyn, neither able to voice a solution to his dilemma. In the distance, the bells continued a slow mournful rhythm.

A knock upon the door interrupted them. Alyn called to whoever it was to enter; a young sentry stepped into the room, bowing low.

"Sire, an Allund messenger has arrived."

Alyn glanced nervously at the other two. "I shall speak with him. If you will excuse me." He strode from the room, neither glancing back nor giving the other two the opportunity to accompany him. Catriona looked towards Astalus. "Should we go with him?" she asked.

"He will call for us if he needs us," Astalus replied.

"He did not like the talk about Drachar," Catriona stated, testing Astalus.

The wizard rose stiffly, going to the window as though finding comfort in the tolling of the bells. It was dark outside and a light drizzle damped the window pane. The light from the palace windows reflected off the black stone outside, making the usual view unfamiliar.

"I have thought long and hard about the Prophecy," Astalus stated matter of factly. "As no doubt many others have. I have prayed that it would never come to pass in my lifetime." Astalus had his back to the Princess, but he could see her face reflected in the pane of glass before him, her silken whiteness exaggerated by the contrasting darkness.

"Only one line of the Prophecy makes sense: *When Tallin's crown once more does shine.*"

"I thought that no one knew what that meant?" she questioned.

Astalus smiled. "Say perhaps that we were afraid to tell people what it meant. Tallin is a constellation. Every five hundred years, or so, a star joins it, making the crown appear whole."

"When does this happen?" Catriona demanded.

"It happened a month ago...."

A look of horror crossed Catriona's face. "Why? Why have you kept this from us?"

Astalus shrugged and walked over to the hearth where he warmed his hands by the fire.

"Who would have believed us?" he asked. "The battle to defeat Drachar was long ago and is now nothing more than a memory. The people want to believe Drachar was destroyed, never to return. My concern though is that Drachar was only defeated because of the Eldric and their Narlassar sorcery."

"But Drachar, too, was a sorcerer," Catriona continued.

"Perhaps that is why the Eldric chose to depart the land. They could no longer live with the shame of their part in the Krell Wars. Don't forget Drachar was an Eldric lord."

316

Astalus turned to face her, his eyes saddened by the look of fear in her face. "Without the Eldric, we are powerless," he admitted. "It has forever been the hope of the Akrane that we would one day unravel the secret of their power before it was too late, but it appears that the sands of time have defeated us. We, the Akrane, were never a match for the Narlassar and our powers are weak by comparison. I doubt we will be able to defeat an enemy as powerful as Trosgarth."

"But surely the Eldric would not have left had they known Drachar might return someday?" Catriona asked hopefully.

Astalus shook his head. "I cannot say. Perhaps the Prophecy was written after they left, or perhaps they were more afraid of their own power."

"Where did they go? Can we not try to find them?"

"People have searched for them for close on five hundred years and yet not a trace has been found. Kaplyn and the others were searching for the Eldric when Vastra betrayed them. He was one of their party and a sorcerer by all accounts."

Astalus had already told Catriona as much as he knew about Kaplyn and the others, which was precious little. Now he wished he had spoken further with Kaplyn, especially concerning Vastra.

"And that leads us to the second line of the Prophecy: *Three princes through time to sleep*. I, like many others, had pondered that line, seeing it as a cryptic verse with the true meaning hidden. How wrong we all were."

"In what way?" Catriona asked.

"The line speaks plainly, or so I now believe; the coincidences are too many. Kaplyn, Lomar and Lars are the Princes mentioned in the verse. Oh, I know the link is tenuous, but then so too is the Prophecy. That is the nature of the beast. I have not spoken much with Kaplyn, so I do not know whether his claim to the Allund throne is true or not, but Lomar says that he is heir to the Gilfillan throne, and I, for one, believe him."

Catriona considered his words for a moment. "Is Lars a prince? I had heard he was from foreign lands."

"I questioned him about his home. It turns out that his father was the Glan-Cran of their village. Many of his people are farmers, choosing to live in smallholdings and only travelling to Lars' village on rare occasions. Since his homeland is so vast, his village is effectively a capital," Astalus concluded with a wry smile. "A Glan-Cran, it seems, is effectively a king!"

"If the Prophecy is fulfilled and Trosgarth is marching, then what allies can we call upon?"

Astalus shrugged. "Allund may be the only immediate ally, if they can be persuaded to side with us. As to the Southern Kingdoms, like us, they have dismissed Trosgarth as a threat. The dwarves of the Northern Kingdom have not been heard from in twenty to thirty years, and no one knows what has become of them. Having seen the krell army that Kaplyn described, I now fear something must have happened to them; they would not have let krell pass through their lands without a fight."

"We are alone, then?" Catriona asked.

Astalus nodded gravely.

Catriona felt as though the rug had been pulled from beneath her feet. She too had considered the Prophecy as an ancient account that would never be fulfilled, and, yet, here she was listening to strange stories that only yesterday she would have dismissed as foolish. Yet, in so many ways, Astalus' story sounded plausible.

Now more than ever, she wished that father was alive. Outside, the funeral bells ceased and, for several moments, the only sound was the patter of rain on the windows. Abruptly, the bells sounded again, ringing forth in a mighty peel, heralding Alyn's succession to the throne.

The King is dead!

Long live the King!

Chapter 17

An Uncertain Dawn

All too soon, Kaplyn was summoned to the Tharn's tent where he was met by a small group of soldiers, most of whom had gone on the peace envoy. Kaplyn was shocked that they had returned already. Quickly he scanned the faces for Tallin, but he was not present. Then he noticed the Tharn. The look on his face was enough to tell him that all was not well.

"The King has been assassinated," Orrin stated bluntly.

"When?" Kaplyn asked, greatly concerned for his friends.

"Last night," Orrin replied. "And what makes matters worse is that the assassins were Priests of Ryoch. Since the priests are only welcome in Allund, the Thracians believe that the assassins were acting under our orders.

Kaplyn was stunned but could not fault the Thracian logic. Absently he fingered his scar.

"If we are outside the walls and the enemy attacks, we will be butchered," Kaplyn announced.

The Tharn nodded. "All we can do is send another envoy in the morning. I suggest we both go and see if we can make sense of this madness."

Tallin felt growing bewilderment as he stood before his new liege Lord, King Alyn, who seemed to have the same short temperament as his father. He had just arrived back and had told the new King about the priests' betrayal of the Allund army, but Alyn simply refused to listen.

"My father has been killed at the hand of an Allund assassin," Alyn was saying. "And now their army camps before our gate demanding entry! For all we know, Allund and Trosgarth are in league."

Tallin remained silent, confused himself about Allund's part in the assassination. He glanced at the other four men in the room, hoping that they might make sense of the situation, but Astalus and the Tharn Commanders remained silent.

"The story of an attack by the priests may be a clever ploy to make us open the gates," Alyn continued, coming to a halt at the end of the table and looking at the others to see if they agreed with him.

Tallin tried to catch Astalus' attention, but failed. Of those present, he felt that Astalus knew King Alyn best of all.

"We cannot even be sure if a krell army exists, and, yet, an enemy lies camped at our very gates for all to see. They are the real threat. I will not betray our people until I am certain of Allund's intent."

"Sire, should we send messengers to the Southern Kingdoms, requesting their aid?" Tharn Ballan asked.

The newly-crowned King shook his head. "We cannot. Not without proof Trosgarth and Aldrace are involved. If your sighting," he continued, turning to Astalus, "is nothing more than a raiding party, then we would have to foot the bill. That we could not afford, especially with the failing of our crops. Besides, no one would believe us."

His voice trailed into silence. Tallin watched his King, hoping he was right and the krell army Kaplyn had seen was nothing more than a raiding party. If not, the Allund army trapped beyond the protection of the city walls could well be in serious trouble.

That night, campfires sprang up around the knoll outside the city. Curious citizens went to the walls to view the army, uncertain whether it was friend or foe. No word had come from the palace; it was as though Alyn's inaction was spreading so that even his commanders seemed uncertain. In one quarter of the city, the people celebrated that Allund was a friend, and yet in another men sharpened their weapons.

In silence, the two forces settled down for the night as a cloak of darkness enveloped the land.

At the crack of dawn, Kaplyn was summoned once again to the Tharn's presence. As he ducked beneath the tent flap into the cold of the morning, he glanced involuntarily towards the north where black clouds gathered on the horizon. Suddenly, a cold wind gusted causing him to shiver.

"A storm comes," his escort said.

"Let's hope it passes us by," Kaplyn answered. His hand fell away from his shirt front. He had not realised he had been fingering his scar.

Outside the Tharn's tent, a small group of men were making final adjustments to their saddles. At their head, sitting astride his mount and looking very much a warrior, sat Tharn Orrin.

Kaplyn swung into his saddle. Orrin signalled and the column set off towards the city, leaving the army to break camp.

Together they rode across the wooden bridge. Once on the other bank, it was only a short distance to the walls.

As they rode towards the gate, Kaplyn and those around him frequently glanced back at the dark clouds to the north. The lead clouds, having been splayed by the wind, looked like fingers reaching out towards them. A strong breeze gusted and in response the pennants on the walls snapped in frenzy.

Movement on the wall caught Kaplyn's attention. He recognised the Tharn Commanders from his previous meeting. Princess Catriona appeared and his heart skipped a beat. King Alyn joined them, wearing his father's crown. Kaplyn hoped that nothing had happened to Lars, Lomar and Tumarl in his absence, remembering King Sharroch's angry words when he had left.

"What is an Allund army doing before the walls of CarCamel, uninvited and arrayed for war?" came a voice from above.

Tharn Orrin grimaced. "We have been betrayed and seek sanctuary. We offer arms in aid of your defence."

"Defence?" came the reply. "We have no need for aid, unless it is from you."

Tharn Orrin was furious. He glanced uncertainly at Kaplyn.

Upon the wall, Astalus came alongside his King and spoke to him. "I would like to cast a spell of seeing to the north," Astalus suggested. "Those clouds worry me."

Alyn nodded and two soldiers brought forward a lighted brazier. By his side, Catriona stirred restlessly. He knew she disapproved of his decision to leave the Allunds outside the city, but he did not trust them.

Astalus looked deep into the flame of the brazier and gasped.

"Sire," Astalus said, but the King remained where he was. "Sire! You *must* look!"

The King's eyes flashed angrily and he stormed across to Astalus. However, as soon as he looked within the flames his face clouded and his frown deepened. He sucked in his breath, groaning.

"How could I have been so wrong?" he muttered.

The Tharns gathered around to see what had shocked him. At first the scene was difficult to interpret. They then realised that they were looking upon thousands and thousands of small individual shapes from above, as though a giant ant hill had been disturbed. Figures marched in disarray across the countryside, completely obscuring the ground.

"We have no choice but to trust the Allunds," Astalus urged. "If we do not aid them they will be massacred."

Alyn could not comprehend what Astalus was saying, so deep was his shock. Catriona joined her brother as he looked within the magical flames; her gasp jolted Alyn's attention away from the fire.

"We *must* open the gates," Catriona agreed, seeing the hordes of krell and men coming towards them. "We don't have much time."

"I cannot order the gates open," Alyn said miserably. "If I do, the city will be lost."

"If you do not then we are certainly lost," Astalus whispered by his side. "We have insufficient men to hold the walls. The Allund army could make the difference between survival and annihilation."

"They *killed* father!" Alyn moaned. "We *cannot* trust them."

"You are wrong," Catriona insisted, trying to still the racing of her heart. "It was the priests who assassinated father. Haft Commander Tallin says that the priests attacked the Allund camp. We have to trust them. Look at the size of the approaching army."

Once more Alyn's gaze dropped to look into the fire. "*By the Kalanth, what must I do?*"

Catriona spun away from the brazier and went to the rear of the battlement. "Open the gates!"

Tharn Shelder stepped forward, his moustache bristling with rage. "No, Sire! We must not."

Alyn could not meet his gaze but seemed happier that Catriona had taken the responsibility away from him. He simply nodded at his sister.

"Open the gates!" she repeated.

Below her, men ran to the gatehouse, and soon they heard the heavy mechanism rotating.

Both Tharn Orrin and Kaplyn kept looking back at the darkening horizon. Half of the sky was now filled with thick, black clouds and the rumble of distant thunder could clearly be heard.

"Bring the army across the river," Orrin ordered one of his commanders. "Cavalry first. Deploy them to our flank, and then the infantry. Bring the wagons last of all."

The man saluted, wheeled his horse around and raced off towards the camp. Others in the group were staring fearfully at the horizon. Before them, the gates slowly opened to reveal the long tunnel leading to the city beyond. The tunnel was empty; Kaplyn had an uneasy feeling as he stared into its blackness.

The sound of horses galloping across the wooden bridge behind them made him turn. The cavalry seemed to take an age to cross the rickety bridge. Once across, they fanned out in good order facing the north. Then, it was the turn of the infantry. Men carried as much as they were able as they marched towards the gates. On the opposite bank, Kaplyn saw the wagons and sensed the frustration of their drivers at having to wait their turn; he did not envy them.

The sky had turned leaden, and dark clouds massed across the heavens as if the war would not to be confined to the land alone. A dark storm was brewing.

"Grakyn," Kaplyn declared suddenly, pointing to the small black shapes in the sky. By his side, Orrin glared into the heavens, a look of fear in his eyes.

By now the front ranks of marching men had crossed the bridge and were heading towards the city. Many had seen the shapes in the sky and were pointing these out to companions. Tharn Orrin urged his horse towards the men, calling for them to break into double time. The bridge was a bottleneck that would be catastrophic if his men panicked.

Kaplyn rode up alongside the Tharn. The black specs flying towards them were clearer now.

"We will lose the supplies!" Orrin muttered angrily.

"Better the supplies than the men," Kaplyn stated. "Do you have any wizards?"

The Tharn shook his head and Kaplyn frowned. "I do not understand: Your troops were hidden from Astalus by a spell of seeing!"

"We have no wizards," Orrin said.

"Perhaps it was the priests who prevented Astalus from seeing your army," Kaplyn speculated.

"If that is true, then the priests would be discredited in Allund," Tharn Orrin replied. "Sorcery was banned many years ago." He returned his attention to the army's progress.

The front ranks had reached the gates but the column still stretched across the bridge from the opposite bank. They were losing the race, and the lead grakyn were fast approaching. Orrin urged the men to run faster. Men sprinted past, racing for the safety of the city. The bridge rattled with the passage of so many booted feet; Kaplyn thought it would shatter at any moment.

A sudden flash of light exploded by the bridge as a grakyn released its power. Others flew high above, hurling spears amongst the men. Those upon the bridge were too tightly packed to defend themselves.

Kaplyn and Orrin mustered as many archers as they could to shoot at the grakyn, which flew higher, but the troops below remained in range of their attack. A bolt of fire exploded on the bridge, throwing bodies to either side. Men screamed as fire clung to their clothing, and many leapt into the water to douse the flames. Others raced across the flaming span, risking the fire to reach the safety of the opposite bank. Kaplyn called to them to hurry as more flames burst around them.

Some soldiers on the far bank unbuckled their armour and threw themselves into the water in an attempt to cross. Quite a few crossed this way while the bridge became crammed with bodies. The queue of wagons upon the other bank was halted by the obstruction, and men were yelling ahead to try to clear the way. A few men abandoned their wagons and ran for the bridge while they were still able to cross.

Bolt after bolt of power pulverised the wooden structure which had already held together longer than Kaplyn had thought possible. Finally, it disintegrated completely in a blast that hurled dozens of screaming men into the river. Many disappeared beneath the cold-looking water, and Kaplyn prayed that they would resurface farther downstream.

The grakyn, having destroyed the bridge, now turned their attention to the cavalry who held their ground as best they could. However, Kaplyn could see that panic was starting to affect the men and horses. Suddenly, one of the grakyn was engulfed in a ball of flame and its fiery form crashed to the earth with a loud thud. More grakyn followed, and Kaplyn guessed the wizards in the city were lending their aid. The grakyn flew higher to avoid the wizards' fire and then, as one, turned and fled.

All around Kaplyn was confusion. Men were swimming across the river whilst others remained upon the far bank, calling across for help. Kaplyn was relieved to see that the bulk of the men were across, and few now remained upon the far bank.

"Go back!" Kaplyn shouted across the river. "Head towards the mountains and get back to Allund." His voice was lost amongst the screaming. He waved his arms in an attempt to make himself understood. A few did turn and started running across the plain. Silently Kaplyn wished them luck.

Orrin rode up beside him, his face stern and marked with soot. Behind them, the gates were still open, and men were crossing the ground for the sanctuary that the city offered. Others dragged themselves from the river. "We are not going to make it!" the Tharn stated flatly, above the background din.

Kaplyn turned to look to the north. Shapes, half concealed by the gloom, were racing towards them. It took his eyes a moment to adjust to the scene. Mounted krell screamed defiance, spears thrust forward towards them.

"What are they riding?" Kaplyn asked

"Chalf," Orrin replied.

"What?" There was little similarity to anything Kaplyn had seen before. They were a mix of horse and hound. Their rear ends were low to the ground, but the legs were well muscled and easily carried the animal and rider at speed. It was clear the enemy would reach the city before all of their infantry reached the safety of the city.

Orrin urged his mount to the head of the Allund cavalry, and Kaplyn followed, stooping down to retrieve a spear from a fallen grakyn. Behind him the cavalry fanned out into a long line facing the oncoming enemy. Calmly the men removed their cloaks, packing them in their saddle straps. The men then buckled metal guards onto their forearms before tucking their lances under their arms and readying their shields.

Seeing his men ready, Orrin gave the order to advance. The troops urged the line of mounts forward towards the howling krell who, sensing that their prey was trapped, in turn urged their steeds to greater haste, eager for the fray. Kaplyn scanned the enemy, realising that in their haste to attack they had spread themselves perilously thin. The main part of the army was still some distance behind the mounted troops.

The order came to charge, and Kaplyn kicked his mount's flanks. The earth trembled beneath the massed hooves. Never before had he taken place in a cavalry charge, and his heart hammered in his chest. The sound of so many running horses was fearful and not just for the enemy. He prayed he would not be unhorsed.

The two forces impacted with a terrifying clash. Lances ripped through armour and krell fell screaming from their mounts. Men fell, too, as chalf pulled down horses, their pitiful cries filling the air. The Allund cavalry, with their long lances, had the advantage, and they broke through the enemy ranks, finding themselves with open fields before them.

Commands were hurriedly shouted for an *about turn,* and the entire line slid to a halt. With a precision borne of practice, the riders wheeled their mounts and within seconds were ready to attack. The enemy was completely disorganised; their chalf reared uncontrollably, and some even started fighting amongst themselves, angrily leaping at their neighbours.

The Allund cavalry's training came into its own as they charged a second time with sabres drawn. Kaplyn struggled with his mount, gripping fiercely with his knees. He managed to turn but couldn't maintain the line with the rest of the troop. He was behind the others as they cut a swathe through the krell ranks.

Kaplyn thrust at a krell, but his spear was wrenched from his grasp. Unarmed, all he could do was duck and twist to avoid the weapons of the demoralised krell who were simply fighting to stay alive. Suddenly the cavalry were through the milling ranks, and before them were the open gates of the city.

Foot troops were still racing towards the gates, and Kaplyn guessed these men were from the wagons, having probably swum the river. Orrin saw the men and ordered his cavalry to pick them up. Some riders peeled to one side but before Kaplyn could help, the ground erupted and by his side a rider and his horse were engulfed in flame. The grakyn were back.

Orrin shouted orders which were swiftly relayed along the line. With military precision, the flanks slowed while the centre maintained its speed, bringing the racing men into file. At breakneck speed the mounted soldiers thundered through the gateway, through the long covered archway and into the city proper. Inside, the infantry scattered, making room for the horses.

High above, the grakyn continued to attack. The wizards on the walls hurled fire and lightning back at the distant shapes, which turned tail and fled as the heavy gates clanged shut with ominous finality. They had made it, but at what cost?

Chapter 18

Preparations for War

Kaplyn dismounted, breathing hard. A Thracian soldier greeted Tharn Orrin, offering to escort him to the King. Looking like thunder, Orrin stormed off with Kaplyn following in his wake. Up several flights of stairs they went to the city's inner walls where they found King Alyn surrounded by his tharns. Alyn also looked angry, as though unable to forgive the Allunds for his father's death.

Kaplyn pushed ahead of Orrin, trying to avert a disaster in the making. "Your Majesty, we are sorry to hear about the loss of your father, and I am sure I speak for the Allund nation when I say he was a great and noble King."

Alyn's shoulders sagged and the anger drained from his face, leaving him looking tired and dispirited. By Kaplyn's side he sensed Orrin was taken aback by the King's open display of grief. Kaplyn had correctly guessed that Orrin was angry it had taken so long to open the gates.

"Your claim to the throne has been accepted?" Alyn asked softly.

Kaplyn glanced sideways at Orrin. "No. But my claim will be put to the Council."

"So I should address myself to you as the representative of the Allund forces," the King said, turning to Orrin.

"Yes, Sire," Orrin confirmed.

The King smiled. By his side, Catriona reminded him that they had not been introduced. Kaplyn was still shocked by her close resemblance to Callan's daughter from so long ago. He found himself staring at her and had to look away embarrassed when she looked back at him.

"I am Tharn Orrin of Allund, Sire," Orrin said, saluting. "And I offer the Allund forces for the defence of this city."

"I suggest your foot soldiers join our men on the outer wall. Do you have archers?" the King asked.

The Tharn nodded.

The King seemed relieved. "Good, that is good news. Tharn Shelder will show you where best to deploy."

With the pleasantries taken care of, they turned to watch the enemy who had slowed their advance now that the gates were shut. Krell lolled around as though uncertain what to do next. Some jeered at the defenders and even a few spears were thrown, but the height of the walls made the attempts look feeble. Behind the krell came disciplined ranks of men, carrying tall banners in Aldracian colours.

"We had a patrol out there!" Orrin exclaimed despondently.

"Perhaps they will evade the enemy and seek sanctuary in the mountains," Astalus said.

"Have you sent messengers to the Southern Kingdoms?" Kaplyn asked.

Alyn shook his head. "We ... I mean, *I* did not believe there could be an army so vast. Tonight, under cover of darkness, I will send men out to seek aid. But I fear I may have hesitated overlong."

"My friends were imprisoned before I left, Sire. Are they free now?" Kaplyn asked.

The King turned to Tallin. "Escort Kaplyn to the prisoners and see that they are released. See to it that they are armed." He turned back to Kaplyn. "You are welcome to watch the battle here or you may wish to join your countrymen. The choice is yours."

"Thank you, Your Majesty," Kaplyn replied. He smiled warmly at Tallin who grinned back at his ex-prisoner, and together the two men departed for the city dungeons.

The news that Allund had come to aid Thrace spread quickly. The delighted people showered the Allund soldiers with flowers, welcoming them as heroes.

Avoiding the crowds, Tallin led them by back routes to a round stone building which Kaplyn guessed was the prison. Inside, a Guard Commander and three men were seated behind a table, discussing what might be happening. They fell silent when Tallin entered.

"The King orders the release of ...?" Tallin started, but then looked blank, turning to Kaplyn.

"Lars, Lomar and Tumarl," Kaplyn offered.

328

"That's right! Well ... see to it!" Tallin said, seeing the look of confusion on the Guard Commander's face.

"Go fetch the three men," the Commander ordered, turning to one of his men.

As the guard left, the Commander asked what was happening at the gate. Tallin told him of the recent events, describing the size of the enemy army. The other man visibly paled at the news.

Then abruptly, framed in the doorway, shielding their eyes from the light, the prisoners appeared. Kaplyn greeted them cheerfully and Lars and Lomar beamed broadly back. Tumarl remained silent, as though it would take a lot more to recompense him for his time in confinement.

Kaplyn introduced Tallin to his friends as their weapons were brought for them. Kaplyn was relieved to see his Eldric sword and bow. As they left, Kaplyn updated them on the events that had transpired since he had left.

When Kaplyn came to the end of the tale and he spoke about the enemy arrayed before the gate, Tumarl's eyes blazed.

"I need a sword!" he announced.

"Come, I will take you to the armoury," Tallin said. "I will get you a sword and anything else you need. After all," he added, looking at Lomar, "it is little enough to offer the friend of one who saved the life of the King."

When Kaplyn looked puzzled, Tallin explained how Lomar had warned them of the assassins and, although the warning had come too late to save the late King, it had saved the Prince's life.

Lomar looked far from pleased by the reminder. On the way to the armoury he told Kaplyn and the others about the rest of his "dream" and the sighting of a second army.

"I cannot be sure whether they received my warning or, even if they did, whether they will heed it."

"Do not worry. When your spirit came to our aid in the KinAnar forest it was very real I can assure you!" Kaplyn said. "I am certain they will have taken your warning seriously."

Tallin looked baffled. "You mean that while you were in your cell you managed to speak with one of your people? All that distance away?"

Lomar smiled as if it had been no great feat, even though it had nearly cost him his life.

Tallin looked at him with respect. "The rumours that you are in league with the demons appear to have some foundation!"

Lars laughed aloud. "Lomar is a man as much as you or I. He is no demon."

At the armoury, they were issued breastplates and helms, although Kaplyn decided to wait until he could be fitted with a spare helm from the Allund stores, if any had survived. Tumarl selected a heavy broadsword, testing the weapon's edge with his thumb.

They could not find a breastplate to fit Lars, but the big man was content with a stout leather jacket braided with metal studs which the armourer found at the very back of his store. Once dressed, they looked formidable, far different from the men who had set off upon a quest so long ago.

Once ready, Tallin led them back to the inner city wall to reunite them with Tharn Orrin who was talking to Tharn Baldor. Tallin excused himself, saying it was his duty to rejoin his own men.

"We lost thirty riders in the charge," Orrin told Kaplyn.

"Thirty?" Kaplyn asked, "I though we had lost many more." It was fewer than he had feared.

"Your first cavalry action is always the worst. We lost more horses than men. Some riders were recovered on our second charge. I fear though for our patrol. They were good men ... as they all are," he said looking out over the walls.

The outer wall was about fifteen yards away. Their position on the inner wall looked down on the outer. Kaplyn leaned over the battlements. A bridge connected the two walls and below him a door set in the inner wall gave access to it. On the outer wall, tall watchtowers guarded the crossing while another bridge, on a second level, linked the watch tower to the inner wall.

"It's strange, isn't it?" Lars commented. "Yesterday Allund and Thrace were on the verge of war. Yet now the two armies stand shoulder to shoulder, facing a common foe no one believed existed until today."

"It's fortunate we discovered the enemy when we did," Lomar said. "Can you imagine what would have happened if Allund had attacked here as they had intended? The enemy would have been able to step in and destroy whoever remained."

"Perhaps that was their plan, to set Allund against Thrace and then finish off the survivors," Kaplyn said. If that was the plan it very nearly succeeded.

"It was the gods who saved the city," Lars stated. "Why else would Tumarl rescue us when he did? Any earlier or later and we would not have seen the enemy."

Kaplyn must have looked unconvinced.

330

"I believe in the gods," Lomar added. "You saw the cave in Gilfillan and the power left there by the Kalanth. How can you doubt their existence?"

"If the gods exist, then why are they not here to help us now?" Tumarl growled.

"Perhaps we have to ask them for their help," Lars suggested. He raised his axe, turning to face the east. "Sarl, god of storms, hear your servant. Aid us in this coming war." He then turned to the south as a low growl of thunder sounded in the distance. "Slathor, guardian of men's souls, aid us."

To the west and then north, "Harlathan and Karlam! Gods of war and famine! Lend us your strength and aid us. If we should die, then let us face death bravely so we can fight by your side at the end of time."

A cold shiver ran down Kaplyn's spine. For once he found comfort in the idea that there might be gods watching over them.

"And may the Kalanth watch over us in the days of turmoil ahead," Kaplyn added softly. By his side Lomar smiled.

Chapter 19

The Siege of CarCamel

For the better part of that day and late into the evening, men and krell continued to arrive, a seemingly endless river emptying into a vast lake of humanity. Fear filled the hearts of even the stoutest defender for, even though the city walls were mighty, the enemy's resources seemed never-ending.

On the western wall, under cover of night, a few brave men were leaving the city to seek aid. King Alyn and Astalus stood to one side, watching the men being lowered by rope, their faces haunted as though expecting to hear the cry of discovery from the enemy at any moment. Once in the river, the current caught the small shapes, propelling them downstream towards the Southern Kingdoms, and hope.

Each messenger carried a letter wrapped in oiled cloths, urging the Southern Kingdoms to send aid. Both Alyn and Astalus knew the task was daunting. It was many miles to the nearest town. Even when the last of the messengers had disappeared from view, neither Alyn nor Astalus could bring themselves to leave. For long moments the two men watched the river, willing the messengers to succeed.

Kaplyn and his friends assembled upon the outer wall, staring at the enemy's campfires that seemed more numerous than the stars. Only Tumarl looked happy with the prospect of the enemy's nearness; a gleam of vengeance shone in his cold brown eyes.

Kaplyn shuddered. While they had been upon the inner wall they had appeared to be relatively safe, but now they were with the front-line troops, their position seemed more precarious.

"What became of Vastra's crystal from the Tree of Life, do you think?" Kaplyn asked Lomar.

The albino shrugged. "Perhaps Vastra used it to cross to another world as he intended. Who knows — perhaps he perished in one of those worlds," the Alvalan prince replied.

Kaplyn shook his head. At some point in the coming conflict, the enemy would summon demons. He had already seen one at the Baron's castle so long ago. He cursed Vastra, his half brother as he had discovered, and wished that they had never met. Vastra had said the crystal could be used to maintain a gateway to another world. It contained pure magic, which could not be destroyed and hence would keep a gateway open indefinitely. He cursed his role in finding the crystal, and guilt threatened as he looked at the Allund soldiers standing fresh-faced about him, knowing many would die in the coming days.

A commotion made Kaplyn turn. A Thracian wizard was coming towards them, a long bow held in his hand. Behind him came two militiamen, one fat and the other thin, struggling with the weight of a lit brazier which sloped alarmingly towards the fat man. Cursing, they dropped it and crouched down, clearly relieved to be free of their burden.

It was a comical sight, causing Kaplyn to smile. The wizard matched his smile. He was an old greybeard, thin as a rake but seemingly full of energy and his eyes sparkled with mischief. The militiamen seemed much more dour by comparison as they tried to recover from carrying their load. The fat man's breastplate looked old and barely covered his girth, while the other was almost lost within his. Both looked afraid to be upon the wall and kept glancing at the wizard, but he ignored them, turning instead to speak to Kaplyn.

"Welcome," he declared, beaming broadly as if it was a casual meeting in more fortunate times. "Perishing night," he continued before Kaplyn could reply. "Much too cold for summer. If I had known it was going to be like this I would have gone south months ago. I have kin there you know! Much warmer," he added conspiratorially.

He continued to prattle while stringing his bow, partially entangling his beard with the twine. The delay as he untangled himself did not appear to bother him too much.

Kaplyn considered reminding the old wizard his chances of going south were slim at best, but thought better of it. Somehow he was sure the old man already knew. The wizard paused in his jabbering as he lit the arrow tip in the brazier.

"There's nothing to shoot at!" Tumarl complained, staring at the wizard as though he were mad.

The wizard ignored the jibe and, with a twang, released the flaming arrow which sailed brightly into the sky. The wizard closed his eyes and started to chant, his hands tracing a rune over the glowing coals. The arrow paused in its descent, hovering eerily in mid air.

Kaplyn marvelled. They could see the intervening ground between them and the enemy, albeit faintly. The wizard grinned.

"Must dash. It's going to be a long night," and with that he left, his companions hurrying behind with their heavy load.

Other flaming arrows appeared all around the city. As darkness retreated, men's hearts were lifted. That night, little occurred except for the hammering of the enemy engineers as they constructed siege engines. It was an eerie sound which grated upon the defenders' nerves with its hypnotic repetitiveness.

Chapter 20

A Rendezvous with Fate

Ariome clung to the dark shadows beneath tall tenement buildings, pulling the hood of her cloak about her face, concealing its whiteness.

The sound of metallic clanking warned her someone was approaching. She paused in a doorway, waiting to see who would pass. A detachment of militia marched by her hiding place, their bright torches forcing her to step deeper into shadow. Fortunately it was militia rather than regular troops. seasoned men would have been more alert. Then, as quickly as they had come, they disappeared, followed a few moments later by the light from their torches.

She needn't have feared detection; the patrol was too caught up in its own importance, thinking that the threat would come from outside rather than from within. Undaunted, she stepped once more into the night and hurried on her way, confident that in the unlikely event of being caught, she would be able to talk her way out of trouble.

A long row of silent merchants' shops caught her attention. She recognised them from a previous visit. Her destination was close. Automatically her hand went to her pocket and slim fingers caressed a glass vial, almost lost in the folds of the soft fabric. She checked to be sure the stopper was in place. The vial contained a very deadly poison, needing only the slightest trace to kill.

Her plan was simple. Poison a well close to the wall and then get a message to the enemy commander telling him of her success. On the morrow, during the attack, the defenders would need water to slake their thirst. When they were either too sick to defend themselves or dead, the enemy could breach the walls with ease.

A smile touched her lips as she stepped into another doorway. A second patrol clanked noisily past. They looked silly in their ill-fitting armour, relics of a forgotten past. She despised them. They would not live long once the walls were breached and krell swarmed through the streets.

Ahead she could make out the outline of a well and, as she suspected, it was unguarded.

Striding to its side, she found it was covered with a stout iron grating, long since rusted. The grating was intended to prevent a dead bird or animal falling in and fouling the water.

It was too dark to see inside, and, from within, a damp smell wafted up. She wrinkled her nose in disgust. Removing the stopper from the vial and taking care not to let any of the contents touch her skin, she tipped the liquid into the well.

A dead animal was not the only way to foul the water, she thought. When she had finished, she put the stopper back before concealing the vial within the folds of her robes. The night was only half gone, and she fell to wondering whom she could invite to her rooms to while away the hours until dawn.

She was far too excited to sleep.

A child's high-pitched scream interrupted the household calm. With her free hand Myra hitched up her skirts as she ran up the narrow flight of stairs to her daughter's bedroom. The young girl was sitting bolt upright in bed, her long blond hair dishevelled. Myra raised her lantern to see what ailed her; only then did her daughter turn away from the window and the darkness beyond.

"Mummy, there is something outside!" she panted.

"Hush now," her mother said, hurrying to her bedside. Taking her in her arms, she stroked her daughter's hair. Her young eyes were wide with fear and tears threatened to tumble down her cheeks. Myra knew that there would be little chance of comforting her daughter that night.

She raised the lantern and peered out through the thick glass, wishing her husband had chosen another house so many years ago. It was in one of the poorer quarters overlooking a graveyard. No wonder her daughter was afraid, especially with the talk of demons. The briefest flicker of movement in the alley outside caused her to hold her breath.

A cat backed away from a pile of rubbish, looked up at the window, its eyes sparkling in the torchlight. For a moment it paused, staring up and then it was gone. Myra breathed a sigh of relief, her breath fogging the cold glass pane.

"Hush now," she repeated, stroking her daughter's head and trying to still her whimpers. "There is nothing out there." The sound of booted feet upon the stair alerted her to her husband's presence.

The big man entered the room looking somewhat foolish. That afternoon he had joined the militia and had since spent the remainder of the day finding his father's armour, which he now wore. He was much too big for the narrow breast plate and the helmet stood at an awkward angle upon his brow. The big man looked questioningly at his wife, his eyes filled with concern.

"What's the matter?" he asked softly.

Myra went on comforting their daughter, trying to suppress a smile at the sight of her husband so ridiculously dressed. She knew better though and her look changed to one of understanding. His heart was in the right place, and, if the rumours were true, the militia might well be called upon to defend the city in the very near future.

"It was just a cat," she assured him. "Would you mind checking out the back just to be certain?"

He smiled reassuringly before turning to go down the stairs, his daughter's soft sobs still ringing in his ears. Grief threatened to overwhelm him and he wished for better times.

From a stairway leading to the eastern wall, a Thracian soldier emerged into the faint light of dawn, carrying his spear sloped across his shoulder and his helm in his hand. Pausing, he looked to the sky, content to have been relieved from the night watch. Behind him, others emerged from the narrow stone archway, fatigue etched upon their faces as they jostled by him eager to get to their beds.

Now that his fear had left him, his mouth felt dry. Stepping to a nearby well he filled a ladle hanging by the bucket suspended from the crossbar. Drinking, he reflected how much he missed his wife and family. Still, it was better for him to sleep in the barracks. At least he would get more rest than at home with his inquisitive children. Stifling a yawn with the back of his hand he replaced the ladle before setting off.

Within the comfort of the barracks, he could barely stand. Throwing himself onto a bunk, he let out a low groan of contentment. He was getting too old to have to stand guard; the battlements were freezing. His companion in the opposite bunk glanced down at him with a look of concern.

"You OK, Lant?"

"I'm all right," he said. "Just tired."

"Well, keep the noise down. We're back on duty in a few hours," replied the other man good naturedly. As soon as his head touched the mattress he fell into a deep sleep. It would not be until much later that morning that he would discover Lant was dead.

In the pitiful light of an uncertain dawn, enemy trumpets sounded. In the city the general alarm rang, calling men to arms.

Kaplyn, Lars and Tumarl were in a street on their way to the eastern command tower when they heard the alarm. They started running, arriving breathless on the battlements to find Tharn Ballan issuing orders summoning more men. At that moment Astalus reached the top of the stair puffing heavily. The cold wind atop the tower forced him to pull his cloak tightly about his throat.

In the distance, four siege engines dominated a dull skyline, and, from within the enemy towers, the lowing of beasts of burden carried upon the frigid air.

"Fetch Gant and Corrin," Astalus said to a nearby runner. The eager boy ran off, almost colliding with another boy carrying a heavy pitcher, coming up the stair. This youth cast the runner a filthy look as he pushed by without so much as a by-your-leave. Returning his attention to the task at hand, the youth with the bucket gratefully dumped his burden down, splashing water over the stone surface.

None of the men noticed the boy who wiped the sweat from his brow, shaking his head as he went to fetch another bucket.

In her tower, Ariome smiled, lounging back upon silken sheets, confident her plan would work.

Nate looked out over the battlements, the wind blowing the hair protruding from beneath his metal skull cap. Although his hair was grey, he was still a strong man, wiry rather than well-built. He knew he would need his strength in the coming days.

"Put it down, boy," he advised, glancing over at one of the younger soldiers who was fiddling with his shield. The other man nearly jumped out of his skin when Nate addressed him.

"It will be a while before the enemy get here! Relax until then," he continued more gently.

The younger man grimaced at being called a boy but put his shield down nonetheless, casting a sidelong glance at the others to see what they were doing. Most were not even looking. They either sat or stood with their backs against the wall, lost in thought while preparing weapons for the hundredth time.

Across the open ground, barely discernible in the gloom, Nate could make out the outlines of siege towers manoeuvring towards the city walls.

"They should have dug trenches," he announced wisely to no one in particular, sighing deeply.

Harlam, the troop's second haft, smiled at the older man. "You are forgetting, Nate! Until a few days ago it was us who were meant to be attacking the city!" The older man looked uncomfortable with the reminder which only served to broaden Harlam's grin.

Nate laughed. It was a refreshing sound against the unnatural silence and Harlam joined in. Their laughter drew the attention of the others who looked at them as though they were deranged.

"Nonetheless, these Thracians could still be taught a thing or two about defending their city," Nate replied leaning heavily against the wall, feeling some security at least in the stout stone.

Harlam nodded. "Aye, but I'm sure that they have a few tricks up their sleeves, too. See that fellow up there in the brown robes standing next to the Tharn?" he said, indicating the tower slightly to their rear.

Nate nodded.

"Well, he's a wizard. See those other two joining him? They are, too. They'll be able to do more than a few trenches ever could. It's a damn shame we Allunds never held wizards in higher esteem..."

"Watch that bucket, boy!" Sarin interrupted. A youth had carelessly slopped water over the floor nearly drenching Sarin.

The two older men smiled at each other. Sarin was barely older than the boy he chastised.

Nate leant his spear against the wall, stretching his arms and back. He hated waiting. It would take time before the siege towers were close enough to be a threat and, in the meantime, all they could do was watch.

Harlam, on the other hand, was dutifully checking their equipment once more. He had recently been promoted, and the burden of command still worried him. Nate felt annoyed. At the time, he had wanted the promotion, but had to admit that Harlam was the better choice. The men respected him. He had a cool head under pressure; perhaps, too, his attention to detail would come in useful. Nate did not have Harlam's patience and he envied the younger man that.

Harlam was making sure the men knew how and when to use some of the siege weapons. Amongst them were long poles with forks on the end for pushing scaling ladders away from the wall. It required at least two men to use these effectively and it was best to topple a ladder when the enemy was already upon it. There were also axes and stout metal rods which could be used either to cut ropes or free grappling hooks.

Harlam was telling the men to wait until someone was scaling the rope. He also warned them not to look over the parapet unless they wanted an arrow decorating their throat.

"Wait until you see the rope become taut, you can tell then that the enemy is climbing."

The boiling oil was another matter. Nate didn't like having the evil-smelling pot upon the battlement. Oil, if accidentally spilt, could be as dangerous to themselves as to an enemy.

"And don't drink so much water, Thad," Harlam called to the other young soldier of his command. Thad belched loudly, grinned broadly, then returned to his post where he sat down with his back to the wall. Sarin joined him, preferring to stand looking out across the intervening ground at the approaching towers.

"When will the wizards attack those things?" Nate heard Sarin ask. The monstrosities were having an effect upon the defenders' nerves, the very sight instilling fear.

"Patience," Harlam replied. "Wait and see. They'll be burning wrecks before long."

Nate couldn't help but shudder. He was in a foreign city, facing an unknown threat. For a moment he wondered what else could go wrong with his life.

Chapter 21

The First Wave

High up on the tower, Astalus sprinkled herbs on the fire while chanting arcane words. By his side, Kaplyn strung his bow and then loosened his blade in its sheath. He was thirsty but decided to wait, knowing if he drank now he ran the risk of cramps. Even so, his eyes kept straying to the bucket in the corner.

Below, Allund troops were spread out along the battlements. He marvelled at their apparent ease sitting around seemingly without a care.

Kaplyn shuddered. It was too cold. The pommel of his sword was icy even through the thick leather binding. He rubbed his hands, trying to get warmth back into his fingers. His scar ached although he was becoming used to its unusual presence.

His dreams were another matter though. His sleep was still plagued by dragons and their persistence was getting him down. He tried to rid his mind of morbid thoughts, looking out instead across the open ground. The siege towers were much closer. Behind him, the wizards' chant grew louder.

King Alyn and Tharn Orrin came up the steps. The two men stood beside Kaplyn, looking out.

Suddenly, a great ball of flame flashed over their heads. Kaplyn ducked, then realised the flame had been cast by Astalus and his companions. Upon the wall below, men leapt to their feet, their voices raised in excitement.

The great ball struck a tower in a shower of flame and sparks. The defenders cheered as an explosion followed. Figures leapt from the tower, their clothes alight and their screams easily heard across the intervening distance. The burning pyre ground to a halt but the remaining three came inexorably onwards.

A whoosh caused Kaplyn to duck a second time. Another ball of flame streaked towards a tower. Grakyn intercepted it, battering it with power of their own. This time when it struck it was feebler than the first and, although some krell were burned, the tower continued to lumber on.

The tone of the wizard's chant changed, and a rent appeared in the ground before the third tower which could not be stopped in time. It toppled forward, gathering momentum until it crashed to the ground in a fountain of dirt.

Two siege towers remained mobile. Their speed across the open ground had increased as the occupants realised they were the next targets.

Kaplyn groaned. The first tower had been doused and already troops were climbing aboard.

Behind the towers came ranks of foot soldiers, carrying scaling ladders and wicker structures. All at once, with a scream of defiance, men and krell surged forward, carrying their frames. A hail of arrows flew from the battlements, but wicker frames were planted in the ground before the arrows struck. Some were poorly made and krell, cowering behind them, fell to the ground screaming as arrows found gaps.

Enemy archers hurried forward to take position behind the frames; from there they exchanged volleys with the archers upon the walls. Grakyn, flying high in the sky, hurled down magical flames onto the walls, causing the defenders to duck back behind the stone.

The defenders tried using fire-arrows against the frames but these proved difficult to torch. Two wizards lent a hand, summoning magical fire and some frames were ignited, forcing a few krell to flee, to be cut down by the defenders' arrows. However, for every frame torched, another two or three were erected. Finally, a cloud of black arrows continually peppered the battlements, obliging the defenders to keep their heads down.

Ariome made her way to the top of her tower. A gust of cold wind greeted her as she approached the edge of the battlements overlooking the eastern defence. She smiled at the sight of the siege towers, although her smile faltered when she saw one in flames and another which had tipped over.

She consoled herself that the poisoned water would soon take effect. It would be a while before these fools realised what had happened and, by then, it would be too late.

She still had to perform the second part of her mission. Before her, on an adjacent tower, she could see King Alyn surrounded by his wizards and two Tharns. She closed her eyes, concentrating on the presence of a grakyn, hovering about the battle's periphery. To her delight she made contact and swiftly she guided it towards the command tower and Alyn.

The men of Harlam's troop huddled behind their arrow slits as flame splashed against the stone wall from a grakyn hovering overhead. Harlam ordered more wood to be placed beneath the oil and an evil smell filled the air.

All at once, Sarin's voice called to him. Keeping close to the protection of the wall, Harlam hurried to see what he wanted. Sarin was crouched by the base of the battlements, cradling Thad's head in his arms.

Sarin's eyes brimmed with unshed tears, confirming Harlam's worst fears. Harlam felt for a pulse. There was none.

"How?" he asked.

Sarin shook his head as the tears finally flowed down his face. There was not a mark upon the body.

The clamour of battle escalated, and a blast from a grakyn caused him to duck instinctively. The enemy were making a concerted attack, and he had to see to his command.

"Leave him!" he ordered, knowing it sounded callous but Sarin either did not hear or chose to ignore him. Harlam grabbed his shoulder, angrily shaking him.

"Leave him! Pick up your weapon! We need you!" he shouted.

Sarin glared back but nonetheless laid Thad's head down. Angrily he picked up his bow and moved to join the others.

Harlam ignored Sarin's flash of hatred, but could not rid himself of the image of Thad's lifeless body. What a waste. He pictured again the young man drinking the water only moments before.

Harlam frowned.

He went to the bucket, picking up the ladle and sniffing the contents. A great cry went up from beyond the wall, but he ignored it.

Dipping a finger into the cold liquid he sucked it. It tasted fine and so he took a tentative sip, rolling the water around his tongue before spitting it out.

There was a distinct after taste confirming his worst fear. Poison!

Spitting repeatedly he looked up at the Commanders in the tower above. Upending the bucket he spilled the contents onto the battlement.

"Nate! You're in charge," he shouted. Not waiting for a reply he raced for the tower. Already his legs were starting to feel leaden.

Astalus, Gant and Corrin were summoning another fireball to attack the remaining towers, and raw energy crackled about the trio. Astalus raised his staff, absorbing the energy and storing it in the crystal atop his staff.

With a sudden cry, he released the power, hurling it at an oncoming tower. The closeness of the tower prevented the grakyn from countering this threat. The tower was immediately engulfed in flame, and screams followed as men and krell burned.

Kaplyn released an arrow; his fingers numb from loosing so many. His bow was more powerful than its longbow counterparts and the arrow pierced a wicker frame. Behind it a man fell back, clutching an arrow in his chest.

A movement by the tower's entrance made Kaplyn turn. An Allund second-haft mounted the stair, his face ashen and his eyes rolling in their sockets. Kaplyn ran to his side, grabbing his shoulders as he fell. There were no visible wounds and so he called to Lomar, struggling all the while against the man's weight.

Lomar appeared by his side and together they laid the soldier down. Lomar drew his kara-stone, placing it on the man's sweat drenched forehead. The albino chanted words of power and immediately swirling circles of light appeared within the stone. At Lomar's command the man's eyes flickered open. He looked confused and then came recollection. He grabbed Kaplyn's cloak.

"Poison!" He arched his back in pain. "The water," he said, forcing the words out slowly to make himself understood. "It's poisoned."

Kaplyn frowned. "Do what you can for him," he said to the albino who nodded, not breaking his concentration as he fought against the poison.

Kaplyn ran over to Astalus who, as yet, had not started to summon more power for his next assault.

"The water's poisoned," Kaplyn shouted above the din, pointing at the bucket.

It took a moment for Kaplyn's words to sink in. "*By the Kalanth....*" Astalus muttered. "Can you get additional men to defend against the siege towers?" Astalus asked.

Kaplyn nodded and ran off.

Astalus explained his plan to his colleagues, and their eyes widened with what he suggested. Nonetheless, they lent their power to his so the pale orb within his staff was once more crackling with energy.

Kaplyn raced from the wall as the din from beyond it reached a crescendo. The enemy were at the base of the wall, and he could smell hot oil being tipped over. Screams assailed his ears. Screams of such intense agony he hoped he would never hear the like again.

He had no idea how he was to find aid. Then he remembered the reaction force others had suggested be assembled for such an emergency. If there was a time for their aid, then it was now. He ran through the deserted streets towards the location of the assembled men, hoping they had not already been summoned to another part of the city.

Nate was more afraid than at any other time of his life. Harlam's sudden absence and the pressure of command were too much for him. Sweat ran down his neck and back in rivulets. Judging the oil ready he took the opportunity to look over the battlements, ducking back instinctively as two arrows skittered off the stone, narrowly missing him.

He had had only an instant to take in the scene, but it was enough to make him shudder. Even though it was unnaturally dark given the time of day, he had seen the enemy in the light cast by burning siege engines and wicker frames. The ground was seething with figures. At that moment ladders clunked against the wall.

Nate did not know what to do. To make matters worse the others seemed to be watching him, awaiting orders. He considered the oil, but did not want to use it too early.

Across from Nate, Allan, an ex-farmer, was about to use one of the wooden poles to push back one of the siege ladders, but Sarin caught his arm.

"Wait!" he said and started to silently count, his mouth forming the words.

Nate realised what he was doing and was suddenly thankful for Harlam's training. The men were not waiting for him, but were doing as Harlam had taught them. Abruptly Sarin gave a shout and the two men pushed out their wooden pole, catching the top of the ladder.

With all their strength, they ran the ladder from the wall. Judging by the effort it took, it was obviously heavily laden. Then, abruptly, the weight was gone and the ladder toppled backwards under the combined weight of the heavily armoured krell upon it. Their screams echoed from the walls as they fell. At the same time, other defenders were repelling siege ladders and cutting grappling lines.

Nate watched as more ladders were raised and more hooks landed atop the wall. When there were too many for his men to handle, he gave the order for the oil to be discharged. The screams from below were terrifying as the burning liquid stuck to exposed flesh, burying itself deep under armour.

For a moment, there was a brief respite, but, then, more ladders were thrown up and a siege engine reached the wall. A loud crash made Nate jump; above his head a drawbridge thudded against the battlements and screaming krell spilled forth. Their swords and spear tips gleamed wickedly in the light cast by the burning fires.

Nate was too busy now to worry about being in charge. With a roar of victory, krell leapt upon the defenders.

T'chark clung stubbornly onto the knotted rope as a large stone whistled by his ear, smashing into the helm of an Aldracian beneath him. The man crumpled and fell backwards. T'chark watched his demise with glee, but, then, Lang kicked T'chark in the temple as he clumsily climbed. Here, being large was a distinct disadvantage; T'chark was in his element.

"Get a move on, you clumsy pig's offal," he called up, only to be rewarded by another kick sending his overlarge helm flying. T'chark bit Lang's leg and was rewarded with a curse as the heavy krell tried to disengage himself from his ferocious subordinate.

Another falling rock made the rope swing wildly as a krell higher up was dislodged. The falling body struck Lang but to his credit he managed to cling on much to T'chark's relief for otherwise he, too, might have been dislodged.

T'chark could think of better places to be at the moment. He glanced back at the burning towers. At first he had been envious of those aboard the siege engines. Now, however, when he saw the burning hulks behind him he was glad he was scaling the wall. He had to admit there were worse places to be.

To his side a scaling ladder was being pushed from the wall. Gleefully T'chark watched as the krell upon it tried to grab hold of the unyielding stone wall. It amused him to see one krell's sudden look of fear as the ladder went beyond the point of no return, falling backwards with gathering momentum, disappearing with a meaty thud within the sea of bodies below.

Meanwhile, Lang had moved up farther. T'chark eagerly gripped the rope, nimbly climbing the few remaining feet. Drawing his slim knife, he scrambled over the parapet after Lang. The scene that greeted him was a macabre dance of death. The image would remain with him for the rest of his (hopefully long) life. Men and krell battled hand-to-hand, each side trying to press the other back from the narrow battlements. T'chark howled gleefully and eagerly joined the press of bodies.

Astalus and the other wizards had no chance to see if their spell was successful. Below them, krell topped the walls. One siege tower had not yet reached the wall, and they turned their attention to this, knowing that if it wasn't stopped the situation could well be lost!

Their power converged and a blast of energy struck the tower, spewing flame and smoke high into the sky. Then they were fighting for their lives as grakyn attacked, hurling bolts of fire. For the moment, all they could do was protect themselves, whilst the siege engine spilled forth its deadly contents onto the city's wall.

Behind the wizards, Alyn and his tharns drew their weapons, their attention wholly upon the scene below. They were, for the moment, protected from the grakyn's attack by the magical shield raised by the wizards, but magic was no defence against arrows or spears.

Tharn Ballan's frustration was obvious. He gripped his sword hilt, and his bushy eyebrows beetled in silent rage. Finally he could stand it no longer; issuing orders to a handful of men he leapt to the tower's entrance to rally his troops. Alyn watched him go, feeling helpless. He was no warrior and had never led anyone else to believe that he was.

High above the tower, a grakyn beat its wings upon the frigid air, holding its position as it drew back its bow. In its mind a woman's voice whispered to it, urging it to its target. Other grakyn hovered close by, their ebony skin reflecting the fires below as they poured fire down upon the tower. The wizards held their barrier, but were hard-pressed to maintain it.

The grakyn recognised its prey, an insignificant-looking man standing slightly apart from the others with dread in his eyes.

With a twang, the grakyn released its arrow. The dart arced towards the figure whoat the last moment looked up. Too late he raised his arm but the arrow pierced his chest. The figure fell, his descent almost graceful as though time had slowed.

In the sky the grakyn was gone.

Chapter 22

Battle in the Balance

Nate pulled his blade from the stomach of a large, evil-looking krell which moments before had tried to decapitate him. For a dreadful moment, Nate's blade stuck in the creature's ribs as others pressed forward to reach the veteran. He pushed fiercely against the corpse. Screams sounded as those krell behind toppled from the wall. With a heave, his blade was free and he shoved the body over the parapet to join its companions.

Only just in time, he parried a blow from his left. The battle was too swift to see who wielded the blade and Nate simply struck out in fear. The blades rang, sending a shock along his arm. Ducking, he butted an opponent in the face.

An arrow from above caught a krell behind the battling pair in the forehead as the defenders upon the inner wall bravely sought to repulse the enemy. However, too few defenders dared to look out over the battlements; in effect, the enemy archers and grakyn had pinned them down.

Sarin leapt to Nate's aid as Allan swept two krell from the wall using his shield. His spear lanced a third as it came at him, its axe raised.

It was not going well for the defenders. Enemy troops were gaining the advantage, forcing the defenders back and increasing their toe-hold on the wall.

With a sharp cry, a figure wielding a bright glowing sword leapt from a stairwell onto the battlements. Those krell battling close by fell back as though scalded by the blade's light. Others shielded their eyes from the Eldritch weapon forged from a forgotten era. A bear of a man followed the first, swinging a great double-headed axe as he protected his comrade's back.

Close behind the pair, from every available doorway, the reserve force spilled onto the battlements. Men from Allund and Thrace stood shoulder to shoulder, shields raised against a common foe. Tharn Alder led them, his helm partially concealing his grim look as his sword rose and fell. The weight of their numbers forced the krell to retreat towards the siege tower, where more krell waited to gain a footing upon the wall.

Kaplyn's blade clove through armour as easily as flesh. The weapon sang eerily as he blocked and counterattacked; the blade's glow brightened with every slain enemy. Krell fell back in despair. With each blow the scar upon Kaplyn's chest burned. From the echoes of his mind he heard dragons roar and he had to refrain from glancing at the sky.

Dragons! His mind screamed.

Battle and blood... Dragons flying silently on gossamer wings, spewing flame and vitriol.

"I am Mad!" he screamed, as he wove a net of steel about himself.

Krell fell before him. But then a giant krell blocked his way, holding a massive double-handed sword. The creature lashed out, and Kaplyn dodged, knowing he lacked the strength to block the blow.

The heavy blade whistled by his ear, barely missing his shoulder. He threw himself bodily at the giant, and was rewarded by the sound of air being expelled from its lungs. Before it could recover, he brought his elbow up under its chin, snapping its head back. The krell snarled, revealing its fangs as it swung its sword about its head. Kaplyn thrust his blade through the krell's armour. Its eyes grew wide as its lifeblood flowed, sapping its strength as the light of the blade damned its soul.

T'chark watched Lang die with a feeling of glee, which was swiftly replaced by fear as the dreaded enemy pushed them back on the slick and bloodied battlements. He dropped to his belly, a plan forming in his mind. Lang had been stupid but, as the saying went, there was more than one way to skin a human.

He lay still feigning death, watching the battle through narrowed eyes, concentrating all the while on the hated human with the bright sword which blurred his vision and made his head swim with pain.

Ah, but he would be a worthy target. Think of the riches for dispatching his worthless carcass to hell. He gripped his knife and waited for the tide of battle to pass over him. In his mind's eye, he was already gutting the stupid human and enjoying his well-deserved reward.

Tumarl fought like a man possessed. With each swing of his heavy blade, he forced the enemy back. Few dared to stand against him for the light of madness was in his eyes. He was no warrior and, instead, he fought as a farmer reaping corn, which was somehow appropriate since the necks of the krell parted company from their bodies just as easily.

For nights he had dreamt of his revenge. Yet now in the thick of battle his lust for vengeance was *not* sated and his anger only burned deeper. Tears rolled down his cheeks and the smoke of battle burnt his throat. The conflict of emotions finally spilled over and, without concern for his own safety, he stepped amongst the krell, screaming defiantly as he hacked and slew. If they had stood their ground, they would have easily defeated the ex-farmer, but his madness terrified them and fearfully they drew back.

By his side, Kaplyn advanced with his sword of death and Lars swung his broad axe with consummate skill. The krell could not face the approaching slayers plainly sowing the seed of their deaths and, as one, turned and fled.

T'chark waited. Two more steps. *Ignore the light*, he thought. His eyes narrowed and his fangs glistened in anticipation. Then the dark-haired man had passed him. As quick as a snake T'chark rose, thrusting at Kaplyn's unprotected back.

He did not see Tumarl's boot, which caught him in the nape of his neck. T'chark tried to turn but was tangled in the press of bodies. T'chark toppled too far and, with a sickening realisation, fell over the battlement.

T'chark braced himself; the pit of his stomach heaved as he plummeted. When the impact came, it was merciful. The force knocked him out and he knew no more.

The defending archers on the inner walls suddenly found that the hail of arrows from the siege tower lessened as the enemy retreat turned into a rout. All at once, they were free to concentrate their own volleys upon the attacking grakyn, successfully driving them back. Astalus and the wizards were in turn free to set fire to the remaining siege tower. With a roar, the protected wood was engulfed in flame and its occupants were forced to leap to their deaths rather than burn alive.

Calm descended as the enemy trumpets sounded the retreat, and the defenders lowered their blood-soaked weapons. Many watched in disbelief as the first serious assault was beaten back; others sought the buckets of water to quench their thirst.

Great cries came from these men who backed from the buckets with eyes wide with fear. Thousands of maggots filled each bucket. Astalus' spell had worked and no one had dared drink the poisoned water.

Sarin held his arm, trying to staunch the flow of blood from a deep cut which stung like blazes.

"Who is that, Nate?" he asked. Nate was also watching the man in the Allund uniform with the blue glowing blade.

"Our King," Nate said smiling. He lowered his sword arm which felt leaden.

"Our King?" Sarin replied. "But we don't have a King."

Nate smiled all the more. "And yesterday you'd never killed a krell either."

Kaplyn returned to the command tower. Everywhere was confusion. The walls were blackened by the grakyn's fire. A few still persisted in their attack but archers kept them at bay. Tharn Ballan was issuing orders for the remaining wells to be guarded and for the poisoned water buckets to be cast over the walls.

Kaplyn found Lomar attending the stricken Allund Haft Commander who had warned them of the poisoned water. The soldier was unconscious, but his flesh looked healthier and his breathing was deep.

"He will live," Lomar said, smiling up at his friend.

"It was fortunate his warning came when it did," Kaplyn replied. "Otherwise the battle would have gone against us."

"It means there's a spy in the city," Lomar answered. "Someone had to poison the water."

Kaplyn nodded. "Good point. I'll warn Ballan."

"And I'll help the wounded," Lomar said, looking about the scene of carnage. Soldiers were attending the fallen while the dead and dying krell were heaved unceremoniously over the wall.

A cry from one of the soldiers searching the corpses for the wounded caused Kaplyn to turn around. The man was standing stock still, looking down at a pile of bodies in disbelief. It was only then that Kaplyn recognised Alyn, lying partially buried beneath the bodies.

Kaplyn and the soldier drew the bodies off the King. An arrow protruded from his chest, and a large pool of blood was thickening on the stone beneath him. Ballan, seeing Kaplyn's desperate attempts to reach the King, came running to his side, a look of shock upon his face.

351

Others crowded around and silence descended over the battlements. Ballan grabbed his beard in his hands, crying out in frustration. "I have failed," he wailed.

Kaplyn took his arm. "No! You have not failed. We succeeded in keeping the enemy from the walls."

"But I should have protected my King," Ballan insisted. He gathered up his King's body in his arms and started a slow walk back to the palace. Men fell back before him, a look of horror on their faces when they recognised their Monarch.

Already the enemy was mounting another attack, and throughout the remainder of that day, thousands of krell and men threw themselves at the wall, but to no avail. Without their siege engines it was doubtful that they would breach the defence. As the darkness became complete, the attacks became less frequent until, by dawn the following day, they had ceased altogether as the enemy withdrew.

The tired defenders stood down. Men went wearily to their beds while women passed amongst them asking for news of husbands or sons.

In her tower, Ariome cursed the luck of the defenders, watching the enemy lines retreating out of range. She would have to be more careful now. Although fools, they could hardly fail to realise there was a spy in the city. She cursed again.

Angrily, she turned from the window, considering her next move. Soon it would be the turn of the Trosgarth sorcerers and their demons. It took considerable power and courage to summon a demon for, if the spell failed, the demon would take the sorcerer's soul screaming to hell.

She smiled. With the demise of the King, her efforts had not been in vain.

T'chark stirred. All around him was blackness. *I am dead*, his mind wailed, but the pain was too real for death. *I am blind then*, he thought. But no — he waved a hand in front of his eyes and saw the faint outline of his talons. He realised it was night. Trying to move sent fresh waves of pain lancing through his bony body.

It seemed his brethrens' corpses had softened his impact. For once he felt gratitude to his larger cousins and thankful, too, that none of their heavy armour had fitted him, for then his demise would have been assured.

Sick and giddy, he crawled away from the wall; Lang's look of surprise when the white-faced man had ended his miserable existence filled his mind. Between bouts of pain he tried not to giggle.

He decided then that he would no longer be brave. Let the bigger fools espouse courage. No, T'chark was too important to be a rotting corpse for the crows. He would be close enough to the battle to boast about his prowess afterwards, but not *too* close. He had learnt that lesson all too well.

Kaplyn stepped out into the chill of night. The tower upon which he stood was part of the main palace building, the highest of four. He had come here to be alone for a moment, hoping to forget the horrors of war and the stench of dragon that seemed to fill the air.

Inadvertently, he fingered the scar on his chest, feeling its roughness and unexpected coldness. Only then did he realise that he was not alone. Silhouetted against the fires of the recent assault, Catriona stood facing away from his position. She wore her cloak pulled tightly to her breast to ward off the chill. Her gaze was fixed upon the distant horizon as though searching for help that they knew might never arrive.

Kaplyn wanted to speak with the new queen, but respected her loss. Backing into the shadows he tried to leave, but something caused her to turn.

"Don't go!" she said softly.

Kaplyn turned to find her looking at him. Once more memories stirred and he sought to quell the disquiet within his soul.

"My apologies, I did not mean to disturb you," he replied.

Catriona smiled although her eyes reflected her recent pain.

"There are many suffering a loss this night. I would be grateful for the company," she answered, and then she looked up as though remembering something else. "I am forgetting that you, too, have suffered a terrible loss — your entire family, and friends..."

"That was long ago," Kaplyn replied.

"But you only found out a few days ago."

"As you say, there are many suffering the loss of a loved one tonight."

"What was it like then," Catriona continued, "in the past?"

Kaplyn was momentarily thrown by her question; it took him a while to think of a reply. "It was warmer," he said, memories drifting to the fore. "Not just the weather has changed though. The grass was greener and the birds more abundant. I remember riding through the KinAnar Forrest with Lars and Lomar; the scent of magnolia filled the air. It was beautiful."

He had not realised until then how bleak the land now seemed. "People were less afraid. No one believed in demons. I certainly didn't. It was only when I fought one that I truly believed."

"You fought a demon?" Catriona questioned.

"I had help," Kaplyn replied. "There was Lars and my friend Hallar, but it was my sword that tipped the balance." He indicated the weapon, hanging by his side. "It's Eldric made and proof against any demon."

"I heard stories today," she went on, "of a marvellous blade that shone like the sun. At first I thought the stories were an exaggeration, but Tharn Shelder told me that he, too, had seen the weapon. Perhaps that is why I came here tonight, in the hope that the Eldric would return."

"We must not give up hope," Kaplyn insisted. "It's not impossible."

"Without them though, we will be lost," Catriona replied bluntly.

Kaplyn wanted to take her hand to reassure her, but felt as though he did not belong in this world, as though it was nothing more than a dream.

"We must hope the Southern Kingdoms will send reinforcements. Together we can defeat Trosgarth." Whether she believed this or not Kaplyn could not tell.

"Come," he said. "We had better go back inside. We have risked being here over long. It would not do morale any good for the Queen to become a victim to grakyn!"

Together they returned to the sanctuary of the palace, seeking bright lights and the company of others to dispel the gloom.

Chapter 23

The Old One

After the funeral, Catriona was officially crowned. The coronation bells sounded throughout the day, although they seemed dull and lack-lustre. At least, the enemy did not attack, preferring instead to lick its wounds. Within the city, rumours spread and, behind each, was a fear of demons.

Many spoke of the Eldric, and eyes turned to the horizon as if hoping for relief to appear. The Prophecy was told and retold, and people tried to interpret the baffling lines until they were weary with the false hope it seemed to offer. To many, the Prophecy only served to remind them that Drachar's shade would once more walk the land, and their fear became unbearable.

Later that afternoon, Kaplyn, Lomar, Tumarl and Lars stood together upon the outer wall, looking north.

Occasional lightning shafts lit up the horizon, followed by deep thunder that rumbled ominously across the land. All about them, a terrible stench filled the air as the corpses outside the city began to rot.

Kaplyn turned as Astalus approached. The wizard looked tired, and Kaplyn realised that he, too, must look similarly weary.

Astalus smiled as he approached and they greeted him warmly. "I've come to look at your famous sword — that is if you don't mind?"

Kaplyn drew it and Astalus scanned the fine, silvery script.

"You can read it?" Kaplyn asked.

Nodding, Astalus said, "It is a wondrous weapon. It's one of the seven forged by the Eldric during the Krell Wars."

"What does it say?" Kaplyn asked.

"It's a spell to enhance whatever powers the bearer wields," Astalus replied deep in thought. "How did you come by it?"

Kaplyn sighed. It all seemed so long ago, and his memory was now clouded by bitterness and loss. Nonetheless, he told Astalus his story, speaking of Vastra and how he had persuaded them to escort him to Tanel, the ancient Eldric city. There they had found a mystical pendant, the sword and Lars' axe. The pendant had guided them to a cavern deep in the heart of a mountain where they had found the fossilised remains of an ancient tree. This had miraculously blossomed and two fruit had formed and then crystallised. Vastra had taken one and Kaplyn the other. Then Vastra had betrayed them, summoning an imp and trapping them in a spell.

"Vastra *must* have been a Narlassar sorcerer," Astalus said when Kaplyn had finished.

"He kept insisting he was a sorcerer rather than wizard. I thought only Eldric were Narlassar sorcerers," Kaplyn said.

"That's true. Only a Narlassar sorcerer could summon an imp. Such an act is impossible for the Akrane. Perhaps a few Eldric remained, or perhaps their offspring are still amongst us," Astalus fell silent for a moment before continuing. "Your story fills me with foreboding though. You say that Vastra wanted to find the Eldric?" he asked.

Kaplyn nodded. "It was something to do with the crystal from the Tree of Life. He spoke about being able to open a gateway to other worlds. He was convinced the Eldric had done that long ago and had passed from this world to another."

"I wonder what became of him?" Astalus asked.

"Something unpleasant, I hope," Lars interrupted.

"This Tree of Life sounds important. What became of Vastra's crystal, I wonder?"

"I don't know," Kaplyn answered. He did not tell Astalus about his scar.

Astalus turned to speak with Lomar. "I also believe that you carry a kara-stone. May I see it please?"

Lomar removed the crystal from his tunic, handing it over. Astalus held it up to the light, peering into its depths.

"Where did you find this?" Astalus asked.

"There is a cave in my city where there are thousands of these stones," Lomar replied. "My people use them for healing."

"So I've heard," Astalus replied. "The surgeons told me that you worked wonders with the injured."

While Astalus held up the stone, Kaplyn caught a glimmer of something trapped within it.

"May I see it?" he asked.

Astalus handed it to him, and the instant it touched his flesh he felt as though static had discharged through his body. His eyes widened and, for an instant, he felt time stand still.

Kaplyn's eyes looked beyond the battlefield, beyond Thrace, and into another world and another time. The sun was high in a clear, azure sky, its warmth welcome after so many days of cold.

He was looking down upon the world as though from the branches of the tallest tree. The land was no longer haunted by fear, but a beautiful green place where the trees somehow seemed more youthful, as though this was the very first spring at the dawn of time.

A forest stretched as far as he could see in every direction.

A great forest.

His forest.

Leaves rustled softly in a gentle breeze. In the distance, between the swaying branches, speckled light reflected from the clear waters of a river wending its way towards a distant sea.

The thought of the sea reminded him of others of his kind he had not seen for a long-long time. An image of a giant wading through the oceans sprang to mind, causing him to smile. Others joined him, wading towards a distant shore for a final gathering. A pang of loss coursed through his veins. He knew he would not see them again.

He looked once more upon the beauty around him. There were no signs of disease or decay, and this gladdened him. Casting an arm over the forest. he sent nourishment deep into the earth, encouraging roots to grow against the time he could no longer feed them. Every millennium exacted its toll, sapping his energy until there was barely any left to give.

Time passed. He remembered sitting down on a small rise. Sunlight filtered through the thick orange and gold forest canopy. A distant memory from another, future time reminded him that he had been to this place before. Looking about, he saw homes built high in the branches and he watched the comings and goings of a people who would come to love his forest as much as he did. He wanted to question the feelings they aroused, but knew his time was at an end.

Lying down upon the soft ground he closed his eyes. At once memories swirled into a myriad of constantly shifting shapes. In that instant Kaplyn saw deep into the expanse of time. He wailed. A dark blackness engulfed him and he knew no more.

Lars watched Astalus hand the kara-stone to Kaplyn. He saw the momentary look of fear upon his friend's face and was already moving to his side as he fell. Catching him under his arms, he lowered him to the floor. Lomar caught the kara-stone as it rolled from Kaplyn's hand, and then, kneeling, he examined the unconscious man.

"What is it?" Tumarl asked. "Is he all right?"

Lomar placed his fingers upon Kaplyn's neck. His pulse was strong and steady. He nodded. "He has fainted; that's all. He's probably just exhausted."

"Take him inside," Astalus suggested.

Together Tumarl and Lars carried Kaplyn from the battlements.

It took only a short while to take him to his room. As they laid him upon his bed, he stirred and his eyes fluttered open. Astalus stopped him from rising.

"Where am I?" Kaplyn croaked.

"In your room," Lars answered. "You passed out and we brought you here."

"It would be wise to let him sleep," Astalus suggested.

The others agreed and, one by one, they left.

Astalus remained, making a pretence of shutting the curtains. When only Kaplyn was left, he turned to face him.

"What did you see in the kara-stone?" Astalus asked. Picking up a chair he went over to the bed, where he sat down, making it clear he did not intend to move.

"I saw one of the Kalanth," Kaplyn said with a sigh after a moment's silence.

"One of the Old Ones?"

Kaplyn nodded. There was no doubt in his mind what he had seen. The memory was still fresh, as was the sadness he had felt at the Kalanth's passing.

"What did you see?"

"Not *see;* it was more as though I *was* the Kalanth. I saw through his eyes and shared his memories. I know it must sound strange, but it was too vivid for a dream.

"I recognised the place. He was in Gilfillan. For a moment, the Old One seemed to recognise my thoughts. It was as if we were one."

"Where is Gilfillan?" Astalus asked.

"It's in the KinAnar forest where Lomar's people live."

"Are you sure it was a Kalanth?" Astalus asked.

Kaplyn nodded.

"Go on."

"He lay down upon a hillock. I think he was dying." Kaplyn's statement was uttered with little or no feeling, but his look conveyed his sadness.

"Surely a god cannot die," Astalus replied frowning.

"That's what I thought. But he was very old, ancient beyond our comprehension. Over the aeons, a small part of his power had gone into preparing the world, feeding the plants and trees, staving off disease and the ravages of age. After such a long time, there was simply nothing left to give."

For a moment, the two men looked at one another.

"You don't believe me?"

"Do you blame me?"

"No," Kaplyn replied, lowering his gaze. "Am I going mad then? First, dragons, and then this."

"What have dragons to do with this?" Astalus asked.

Kaplyn looked up. He had told no one about his dreams.

"I do not know. Every night I dream about them. I never see them! It's more as though they are nearby. The dreams are terrifying."

Astalus looked perplexed. "I don't think that you are mad." He rose from his chair and went to the windows where he drew back the curtains, letting a trickle of light in.

"I do not understand what you have told me though. Dragons are a myth. I don't believe they ever existed in this world. But the Kalanth are another matter. Our belief in them is very strong. You say that this Kalanth died? But was it just its physical form passing on? Could its spirit have moved on to another world?"

Kaplyn nodded. "There is something else," Kaplyn continued. Astalus returned to side of the bed and looked down upon the recumbent man, leaning wearily against his staff.

"Lomar showed us a cavern where his people harvest kara-stones. This was the spot where the Kalanth lay down to die."

Astalus rose from leaning on his staff, his eyes wide as he absorbed the information. For a moment he stood stock still. Then his eyes widened as though he suddenly understood.

"Of course, and why not?"

It was Kaplyn's turn to be baffled so the wizard went on to explain.

"Some believe that kara-stones are the remains of dead wizards. Why not, then, the same for a Kalanth? That may well explain what you saw, for if this stone was once part of a Kalanth, then its memories may well persist."

"It was more than a memory," Kaplyn reminded him. "I am certain the Kalanth felt my presence!"

Astalus frowned. "*That*, I do not understand."

Kaplyn was looking at Astalus' staff and his kara-stone.

"Perhaps if I was to touch your kara-stone, I would see into its history."

Astalus shook his head, although the idea was tempting. "No. Not if what you say is true. The Kalanth, we must presume, were good. But consider a kara-stone from an evil wizard. If you did see into his mind, and he into yours, you might then alert evil to our intent; say to the disposition of our troops in the city."

Kaplyn's pallor turned grey.

"It would be wise if you avoided such a temptation. It does raise the question as to why this happened to you?"

Kaplyn did not reply. What Astalus had just told him had raised several questions of his own — not least about dragons — but, for the moment, he preferred to remain silent. He also felt there was some kind of connection between his scar and the Tree of Life, which might yet answer some of these.

"You should sleep for a while," Astalus suggested, rising. "I shall prepare a potion to protect you from dreams."

As the door closed behind the wizard, Kaplyn lay back, but his mind was too active to sleep. He felt as though he was a pawn being manipulated by others, and the thought alarmed him. Eventually, however, sleep did come and with it came the all too familiar sounds of dragons in flight.

Chapter 24

A Startling Discovery

During the next few days, the enemy was content to let its artillery take its toll. Heavy rocks struck the walls with tremendous force, shaking the earth and sending stone splinters flying in all directions. After a while, the enemy used another weapon. Dark-green vitriol splashed the walls, eating into the stone, leaving large smouldering stains.

Queen Catriona ordered the majority of troops to be withdrawn to the relative safety of the inner defence, leaving only a few soldiers upon the outer wall. These brave souls cowered in fear as heavy rocks and acid landed all about them. The wizards, too, were kept busy using their magic to strengthen the walls against the acid attack. It was a tiring, but necessary, work.

Deep within the stone, ancient spells set long ago by the Eldric awoke to strengthen the walls, but it could not protect the men. Many were splashed, and their flesh melted.

At the edge of the enemy camp, krell started to dig a deep trench. The defenders fearfully watched its progress towards the city, drawing closer with each passing day.

After three days of digging, the trench was midway between the enemy and the city. Its purpose soon became clear. In the early morning the first missiles from a catapult hidden in the trench cleared the city walls, landing in its heart.

The missiles were the decaying corpses of either krell or men hurled into the city to spread disease. A detail had the gruesome task of collecting the bodies and transporting them to a fire. The men assigned to this task wore thick, damp cloths wrapped about their faces to shut out the stink. It was a terrible job, made worse when one of the bodies was found to be still alive, if only just.

Astalus and the wizards were given the immediate task of silencing the catapult before plague took hold. Kaplyn joined the wizards upon the outer defence and, instinctively, the group ducked as more bodies cleared the walls.

"We could use your sword's power," Astalus said, picking himself up from the battlement. "If you don't object!"

"Yes, of course. What must I do?" Kaplyn asked.

"Draw it and join us by the fire," Astalus said, indicating a brazier close at hand.

Kaplyn drew the blade, which glowed brightly with the presence of so many enemies. The runes seemed to dance along its length; whether by some trick of the light or not Kaplyn could not tell. Silently the wizards formed a circle about the fire, their faces grim, and then Astalus asked Kaplyn to hold his blade over the flames.

The wizard sprinkled a liberal quantity of herbs upon the fire. The flames briefly turned from orange to green. Kaplyn felt a tremor in the hilt, the unexpected feeling nearly causing him to drop it.

Astalus had said that the runes would enhance the power of the user, and he wondered whether Astalus would be able to direct his power through the weapon. Beside him, the wizard's chant grew to a crescendo.

Then all at once, his blade heaved, forcing him to his knees. The wizards, too, fell back as though struck by an invisible force.

Astalus was the first to his feet and he ran to look out over the battlements. All about the trench the ground heaved like waves in a stormy sea. Men, krell and wood were crushed as the ground bucked in frenzy. Gradually, the ground became still, and a silence descended as both sides looked on in horror.

A ragged cheer went up from the defence. It would be a while before the enemy could construct another trench and, after what had just happened, they would find few volunteers to man it.

The wizards started to talk excitedly amongst themselves before Astalus turned to Kaplyn, a look of wonder upon his face.

"We should not have been able to achieve such power, even with the wizard's orb. Truly the Eldric were powerful," he said shaking his head, staring at Kaplyn's unsheathed sword, which continued to glow eerily in the half light.

"If only we had more such weapons," one of the other wizards wished.

"And what, I wonder, would we do with such power?" Astalus replied.

Beyond the wall, the cries of wounded continued long into the night.

As the day drew to a close, a sentry upon the city wall overlooking the river Torrid was alerted to a noise from below. He peered out into the growing gloom but could see nothing. Knowing better than to delay, he called softly to his companion.

"Sound the alarm and fetch a wizard," he ordered. The other did not question his authority as he hurried away.

A few moments later the sounds of footfalls assured him that others were coming. An enemy assault on this part of the wall would be difficult as this side was protected in part by the fast flowing river. However, for this reason, the wall had been deliberately left under strength...

The first man to arrive was Tharn Shelder, looking gaunt. Even his moustache drooped, although his expression was resolute. Behind him, his troops followed, silently spreading across the length of the wall, nocking bows and hefting spears.

"What is it?" the Tharn whispered.

"I heard a noise, sir," the young man answered, pointing into the darkness.

At another time Shelder would have dismissed the soldier for wasting his time, but after recent events, he had become more tolerant. Absently, he stroked his moustache as he listened. The troops along the wall fell silent, knowing their lives depended upon detecting an enemy attack before it was launched.

Astalus joined them, his brown robes billowing behind him as he ran. Two soldiers had already lit a brazier for Astalus' use and as a warning against demons.

Astalus strung his bow. Taking an arrow from his quiver he placed the cloth-wrapped tip into the hot coals until it caught fire. Nocking the weapon he shot the arrow into the dark sky. At the top of its trajectory it slowed until it hung eerily in position, softly illuminating the scene before them.

On the opposite bank, enemy troops were sliding boats into the river; others, already upon the water, were rowing towards the jetties beneath the wall.

Tharn Shelder sucked in his breath. Now they had been detected, a shout went up. Krell struggled to keep the boats in a straight line as arrows landed amongst them, thudding into exposed flesh or hammering into wet planking.

One boat overturned as its occupants tried to cower beneath the gunwale. The enemy archers on the opposite bank returned fire, their arrows skittering off stone. Some found a mark and more than one defender fell backwards, arrows protruding from flesh, emitting cries of agony as sharp barbs bit into muscle and bone.

Astalus took in the enemy's disposition before ducking back behind the parapet. Hurriedly, he tipped some herbs onto the coals, summoning power to his staff. The spell he was going to attempt was difficult and required some moments to prepare; in the meantime, his staff's orb absorbed the power he would need.

Already some of the boats had made it to the near bank. Yelling krell ran for the wall, hoisting ladders and throwing grappling hooks. The defenders pushed the ladders back or chopped at ropes. Tharn Shelder ran amongst them yelling encouragement, lending a hand wherever needed and directing the reserve troops to the weakest point.

Astalus chanted his spell, holding his staff aloft. It glowed whitely against the dark sky.

All at once the krell in the boats shouted in fear, not comprehending at first what was happening. The river started to slow, thickening about them as the water turned to ice. In a few heartbeats, a large proportion of the attacking army was locked within a thick solid mass. For the time being, the enemy lost its momentum, allowing the defenders brief moments to counter the threat.

Spears and arrows exacted a heavy toll as those krell already at the wall were forced to retreat onto the ice. The krell waiting to board boats on the opposite bank suddenly charged, having been ordered to cross now that the water was frozen.

Those krell still in boats joined the attack, clambering from their small craft and racing for the temporary protection of the wall. For a moment, there was confusion as the retreating krell mixed with those trying to advance.

Astalus continued chanting as he watched the nature of the threat change. Then he stopped his chant. Almost instantly, the ice melted as though it had never existed.

Enemy troops fell into the deep-flowing water, their heavy armour pulling them under while unmanned boats were swept away. Others, still in their boats, out of a spirit of self-preservation, tried to prise away the fingers of krell clinging to the sides; many capsized with the weight.

All along the line, the attack faltered as those at the water's edge watched their comrades being swallowed by the greedy water. Suddenly the attack faltered, and the enemy was in flight. Astalus' flame arrow continued to sink slowly in the dark sky as the krell retreated.

Astalus sank to the ground in a fitful slumber. Tharn Shelder came over to the unconscious wizard to examine him.

"He sleeps," he said simply. It was apparent that the spell had sapped all of his reserves.

"Carry him back to his quarters," the Tharn ordered. "Tonight, he has earned a rest."

As two men carried him from the fray, others collected the dead and dying, taking them back to overflowing mortuaries and hospitals. The Tharn shook his head, silently praying for aid from the Southern Kingdoms.

Malok lounged back in his cushions, lulled by the gentle rocking of the wagon. Briefly he took in the rich trappings of the interior and cursed at having to make this abominable journey. Still, needs must and all that. He was one of the wealthiest merchants in West Meath and yet he always travelled with his caravans. Times were hard and he didn't trust anyone else to get the best prices for his silks and perfumes.

Abruptly, and not for the first time that day, the wagon rolled to a stop. Fretting, Malok threw back the curtain, searching for the Guard Commander.

"Why have we stopped?" he asked of the nearest guard, sitting sullenly on his horse. The man shrugged his shoulders before realising his error. It was not wise to disrespect one's employer.

"I will f...find out, sir," he stammered. Taking up his reins, he urged his mount into a canter.

Malok raised a handkerchief to his nose, irritated by the damp. Looking towards their destination, he shuddered. The entire horizon was dark as though a storm had blotted out Thrace in its entirety. Being a practical man, he hoped to reach CarCamel before the storm broke.

The rider returned, accompanied by the Guard Commander who dismounted and approached the merchant's carriage.

"I'm sorry for the delay, sir. There's a body on the road ahead and I've sent men forward to investigate."

Malok nodded, although he sighed wearily. This commander was too cautious for his liking. On his next trip he would see to it that he was replaced. Patiently they waited. Two riders appeared, carrying a body across one of their mounts. A black, quilled arrow protruded from the man's back.

The Guard Commander rode over to examine the body. "He's alive, but barely."

"Well, we can be on our way then," the merchant demanded.

The Commander was examining the shaft. "I've not seen anything like this before," he announced.

The merchant rolled his eyes, hating what he called *professionals*. "Get the physician to look at him," he insisted. "I want to be in CarCamel by nightfall."

At that moment the wounded man stirred; a low moan escaping his lips. The Commander bent close to hear what he was saying.

Frowning, he removed a package from within the injured man's tunic. Unfolding the oiled cloths he took out a sealed letter which he handed to the merchant.

"It's not addressed to anyone," Malok announced, breaking the seal. His face turned pale as he read.

"We must return at once," he announced when he had finished reading the document, which he swiftly stowed in his breast pocket as though its very sight offended him.

The Commander looked puzzled. The news must be grave indeed to keep a merchant from his money.

Chapter 25

Sorcery

In CarCamel, the alarm sounded, sending men scurrying to their posts. Kaplyn and his companions joined Tharns Orrin and Ballan on the battlement. Many took heart at seeing the two commanders working together; both seemed undaunted by the sight of advancing siege engines.

Suddenly, a loud explosion at the base of the wall made the defenders duck. Shards of rock flew in all directions, and the very foundations shook.

"Sorcery," Tharn Orrin spat as he and Kaplyn risked looking over the battlements. A crack had appeared in the stone

Astalus and the wizards had already gathered. "Protect the walls," Orrin demanded. "Another blast of that magnitude could split the stone."

Astalus nodded and, together, the assembled wizards sought out the enemy sorcerer to block his spells.

High in the sky, grakyn attacked the inner walls, forcing the defenders to take cover, preventing them from aiding their fellows below. Several grakyn were killed, but their numbers were many, and they could fly high, out of the range of bow shot.

Some wizards tried attacking the towers with balls of flame, but this time their spells didn't work as well as before.

"They've protected them with magic," Lars grumbled, standing by Kaplyn's side.

"They haven't protected the occupants though," Kaplyn said grimly. Men and krell were leaping from the tower, in flames. At least for the moment, one tower was out of action.

No further blasts occurred against the wall, and Astalus was kept busy repelling the enemy sorcerers' spells, leaving fewer and less powerful wizards to deal with the remaining towers.

Lomar joined Kaplyn, Lars and Tumarl upon the battlements. "I have an idea," he said. "Fetch a brazier," he ordered of two men standing by their side.

"What are you going to do?" Kaplyn asked.

Lomar smiled. "I don't know if it will work, but it's worth a try. Let me show you."

The two men returned, carrying a lighted brazier. Lomar took out his kara-stone and chanted.

An image of one of the siege towers appeared magically within the orb. Lomar's pale complexion was a picture of concentration as, in the next instance, an image of the brazier's hot coals also appeared within the stone. Abruptly, one of the siege towers burst into flame, grinding to a sudden halt as its occupants leapt from its burning hulk.

"How did you do that?" Kaplyn asked.

Beads of sweat dotted Lomar's brow as he spoke. "I drew together two images within the stone," he declared. "One was of the siege tower and the other fire. Magic could not prevent the fire from destroying the tower because, by focusing one with the other, the two became one."

Kaplyn shook his head, knowing that further questions would have to wait. Lomar concentrated once more, and the image of another tower appeared within the orb. He only had time to destroy one more tower before the remainder reached the walls. With a blood curdling scream, krell spilled onto the battlement as scaling ladders were thrown up against the wall.

A general alert was sounded within the city; everyone on rest detail was roused to deal with the crisis. Many women and older children took up arms, knowing defeat would mean death.

Kaplyn fought like a man possessed.

Tiredness did not seem to affect him as he swung his sword with increasing accuracy. The dark blade twisted and turned within his grip, seemingly with a power of its own. No enemy blade could match it, and many weapons simply broke as Kaplyn blocked their attacks. With each kill, an eerie crooning emanated from within the metal's blackness, and strength seemed to flow into him.

By his side, Lars fought with brute strength: his double-bladed axe clove swords and limbs alike, tearing deep into armour and hurling krell back.

Tumarl fought out of a bitter desire for revenge. His wide, sweeping strokes scattered the enemy, so few dared approach. Aloud, he counted each

368

enemy he slew as if eventually the tally would make amends for the death of his family and friends.

Lomar brought up the rear, fighting with grace and speed, favouring a short blade and a small oval shield. The enemy found the sprightly albino a difficult target as he danced amongst them, sowing the seed of their death.

Behind the small group Tharn Orrin saw Kaplyn's blade glowing like a star amongst the enemy. He urged his troops forward to protect Kaplyn's flank. Krell toppled from the walls to their deaths below, but more scaled the walls. With a massive bellow, Orrin fought on with grim determination. By his side, his men responded as best they could.

Nate cursed aloud as a spear all but caught his shin and toppled him. Harlam leapt to his aid, impaling a large ugly krell who, only moments before, had been about to decapitate the older man. Nate clambered shakily to his feet, nodded his thanks and was then swept up once more into the terrible slaughter.

Kaplyn glanced around, suddenly realising he had overcommitted himself and his friends as his battle-rage cleared. All around him, Allund and Thracians were dying as krell pressed them from both their front and flank, as more gained the wall. By his side, Lars bellowed a savage oath to Karlam, his god of war, and Kaplyn heard how tired he was.

The tide of battle was turning, and they had to retreat to the inner wall before it was too late.

"Withdraw!" he cried to those around him.

Slowly they fought their way back to the narrow crossing and the safety of the inner wall. Above them, in the tall towers, the few defenders not pinned down covered their retreat. Krell poured over the battlements like a flood-water, snapping at their heels as they hurried across the narrow, rickety bridges which swayed alarmingly as men fought desperately to retreat. After the last man had crossed the retaining pins were drawn so that the bridges tumbled into the chasm below, spilling heavily-armoured krell to their deaths. The doors through the inner walls slammed shut. The towers and upper bridges held as their occupants fought bravely to deny the enemy access, pouring a heavy volley of fire into its troops.

Through doors set deep in the city walls, the Allund and Thracian soldiers withdrew, abandoning the lower wall. From slits cut deep into the stone archers directed a deadly fire. Having gained a foothold, the enemy troops wavered, failing to press their advantage. Now that they were upon the outer wall they saw just how formidable the ancient defences were; the next walls were easily as high as the one they had won.

High above, the grakyn were also starting to falter. Drained of power through continuous assault, they were forced to flee. This gave the defenders a much needed respite and, once more, they started to loose arrows upon the enemy, who tried to flee but met those coming up the walls. In the confusion, many of the enemy troops fell to their deaths. Fights broke out amongst them until eventually order was restored.

Except for the majority of the towers, the enemy held the outer wall.

Kaplyn, Lars, Lomar and Tumarl made their way up the poorly lit stair within the inner wall, past the firing bays, where the defenders continued to shoot arrows.

Kaplyn had to squint when they came out once more into the comparative brightness of the open air. Queen Catriona greeted them coldly; to their surprise, she wore armour and carried a sword. The loss of the outer wall was clearly a heavy burden.

"The grakyn have retreated for the moment. If we are to retake the wall we should do it now," Catriona announced.

By her side Ballan agreed. His face was etched with deep wrinkles; his eyes were sunken and his complexion pale. Yet the light of battle was in his eyes.

Astalus joined the group and heard the Queen's comment. He understood what was being asked but could not see how they could achieve it. "How can we attack the wall when all the bridges have been destroyed?"

"From the towers," Queen Catriona declared. "We still hold the upper levels, and the bridges to these are intact."

Kaplyn had a sinking feeling, knowing many would lose their lives in the attempt. However, if they were to survive, there was no alternative for, while the enemy held the outer wall, the city's defence was in the balance.

"We might be able to create a screen to hide our troops," Astalus suggested. The Queen nodded and he took his leave to make preparations. Her face was drawn and her complexion pale as she turned to look determinedly over the inner wall.

Swiftly, men were summoned to await the order to counterattack. Out of the gloom, a thick fog filled the air until it was difficult to see a hand waved in front of a face. In silence, the order was given, and the troops crossed the bridges into the upper levels where gaunt soldiers greeted them silently with nods. With screams of rage, men spilled from the towers, falling upon the

370

unsuspecting enemy. The enemy were bewildered by the sudden attack from within the fog, made worse by ghostly forms added by the wizards.

Kaplyn's blade glowed like fire, and the enemy fell before him until word spread that the Eldric had returned. Krell fled in terror from the wall they had so recently fought so hard to take. In parts, the enemy defence was stubborn and many men of Thrace and Allund fell before the wall was finally retaken.

As the fog lifted, the defenders stood wearily upon the outer wall, with barely enough energy to stand. The enemy retreat became a rout as the reinforcements fled with their brothers. The dreaded siege towers perched against the city walls were fired so that they could not be reused, and the smoke from the wreckage blackened the walls so that they would never again be clean.

Behind the fleeing enemy, a stillness hung over the city. Life slowly returned to numb arms and legs as men assessed the carnage. Kaplyn felt incredibly sad when he saw all the bodies. He despised himself for his part in their deaths. Then his feelings changed to concern for his friends, standing nearby. Fortunately none of them were seriously injured though most had minor cuts and burns.

Looking about, he realised how close they were to failing. If the enemy were to counter attack now, then no one would be able to withstand them. Everyone looked shattered; their eyes were red and their complexion pale.

Civilians joined the soldiers looking out from the walls. Mothers looked for sons and wives searched for husbands. All about the smoking city, sorrow was mixed with joy.

At that moment the fate of the city hung in the balance. Tired, over-weary soldiers had experienced their first real taste of disaster. Many were terrified by the experience, recognising how vulnerable the city truly was. Even the bravest quaked at the thought of facing more danger on the morrow. Doubt, fear and dread ate at their hearts like a cancer.

If the enemy had known of the city's fear, he would have attacked again. However, fortune smiled upon the defenders as, instead, the enemy retired to contemplate their stubbornness. For the remainder of the day and that night, the battlefield remained silent save for the sobbing of the bereaved.

Chapter 26

Demons Summoned

As dawn broke, weak sunlight revealed a more resolute city. After stalking the city like dreadful ghouls for most of the night, doubt and fear had gone. The sun found the defenders standing staunchly resolute, waiting with grim determination. Legs were planted firmly on stone, and the message of defiance was clear as every person who could wield a weapon stood waiting for the enemy to attack.

Anger had replaced the previous night's fear. Their homes, their lives and those of their loved ones were threatened. As a result, the armies of Thrace and Allund found a new determination.

That night, a king had been born, baptised in blood and fire, and cocooned in death. Now many accepted Kaplyn as their Monarch, looking to him with renewed hope. Orrin, too, noticed this, even if Kaplyn did not. Quietly, he encouraged it, seeing signs of hope in the young man.

Astalus joined the group upon the watch tower, grimy from the previous day's battle. It was clear that, like everyone else, he had not slept that night.

"He's tried his army and failed," he said softly, looking out at the enemy. His eyes focused on the small knoll upon which he sensed the enemy commander. "And now it's the turn of his necromancer."

How Astalus knew this, nobody could say. Standing high upon the city wall, buffeted by cold winds while vast enemy hordes surrounded the city, was justification enough that demons might be next.

Kaplyn realised how isolated they were. He hoped that, by now, messengers had made it to the Southern Kingdoms and help was on the way. They situation seemed hopeless. The enemy was too strong.

A deep thrumming started, startling Kaplyn and he found himself holding his breath while he tried to identify the noise. Clutching his cloak tightly about his shoulders he leant against the cold battlements as he peered into the surrounding gloom. The others, too, strained to hear the noise. It was a drum, and with a hypnotic repetitiveness each note trailed off faintly as the next sounded.

"It comes," Astalus declared.

"Can we stop the demon before it is summoned?" Queen Catriona asked, gripping her sword firmly as if seeking reassurance in the cold metal. To Kaplyn's ears she sounded afraid, her voice small and insignificant.

Astalus shook his head bleakly. "I am a wizard, not a necromancer. This is my world," he said, gesturing to their surroundings, "I cannot affect the dead." He looked grim.

"Tharn Alder, are the archers standing by?" The Queen asked.

He nodded; the archers had been positioned about the city. The Tharn had lost considerable weight over the last few days, but he looked resolute. He had gained the respect of his men, having been in the thick of the fighting, and his blade had proven deadly to the enemies of Thrace. Legends told that demons suffered pain in this world and the very earth hurt them. With this hope, their arrow tips were encrusted with jewels in the belief their purity would be fatal to the demons.

"Our only hope now is that the enemy sorcerer will fail, and the demon will take *his* soul to Hell," Astalus said hopefully.

By his side, Lomar took out his kara-stone. "I might be able to distract him while he summons the demon. It might encourage him to make a mistake."

Astalus smiled, crouching down besides Lomar. "It's worth trying."

Lomar stared into the crystal's depths. The others backed away, watching them with a mixture of feelings.

As Lomar traced a rune over the stone, an image of the knoll formed, and then the scene changed. A fire appeared alongside it. Lomar tried to merge the two images, but, try as he might, failed. Cursing he sat down, looking dejected.

"They have protected the knoll well," Astalus admitted, looking equally despondent. With renewed determination and knowing that any attempt to distract the enemy sorcerer was worth trying, he arose and walked towards one of the lighted braziers. He spilled a good portion of herbs from his pouch onto the burning coals, which consumed the small leaves in a fountain of colours. A sweet aroma filled the air.

Closing his eyes, Astalus started to chant. His voice rose and fell in time with the rhythm of the enemy drums. As he trailed off into silence, there was a sudden high-pitched scream and a blinding flash from the enemy camp. All eyes turned in that direction. No one could be certain what had happened, it was so quick. On reflection, however, Kaplyn thought that a great fireball had appeared in the sky and slammed against the knoll only to be diverted at the last moment as if it had come up against an invisible barrier. A shower of sparks and flame cascaded into the enemy ranks, which fell back with shouts of surprise. A ragged cheer arose from the defenders.

"It won't harm the necromancer," Astalus explained, "but it might cause him to make a mistake."

"Did it work?" Lars asked uncertainly.

Astalus shrugged, "I don't know," he admitted.

As if in defiance to Astalus' optimism, a green glow emanated from the knoll.

"I have failed. It is here!" Astalus proclaimed.

As suddenly as it had appeared, the glow winked out, leaving the knoll in semi-darkness. Abruptly the flames within the brazier turned blue and, with fear in their eyes, the Commanders knew a demon had been summoned.

Deep within the city's heart, a scream sounded. In a deserted street, a well-armed group of militiamen ran as fast as they were able towards the scream's source, their ill-fitting armour clanking as they jogged along the cobbled street. With nervous looks, they took in the rows of silent houses and dark alleyways.

As one, the men skidded to a halt as a huge creature leapt into the street before them. In one terrifying instant they saw the demon's horrific form. It was over eight feet tall with ungainly-looking limbs and a long flickering tail. Its skin was green-tinged and looked as thick as a bull's hide. The demon's small eyes glinted maliciously, and an evil grin spread across its face as it approached the unfortunate troops, who froze in terror.

Before the soldiers could react, the creature pounced, covering the distance separating them in a single bound and landing amongst the startled men in the blink of an eye. In an instant two soldiers lay dead whilst those remaining fled screaming, throwing down their weapons as they ran. For a moment, the demon remained where it was, gorging itself upon the warm remains.

The news of the demon's arrival spread like wildfire, and, on its heels, came terror.

A runner came panting up the stairs.

"My Queen, a demon is attacking in the heart of the city."

Queen Catriona looked to Astalus for guidance.

"I will go," Kaplyn announced. "My sword has killed a demon before." The blade burned blue, matching the flames of the surrounding fires as if in anticipation of tasting the demon's blood.

Accompanied by several archers, Kaplyn, with the messenger showing him the way, raced off. Lars, Lomar and Tumarl were about to follow but, just then, a great cry went up from the enemy position as thousands of krell and men started to advance. Another louder cry sounded from below their position, making them jump. Then the sound of muffled fighting came to their ears, intermingled with shouts of terror.

"The main gate!" Astalus shouted above the din. Without waiting, he started down the stairs towards the source of the commotion.

Kaplyn sprinted down narrow streets with the archers following. Most of the citizens were locked indoors, and windows had long since been boarded over, making the once-thriving city seem deserted.

Abruptly, five militiamen came stumbling around a corner towards them. Most had discarded their weapons and some were unbuckling armour as they ran. The look of fear upon their faces was enough to make Kaplyn slow down. The archers caught up, breathing raggedly, their eyes wide with fear.

"Prepare yourselves!" Kaplyn hissed. "Draw!" he said, pointing down the street with his blade.

The archers nocked their arrows and drew back their bows. The tiny jewels embedded in the arrow tips sparkled in the faint light. Kaplyn stood to one side, his sword glowing eerily.

Long moments dragged by and, just as Kaplyn was debating whether to press on, the demon appeared, its long tail thrashing from side to side.

Kaplyn's blade sliced down. "Loose!" he shouted.

In unison, five arrows flashed through the air. Four struck the demon, slicing deeply into its flesh, and one missed completely, bouncing harmlessly off a nearby wall. The jewels had done their work and at least the arrows had penetrated the demon's hide, wounding it and causing it to scream in pain. Recovering, its hate-filled eyes fastened on its tormentors. The look was sufficient to cause one of the archers to flee, dropping his bow as he went.

A scream of rage rent the air, and another archer turned tail and fled after the first man.

"Shoot again," Kaplyn bellowed.

Before they could take aim, the demon raced towards them, pointing a taloned claw and barking arcane words.

Kaplyn could only watch in horror as the remaining archers fell to the ground. White, evil-smelling froth bubbled from their gaping mouths as the men died a terrible death. Why Kaplyn had not been affected he did not know. Perhaps his scar protected him.

He raised his sword, and the demon shrank back, howling in pain and shielding its eyes. Then, with extraordinary speed, it launched itself at Kaplyn. Before he had time to think, his sword rose to parry the attack. The demon struck, intending to tear Kaplyn limb from limb, but his sword met the blow, effortlessly slicing through the demon's wrist, severing the limb.

Instinctively, Kaplyn ducked, narrowly avoiding a spray of green blood which hissed as it splashed against stone, leaving a dark green, glowing wound.

With a massive leap, the demon was gone. Kaplyn spun about, his heart beating wildly. Its screams of agony continued, coming from the rooftops by his side. Kaplyn ran to a nearby building, wrenching open the door.

Determined to prevent the demon escaping, he ran up a narrow flight of stairs, passing a number of doors along the way. Finally, he came to a door blocking the stair. Without pausing, he shouldered it open, diving through onto a flat roof.

The demon was facing him, gripping its bloody stump, screaming in pain. When it saw Kaplyn, it quietened; its eyes widened in anger, and its forked tongue shot out through thin lips.

It attacked suddenly, screaming to paralyse him. Kaplyn's sword met the charge, slicing deeply into the demon's body. The force of the blow, combined with the speed of the demon's attack, wrenched the blade from Kaplyn's grip. He rolled to one side. The demon raced by, trying to knock the weapon away with its stump.

Kaplyn completed his roll and, in desperation, drew his dagger. The demon looked up, its eyes glazed with pain and hate. Seeing its enemy so vulnerable, it screamed and launched itself at him, either hoping to hurl him from the roof or crush him under its weight.

At that moment, the air was filled with arrows. Several hammered into the demon's hide and it came to a halt mid-stride; its legs buckling beneath it.

Kaplyn darted forward, wrenching his blade from the demon's body. With a cry of rage, he thrust it into the demon's throat. The demon convulsed but Kaplyn hung on as it toppled backwards. Kneeling on the demon's chest he drew the blade before plunging it deep into the demon's heart, or at least where he supposed its heart was. He must have been successful for gradually the demon's convulsions lessened until finally it lay still.

Slowly he got to his feet, backing warily away from the corpse. Satisfied that it was truly lifeless, he risked a glance over his shoulder towards the opposite building from where the arrows had come.

Lars stood with a group of archers who were shouting triumphantly, arms raised and fists punching the air. Kaplyn grinned and waved back. His own celebration was abruptly cut short when he heard a soft hissing coming from his chest. To his horror some of the demon's blood had splashed onto his breastplate and smoke was issuing forth from a growing hole. Slicing through the leather straps he let the armour fall with a clang to the rooftop.

At that moment, a loud explosion rent the air and the building shook beneath his feet.

"The gate!" one of the men on the other rooftop shouted above the din. A second explosion shook the ground as a great cloud of smoke erupted skyward. From their vantage-point, Kaplyn and the others could see the gate clearly.

Before it stood another demon. It was massive, standing nearly as tall as the gates themselves. Its arms were as thick as tree trunks, and its fists looked like giant hammers. With slow deliberate blows, it struck the gates, sending shock waves reverberating around the city.

The wood buckled and, with a loud splintering, the gate shattered. Without pausing, the demon set about smashing the granite towers either side. Like the gate before it, the stone proved no match for the demon. Large chunks of masonry gave way before each massive blow as, gradually, the creature revealed the long, dark tunnel leading to the outer wall and the only gate which remained between the city and destruction. Kaplyn cried out; he was too far away to save the gate and could only watch in horror.

Chapter 27

Defeat

Ariome felt the build up of energy from the Narlassar sorcerer as he drew power to summon the demon. She also felt his shock when Astalus hurled the fireball against his magical barrier, but the sorcerer had succeeded and the demons had come.

Ariome shuddered and closed her mind to the kara-stone, releasing the spell of seeing. Almost crying, she sought sanctuary in the darkest corner of her room. Sitting upon the floor, she pulled her knees up to her chest and hugged them tightly.

Now was her time, her moment of glory when CarCamel would finally fall.

Feelings of both elation and fear flooded through her.

In the very moment of her glory, she knew terror. The summoning appalled her, blunting her victory; the enemy had summoned a very powerful demon. At that moment, the soul of every citizen in CarCamel was at risk, including her own.

Astalus raced towards the main gates that were such a vital part of the city's defence. His legs felt weary after the unremitting exertions of recent days. Physical effort was alien to the young wizard, and now he had to will himself on with every painful stride.

Passing swiftly through the once vibrant streets, wild thoughts tumbled through his mind. Although the gates were formidable, comprising a stout inner door connected via a long tunnel to an outer one, beyond them there was no other defence. If the gates fell, an enemy would be free to sack the city at will.

Shouts of surprise and the clanging of metal on stone came from ahead, followed by several fearful screams. Astalus slowed and, as he turned the final corner, his heart lurched.

A huge, powerfully-built demon crouched in front of the gates. Before it several soldiers were fighting for their lives — and souls. The devil was methodically killing each man with unabated fury. Astalus wanted to cover his ears as the men's screams echoed from the granite walls.

All this Astalus saw in an instant. Within the space of a few heartbeats, an incantation formed in his mind and archaic words of power tumbled from his trembling lips. He could only watch the carnage in horror as he recited the spell, summoning power to his staff. As the power grew, so too did his fear; never had he confronted a demon before.

The demon, as yet unaware of him, had started striking the gates. After a few blows, they shattered, hurling wood and stone in all directions. Next it turned its attention to the towers at the gate's side, and its club-like fists rose and fell in unison.

All at once, the demon sensed the build up of energy behind it and all thoughts of the gate were banished. Shrieking, it turned to locate its nemesis and, too late, its glare fell upon the brown-robed wizard.

Astalus pointed the tip of his staff at the devil-spawn. Instantly a great wave of vitriol struck it from all sides. The creature howled in agony as acid seeped beneath its protective scales, burning deep into its eyes and flesh, leaving it blind.

The attack was good, but not good enough. The demon, though sightless, still lived. Worse, it had seen where its assailant was. Picking up a hay-packed cart it hurled the improvised weapon with all its brute strength.

Astalus saw the demon's intent but was spent and could not summon more power. He tried to run but was unsure where the demon was going to throw the missile. In indecision, Astalus swung from side to side, trying to anticipate which way to turn. At the last moment, he made up his mind, throwing himself to one side, willing his legs to respond.

However, luck was with the devil. In a shower of dust and debris, the heavy cart slammed into the cobbled road just in front of the wizard, skidding into him in a terrifying din of metal grating on stone, bowling him over and burying him beneath its heavy load.

The demon started to stride towards Astalus, but then a silent command forbade it. It screams shook the ground as its summoner forced its attention back to the gate's destruction. Reluctantly, it turned to pummel the gate posts with its massive fists, not caring where its blows fell, its rage made uncontrollable by the acid.

379

One of the towers protecting the inner gate collapsed as the demon shattered it as effectively as if it were wood. Masonry fell from the surrounding walls, smashing onto the cobbles below. The demon roared its success, pushing through the broken portal, dragging the wooden frame with it. Through arrow slits in the tunnel, archers poured down a hail of fire. Their arrows skipped off the demon's scales, and it barely broke stride as it heaved against the stone. Suddenly, the tunnel collapsed, scattering bodies like leaves.

Unable to see, the demon collided with the outer gate, and the planking groaned beneath its weight. With a roar, the demon charged the obstruction, shattering it. Screaming its success, it hammered at the remaining tunnel walls, throwing out a shower of rock and dust.

A great yell went up from the hordes waiting outside, and brazen trumpets sounded the charge. The city's defences were breached.

Chapter 28

Dragon!

Kaplyn watched the smoke over the gate slowly settle. While the gates had held, the city had had a chance, but now that chance was lost.

Howling enemy hordes, waving spears and swords, leapt over the fallen masonry, swarming through the broken portal. Their numbers were a trickle at first, but soon thousands would pour through the shattered gates. Ignoring them, the demon continued its unrelenting attack on the walls on either side of the gate, widening the gap ever more while defenders fled in panic.

Kaplyn watched in mounting despair. He cried out against the terrible feeling of hopelessness.

No one could stop the enemy now.

His vision dimmed as unshed tears brimmed his eyes. He held his blade aloft shouting his defiance, knowing the fight would be to the death. Nothing else remained. He thought of his friends and hoped their deaths would be swift. In his mind's eye, an image of Catriona formed, and he knew then that he loved her and felt robbed to lose her in this way.

His scar throbbed as his heart hammered. It felt as though it was about to burst. He wished it would; anything to end this torment. From his scar, a terrible pain lanced through his chest, as if he were being torn in two. He screamed aloud in agony.

Opening his eyes he looked at his outstretched blade. The runes danced along its length, taunting his ignorance. All at once, strange words of power came unbidden to his mind, and Kaplyn could hear Astalus reciting the spell he had used to summon power from his blade.

For that brief instant, Kaplyn understood the runes.

In a deep voice, he shouted, chanting in time with the voice within his mind. His senses reeled. A strange sensation swept through him and then his vision swam.

All at once, he was seeing two different landscapes, one superimposed on the other. In one world, he was standing upon the familiar rooftop with the body of the demon by his side. In the other, he was standing upon a steep mountainside, facing an alien landscape.

With mounting panic, and knowing he would be lost if his vision did not clear quickly, he tried to make sense of the images. Squinting into the other world, his senses reeled and he almost overbalanced. Cold winds from both worlds gusted, making him shiver.

Suddenly, he smelt the terrible odours that had haunted his dreams. His heart quailed as he recognised the scent.

Dragon!

Instantly he felt an overwhelming urge to hide, but dared not move.

A name sprang to mind.

Shastlan!

Destroyer of your people.

He knew this other world was very real and equally as deadly as the enemy pouring into the city. Wailing, he lifted his eyes to the heavens and beheld a faint, but familiar, spot he knew would be there. The speck increased in size, drawing steadily nearer. The desire to hide grew stronger, but he remained stubbornly rooted to the spot, transfixed. The speck grew, becoming a long, red serpentine body with outstretched gossamer wings. A broad head searched the ground below; then its eyes alighted upon him. He recognised the dragon as it glided effortlessly on the thermal currents. He remembered flying it, and his fear turned to joy.

The serpent landed with a grace belying its size, coming to rest alongside Kaplyn on the rooftop. Strangely, the dragon was the only thing that was not blurred, as though it existed in both worlds.

The dragon waited as though willing Kaplyn to step forward into the strange world, but something held him where he was.

Shastlan.

Remember your people.

Betrayer.

Slowly Kaplyn took a step backwards.

Palpable fear emanated from the dragon, and, reluctantly, it followed. Kaplyn backed up until they were both standing upon the rooftop. The other world faded, leaving Kaplyn's vision clear at last.

Well? the dragon declared, its thoughts tumbling through his mind.

Suddenly Kaplyn's blade felt heavy. He realised he was still holding it aloft. Lowering it, the smoke from a dozen fires wafted about them. The dragon inhaled deeply, enjoying the reek of war. Beyond them, the cries of battle rose and fell.

Kaplyn risked glancing towards the gate. Dark figures were clambering over the wreckage, swarming into the city. Beside him the dragon stirred impatiently.

Fearing an attack, he raised his blade, but it was merely watching the demon. Kaplyn sensed the dragon's anger rise like a flaming beacon, and he knew — as their eyes met — that the immense creature would aid them.

Come! the dragon ordered. *Mount!*

"Mount? How?"

The dragon raised a foreleg and seemed to grin as though daring him. Kaplyn was reluctant, but with every passing moment, his friends were in danger.

Once astride the dragon, he felt secure, as though the base of its long neck had been made for a rider. He could almost say that it felt comfortable. With a jolt the dragon launched itself skywards. Its huge wings buffeted the smoke-filled air as it climbed into the sky until the city was nothing but a bare speck far below.

Kaplyn looked fearfully down at the receding city. Desperately he sought a handhold but could only grasp the long strands of thick orange hair growing like a mane from the dragon's neck. He used these as reins, keeping his grip on his sword.

His thoughts returned to the dragon.

For the moment at least the great beast was intent upon the scene below as if seeking how best to attack. When Kaplyn finally realised he was not going to be betrayed, he thrilled at the feeling of flying. His dark hair streamed out behind him in the cold air.

The feeling of euphoria did not last. Without warning, the dragon tucked in its wings, plummeting like a stone. Kaplyn's stomach lurched skyward and he gripped the dragon's neck for all he was worth. Beyond the head he saw the ground rushing up towards them. Fearing they would crash, he squeezed his eyes tightly shut. Screaming, he willed the dragon to spread its wings and fly. Air buffeted him, threatening to dislodge him from his precarious perch. He regretted holding onto his sword, wishing he had both hands free.

A distant memory replaced his fear, and he recalled other dragon flights but knew *that* was impossible. He had never even seen a dragon before. Perhaps once he thought he had, hidden in icy depths on his journey into BanKildor, but that was not the same as coming face to face with a real one.

With a sudden lurch, his thoughts were instantly scattered. He felt as though he had been slammed between two great weights, and his stomach leapt to his throat. Then he opened his eyes, instantly regretting it.

Below, the upturned faces of Allund and Thracian soldiers stared wide eyed with fear at him as they fled down the main street. Ahead of the speeding dragon, thousands of krell and Aldracian troops were in hot pursuit, while behind them the ruined gates of the city rose like an obelisk, shrouded in smoke of a sacked city.

A great burst of flame and vitriol spewed from the serpent's gaping maw. Acid raked both armies, killing men and krell in an instant. A ball of heat engulfed dragon and rider, singeing Kaplyn's hair and forcing him to duck behind the dragon's head. He wanted to cry out that it had killed friendly troops, but there was no time.

He clung on as they sped at breakneck speed towards the gate and the blinded demon. He sensed the demon's confusion as it scented the air, searching for the approaching power. Their speed was so great that they were upon it before it had time to react.

Dragon fire engulfed both the demon and krell pouring through the gate. The krell perished instantly but the demon's scales protected it, although vitriol slowly seeped beneath its armour, burning its already damaged flesh. The demon howled in torment.

The dragon tucked in its wings, its forward momentum propelling it through the narrow opening in the outer wall. Kaplyn lashed out with his blade, the force of the blow severing the demon's head from its body.

Instinctively he tucked himself behind the dragon's neck, and they shot through the wreckage of the gate, coming upon the advancing hordes like an avenging angel of death. The dragon snapped its powerful wings, and krell cried out in fear as their hopes of victory were replaced with terror. Flame splashed about them, searing their flesh and boiling their blood. The dragon ceased its attack, climbing high into the sombre grey sky, seeking height to launch its next assault.

Below, the krell army was suddenly halted as the dragon shot like a thunderbolt of death from the shattered gates. A great cry of fear went up. Those following behind crashed into the backs of their comrades, trampling them underfoot.

Again the dragon struck, breathing death and destruction. There was nowhere for the enemy to run; the press of bodies was too great. For terrible moments, the dragon wreaked havoc until the ground was covered in a mass of boiling flesh. With a roar of success, it rocketed skywards.

So far, its attacks had been too low and sudden for the enemy commanders to realise what was happening and, as yet they were ignorant of the threat.

From his vantage point, Kaplyn saw the small hill and the enemy standard flapping in the cold wind. As the dragon paused in its flight, Kaplyn shouted above the wind's rush, pointing down towards the enemy commanders.

Instantly the dragon fell, attacking low and at an angle away from CarCamel. It glided scant yards above the upturned faces of a vast sea of krell and men of Aldrace, skimming across the ground, aiming like a bolt from a bow at the heart of the enemy command.

The Commanders were confused by the battle's lull. At the instant of the demon's demise, the Narlassar sorcerer screamed aloud as his power was abruptly shattered. The others looked on helplessly as the sorcerer squirmed upon the ground, his tongue lolling from his mouth and his eyes bulging with pain.

Screams from their army added to the confusion. Without the sorcerer's help, they were blind to the events transpiring about them. Calling for runners, they sought news of the attack. They were so *close* to victory; the city was *sure* to fall.

Suddenly, the dark silhouette of the dragon loomed up before them as though it had risen out of the very ground. Men and krell screamed in terror as a blast of fire and venom engulfed them. Then the dragon was gone, leaving only charred remains and a burning standard. No spells could withstand dragon fire.

The dragon rose high above the battlefield, exulting in the surge of power it felt from the destruction of a sorcerer. *A Chantrall!* Kaplyn's mind echoed. He did not know what this meant, but guessed it was the dragon's word for necromancer.

In sheer joy, it twisted and turned in a victory roll. Kaplyn clung on to the neck in terror, screaming at the top of his voice for the dragon to stop. Finally the serpent acknowledged his cries, reluctantly levelling off and skimming fearlessly across the heads of the enemy.

Across the entire front, the enemy was in flight.

Kaplyn looked down and, for a moment, his heart stopped beating with the enormity of their success. Only moments before, he had been in total despair. Yet now ....

Swiftly the dragon rose until Kaplyn could see nothing below but clouds. Abruptly, it went into another steep dive aiming at a formation of grakyn. The grakyn were intent upon the allied cavalry, issuing forth from the city. If the grakyn had struck, the cavalry would have been annihilated.

Once more, the dragon saved the day. It flew straight at the grakyn, distracting them from their target; but if Kaplyn thought the dragon was going to destroy them, he was mistaken. At first it toyed with the startled creatures that scattered flying this way and that. The dragon gave chase as though it were a game.

Kaplyn lashed out with his blade, slashing futilely at the air where a grakyn had been moments before. He was too slow and his reach too short for this type of aerial battle. A ball of flame flew by his head as a grakyn turned to attack. Another bolt of flame splashed harmlessly against the dragon's scales. Many of the grakyn had become confident and were now turning to fight.

Kaplyn realised why the dragon could afford to play with the grakyn. Its scales were impervious to their attacks. He was not, though! He was an easy target sitting astride the dragon's neck. A blast of energy passed so close he felt its heat on his neck. His mind wailed in fear, and he sensed the dragon's enjoyment of his terror as it continued to dart in and out of the flying demons.

Kaplyn swore, placing the tip of his sword beneath one of the dragon's scales, pressing firmly. The dragon abruptly rose and immediately flame engulfed several grakyn, burning their wings as their bodies plummeted from the sky. The dragon twisted and more grakyn were consumed by flame. The remainder scattered and, for a while, the dragon gave chase, killing several more before becoming bored. Kaplyn watched the dark bodies writhing as they fell, before bouncing from the spongy turf. He was panting as the dragon rose into the sky. For his own security he left his blade where it was.

From height, he surveyed the battle. The cavalry was cutting a great swathe through the enemy ranks. Small knots of krell formed islands which the cavalry flowed around. Kaplyn guided the dragon in a steep attack. The immense creature spewed flame, scattering the krell and forcing them to join the ranks of their fleeing comrades. Then the dragon rose steeply before going into another dive, killing hundreds more in one pass.

The enemy were now all too aware of the threat; their screams reached Kaplyn and the carnage sickened him. He forced the dragon to rise and reluctantly it obeyed. Behind them, Kaplyn could see a dark swathe of blackened corpses.

A roar, followed by screams, caused him to turn and look to the enemy's rear. A wall of figures, carrying what looked like lanterns, was advancing. Fearing a new menace, Kaplyn guided the dragon towards them. And then, all at once, his hopes were renewed. Below him another army was attacking the fleeing enemy. Long lines of troops were advancing and the enemy were breaking upon its ranks.

He looked on in disbelief, holding the dragon in check. For a moment he thought that they were Eldric ghosts resurrected from the distant past. Magic bolts of power leapt from their ranks, flaying the enemy.

Kaplyn wanted to find out who they were but did not trust the dragon. Abruptly he was afraid of the large creature, sensing its malice. A voice seemed to urge him to distrust the beast. Again he felt a familiarity about being on dragon-back, but this time he did not feel exulted; instead, a wave of nausea swept over him. He forced the dragon to turn and headed back to the city, flying high over the broken gates.

Kaplyn guided it towards the rooftop they had taken off from moments before. Below, people scurried from the streets in fear of the great serpent. Lazily the dragon descended and, graceful as a cat, alighted upon the roof.

Warily Kaplyn dismounted. Anger coursed through his veins as he looked at the beast. Once more his vision swam, and he saw two worlds superimposed on each other. One world was his, a city shadowed by the smoke of battle. The other was that of lush mountains overlooked by a blue, peaceful sky.

"Go!" Kaplyn commanded, raising his sword.

The dragon looked over Kaplyn's shoulder at the smoke of battle and, for a moment, Kaplyn feared it would disobey.

"Go!" he repeated, and the dragon's eyes locked on his. Kaplyn's legs felt weak and his blade heavy in his grasp. He returned the dragon's stare and did not falter.

Farewell, the dragon's voice echoed in his mind. *We shall meet again*! It sounded like a threat.

With that, the lizard turned and, with a snap of its mighty wings, lifted into the azure sky. Kaplyn's vision blurred; all at once he was looking across at the tall towers of the rich part of the city. Smoke drifted across his view, its acrid smell making him retch. His throat felt as though he had swallowed razor blades.

He looked down at his sword. The glow had diminished and the runes were unintelligible. He tried to recollect how he had summoned the dragon but his memory was already fading. Sheathing his blade, he made his way back down the stairs to the cobbled street. Through deserted alleys, he hurried towards the main gate, eager for news. His pace slowed when he entered the main street through which he had flown on dragon-back only a short while earlier.

Dragon fire had ravaged the stones and blackened bodies littered the road. Small fires still burned and smoke rose lazily into the darkening sky as night approached. A stench of cooked meat filled the air.

Kaplyn looked with horror upon the allied troops amongst the wreckage. A pang of guilt stabbed painfully into his soul as he walked the length of the macabre funeral pyre.

People were starting to return to the streets. They looked upon Kaplyn with fear. Nearing the gates, he came alongside the demon's headless corpse. Lars stood to one side, his broad axe in his hand. With relief, Kaplyn saw Lomar and Tumarl entering the city. Tumarl was limping and deep red blood soaked his leggings.

Lars hailed Kaplyn, clearly relieved he was all right.

As Kaplyn approached, the big man's look of relief changed to confusion. By Lars' side Tumarl gasped. Others were looking at Kaplyn, horror on their smoke-grimed faces.

When Kaplyn saw their stares, he looked down at his chest. His clothes, burnt from his recent flight, hung in tatters from his body and his scar was plainly visible for everyone to see. It was blazing with silver light. His finger traced the rough surface; it was cold and lifeless as though made of stone rather than flesh.

The light shocked him, as did the horror upon his friends' faces. He tried to cover the wound with his shirt but the pieces crumbled in his hand. In despair he gave up, his hands hanging by his side. People muttered and he saw one man making warding signs against evil.

Removing his own jerkin, Lars strode over to Kaplyn's side and handed it to him. Kaplyn accepted it and, putting it on, even though it hung to his knees, he hugged it tightly shut.

"Come," Lomar said. "Let's find the healers and have Tumarl's wound seen to."

Tumarl stood transfixed with his mouth open, staring in disbelief at a spot on the front of Kaplyn's jerkin. Lars shoved him to get him moving.

Gratefully, Kaplyn allowed Lomar to escort them back into the city. He suddenly felt bone weary, wanting above all else to rest.

Together, they made their way to the hospital. There they left Tumarl. Lomar volunteered to remain to tend the wounded.

Once inside the palace Kaplyn took his leave of Lars. He could tell by Lars' expression that he wanted to talk, but Kaplyn ignored him. Once inside his room, Kaplyn slammed the door shut and tumbled onto his bed, falling asleep immediately.

Dragon dreams returned to haunt him and he tossed and turned restlessly. This time there was an urgency about the dreams. Across a great distance, Kaplyn thought he could make out a voice warning him, but the more he concentrated on it the more it receded. Finally, even the dream was forgotten. Exhaustion quieted his restless mind. Sighing, he slipped into a deep dreamless sleep.

Chapter 29

Victory

Kaplyn awoke to find Lomar standing over him. The albino was smiling, although Kaplyn saw confusion within his eyes. Gone were the trappings of war; instead he wore silk finery, reminding Kaplyn of the time when they had first met.

"How's Tumarl?" Kaplyn asked, holding onto his aching head as he raised himself into a sitting position.

"Fine. The wound was shallow and will heal quickly," Lomar replied. He paused for a moment before continuing.

"How is your scar?" he asked.

Kaplyn remembered the wound glowing and everyone staring. With a grimace, he looked up at the albino. The only emotion in his friend's face was that of concern.

"It would be wise to let Astalus look at it. His opinion would be valuable." Lomar seated himself opposite his friend. Kaplyn remained silent, not knowing what to say. The strange looks he had received after the dragon flight were still too fresh in his mind.

"My people are here," Lomar said.

"Here? In CarCamel?"

Lomar nodded. His eyes sparkled with excitement. "They received my warning about the enemy coming through the Turn Marshes and they destroyed them."

"Destroyed them! That's incredible. But how did they know to come here?" Kaplyn asked uncertainly.

"I don't know. They seem to have learnt to use the kara-stones for more than healing. My departure seems to have made them realise how little they knew of the outside world and, apparently, my mother, the Queen, insisted that they prepare for war."

Kaplyn shook his head and smiled. He remembered seeing the line of figures from dragon back and the bright flashing lights as they blocked the enemy's retreat.

"So the Eldric haven't returned?" he asked. In a way he was disappointed.

Lomar shook his head. "No, it was my people, the Alvalah." Lomar arose. "If you feel up to it, we could go out and meet them."

Kaplyn agreed. Hurriedly he washed, shaved and then changed his clothes. He felt incredibly light without the thick padding and metal breastplate, and it felt good to be clean after so many long days of battle. As they left his room, Kaplyn experienced a sense of well being he had not felt for some time.

They passed others along the corridor. Everyone greeted them cheerfully although some cast Kaplyn a backward glance; rumour, fuelled by speculation about his dragon flight, had clearly spread.

Entering the main dining hall they saw a lone figure dressed in a sombre brown robe sitting with his back towards them at a long table and heartily tucking in to a large breakfast.

"Astalus!" Kaplyn called out, genuinely pleased to see the wizard who turned and waved back with his good arm, the other being bandaged.

"What happened to your arm?" Kaplyn asked, taking a seat by his side.

Lomar joined them as a servant entered, heavily laden with a tray piled high with hunks of warm bread covered with hot melted cheese. On the servant's heels, Lars entered. Clapping Kaplyn on the shoulder, he sat down, never once taking his eyes off the food.

"My arm? Oh, it's nothing, just a sprain," Astalus said. "It should be back to normal in a week or so." He then told Kaplyn of his battle with the demon and how he had been buried beneath the hay cart.

"We found him several hours after the battle ended," Lomar interrupted, laughing. "Queen Catriona was riding by and noticed Astalus' feet sticking out from beneath the hay. We thought he was dead until we moved the cart. You should have heard his language, and in front of the Queen, too!"

"You ought to try being buried for several hours, not knowing whether an irate demon was about to stamp on you!" Astalus snapped back, scooping up a piece of bread from the platter.

"The Queen is well?" Kaplyn asked.

"That she is," Astalus replied. "And what about you?" he said, looking intently at him. "Where did you find a dragon in the midst of battle?"

Kaplyn looked uncomfortable and Astalus' smile faded.

"You saved us," he continued seriously. "With the gate breached, the city was doomed."

"That may be so, but people look at me like I am possessed," Kaplyn said softly.

"I suppose that's to be expected; after all it's not every day a man rides a dragon and defeats an enemy we only thought existed in legends," Astalus assured him.

"And the scar...?" Kaplyn asked.

Astalus remained silent. He had been told about the mysterious scar and could see for himself the look of fear as people around them whispered about Kaplyn.

Unaware he was being talked about, Kaplyn looked out of the window at the grey clouds. "I have no idea where the dragon came from. Before it appeared, I felt as though I was standing between two worlds: ours and another alien place. It was a beautiful world with tall mountains. The trees and plants seemed strange and even the sun was different. At first I thought that my eyes were playing tricks; now I know differently."

Astalus looked puzzled. Warm cheese dripped from his forgotten bread, forming a yellow pool upon the table.

"Seeing a demon for the first time confirms their world exists. So why not others? We must speak further about this when you feel rested. I would also like to see your scar, if you don't mind," Astalus offered.

Kaplyn nodded although the prospect made him feel uncomfortable. At that moment the door opened and several Alvalah, Lomar's people, entered accompanied by Tharn Orrin. He was talking loudly in his deep baritone. At first Kaplyn was relieved by the distraction, but his relief was soon dashed.

"There he is," he heard Orrin declare, pointing at Kaplyn. The large Tharn suddenly looked uncertain, as though he had committed a grave offence.

"My pardon, Sire!" he said more quietly as he escorted the newcomers to their table. Kaplyn cast him a confused look as he and the others rose to their feet to greet the albinos.

"My Liege, allow me to introduce Kaplyn, King of Allund," Orrin declared abruptly, bowing towards Kaplyn.

The newcomers also bowed.

"Sire," one of the Alvalah said. "We have heard about the dragon and how you defeated the demons — it's a story that will be told throughout the land."

Kaplyn looked embarrassed. "There is s...some mistake," he stammered. "I am not a king, unless Tharn Orrin has forgotten a Council still rules Allund."

Orrin shrugged. "To every Allund here, you are our King. Once we return to Dundalk, we *will* convince the Council, believe me!"

One of the Alvalah was scrutinising Lomar, a confused expression upon his face. "It's surprising to find one of our own people in CarCamel," the Alvalan stated.

Lomar smiled. "I am Lomar," he said, extending his hand.

The Alvalan took his hand, looking stunned.

"Our history tells of a Prince Lomar who left Gilfillan over sixty years ago. Your portrait occupies pride of place in the hall of your ancestors."

Lomar bowed with the acknowledgement.

"Your mother, the Queen, said that you would return and, yet, few believed her."

Lomar smiled sadly, knowing his mother would be long since dead. "It's not the first time that we have met, is it?" he asked.

It was the newcomer's turn to look embarrassed. "In a way, it's easier to think of you as a ghost. Your warning came at an opportune moment. Without it, and your mother's insistence that we learn to defend ourselves, we would have been destroyed."

A silence descended before Orrin said somewhat flustered, "My pardon. May I introduce King Palastor of Gilfillan."

The albino held up a slender gloved hand, "It appears there may be some dispute about my right to the throne."

Orrin looked confused.

"If there is, then this is neither the time nor the place to discuss it," Lomar replied.

Palastor's eyes flashed for a moment as if he were about to reply. Instead he smiled and bowed fractionally as he removed his gloves.

Kaplyn felt events were happening too quickly. Palastor was right. Lomar was probably the rightful heir, but he hoped there wouldn't be a rift over who should rule. Enough kingdoms had already fallen over far lesser grievances.

The remainder of the breakfast passed uneventfully. Kaplyn was asked numerous questions about the dragon, many for which he had no answers. He was deeply troubled. He did not trust the beast and, yet, at the same time, it had saved them.

Talk turned to news of the battle. Orrin spoke of the more notable casualties of the war. The most noteworthy was Tharn Shelder. He had fought bravely, leading the reserve troops against the breach in the gates. He and many of his men had been killed when the dragon had attacked so unexpectedly. No one reproached Kaplyn, but he closed his eyes and clenched his fists as despair washed over him.

"What will happen now that the battle is over?" Lars asked.

"We have won a significant battle," Astalus answered. "However, I find King Palastor's report of krell crossing the Pen-am-Pelleas Mountains of concern. It shows how strong the enemy is.

"Trosgarth and Aldrace have had over five hundred years to prepare for war and we can only guess at their strength. Of the two nations, we know most about Aldrace, the closer of the two countries."

"What of Trosgarth though?" Kaplyn asked.

"We know very little, if anything, about that country," Astalus answered. "In the recent battle, apart from their standard, there were no other signs that Trosgarth was present. I, for one, find that worrying and believe we have yet to face the real threat."

"Surely you must know something about Trosgarth?" Lars questioned in disbelief.

Astalus shook his head. "After the Krell Wars, the enemy sealed their borders. Chalynth lies between us and Trosgarth. That was once a prosperous nation, but now it is a wilderness, a vast plain upon which anything that moves is easily spotted. Beside the open plains, there is KinKassack forest, which lies upon our own borders to the north. It is said to be evil beyond measure and few can pass through it."

The one question that remained was, had Drachar's shade indeed arisen as the Prophecy foretold? The men continued to eat their breakfast in silence whilst beyond the palace the people started the grim task of burying the dead.

For several days the inhabitants lent themselves to the task of cleaning up. Stonemasons were set to repairing the city walls, the most difficult task being the rebuilding of the gates, which had been very badly damaged. Because so many had died, a large communal grave was dug upon the Plain of Rhye. Many attended the funeral, for there were few in the city that had not lost someone.

Another mass grave was dug farther from the city for the enemy dead; few wanted their ghosts to overlook the city walls. Years later, the site of the enemy grave was still dark, as if the very land were tainted. Many commented on this; it was suggested that the bones of the enemy krell were poisoning the land. The more learned recognised it was more probably due to the iron weapons and armour buried with the corpses. However, being wise, they held their tongues and agreed with popular opinion.

Chapter 30

The Southern Kingdoms Respond

When the dead were buried and repairs started, life started to seep slowly into the city. Friends and families came to the realisation that their lives must continue. The weather, too, seemed to improve if only slightly. The dark clouds which had hung over the city during the conflict lifted, and, although they did not disperse completely, the change was enough to boost morale. Still, a cold wind blew from the north, an evil portent of dark days to come.

On the fourth day after the battle, a cry went up from a sentry upon the outer wall. All those in earshot froze in fear as they looked out. A line of riders could be seen approaching the city from the east. The gates were a long way from completion, and, if an enemy launched an assault, they would be hard pressed defending themselves.

Queen Catriona went personally to the walls accompanied by Astalus, Kaplyn and Orrin. It was the first time Kaplyn had seen Catriona since the battle's end. An endless stream of court protocol had kept her busy. She smiled when they met, although her look was distant. Kaplyn felt hurt by her coldness and did not know how to respond.

Together they watched the approaching shapes. Two soldiers were tasked to fetch a brazier and, when they returned, Astalus cast a spell of seeing. As the image took shape, they saw horsemen riding four abreast. The men wore scarlet cloaks, pinned at the shoulder, and tall helms. Each carried a long lance decorated with a scarlet pennant.

"Men of Bhutan," Queen Catriona said as she rose from her position overlooking the flames. She glanced at Astalus, seeking confirmation.

"It's Prince Fiad at their head," Astalus announced.

Catriona looked relieved. Turning, she ordered Orrin to prepare a guard of honour. She then left to make her own arrangements, leaving Astalus and Kaplyn on their own.

"Astalus, do you know Prince Fiad?" Kaplyn asked, seeking to lift his own mood.

"Yes, everyone has heard of Fiad," he answered, "although few have actually met him. His people treat him as though he is a god. From the way they talk, you'd think there was nothing he cannot do. They believe he is the *one* the Prophecy speaks of. There may even be some truth to the claims, except that Fiad is only a prince and not a king as the Prophecy requires. However, his father is old, and it's rumoured he may not last long."

"In what way does he fulfil the Prophecy?" Kaplyn asked.

"On the day of his birth, a comet appeared in the night sky. That was a powerful portent, especially since he was born under one of the water signs and his home is in the mountains," Astalus continued, leaning on the parapet.

Kaplyn looked confused. "I do not see how this fulfils the Prophecy."

Astalus smiled. "The comet had a tail of fire, his birth sign is water and his home is in the air. *Of air, fire and water he will be born.*"

Kaplyn shook his head, "Well I suppose it fits, but it's a little tenuous."

"Try telling his people that, especially now the enemy is on the move."

They remained on the battlements until the horsemen rode through the gates. By that time, a large crowd had gathered, lining the streets. The people cheered as Fiad and his men entered through the ruined gates, their horses' hooves clattering noisily upon the cobbled streets. Close up, the riders looked weary from their long journey, although they held themselves proudly erect in their saddles.

At their head rode Fiad. He was a young man and, like most of the men of the Southern Kingdoms, his hair was almost blond. As he passed by, the cheering increased. He was clearly popular, especially amongst the women who leapt up and down, trying to get his attention. He raised his hand to acknowledge the cheers, and women screamed in rapture.

"I'd say about two thousand horses," Astalus estimated. "It's probably his vanguard. No doubt it will take some time yet before the armies of Bhutan and West Meath can be mustered."

"They are brave coming here with so few men, not knowing if the enemy was successful or not," Kaplyn stated, watching the troops disappear down the broad main street.

"With Fiad leading, they probably had few options," Astalus replied ruefully.

On the following day Queen Catriona called a meeting of heads of state and Tharn Commanders. Kaplyn and Tharn Orrin were invited as the Allund representatives. When they arrived, most of the others were already present. At the sight of Kaplyn, a silence fell, and he saw fear and uncertainty in their looks, even in those whom he considered friends.

At that moment Queen Catriona entered accompanied by Prince Fiad. She sat down, indicating to the others to do likewise. Chairs scraped noisily as they were drawn back from the long table and men settled into place.

"I have asked you here to consider our situation and that of the enemy," she started. "As you are no doubt aware, we have won a battle, but I think that the threat of war still exists. So far, we have been fortunate. If Kaplyn had not warned us of the threat from the enemy and helped to unite Allund and Thrace, things might now be very different."

Many eyes turned to look at Kaplyn and he felt distinctly uncomfortable. His scar itched as if reminding him of its presence.

"The enemy has been driven back," Catriona resumed, once more gaining their attention, "but we do not know what they plan next. Over the last two days, Astalus has spied on the enemy, using spells of seeing." She gestured to Astalus to speak.

Astalus stood, trying to look dignified beneath the gaze of so many high-ranking men. "I have tried to spy on both Trosgarth and Aldrace, but with little success. It's difficult to cast a spell of seeing over such a distance, and I would not normally expect much success." His brown robes rustled as he moved uncomfortably under their gaze.

"As always, a dark cloud hangs over Trosgarth, and there is no way to spy on that land using sorcery. Aldrace, on the other hand, has no such protection and I have been able to catch glimpses of Drishnack, their capital."

The others in the room were very quiet, enthralled by Astalus' news.

He resumed his narrative. "The city is very active; riders regularly come and go, probably with news of their defeat." Astalus looked momentarily pained by his next admission. "However, the images I see are of little value, and I have a feeling my spells are being manipulated."

"Is that possible?" interrupted Tharn Ballan.

Astalus shrugged. "To control someone else's spell is a remarkable feat, if that *is* what is happening. A wizard trying to control the spell of another would have to know precisely when to manipulate the spell and from where it originates." Astalus looked sombre as he finished speaking. A nervous murmur arose from the assembled throng.

"What about the spell of concealment the enemy army used when they were in hiding in the mountains?" Kaplyn asked. "Isn't that controlling another wizard's spell?"

Astalus shook his head. "That spell affected only a local area and anyone looking saw the view that the sorcerer had prepared. This is different. We are dealing with a very powerful sorcerer if he can control another's spell."

"Drachar?" Catriona muttered uncertainly.

"Possibly, or a powerful Narlassar sorcerer. I cannot begin to comprehend how someone could foresee another wizard's spell and control it in such a way. Unfortunately the visions reveal nothing of value. When I try to see high-ranking officers, I see the lowest of soldiers performing menial tasks. It's almost as if someone is playing with my thoughts — and amusing themselves, to boot."

Queen Catriona turned to address the assembled men. "It's imperative that we get more information about the enemy. We must send spies both to Trosgarth and Aldrace."

Silence hung over the room. Fiad shifted in his chair and most eyes turned to him.

When he spoke, his voice was firm. "Sending spies into our enemy's land is a sound plan." Many around the table nodded in agreement. "Even now the armies of Bhutan and West Meath are mustering." Muttered approval greeted the Prince's words. "Within one month over one hundred and fifty thousand troops will be assembled *here* at CarCamel. Word has been sent to the mountain dwarves, and it is hoped that they, too, will send an army. The question we must now ask is, what should we do after our spies return?"

The room was instantly silent. No one wanted to express a view on so weighty a matter.

"Within six weeks, we will have assembled the greatest army this land has ever seen," Fiad continued. "We have the might not only to oppose Trosgarth, but to smash it forever."

Fiad's words hung in the air for several moments before the assembled men realised what he was driving at.

"You mean that we should march on Trosgarth?" Tharn Ballan asked, the tone of his voice expressing incredulity. Several voices were immediately raised in protest, but Fiad stilled them, raising his hand. His steel-grey eyes locked on Ballan's.

"We do not have the power of the Eldric to march on Trosgarth," Kaplyn interposed, feeling eyes turn upon him. "Without sorcery we cannot hope to oppose an enemy who can summon demons."

Fiad turned to look at Kaplyn as though questioning his right to speak. "We do not need the Eldric. We have the Alvalah and their kara-stones.

With the Akrane wizards of all our lands, that makes us powerful enough to defeat the enemy. The signs of battle here prove that we can win!"

"We were lucky," Kaplyn said, raising his voice to be heard above the mutterings around the table. "Even with the forces you mentioned, we are still not powerful enough to defeat an enemy if it is indeed led by Drachar."

"There is also the dragon!" Catriona said softly.

Kaplyn felt his face flush as eyes bored into him. He wanted to stand up and tell them that he didn't trust the dragon, but knew that he couldn't dash their hopes simply on the strength of his own fears.

Fortunately Astalus came to his aid, "If I may speak?"

Catriona nodded for him to continue.

"Marching into Trosgarth would be suicide until we know more about the enemy. Kaplyn is right; if Drachar has returned, then we do not know what to expect. We have six weeks before the armies are assembled and then a few weeks more to organise into an effective force. I suggest, in the meantime, we send a number of small groups to Trosgarth and Aldrace to see what they can learn. There is also the question of the Eldric. We would be fools to ignore them and the aid that their power could give us. Kaplyn has given me hope that they can be found. He has entered one of their cities, and I intend to do likewise."

Several people tried to speak at once and Astalus gestured for silence, raising a slim hand until all was quiet. "I accept that this journey may prove to be folly. When the Eldric left our lands, they sealed their cities and hid them from us in such a way that there seems to be nothing left but ruins. But Kaplyn, with help, successfully entered one. My concern is that I may not be able to summon the true city, for I am a *wizard,* not a sorcerer. However, the rewards may be great. Many of you have seen Kaplyn's Eldric blade; other such weapons may exist. There is the site of an ancient Eldric citadel at Namthrall, only one week's ride from here. I can be there and back within three weeks, leaving plenty of time to be here when the armies assemble."

At first Queen Catriona was opposed to it, not liking the idea of losing Astalus on a fool's errand. The roads were dangerous and enemy krell (many had escaped the slaughter) might still be lurking in the foothills. However, Astalus was very persuasive and, for the moment, none could gainsay him.

The remainder of the meeting was turmoil with many alternative plans offered, but none had any merit and by the meeting's end, the only consensus was that spies should be sent out as soon as possible and that Astalus *should* leave on his quest. As people filed out, Astalus came over to speak with Kaplyn.

"Would you accompany me to my laboratory? There is something there that you might be able to help me with."

The two men made their way to Astalus' laboratories. When they entered, the aroma of herbs and chemicals greeted them. Gant was busy performing a spell whilst consulting a very large book, the like of which Kaplyn had never seen before.

"Gant, have there been any changes in the visions?" Astalus asked.

The older man looked up and shook his head. He seemed grateful for the interruption. Astalus led Kaplyn to the brazier, where Gant joined them. Kaplyn was by now familiar with the way in which wizards performed a spell of seeing. Looking deep into the flames he waited patiently for a vision to form.

"What are we looking at?" he asked.

"Drishnack, the capital of Aldrace," Astalus replied, as though from across a great distance. "You will see the images I told the others about."

Blurred shapes gradually turned into a clear image. They were looking into an immense hall, and, judging by the height of the statues flanking it, the ceiling must have been at least thirty feet high. The room was stone-built. Shafts of light from stained glass windows formed bright pools of colour on the otherwise mundane floor. Elsewhere, dark shadows obscured much of the hall.

The viewpoint drifted towards a distant corner where a golden cage had been erected on a raised dais. The contrast with the stone surroundings was very marked. Kaplyn frowned at its beauty; the cage shone with encrusted jewels.

Suddenly, Kaplyn became aware of the figure of an old man hunched within a corner of the cage. He wore coarse brown robes. Long, grey hair obscured his face. For the moment he appeared to be asleep.

Kaplyn felt sorry for him and he wondered why he was being held captive in such a bizarre way.

Abruptly the figure jerked and sat up, looking as though he had just woken from a bad dream. Kaplyn studied his face as he brushed away strands of his hair. His eyes were rheumy while his nose was long and hawk like. His face was grey due to lack of sunlight. An unkempt beard, matted and filthy, hid the lower half of his face.

With a shock, Kaplyn recognised the weeping scar running diagonally across the man's cheek. It had healed poorly and even now appeared to give the old man discomfort. Kaplyn looked at the eyes, recognising them this time.

It was Vastra, the man who had betrayed him so many years ago.

The old man frowned as though deep in thought.

400

Kaplyn felt faint just as the scene within the fire started to swirl and shift once more. He cried out, trying to hold onto the last image. He did not want to believe his own eyes.

Within the fire, vast armies camped outside tall city walls, but these images were not important. He turned instead to face Astalus. The wizard, his eyes haunted with fear, simply returned his look.

Chapter 31

Preparations for Departure

"You recognise him, don't you?" Astalus asked at length, looking hard at Kaplyn.

Kaplyn nodded. "It was Vastra. But it c…cannot be!" he stammered uncertainly. "He would be close to a hundred years old by now."

Astalus pulled up a stool, offering it to Kaplyn. He sat down as though his world had been shattered. Astalus brought up another stool and sat down opposite him.

"I had a feeling that this image was meant for you," the wizard said. Kaplyn looked up, feeling somewhat bemused.

"Oh, don't ask me how I knew. It was as if the thought was deliberately planted in my mind. That's what worries me! We need to talk about your journey to BanKildor. Start when you met this Vastra, and try to omit nothing."

Kaplyn glanced into the flames. Shapes paraded before his eyes, but his attention was already lost to the past. He told Astalus about his earlier adventures with Lars and Vastra, and, as the tale unfolded, he gradually found it easier to talk.

Astalus showed interest in Kaplyn's story, especially in those parts that concerned Tanel, the Eldric city. He questioned Kaplyn about the trap by the window within the tower, and frowned when Kaplyn told him that it was clearly visible once he had put the Eldric pendant on.

"Lars very nearly fell into it; he clearly hadn't seen it." Kaplyn smiled at the memory of the big man perched on the narrow windowsill. "Later, Vastra explained that the pendant nullified magic."

"And Vastra said that the city was hidden in a different time?" Astalus asked.

Kaplyn agreed.

"Do you remember how he summoned it?"

"No. The words from his spell seemed to fade as soon as he spoke them. Within seconds, I couldn't remember what he had said."

Astalus looked thoughtful before asking Kaplyn to continue.

When Kaplyn came to the part about the Tree of Life, Astalus once more showed considerable interest. When Kaplyn described Vastra's betrayal, Astalus questioned him about his memory before and after the spell. He was vague about this since his memory of these events had dimmed. However, he tried to remember for the wizard's sake.

"I discovered the scar when I awoke from the spell," he said, unbuttoning his shirt to show Astalus. "Lomar thinks it might be, in part, due to the crystal from the Tree of Life. Perhaps Vastra tried to take it from my pocket after I was turned to stone, or maybe it happened as a result of the Eldric spell. The pendant had also gone, and I have no idea where."

Astalus looked at the scar in disbelief; it was the first time he had seen it. It was milky white, more like crystal than skin tissue. He asked Kaplyn to move to the fire where he traced a rune over the pale embers. Nothing happened although Kaplyn was not sure if anything was supposed to.

"It contains magic," Astalus explained at last. "It's very strong. So strong that I am surprised you do not stand out like a beacon."

"What do you mean?"

"To a wizard, magic is visible. I can feel its essence especially when casting a spell. And yet, with you, there is nothing."

"Vastra explained the crystal contains magic but that it could not be used. He said it was like a kara-stone except, instead of being empty, it was full. He hoped to use it to find the Eldric and with it he would be able to hold open a gateway between the worlds, with the crystal to keep it open."

A look of comprehension dawned on Astalus' face and he slapped the tabletop. "Of course!" he said excitedly. "Magic cannot be destroyed. While the crystal is within the tunnel it cannot collapse!"

He rose and started pacing. "That does not explain how you managed to open a gateway to the dragon's world. However, once it was open you only had to stand inside it to keep it open. Oh, but that doesn't bode well...." Astalus said, putting his hand to his head.

He turned to Kaplyn. "You must be careful! There is a chance you could become trapped if the magic from both worlds equally attracted yours."

It was a very sobering thought. Perhaps the dragon had deliberately tried to delay him between the worlds for that reason. Astalus sat down as if his declaration had left him weary.

"What do you think happened to the crystal that Vastra took?" Kaplyn asked.

Astalus said nothing. Then a terrible look of fear crossed his face. "*By the Kalanth*, but I hope I am wrong! His face was suddenly drained of colour.

"What is it?"

"If the enemy were to obtain it, then he could then open a *permanent* gateway to the demon world."

Kaplyn's heart sank. He had defeated two demons with the help of others and his Eldric blade. He, of all people, knew how difficult they were to kill. The prospect of hordes of them was more than alarming.

"So far, demon attacks have always been limited. They can only be summoned for a relatively brief time before they have to return to their own world. The process requires considerable effort, and only the most powerful of sorcerers can summon more than one demon at a time. However, if a permanent gateway could be opened, then demons could be summoned at will."

It was a nightmare scenario, and Kaplyn could only hope that Astalus was wrong.

"Perhaps that was why Vastra wanted the power from the Tree of Life in the first place, and he never intended finding the Eldric."

"Then it is even more imperative that I locate an Eldric city!" Astalus replied, going over to the window. "I am convinced there may be useful information, hopefully, about the Tree of Life, or even details about the Eldric.

"It would be wise if you did not use your powers again until we are more certain about what we are dealing with. In fact," Astalus added, turning to face Kaplyn, "your very presence in CarCamel may well be dangerous."

"In what way? I don't know how I managed to summon the dragon, and I doubt I could do it again — even if I wanted to."

"That may be so, but what if you managed to open a doorway to another world unintentionally — in your sleep, say? You could open a gateway to the demon world, allowing its minions access to the very heart of our city!"

It was a point Kaplyn had failed to consider. The terrible prospect stayed with him as he left the wizard's tower, his thoughts in turmoil.

Later that day, Kaplyn was summoned to a meeting in the Queen's audience chambers. There, Astalus described some of the key events of Kaplyn's previous journey to find Tanel, the Eldric city, and his subsequent incursion deep into the heart of the mountains where he had found a crystal from the Tree of Life.

"I have recently investigated the remains of one of these crystals, which now forms scar tissue upon Kaplyn's chest," Astalus announced to the grave assembly. "I have never seen its like before and, from what Kaplyn has told me, I believe that it is the very essence of pure magic. If it were placed within a gateway to another world, that gateway would not collapse. It is my fear that the enemy has one of these crystals."

The men around the table were clearly stunned by the news. Their voices rose in anger. Tharn Ballan thumped the table, calling for silence.

"What do you suggest we do?" Queen Catriona asked, addressing Astalus.

"I must leave immediately for Namthrall where I hope to gain access to the Eldric city. In the meantime, spies should be sent into Aldrace and Trosgarth to search for news of the missing crystal."

"Very well," Catriona conceded, although she sounded far from happy with his decision to leave. "Make whatever preparations you require and be ready to leave in the morning. Tharn Ballan, you will arrange a haft to accompany Astalus.

"Astalus, we will expect you back in three weeks. If what you say is true, then it is more important than ever that we strike at the enemy before they can prepare further. I have spoken with Fiad on this matter, and he has convinced me we will have the strength to defeat Trosgarth once and for all. With a dragon at the head of the army, we cannot fail."

Kaplyn shuddered. He felt as though somebody had just walked over his grave. If there was one thing he was certain of, he would not summon a dragon again unless their lives depended upon it.

For Kaplyn, the remainder of that day dragged slowly by. He met with Lars, Lomar and Tumarl in the dining hall and, briefly, he spoke about the visions and of Vastra.

Lars started ranting about Vastra and what he had done to them. Lomar tried to calm him while Kaplyn watched them, somewhat detached. He was in a quandary. On the one hand, he wanted to go with Astalus but, on the other, he could not dispel the image of the old man in the cage.

Vastra, who had caused them such pain.

Kaplyn realised suddenly that he could not go with Astalus. But for the moment, his alternative options seemed few.

Later that day, the small group went for a walk through the city. Almost immediately, a crowd started following, talking excitedly but remaining at a discreet distance.

Kaplyn saw several people pointing at him and heard the word *dragon* mentioned more than once. He quickened his pace but the crowd remained doggedly in pursuit. It was a far cry from recent days when people had looked at him with fear.

The crowd's attention galled Kaplyn and only served to increase his fear of dragons. He could not even explain why he felt so afraid. Deep down, he knew dragons could not be trusted, and, yet, people needed him to protect them by summoning one.

It was with relief that the group returned to the sanctuary of the palace, leaving the crowds behind.

In the morning, Kaplyn arose early and went to find Astalus. The day was grey and cold. A bitter wind blew, forcing him to pull his cloak tightly about his chest as he made his way down deserted streets. To his surprise the wizard was already there; his horse and gear were packed. Kaplyn joined him and together they walked his mount to the garrison stables to meet up with his escort.

"Ah — I can see by the lack of a pack that you've decided not to join us," Astalus said.

"I'm sorry," Kaplyn replied. "I don't know what to do for the best. The image of Vastra worries me."

Astalus smiled, trying to reassure his friend. "Perhaps it was unwise showing you that," he admitted.

Along the street, by the barracks, a group of soldiers and their mounts were assembled. The horses were skittish and the sound of iron-shod hooves on cobbles echoed in the narrow street.

"Tallin, good to see you," Kaplyn called out.

Tallin, leading his horse by its reins, walked over to Kaplyn and the two men shook hands.

"It seems a long time since last we met," Tallin said, smiling broadly. "It appears we were wise to trust you, after all!"

Kaplyn smiled back. "So you drew the short straw to escort Astalus!"

"No short straw. After the recent battle, it will be good to be out in the countryside, not surrounded by stone."

Kaplyn understood how he felt and, suddenly, he experienced an urge to be away from the city himself.

Tallin turned to Astalus. "Are you ready?"

Astalus nodded although he looked pale at the prospect, clearly not relishing the idea of the long ride ahead.

"Well, we had better make tracks. If you will excuse me . . ."

Tallin gave the order to mount. Astalus pulled himself into the saddle where, even though his horse waited placidly for him to settle, he swayed uncertainly.

When Astalus was certain he was secure, he looked down at Kaplyn. "Farewell. And remember to heed my warning. Do not try to investigate other worlds, at least not until I return. With any luck, I may find something useful within the city to help us."

"Keep yourself from harm. And I wish you success."

Astalus smiled, raising his hand in farewell.

"Forward, walk," Tallin ordered.

With impressive precision, the men wheeled their mounts into double file and headed out of the safety of the barracks.

For several moments Kaplyn watched as the file of men rode by with Tallin and Astalus at their head. With a heavy heart, he made his way back to the palace, his mind chewing over the problem of what to do next.

From a window high above, Ariome also watched the troop clatter through the narrow streets. Lights appeared in the windows of the building opposite. Probably a few of the hardier citizens looking out to see what the disturbance was at such an early hour.

Ariome drew back farther into the shadows, making a note of the patrol's number for her report later that day. She wondered where they were going. Over the last few days, several patrols had been sent out into the surrounding countryside, mainly to search for krell. This was more significant though, for she recognised Astalus at the head of the troop. Previously, she had written him off as a fool. Now, after recent events, she had a grudging respect for him.

She thought back to the final day of fighting. She hadn't learnt until later that a dragon had appeared at her moment of triumph. She had been furious, on the one hand, and terrified on the other, for she knew that she had to send her masters news of the defeat.

She had been surprised by their calm. *Remain where you are,* they had urged. *Continue to spy upon our enemy and we shall send word when we want more from you.* The message had been brief and had left her wondering whether defeat had been expected.

Now, she looked down upon the lone figure below.

Kaplyn.

Dragon Rider.

Orlastor.

She and her masters knew now who he was, and it was her privilege to make certain that he would trouble them no further.

Quickly, she ducked back out of sight as the figure below looked up at her window, as though sensing her presence. She only saw his handsome face for a moment, but it was stamped indelibly upon her mind. A pity, she reflected. But pity did not stop her from considering ways of eliminating the troublesome Allunder.

As her mind worked on the matter, she found herself becoming almost cheerful. After all, she did enjoy her work.

Chapter 32

Departure to the Wilderness

Kaplyn lay on his wooden cot, looking up at the ceiling as the darkness within the room became complete. Outside his window, he could hear people rejoicing. It had taken them several days, but, at last, they were forgetting their recent losses, finally coming out into the streets to celebrate their hard-won victory.

Kaplyn felt terrible.

There was nothing wrong, as far as he could tell, but he did not feel particularly happy. It had something to do with the image of Vastra that Astalus had shown him. If Vastra was now a prisoner in Drishnack, the Aldracian capital, then that meant the enemy now possessed the crystal from the Tree of Life. Wearily, he swung his feet off the bed.

He listened a little longer to the voices outside. A woman called out to a friend who laughed. Their voices faded into the distance as they passed beneath his window.

These people were expecting him to summon a dragon and lead the army into Trosgarth. His fear of dragons escalated with the very thought, and, yet, when he had ridden one, he had been completely unafraid.

He could not do it!

He could not summon a dragon! Nor then could he lead the army to Trosgarth.

A knock at the door startled him. "Enter," he said when he had recovered. Inwardly he cursed the intrusion for, although his mind was made up, it was a fragile peace.

Lomar entered wearing a resolute look.

Kaplyn got up and strode over to the lamp on the table, which he lit using the tinder by its side, adjusting the wick so they could see. Behind him, Lomar softly shut the door.

"You are leaving? he asked simply.

Kaplyn smiled, knowing how difficult it would be to hide the truth from the albino.

"Tonight?" Lomar asked.

Kaplyn nodded as though speaking might somehow shatter his resolve.

In a way, Lomar looked relieved. "I shall go with you."

His tone suggested his mind was made up.

"What of your people?" Kaplyn complained. "Where I am going will be dangerous. You should remain here where you are needed."

"I could say the same of you," Lomar stated softly.

Kaplyn paused. He *would* appreciate the company but had no right to ask Lomar to risk his life on a futile venture.

"I am going to Aldrace," Kaplyn stated, hoping that his bluntness might put the albino off. "I want to find Vastra."

"You are sure then, that he lives?"

"Yes."

"It's a considerable risk!" Lomar suggested, watching Kaplyn's response.

"The enemy may have Vastra's crystal, and Astalus told me it could keep open a gateway to the demon world. It's my fault he had it and it's my responsibility to see that the enemy cannot use it."

"Then you will need help," Lomar replied.

Kaplyn smiled, grateful for the albino's offer. "Meet me in one hour and we'll leave then. Pack what you can carry. We'll take horses."

Lomar left the room, leaving Kaplyn alone to pack. Once ready, he made a forage to the palace kitchens where he grabbed enough rations to last a few days.

On returning to his room, he opened the door and, to his surprise, found Lars and Tumarl waiting by Lomar's side. At first Kaplyn was angry, and it must have shown for Lars immediately started to explain why he would not be left behind.

Lars' attempt to defend himself amused Kaplyn. He turned to look at Tumarl. The ex-farmer stood impassively, his stance suggesting that he would not be swayed.

Kaplyn was concerned for Tumarl; his hatred for the enemy and his desire for revenge were driving him too hard. And, yet, he felt loath to leave him behind; there was nothing for him here. His friends and family had long since perished — like Kaplyn's.

Kaplyn raised a hand, signalling to Lars that he had heard enough. At last, the big man stopped.

410

"Very well," Kaplyn conceded. "You may come, but I think you will regret it."

The four men shouldered their packs and left the palace through an infrequently used exit. As they walked down the busy streets, people called to them, waving joyfully and inviting them to join them. Each time Kaplyn waved back but gracefully declined.

Fortunately for them, the stables were deserted. Quickly they saddled four mounts, taking two spare for their packs. Once ready they set off, walking towards the city gates.

The guard waved them through without question. Many others had also left that day, travelling back to outlying farms to assess the damage.

Once beyond the gate, the four men mounted.

A cold wind blew from the north as though reminding them of what lay ahead. Turning their mounts into the wind, they rode off into the night, swiftly disappearing into the gloom as darkness closed in around them.

In her room, Ariome stirred from her afternoon sleep. Smiling, she stretched languidly, then got up from the warm bed and dressed swiftly. She had rested enough and — judging by the darkness — the time was now ripe to perform her task.

She walked softly to her chest of drawers, opened the top drawer and searched the contents for the object she required. With a satisfied grunt she took out a pale blue kara-stone. Normally she did not require such baubles, but tonight, late as it was, she would allow herself this one luxury.

She returned to the dining room table, placed the kara-stone on it, then sat down.

Kill Kaplyn.

That had been the command from Trosgarth. Tonight, she would fulfil that order. Sprinkling a white powder upon the wooden surface, she traced a rune, revealing the dark wood beneath. Instantly a fire elemental burst into view. It was confined within the rune's lines as it spun violently in its death frenzy.

Speaking arcane words Ariome forced the sprite to enter into the kara-stone. As the flame disappeared, she leant over the orb tracing runes over its pale surface. Instantly Kaplyn's room appeared. Seeing the narrow bed with blankets heaped in disarray upon it, she smiled. The room was dark but she did not need light for what she intended.

Tracing a rune and speaking more words of power, she slammed her hand down on the table. Instantly, the bed burst into flames. If there had been anyone within it, they would not have escaped. However, at the moment of her victory, a sudden look of doubt crossed her face. Even though the victim could not escape, there were usually screams. She peered more closely into the orb, searching the room more carefully.

Kaplyn's possessions were gone she realised with mounting rage. Looking back towards the burning bed, she realised that it had been empty.

In haste she traced a different rune over the kara-stone. Searching the depths of the orb, she scoured the city but found nothing. More frantically she extended the range of her spell, but, to her frustration she could not find any sign of her intended prey. Cursing, she hurled the kara-stone from the table. As it clattered noisily across the floor, her scream of frustration rent the cold night air.

Chapter 33

Journey to Namthrall

Astalus looked over his shoulder one last time at the city's war-ravaged walls. His horse followed Tallin's as the long file of riders snaked across the lush countryside.

For a moment, he was tempted to return to the stout walls and the sanctuary they offered. The prospect of riding into the wilderness was far from attractive. Queen Catriona had assured him that the way should be safe. Patrols had been sent out to scout the land for some miles, but he was far from convinced. The recent conflict had left him shaken, and the mental scars would take many years to heal. A dreadful battle had just been fought and they had barely won.

He turned to look forward, concentrating on the ground ahead, striving not to think of the safety he was leaving behind. Ahead of him, Tallin's broad shoulders and confident manner were reassuring. Tallin, a Haft Commander, had more than proven himself in the recent battles. There was no doubt he was a brave commander, judging from what he had heard of his part in the battle.

The haft consisted of one hundred and twenty riders. They intended to follow the river Torrid for several miles to the Lost Hest's Gorge, after which they would journey west for two more days, taking them close to the Chanteal Mountains. There, they would find the remains of Namthrall, the ancient Eldric city. Astalus was not sure what they would find there, and he regretted that Kaplyn had declined to join them.

For a moment he listened to the horses' hooves on the soft ground, reassured by the sound of so many mounts. Only a determined enemy could attack them with any hope of success. Then he gripped his staff more tightly as he remembered the battle and the cries of the enemy krell as waves of them broke against the city wall, like the sea crashing against unyielding rock.

He realised he had every reason to be afraid.

That day's ride was uneventful.

At night they camped in a small copse that crowned a hillock, which was surrounded on one side by a stream and on the other by a long line of tall beech trees. The wood offered them concealment both from prying eyes and the chill wind that seemed to be following them.

When they were deep enough into the wood, the men dispersed silently in small groups, seeking sufficient space to spread their cloaks. The men set to preparing cooking fires whilst Tallin went amongst them posting sentries, securing their perimeter.

Astalus sat aside from the other men, unrolling his own blanket and clearing aside rocks, twigs and cones from his bed space. More than once, he caught one of the men casting him a fearful look although deep down he knew that they welcomed his company, or at least the power he wielded. His prowess on the battlefield had proved his worth. But now, away from the safety of the city, rumours about where they were going and why the Master Wizard was accompanying them were spreading.

Astalus continued to clear the rest of his small area, hoping that the ground would be comfortable. After a while, feeling somewhat foolish, he glanced towards the others to see what they were doing. To his relief, Tallin was pushing his way through the thick undergrowth, carrying two wooden bowls heaped high with a thick meaty stew. A large loaf of bread was tucked under one arm.

Tallin smiled as he handed Astalus a bowl. He then spread his cloak upon the ground before sitting down, emphasising the luxury of being off horseback as he settled into a cross-legged position. Blowing on the stew, he ate a full spoonful, seeming to relish the taste as he chewed.

"Tomorrow we go through the gorge," he announced. He offered some of the bread to Astalus before tearing at his own with his teeth. Astalus accepted his portion, in turn biting off a much smaller piece. Astalus could not understand Tallin's look of relish as he ate, the stew looked less than palatable. Still, he was certainly hungry enough. He forked a small portion, examining the meat before risking a taste. He noticed Tallin smile at his caution.

"Do we need to go through the gorge?" Astalus asked after a moment. He had to wait for a reply while Tallin finished chewing.

"I'm afraid so," Talin answered. "Tharn Ballan told me of the need for haste. To go around the gorge would take extra time, time that we do not have."

Astalus nodded. He had hoped to persuade Tallin to take an alternative route.

"It's not too bad a journey," Tallin continued. "I've been that way before and it's an inspiring sight, under normal circumstances."

Astalus' frown deepened; that was not exactly the reassurance he had wanted. "I'm sorry," he apologised, realising that Tallin must have seen his look of fear. "It's just that I'm not very good with heights."

"Don't worry. We will not let you fall."

"How long will it take?"

"We will set off at dawn and arrive at the gorge by mid-morning. Hopefully, we will be through it by mid-afternoon."

Astalus spooned another morsel of meat up to his lips, then paused, lost in thought.

"What will we find at Namthrall?" Tallin asked. "There are rumours spreading, and it might be wise to quash these before they get out of hand."

Astalus put his bowl of half-eaten stew down on the soft moss, carefully placing the spoon on top before giving the Haft Commander his full attention.

"I expect to find only ruins," Astalus said. "However, Kaplyn told me something that leads me to believe that the real city has been hidden, using sorcery. If possible, I intend to summon it."

It was Tallin's turn to frown. "Why? I mean, if the city has been hidden, what do you expect to find?"

"I hope to find books that might help us defeat the enemy," Astalus replied.

Tallin looked unimpressed. It appeared that, from a soldier's view point, books were of little value.

"We might also find Eldric weapons like Kaplyn's sword," Astalus continued, noting with satisfaction the sparkle in Tallin's eyes. He had read the young commander correctly; the chance of getting more Eldric weapons was something he understood.

Tallin rose wearily, brushing aside low branches so that he could stand. "I need to check the men before nightfall. You'd better get some rest. It's an early start and a long ride. I'll see to it that your horse is fed and watered. I'll send someone over later to see if you need anything." Bidding him a good night, Tallin departed, swiftly disappearing into the thick wood.

As Tallin predicted, the haft entered the gorge late that morning. Astalus was weary from his short night's rest. It had seemed that no sooner had the sun set that it was dawn, albeit a grey one.

Activity within the camp had started shortly before daybreak when patrols were sent out to check their perimeter. Then, all too soon, one of the soldiers, a fresh-faced youngster, had been sent to waken Astalus. Clearly afraid to approach the sleeping wizard too closely, he had called softly to him and, as soon as the wizard had mumbled a reply, had scurried away. Astalus had smiled at the soldier's panic, but now he had fears of his own to contend with.

For the initial part of the journey through the gorge, Astalus was not afraid. All too soon, it became sheer. One side of the path plunged steeply into the raging waters, and the other rose sharply with only a narrow path between them.

Astalus was already scared but took comfort from the belief that things could not get any worse. After a short while, the path narrowed even more so that his left knee was almost brushing the steep rock wall while, to his right, the ground dropped alarmingly into the river. Apart from the occasional tree growing stubbornly from the cliff face, there was nothing to prevent them falling.

Tallin's earlier warning to keep his eyes on the trail was unnecessary: Astalus kept his eyes glued to the hooves of Tallin's mount for the entire journey and was too afraid to look anywhere else. He kept remembering the story about the lost patrol which, while trying to negotiate the winding trail in midwinter, fell into the river below and perished. His fear of heights and the thought of ambush nearly made him panic.

The ride seemed to take an age. He suppressed the urge to call to ask Tallin to stop. Each time he was about to do so, his courage failed and he remained silent.

By late afternoon, the trees to the right of the narrow path were much thicker, so that at least he could no longer see the fearful drop to the river. The vegetation helped to muffle the sounds of the river, and, suddenly, he became aware of birds singing.

Eventually, the noise of the river faded, and then they crested the top of the gorge. Immediately the trail widened and headed away from the river. At the front of the column, Tallin slowed, coming alongside Astalus, grinning broadly at the sight of the wizard's pale complexion. Astalus smiled weakly back, glancing momentarily behind to see the long line of soldiers, some equally pale, reaching the top.

"Quite a path, isn't it?" Tallin said.

Astalus could only nod. His mouth was so dry he could barely speak. "I hope we don't have to go back that way. I don't think I could manage a second attempt."

Tallin grinned. "No. I think we can afford to return by the longer route. It's not wise to travel the same path twice. Anyone seeing us coming this way might be tempted to set an ambush."

Astalus relaxed visibly with the news.

Smiling broadly, Tallin gathered in his reins. Turning his mount, he rode towards the rear of the column to check their progress.

Astalus was convinced he would remember that part of the journey for the rest of his life.

Later that day, they entered thick woodland with only narrow animal trails to follow. The light beneath the trees was poor, and dark shadows obscured large parts. The riders were overcome by a deep gloom that seemed to match the darkness. Even their horses seemed nervous, flinching with every crack of a dry twig.

The thick undergrowth seemed to stifle other sounds, and, if there were any birds, they did not hear them. Dark moss covered the trunks, making the air damp and full of spores.

That night the men slept fitfully, too fatigued to remain awake. Those unfortunate to be chosen for the first watch looked at the sleeping forms of their comrades with envy, until it became so dark they could not even see the shapes of the trees about them. When the time came to change the watch, chaos reigned as men stumbled over one another, trying to find their blankets. The new watch sat at their post, clutching their bows, surrounded by darkness. Eventually, the diffuse rays of the morning sun faintly tinged the trees with a pale orange glow, heralding the start of a new day.

On their fourth day out of the city and the second in the wood, they topped a small rise thickly overgrown with sharp briar and tall weeds. To their relief, the wood came to an abrupt end. Their eyes, having grown used to the seemingly perpetual darkness, found the light almost too much to bear.

Tallin rode silently to the head of the column cautiously approaching the edge of the wood. Concealed behind a large oak, he searched the open ground. A large scar ran down the side of a hill whose summit was crowned with dark, sombre-looking evergreens. Behind the hill, vast, cloud-wreathed mountains loomed tall.

Within the re-entry, the crumbling remains of the Eldric city littered the green sward like broken teeth. From a wood-line behind the city, a small stream descended the rocky slope, wending its inexorable way towards some distant shore.

Oppressive as it was, Tallin did not like leaving the safety of the forest. Looking to his right, the tree line they were emerging from contoured around from their present position, leading partway towards a smaller hill in the centre of the open ground. This hill was also wooded although not as thickly as the one from which they had just emerged. Tallin immediately recognised its benefits. It was defensive and close enough to the ruins to allow Astalus to carry out his task.

Signalling for the column to advance, he lead the way, skirting the forest's edge and taking the shortest route across the open ground. Once inside the wood, he whispered orders, dispersing the men into a defensive position. Next, he summoned his second in command, Chanathen, instructing him to send out patrols to secure their perimeter.

Satisfied that the tasks were under way, he sent for Astalus. The wizard soon appeared, coming between the trees, his brown robes blending in with the surroundings.

"Can I go down to the city now?" Astalus asked.

Tallin would have preferred to wait until nightfall. On the other hand, if he allowed the wizard to perform his task now, they could be under way all the sooner. He called two of his men to escort Astalus to the ruins. Neither looked happy with the task and, with soft mutterings, they led the way.

Chapter 34

Namthrall

Astalus approached the ruins, using what little cover there was to cross the open ground. To his front, a bird took flight, calling shrill warnings and causing the young wizard to jump. He raised his staff and traced a rune in the air with his free hand, feeling familiar warmth as he cast a spell of seeing.

Behind him, the two soldiers paused, hands on their hilts. Both looked startled by the wizard's use of power. When Astalus shook his head and continued on towards the ruins, the men looked nervously at each other before following. Astalus halted at the ruin's edge. The two soldiers stopped a few paces behind.

The magnitude of the problem confronting Astalus threatened to overwhelm him. Before him were only rocks — nothing more, nothing less.

He concentrated, trying to make sense of the broken shards littering the greensward. Behind, he heard his escort moving away to find some degree of comfort while they waited. The soft sound of their hushed whispers threatened his concentration and started to irritate him. He considered telling them to be quiet, but realised he was angrier with himself than with them.

Sitting down, he took the strain off his travel-weary legs, rubbing his thighs to relieve the pain from the long ride. Gripping his staff, he tried to think of the best approach. His spell of revealing had failed to show anything unusual, and he had cast the spell to see if there were any obvious traps. He had also hoped that the spell would reveal the true city, but it hadn't.

He remembered Kaplyn's description of Vastra's summoning. It had not sounded overcomplicated nor had it taken long. On the other hand, Vastra had been a sorcerer, capable of much more powerful spells than Astalus. Concentrating, he tried a different rune, tracing the intricate symbol upon the ground. Patiently, he waited for a few moments, but again nothing happened.

He needed a medium to work through he decided at length. Rising, he looked about in the grass for firewood. Seeing Astalus stand, the two soldiers also stood, hoping they were going back to the camp. When it became clear he was only collecting wood, the two men sat down, sullenly resigned to a long wait.

In the wood, Tallin walked the perimeter of the camp with Chanathen, checking that none of the men could be seen. As he passed along the tree line closest to the ruins, he looked down to see the brown-robed wizard stooping low over a small fire. His two men sat to one side, clearly bored with the proceedings.

"Chanathen, get two men to take food down to Astalus and relieve his guards," Tallin said.

Chanathen nodded. "I don't like this place, Sir. It's dismal and krell probably live in those mountains."

"Unfortunately we have no option. Astalus wants to search the city for Eldric artefacts which may help defeat the enemy."

The two men continued to survey the area. "I think we should have a patrol sweep the woods to our right though," Tallin continued.

"Shall we set some traps as well, just in case?"

"Yes, but make sure the men know where they are."

Chanathen left to carry out his orders while Tallin remained where he was. He tried to raise his own flagging spirits, knowing that he at least had to present an optimistic front. He would inspect their defences later, and perhaps he would feel better once their perimeter was secure.

As night closed in, he sent his second in command to bring Astalus back to the camp. Astalus returned a short while later, clearly dejected by his failure.

Gloomily, he sat apart from the others as they continued their labours late into the night. Tallin, not wanting to disturb his concentration, deliberately stayed away from the wizard. As the night thickened about them, a persistent drizzle set in. It was going to be an uncomfortable night, he reflected soberly.

"Sir!"

Tallin jumped. He had been fast asleep, and the hand on his shoulder had roused him from a nightmare.

"I'm soaked," he complained. Inadvertently he had rolled from beneath his shelter.

"Aye, it's a wet one," Chanathen said. "But it looks like it's clearing."

"What is it?" Tallin asked, knuckling sleep from his eyes.

"Astalus has gone. He's back at the ruins."

"*By the Kalanth*, did anyone bother to show him where the traps had been set?"

Chanathen looked guilty. "Last night he came in late and I didn't think to."

"Don't be hard on yourself; I didn't either. You'd better send two men down to keep an eye on him."

Tallin went in search of his pack and a change of clothes. He had a feeling it was going to be a long day.

Astalus had been too excited to sleep. He sat at the edge of the ruins with his staff raised, watching the light from the rising sun. He had decided on a number of approaches and was eager to try them. Tallin had warned him against the use of a fire, so he would have to rely upon the power of his staff to perform the magic.

Firstly, he drew a complex rune on the soil. Then he mumbled arcane words and made intricate patterns in the air. From his pouch, he sprinkled herbs on the rune and waited.

Nothing happened.

Without further ado, he changed tack and made a small pyramid of stones. Placing a hand upon the top stone, he invoked an ancient spell, long since forgotten by most wizards. Applying a light pressure to the stones, they crumbled to dust. Taking a pinch of dust Astalus drew a rune. He repeated the procedure with a branch from a tree, reducing the wood to dust. Drawing another rune on top of the first, but with the wood dust this time, he again waited as if expecting something to occur. Nothing did.

A noise behind him caused him to turn. Two of Tallin's men were crouching a few yards away, watching him.

Astalus returned his attention to his work. For the better part of the morning, he summoned power in different forms, probing every rock and crevice for a clue to the release of the ancient city from its hiding place. By mid-morning, he was exhausted. He sat back on his haunches and glared at the ruins with no further ideas of what to do. He had been defeated at every turn and now he was at a complete loss.

He could only assume that his Akrane magic was too limited and that only a sorcerer could complete the task. The thought angered him. Why should the Narlassar be so powerful? After all, it was their fault that Trosgarth's might had grown and evil abounded.

A noise startled him, and he turned to see Tallin approach accompanied by one of his men. The two men used cover to approach the wizard's position.

"No luck?" Tallin asked.

Astalus' pained expression was a sufficient reply. The soldier accompanying Tallin handed Astalus a large hunk of bread, which he took graciously, even though he did not feel like eating. He had not realised it was so late. Glancing around, he saw that the previous sentries had gone, replaced by a different pair. Sighing, Astalus sat back and started to eat his meal. The taste was strong and he opened the bread to see what was inside.

Tallin smiled. "Sorry, but we are on rations. I dare not send anyone out hunting; we need to keep our tracks to a minimum."

The bread was filled with thick slices of cheese, some pieces of which were age-hardened. Astalus broke off some of the harder pieces and scattered them onto the ground before closing the sandwich and taking a thoughtful bite. On the ground the cheese stood out in stark contrast to the green of the grass. He shouldn't leave the pieces there. They were a telltale sign of their presence. However, he was too fatigued to pick them up; instead he sat, chewing as he stared forlornly at the cheese. He realised Tallin was talking, but was lost in daydreams.

Perhaps the birds would eat the cheese. He doubted that, however. If it was left long enough, it would grow mouldy and, after a while, would disappear of its own accord. Suddenly he stopped chewing, the thick hunks of bread in his hand abruptly forgotten, as a broad smile crossed his face.

"It's so simple!" he exclaimed softly. He remembered then Kaplyn saying the city was hidden in time.

Tallin stopped speaking, realising that Astalus had not heard a word of what he had been saying. The wizard dropped his meal onto the grass and hurriedly traced a rune.

"Did you hear that?" Astalus asked.

Tallin frowned uncertainly as though not understanding what he was supposed to hear. "No." he replied.

Astalus traced the rune again.

"Did you hear it that time?" Astalus asked.

Tallin shook his head.

"Something that sounded like a fly?" Astalus suggested, staring intently at the young commander.

Tallin looked uncertainly back, thinking that the wizard was teasing him. Astalus' expression was earnest and his eyes sparkled with excitement.

"No, nothing," Tallin assured him.

Astalus paused in thought. "Not a fly, but words spoken very quickly." He traced a rune, feeling his strength fade with every spell as his reserves were used up. This spell would slow down whatever happened next. He repeated the previous spell and was rewarded instantly as a voice spoke to him in the common tongue, telling him the words of the spell to summon the city.

In excitement Astalus traced the necessary runes, feeling the power of his spell forming within the orb of his staff. Briefly, the air shimmered. Then they were looking through a pale tunnel of diffuse light at tall city walls broken only by a stout wooden gate, which seemed to beckon for Astalus to enter.

Tallin swore. Behind them, the two men shuffled backwards, nearly tripping over each other in their haste to escape.

"What is this place?" Tallin asked, fear born through years of superstition evident in his voice.

"Namthrall!" Astalus replied in awe without taking his eyes off the distant city. It was like looking through a tunnel. It was a portal to another time.

He arose slowly; his joints ached from squatting for so long. Before he had chance to stand, Tallin grabbed his arm. The young commander's face was full of concern. "Where are you going?"

Astalus shrugged off his grip as he stood. He looked towards the city, the eagerness of his intent reflected within his dark, brooding expression.

"Wait here for me, I shall not be long." He remembered Kaplyn's strange story. "If I am not back within two days, you must return to inform the Queen that I have failed."

"You cannot go in there," Tallin insisted. Behind them, the two soldiers arose and backed away several yards, making it clear that they also would not enter.

"I'm going," he said simply. "I have to. There is too much at stake."

With that he walked towards the circle of light.

Tallin looked up at the mountains which, framed against the cold grey sky, formed a sombre background to a city seemingly resurrected from thin air. A cold wind gusted, making him shiver. Drawing his cloak tightly about his shoulders, he hurried after his men, only once glancing back.

There was no doubt now, if there was anyone in the mountains, they would be alert to their presence thanks to the city's magical appearance. To all effects, they had just lit a beacon in the dark of night.

423

Chapter 35

In Search of Truth

Astalus paused uncertainly before the tunnel of shimmering light beyond which he could see the tall city walls, marking Namthrall's boundary. Summoning his courage, he stepped into the tunnel. For a brief instant, his way was barred as though held by an invisible hand. He struggled forward and, to his relief, was abruptly released. His heart laboured heavily, and he glanced back uncertainly, but the shining tunnel appeared the same from both sides.

His legs responded mechanically as he approached the large wooden doors, towering over him like silent sentinels from a forgotten era. He traced a spell of seeing using the power stored within his staff. Immediately, the gate shimmered, alerting him to potential danger beyond. The gate concealed a trap!

He cast a spell of opening and, as a precaution, stood back to watch the large doors as they swung silently inwards, exposing a dark tunnel. The air in front of the gate continued to shimmer, showing the outline of a spell protecting the entrance. It was incomplete, allowing someone with the ability to do so to pass.

Astalus remembered Kaplyn's warning that Vastra had feared to enter the city, and hoped that his Akrane magic would not be detected; in their arrogance, the Eldric had never considered the Akrane a threat. With a heavy heart, he entered the darkness where he paused. Nothing happened, and so he continued through zigzagging defences. Upon turning a corner, he found himself standing before a dark and forbidding gate, nearly as large as the one in the outer wall. It was locked, and so he was forced to repeat the spell of opening. As these gates swung inwards he found himself holding his breath in anticipation.

A long street, flanked by tall imposing buildings, stretched before him, pointing like a dagger towards the very heart of the ancient city. It was almost too much for him to comprehend, and he realised how Kaplyn must have felt when he had stood on Tanel's threshold, the only other Eldric city to be violated since their people had mysteriously vanished from the land.

Astalus quickened his pace, aiming for a large tower that dominated the skyline. It somehow seemed to epitomise the Eldric's power; taller than any other building, straight as a needle and perfectly round. He decided he would start his search for a library here and approached a small wooden door set beneath a stout stone lintel.

When his spell of seeing did not reveal any danger, he tried the handle. It refused to open, forcing him to use his magic. Immediately, the door sprang inwards. Cautiously Astalus entered a long corridor flanked on both sides by dark wooden doors, each of which seemed to demand his attention. A thick woollen carpet cushioned his footsteps. He tried a door. It wasn't bolted, and he peered within, taken aback by the grandeur even though a thick layer of dust covered most of the furniture.

He continued to the end of the corridor where a broad flight of stairs led up to the next level. He climbed these, enthralled by tall arching ceilings inlaid with ornate gold and silver decorations. He went on casting spells of seeing as he opened each door on this level, slowly draining his power.

The corridors were surprisingly wide and bright. Astalus was amazed to find that the windows were so large and frequent; clearly the tower had not been built for defence. As he ascended, the rooms became even more elegant and richly furnished with large tapestries covering the otherwise bare walls. He was saddened that he could not stay longer to look at the rich scenes. He was witnessing art that had been lost to the world for centuries, the like of which would probably never be seen again.

There were six floors in total, and, just when he was about to despair of finding the library, he did. It was on the top floor and practically took up the entire level. In awe, he walked along the rows of silent volumes. Pausing, he selected one at random and blew away centuries of accumulated dust. To anyone else, this was simply an old book; to Astalus it was the lifeblood of civilisation.

Reverently, he opened it and waited as several sheets wafted open, then settled as if by magic. He read the words, elated that he understood the thin spidery letters. To his surprise, it was nothing more than a gardening book and the discovery made him smile. It was hard to imagine anyone taking the time to write about such a trivial subject. Then he realised how much easier those times must have been.

He glanced back at the other neatly stacked volumes, observing belatedly that they were arranged according to subject. Swiftly he located the History section and was momentarily taken aback by the sheer number of titles. He walked down the brightly-lit aisle, taking only a cursory glance at the covers. When he reached the end, he checked through the window to make sure there was still sufficient daylight to continue his search.

Turning, he retraced his steps more slowly, pausing occasionally to take down a volume and search its contents. When he had selected a few and could carry no more, he went to the end of the aisle where he found a stool set before a sturdy table. Reverently, he laid the books down in a neat pile. Then he sat down and, drawing the topmost book towards him, he opened it at the first page.

After a while a particularly large volume proved more than interesting. A look of disbelief crossed his face as he silently spoke the words that stood out so starkly against the pure white of the vellum:

This is a true account of the fateful day when our liege Lord Darwyl was mortally wounded in combat with that foul traitor, Drachar. It is written by my own hand — I being Cralan, the King's friend and companion for nigh on twenty years.

I tell this account three months after the conclusion of the battle of DrummondCal, and even now my hand shakes to recall the tragic and terrible events of that dismal day. Forgive then my writing, but have sympathy in your heart when reading my tale — for we, the Eldric, suffered greatly in what have now become known as the Krell Wars.

If there are gods, which I doubt, then I believe they forsook us on that day, perhaps forever. Many now no longer smile and a dreadful weight seems to have descended upon the hearts of my people. We do not know how much longer we must endure the terrible sadness of these last few months, but I hope that I may gain some solace from writing about our tragedy.

That I was witness to Drachar's demise has done little to lift my mood, for on that day I also saw my Lord pass on to whatever fate awaits our souls after our long journey upon the road of death. I shall never forget that battle.

Demons strode amongst the combatants, taking souls to their dreaded world for eternal damnation. Whether they were a boon to the enemy or not I do not know, for to me it seemed as though friend and foe alike perished at the hands of these foul creatures.

For my part the battle was nothing more than a dreadful haze. There seemed to be no plan. Men from both sides simply fought and died, and if that was the plan, it was successful beyond measure, for the slaughter was terrible. Krell, as many as the ears of corn in a ripened field, attacked us time after time. After each assault they were ordered to attack again, the fear of their own commanders being greater than fear of our swords.

At that time, Darwyl and the other lords were beacons to our troops. Their shields shone like the rising of the sun, dispelling the darkness that surrounded the enemy host. Even so, we were outnumbered and to my untrained eye, it looked as though the battle would be lost. Trolls, as tall as trees, lumbered into the attack, crushing our front ranks like wheat beneath the farmer's boot. Behind them came krell and knights of both Trosgarth and Aldrace.

It was at this time that an enemy wedge divided our line, so that Darwyl and his command, myself included, were separated from the main force and were quickly surrounded by a living sea of enemy. At that moment, the light in Darwyl's eyes shone as though he was a god, and few enemies could stand before him. But he was one and they were many. For each enemy his enchanted blade slew, one or more of our small force fell, so that it looked as though we would be swiftly finished.

That is why I believe Drachar risked coming so close: to gloat. I had heard that he had sworn to kill Darwyl, but he dared not face him for no greater coward strode the earth. I do not doubt that he hoped to deliver the final thrust but not until he had sacrificed an army of krell to ensure that Darwyl was already weakened, if not mortally wounded.

At that point the dwarves came to our aid. A great shout went up to announce their arrival. By all accounts, their King wore dragon armour, which no earthly weapon could pierce. His kinsmen carried great double-headed axes that clove a gaping path through the enemy ranks.

I remember being told that every battle has a turning point, and a great commander will seize that moment, using the slightest change in the winds of war to ensure victory. That is what Darwyl did. In that brief moment of confusion, instead of retreating into his own ranks, he attacked, leading his men like an arrow into the enemy's flank. Drachar had over committed himself, a fact he learned too late.

Darwyl drove us on, aiming towards the dread Lord. I shall always remember the dark shroud of night that surrounded his earthly form. As we came closer, the light from Darwyl's shield dispelled the gloom. We could see Drachar, standing at the heart of his elite guard, wearing the black armour that some say was forged in the very depths of hell.

With a fearful cry, we fell upon them, for there was no way back, and, behind us, the enemy ranks had closed as the dwarves pressed them from one side and the allies from the other. In desperation, we fought like men possessed, and not even Drachar's elite could stand before us.

And then they met, Darwyl with his shield of light and Drachar shrouded in gloom, with spells of death and destruction impregnated into the very air about him. No one else could have stood before him, but Darwyl's shield countered Drachar's vile magic.

Instantly, their eyes locked and they knew this was the fight that would decide the war. The battle around them abated as combatants on both sides paused in their slaughter to watch the ensuing struggle.

Drachar struck first. He carried a weapon which, having been forged and tempered in the blood of men, was equal to Darwyl's blade. Kastral, he had named the dread weapon, Harbinger of Death. Kastral's aim was true, forcing Darwyl to use his shield to protect himself. Under the impact, the shield shattered into a thousand pieces, momentarily blinding the two combatants.

Darwyl's arm took the full force of the blow, and I could tell from his grimace that he was in pain. Before Drachar's darkness could close in to finish Darwyl, he swung his own blade around in a titanic arc of whistling steel. The enchanted metal burned fiercely, reflecting the blue fires of the battle surrounding them. Drachar was off balance and could not protect himself properly. However, unfortunately for Darwyl, his own aim was poor; his blade struck a glancing blow, shattering his enemy's helm.

In fear, Drachar summoned a spell of binding and hurled it at Darwyl, successfully ensnaring him. Whether Drachar was dazed from the blow or not I cannot say, but he failed to take advantage of the spell that trapped his opponent. Instead, he stumbled about the small arena while Darwyl struggled to free himself, shouting counter spells of his own. In those precious seconds, Darwyl finally managed to unravel the spell. With a cry of rage, he leapt at the evil sorcerer, casting his own spell of binding at the black-hearted traitor.

Drachar countered the spell, sending forth a dark cloud to ensnare Darwyl, perhaps by then hoping to escape the battle altogether. But even though the shards of Darwyl's shield lay broken on the battlefield, its magic was still intact — the bright light fought off the evil fog.

The combatants exchanged fierce blows. Then Darwyl saw an opening and swung his enchanted blade at his opponent's unprotected head; However, with Kastral's aid, Drachar blocked the blow. Lightning flashed along the length of the two weapons, showering sparks in all directions. Both men stood toe to toe, battle-weary and too exhausted to do much more.

My Liege Lord braced himself defiantly. The pain from his arm clearly showed as he somehow found a hidden reserve with which to force Drachar back. At that moment, Drachar felt his enemy's strength and knew that he *might lose. Backing away he sought to escape. However, although the fighting had stopped locally, the battle still raged all about and Drachar had no where to go.*

Invoking spells of strength and speed, he launched a blistering attack, delivering blows that he hoped even Darwyl's blade could not withstand. He had forgotten the shards of the shield lying broken on the ground. The light from one caught his eye, distracting him for the briefest moment. Darwyl sensed an opening and ducked beneath Kastral, plunging his own blade deep into the sorcerer's chest.

I could see the terrible pain in Drachar's eyes as the steel pierced his flesh. He knew it was a mortal blow, but had made evil pacts with Darkness so that his spirit was forbidden to leave his wounded body. I watched with horror as, with slow deliberate moves, Drachar pulled out a hidden dagger and stabbed Darwyl in his side.

My Lord cried out as the cold metal bit deep. With all of his remaining strength he forced his own blade deeper into Drachar's chest. This was a blow that even the darkest sorcery could not withstand. Drachar crumpled lifeless at my Lord's feet. I rushed to his side as a terrible wail started amongst the enemy ranks.

My Lord was only wounded, and yet the pain in his eyes revealed that the wound was worse than it looked. Others rushed forward to help, but we later learned that Drachar's accursed blade was poisoned. To my eternal shame, there was nothing that we could do to save him, and all that remained was to comfort him as the poison spread.

As to the remainder of the battle, I must confess that I know little. Drachar's defeat must have been enough to break the spell keeping the enemy together. Where before they had advanced, they now retreated. His sorcerers fled first, too afraid to summon demons, and the rest of his army followed upon their heels. I remember the cheering from thousands of battle-hoarse throats as the enemy took flight, both demoralised and beaten.

At that moment, Darwyl died, content at least that we had won. I remember his eyes glazing over, and I could see the light of his life, usually so vibrant, extinguished at the last.

Those around me cried out in frustration. A shield was brought forward and my liege Lord's body placed upon it, to be carried from the field.

It is odd; some years later I heard a rumour that Darwyl did not truly die and will one day return from his mountain tomb when the land is once more threatened. It is a pleasant tale in its way, for it maintains that my Lord will live forever.

That he will is undeniable — in the hearts of his people.

429

Forgive me, for I had to stop for a moment; my eyes, so filled with tears, prevented me from writing. My tale is not yet told. Of Drachar, I must yet speak.

As I mentioned earlier his soul was forbidden release from his earthly body. Do not ask why. My people assumed it was because of his alliance with the demons, believing that while the sun was still in the sky, his soul could not escape its mortal bounds.

Our sorcerers took up his body and carried it to a secret destination, close to the battle site. There, they wrested his soul from the corpse, forcing it to step into the world to face their wrath. So that his evil could never again threaten the land, they banished his shade into oblivion in the nether-regions between the worlds. A fitting end to the Prince of Hell.

Finally, two weeks ago, a lesser noble, Prince Ellard, returned to Namthrall. He had left DrummondCal after the battle on a secret quest into the mountains. There he has found a power with which it is hoped that my people will finally find peace. I feel that it is my duty to tell of this power for, if it does indeed do what Ellard claims, then my race will no longer live in this land.

For some time now we have been aware that there are other worlds separated from ours by a dark region to which Drachar's ghost was banished. The demon world is one of these. It is reputedly a cold and lifeless place where the sun has long since perished.

I am assured that other worlds also exist, and this is our salvation for we cannot continue to live in a land burdened by our own guilt. Our shame is too great in this matter. It is hoped that the power that Prince Ellard found is sufficient to keep open a passageway between the worlds, allowing our people to escape. We shall seek a world devoid of magic; that is, assuming that such a place exists!

Prince Ellard will remain behind, taking with him the power to the other Eldric cities so that they, too, may join us. We have already spoken with our kin in these cities and we are of one accord in this matter.

One day perhaps we shall return, when the people left behind have learnt to forgive us.

Astalus sat back in the chair. His neck was sore from leaning over for too long, and he rubbed it now, temporarily relieving the pain. To say that Cralan's account shocked him was an understatement. He was possibly the only person in the realm to know what had become of their race, and the discovery left him feeling both cold and numb.

Chapter 36

Fear

Rubbing his eyes, Astalus realised that the light outside was fading. He could not leave just yet; too many questions remained unanswered.

He assumed that the power Prince Ellard had uncovered had something to do with Kaplyn's Tree of Life. Rising from his chair, he looked about the long room for signs of a torch. He walked along the silent rows until he found a small table lamp and, gratefully, he removed the delicate glass cover, using his dwindling power to light the wick. With his staff in one hand and the lamp in the other, he worked his way along the rows of books, reading the spines and occasionally pausing to take one down and flick through its contents.

After a short while, he returned to the desk with three volumes. Sitting down he rearranged his robes more comfortably before opening one. It was not long before he was totally immersed in the fine script, spellbound by its beauty.

Fortune was with him, he had found a volume describing the other worlds seen by the Eldric sorcerers. In one chapter, to his amazement, he read about a world populated entirely by dragons. Astalus was immediately interested, but the text told him little other than the world's geography. Fortunately, there was a cross-reference to another book. Astalus started to search for this, returning moments later with a large, dusty volume. Eerily, the book fell open at the correct page almost as if by command.

Astalus held his breath as he read, only exhaling when he had finished the first paragraph. He could not believe his luck; the volume contained a list of Narlassar spells, including one for summoning dragons. It was more than he could possibly have hoped for. His mind was immediately filled with questions. If the Eldric knew about dragons, why had they not summoned them during the Krell Wars?

He returned to the front pages to determine when the book was written. The date was meaningless; he could not tell whether the book had been written before or after the war. He shook his head in dismay. It might take him ages to find an Eldric date for the start of the Krell Wars.

Abruptly, the light within the library dimmed. Astalus looked up from his reading, not quite comprehending why this had happened. As his eyes fell upon the lamp, he saw to his horror that the flame was now burning with a blue flame. Instantly, he rose from the table and turned, becoming aware of a stench within the dusty library. His heart almost failed as comprehension dawned.

A demon.

To his dismay, his power was already expended.

A movement in the shadows caused him to start. He turned to face his danger. A man stood motionless at the edge of the faint radiance as though afraid to let the light touch him. His clothes were rich and fine, much too fine for a soldier.

The figure smiled, though not reassuringly. His red eyes glistened with evil anticipation.

Astalus backed away, his senses confirming his worst fears. He was facing a demon, probably one of the most powerful he had ever seen for it was able to take the guise of a man.

With a roar that caused Astalus to stumble and nearly drop his staff, the demon threw forth his arm, pointing accusingly at the wizard. A small orb flashed from his grasp, spinning towards him. The startled wizard responded more quickly than he would have believed possible, screaming words of power.

The two powers collided in a blinding explosion, throwing Astalus back against one of the bookshelves and showering the room in a fountain of dust and flame. The force of the blast threatened to render him unconscious, and he fought against the ringing in his ears, bright lights blurring his vision.

As he lay on the ground trying to gather his wits, the ringing in his ears gradually changed into hollow laughter. He looked up. From within the burning wreckage of books, the demon stepped towards him, unaffected by the terrible blast that had robbed Astalus of his senses. In his semi-conscious state, the wizard could only watch, half mesmerised by the demon's eyes as it approached, fighting the horror and trying to force his limbs into action. He was exhausted. He looked at the demon's face, hoping to see pity reflected there. Instead his heart quailed at the vindictive look of triumph upon the demon's handsome face.

The monster stepped deliberately over the fallen wreckage, taking its time and revelling in Astalus' fear. Its blood-red lips formed a cruel smile as he conjured a long, wicked-looking knife out of the air, testing the blade's sharpness on his finger as he looked down at the fallen wizard.

Astalus felt life slowly seep back into his limbs, but his own terror held him confined as effectively as if he had been bound with rope. His mind screamed at his body to move, but like countless nightmares before, he remained helplessly pinned to the floor. The demon reached his outstretched legs, its smile even broader as it crouched down by his side, running the knife threateningly but gently across the stricken man's thigh.

Astalus locked his gaze upon that of the demon. As if in response, its eyes seemed to grow until he was lost in their dark, unfathomable depths. At the back of his mind, his fear urged him to respond. A sense of urgency coursed through his veins.

With renewed energy, he struggled to rise, but failed. Suddenly, to his horror, he felt as though there was something pulsing inside his head. His breathing, already ragged with fear, stopped altogether as he felt a second more deliberate push, followed in quick succession by more determined probing. The demon blurred before his eyes, and a dark mist descended over his own vision, shutting out the light from the minor fires. A cry of perpetual terror escalated through his mind as his consciousness fled into the remotest part of his being.

For long seconds a terrible wail filled every dark recess of the tower; and then there came silence. The hollow silence of the grave.

Chapter 37

Sorely Missed

From the concealment of the wood, Tallin looked out upon the city walls.

Where was Astalus? What was keeping him? A noise alerted him to someone's presence, and, looking to one side, he saw one of his men approaching. He recognised Tharlan by his thick beard and broad shoulders. Tharlan was one of the scouts he had sent out earlier to check the wood behind them.

"What have you to report?" Tallin asked in a low voice.

Tharlan shook his head and looked uncomfortable. "We scouted out to about a mile and then circled back to the east before returning here, following a gully for some of the way. The trees were dense and we saw nothing."

Tallin could tell there was something else and waited patiently for the other man to continue.

Tharlan glanced over his shoulder, evidently worried by the closeness of the Eldric city. When he looked back, his eyes reflected his fear.

"We felt something though. I'm not sure what. It was quiet, as well; no birds were singing and there were very few animal trails, none fresh."

Tallin shifted uncertainly. If Tharlan said there was something amiss in the forest, then he believed him.

"Return to the camp, set the traps early this evening and get everyone within the perimeter," Tallin ordered, rising to his feet. He waited for a while longer, but there was no sign of Astalus. By that time it was too dark to see very far, and he decided to return to camp and send men back to guide the wizard later.

By the time he returned, it was completely black. Most of the men were relaxing as best they could. Tallin sat down by his shelter, but, before he could start eating, a soldier came to his position.

"Sir, Chanathen says that there is something moving beyond the perimeter," the soldier whispered. He was very young and looked afraid.

Tallin laid the uneaten meal down, picking up his long bow.

"Stand-to," he called softly to the men nearest him. Accompanied by the young man he went to find Chanathen, repeating the command to stand-to as they went. If there was ever a time when they needed Astalus and his magic, it was now.

Suddenly, voices were raised in front of him and he heard several arrows loosed. Shouts from the trees ahead confirmed the enemy's presence. Krell voices cursed out loudly as they triggered traps, their oaths turning to screams as they were impaled upon spikes.

From the sound of their voices, they were being attacked along a wide front. Ahead, he could see Chanathen and a group of men rapidly firing arrows into the trees. An arrow flew over his head, imbedding itself in a trunk just above him. Instinctively, he ducked, not risking getting too close to the fighting so that he could still issue orders. His second in command and a runner joined him, each crouching low behind a trunk.

At the moment, it looked as though the attack had failed as the number of arrows fired had dwindled to just a few. Then silence descended.

"They probably meant to creep up on us," Chanathen whispered by his side.

Tallin nodded, "How did they get so near?" the runner asked fearfully. It was clear that the presence of the recently summoned city was having a detrimental effect upon morale.

"The woods are thicker beyond here; it wouldn't be difficult to get this close," Tallin replied. He was thankful that there was at least a short stretch of open ground between them and the wood opposite. Fortunately, the traps had served their purpose in warning them.

He gave orders for the men to be concentrated along this edge of the tree line with a small rear guard looking after the horses. As men filed silently by his position, a cry went up from the trees beyond and swarms of dark figures raced across the open ground.

Scores of arrows flew to meet them, bowling over the first rank. Screams and battle cries from the krell ranks filled the air, while only silence and death greeted them from the wood ahead. Silently, Tallin prayed that Astalus would return. With his magic, they could at least see the enemy.

All at once, the enemy was across the open ground, and sporadic hand to hand fighting broke out. Tallin, fearing they might be flanked, called in his own flanks, forming a semi circle and brought in the rear guard to fill the gap.

Before they could be brought into the circle, the horses neighed loudly in terror and their nostrils flaring with the scent of blood. They reared up, seeking to escape and then, suddenly, they were free, racing through the wood, throwing men and krell alike to the ground. For a moment, confusion reigned as men and krell parted, allowing the horses to escape. Then, as swiftly as the battle had ceased, it resumed. Dark shapes flitted from tree to tree until it looked as though the wood was alive.

Tallin saw two of his men fall. With a cry, he urged the reserves forward and was soon lost himself amongst the melee. It was impossible to swing his sword in the thick confines of the wood, and instead he was forced to use the point to stab the enemy. Their numbers were too great. Slowly, step by step, his men were forced to retreat.

All at once, their flank folded and krell leapt over the bodies, screaming gleefully as they threw themselves upon the soldiers' rear. Tallin had lost control of his command. In desperation, he shouted orders for his men to fall back to the open ground before the citadel, still hoping Astalus would save them. If all else failed he was thinking he could lead his men into the city.

A horn, brash and harsh against the thick tangle of wood, sounded the retreat. Men turned on the krell behind them, stabbing and thrusting at the enemy in a desperate attempt to avoid being caught in a stranglehold. Tallin reached the tree line in time to see the remnants of his command break free. Krell emerged alongside the men but paused before the open ground, allowing his men time to regroup.

They were breathing hard and many were wounded. All along their line, shields were defensively interlocked. Men peered over shield tops as more krell poured from the wood, jeering at them. The occasional spear flew from the krell ranks, but these were easily parried by a sword or shield.

"Chanathen," Tallin shouted. "Get the men into the city."

"Fall back!" Chanathen shouted and others took up the command.

Men cast fearful glances behind and Tallin knew what they were thinking — better to die a clean death in the open rather than in a city of ghosts.

The delay was their downfall.

All at once the men on the left flank gave out a great cry. Tallin looked where some of the men were pointing, goggle-eyed. It was as though a giant rock was striding forth from beneath the trees. The krell parted before it, forming a corridor down which the creature advanced. The faint moonlight, penetrating the thick cloud cover, reflected from its thick hide.

Tallin realised it was a troll. Desperately, he called to the men to retreat to the city, but already krell were swarming to cut off this avenue of escape. Like a thunderbolt, the troll launched itself at the small group of men, bowling aside the front ranks and crushing many beneath its heavy body. Its small arms flayed out, breaking arms and backs with a single swipe.

Immediately, sensing victory, the krell attacked, their wicked spurred swords ripping through flesh and bone alike. Tallin saw Chanathen felled by a krell whose sword jammed in the big man's armour. Tallin decapitated it with a single sweep of his sword.

There was nowhere now for the men to go. They were surrounded.

The troll bellowed angrily as it thundered amongst them, trampling the fallen and wounded beneath its broad feet. Tallin tried to lead his men away, desperately striving to breach the wall of krell in an attempt to return to the forest, but it was no good; slowly the circle of men was reduced as more and more fell.

By now, Tallin's arm was leaden. He was slipping on the slick grass, made greasy by the blood of men and krell. As he slipped for the last time, a krell loomed over him, its sword raised. Tallin pierced its armour in a desperate uppercut, but before the dark creature died it completed its blow, knocking aside Tallin's helm. Sparks burst in his mind. He fell to the wet ground, his head exploding in waves of agony. As his eyes grew dim, he thought he saw a bright light issue forth from the gates of the city. Astalus, he thought, watching with faint hope as krell fell back before the blazing light. But then he knew no more as blackness engulfed him.

Chapter 38

Awakening

Grey shapes filled Tallin's fog-enshrouded mind.

A splitting headache made him realise he was not dead.

A voice spoke to him from afar. He tried to concentrate on the words, but could not understand the language. He strove to open his eyes, but failed. The lids remained unbearably heavy.

Once more his mind tumbled into oblivion.

The next time he awoke, the headache had subsided. Opening his eyes, he saw branches swaying gently against the backdrop of a grey, leaden sky. Sounds returned and he listened to the gentle piping of songbirds as they heralded the start of a new day.

A figure leant over Tallin and rough fingers probed his skull. He could not see the figure's face for it was shadowed by the brightness of the sky and his cowl.

"Astalus?" Tallin asked, surprised by the hoarseness of his own voice.

The figure drew back as though burnt.

"Yes," came an abrupt reply.

Tallin raised himself wearily onto his elbow, looking fearfully about. Trees surrounded him.

"Where are the others?" he asked, looking to the wizard for an explanation.

Astalus was busy saddling a horse. A second horse was already saddled and stood patiently to one side, its head lowered to the ground as it chewed the short grass of the forest floor.

"Dead," came the reply.

Tallin's head throbbed sharply, and he had to close his eyes as another stabbing pain ripped through his skull. As the pain subsided, Astalus' words slowly sank in. Tallin's eyes flew open; a look of pain and disbelief etched upon his face.

"Dead? All of them?" He could not believe it. He started to rise, but the pain returned and he almost passed out. Strong hands helped him to his feet where he stood swaying until the giddiness passed.

When he looked, Astalus was strapping a large book onto the saddle.

"I must return," Tallin insisted bravely. "Somebody may have survived."

Astalus turned angrily to face him, "They're all dead," he hissed from within the shadow of his hood. He, too, looked unsteady and for a moment he swayed alarmingly. "I saw them!" he snapped. "None lived — take my word for it. Now we must leave before the krell return!"

For a moment, Tallin realised he was being selfish. "Are you wounded?" he asked.

"Can you ride?" came the reply. It sounded sarcastic, full of hidden menace.

Tallin frowned.

The figure paused for a moment. "No, I am uninjured," he replied more softly this time. "Now we must leave. I have urgent news for the Queen." He patted the book.

Tallin nodded. "I can ride," he said, not knowing if he spoke truthfully.

"Let me help you," Astalus offered.

Tallin walked unsteadily towards the wizard who took his arm in a firm grip, steadying him as he clung to the horse's saddle. He felt both giddy and sick. The loss of his men was a terrible burden, and, for a moment, he felt as though he could not continue. Already, he saw their faces floating before his vision, which blurred as tears threatened.

By his side, he sensed Astalus' impatience and so tried to mount. He was too weary and his head ached. His legs gave way beneath him, but, before he fell, Astalus caught him and, with a strength Tallin hadn't known he possessed, boosted him into the saddle.

Clutching his reins, Tallin saw Astalus' face for the first time that day. The wizard turned away as though afraid to let Tallin see him, but the image was already indelibly burned into the soldier's memory. Astalus was pale, almost a deathly white, and his eyes were scarlet as though reddened by the smoke of battle. At that moment, he looked like one of the Alvalah, Lomar's people.

He's ill, Tallin realised with shock as Astalus mounted, turning his horse's head in the direction of CarCamel. He was feeling none too well himself. With his free hand, he tenderly probed his skull, touching his hair, matted with congealed blood. He winced at the touch. His head hurt like hell. He would have to bathe the wound later when they stopped.

Calling to Astalus in a hoarse whisper, he asked which way they were going.

"Through the gorge," Astalus replied. "We shall be in CarCamel within a few days."

Doubt nagged at Tallin, but he could not put his finger on why. He felt sick. His head throbbed and his mouth was terribly dry. After they had ridden a few yards, his chin dropped onto his chest and his head bounced uncomfortably back and forth. They had not gone far before Tallin mercifully blacked out.

Before him Astalus rode as though a pole had been inserted down his spine. There was a terrible air of purpose about the wizard; if Tallin had seen it, he would have been alerted to their danger. Unfortunately, however, he did not.

Astalus glanced back only once. The light caught his eyes, which shone red with hidden malice, as the demon allowed itself a rare smile. Sensing his presence, animals fell silent until he had passed, and, even then, the usual sounds of life seemed dull as though tainted by his evil, a foretelling of what the future held should the demons win.

Epilogue

T'chark lay beneath the overhanging branches of a thick bush, staring out into the fading light at the distant mountains. The pain in his side throbbed, and he bit back a curse in case another of the enemy's patrols was close at hand. He had already witnessed the demise of several of his kind, hunted down and exterminated by mounted patrols.

Not T'chark though. He was too clever.

A fresh burst of pain lanced through his emaciated form. He cursed the man who had wounded him as he had fled the battle. This time he had not been at the front, fighting with his larger cousins, but had remained at the rear where he felt he had a better chance of surviving to take part in the sacking of the city. It had mattered little where he was once the rout had begun.

Now he licked his dry lips as he looked up at the mountains, dreaming of home and safety. It was a long way across open ground, offering little or no concealment. Laying his head upon his arm, he decided to sleep for a little while to let the darkness become more complete.

A smile spread across his face. He was tired. His talon went to his wound; the grass about him was already slick with blood.

But it had been a glorious battle.

And Lang. An image of the giant krell came to mind. He watched again with glee as Lang dies. He realised then that he missed the others, even Lang.

Gradually a grey mist descended over his eyes and unaccustomed warmth spread through his tiny frame. From within, the mist figures gathered, beckoning him to join them. At their fore, stood Lang, grinning wickedly, fangs glistening in the dying light.

In the branches of a nearby tree, an owl hooted welcoming once more the night and caring little about war or the acts of men or krell.

Thus ends Dragon Rider. The story concludes in Shadow of the Demon

The Prophecy of the Kings

Book 3

Shadow of the Demon

By David Burrows

Chapter 1

An Unexpected Encounter

Kaplyn wearily shifted his weight as he kept watch over the small camp. It was dark. Not the complete blackness he had become accustomed to during the recent battles — that had been unbearable. Now faint moonlight bathed the land, enabling him to see the silhouettes of the surrounding hills and thick gorse that grew in profusion in this part of Thrace.

Even though he could see, he still glanced down at his unsheathed sword. The onyx metal remained dull, reassuring him there were no krell or demons in the vicinity. If there had been, then it would have glowed blue in warning. The wild was a dangerous place, made more so after the recent battles. Roving bands of defeated enemy had fled to the surrounding lands, seeking to escape to their homelands. Kaplyn and his companions were far beyond the range of any help, and, to make matters worse, their journey was taking them north, deeper into enemy territory.

Absently he fingered the scar on his chest, the cold, crystalline surface felt alien. He shuddered as he recalled the final days of the battle at CarCamel and being spurned by those closest to him. His thoughts turned to Catriona, the newly crowned Thracian Queen, and her memory tugged painfully at his heart.

He tried to dispel his gloomy thoughts, contemplating instead the men who had chosen to accompany him: Lars, Lomar and especially Tumarl, who was such an enigma. He had sworn vengeance against the krell for the death of his family, a tortured soul who could find no peace. And yet strangely, of the three men, Kaplyn felt he understood Tumarl the most. The loss of Kaplyn's family and friends was a difficult burden, and he felt guilty that he could have prevented their deaths. It would be too easy to become like Tumarl, to live only for the moment, seeking war against his enemies and losing himself in that single goal.

Kaplyn tried to focus on the task at hand and his eyes searched the surrounding night. Suddenly, a nagging feeling that he was not alone swept over him. His blade remained dull but, even still, his discomfort grew. He laid down his sword, taking up his bow and reaching for an arrow.

"Hold," a voice commanded from somewhere alarmingly close. Kaplyn's heart was racing and, although his bow was strung, he did not have an arrow to hand.

"Put your weapon down and back away," the voice said.

Kaplyn hesitated and considered calling to his friends. "A bolt is aimed at your heart," the voice growled.

Kaplyn stood, backing away from his weapons, inwardly cursing himself for daydreaming. A shape detached itself from the gorse closest to Kaplyn. The silhouette was shorter than Kaplyn but much broader across the shoulders. Other shapes peeled away from the shadows.

Behind him he heard firstly Lomar's and then Lars' voices as they were woken. Tumarl's angry shouts filled the air, and there followed sounds of a scuffle before silence abruptly descended.

A fire was lit and Kaplyn was forced to sit close to the flames. Lars was jostled to sit opposite him and two of their captors appeared dragging Tumarl's unconscious body between them. Then Lomar joined them, his pale complexion standing out in stark contrast to the dark of the night.

In the light of the flames, it was the first chance Kaplyn had to see their captors and the realisation sent a shock through his soul.

Dwarves.

He did not know whether they were friendly or not for recently there had been little contact between the races.

"Well — they are not krell," one of the dwarves stated, joining the others by the fire. His tone suggested disappointment. "But I'll warrant that fellow is a demon," he said, pointing his axe blade at Lomar whose scarlet eyes marked him in stark contrast to the others.

"He's not a demon," Kaplyn interrupted, seeking to dispel their fears. "We are enemies of Trosgarth."

One of the dwarves snorted. "Then more fool you, travelling abroad with so many krell about."

More dwarves joined them about the fire, carrying the captured weapons. One dwarf held Kaplyn's blade in his hand and he looked on it in wonder. "It's Eldric made!"

"Let me see it," demanded another. Kaplyn tried to turn to see the dwarf who spoke but was shoved by one of the captives. "Keep facing the fire," a voice warned.

Behind him several dwarves muttered in surprise, but he could not tell what was said. Instead he looked at the dwarves opposite. They were not as he had imagined; they were too grim for one thing. They were also taller than he imagined, although the tallest still barely reached Kaplyn's shoulder. Otherwise, they were similar to that in his imagination; each wore a long beard, plaited and tucked into broad leather belts from which hung decorative pouches and other objects that Kaplyn did not understand. Their tunics were of tanned leather, their trousers were made from wool and they wore sturdy boots, laced up to their knees. They favoured dark colours, possibly to help them blend into the night, and each carried a double-headed axe.

A gasp by his side made him want to look around, but after his earlier warning he refrained. "That one there," he heard one of the captors saying.

Two dwarves came to stand in front of Lars. One was carrying the big man's axe in his broad hands and, even though it was huge by comparison to his own weapon, he looked more than comfortable with it. Lars looked up from where he sat, remaining silent, the fire highlighting the ginger streaks in his otherwise blond beard.

"Where did you get this?" one of the dwarves asked.

"We found it in Tanel, an Eldric city," Lars answered.

The dwarves murmured excitedly.

"Are you one of the Eldric?" the dwarf questioned.

Smiling, the big man shook his head.

"You are certainly not a dwarf," the other stated. Lars stood and he towered over the dwarves, causing them to take a step backwards. "If it was not for your height, I would have judged you to be one of us," the dwarf stated. "Never before have I met a race who favour the axe." The dwarf bowed before Lars, although the others still eyed the group darkly, clearly not yet convinced they were friends.

One of the dwarves stepped forward and Kaplyn marked him to be their leader. He was older than the others were and his beard was greying. "You are our prisoners and must be judged by our King."

"We cannot," Kaplyn stated bluntly. "We are on an important quest. The people in CarCamel are relying on us."

"Bind and gag them," the dwarf ordered, ignoring Kaplyn. "Free their horses. We dwarves prefer to walk!" Strong hands grabbed Kaplyn, nearly lifting him from the grass as his hands were bound behind his back. A coarse cloth was pushed into his mouth. He could hardly breathe; inwardly he cursed.

Some of the dwarves tried to rouse Tumarl, shaking him until he came around and then setting him on his feet where he swayed alarmingly.

Then the fire was doused, plunging them back into darkness. With dwarves flanking them, they set off into the night. Occasionally, Kaplyn stumbled and each time strong hands prevented him from falling, but there was little compassion in their grip and swiftly he was herded on. He tried to remember what he knew about the dwarves, but his knowledge was scant. For many generations contact had been lost between the races, partly due to the remoteness of Thandor, the dwarves' ancestral home.

Much later the column stopped, and an outflanking scout appeared from out of the darkness by Kaplyn's side, making his way to the head of the column. The prisoners were forced to lie down on the damp ground. The rest of the dwarves crouched where they had stood.

After a moment longer a party of about ten dwarves left the column, swiftly blending into the night. Kaplyn listened but could hear nothing and then the silence was shattered by hoarse cries of alarm.

Krell voices, Kaplyn realised fearfully.

Abruptly silence returned and, within moments, a dwarf returned for the prisoners and their escort, ordering them forward. They entered a deep hollow within which Kaplyn saw several shapes which he initially mistook to be boulders. He soon realised his mistake. Small bolts from the dwarves crossbows protruded from the shapes, which he now realised were krell bodies. Some lay on the rim of the hollow where they had been killed, trying to escape. A krell lay close to Kaplyn and he stared at it in revulsion. It looked gaunt, as though it had not eaten for some time, and its clothes were rags.

They didn't stop and were led out the other side of the hollow. Kaplyn felt a sudden urge to look up, and then heard soft flapping of wings overhead. One of his captors pushed him in the back. Kaplyn planted his feet firmly, and desperately tried to nod in the direction of the sounds, hoping the look of fear in his eyes would be sufficient warning.

The guard pushed him harder, forcing him on.

A bolt of blue light streaked down from the heavens catching Kaplyn's guard full in the chest and narrowly missing Kaplyn. The dwarf was thrown back by the blast, and Kaplyn hurled himself to the ground whilst all around him pandemonium broke out. A second and a third bolt followed, accompanied by loud explosions.

Kaplyn crawled to the dwarf's body and found that, in his death grip, he was still clutching his axe. He rolled onto his back and felt for the sharp blade with his hands. As bright lights danced before his eyes, he sawed at his bonds which swiftly parted. With relief he pulled the gag from his mouth and, scooping up the dead dwarf's axe, ran to find his friends.

The flapping of wings was more obvious now and a shrill scream of rage split the night air. Kaplyn knew that a grakyn had found them. The dwarves were busy returning fire, and several crossbow bolts streaked skyward in the vain hope that, in the darkness, they might hit it. More explosions shook the ground as the grakyn continued its attack.

Kaplyn realised it was futile trying to find the others in the ensuing pandemonium. Crouching on one knee, he concentrated on the flapping of the grakyn's wings with the intention of throwing his axe, but the dwarves' shouts and the explosions confused him. He gripped the axe and was preparing to make a desperate throw when a ghostly spectre materialised from the darkness by his side. His immediate thought was that a demon had found them, but then he recognised Lomar, or at least his shaol. None of the dwarves close to Kaplyn seemed able to see the spectre.

Another explosion erupted, killing another dwarf whose body hit the earth with a sickening thud; his skull cap rolled from his head and came to a halt a few feet from the body. Lomar's shade frowned down on Kaplyn uncertainly, and, for a moment, Kaplyn sensed that the albino was looking at something by, or close to his side. So convinced was Kaplyn that he, too, glanced by his side but there was nothing there.

"What is it?" Kaplyn asked, turning to face Lomar's shaol..

"I thought I saw something by your side," Lomar answered. "I must have been mistaken."

Kaplyn sensed that Lomar was still troubled by what he had imagined, but given their present dilemma he dismissed the incident.

"Kaplyn, I can see the grakyn," he stated. "With my help you might be able to kill it."

Kaplyn nodded and Lomar floated close to his side and pointed into the sky over Kaplyn's shoulder.

"Throw along my point of aim when I tell you to."

Kaplyn drew back the heavy axe and waited.

"Now," the albino shouted all at once. Kaplyn hurled the axe with all his strength and the weapon flew into the sky, unintentionally spinning end over end as it went.

A cry of pain followed and a few heartbeats later, a dark shape hit the ground only a few yards from Kaplyn, bouncing on the hard earth. The grakyn stirred and tried to rise, but shadowy shapes arose around it and axes descended, severing the neck and splitting its wings before the creature had time to recover.

Kaplyn was immediately surrounded by dwarves, their weapons raised, but there was no menace in their eyes. Kaplyn rose, spreading his arms wide, making it clear he was unarmed. Glancing around, to his relief, Lomar's shade had disappeared.

The dwarf he assumed to be their leader came over to him.

"He brought down the grakyn with an axe throw I would have been proud of," one of the dwarves standing by Kaplyn's side stated by way of explanation. The leader nodded and looked back at the body, its black skin glistened oily in the faint light.

"Untie them," the dwarf said. "You will come with us. You will not be bound again unless you attempt to escape."

Kaplyn agreed as Lars, Lomar and Tumarl were herded from the surrounding darkness. Tumarl was rubbing his wrists, trying to get the circulation back, his eyes blazed angrily, but, for the moment, he held his frustration in check. When he saw the grakyn's corpse, his gaze fixed on the body as though feeding his hatred.

"I have agreed we will accompany the dwarves to their home," Kaplyn explained to the others who nodded, although their eyes reflected uncertainty.

The dwarves took stock of their situation. In all three were dead and two badly burned. Quickly, the column was formed and, without delay, they set off; the dwarves carrying the dead and wounded as though their bodies were no heavier than their axes.

Lomar reflected on his out of body experience. It chilled him for he had never done this before whilst awake. It was the urgency of the situation that had forced him to consider the possibility. He had concentrated hard, seeking the elusive link with his shaol, his guardian spirit, and almost as soon as he did so, he had felt his spirit slip from his body, abruptly finding himself by Kaplyn's side. At the time he had been convinced that something was standing beside Kaplyn. Something indistinct, like the ghost of a man. He had seen other people's shaols before, but they had always looked vague, more akin to an indistinct fog. This time the shaol had looked as real as Kaplyn although it had shimmered in and out of view as though his presence in this world was tenuous.

The spirit's attire was bizarre, unlike anything Lomar had seen before. An ornate breastplate covered a bright tunic, flaring excessively at the wrists with cuffs decorated with gold thread. He wore long riding boots and baggy trousers, tucked into the tops of his boots. A dagger and several pouches had hung from a thin belt. His hair was long and fine and he wore a tall conical helm, ornately wrought with fine carvings. The spectre's gaze was intense and his eyes penetrating. His bearded face had been long and angular, and his look almost regal, but his eyes suggested an intense cruelty that had caused Lomar to hold his breath.

As he had studied the figure, he had realised that it, too, was studying him. That came as a shock. But then the figure had flickered from view as though it had never really existed. Lomar had been left looking bewildered upon Kaplyn before he had remembered the grakyn. Now, as they walked in the complete darkness of a moonless night, Lomar glanced back at Kaplyn who was walking mechanically with weariness reflected in his eyes. There was no sign of the spectre by his side, although Lomar somehow knew he would not see it unless his own spirit travelled on the astral plane.

He turned his attention back to the column ahead. Should he tell Kaplyn what he had seen? That was his dilemma, for he doubted Kaplyn would believe him. He had a premonition that worse was yet to come. As he walked, he pondered upon why he could only see Kaplyn's and the priests' shaols, sensing an urgent need to solve that riddle.

They walked for the remainder of the night and, at the first signs of dawn, the column took shelter in a small wood. As soon as they were settled, the leader of the dwarves approached Kaplyn.

"I'm Thaneck," he said holding out a hand.

"Kaplyn," he replied taking the dwarf's hand in a firm handshake.

"Why are you travelling in our lands?"

"We have come from CarCamel. Recently there was a battle against an army we believe was sent by Trosgarth. The krell you slew last night were probably remnants from that army, trying to return to their homes.

"We are going to Drishnack, the Aldracian capital, to find out how large their army really is." Kaplyn continued. He refrained from mentioning that he was drawn to Drishnack by a vision of Vastra, now an old man, captive in a golden cage. Vastra was a wizard, or sorcerer as he had always insisted, who had led the group when they had searched to discover the fate of the Eldric so long ago. Vastra had betrayed them after taking a crystallised fruit they had found hanging from a fossilised tree deep in the heart of BanKildor, one of the tallest mountains in the PenAmPeleas range. Kaplyn bore the remains of another crystal, now a crystalline scar embedded in his chest. Inadvertently, his hand had strayed to it and absently he rubbed it beneath his shirt. How he had got the scar he did not know, but suspected Vastra was to blame.

Kaplyn feared if Vastra's crystal fell into enemy hands, the enemy would be able to open a permanent passage to the demon world. The thought made him shudder. He was nervous enough having told only half the truth, but he held the dwarf's steady gaze, hoping that his deceit would not be discovered; the scar on his chest itched uncomfortably as though it, too, was part of the lie.

"You and your friends look nothing like Aldracians," the dwarf snorted, eyeing particularly Lars and Lomar. "Put one foot in Aldrace and you will be arrested."

Kaplyn smiled, knowing that the dwarf spoke truthfully. Neither Lomar nor Lars could ever hope to enter the enemy city, both were markedly different to the other races: Lomar with his white complexion and hair and Lars with his blond hair and sheer size.

"It's a problem we have yet to solve," Kaplyn admitted.

"And how do you intend getting through KinKassack? That forest will eat you up and spit you out."

Kaplyn had not formulated a plan and was embarrassed by the dwarf's questions. "Tumarl has travelled through KinKassack or part of it, at least."

Tumarl's gaze never faltered even though this was the first mention of the fact they would travel through the forest that had so nearly killed him.

The dwarf looked at Tumarl in disbelief. "That's impossible," he said "KinKassack is evil. No one could pass through it. It's an unholy place; krell and trolls live there and even the trees are evil. Namlwyn tried, he was my friend. He took with him over a hundred dwarves, intending to cut a passage to Thandor, our ancestral home. Neither he nor his men were heard of again."

"We live in dark times," Kaplyn agreed.

"Your tale suggests we need to make haste," Thaneck decided. "Do you have a head for heights?" he continued with an impish grin. Behind Kaplyn, Lars groaned which only served to broaden the dwarf's smile. With that he walked off towards his fellows who had gathered together a short distance away.

"What did he mean by that?" Lars asked uncertainly.

"I don't know," Kaplyn answered, also concerned by the dwarf's glib statement.

Thaneck spoke to another dwarf who removed an object from his pack before walking to a tall tree, which he commenced to climb. He shuffled on to a large branch high above the ground where he unwound a length of cord at the end of which dangled a small object. Slowly at first, he swung the wood in a circle by his side, and a low eerie whistling started which gradually grew in intensity as he increased its speed, alternately increasing and decreasing in pitch as it sailed through the air.

Kaplyn and the others felt uneasy and they glanced about the treetops. Thaneck approached and, seeing their apprehension, grinned wolfishly. "Do not fear, we are merely calling to our steeds. You might have heard of them — dristal?"

Kaplyn remembered the name from childhood tales. "I thought that they were a myth."

The dwarf shook his head. "Many dristal live in the mountains of our homeland, but their numbers are dwindling," the dwarf said. "They are difficult to catch and even harder to train, so we rear them from hatchlings."

"What is a dristal?" Tumarl asked. As though in reply to his question, a plaintive cry echoed through the wood, causing everyone to look up.

"Come and you will soon find out," Thaneck said, leading them to the edge of the wood. In the distance they could see several small specks against a dark and forbidding sky. As they watched, the shapes grew in size until they could clearly see giant wings beating against the chill air. Tumarl sucked in his breath in awe.

They were gigantic birds of prey, very similar to an eagle, but much larger. The first alighted gracefully on a small grassy knoll not far from the wood. Its talons were huge and Lars could not help but stare uncertainly at the massive birds. A dwarf ran out to greet the dristal, running his hand through its neck feathers.

"*No!*" Lars said. "There's absolutely no way that I'm going to ride one of those. If Valra had meant us to fly, he would not have asked Kantral to give us legs."

"Valra?" Kaplyn asked.

"The god of the air," Lars pronounced, making a sweeping gesture with his arm.

"I agree," Lomar said. "They look like they would rather eat us than carry us."

"It's the dristal or KinKassack," Kaplyn said.

Tumarl grimaced. "I'll take my chance with the dristal," he said. "Besides, dwarves ride them and survive."

"Maybe the dwarves taste bad," Lars said, his eyes wide with fear.

They watched as the dwarves unloaded some of their heavy packs. They then unrolled leather saddles that looked too fragile to support them. A short while later, six dristal were ready for the dwarves to ride, each bird now wore a double saddle and harness.

"A dristal normally carries two dwarves," Thaneck explained, re-joining the group. "One controls its flight — well as much as possible," he admitted somewhat sheepishly. "The other rider is armed with a crossbow and watches the sky in case of attack; the grakyn have become bold of late."

Behind him, five dwarves mounted the giant birds and adjusted the flying harnesses. Clearly, the bulk of the patrol was remaining where they were. Thaneck led them towards the great birds. "Do not worry about your supplies, I have asked Delbarl to follow us." A dwarf standing by Thaneck's side bowed low to Kaplyn at the mention of his name.

Kaplyn thanked him and then approached the foremost bird, eyeing it warily. Thaneck mounted first, making it look easy. Kaplyn found a stirrup and put a foot in it and, taking Thaneck's proffered hand, he climbed up. Once on the bird's back he grinned down at his companions, but no one returned his smile.

"Valra," Lars said solemnly. "Hear my prayer and do not let this bird fall from the sky. And, if you are listening, do not let it eat your servant."

Kaplyn smiled. The stories that he had heard about Lars' gods suggested they were likely to ignore the big man's prayers in any event. Lars mounted and sat on his dristal looking completely miserable. The others also mounted and, without waiting, the great birds launched themselves into the sky. They were much slower and less graceful than the dragon Kaplyn had ridden and he, at least, felt at ease.

He looked down at the ground far below and watched as the small wood receded into the distance. Glancing around at his companions, he saw that they were coping, although Lars' eyes were tightly shut. Tumarl had overcome his fear and was looking around wide eyed with curiosity whilst Lomar sat erect, seeming indifferent to the experience.

Flying only served to remind Kaplyn about his dragon flight and recurring nightmares. Thinking about them now, he realised that he did not even know how he had actually summoned the dragon. He cast his mind back to the rooftop in CarCamel with the smoke of battle partially obscuring the breach in the wall and the enemy flooding through. He had raised his sword and for a moment the runes on the blade had seemed to dance, unless it had been a trick of the light. To his surprise the dragon had not appeared evil as in the dreams, and yet a voice within his mind seemed to urge him not to trust it.

After the battle, he had been asked to lead an army against Trosgarth, riding on a dragon at the army's head. Kaplyn could not explain his concerns but the prospect had terrified him. That was one reason why he had left the city; the other was Vastra. Thinking about him made him angry. If it was not for him, Kaplyn would have returned to his family and perhaps could have saved them.

Abruptly he noticed a mountain range looming up on their right and was distracted from his melancholy by the mountain's bleak magnificence. Each peak rose sharply into the sky whilst rocky crags plunged steeply into deep valleys. Unlike other mountains he had seen, these were bare and forlorn, being mainly rock; nothing seemed to grow on their sheer slopes. Each summit they flew over seemed to be more perilous than the last, and vast screes marked ancient rock falls.

Kaplyn was riding with Thaneck and, throughout the journey, the dwarf had remained silent. Now he pointed down and shouted above the noise of the wind. "Kaldor," he said simply.

Kaplyn looked where he was pointing. Below was a narrow plateau. Three sides of the plateau were surrounded by cliffs, on the fourth side the mountain rose sheer, disappearing high in the sky, wreathed in sombre looking clouds. Small, dark openings in the mountain marked windows and doors overlooking the plateau and Kaplyn guessed that this was a city. To Kaplyn the rock walls were dark and gloomy, but Thaneck beamed down at the city with obvious pride.

The dristal spread their wings and spiralled down toward the high walls and, as Kaplyn's stomach lurched at the sudden descent, he suppressed a growing feeling of dread.

Chapter 2

Discovery

Guided by their riders, the dristal spiralled down in a tight arc, aiming towards the plateau within the high walls. Below, small figures scurried about, clearing a landing space for the incoming flight. In the last few seconds of their descent, the ground suddenly seemed to speed up towards them, causing the inexperienced passengers to recoil in fear. However, with only a slight jar, the great birds alighted, folding their wings beneath their bodies and cocking their heads as though awaiting further orders.

The riders climbed down, the dwarves descending nimbly with their passengers following as best they could. Lars staggered towards Kaplyn, looking unsteady as though his legs were unaccustomed to the motionless ground. Even still, he was smiling broadly and had a look of wonder in his eyes. Tumarl also seemed visibly moved by his experience and even managed a rare smile. Lomar's bird alighted last of all and he joined the others His pale complexion and scarlet eyes made his expression uncertain so that Kaplyn could not decide how the journey had affected him.

A knot of excited dwarves formed around the four men. Many carried weapons although at the moment they seemed more curious than threatening. Kaplyn realised the dwarves probably had little contact with the outside races.

Thaneck spoke briefly to the crowd, assuring them that the strangers were friends. With reluctance their ranks parted, allowing Thaneck to lead the small band towards a large portal set beneath an embellished stone archway. Small globes, set at intervals, faintly illuminated the passage.

"I recognise these," Lomar said, walking over to one of the globes. "Look, they shine like the cavern walls we saw in BanKildor. You remember, the walls glowed just like these lamps."

Thaneck smiled. "Inside the glass, lichen feeds on damp and minerals within the rock, and as a result emit light."

The tunnel was broad and beautifully shaped and the walls shone like mirrors. Tall carvings depicted all manner of landscapes, and Kaplyn was surprised by the abundant forest scenes. Shortly afterwards the passageway changed and the carvings were replaced by colourful tapestries and huge plants in tall clay vases.

"These plants are the only flora that will grow in these conditions," Thaneck explained.

They passed by a few dwarves, but far fewer than Kaplyn expected for such a large habitat. Then Thaneck led them up some winding stairs, at the top of which they entered another tunnel, heading which way they could not tell.

"Here we are," Thaneck declared at length. "I think this part of the city will be most suitable to your tastes." Daylight filtered through tall windows hewn in the rock face. "Come, I'll show you the view," he offered.

Thaneck opened a wooden doorway; drawing back a heavy bolt rusted with age, and went out onto a balcony surrounded by a stone battlement. They ascended a stone stair to the parapet. Looking over the wall, Kaplyn was astounded by the scene before them. They were high up on a cliff-face, overlooking a vast forest that stretched as far as the eye could see. The tops of the trees were a light green, but in the distance darkness obscured the forest as though a giant hand stretched over it, blotting out what little light there was.

"When we first came here there was no need for a defensive wall since the forest served to protect us," Thaneck explained sadly. "However, over a few generations, a cancer has spread and the forest is now a dark and malevolent place where not even the dwarves dare to go. It is a great shame, for, although we love our caverns, we also love forests, but this one has become tainted..."

"It is KinKassack," Tumarl stated flatly. His breath was short and his eyes wide as he surveyed the place that had very nearly become his grave.

Kaplyn, Lars and Lomar each looked shocked by Tumarl's statement.

"I had not realised we were so close," Kaplyn said in a hushed voice as though afraid the forest might hear.

"Over the past few years there have been several attacks by grakyn," Thaneck continued as though he had not heard Kaplyn. "We have to be careful and seldom venture far from the city. Even here on the battlements it is no longer safe. Fortunately, in daylight, we can see an attack coming. The grakyn have also learnt to respect our dristal patrols."

Thaneck saw their looks of concern as they glanced uneasily skyward. "Come, you must be tired. It was a long night — let me take you to your quarters."

With that the dwarf left the narrow battlement and, descending the stair, led them through the doorway into the city once more. Thaneck shut and bolted the door and escorted them along the corridor, turning off the main tunnel into a smaller side passage. He entered a house cut into the rock. The first room they entered was large and furnished with several comfortable-looking chairs and, more importantly, beds. Fruit had been piled high on a stone table and a jug of mulled wine filled the air with a delicious aroma.

"Make yourselves at home," Thaneck said. "I have to report to the King. Eat and then rest; I will return early this evening."

They thanked the dwarf who promptly left. Lars poured four goblets of wine and then selected some fruit. Kaplyn and Lomar looked about the room, enjoying the tapestries and marvelling at the craftsmanship of the furniture.

"They have not returned our weapons," Tumarl noted bleakly.

"Don't worry," Kaplyn replied. "I am sure that they mean no harm and, besides, there is no guard."

"Where would we escape to anyway?" Lomar said, picking up his wine and warming his hands. "You saw the forest."

"Well I for one am tired," Kaplyn admitted. However, the seed of doubt Tumarl had sown was now causing him concern. "Let's sleep for now and we will see what happens later."

They were woken some time later by Thaneck, accompanied by several heavily armoured dwarves. At first Kaplyn thought they were in danger, but the dwarves returned their weapons, although they asked them to leave them in the room until after their audience with the King.

Kaplyn checked the sword was his and as he drew it there was no mistaking the dark metal and the flowing inscription. Satisfied, he re-sheathed it and agreed to leave the weapon behind.

They entered a long hall, stretching far into the distance. A thick carpet softened their footsteps, and a faint smell of burning oil filled the room from the many torches that hung in iron brackets. Beneath rich tapestries, guards stood to attention, each holding a tall axe

The King sat on a throne at the far end of the hall. He was an imposing figure. His clothes reflected great wealth; gold thread decorated the collar and cuffs of his scarlet robe of state and pearls were sewn around the lapels. A fur stole was wrapped about his shoulders and he held a stout gold mace in his ancient hands. However the King looked far from content. His shoulders sagged and his eyes harboured a terrible sadness.

"Sire," Thaneck said, bowing low as he came before the throne. "These are our guests."

Kaplyn and the others bowed respectfully.

Thaneck turned to the small group. "May I introduce King Elador, Monarch of Kaldor and the dwarven kingdom east of the Mountains of Mist. It is our custom for newcomers to announce themselves so that all might hear their voices and know that they come in peace."

"I am Kaplyn, King of Allund," Kaplyn announced, stepping forward. He had not acknowledged his title before but after the battle of CarCamel he had become accustomed to the fact that his family was gone and the title was his. Now he must bear it with pride.

Lomar stepped forward and bowed. "I am Prince Lomar, an Alvalan from Gilfillan," he said softly. There was a dispute over his title at present. Otherwise he, too, could claim to be the monarch of his people.

Lars was next. The big man stepped forward uncertainly. "Lars," he said, "Glan-Can of Gorlanth." He too had not acknowledged his title before, but he must assume his father was dead and therefore he was indeed the Glan-Can, even though he was far from home and unlikely to ever return.

Tumarl looked uncertain as to what he should say and then he stepped forward blushing. "Tumarl, a farmer from Thrace."

"You travel in high company," King Elador said after a moment's pause. "If I had known I had such exalted guests you would have been quartered in the royal wing.

"You and your companions have my thanks for helping my people when the grakyn attacked. Thaneck has told me of your mission and we shall not prevent you from entering Aldrace. Indeed, I offer you our help and hope that, after a rest, we will be able to speed you on your journey.

"I was aware of the army from Trosgarth as it marched south to attack your lands," he continued less certainly. "As you can see around you," the old monarch said, sweeping his arm about the hall, "my people are few and we could not help against the full force of Trosgarth. However, I am relieved to find that the enemy was defeated. Be assured that we have done much to ensure that as few krell as possible have managed to return home."

"Your Highness is gracious," Kaplyn said bowing. "I am sure that the people of Thrace will send an envoy to thank you personally when they hear of your help."

The King smiled as though, for the moment at least, his cares were fewer. "I have something I would like to show you." His mood seemed to lift as he rose and motioned for Kaplyn and the others to follow.

Several guards left their posts to follow behind. The group left through a narrow door concealed by tapestries hanging behind the throne and followed a tunnel that plunged steeply down into the heart of the mountain.

After a short while they came to a small, circular chamber with an altar at its centre where four fully armoured dwarves solemnly stood guard. Upon the altar rested a suit of armour, held upright by a golden cross. Glow globes were positioned around the armour and their faint light reflected from the interlocking plates. This was unlike any armour Kaplyn had seen before.

"Dragon scales," Kaplyn announced incredulously. His eyes shone brightly as he strode over to the armour. "This must be Hanet's armour. He was the dwarf king who fought at DrummondCal, helping Darwyl and the Eldric to defeat Drachar."

"A long time ago," the monarch nodded sagely. "Much has happened since then and not all good — we have lost Hanet's axe."

Kaplyn realised then that the armoured gauntlets held in front of the dragon armour were set in such a position that the haft of an axe could be slipped inside them.

"That was the axe given to the dwarves by the Eldric?" Kaplyn asked.

"Yes," the King acknowledged. "It was lost long ago. Once, this was a thriving city with dwarf children aplenty, running about the caverns and causing mischief — a city to be compared with Thandor, from which my people fled so long ago and which is forbidden to us. Now our city is quiet, it is as if some curse has been cast against us."

The King looked sad as he continued. "Thandor has now become but a dream. That is a terrible burden for our people. Perhaps that is why our numbers dwindle. I, like many others, long to see our ancient home. We have sent several emissaries there, seeking pardon for our people, but none have returned. I do not think that it is purely the evil of KinKassack that keeps our homeland hidden from us. I believe a greater evil is at work.

"It is partly due to our own folly after the Krell Wars. We assumed Drachar was gone completely from this world, and we relaxed our vigil on our borders, concentrating instead on finding gold and other wealth. Before our people left Thandor, we were content, and then a rumour sprang up that if we dug deep enough we would find Tel-Am-Nythryn at the heart of the mountains."

"What is Tel-Am-Nythryn?" Kaplyn asked.

The King's eyes shone. "Nythryn is a jewel unsurpassed by any other, the greatest treasure of the dwarves. Our legends tell us that the Kalanth hid Nythryn deep in the mountains, knowing that we would find it one day. Everywhere we dug, and yet we found only gold and diamonds. These we ignored, so great was our desire to find Nythryn. Can you imagine? A dwarf — ignoring gold." Elador said, looking at Kaplyn.

Kaplyn nodded, allowing the King to continue. "One day we found an especially long vein of gold. It was as though it was placed there to guide us. For long days my people laboured to reach its heart. It was then that we discovered our bane." The King hung his head. "We found a jewel beyond compare and its beauty was immeasurable. And yet a cold green light shone from its heart. We knew it was not Nythryn for green is associated with the demon world. But even still, it was like looking upon heaven.

"At first it was set in the market place where everyone could see it. It was named Tel-Am-Talwyn — the healer, for all that looked upon it felt as if their soul was released from torment. We kept digging seeking Nythryn but no other jewels were found. Then, one day, a calamity befell us; Talwyn was stolen. A search of the kingdom revealed that a noble called Wynthren had stolen it for his own and hidden it within his hall. Greed seized our once great nation, and immediately all work ceased and a terrible civil war beset our kingdom. Armies were summoned from the other dwarven kingdoms and they marched to Thandor to fight in the Dwarven Wars as they are now known.

"The king at the time was Nynvanar, a good and noble monarch directly descended from Hanet himself. He tried his best to stop the war, calling on the dwarves to lay down their arms. But a great hatred had taken hold of their hearts and a deep desire to see Talwyn drove them onwards so that no one would stop to listen to reason.

"Unfortunately Wynthren, the noble who had stolen Talwyn, was very powerful and had allegiances in other dwarf kingdoms who rallied to his call for help.

"King Nynvanar was left with no choice but to take sides and end the conflict. Otherwise his kingdom would be divided forever. At the head of a great army, he laid siege to Wynthren's fortified home. Seeing the King in full dragon armour and carrying Hanet's axe, Wynthren knew that his forces could not hold out for long. One night he disguised himself, and, carrying Talwyn, he escaped his fortress and went unrecognised through the surrounding army. Wynthren left Thandor and set off across country, hoping to meet with dwarves he had summoned from the Southern Kingdoms.

"With their leader gone, Wynthren's followers laid down their arms and sued for pardon. The King, in a rage, ordered these dwarves exiled. With a large army the King immediately went in pursuit of Wynthren.

"It was said that Wynthren made his way into KinKassack, which at this time was still a wholesome place. The King's army was hot in pursuit when an army of krell and grakyn attacked. It was a well-laid ambush and the King's forces were completely ensnared. The King wrought havoc upon the enemy, for his armour was impenetrable, proof against even the strongest magic.

461

"Even though many dwarves were killed, it looked as though they would be able to hold and eventually turn the tide of battle. At that moment, a new force arrived from Trosgarth, led by death knights."

"Death Knights?" Kaplyn queried, "I have never heard of them before, not even in legends."

The old King nodded. "Neither had we. It was a new enemy from Trosgarth. I do not understand what evil managed to create such a being, but they were a terrible foe who could only be banished from this world by chance. Apparently iron through the heart killed them, but few managed to deliver a mortal blow, especially since they were armoured. My father, a cousin to Nynvanar who was at the battle, told me of this horror."

Kaplyn had forgotten that the dwarves lived much longer than the other races and was shocked to think that Elador had a first hand account of a battle so long ago. He realised that the old dwarf was speaking once more and he listened to the tale.

"The death knights proved too strong for the dwarf army and few could face them. Nynvanar himself fought their leader, a dark knight called Straum. They fought for a long time, but Straum could not be wearied and only one blow could kill him. Nynvanar's dragon armour turned even Straum's evil blade whilst the axe of Hanet clove the death knight's armour. But the death knight was also a sorcerer and, as Nynvanar weakened, Straum summoned the *dead;* unseen hands wrenched the ancient weapon from Nynvanar's grasp, leaving the dwarf King defenceless. Any other magic would not have worked on Nynvanar because of his dragon armour, but the dead Straum had summoned were tangible beings, and they held the King while Straum lifted a plate of the dragon armour and thrust his immortal blade deep into the King's heart.

"The dwarves were lost then. Many sought to escape, carrying the King's lifeless body with them. They went into KinKassack, forsaking their comrades who were butchered to the last. Hanet's axe was lost, but the dragon armour was saved and brought here. This was a minor kingdom, but the arrival of the defeated army swelled its numbers so that in its day this was a thriving city.

"What became of Thandor is not known, nor is the fate of Wynthren and the Talwyn, the stolen jewel. Since then, we have often tried to make contact with Thandor, but no word of the city ever comes back to us and our messengers simply disappear."

A silence fell over the group. "Have you searched for Hanet's axe?" Kaplyn asked eventually.

The King nodded, but his look conveyed his doubts that it would ever be found again.

"You want us to see if the axe is in Drishnack?" Kaplyn guessed, knowing that the King's tale was leading somewhere.

The King paused before speaking, knowing that he was perhaps expecting too much. "That was my hope," he admitted at length, speaking softly.

"What does the weapon look like?" Kaplyn asked. "I mean, how do we distinguish it from other axes?"

"It was an Eldric weapon. The metal is black and there are fine silver runes inlaid into its surface, very like your sword. Your pardon," he continued, "I took the liberty of looking at the weapon whilst you slept."

Kaplyn did not mind and he told the King so. Smiling, and somewhat relieved, the old King escorted them from the chamber and they retraced their way back to the throne room where Thaneck took his leave of his monarch and escorted Kaplyn and the others back to their room.

That night Kaplyn lay awake, unable to sleep. He dreaded the dragon dreams that haunted his sleep and instead refused to succumb to weariness. In the dead of night, frustrated by the lack of sleep, he swung his legs out of his bed and dressed hurriedly leaving their house. It was late and few dwarves were about; those who were gave him peculiar sideways looks as he went by.

He had no idea where he was going. He only knew that he did not want to dream about dragons. After a short while, he found himself in a dark, narrow passage that descended steeply. His heart was racing although he did not know why.

"Why are you not abed?" a voice asked from behind.

Turning, Kaplyn saw Thaneck. The dwarf looked concerned, perhaps worried that Kaplyn had betrayed his confidence. "I could not sleep," Kaplyn replied. His attention returned to the tunnel in front of him. "Where does this lead?" A strange sensation swept over him; he felt he knew this place.

"It's a dead end. Our people started to excavate it but, when our numbers dwindled, there was no further need."

Kaplyn started down the tunnel. Thaneck took a nearby glow globe and followed, calling to Kaplyn to return. The dwarf caught up with him only a short way ahead, standing in the tunnel, a strange expression on his face.

"Fetch others," Kaplyn commanded. "Bring digging tools."

"*What?*"

"Just do as I say, trust me."

Thaneck frowned, but sensed the excitement in Kaplyn's voice. Turning, he returned along the tunnel, leaving the glow globe by Kaplyn's feet.

Kaplyn could not explain his feeling. The scar on his chest started to itch furiously. Unbuttoning his shirt his scar was radiating a strong white light akin to the time he had ridden the dragon.

The dwarves were coming and so he hurriedly buttoned his shirt. Behind the dwarves came Thaneck. All were burdened with digging tools although they stood staring uncertainly at Kaplyn as though he had lost his mind.

"Dig here," he said.

"Why?" one of the dwarves grumbled. The others looked at Thaneck, waiting for him to confirm the order.

Kaplyn turned to Thaneck. "I do not know why," he admitted. "It's merely a feeling that something is here."

The dwarf looked at Kaplyn but then smiled. "Come," he said to the others, "Are we not dwarves? Were we not born to dig?" With that he took up a pick and started to attack the cavern floor as though it was a personal enemy. Kaplyn also took up a pick and started to dig alongside him. The others joined in until the cavern rang with the sound of metal on stone.

Kaplyn could not keep up with the dwarves whose endurance kept them going long after he had stopped. His hands ached after digging for so long and yet the dwarves showed no signs of weariness. By now the dwarves were digging in a hole deep enough to stand in and not be seen. Kaplyn was not sure what they were looking for, but a strange feeling of familiarity persisted.

Several times Thaneck glanced towards Kaplyn, his eyes suggested that he hoped Kaplyn knew what he was doing. Just as Kaplyn was beginning to wonder if his senses had betrayed him, a dwarf at the bottom of the hole gave an excited yell. Those not digging crowded around the lip and peered intently into the hole. A large crystal had been partially unearthed and a deep ruby light emanated from it, filling the hollow with its gentle radiance. The dwarves fell silent in respect.

"It's a kara-stone," Kaplyn said, breaking the spell that held them. Thaneck dropped down into the hole and timidly touched the jewel as though expecting it to react in some way. Reverently he dug at the loose rock surrounding it, using a knife from his belt to work the jewel free. Eventually it loosened and he raised his prize for the others to see. As the light from the crystal lit the tunnel a smell of spring seemed to surround them. The dwarves grinned broadly as they looked with marvel upon the orb. Thaneck climbed from the hole and presented it to Kaplyn.

Kaplyn tentatively placed his hand on the stone. The scar upon his chest itched more furiously than before, and he feared that its light might actually shine through his clothing. He knew that he was taking a risk touching the jewel. When he had held Lomar's kara-stone, he had a vision through the eyes of one of the Kalanth. Then he had seen the world, many aeons past, and had known that at the end of the experience that the Kalanth had lain down to die, if that was possible.

As his hand rested on the orb he was filled with a great sense of wonder. There was no vision this time. Perhaps, if it was the remains of another Kalanth, it had gone too far beyond the world for him to feel its presence. He remembered a name though, and the part of him that had joined with the Kalanth from Lomar's kara-stone wept with a mixture of joy and sorrow. It was with great reluctance that he finally removed his hand.

The stone was not evil. Of that he was certain.

"We must take this to the King," Thaneck announced seriously. "It is a wonderful discovery." Turning to one of the other dwarves, he bid him fetch Kaplyn's companions. Together the dwarves, led by Thaneck and Kaplyn, headed for the royal apartments, calling on others to awaken as they went. They approached the King's audience hall with a large excited crowd following. Thaneck held up the kara-stone for all to see and a hush fell over the assembled throng.

Two dwarves of the royal guard left the hall to summon the King, who returned some moments later, still arranging his robes. "What is it, Thaneck?" he asked.

The dwarf raised the kara-stone for the King to see. His eyes nearly popped out of his head as he reached for the orb. "It is beautiful," the King confessed earnestly. "Who found it?"

"Kaplyn," Thaneck replied.

Lomar, Lars and Tumarl came to stand beside Kaplyn. Their eyes shone with wonder as they looked at the jewel resting in the King's broad hands.

"A kara-stone," Lomar said.

Kaplyn nodded.

"It will take time to study and unlock the magic within it," Lomar continued. "Your Highness, my people would be willing to help you in this task," he offered, addressing the King.

The King thanked Lomar, welcoming his people's aid.

"Could I have a look?" Lomar asked. The King handed the stone to Lomar who held it in cupped hands and peered into its depths. He felt the heat within the stone and used this warmth to drive his consciousness within. His experience was different from Kaplyn's. Lomar peeled back the structure within the orb like lifting the petals from a rose. As Lomar probed, the light within the stone grew until the room was filled with its warmth. The dwarves gasped in awe and a loud cheer sounded about the room.

An immense peacefulness emanated from the jewel and a fresh loamy fragrance of freshly dug earth filled the air. All within the chamber suddenly felt young and vital.

The dwarf King's eyes shone with pleasure. "This is a magnificent gift you have discovered," he said addressing Kaplyn, after Thaneck had described how Kaplyn had found it. "We are deeply in your debt. Tonight we will celebrate. It has been a long time since we had a feast worthy of a tale. Let us make this one to remember, for perhaps we have reached a turning point in our history."

Kaplyn and the others found themselves guests of honour in a large banquet hall. The room was filled with bright flowers, hurriedly gathered that morning from the forest. Kaplyn yawned broadly. He had not slept all night, but the heady atmosphere kept him awake.

The dwarves looked resplendent in their burnished armour, and their beards had been groomed and freshly braided and tucked into large ornately decorated belts, crowded with gold and jewels. Wives or companions accompanied many of the dwarves and they, too, had been meticulous with their preparation. Dwarf women took as much pride in their hair as their men-folk did their beards. Indeed, if a dwarf committed an offence, either his beard or her hair was shorn, which was an act of great shame, so that their guilt was known to all.

All at once the dwarves stood, and Kaplyn and his companions did likewise as a respectful hush descended over the hall. At the head of a long procession, the King entered accompanied by nobles and their ladies, bearing more gold and jewels than Kaplyn had seen in his lifetime.

There was a gasp of awe as the assembled dwarves recognised the dragon armour the King wore. Behind him came a group of dwarves carrying the recently discovered kara-stone, held aloft upon a cushion. As the group passed by, glow globes dimmed as though they could not compete with the light from the jewel.

The King seated himself next to Kaplyn and commanded that the feast commence. There were many courses and the food was both varied and rich. Wine, as cool as a mountain spring, was in abundance and, after tasting it, Lars declared he would never drink ale ever again.

As the meal progressed, the dwarves became more and more boisterous, with songs breaking out at many of the tables. A troop of dwarfish acrobats performed about the tables to great applause. The act was more of a comedy as the dwarves tumbled around the chamber in a series of feats that left Kaplyn and the others stunned. Kaplyn watched amazed as dwarves climbed a tower of precariously placed chairs which promptly collapsed in a heap of wood and bodies much to the approval of the on-looking dwarves who roared with laughter. Kaplyn was amazed that no one was killed.

A dwarf carrying an immense axe followed the acrobats and he called on Lars for his aid. From the amount of wine that Lars had consumed, Kaplyn was concerned about his abilities to throw an axe straight. To Kaplyn's horror, Lars' target was the dwarf's wife who was to be punished for some misdemeanour; her hair was to be ritually cut. She stood in front of an upended table and her long plaits were fastened to the wood either side of her.

At this point, Lars had sobered enough to realise what was being asked of him, and he cast worried looks to Kaplyn who shook his head. Lars tried to decline the dwarf's offer to let him cut his wife's hair, but the dwarf refused, claiming that it was a great honour he was bestowing on him.

The dwarf bid Lars to continue, handing him the axe and positioning him several yards from the woman. The big man hefted the axe, testing its balance. With a fluid motion, the big man drew his arm back and hurled the axe. With a roar of approval, the axe parted a braid of hair and the dwarfish woman shrieked in frustration; if he had missed she would have been allowed to keep her hair long. Sensibly she held her position as her husband recovered the axe.

A silence descended as Lars took aim for his second throw. The axe parted the second braid and a great roar split the air once more. Several flagons of wine were thrust towards the big man who sagged with relief as the woman fled in tears. Dwarves patted the big man on the back and he stood grinning at the assembled throng.

It was much later, when the festivities started to die down, that Kaplyn and the others finally managed to take their leave. Tumarl was in a black mood and the festivities had only served to fuel his despair. He was remembering all too clearly the happy times with his wife before she was killed by krell. Kaplyn and Lars tried to cheer him, but nothing they said seemed to help. Tumarl's depression served to remind Kaplyn that they had to continue their journey and it was with a heavy heart that he lay down to sleep.

Chapter 3

Flight of Fear

They slept through the morning and in the afternoon Thaneck came to talk to them. He told them they were welcome to stay for as long as they liked. Kaplyn was reluctant to leave, but knew they had to. His dreams had been troubled, but not only by the fear of dragons. He had seen again Vastra in his golden cage, and the dream had served to fuel his fear that the enemy might now have a crystal from the Tree of Life.

Thaneck was genuinely sorry when Kaplyn told him that they would be leaving, and he left them as they packed their meagre belongings. Later another dwarf appeared to escort them to the main gate.

Their spirits picked up marginally when they left the tunnels and stood once more in daylight but this was short lived. Low, menacing clouds darkly threatened from horizon to horizon. Most of the mountains were obscured and lightning occasionally flickered across the heavens, briefly illuminating distant lands. The storm was too far away to hear the thunder and the silence was ominous.

The King, accompanied by a retinue of armed guards, came out from the city to bid them farewell. Thaneck followed the King, dressed in mail and carrying an axe at his belt.

"Well met," the King said. "As I promised, we will aid you on your journey. Thaneck has offered to accompany you, at least as far as Thandor should your path take you that way." By his side the dwarf nodded grimly. "I should warn you though," the King continued. "He is stubborn and has made up his mind on this matter so it would seem that you have little choice."

Kaplyn was surprised that Thaneck was willing to follow them into danger, but did not mind the extra company. "Thaneck is more than welcome to accompany us," he said.

Lars smiled warmly and gave the dwarf a friendly pat on the shoulder.

Five dwarves appeared, each leading a dristal by their flight harnesses. The birds were clearly restless, eager to take to the skies. Unlike before, the dristal were dressed for war; leather bonnets, with large eyeholes cut in them, covered their heads and steel blades were attached to their talons. Stout looking crossbows and a full quiver of arrows hung from the saddles.

The birds' huge black eyes fixed on the company, eagerly awaiting them to mount.

Kaplyn once more felt a nervous fluttering in the pit of his stomach. The thought of flying still unnerved him. Lars was putting on a braver face than last time, possibly so as to not disappoint his newfound friends; the dwarves seemed to have adopted Lars as a long lost cousin.

Swiftly the group mounted, with a dwarf taking control of each of the large birds.

"Farewell," the King called up. "Remember, you are always welcome in my halls."

They waved farewell and, with a great cry, the lead bird launched itself into the dark overcast sky. Soon they were high over the city with a spectacular view of KinKassack, stretching far into the horizon. They flew below the dark, brooding clouds. Occasionally lightning flared across the sky and thunder rumbled, reminding Kaplyn of Lars' tale of his god, Sarl, who hunted during storms with his great bow and arrows of fire. Silently he prayed that Sarl would ignore the flight of birds.

Kaplyn was riding with Thaneck and tried to talk to him, but it was difficult. The dwarf's voice was lost in the rush of air so Kaplyn fell silent and, instead, took in the forest scene below. There was little to see other than the canopy. Then, abruptly, something caught his eye and he concentrated on a particularly dark region where he thought movement had occurred. Unfortunately the dristal's wings kept getting into the field of view and the changing air currents caused the dristal's flight to be erratic.

Then Kaplyn realised shapes were moving against the dark foliage of the forest and fearfully he realised he was watching three grakyn in flight. Kaplyn tapped Thaneck's shoulder and pointed down at the grakyn and, at that moment, the grakyn started to rise from the forest in pursuit.

Thaneck signalled to the others, alerting them to the approaching menace. Kaplyn and the other passengers felt helpless even though they had crossbows. They cocked these and loaded bolts. The thought of an aerial battle was discomforting; it was hard enough just keeping their balance. Kaplyn cursed the cloud cover and wished that the sun would break through; being creatures of the demon world, the grakyn would then be disorientated.

A sudden change in the air currents caused Kaplyn to overbalance sufficiently to drop the bolt from the crossbow. Frantically he fitted another and waited for the grakyn to come into range.

All too soon the dark specks became more recognisable and it seemed that their speed increased. Kaplyn could clearly see the large bat-like wings as they beat against the turgid air. Lightning flared and thunder sounded only seconds later, much louder than before.

At that moment the lead grakyn drew back its arm, no doubt to launch its attack. Kaplyn took aim and squeezed the trigger. The bow bucked in his hand and, with a zing, the missile streaked towards its target. Kaplyn had never fired a crossbow before, and the unfamiliarity of the weapon and the constant motion of the flight threw off his aim. The closeness of Kaplyn's bolt caused the grakyn to swerve so that its own aim was spoiled. Kaplyn ducked as a thick, vitriol projectile hurtled past the riders before falling in a low graceful arc to the forest below.

On cue with Kaplyn's attack, the other passengers fired their weapons. Small darts streaked towards the grakyn which dodged frantically to avoid the missiles, screaming in frustration as they did so, causing them to fall back in their pursuit.

Thaneck bent low over the giant bird's neck, urging it to greater speed. A screech of delight erupted from the bird as its powerful wings propelled it forward. Thaneck was trying desperately to keep the bird's attention from the grakyn, hoping the thrill of flight would distract the birds so they could make good their escape. Dristal were territorial creatures who didn't like anything flying within their domain and, since they had tremendous courage, it was very likely that they would turn to attack. So far the plan was succeeding as the gap between the grakyn and the dristal widened.

A sudden bolt of lightning forked brightly in front of the birds, momentarily blinding the riders and causing the dristal to hang momentarily in the air in sudden confusion. A loud clap of thunder followed so that Kaplyn's ears rang and bright lights danced before his eyes. He shook his head and rubbed at his eyes. A bolt of a different type exploded close to Kaplyn's side. His dristal's sudden confusion was gone and its attention was riveted on the grakyn. It didn't recognise the half-demons for what they were; it only saw other creatures flying in its domain. Smaller birds it accepted but these were much too large to ignore.

A high-pitched scream split the air as the great bird launched itself at the demons. The other birds, seeing their leader attack, followed suit. Everyone was thrown into confusion — no less so the grakyn. One moment they were chasing an enemy fleeing before them. Next they faced an all out assault. So intent were they on chasing their prey they had not had time to defend themselves.

The lead dristal's onslaught was devastating. The grakyn were in a ragged line as it struck. One managed to dodge but the other two were caught by the dristal as its razor sharp talons ripped through their wings, sending their bodies tumbling from the sky.

Kaplyn chanced a shot at the remaining grakyn and was rewarded with a hit. The grakyn hovered in the sky, clutching the projectile protruding from its side. Then its wing failed and it, too, followed its brothers.

Thaneck had already turned the lead bird's head back to their original direction, and on cue the other dristal followed. At that moment Thaneck cried out in alarm and pointed below. A dark shape had detached itself from the forest and fear, mixed with dread, seemed to follow in its wake.

Kaplyn realised he was looking at a very powerful demon. Its span was much larger than that of the grakyn and a green aura surrounded it. Thaneck was urging the dristal to greater speed but Kaplyn was not convinced that they would outdistance it. Already the gap between them had narrowed. It seemed to move as if in a different plane of existence; its very motion a parody of evil.

Thaneck realised that flight was impossible and looked toward the cloud for cover, urging his steed to fly higher. Abruptly the sky lit up in a blaze of silver and, for an instant, it was as if the hand of one of Lars' many gods had intervened, parting the fabric between heaven and earth. A massive clap of thunder followed, deafening the riders and steeds alike.

When Kaplyn's vision returned he frantically searched the skies for their pursuer — to his relief whatever it was had vanished. He prayed that it had been struck by lightning and sent back to the underworld from which it had emerged.

At that moment the heavens opened and a torrential downpour started. The dristal were furious. They did not normally fly in rain, preferring instead to seek shelter, but their riders urged them on.

The remainder of the flight was dismal. The passengers tried to shelter as much as possible, but, whichever way they turned, rain lashed their faces. The dwarves were hard pressed to keep their mounts flying and eventually Thaneck decided it would be better to land. The ground was getting harder to see and they could soon be lost.

The great birds spiralled down, glad to be leaving the inhospitable skies. As they lost height, the land became more distinct and Kaplyn was relieved to see that they were well beyond KinKassack. Thaneck directed the flight towards a small wood that was the only cover in the otherwise featureless landscape. Landing, they took shelter beneath the trees. The great birds immediately started to preen themselves and gradually their tempers lessened.

"Where do you think we are, Kaplyn?" Lars asked.

Kaplyn shrugged; he was totally lost.

"We're in Aldrace," Thaneck replied on his behalf. "And, if I am not mistaken, Drishnack is only a few hours walk from here. It is probably as well that we landed here; any nearer and their patrols might have spotted us."

"You have done well," Kaplyn said.

The dwarf grinned mischievously. "It was close," he admitted. "We must have travelled farther than I'd anticipated."

"What now?" Kaplyn asked.

"When the rain lessens the others will return to Kaldor with the dristal. If they fly high enough then they should not encounter any difficulties. How, though, do you intend to enter Drishnack?" Thaneck asked.

Kaplyn was not sure. He was taking their journey one step at a time.

By the time the rain had lessened, it was too late for the dwarves to leave, and so they made camp for the night. By nightfall it had stopped raining and so they tried to dry their clothes by a small fire.

In the morning, after a hurried breakfast, they bade farewell to their dwarven companions and watched as they flew high into a grey sky.

Kaplyn was still no nearer to a solution to his problem of how to enter Drishnack. It still seemed distant and they decided to keep travelling until they could at least see the city. The image of Vastra that Astalus had shown him came back to haunt him and he felt despair. They might never be able to get into the city, but he had made his mind up that they would at least try. Vastra held the key to what happened to his crystal from the Tree of Life, and Kaplyn was determined to wring an answer from him.

After a while the wood thinned and, before them, was an open expanse of undulating ground across which a narrow road wended its way towards the horizon. Unlike the lush lands they had left, Aldrace was bleak and sparse. Sage grass grew high, covering most of the land and tall brambles interrupted the otherwise spartan landscape. It was a weary place lacking the health and vitality of other lands they had travelled. Lomar seemed to be the most affected by the transition, and his eyes had a weary haunted look to them as though he could see the illness deep in the heart of the country. The pact Aldrace had made with Trosgarth had been an unholy alliance and evil was seeping into the land.

Kaplyn halted the group and they lay on the lip of a small rise surrounded by sparse trees. Almost immediately a figure appeared in the distance, moving along the track. The onlookers crouched lower in the rough vegetation and in silence waited. After a while longer they could make out a horse and rider.

"A Priest of Ryoch," Lars hissed. Kaplyn could see the familiar ochre robes of the priest's order. A knot formed in the pit of his stomach as he thought about his people in Allund held under the sway of the self-appointed priests. As if sensing his anger, Lars placed a hand on his shoulder, seeking to pacify him.

"Let's take him prisoner and question him," Kaplyn said through gritted teeth.

Lars nodded and crawled around the hillock, down into the gully at the side of the track where he hid among the long grass. Soon they could hear the horse's hooves.

As the horse and rider passed Lars' hiding place, the big man leapt out, grabbing the reins. The sudden appearance of the big man threw the rider and horse into panic. Kaplyn and the others charged down the slope to be at Lars' side, but there was no need. The horse reared and fell onto its side, toppling the priest from the saddle. For a moment the priest lay winded on the ground, but then frantically sought to stand. Kaplyn was too quick for him and, in an instant, his blade was at the priest's throat.

The priest froze, a look of pure hatred upon his face although the rattle of his breathing betrayed his fear. Kaplyn judged him to be young, but his shaven head made it difficult to guess his exact age.

"Beware," Tumarl warned by Kaplyn's side. "He might take his own life rather than be taken captive."

Lars held the priest's arms while Kaplyn searched him. He found a small knife concealed within his robes. Kaplyn took the weapon and tucked it into his belt. Lars then bound the priest before lifting him onto his shoulders. Leading his horse, they went deeper into the wood.

There was something about the priest that puzzled Kaplyn. He seemed less sure of himself than other priests Kaplyn had encountered and his eyes darted nervously about the wood. Perhaps he was new to the priesthood.

They came across a small ravine that offered an ideal campsite, surrounded by trees and hidden from prying eyes. The priest was sweating freely; beads of sweat spotted his brow and flies crawled around his face. Since his hands were tied behind his back, he was forced to shake his head to rid himself of them. Lars tied him to the base of a broad tree while the rest made camp.

Kaplyn considered their options. The sudden appearance of the priest seemed to be more than a coincidence, and he now realised he had a way of entering the city, but it would mean going alone. The more he thought about it, the better his plan seemed and eventually he decided. Softly, since they were deep in unfriendly lands, he called the group together and took them beyond hearing of the priest who was bravely trying to ignore everyone.

"I have decided on a plan to get into Drishnack," he said.

"You are planning to go alone, aren't you?" Lars asked.

473

"I have to," Kaplyn replied. "You, Lomar and Thaneck cannot come, you would attract too much attention." By their side Tumarl looked eager to go. However, Kaplyn did not want Tumarl with him in case he behaved rashly. "I must go alone," he insisted. "I'll enter the city dressed as a Priest of Ryoch and, since there is only one robe, only one person can go."

"You cannot go to Drishnack on your own. It is far too dangerous," Lars argued.

"It would be dangerous for all of us," Kaplyn admitted. "But at least I have an Allund accent, and we know that the priests have been recruiting there. I also know many towns and cities in Allund so if anyone questions me I can at least answer honestly."

With some reluctance Lars finally agreed that Kaplyn should go.

"Tumarl, search his saddlebags," Kaplyn asked.

The others forced the priest to strip. Naked, he squatted by the tree, shivering in the cold morning air. Tumarl returned with his saddlebags but they contained nothing of consequence. Wrapping a blanket about the priest, they tied him once more to the tree.

Kaplyn shuddered at the prospect of putting on the priest's clothes. They smelt vile and he was sure he saw a flea. Then he asked Lars to shave his head.

Tumarl questioned the priest but could get nothing from him. In disgust Tumarl gave up just as Lars finished shaving Kaplyn. The others grinned broadly as Kaplyn stood.

"What do you think?" he asked.

"Try on the robe," Thaneck suggested.

Kaplyn didn't want the others and, especially the priest, seeing his scar. Feigning modesty he went behind a bush to change. The robe was more disgusting than he had realised. It was coarse, damp and it itched. When he returned he felt foolish, but the others assured him he would pass for one of the priests. Kaplyn didn't take that as a compliment.

"I had better go," he said. "He may be expected today, and besides I would be better off entering the city at dusk when the guard will hopefully be less alert. The rest of you had better wait here until I return. There should be enough game hereabouts to keep off hunger. If I'm not back in a week, you'd better make your way back to CarCamel."

Lars shook his head and the others looked uncomfortable.

"Rest assured, if you do not return, we will come and find you," Lomar replied.

Kaplyn smiled. "I hope that's not necessary."

They bade him farewell and, with a heavy heart, Kaplyn led the priest's horse through the wood to the track, reluctant to leave his weapons behind but there was little choice. Mounting, he set off alone towards the distant city.

Chapter 4

Drishnack

It didn't take long before Kaplyn caught sight of Drishnack, and he drew rein for a moment to look at the formidable walls. It was growing dark and the sky was overcast with little light filtering through the sombre clouds.

All at once he felt very much alone. His only friends were several miles away, hiding in a wood which he was starting to fear he might never find again. His robes itched and the crystal in his chest felt strange. He turned his thoughts to Catriona, the Thracian Queen, and his heart turned leaden with the prospect that he might not see her again.

"Let's get on with it," he muttered to his horse as he urged the animal on. He rode towards the city gates that towered over him like the maw of a huge dark beast. Above, he could see figures on top of the wall. By now they had surely seen him, and he tried to ignore his growing fear as he entered the city.

A guard by the gate hailed him and he made his way towards him. He was a tall, broad-shouldered man, dressed in heavy armour that clanked noisily as he moved. A broadsword and dagger hung from his waist and he carried a long spear.

"You are lucky to make it before we shut the gates for the night," the guard rebuked in good humour.

Kaplyn relaxed marginally. "It's been a long ride."

"Do you know where to go?" the guard asked.

Kaplyn shook his head.

"The other priests are billeted in the eastern sector of the city — you will need an escort though. If you wait here I will go and find somebody."

Kaplyn had hoped to be able to wander freely through the city, and his look of alarm must have shown for the guard spoke again.

"Don't worry; it's for your own protection. Not many Aldracians like the priesthood."

At that, the sentry turned and disappeared within the guardroom. Kaplyn heard his voice calling for a volunteer. Briefly he considered riding into the city on his own but quickly discounted the idea for it would make the guard suspicious. At least for the moment, he was accepted as a priest and as long as the disguise held he was safe.

The guard returned accompanied with another fellow, a surly looking, unkempt individual who was moaning at having to escort a novice at that time of day. Without a word his escort set off into the city, muttering beneath his breath as he went.

Kaplyn dismounted and led his horse after the fellow just as the gates started to shut ominously behind him. He couldn't help looking back at his last sight of freedom for only the Kalanth knew how long, and he wondered if he was making a big mistake.

He was hard pressed to follow his guide who had set off at a fair pace. He fixed his attention on the man's broad shoulders. It was quiet and Kaplyn saw few people. To either side of the street the buildings were tall and narrow and, on close inspection, were in a bad state of repair. He also noticed that many of the windows were shuttered which gave the city an eerie feel. Abruptly his guide stopped and Kaplyn nearly collided with his back.

"In there," the fellow said. "Horse to the left, billets to the right." With that he turned on his heel and was off.

The opening led into a dark courtyard. Once again, Kaplyn considered going off on his own, but worried that a lone priest wandering the city might bring unwanted attention. He decided to trust to his disguise and luck as he led his mount into the courtyard. The stables were nearly full. However, he found one stall empty and, after attending to his mount, he went in search of his quarters.

Entering through an arched doorway, he stepped into a brightly-lit hall and his heart lurched. The room was crowded with men wearing ochre robes and each man's head was shaven. All eyes turned towards him and he froze, suddenly unsure of himself. It was a dormitory judging by the number of beds, and the priests were either standing or sitting in small groups.

"Well man? Shut the door; you are letting the cold out," a deep voice rang out. Its owner, a big fellow with a long, hooked nose, stared intently at him as if daring him to reply.

Several others laughed and Kaplyn realised the door was still open. He shut it quickly which resulted in a loud bang as a gust of wind caught it. He had certainly made an entrance and, far from being unnoticed, he was now the centre of attention.

Kaplyn's eyes searched the room for a spare bed, and he saw one about half way along the room. Blood rushed to his cheeks as he made his way towards it. His mind was in turmoil as he considered his options. For the moment at least he could only focus on the bed and getting there without gaining more attention. So intent was he that he failed to notice one of the priests who stuck out a leg. Kaplyn fell in an untidy heap as laughter filled the room.

In a way it was a good thing that he had been tripped; the other priests mistook his red cheeks for anger. Slowly he picked himself up and dusted himself off. Turning, he gave the fellow who had tripped him up a long hard look. The other man stopped laughing, seeing the dangerous glint in Kaplyn's eye.

"No offence," he said raising his arms. "You just came in at the wrong time."

Kaplyn nodded and risked looking about the room at the others who were returning to their idle chatter, leaving him free to get to the bed in peace.

He lay his saddlebags down and sat on the bed, not knowing what to do or say. A young man sat on the bed next to Kaplyn's and he decided to speak to him. "How long have you been here?" he asked.

The man looked surprised to be addressed. He was younger than Kaplyn, probably in his early twenties.

"Two days," he said. "Where are you from?"

Kaplyn had been prepared for this. "Pendrat, it's a small town," he said quietly hoping nobody else would overhear him.

The other man didn't show any signs of recognising the name and Kaplyn breathed more easily. "Are we confined to this room?"

"Yes. Until we are invested into the priesthood."

Kaplyn suddenly felt very cold. A thousand questions tumbled through his mind, but he was afraid to ask in case the other man became suspicious.

"Do not worry. At least we don't have long to wait," his new companion told him. "The ceremony is tomorrow."

Kaplyn looked perplexed. "*Tomorrow*?" he repeated.

The other nodded. "I'll be glad when it's over. I couldn't put up with this fleapit for much longer."

Kaplyn was surprised by the other's candour and was finding it hard to believe that this man was a Priest of Ryoch; he found himself warming to him.

"What's your name?" the priest asked.

The question took Kaplyn by surprise. He had anticipated most things and overlooked the obvious. "Kaplyn," he replied, aware that he had already hesitated sufficiently. Here, his own name was as good as any.

The priest grinned broadly, "Mine is Rodric. I'm from West Meath," he said. "Do you have any idea what is going to happen tomorrow?"

478

"No," he admitted, knowing that a lie claiming to know otherwise was likely to catch him out.

"Neither do I," the other agreed.

"They are going to introduce us to Ryoch himself," a man on Kaplyn's other side announced, joining in their conversation. At the mention of *that* name several others around the room took interest, and Kaplyn found himself the centre of a large group all debating what was going to happen. No one seemed to know and the guesses being bandied about surely had to be wide of the mark.

Where before there was relative quiet, now everyone was talking, expressing their view of the coming events. The banter in general was friendly and, amongst the many voices, he recognised different Allund accents, bringing memories of home flooding back.

He jumped when the door behind him slammed with a bang. The room fell silent as everyone turned to see who had entered. Framed within the doorway stood a priest who positively glared at the novices. He was a large, well-built man whose bushy eyebrows and equally bushy beard were flecked with grey. He looked intently at each man in turn and, when his gaze alighted on Kaplyn, he felt sure that he would be discovered but the stranger soon turned to look at another.

"No doubt you will be wondering about tomorrow..." he said, deliberately pausing to let his words sink in. "So far, life has been easy for you, but rest assured *that* is going to change. *You* have been chosen, but that is only the start...." All eyes were on the figure now and he held their attention like mice spellbound before a cat.

"You are older than we would like. Most priests are selected at a much younger age. Tomorrow you will have to pass the initiation to test your shaol," he continued. "You will face your worst fears, and not everyone will pass."

Silence.

They listened intently now.

"If you succeed, your reward will be great. But if you fail, you will wish you had never been born." He looked about the room slowly, looking at each man in turn. "Now, for what remains of this night, I suggest that you sleep."

Kaplyn was completely stunned. All thoughts of sleep were banished as he considered his plight. He had to escape, but had no idea where to go. Looking around, he saw the same terror he felt etched plainly on the faces of the others.

Some of the novices lay down and so Kaplyn followed suit, covering his eyes with his arm and peering at the priest by the door under the crook of his arm. The priest remained where he was and Kaplyn cursed; he would not be able to leave until the priest did.

After a while, someone picked up the courage to speak. "How is the war going?" Kaplyn heard. He expected a swift rebuke for breaking the silence but their guard seemed content to talk. Perhaps he realised it would be a long night and talking would relieve his boredom. Like many other around him, Kaplyn uncovered his eyes and sat up to listen.

"The war is going as expected, although there has been a setback. As you know Thrace has rebelled against us, refusing to trade whilst many in Allund starve due to severe winters and a succession of poor harvests," the priest said. "What you won't know is that an Allund delegation was sent to Thrace, seeking repatriations for lost trade. Unfortunately, they were ambushed along the route." Instantly there were angry mutters around the room.

These were not the same events Kaplyn remembered, and his own anger escalated as the priest continued to rant.

"Thrace destroyed the delegation, and those few who survived were conscripted into the Thracian army, under penalty of death." Angry murmurs arose around the room. Kaplyn looked around, frustrated that the others were taken in by the lies.

"We will show them when we get a chance," shouted the man who had tripped Kaplyn up, and many of those present murmured their approval.

"What happens in the initiation?" another novice asked, confident now that the priest was chatting freely, a gleam of anticipation in his eyes.

The older priest looked suddenly weary as though remembering his own initiation. The others in the room fell silent, giving him a chance to speak. "You have each been examined by one of our order, looking for boys and young men with a strong shaol. Everyone has a shaol, or guardian spirit, but you have particularly strong links to yours, and that will be important in your coming training."

"Is a shaol like a ghost?" Rodric questioned.

The priest nodded. "Sort of…. We believe it is the spirit of one of our ancestors. As I stand here, I can see each of your shaol, although weakly. It is like looking at a person through a thick fog."

Several of the novices glanced at their neighbour as though expecting to see something hovering eerily over their shoulder.

"Tomorrow, the ceremony will strengthen the bond with your shaol. Then, with varying degrees, depending on your abilities, you will be able to communicate with it."

Several voices exclaimed surprise. The priest held up his hand for silence.

"Do not misunderstand me — you will not have long conversations with your shaol. At first the link is nothing more than a feeling. With practice however, this bond will strengthen. For example, before you enter a room you will be able to anticipate how many people are present. For the strongest amongst you, you might also be able to tell where the occupants are within the room. After many more months of practice, you will be able to sense orders as they are passed between our brethren during battle."

Silence followed. "You mean we will be able to talk to the dead?" one fellow piped up.

The priest shook his head, "No, but with any luck, *they* will talk to you." His eyebrows seemed to protrude as he finished his sentence. "Now sleep, for tomorrow you will need all of your strength."

No one made any move to lie down. He had whetted their appetites and they were eager for more.

Kaplyn shuddered, suddenly deeply afraid. He believed in shaols, having seen Lomar's. The problem for Kaplyn was, if he *had* a guardian spirit, it was likely to be a weak link and then he would be found out. From whatever angle he considered his current predicament, he was in serious trouble.

His attention came back to the priest who was talking again although the conversation had turned to more mundane subjects. By his side Rodric's eyes shone. "We will pass tomorrow; you and I, Kaplyn. Then we will show the Thracians a thing or two."

Kaplyn forced a smile and lay back. It occurred to him that the priest at the door was there for another reason; he was their guardian, ensuring that no one attempted to leave. All at once Kaplyn wished he had listened to Lars and had found another way to enter the city. He was trapped!

Chapter 5

Initiation of the Damned

Kaplyn awoke with a start. He had not meant to fall asleep but had clearly been too tired to remain awake. Other novices were rousing and one or two were already up. The older priest was standing in the centre of the room, and Kaplyn surmised he had stood guard all night. Silently Kaplyn cursed himself for not staying awake and, with a groan, forced himself from the bed.

The priest started to arouse the novices still abed whilst servants brought in breakfast. Few could face food and those that did, ate like condemned men. Kaplyn chewed on a dry crust but could barely swallow. Putting his bread down, he want to the privies. Others were relieving themselves in buckets and the smell in the confined space was vile. Wrinkling his nose, Kaplyn looked around the room for an escape but there wasn't even a window.

With a grim finality, Kaplyn realised he had walked into a trap as easily as a lamb to slaughter. His options seemed non-existent, and he had no alternative but to wait until some avenue of escape presented itself.

All too soon the priest called them to follow him. Kaplyn joined the others as they were led from the room, out through the courtyard and through another opening into a long dark corridor. There were no windows and the ceiling disappeared into the gloom high above their heads. The low murmur of many voices echoed along the corridor, and Kaplyn realised that somewhere unseen priests were chanting. The sound made Kaplyn frantic; the chance to escape was diminishing fast.

The procession approached large wooden doors set in a stone arch. The doors were shut and yet the sound of voices still penetrated the thick beams. With obscene slowness, the doors swung inwards and the chanting grew louder. The effect on Kaplyn's nerves was electrifying, and he considered one last time making a break for it. But, surrounded by so many enemies, he realised flight was impossible. He would have to go through the ritual and seek an escape afterwards. Just then, the line continued to move once more, accompanied now by the silence of the grave.

They entered a large cathedral. Kaplyn immediately thought of Vastra but this cathedral was not the one in his vision. The roof towered high above, making Kaplyn feel giddy as he stared into its vastness. Magnificent windows illuminated large tapestries, depicting heroic scenes, their sheer size making the figures seem all the more heroic.

Slowly, the procession passed rows of seated priests who stared up at the novices with the vacant expressions of those bored beyond measure. Kaplyn noticed a green glow emanating from the front of the room, and his thoughts immediately turned to demons, remembering all too clearly that a green glow had accompanied the one demon he had encountered. His eyes went to the torches, hanging in brackets on the walls, but to his relief they burned with an orange flame. If a demon was present, they would burn blue.

The procession slowed and then came to a halt. Fear nagged at Kaplyn and he glanced around to see Rodric, who looked as worried as Kaplyn felt.

Kaplyn felt sick.

He tried to peer ahead but there were too many novices in the way. Gradually their numbers diminished and shortly there were only a few in front of him. He now had a clearer view of the proceedings. An ancient priest stood on a low platform. His face was grey and wrinkled, and his hands arthritic claws. By his side a wooden altar supported a brightly glowing crystal. A novice approached, looking terrified, and in a low voice the old priest bade him lay a hand upon the crystal. Even at this distance, Kaplyn could see beads of sweat on the novice's brow.

It was a kara-stone, or so Kaplyn assumed, which immediately caused him considerable dread. He had touched a kara-stone in CarCamel and it had caused him to pass out. He had seen the world through the eyes of a Kalanth. How, he did not know.

The novice was raising his hand but was clearly too afraid to continue.

"Go on," the old priest urged impatiently.

The novice touched the stone and immediately went rigid. Priests standing to one side rushed forward to support him and then help him from the chamber. His eyes looked terrified as he passed by Kaplyn.

All too soon Kaplyn found himself at the front of the queue. So far, he had not seen anybody fail and then all too quickly it was his turn.

Kaplyn mounted the platform and stood before the old priest. There was no compassion in his old eyes and, too late, Kaplyn realised the old man was looking for Kaplyn's shaol (if he had one). An unreasonable urge prompted Kaplyn to confess, to tell him then that he was a traitor and not a novice, but a stronger voice at the back of his mind stilled his fears.

As with the previous novices, the priest told him to put his hand on the kara-stone. Kaplyn's mind wailed a warning but he had no choice. As he laid his hand on the stone a burst of pure agony hit Kaplyn like a thunderbolt. The pain flashed along his arm, penetrating deep into his chest, seeming to burst through his scar. A silent wail of agony issued from his parched lips. As his eyes dimmed he saw a look of horror reflected on the old priest's face.

Chapter 6

Dreams

Silence.

Nothing.

Death hovered in the skies.

His eyes flew open.

Dragons!

He was flying and he glanced around. Behind him followed a flight of dragons and he waved to the nearest rider. A feeling of elation caused him to shout with joy, but his voice was lost in the rush of air. He had the power to destroy a dozen cities and it was his to command. He revelled in the flight; the wind felt good on his face even though it made his beard itch. Absently he scratched with his free hand.

For some reason, he didn't remember having a beard before and then he felt foolish. In TorLanyar, every male over the age of twelve had a beard. He breathed deeply, relishing the scent of dragon. His mount, a magnificent red, was unstoppable, far superior to the other dragons in the flight. Being black, they were lesser beasts.

Abruptly a dragon behind drew alongside and its rider pointed below. He stared at the other man confused; his armour seemed alien. The helm was much too tall and embossed with a decorative script that was unfamiliar. His cuffs were embroidered with gold thread and he barely recognised the royal crest. It took some moments for the fog to lift from his mind.

And then he roared triumphantly. "I am Shastlan!"

He glanced down to where the other man was pointing. A city appeared in the distance, a tiny speck in the surrounding landscape. Waving his arm he gave the command to attack and felt growing excitement as the dragons tucked in their wings to dive.

How many were there? He counted six others as they fell from the sky. In reality, the task at hand needed only one dragon, and he had perhaps fifty at his command, although he never took more than seven with him as a rule. He could reduce hundreds of such cities to rubble, and his armies would later follow to claim the rubble, putting any survivors (there would be few) either to the sword or in chains.

Below, the city's marble walls reflected the early morning light, staining them crimson as if awash with blood. (How appropriate, he thought.) Banners fluttered defiantly from the walls; rich colours, depicting many ancient houses with long histories ... and short futures. A few sentries had brief moments to look startled as death swept from the skies to claim their pitiful lives in a fury of vitriol and flame. Their screams of terror reached Shastlan and eagerly he listened to the fanfare of death.

The dragons broke formation, spreading out around the sleeping city. Flame and venom spewed down from the skies, creating an acrid fog that obscured the riders' view. Shastlan felt frustrated that he was not killing directly. He could not see them die, only imagine it and he urged his dragon lower. The great serpent complied with a broad grin splitting its long snout.

All too soon they reached the opposite walls of the city, and the dragon lifted effortlessly into the morning sky just as the sun crested the distant horizon as if greeting the dragon and its rider. Exultation spread through him as he saw the city awash with flame. He heard the cries of people as they rushed into the streets only to be consumed by dragon fire.

"Again!" he urged, "Again! Attack! Attack!"

The dragon's head turned on its long neck to face the rider. *Patience*, he heard its voice echo in his mind. *This is but the beginning. Your enemies will be destroyed, but be patient! Let them wait and let them tremble. When they hear that two cities have been destroyed, they will be all the more eager to surrender when they hear your name.*

It unnerved him that the dragon could speak to him so. Behind them, he could already see a long line of foot soldiers, crawling toward the stricken city. He smiled. His people would adore him for his victory; he could already hear their chants as they proclaimed him their saviour.

Shastlan! Shastlan! They would cry, but already his eyes were turned towards other cities and enemies.

Kaplyn awoke.

The smell of dragon mixed with battle and death was abruptly gone. Confused he looked about. He was within a small room, sparsely furnished, with just the bed he was lying on and one chair. A single door was the only exit and there were no windows.

He had a massive hangover and his head thumped hard as though in time to a hammer beating his brow. Moaning, he put a hand to his head and felt his baldness, remembering then the cathedral and the old priest. In alarm he sat up, realising that he must have passed out. Fortunately he was still dressed in his robes; he didn't want anyone to see his strange scar. That had to be kept a secret. He could not explain it otherwise.

At that moment the door opened and the old priest from the cathedral entered.

A sudden rage took hold of Kaplyn. "How dare you enter without knocking!"

The priest stood framed in the doorway. A smile formed on his lips that seemed to make him all the more threatening.

Kaplyn suddenly felt afraid. The priest could very well be his executioner.

"Don't worry. The stone often affects novices this way," the old man assured him. "I will forgive your outburst, this once. Now sleep. You will feel better in the morning."

Kaplyn could not argue and felt a great weariness wash over him.

He had lots of questions; many he dared not ask. Sleep stole over him; he was tired — dragon flight and war did that to him, he realised.

He was awakened almost immediately. He was lying in his bed looking up at the canvas roof of his tent. Captain Thral stood framed in the entrance, looking uncertain as to whether he should have woken his King.

"We have him, lord," he said with exuberance.

Shastlan shook his head. He had been dreaming and was confused. "Who?" he asked uncertainly. The dream had been important and he was angry to be disturbed.

"Prince Antlak," Thral declared triumphantly. "He escaped the palace through a secret passage but we caught him. He was dressed as a woman, fleeing the city wearing a dress, lord." Thral grinned broadly as though it were a great jest.

Immediately sleep left him and Shastlan sat up.

"Let me get dressed and then bring him in, Captain." Hurriedly he pulled his tunic and trousers on. Lastly, he buckled on his silver breastplate, wanting his enemy to see his wealth.

A pitiful wreck of a man was thrown into the room. He tried to arrest his fall but the dress he was still wearing tangled his feet and he fell to the ground where he remained, his sobs the only sound. Two guards followed and stood to attention behind the prostrate figure.

With disdain, Shastlan looked down at the man. "Only a coward would flee dressed as a woman." he said scornfully.

Antlak stared at the ground, too afraid to look at his enemy.

Shastlan was annoyed by his silence. Anger flooded through him and a red haze obscured his vision. Without realising what he was doing, his sword was suddenly in his hand aimed menacingly at the prostrate prince.

Prince Antlak, seeing the blade, started pleading for his life. The more he grovelled the more angry Shastlan became; lowering his sword, he shouted at the prince: "You and your entire race are snivelling cowards and the sooner we are cleansed of Bosra the better. At least have the decency to die like a man."

The prince continued to plead as though he had not even heard. Shastlan could take no more. In frustration he plunged his blade into the prince's chest. The young man convulsed, blood dribbling down the corners of his mouth. Not satisfied, Shastlan commenced butchering him, and the sounds of splintering bone and the hacking of flesh carried beyond the tent.

Fearing their king was being attacked, more sentries entered but they paused, astounded by the sight that confronted them. Silently they withdrew, not wanting to bring attention to themselves lest it be their fate in the future. Captain Thral turned his back on the scene, wondering what had become of his Lord.

Chapter 7

A Waking Nightmare

Kaplyn awoke, crying out in a strange language. For a moment he wondered at the words but then dismissed them. He shook his head to clear it of sleep and rubbed absently at his beard. His fingers caressed his smooth chin and only then did he realise that he didn't have a beard. A frown creased his brow, a meaningless name echoed in his mind.

Shastlan.

He hugged his head. *What was happening*? Arising he crossed the room to a small dirty mirror hanging on the wall where he peered intently at his reflection, barely recognising himself. He looked both pale and haggard, and dark circles rimmed his eyes. His baldness made him look worse, seeming to accentuate his sickly pallor.

Kaplyn shook his head, looking away. Shastlan — *who*, by the Kalanth, was he? He remembered his first dream about Shastlan the night (or was it the day?) before. He remembered there had been dragons in that dream and his heart sank. For too long he had dreamt about dragons and he had almost become used to them by now, but his dreams and their clarity meant that they had taken on a new, more sinister, meaning. There could be no doubting that his dreams were real. Was he going mad?

Behind him the door opened and, instinctively, Kaplyn grabbed a boot from the floor and hurled it towards the door with an angry cry. A priest entered, carrying a tray of food. The boot sailed past his nose, barely missing him and crashing against the wall by his side. Kaplyn had to suppress his mounting rage; he really wanted to hurt the man.

The priest's eyes widened by his near miss and, for a moment, he looked ready to flee. "I was t-told to bring you your breakfast," he stammered, almost apologetically, which angered Kaplyn even more, but then he suddenly felt foolish for losing his temper. What was wrong with him?

Another priest entered. He glanced at his colleague who shuffled towards the small table by the side of Kaplyn's bed. With a fearful look at Kaplyn he placed the tray down and scuttled from the room. The other priest quickly followed, leaving Kaplyn to survey his breakfast of bread, jam and milk. He was famished and with gusto ate and drank as though it were his last meal. Simple though it was, it tasted good and, after only a short while, the plate and jug were empty; he belched loudly in appreciation.

The old priest from the cathedral entered and Kaplyn suppressed a sudden urge to hurl the tray at him.

"Today your study begins," he said from the safety of the doorway. "You must train with the others until you have mastered control of your shaol. Now dress and I will await you outside." Without further ado, the old man turned and left.

Kaplyn dressed and had to search for his boot, which he found under the bed. He then remembered Lars and the others were waiting for him in the wood, and he had less than a week before they would leave — or worse still, start looking for him.

A priest entered to clear the remains of his breakfast.

"How long have I been here?" Kaplyn asked.

"A night and most of a day," the other man replied.

Kaplyn cursed.

The priest frowned. "What language is that? I've never heard it before"

"*What*?" Kaplyn frowned, not realising he had spoken any language other than Allund. Alarmed that he was loosing control, he strode from the room, ignoring the other man. The old priest was waiting outside the door and, smiling, he led the way along the corridor. Kaplyn felt a storm brewing behind his brow and, with effort, tried to suppress it.

The priest stopped by a door which he opened and held open for Kaplyn to enter.

Kaplyn paused on the threshold, experiencing a strange sensation that seemed to sweep through his very being; for some unexplained reason he was very afraid to enter the room. He glanced at the old priest whose smile seemed to be mocking him.

Pride would not let him falter so he stepped forward.

Danger, he heard.

Pausing, he looked around for the source of the warning but no one was there. Kaplyn felt the presence of others within the room, even though, from where he was standing, the door blocked his view of the interior.

Cautious now, he went forward a short way to where he could see inside. It was full of priests wearing their distinctive ochre robes, sitting in a semicircle on the floor. He recognised Rodric and the sight of someone he knew helped to restore his confidence and, so he stepped inside.

490

Immediately his senses screamed a warning. Instinctively, he ducked, lashing out to his right. His fist connected with something soft and yielding. The feeling of danger remained and he threw himself forward into a roll; then instinct made him kick out. He was rewarded by a loud crack, like the breaking of a stout branch. Already he was on his feet, breathing hard with the sudden exertion. By his side two figures lay on the floor. One man held his leg which was at an awkward angle, a grimace of agony etched upon his face while the other lay on his back, his face turning a sickly shade of blue. This man lay terribly still and Kaplyn knew that he was dead.

Kaplyn looked about in alarm, expecting the others in the room to attack him for harming their comrades, but they just continued to watch in awkward silence.

Behind Kaplyn the old priest entered. "*That* is what you, also, can do," he said, ignoring Kaplyn and addressing the stunned crowd. "And *he* has had no training!" he pronounced angrily, pointing at Kaplyn. "Whereas *you* have been training for a day with little result."

"Remove these," the old man gestured to the bodies on the floor. Several priests rushed forward to get rid of the bodies. Kaplyn still couldn't believe what had occurred. He had killed someone without even a second thought. Of course, he had killed during the recent battles at CarCamel, but that was a different matter. There he had been forced to.

"Who warned me?" he asked, remembering the forewarning.

The old priest looked at him. "Your shaol," he answered.

Kaplyn shook his head, stroking his chin. "*Shaol?*" he echoed. Lomar had talked at length about his own shaol and the strange link that enabled him to see and hear things whilst his body slept.

The priest nodded. "You have the strongest link with a shaol I have ever come across. Further, I believe your shaol is a dragon rider, and never has such a thing happened before. Of course, we believe dragons existed many years ago, but that would normally mean a very weak link with your shaol as it is such a distant relative; this is a very great puzzle."

Kaplyn grimaced, caring nothing for puzzles at that moment, still reeling from the fact he had killed someone so easily

"It was your shaol who spoke with you," the priest continued, mistaking Kaplyn's frown for one of confusion. "We awoke the link between you and your guardian when you touched the kara-stone. This link now enables your guardian to communicate more clearly with you; although it is rare to *actually* hear one's shaol, as you described. With such men as you, we can forge the greatest army in the world," the old man's voice had reached a fevered pitch and spittle ran down his chin.

Kaplyn was horrified. He had been turned into a monster.

491

That night, after an arduous day's training, Kaplyn returned to his room. Both the priests and novices treated him with considerable respect. He was the only novice with his own room. Without thinking, he ordered a nearby priest to fetch him water, so he could wash, and a clean robe. Without comment the man hurried away to obey.

Kaplyn was behaving out of character, saying things before actually thinking through the consequences. He had to be more careful and try to draw less attention to himself; after all he was a spy and, if discovered....

The memory of the corpse being carried away earlier that day returned to haunt him. In despair, he sat down heavily on the bed.

When the priest returned he suppressed the urge to reprimand him for taking his time. Putting the pitcher and robe down, the priest fled as though sensing his ire.

Stripping off the disgusting robes he had worn since arriving, he started to wash, only then realising that the silver light from his scar had been replaced with a baleful green glow, the same colour as the kara-stone he had touched. He froze in fear. He associated that colour with the demon world and evil. He rubbed at the scar, but the light persisted. A cry of frustration escaped his lips and he sat forlornly on his bed.

That night he was too afraid to sleep, remembering all too clearly the horror of the previous night's dreams. That day, he had tentatively asked others about their experiences. A few had admitted they, too, had experienced dreams about their shaol's lives, but none were as vivid as Kaplyn's.

Of one thing he was convinced.

Shastlan was evil.

Any man who could butcher another, in the cold-blooded manner Shastlan had, must be evil. Kaplyn suppressed another shudder, remembering the words of the old priest. He had assumed that Kaplyn's shaol was from their past; Kaplyn was not so sure. Vastra had spoken about other worlds and Kaplyn had a strong feeling that his shaol was not of this world, but how he had acquired a shaol from another, he did not know.

He *had* to find Vastra and leave the city at all costs, but it was too light outside and he would be better off waiting for darkness before exploring the city. Grateful for the excuse, he sank back into the bed, intending, as he did so, only to rest for a short while. Anxiously, his thoughts turned to Lars and the others and wondered if they were all right. Gradually, his mind became tired and all too soon he fell asleep.

The murdered body of the prince had been removed and Shastlan was already planning a campaign against the other kingdoms. His generals were currently arguing, saying there was little point continuing the war. After all, they had defeated their enemies and the remaining kingdoms were friendly. He was frustrated with their lack of vision.

"Think of the plunder," he yelled above the hubbub, and a silence descended.

"That may be well, but what plunder remains after the dragons incinerate a city?" one general complained. Shastlan made a mental note of the man who dared to speak so openly against him, deciding to replace him later.

His thoughts were instantly scattered as, within his mind, his dragon sent him a silent summons. Shastlan thrilled at the sensation of the dragon's thoughts. Excusing himself he left the tent and was immediately engulfed by darkness.

The night air carried with it the scent of exotic plants and, to his ears, came the faint chirrup of crickets, but he ignored these as he made his way to the dragon's temporary shelter in a tall marquee.

Standing before the dragon, he felt in awe of the great serpent while heavily hooded eyes regarded him lazily, seeming to see into his very soul.

When do we leave? a voice echoed in his mind, causing him to jump in fright.

"Soon," he said, forgetting he didn't need to speak.

A thin wisp of smoke rose from the dragon's maw and he watched as it dispersed on the night breeze.

We have been waiting for a week. You did not summon me from my home world just to keep me waiting. What is the delay? he heard.

"*Delay!* There is no delay. It is important we consider our next move carefully; otherwise we could be vulnerable to attack."

Who would dare attack you with dragons at your command?

Shastlan smiled. Was he being over cautious? "Very well," he conceded. "We will leave at dawn." With a growing feeling of excitement he made his way to back his tent to tell his commanders his decision.

The next morning seven dragons took flight, rising high into the dawn sky. Shastlan felt exhilarated to be in command. In the sky he felt invincible and he laughed out loud. "Come dragon," he shouted into the wind. "Let us find an enemy to kill."

Shortly before noon they spotted a small column below. Gleefully, they swooped down on the enemy and just before they struck, figures looked up. Pointing at the sky, they yelled warnings and in panic many scattered, screaming in fear, throwing down their possessions whilst others,

493

recognising flight was futile, crouched beneath their wagons, praying to be spared. The people's screams were soon lost in the ensuing blasts that accompanied dragon fire.

The battle raged for only a short while, and soon Shastlan ordered his dragon to descend to personally view the field, his boots crunching on charred bodies and burnt flesh.

"We have won a great victory," he announced to the other riders who had landed to inspect the carnage. Shastlan failed to notice their pale faces and looks of horror. One man turned away, retching noisily. In his search for glory, Shastlan had overlooked the fact that the enemy was nothing more than a refugee caravan, comprising mainly women and children.

Shastlan bade them mount. Reluctantly they complied and the dragons leapt into the sky, eager to find another enemy.

Kaplyn awoke sweating, "I can't sleep!" he screamed. "I will *not* sleep!" He was so weary and depressed; arising he dressed woodenly. His shaol's presence was horrific and he wished he could break the link. He understood now his previous fears of dragons and why they had haunted his dreams. Thinking back, he realised the nightmares had started soon after Tumarl had freed them from the Eldric spell.

That was the link.

In some way he had been altered by the spell. Somehow a spirit from another world had become his shaol. He wanted to get out from his room. He needed something to occupy his mind. By now, Lars and the others would be getting worried; he had to find Vastra and escape.

His training the previous day had proven useful and his ability to see things via his shaol, good though it was, was improving: He could sense when someone was present without actually seeing them, provided, of course, that they were relatively close and he did not ignore his shaol's warnings.

Shastlan did not talk directly to Kaplyn; communication was much more subtle. Clearing his mind resulted in an indistinct image of his surroundings, like looking through a ghostly fog.

Calming himself, he tried to sense anyone within the corridor. It felt empty and so quietly he slipped out of the room. A small window at the corridor's end let him see outside. It was still night and he judged there were a few hours yet until dawn.

He went along the corridor, down a flight of stairs and then retraced his steps toward the school's entrance, for that was how he saw the building. Stepping into the street, he made his way towards the heart of the city. He knew there was a curfew but, even still, it was strange to see streets so devoid of life. Pausing for a moment, he sensed his link with Shastlan to see if the way was clear. Once assured, he hurried along the dark street.

The buildings to either side seemed menacing, dark and brooding. Frequently he glanced up at the unlit windows, but nothing stirred. He would have preferred it if there had been signs of life for that at least would have been a comfort; as it was, it was like a city of ghosts. The street he was following joined another and he sensed someone coming. Quickly he stepped into a deep alcove. Peering from within the shadows, he tried to determine who it was, but it was too dark to see far.

Nothing happened and he began to doubt the warning. Just as he was about to leave he heard voices and the clanking of metal and he held his breath to hear better. He sensed five people approaching and he shrank deeper into the shadows.

A pale radiance preceded the group and, as they came into view, Kaplyn saw five men, carrying a single torch, the light from which grew in intensity as they came closer to Kaplyn's place of concealment. He turned his face into the shadows so its whiteness did not betray him.

The soldiers were overconfident and seemed more interested in talking than looking for an enemy. Only when they had passed did Kaplyn breathe more easily and, as the clink of their armour receded, he detached himself from the shadows to continue his journey. He wandered down several more streets before he again had the urge to hide. Quickly he stepped into a doorway, concealing himself in shadow.

A lone figure appeared, walking rapidly and keeping close to dark recesses. He was a tall man, dressed in sombre clothes as though he had anticipated his need to be out late. *Somebody else disobeying the curfew*, Kaplyn thought, *probably a soldier returning from the embrace of a lover*. The man passed very close to Kaplyn's hiding place and then was gone from view. Kaplyn waited for several moments before continuing.

Some time later he found himself standing before a large square, probably a market place. In the centre of the square loomed a tall, stone-built cathedral. Unlike the Cathedral where he had been initiated, this looked derelict. At one time, it would have been a magnificent building, but now there were clear signs of neglect. Many of the windows were boarded and roof tiles lay scattered about the ground. Excitedly, he crossed the street, heading towards the deepest shadows.

He skirted the building's perimeter, searching for an entrance. There was no obvious way in and, conscious that he was vulnerable in the open, he tested one of the boards covering a window. The mortar was loose and the nails came away easily, leaving a hole large enough for him to climb through. Scrabbling inside, dust, undisturbed for years, clung to the back of his throat, leaving an unpleasant taste in his mouth.

Gradually he became aware of a faint glow emanating from the room's farthest point. Skirting a maze of fallen masonry, he made his way towards the light, recognising the golden cage as it came into view.

Immediately the hackles on the back of his neck rose and he crouched momentarily in the shadows. Up until that moment he had not truly considered his actions if he should find Vastra. He had only wanted to discover what had become of his crystal from the Tree of Life, but now he wanted vengeance. He realised how badly his dreams were affecting him, and with a great difficulty he fought to control his mounting rage, telling himself it was Shastlan's anger he felt, not his own.

Fixing his gaze on the cage, he moved closer. Several candles stood at each corner, illuminating the occupant who was huddled in the corner, just as Astalus' vision had revealed. It was then that Kaplyn saw a subtle haze around the cage and realised that magic surrounded it. The haze did not extend very far so he approached closer. The figure stirred, turning to face Kaplyn, a look of surprise crossing his face.

Kaplyn recognised Vastra. His skin, wrinkled with age, was ashen probably due to lack of sunlight and his hair was long and grey, matted with grime. He had a haunted look as he surveyed Kaplyn through red and rheumy eyes. Then, suddenly recognition dawned, and the old man's surprise was replaced with fear as he scrambled pitifully to the back of the cage.

Kaplyn was fighting for control of his own emotions, torn between restraint and wanting to tear the vile old man's heart out. Vaguely, he became aware of a warning at the back of his mind, but he had been so intent on Vastra that he had failed to listen to his shaol and, now, he realised that was a costly error. Too late, he whirled to face the danger, realising that he was already surrounded as shapes stepped from the shadows.

The flapping of wings announced the arrival of several grakyn that landed in front of the advancing guards who held their spears at the ready. Kaplyn had a knife but all thoughts of drawing the weapon were banished; there were too many of them.

Another figure approached through the shadows, a more sinister shape that seemed to demand his attention. The darkness about it shimmered eerily.

It was a man, he realised as the figure finally stepped into the light, but something warned him he was wrong. He was handsome, probably the most perfect specimen of manhood that Kaplyn had ever seen, but there was an intense, almost wild look in his eyes.

"Well! Well! Well! What have we here, a priest." said the figure. "Not at all what I was expecting, but, then again, appearances can be deceptive." As he spoke his face appeared to blur momentarily and Kaplyn looked on in horror. He realised he was looking at a demon and, as if reading his thoughts, the demon smiled.

"Put down your knife," he suggested with a wave of his arm. Kaplyn had not even been aware that he had drawn it. Whether he complied of his own volition or not, he never knew, but the blade simply fell from seemingly nerveless fingers.

The grakyn beat their wings, eager to be let loose to finish him, but the demon was clearly in no hurry. "What are you?" he asked more to himself than to Kaplyn as he paced to and fro in front of him, like a cat intent on its prey. "A spy perhaps?" he suggested, looking darkly at Kaplyn.

Kaplyn felt transparent at that moment, as if the demon could read his thoughts. He glanced at Vastra and the direction of his look seemed to pique the demon's curiosity. "And what is your connection with the old man?" he asked softly. Vastra meanwhile cringed at the back of the cage as though the bars might offer him protection.

"You couldn't reach him you know," the demon said matter of factly. "He is confined by more than metal bars." The demon turned to the grakyn. "Take him to the dungeons," he said with a dismissive wave of his hand. "But make sure he is kept safe. I will want to talk to this one personally upon my return."

Kaplyn was led away from the golden cage. His shoulders sagged in defeat and his eyes desperately searched the surroundings as though seeking a means of escape. Dark anger flooded through his body as he was escorted from the cathedral into the night. On the horizon the sky was showing faint signs of brightening and Kaplyn wondered if it was the last daylight he would ever see.

Chapter 8

Captive

The grakyn escorted him to a tall, brick-built tower guarded by two sentries armed with long spears. Rough hands pushed Kaplyn through the entrance into a circular room with two doors leading from it. One was open and, beyond that, a stair plunged into darkness. Kaplyn was forced forward and he had to catch himself from toppling headfirst into blackness. His heart lurched and, as swiftly as he dared, he descended lest his captors shove him again.

The stairs seemed endless and, the deeper he went, the more the air smelt like a crypt of damp and decay. Soon, all light failed and he couldn't see a thing. Abruptly, as he reached the bottom, his legs buckled, but the grakyn following didn't give him any time to recover. Instead, he was roughly herder along a long corridor that twisted and turned until he was completely disorientated. Stumbling, strong hands from behind halted him. A key snicked in a lock and then he was shoved forwards. His heart lurched as he fell down some steps, cracking his knees on a stone floor and skinning his hands.

Behind him the door banged shut.

Only silence and darkness remained. For several moments he knelt there, too afraid to move and then, like a blind man, he felt his way around his cell. The walls were circular and slimy. He smelt his fingers and wished that he hadn't. Wiping his hands on his trousers, he forced himself to continue the search, hardening himself to the task. It did not take long and there was no sign of any exit other than the door he had entered. He reached up, but the cell was too tall and his fingers caressed nothing more than air. If the corridor smelt vile, then this was much worse. The air clogged his nostrils so that he hardly dared breathe.

Hope left him and, with a groan, he sat down and a bleak despair washed over him. He was trapped.

The ancient priest sat in his office surrounded by books of all shapes and sizes. These were his only vice and it was a magnificent collection, spanning many generations.

Suddenly the door burst open and the old man jumped with fright. Urgently he felt for his shaol's presence but, unusually, it remained silent. It was then that the demon walked in. The priest cursed silently for this fiend was immensely powerful, which explained his shaol's silence; it, too, was clearly in terror of the demon. The priest pulled himself upright and tried to look as if he had expected the demon, but the figure standing before him smiled back, all too knowingly.

"We have taken one of your priests prisoner," the demon said gloating.

This was news and the ancient priest couldn't suppress a look of surprise. "What do you mean?"

"We found one of your priests in the old cathedral. I suspect he was spying."

"Impossible" the priest replied. "All of my men are handpicked. Their shaol would not betray us."

"And yet it seems that one has managed to persuade his shaol to turn a blind eye." The demon paced the room slowly. "Do you have a priest missing at present?" the demon asked, picking a particularly old volume from the shelf and examining it.

"Yes. One of our newest students was not in his room this morning."

The demon waited for him to continue.

"He is called Kaplyn. He is one of our most promising recruits." The priest suddenly realised what might have happened. "I think I understand. This man has a particularly powerful shaol. Usually there is a period of adjustment after the link is awoken. Many are disorientated and, on occasions, the shaol tries to gain mastery. I saw this happen once, several years ago. A very nasty business…"

"Tell me about his shaol," the demon asked, dropping the book he held before picking out another from the stacked shelves.

The old priest stared at his beloved volume on the floor. The spine had cracked and pages lay scattered. Knowing a confrontation was useless, he suppressed his anger. "His shaol was very powerful in his former life. I found it hard to believe, but he was a dragon rider or, at least, the sense of dragons was very great."

It was the demon's turn to look surprised and he turned to face the priest, the book in his hand immediately forgotten. "*Dragon*? And you did not think to report this!"

The old man cringed. "I did not think to. We have long since known there might, at one time, have been dragons, and we even have some old

499

bones to suggest this. I was hoping to study Kaplyn and his shaol further once his training had progressed." His tone was hopeful but his eyes suggested that he already knew this was now impossible.

"He is *mine* now," the demon said simply. His tone conveyed a hidden menace and his eyes glittered dangerously.

"I'm going away for a while," the demon continued. "I have other business to attend to. I shall speak further with the prisoner when I return. That will give him time to reflect on his deeds, and he will be more compliant to my questions." Then he was gone.

The priest turned in his chair, suddenly wishing that Kaplyn had never attended the ceremony, and his recent euphoria at seeing such a powerful shaol was replaced with regret.

"Damn!" he said, slapping the tabletop.

In complete darkness Kaplyn stirred. The silence and staring into the gloom made him feel giddy. He closed his eyes and immediately saw a dragon in his mind's eye; its familiar scent seemed to pervade his very being. Then, an image of Shastlan replaced that of the dragon and thoughts of war and death tumbled through his mind. With a groan, he opened his eyes and at least the images were banished.

"I don't want to sleep!" he screamed.

Suddenly, a grating noise sounded in the cell and Kaplyn became alert. Nothing happened. He groped his way about the cell, feeling the floor with outstretched hands. He knocked over a bowl and he felt the wetness, realising it was water. Desperately he found the bowl and righted it. There were still a few drops and he licked these with a parched tongue. Groping around, he found another bowl containing bread. Realising how hungry he was, he wolfed this down.

Once he had eaten, he tried to figure out where the food had come from, but he could not feel anything that would suggest a trap door within the main door. He traced the cell several times, but it was completely bare.

The isolation was terrible, but not being able to see or hear anything was even more terrifying. He banged the metal plate on the floor, reassured by the noise. At least he was not deaf, he thought. His eyes were another matter though. It was so dark that he started to wonder if he was blind. Panic grew inside him and he yelled in frustration.

Vastra sat alone in his cage as daylight flooded into the cathedral. It was apt in a way to be held captive in a building once dedicated to the gods, especially the very gods he didn't believe in. He had been a prisoner for almost as long as could remember. His stomach growled and he hugged his chest hard. Since his incarceration he had not eaten — how many years ago was the last time, he wondered? He was held in a magic prison. The golden cage was not actually locked, but he could not get out; he had tried often enough. It was enchanted, deliberately set to mock him of his own futility. It was as if time had stood still. He aged more slowly than he should have and yet the magic of his cell kept him alive.

He remembered his recent visitor. It was the first time he had seen anyone for years and, more to the point, he recognised him from his past. The name was one that he would never forget.

Kaplyn.

He remembered betraying him and the others. And now, after all this time, Kaplyn had come for revenge. Vastra closed his eyes. He deserved death and part of him yearned for it, but he was terribly afraid to die. He snorted. Common sense dictated that it could *not* have been Kaplyn — that was simply too long ago.

He thought back, recalling an image of the visitor. He had been dressed as a Priest of Ryoch; his head was shaven but his eyebrows were dark, without even a trace of grey, and his flesh tone had been youthful, not more than twenty-three or twenty-four, he guessed. The Kaplyn he had known would have been at least as old as *he* was. More so! For Drachar had ensured he aged more slowly than others did. He looked down at his own hands, wrinkled with age. No! It could not have been Kaplyn. It was nothing more than a memory sent to haunt him.

"What have *I* done?" he wailed, but silence was his only reply.

Burying his head in his arms, he wept. The tears were not selfish. Not this time. He realised the enormity of his actions and he wept for humanity.

Lars awoke.

It was still dark and the campfire, which had burned low, cast little light. He looked across to the prisoner, tied to the tree, trying as best as he could to get comfortable and sleep. Already the bald plate had sprouted hairs and a thin stubble covered the youth's head.

Something felt wrong. Lars sat upright trying to place the feeling.

Across from him Thaneck, Tumarl and Lomar were sleeping. Something still preyed on Lars' mind, so much so that he was forced to rise. He went over to Lomar, shaking his shoulder, calling his name.

Lomar did not stir.

It always bothered Lars that Lomar was an albino; he associated his paleness with death. Now, in the faint glow of the fire, he looked worse than ever. Lars was reminded of the terrible time in the dungeon in CarCamel.

Lomar had gone into a trance and it had taken Astalus and his powers to waken him.

Desperately Lars felt for a pulse but could not find one. He bent over the body and felt for signs of breath on his cheek. Nothing. Panic gripped him and he shook Lomar harder, urgently calling his name.

Awoken by his calling, both Tumarl and Thaneck came over to the big man.

Lars looked up at them with dread in his eyes. "I think he is dead," he stated flatly.

Shastlan.

He stood in front of a long, tall mirror proudly admiring his image. He was dressed in a long, flowing ermine robe, and a gold crown adorned his brow.

"Emperor!" he mused. That was not quite true — not yet at least. But already his people were calling him that. The wars were going well, though a few still tried to oppose his dragon-led armies, but none could.

Most cities surrendered at the first sight of a dragon.

Many were sacked nonetheless.

It boosted morale.

Soon he would be proclaimed emperor. He would rebuild the cities, appointing his most faithful generals to oversee them. Competition amongst his men was to be encouraged, especially since the attempt on his life. One general, Zoreal, had waited in the shadows as he had passed, and it was only Shastlan's luck that had saved him. Luck and the mail he wore beneath his robe.

The knife had broken with the force of the blow and Shastlan's personal guard had done the rest. He had been furious to find they had been overzealous; he could not interrogate a corpse.

Once more he looked in the mirror and, to his horror, saw someone else reflected there, someone he did not recognise. A dark haired youth stared back, a wild, fearful look in his eyes. Then the image was gone, but in his mind's eye he could still see the youth dressed in a leather tunic and high riding boots.

"*What is it?*" Shastlan whispered. "*An omen?*" For a moment, he looked uncertain and then his furrowed bow cleared. "Ah!" he sighed. "A vision from the gods. Clearly, this man will try to destroy me?" He memorised the image. "Beware, whoever you are, for I will destroy *you* first."

Kaplyn awoke. Darkness surrounded him and despair engulfed him. His head, neck and shoulders ached and he felt damp all over. In pain, he pushed himself upright and searched for a meal. He was rewarded with empty plates.

A sob escaped his lips.

He had no concept of the time. Had he slept for hours or days?

"Kaplyn!" came a soft voice.

He looked around baffled. Again he heard his name and he called out in reply. "Who is it?" Silence greeted him. "Am I going insane?" he groaned.

"Kaplyn!"

Looking up, he saw the faint form of Lomar standing over him. Relief flooded through him. "Lomar," he said half choking.

Lomar smiled. "Only in spirit form," he answered.

Kaplyn looked more closely and recognised the translucence of Lomar's appearance.

"How long has it been?" he questioned. His voice cracked as he spoke and he was forced to repeat the question.

"It's over a week since you left us," Lomar replied.

"Can you help me?" Kaplyn asked, rising unsteadily to his feet. Lomar did not reply immediately; instead, he appeared to be listening.

"I will try," he answered, although his tone reflected uncertainty. "First, I must get back to Lars and the others and report that I have found you."

Then he was gone.

"No! Don't go!" Kaplyn cried out, but he was alone. Had he imagined Lomar's presence? In despair, he sat down on the floor, hugging his knees to his chest.

Chapter 9

Rescue

Lars stood over Lomar's body, staring down at him as though he could not believe that his friend was dead.

"We had better bury him," he announced. Tumarl and Thaneck stood by his side, a look of shock on their faces.

"What did he die of?" Tumarl asked.

The big man shrugged.

"We bury our dead under a cairn," Thaneck suggested.

Lars looked around. "There aren't enough stones." He looked down at Lomar one more time. The Albino's white skin seemed as pure as alabaster in the dwindling light. Lars felt saddened; they had been through difficult times, and to see him die for no reason seemed so very wrong. Bending down, he took Lomar's hand to raise him up.

Lomar stirred, groaning aloud.

Lars leapt back, his eyes wide.

Lomar sat up, swaying. "I've found him! I have found Kaplyn!"

Lars froze in disbelief, "You're not dead?"

Lomar looked surprised, "You sound disappointed."

"We thought that you had died; there was no pulse," Tumarl explained.

Lomar smiled, "I feel like I've died, but I will recover."

"What did you say about Kaplyn?" Lars asked.

Lomar stood. "I have seen him. You remember the dungeon in Thrace when I saw the assassins searching for the King — it was like that. My spirit left my body and I was able to search the city, but it is far away and I nearly lost the link back to my body."

"Where is he?" Tumarl questioned.

"He's in a dungeon."

"Can we get to him?" Thaneck asked.

"No." Lomar stated. "There's also a lot of activity between the encampment and main gates, and there's an army camped on the city's outskirts."

Lars shifted uncomfortably. "Will you go back? You might be able to find some way to get us in."

Lomar nodded. "But first I need food, drink and rest."

Lars remained where he was, staring at the albino as though expecting to see his spirit detach itself from his body before his very eyes.

Thaneck shook his head and, smiling, went to prepare food.

Lomar called Kaplyn's name, but the figure on the floor did not stir. In the eerie spectral light cast by Lomar's shade, he looked terrible. His flesh was an unhealthy pallor and dark rings circled his eyes. Repeatedly he called, but Kaplyn remained asleep, although his dreams caused him to groan. Eventually, however, he stirred, and Lomar called his name again.

Kaplyn sat up, comprehension dawning on his face.

"Lomar, you're back."

"Yes, and I've found a passageway behind the wall, leading back to the city," Lomar told him. "It's probably an old entrance, used to bring special prisoners to the dungeon, or to dispose of them."

"How does that help?" Kaplyn snapped.

"I've found what looks like a trigger mechanism. It's old and I am not sure if I can activate it from the spirit world."

"Why are you waiting then? If you cannot open it then you are of no use to me," Kaplyn croaked.

Lomar considered his options, which seemed too few. Reluctantly, he faded, going to inspect the mechanism once more and leaving Kaplyn wishing he had not been so angry.

Time passed and, then, with a suddenness that made Kaplyn jump, a section of stone swung inwards. Lomar was standing in the opening looking exhausted.

Wearily Kaplyn stood and, without comment, made his way through the opening. Lomar pointed to the trigger mechanism. "You'd better close it," he said.

Kaplyn nodded and swung the lever, watching as the door closed. "That will give the guards something to think about," he growled angrily. "Lead the way."

The tunnel was narrow and not very tall so Kaplyn was forced to stoop. Grime from centuries of disuse coated the walls and floor.

"While I was searching for you, I investigated the city," Lomar said. "I know my way around a little, but unfortunately I don't know where this leads."

Kaplyn shook his head. "I should not have come here. They've done something terrible to me. We should have relied on your talents to find Vastra."

Kaplyn's statement that something had happened to him caused Lomar genuine concern. As he glanced at his friend, he saw how thin he had become. His gaze was drawn to Kaplyn's side, looking for his shaol that he had seen when the dwarves had captured them and, as if upon command, a figure appeared, walking by Kaplyn's shoulder.

The figure stared intently at the albino, a look of surprise on his face as though he, too, could see Lomar. All at once the figure disappeared. There was little doubt that the shape had been there and, to make matters worse, it seemed more distinct than before. The intensity of the man's look had frightened Lomar.

"Kaplyn, this may seem odd but there seemed to be a man's ghost, standing by your shoulder a moment ago," the albino said. He expected Kaplyn to be shocked by his statement; however, he merely continued along the corridor, although his step faltered for a moment.

"Describe him to me."

Kaplyn listened to the description. "You can *see* him?"

Lomar looked by Kaplyn's side as once more the spirit came into view. "Yes, but sometimes he is there, and the next he is gone."

As he walked, Kaplyn told Lomar about what had happened during the initiation and how he had touched the kara-stone. He also told him about his dreams and Shastlan. The albino listened in silence; a feeling of unease growing within him.

Soon they came to wooden stairs worn with age. Wearily, Kaplyn ascended, panting for breath.

"Do you think that they have permanently altered me?" he asked between gasps.

Lomar shook his head. "Hopefully not. Once we are back amongst friends, you will feel better."

"We must return for Vastra," Kaplyn continued. "I found him, but a demon took me captive."

"It's too great a risk. The city is crawling with soldiers and you are not well. You need to return with me."

Kaplyn shook his head and Lomar sighed, "Very well, but we must hurry." His spirit had already been away from his body for a long time, and the link back was growing tenuous. He had expended considerable energy, opening the mechanism to Kaplyn's cell. How he had done that, he did not know. Somehow, he had focused his mind and the lock had sprung. Never before had he been able to do anything physical in the spirit world, and the consequences were enormous.

At the top of the stair, they came to a doorway where they paused while Kaplyn caught his breath. Shastlan enabled him to see through the wall and to his satisfaction, the way was clear.

Tracing the mechanism, Kaplyn found the release. Triggering it, the door swung noisily inwards. The exit led into a cellar and a flight of stairs at the farthest wall led up to a wooden door. As a precaution Kaplyn shut it behind them.

Lomar went ahead to investigate and came back only moments later. "We are in a cathedral," he said.

Kaplyn was not too surprised, for the priests of Ryoch were evil and, even in their past, were likely to want access to the prisoners.

"I saw Vastra in a golden cage. There was no one else with him," Lomar continued. Kaplyn nodded. He climbed the stair and entered through the door. Lomar followed him into the room.

The golden cage was nearby and, within it, Vastra was sitting upright, his eyes fixed intently on Kaplyn. He looked terrified, as though fearing the worse.

"Peace, Vastra," Kaplyn said, holding out his empty hands. "I seek your help, not your death."

"It *is* you!" Vastra managed. "Kaplyn — I had not thought it possible," his voice was hoarse as though he was unused to speaking.

Kaplyn looked at the shimmering curtain surrounding the prison. "What is it that surrounds the prison?"

"It's a spell of confinement. A powerful one at that. You would be wise to leave me whilst you can."

Kaplyn shook his head. "If I free you, will you help us?"

Vastra nodded.

Kaplyn undid his shirt and bared his scar that burned with a fierce green glow.

Vastra's eyes widened. "The second crystal from the Tree of Life. I thought it destroyed."

Lomar saw a flicker of anger cross Kaplyn's face, but swiftly he controlled his temper. Lomar's gaze was drawn to the crystal. The last time he had seen it, it had glowed white, but now it burned green and that scared him.

"Tell me how it affects me and if it's of any use now," Kaplyn said.

Vastra nodded enthusiastically. "The crystal is the essence of pure magic, it cannot be destroyed. If you stand in the field it will create a gateway through which I would be able to pass."

507

Vastra's eyes betrayed his hope and Lomar sensed Kaplyn's reluctance. After all, why should he aid the man who had tried to kill him?

Vastra also saw his hesitation. "I promise that I will do what I can to make amends." Anger showed in his eyes. "I admit now my folly: I was an ambitious fool. Give me this chance, I implore you."

Lomar was afraid. They were pressed for time. He knew that his shaol could not be away from his body for too long, otherwise he might not be able to find his way back. Either they trusted Vastra or they left him there to rot. "Kaplyn, either way we must leave now."

Kaplyn nodded, causing Vastra to frown.

"What about the demon. Will he know if I have broken the spell?" Kaplyn asked, remembering all too clearly the demon that had taken him captive.

"No," Vastra replied. "Before, he was waiting for you with the guards and grakyn. Somehow he knew that someone was coming, but now he has gone."

Kaplyn walked towards the shimmering curtain. Standing next to it he placed a hand in the light as if expecting to meet with some resistance. Instead his hand passed effortlessly through. Satisfied, Kaplyn stepped forward.

Even when Kaplyn stood completely within the spell, Vastra hesitated. Lomar understood his dilemma; he would have to pass close to Kaplyn to gain his freedom. There was trust being offered on both sides. Vastra stood and then walked uncertainly from his cell, a look of disbelief on his face. Then his shoulders shook as silently he sobbed.

Kaplyn stepped back and turned to Lomar. "How do we get out of here?"

Lomar looked at the tunnel through which they had entered. "There were no other tunnels between here and the dungeon so I assume that there is no way out that way. You will have to cross the square and leave by the main gate."

"Who are you talking to?" Vastra croaked, drying his eyes with his sleeve.

Kaplyn explained about Lomar's shaol and what the albino had said. Vastra looked crestfallen with the news that his escape was not yet guaranteed.

Kaplyn felt his temper rising and fought against it. "Lomar, we need a diversion."

"I might be able to help," Lomar managed and then disappeared.

Tarn Molach was a big oaf of a man serving in the sixth division of the Aldracian foot infantry. He had never been very bright, and his mates often teased him about his slowness, although they were always careful not to goad him too far. He could break a man in half in his powerful arms.

Hundreds of tents surrounded Tarn and the others in his heft, many flying bright coloured banners and each denoting a different tribe. Tarn and his companions were currently playing quats; a game where coins were tossed to see who could get closest to the side of a helmet placed on the ground.

"When are we going to leave this place and bash a few Thracian heads?" Larnak asked, growing bored of the game. He was one of Tarn's closest friends.

"You'll get your chance," replied Stonar, the group's haft commander, a skinny weasel of a man who used Tarn's strength and lack of brains to his advantage.

"Look at those Dracs," Larnak continued. He didn't like Stonar and often cautioned Tarn against helping him. "They're a thick-headed bunch of country yokels who smell of sheep. Why were we billeted so close to them?" A group of Dracs was watching the game, but there was no menace in their intent. They were part of the eighth division and there was no love lost between the two units.

Some of Tarn's group laughed at the mention of sheep and Tarn "baaahed," increasing the laughter. The Dracs, sensing they were the butt of a joke, scowled back.

Tarn's group turned their attention back to the game. Abruptly a stone hit Stonar on the back of the head. The little man turned, rubbing the wound.

"Who did that?" he demanded, looking at the Dracs. No one had seen anyone throw a stone and so he reluctantly turned his attention back to the game.

Almost immediately another stone hit him with a meaty thwack. He collapsed in a heap, hugging his injured head. Quiet descended as all eyes turned to the Dracs, some of whom were laughing. Their laughter was enough to convince Stonar of their guilt. Rising he strode over, his eyes blazing angrily. As he approached he slowed his pace sufficiently to ensure that Tarn and the others were following.

"What's the meaning of throwing stones — you Drac sons of dogs!" The Dracs looked nervous; the sight of Tarn standing by Stonar's shoulder was enough to still their laughter.

Stonar took their silence for respect of his rank and that fuelled his courage. Pulling himself to his full height, he prepared to rebuke the Dracs further, relying on his companions (and Tarn) to keep him safe. Before he could utter a word the nearest Drac fell over in a heap. The others looked at

Stonar angrily, assuming he was responsible. The fallen man sat up, also staring angrily at the smaller man.

"Why'd you push him?" Tarn asked by his side.

Stonar was going to deny it when another rock hit him in the centre of the forehead, leaving a bloody patch. He collapsed in an unconscious heap. That was enough for Tarn who always protected the diminutive haft commander.

Bellowing, the big man launched himself at the Dracs who scurried for their weapons. Tarn's friends had no alternative; drawing their own , they launched into the fight. Within moments a hard, hand-to-hand battle raged between the tents.

Stonar, coming to and seeing the bedlam, retreated from the skirmish, calling on the sixth division to save their comrades. Soon the fight spread to the other divisions as old feuds and hatreds came to the fore.

The clamour and din of battle could easily be heard within the city where the citizens, thinking they were under attack, manned the walls. For the moment at least chaos ensued.

Lomar returned to Kaplyn and Vastra. The other two men had heard the commotion and had risked peering through a broken window. Lomar's reappearance was more than coincidental, and a large grin indicated that he had been up to no good.

"Your doing?" Kaplyn asked.

Lomar's grin broadened. "I think I might have delayed Aldrace's war effort," he pronounced. "We'd better leave while we can."

Kaplyn and Vastra left the cathedral through the window Kaplyn had entered over a week earlier. The main square was relatively quiet and a few troops rushed by, but none paid Kaplyn and Vastra any notice.

Both men squinted against the glare. Neither was in good physical condition; Vastra hobbled as best he could, considering his age, whilst Kaplyn fared little better.

"We need horses," Kaplyn said.

"That way," the albino said from behind his friend. Kaplyn glanced back and followed in the direction that he was indicating.

They limped towards the open doorway of an old barn. Inside the pungent smell of horses and hay filled the air. Several horses stamped impatiently, eager to be out of their stalls. Kaplyn selected two and as swiftly as he could he saddled them. Just as they were about to mount, to his shock, Kaplyn experienced a shrill warning from his shaol. He would have to get used to this new phenomena. He concentrated and felt a presence outside. Urging Vastra to hide, they just managed to conceal themselves behind a stack of hay bales as the door opened. To Kaplyn's dismay, framed against the light outside, he saw two Priests of Ryoch.

Lomar realised with a sinking feeling that the priests would be able to sense their presence in the barn with their shaol's aid, and it was only a matter of time before Kaplyn and Vastra would be taken prisoner.

Kaplyn pressed himself against a hay bale, casting Vastra a worried look. He pointed at the priests, hoping that he could do something to help, but he shook his head.

Kaplyn was furious and he fought to keep control. He was just considering tackling them when the priests abruptly turned and left.

After a few moments Lomar's spirit appeared.

"You helped?" Kaplyn asked.

Lomar nodded. "Fortunately, the link between the priests and their shaol was tenuous. It was a simple task to confuse them."

"Well done, now let's go," Kaplyn said, taking hold of the horses' reins.

Lomar stopped him. "I must leave. I need to return to my body before I lose contact with it entirely."

Kaplyn agreed and Lomar faded. Kaplyn explained to Vastra that Lomar was gone.

Together they led the horses from the barn. There was no alternative other than to walk towards the gate as though they had every right to do so. In the distance they could hear the metallic ring of weapons as the battle Lomar had fuelled continued to escalate.

At the gate, the guards looked nervous and Kaplyn suspected they might be stopped.

"Open the gate," he ordered, not pausing.

The two men looked at each other uncertainly.

"Open the gate or I'll have you flogged," Kaplyn continued using his most commanding tone.

Both men nearly fell over each other in their haste to comply. Clearly they both feared the priests.

Vastra and Kaplyn mounted and, as soon as the gates were wide enough, rode their horses through. The strain was too much and, as soon as they dared, they broke into a canter, but after a while weariness forced them to let the horses slow to a walk.

The ride back to the wood was uneventful, and Kaplyn shortly recognised the spot where they had ambushed the priest and stolen his robes. He and Vastra dismounted so that they could better travel beneath the trees. Kaplyn was near to dropping with fatigue when finally they entered the camp. The others were surprised to see them, and Lars beamed broadly when he saw Kaplyn, although his smile was short lived upon seeing Vastra.

"Where's Lomar?" Kaplyn asked, pre-empting any questions that Lars might raise. He saw him then, lying on the ground apparently asleep, but when he tried to find a pulse it was weak and erratic.

"Vastra, we need your help," Kaplyn said turning to the other man.

Vastra nodded, kneeling down besides Lomar. He traced runes over Lomar and called his name. When there was no response the old man looked worried. He repeated his actions, calling his name louder this time. Lomar's eyes fluttered then opened, although there were no signs of recognition. "Sleep," he croaked and with that his eyelids promptly closed.

Vastra sat back.

"Will he be all right?" Thaneck asked.

Vastra nodded before rising and looking around at the mixed group.

"I'm Tumarl," Tumarl said, his tone reflecting his distrust.

"And my name is Thaneck," the dwarf said, holding out his hand.

Vastra limply shook the dwarf's hand. "I'm Vastra," he replied, sounding weary.

Kaplyn was very close to falling asleep himself. He allowed himself a few moments more to change into his own clothes, keeping his back to the others to conceal his scar which still gave off a baleful green glow. Kaplyn suppressed a shudder. The light made him feel unclean, but there was little he could do about that now and, at least, he felt more comfortable in his own clothes.

They covered Lomar with extra blankets and Kaplyn made a bed close by. He had only just lain down when he fell instantly asleep.

Late into the night Kaplyn was startled from his dreams. He had another nightmare involving Shastlan who, since the attempt upon his life, seemed to have lost control of his senses. Friends and enemies alike died at his command, regardless of what they had done. No one could oppose him, not with the threat from his dragons. Kaplyn saw many men executed and Shastlan seemed to revel in their demise, convinced they were all traitors.

Sobbing Kaplyn sat up, hugging his knees. It was too dark to see. His scar ached, and he felt sick. He refused to even try to sleep, preferring to remain awake rather than experience again the terrible nightmares. His thoughts turned to Catriona, but he could not picture her, and this only served to fuel his frustration.

By morning his clothes were damp with dew. Stiffly he arose and nearly fell. His thoughts turned to food. The others were still sleeping and he noticed then how gaunt even Lars was. Taking up his bow and quiver he set off into the wood.

He returned some time later, carrying three rabbits and a squirrel. The others had arisen and Lars was sitting by a campfire, warming his hands. By his side Thaneck chopped wood.

To Kaplyn's relief Lomar was awake and sitting by the fire. He looked weary and his smile seemed to drain him of his remaining strength. Kaplyn thanked him for his help in their escape and, this time, Lomar's smile returned more easily. Vastra was sitting apart from the others, hugging his knees to his chest and, for a moment, Kaplyn felt sorry for him. Then he was distracted by Tumarl entering the glade, carrying a pan of water which he hung over the fire, using a framework of branches and rope.

With a start Kaplyn remembered the captive priest, and his eyes searched the glade, finding him still tied to a tree. He had a blanket which he was clutching tightly about his throat. He cast Kaplyn a baleful look.

A sudden urge swept over Kaplyn to kill him and, in his mind's eye, he saw himself butchering the other man; he fought the craving with all his might. His dreams were affecting him badly. He couldn't understand any of it. Was he becoming evil?

Behind him, Lars called out cheerfully, offering to take the rabbits from Kaplyn who realised he had forgotten about the game. Looking at Lars, he saw the hungry look on his face and felt a pang of guilt as he gave him the rabbits and the squirrel. He should not have brought his friends on such a hazardous journey. Tumarl took a rabbit from Lars and started to skin it.

Kaplyn decided it was time to talk to Vastra and called for him to join them. With difficulty Vastra arose, very much an old man.

"What happened after you betrayed us and left us in the tunnels?" Kaplyn asked.

Vastra stiffened, clearly uncomfortable talking about his disloyalty. "I took the crystal and left BanKildor. At the time I had hoped to gain power with the crystal and even perhaps to have revenge on your father, the King."

Kaplyn looked surprised. "You know, then, that we are half-brothers?"

Vastra nodded. He crouched like some great hawk, uncomfortable in its master's presence.

"I guessed in Kinlin castle. Both you and Hallar were clearly close friends. I wondered long and hard how you knew him. Later, I asked the imp who you were and it found out for me. It seemed ironic, two half-brothers travelling together, initially not even knowing we were related..."

"Go on," Kaplyn ordered.

Vastra snorted. "I travelled for a few days and finally came to the foothills where I made camp, commanding the imp keep watch. I, too, was betrayed and, in the dark of the night, a grakyn ensnared me.

"For years the imp was playing me for a fool and I, in my arrogance, never guessed. The imp's true master was a very powerful demon. It was sent to help me find the Tree of Life, and, all the while, I thought it was my doing.

"You see now why I am willing to help you! I seek revenge on the demons. The imp, for its own ends, fuelled my bitterness of our father. For years I let it nurture my hatred until its feelings became mine. Now I seek retribution, against evil."

"Revenge is a strong motivation, but it could cloud your judgement," Kaplyn interrupted, eyeing Tumarl. He looked back at Kaplyn, his face devoid of expression.

"I have a hatred born from more than sixty years of captivity. My life has gone. I have *nothing* left!"

"What of Drachar?" Kaplyn asked. "Does he exist?"

"Yes, his spirit lives, trapped between the worlds. Now his spirit grows stronger and he has gained partial access to this world, through men's minds. I know this all too well, for his thoughts came to me often in my captivity.

"For the first twenty years he simply mocked me. His spell prevented my ageing too swiftly, for he wanted to gloat over my petty ambitions. However, after a time, he became over confident and started to confide in me. He even asked my advice, although I never really knew whether he was testing me or not. I learned a great deal then so that I am now probably the strongest sorcerer ever to live, and, yet, I dare not use my powers." His head hung miserably.

Kaplyn was curious. "Why not?" he asked.

Slowly Vastra's head came up and his eyes were terrible to behold. "Drachar wanted to be certain that I would never betray him."

They waited for him to continue, spellbound by his tale. Finally he cleared his throat; his voice husky from lack of use.

"He has taken my soul. Even now it walks a world of darkness, confined to the demon world where I know that I will eventually join it. When I sleep, I dream of that vile place. I have witnessed sights that no man should ever see and evil beings whisper to me, promising a pain of a thousand deaths.

"I was taken to Trosgarth where they made me pay homage to Drachar's shade. I saw death knights being initiated. *That* sight will haunt me for the rest of my life."

"From Trosgarth, I was sent to Drishnack as bait, but I was not told who for. For the last year I was imprisoned in that golden cage, but why I was put there, I did not know. Not until you appeared, that is."

"Did you hear about the battle at CarCamel?" Kaplyn asked.

Vastra nodded. "Drachar's plan was to turn Allund against Thrace, hoping they would destroy each other, and then he intended marching on the Southern Kingdoms, his armies intact. Over many years, he sought to undermine the good will between Thrace and Allund. His plotting led to the downfall of the Allund Monarchy, and the Council now comprises his most dedicated servants.

"From what I hear he was very nearly successful, but, for some reason, Thrace was forewarned and combined forces with Allund to defeat his army. That must have been a considerable achievement, for one of Drachar's best sorcerers led it.

"I was forced to watch the huge armies gathering. Drachar was so very confident that his armies would succeed. Somehow, he has eliminated the dwarves, although he never revealed how he achieved this."

By Kaplyn's side Thaneck growled.

Kaplyn shook his head sadly. "What became of your crystal?"

"I don't know," Vastra replied. His face turned pale. "But I think it is in Trosgarth."

"Do you know of what it is capable?" Kaplyn questioned further.

Vastra nodded slowly. "With it, Trosgarth can open a gateway to the demon world — a permanent one."

"And this time there would be no Eldric to save us," Tumarl said softly.

Thaneck muttered into his beard and his eyes blazed with suppressed fury.

"So what do we do now?" Lomar asked, looking at Kaplyn.

Kaplyn could not meet the albino's scarlet eyes and deliberately kept his gaze on the cooking rabbits. "Eat," was all he managed and the others remained silent.

Chapter 10

Flight

After they had cleared away their breakfast, Kaplyn called them together. "I have decided to go on," he announced. His companions glanced uneasily at each other.

"Where to?" Tumarl asked.

Kaplyn took a deep breath. "Trosgarth."

Tumarl smiled, clearly pleased at the prospect of striking at the enemy's heart.

A light shone in Thaneck's dark eyes. "That will take us close to Thandor," he declared almost reverently, clearly wanting to visit his ancestral home to discover the fate of his people.

"Why Trosgarth?" Lomar asked.

"To recover Vastra's crystal from the Tree of Life," Kaplyn answered.

"Why?" Lomar countered, facing Kaplyn. "You could summon dragons, like Queen Catriona and the others want, and with their aid, defeat the demons."

Kaplyn looked horrified. "No!" he said simply, although his heart laboured in his chest at the mere mention of dragons. "They are evil and we would only be replacing one enemy with another." Briefly, he told them then about Shastlan and his dreams.

"But *surely* they are only dreams," Tumarl said.

Kaplyn shook his head. "I don't know," he replied. Tears filled his eyes and his voice shook. "Do not forget the dragon I summoned. And the dreams are so real. In Shastlan's world I have seen such slaughter — men, women and children."

For a moment they were silent. "We do need to leave," Vastra said at last.

"What do we do with the priest?" Thaneck asked.

Kaplyn looked at the prisoner who tried to avoid his gaze. He was young, a novice not yet indoctrinated into the ways of the priesthood.

516

Kaplyn's initial thoughts were to kill him, and what was so scary, it seemed so easy. He reasoned it was Shastlan's presence that made him feel that way, but the knowing that did not ease his conscience.

He walked over to the young man who stared up defiantly, although his eyes brimmed with unshed tears.

"You are from Allund?" Kaplyn asked.

The prisoner nodded.

Kaplyn drew a knife and the prisoner tried to draw back. "We have two choices," he said. "We could let you go, but no doubt you will betray us. The alternative is that we kill you."

A tear slid down his face and his eyes turned pleadingly towards the others, seeking signs of mercy.

"There is perhaps another choice," Kaplyn continued. The priest turned to look at him. "We could let you go and you could return to Allund and leave us in peace."

Renewed hope appeared in the prisoner's eyes.

"Some years ago the people of Allund could be trusted," Kaplyn continued talking. "Can you?"

The priest nodded enthusiastically. Kaplyn fought an urge to bury the knife in his throat; it was so strong, his hands shook. Instead he cut the prisoner's bonds and, rising, turned his back on the stunned prisoner who slowly arose, rubbing his wrists and looking at the others in confusion. Even then he expected to die. It took a great deal of courage to turn his back and walk away.

Tumarl cursed and cast Kaplyn an angry look. "We should kill him," he declared bitterly.

The others remained silent and, instead, set about breaking camp, but before they had extinguished the fire, a strange sensation swept over Kaplyn.

"Grab your weapons," he hissed, dropping his own pack and drawing his sword. The others stopped what they were doing and took up their arms. Tumarl had a crossbow that he had borrowed from the dwarves and, with considerable effort, he cocked the weapon and fitted a bolt.

By his side the fire turned a deep blue, causing the onlookers to glance at each other in horror.

A demon.

At the same moment Kaplyn's blade flared, matching the colour of the fire.

In the middle of the group, a jagged rent appeared, emanating a cold green light. How their camp had been discovered none could guess, whether a grakyn had spotted their small fire from above or perhaps they had simply lingered over long. It was too late to speculate now; already the evil odour of a demon assailed their nostrils.

A shape hurtled through the opening, causing the group to recoil at the suddenness of its coming. Tumarl was the first to react; levelling his crossbow he squeezed the trigger. The bolt hissed through the air. The demon had paused, assessing them before attacking. It was similar, but not quite identical, to the demon that Kaplyn had killed on the rooftop in CarCamel. Its arms were long and thin, ending in talons that shone like steel in the faint light of the wood. Its eyes were large and the pupils cat-like. A long tail flickered angrily behind the demon; at its tip was a deadly looking sting.

The demon waved its arm at the oncoming bolt, which flashed brightly and disappeared. Then it screeched, leaping at Kaplyn and Lars. Tumarl desperately tried to reload his weapon, but his shaking hands made it all the more difficult. Lars was closest and his axe flashed through the air, but the demon blocked it and then struck Lars a terrific backhand blow, lifting him from his feet, flinging him through the air.

Kaplyn cried out, swinging his sword at the demon's head. Fast as lightning the demon blocked the blow, but the blade bit deeply into the creature's forearm, slicing through its thick green skin before hitting bone. It screamed in pain, recoiling while striking out with its other talon. Thaneck threw up his axe to block the blow, but was thrown from his feet, colliding with Lomar who was trying to get behind the demon with his slender blade.

The demon stared at Kaplyn, a look of intense hatred in its eye. Never before had anyone inflicted such an injury. Crying words of power, it flung a spell at Kaplyn, but its power was deflected by his scar. For a moment, the demon hesitated, not understanding why its spell had failed. Kaplyn, seeing an opening, leapt forward, thrusting his sword at the demon's chest. Its tail swung around, trying to sting Kaplyn, but Lars stepped in to block the tail with his axe.

The demon screamed as Kaplyn's blade pierced its chest. With all his might, Kaplyn thrust harder, but the demon was turning and the blade simply cut across its chest. Its forearm smashed into Kaplyn, sending him reeling into a tree. The power of the demon's tail felled Lars who rolled away from the sting as Kaplyn collapsed groggily against the tree.

Kaplyn was dazed and barely registered the demon's attack. His sword came up automatically, but even with the Eldritch blade, his reactions were slowed by his fall.

With a scream of victory, the demon lunged. Suddenly a flash of light exploded in front of its face, causing it to draw back, howling in pain. An imp appeared before the demon, hovering in the air, hurling stinging shards that exploded into the demon's skin.

The attack was nothing more than an irritation, but it was enough to take its mind off Kaplyn and he was quick to recover. Bringing up his blade, he pierced the demon's belly. The sword crooned as it slid deeper, exulting as it claimed the demon's soul.

Falling backwards, the demon screamed a piercing cry that abruptly stopped when it hit the ground. Kaplyn let go of the sword so as not to let any blood touch him, having seen the effect of demon blood on stone and having no desire to see what happened with flesh.

The demon twitched and then lay still. Fearing a trick, Kaplyn ran forwards, grabbing the hilt of his sword and plunging the blade into its heart.

"I hate demons," he hissed, panting heavily. The others came up to Kaplyn and the imp hovered in the air above them. It was much smaller than its cousin Kaplyn had killed, more like a cat, although it was hairless except for a long mane running down its back.

Vastra turned to it. "Go! Do not return until I summon you. Hide, but follow and screen us from detection."

The imp bowed before disappearing.

"Will it betray us?" Kaplyn asked.

"No," Vastra replied. "As I have said, I am probably the greatest sorcerer alive today. The imp obeys *me* now and no one else."

"If you are so great," Tumarl spat, "then why did you not simply banish the other demon?"

Vastra's anger was palpable, "No sorcerer can interfere in the summoning of another. That is a basic law."

Wishing to prevent further argument. Kaplyn reminded them of their plight, "We need to leave — there might be other demons."

Hurriedly they hoisted their packs onto their shoulders, setting off through the trees and leaving the demon's corpse behind. As they departed, Vastra cast runes about the group to confuse anyone who might follow.

Initially, the trees were fairly well spaced and their progress was relatively good, although it was clear that Kaplyn and Vastra could not walk for long. Lars was concerned for Kaplyn whose eyes were sunken. He could see how little sleep he was getting, and, more often than not, he stumbled as though his concentration was elsewhere. Eventually, the trees thinned and they stood at the edge of the wood with open ground before them.

"There's not enough cover to cross. We should wait for dark," Thaneck growled.

"I could cast a spell of concealment." Vastra suggested.

While they argued, Kaplyn sat down heavily, grateful for a moment's pause.

Seeing his pain, Lomar came over. "I may be able to help you with my kara-stone." The Alvalan used the stones for healing. Kaplyn nodded, knowing he had little to lose.

Lomar withdrew his stone. It fitted his hand, radiating a gentle white light. As Lomar brought the stone towards Kaplyn, the glow from the stone was replaced by a baleful green glare, reminiscent of the light that had accompanied the demon.

Kaplyn drew back, a startled look in his eye. Lomar stayed his hand and the stone's glow returned to normal.

"Take it away," Kaplyn snapped. His eyes reflected his rage and, at that moment, Lars half expected Kaplyn to strike Lomar. The albino glanced uncertainly at Lars before putting the stone back within his tunic.

Rising on shaking legs Kaplyn started out into the open. Without a word the others followed. They had little choice. Immediately it was rough going. The ground was boggy and small stunted bushes with sharp needles grew in profusion.

As the day wore on, the scenery changed little and, as night fell, darkness grew about them. To their frustration, they were still in the marsh with zelph doggedly following, the small insects eagerly feeding off their blood. Lars swatted at them, but there were too many.

To add to their discomfort, it started to rain, the only bonus being that the zelph disappeared. Vastra, Lomar and Kaplyn fared worse as they had suffered the most recently and, as the rain soaked into their clothing, they started to shiver uncontrollably. They had no alternative but to stop. They sat down on their packs and huddled together for warmth, using their blankets for shelter.

"Why did only one demon attack us?" Tumarl asked.

"They were perhaps hunting by chance, investigating areas that seemed likely to conceal us," Vastra replied between shivers. "They could not search everywhere; it expends a lot of power to summon a demon. I was foolish. I should have thought to conceal us earlier. It is a simple enough spell."

At that moment the rain increased in fury. "Why can't you shelter us from the rain if sorcery is so *simple*," Tumarl hissed. By his side, the dwarf muttered in agreement.

"Because, in the demon world, that would be the same as lighting a beacon with *I am here* in large letters," Vastra answered.

Tumarl glared at Vastra but let the matter rest.. They were too cold and wet to remain where they were and so they decided to press on. They journeyed late into the night. They were a sorry sight, limping along at a weary pace, fatigued to the point of exhaustion.

Eventually the rain ceased, but it remained cold. A cloud of zelph appeared from nowhere, persistently following them. The tiny insects crawled under their clothing and into their hair. The group swatted and scratched. It was a miserable night for all.

Later, they noticed a change in the land. The ground started to rise and they found themselves on firmer footing. Large rocks appeared out of the darkness and they were forced to skirt around these. They came to a dip in the ground and with a great weariness sank down, simply unable to go any farther. Their surroundings at least gave them some protection from the wind and, even though they were soaked and miserable, they swiftly fell asleep.

It seemed as though Shastlan was waiting for Kaplyn to enact his nightly drama. He was riding on dragon back, high in a clear autumn sky. Below, farms and meadows were mere specks. Exulting in the thrill of flying, he laughed aloud. Behind him came ever more dragons; a flight of twenty, more than he had ever assembled before.

Shastlan was reminiscing about his earliest encounter with a dragon. He had acquired a spell to open a gateway to the dragon world from a travelling wise man. The spell had cost him dearly and the man who had sold it had been well recompensed — once the spell had been proven, of course. Shastlan had, at first, not believed it possible to summon a dragon, and his scepticism continued until finally a great red serpent had stood before him, almost as soon as the spell was cast. All too keen, Shastlan bid the dragon enter his realm and on its belly, the red serpent had crawled through the gap between the worlds.

The dragon had spoken with him for a long time, offering its service to aid Shastlan in a minor war that had been dragging for many years, making the monarch unpopular amongst his people. From that moment, he had found it difficult to comprehend what was happening. It was as though a fog had befuddled his mind and held him captive while the dragon spoke to him of the power he could achieve.

In his first skirmish, Shastlan had ridden against a local lord and, within moments, the enemy troops had been put to rout. True, some of his own people had died but many more of the enemy had perished.

Then the dragon had convinced Shastlan to summon its brethren. Only one dragon at a time could be called into his world, something to do with the balance of magic. However, the more dragons there were, the more they seemed to be required. War spread to different fronts and all too soon his men were soon scattered, fighting in foreign lands.

Now, as kingdoms crumbled, he had dragons in excess. This made victory ever easier but Shastlan's dragon counselled him against taking cities without a fight.

Their people will not respect you, the dragon's thoughts had tumbled through his mind. *You must set an example; otherwise, as soon as your armies march on, the people will rise against you, cutting off your supplies.*

The dragon's words had made sense and, after several cities were brutally sacked, others submitted meekly to his will. He now chose to ride at the head of his army to ensure that cities were suitably chastised prior to being subjugated.

He saw then the tall spires of GarLanar, reaching high into an azure sky specked with tiny clouds. Upon the walls horns sounded and gongs rang at the dragons' approach. Shastlan waved the command to attack. It was unnecessary for dragons communicated telepathically and already the command had been given. As one, the flight started the assault.

GarLanar was a beautiful city, famous through the lands for both its awe-inspiring architecture and its culture. It was not a city used to war, and its defences had been hurriedly erected after the fall of a neighbouring kingdom. The city was a marvel. Huge windows, designed to let in an abundance of light rather than protect its inhabitants, caught the early morning sun, dazzling the riders and dragons.

Shastlan's dragon struck first, spewing flame on a group of soldiers who huddled together behind a stone parapet; too afraid to even look at the attacking foe. They died without loosing a single arrow, and the tower burned fiercely as Shastlan's dragon arose, searching for other targets while around him dragons swooped down to attack. He watched as arrows bounced harmlessly from scales or flew wide of their mark, but there were simply not enough missiles to deter the attack.

From his vantage point high in the sky, Shastlan watched the battle flow. Some defenders tried to flee, dropping their weapons, but a dragon saw them and attacked, leaving charred remains where once had been men. Other defenders saw their colleagues die and at that point many lay down their weapons, searching for someplace to hide.

Growing bored, Shastlan urged his dragon to descend, electing to land on one of the towers guarding the ornate royal palace. Dismounting, he unfastened his cloak, letting it slip to the ground before drawing his sword.

A figure appeared from a smoking doorway. His face was black with soot and his clothes torn and singed. Nonetheless, Shastlan recognised Theal, a prince who had visited Shastlan some months earlier, seeking peace. Shastlan had made promises, of course, but that was before his army's situation had changed; their supply lines were dangerously stretched and he dared not leave a stronghold so close intact.

Theal threw down his sword. The metal rang loudly on the stone surface as it skidded before coming to rest. Until that moment Shastlan had not even realised that the prince was armed. The other man gave Shastlan a look of hatred before glancing sideways at his dragon which remained ominously still, as though cast from stone.

Shastlan walked slowly over to the prince enjoying the other man's uncertainty until they stood only a few feet apart. The prince stood bravely before his foe, his eyes locked on the other man's in defiance. Shastlan smiled and unexpectedly plunged his sword ferociously into the other man's unprotected belly. The prince doubled over, sinking slowly to his knees, his lifeblood staining the stone in a growing pool of crimson.

Kaplyn awoke screaming.

"I am not evil," he shouted. "Shastlan — you *bloody* murderer!" The others leapt from their blankets, grabbing for their weapons. Lars was the first to realise that Kaplyn had been dreaming, and he went to comfort his friend who was hugging his knees and rocking back and forth in anguish.

"Go *away!*" Kaplyn cried out as the big man came close to comfort him. "Leave *me* alone!" he screamed. Lars withdrew, stunned by Kaplyn's venom. The others looked at the big man with sympathy in their eyes, before looking back at Kaplyn with uncertainty. He had changed since entering Drishnack and not for the better.

Wearily Kaplyn arose and woodenly packed his gear. The dark circles beneath his eyes made him look haunted. He was clearly close to both physical and mental limits. Lars could not help but wonder for how much longer his friend could go on. The others packed and had to hurry for Kaplyn made no sign that he would wait. It was about mid-morning, and the marsh that they had recently crossed was behind them while before them low foothills gave way to tall mountains. They were still soaked from the overnight rain and their packs were sodden.

As they climbed, walking became more difficult, and, as the day wore on, it became obvious by his frequent stumbles that Kaplyn was suffering from the exertion and the lack of a deep sleep. He looked as though he was fighting an inner turmoil; his brow was creased as he scowled at the ground, toiling with the weight of his pack. Lars offered more than once to take it from him but Kaplyn refused. Occasionally he flinched and his eyes searched the sky as though expecting to see something there.

By mid-afternoon they came across a large number of boulders and Lars noted a dark opening behind one. He called to the others and went to explore. It was a cave and he beckoned to the others to come over. To their relief, Kaplyn did not object when Lars suggested stopping. He simply walked past them into the awaiting darkness like a man treading the path to his own execution.

As they entered a smile crossed Vastra's face. "Iron!" The others looked to him for an explanation. "The rock is an iron ore and that means I can use sorcery without fear of detection."

He traced a rune and immediately they were bathed in a soft silvery light and a small fire appeared at the centre of the cave. The warmth felt marvellous and they crowded around the fire, drying their clothes as best they could, spreading spare clothes on the floor.

After only a short while the cave became pleasantly warm. They removed what little food they had in their packs and shared out their meagre fare.

"Can you summon food?" Lars asked when they had finished. "I'm starving." What little they had left would normally have fed one of them.

Vastra shook his head sadly. "I cannot create food, but if there is game nearby I could try to attract it closer; that might, however, take time."

Lars looked crestfallen. With stomachs grumbling, they settled down to sleep for no one had slept well during the night due to the damp and cold.

Kaplyn lay on the hard floor stubbornly refusing to sleep, and, as time crept by, his mood became ever bleaker. He thought of his father, family and friends, all dead — and the weight of responsibility threatened to crush him. Terrible notions piled one on top of each other until he was caught in a spiral of self-doubt and loathing.

He fought his fatigue lest dreams overtake him. Shastlan's presence seemed to threaten as though his shaol was a tangible being, as real as his friends in the cave. Listening to their soft snores angered him, and he envied them their sweet surrender to forgetfulness. Sweat bathed his body, even though the fire had burned low and the air was chill.

After what seemed an age, he could no longer resist and sleep closed in about him. Immediately dreams crowded into his mind and the terror grew as, once more, he saw Shastlan's life enacted for his benefit.

In a tall cathedral decorated richly with gold and silver tapestries, Shastlan was finally proclaimed emperor. However, the newly crowned emperor did not hear the muttering of his own people, nor did he see the fear in their eyes as his coronation procession wound its way from the cathedral.

"The dragons are out of control," they muttered darkly. "Shastlan is a puppet leader — it's the serpents that rule."

Whenever Shastlan was away from the dragons, which was seldom, he craved their presence as though they were a drug. It was an addiction but, like any addict, he refused to acknowledge their spell.

Nathran, one of the few Generals that had survived the many recent purges, realised the effect that the dragons were having on his liege lord. He had been Shastlan's friend from childhood and that was possibly why his life had been spared.

Over the years others had begged Nathran to help to stop the slaughter, but he dared not and, now, his conscience wouldn't let him sleep. Even though the war was officially over, and all the kingdoms subjugated, there was still an excuse for massacres. Dragon riders searched fervently for enemy troops who had escaped the war, and, when these couldn't be found, they preyed on the refugees still struggling to find a home.

Finally Nathran could take no more, and, when the opportunity arose, he persuaded the emperor to accompany him on a journey, forsaking the dragons for a while, saying that his greatness would be diminished by their presence. Being vain Shastlan readily agreed.

Accompanied by a large retinue, they left the city, riding for many days. The weather was beautiful, mild with clear skies. At first, Shastlan was buoyant and good-tempered, but, as the days passed, he kept glancing backwards as though he longed to return. During this time, his mood became bleak and he threatened a great many people, Nathran included.

After a week Nathran saw further changes come over his emperor. It was as though he was awakening from a dream. Deep lines scarred the once youthful face and overnight grey hair appeared at his temples. When he slept, there was no escape from his own guilt and often Shastlan awoke, screaming and bathed in sweat.

One evening, Nathran found Shastlan standing alone by a river, looking into the shallows as the sun dipped lazily in the sky, casting beautiful shades of orange and red across the horizon. The shallow water bubbled over small rocks, soothing his weary mind. By the set of Shastlan's shoulders, it was clear that he was deeply troubled and Nathran, sensing that the time was ripe, questioned his once friend.

"Is something wrong?" he asked.

A look of chagrin crossed Shastlan's face and he fidgeted nervously. When he looked up at his general, his face was contorted with doubt. "Was the war right?" he asked, so quietly that Nathran was not even sure that he had spoken.

Nathran shook his head. Shastlan's eyes darkened and Nathran suddenly feared for his life.

"It's the dragons," he explained swiftly. "They're evil! They are controlling you!"

Shastlan's face turned crimson and his eyes burned fiercely, causing Nathran to step back in fear.

"No, the dragons were summoned by me to do my bidding," Shastlan stated. "I am in control," he shouted, his face red. Others in the camp glanced around, but returned to their assigned tasks, for it did not do to offend the emperor; not if you wanted to live.

All at once Shastlan's sword was in his hand, even though he had not realised that he had drawn it. Nathran did not draw his own weapon for this was his King and one-time friend. Even though he was terribly afraid, he knew he had to press Shastlan; the killing had to end.

"You are being used. Look around you. You and the dragons have destroyed nearly every kingdom, slaughtering their people; those left alive are scattered to the four winds and are hunted even now like vermin. Dragons have killed even our own people, by mistake you tell us, but *you* refuse to see the truth."

A dark rage swept over Shastlan. Nathran raised his hands, whether to show Shastlan that he was unarmed or in self-defence it mattered not. Shastlan plunged his sword deep into Nathan's stomach. For a moment the other man remained standing, a look of confusion upon his face. Slowly his eyes glazed over and the sparkle of life dimmed as he sank to his knees, clutching at Shastlan's cloak before falling onto his face. Shastlan retained his grip on the hilt of the sword and the blade came away free of the body, bloody and forever stained.

For several moments he stood over the corpse, a grotesque statue dedicated to an evil cause. The mists of anger faded from his eye and a terrible realisation came over him. He sank to his knees by his friend's side and wept openly. Unaware of what had just happened by the river, the rest of the emperor's retinue carried on with their tasks.

A sentry at the camp's perimeter glanced at the sky and saw four small specks. There was no mistaking the dragons, even at that distance, but the sentry simply assumed that they had been summoned by his emperor. When the dragons attacked, the sentry was the first to die.

Within moments the camp was ablaze as dragons swept down, one after the other; their shadows casting a premature darkness over the camp. A few troops fled from burning tents, escaping to nearby woods. The dragons let them go, knowing that there was nowhere for the men to hide; they would make good sport later.

By the river, Shastlan looked on in horror, too shocked to move. The horses made a fearful din before breaking free and bolting for freedom. At once the spell holding Shastlan broke. He ran to the camp, waving his arms, calling to the dragons to stop. He thought simply they had mistaken his camp for an enemy one; it never occurred to him that the dragons knew he was there.

A large red shape landed in front of Shastlan, making him stop and stare open-mouthed. It took a moment to recognise his own dragon, the first he had summoned to the land.

"You are killing my people. Stop it!" he commanded.

The dragon remained where it was, clearly not intending to do anything. Shastlan looked on as the horses were incinerated and their cries filled the air.

Finally he understood. "Why?" was all that he could manage.

We grow bored with you, the dragon's thoughts stated.

Shastlan's ire mounted. "I summoned you!" he shouted in frustration.

Yes. Our world was dying. This is our world now. You could have defeated us, if the people of the lands had united, but you did not, and now we are stronger. We really could not have managed without you and, for that, we are grateful.

Shastlan recognised the truth in the words. If it had not been for the might of his armies, the combination of the other nations might successfully have overcome the dragons and destroyed them. Now his armies were scattered across the land and would easily fall prey to the dragons.

Shastlan remembered then his sword and a desire for vengeance swept through his very being. Crying his battle cry, he threw himself at the dragon with a fury born of desperation. It was a useless gesture and he felt like a mouse turning on an owl. His sword felt heavy and his arm leaden. The futility nearly made him smile; dragon scales were impervious to swords.

In the cave Kaplyn thrashed in his sleep. Constantly his hand went to his side as though seeking his sword. Strange oaths leapt to his lips and abruptly he screamed into the night. His voice echoed about the small chamber before receding into the distance. The others awoke, terrified by the inhumane cry.

Lars scrambled from his bed and ran to his friend's side, but Lomar was there before him, preventing him from reaching his friend.

"Do not wake him," he said. "Perhaps if he confronts his fears, he will be whole once more."

"He needs our help," Lars complained.

"No. He needs to see this nightmare through to its conclusion," Lomar replied. His tone was firm and Lars felt that he could not object. It was a hard thing for him to do, but he sat back and watched Kaplyn struggle with his inner demons.

Shastlan didn't even make two strides. A blast of dragon fire engulfed him in a searing wall of flame.

In his dreams Kaplyn felt Shastlan's pain as flames washed over him. Even in his agony, Shastlan managed to take a couple more strides, determined to at least reach his nemesis. The smell of his own seared flesh assailed his nostrils as the flame continued to burn into his very soul.

A terrible cry rang through the cave, a cry of anguish and remorse. The cry carried with it the deaths of thousands and through it, souls cried out in torment until the cave echoed with their pain. Tumarl covered his ears and the others cringed in terror — fearful of the inhuman cry.

At that moment Shastlan died. However, his soul lingered, transfixed to the very world he had betrayed. A blinding light appeared, and he knew that he was looking at the exit from his world to whatever fate awaited his soul. He tried to take a step forward, but remained motionless and, with despair, knew that he was refused entry, not realising that it was himself denying his soul's release. Looking into the light, he sensed peace and tranquillity, yet, he was compelled to turn away, searching his own world for forgiveness, his own guilt driving him on.

Kaplyn sighed and, as the others looked on, the lines that had etched his face since his return from Drishnack seemed to fade, as he fell into a deep, dreamless sleep, his first for many weeks.

Lomar saw Kaplyn relax and, after the inhumane scream, thought that perhaps his friend had died. His slender fingers probed Kaplyn's throat for a pulse and, to his relief, found it, but in so doing he inadvertently revealed Kaplyn's scar. It no longer glowed with a green light and had returned to the same silver glow they associated with the Tree of Life.

"He's sleeping," Lomar said to the others.

Lars looked at Kaplyn with concern in his eyes. "Will he be all right?"

Lomar nodded. "He has faced his demons and survived. The scar changing colour is also significant. Perhaps he has managed to shrug off the effect of the Drishnack kara-stone. There is nothing more we can do for him now. He should sleep and I suggest we do the same."

Lars and Lomar returned to their beds, seeking a temporary release from the harsh realities of life. Vastra remained by Kaplyn's side moments longer, his eyes fastened on the crystal and its silver radiance while Tumarl sat by the fire, feeding kindling onto the embers. Gradually warmth crept into the cave, dispelling the chill that only moments before had held sway. A look of peace came over Kaplyn's face and, from his bed, Lars saw the look and recognised at last the Kaplyn of old.

Shastlan turned his back to the light as dark mists swirled about him, but he rejected these searching for something else. He saw then his world and what it had become. Humans were scarce now, if not destroyed altogether. Dragons regularly swept the skies, their cries of anger and frustration echoed through Shastlan's soul.

Once again they ruled a dead planet. In their own greed and lust for death, they had destroyed everything. Eventually, he assumed, they would destroy themselves in their folly and he prayed that would be the case. If they found their way to another world, then the slaughter would start all over again.

Shastlan wept. Phantom tears of real sorrow coursed down his ghostly cheeks as he watched the dragons squabble over a corpse. He resigned himself to an eternity of sadness and self-hatred.

And at that moment, a rent had appeared between the worlds. He felt a collision of immense power and, beneath his feet, the ground shook so hard that he thought that the end of the world must be nigh.

In Kaplyn's world, as he was being turned to stone in the tunnel beneath BanKildor, the Eldric spell had collided with the power of the crystal from the Tree of Life, and the force had been sufficient to tear through the very fabric of space.

Wearily and with resignation in his heart, Shastlan stepped through the void, accepting whatever fate awaited him.

Chapter 11

The Demon World

In his dream, Kaplyn found himself standing within a complete and unfathomable darkness. It took his weary mind long moments to realise that he was still asleep, and yet his surroundings seemed to be too real to be a dream. Abruptly he realised that another figure stood close by. Shastlan was staring back at him in wonder.

Kaplyn felt no fear as he willed himself to approach the other man's ghost. Shastlan's haunted eyes looked infinitely deep and harboured a terrible grief. Kaplyn spread his arms, embracing the shade and Shastlan returned it. For an instant, their embrace was real and for the first time in centuries Shastlan knew forgiveness.

It was a sense of forgiveness for Kaplyn as well. For so long now, ever since the dreams had started, Kaplyn had feared he, too, was evil. The killing of the priests in the training practice had shaken him severely, but now he accepted it had not been his fault.

Kaplyn suddenly sensed that somebody else was present and, turning, he recognised Lomar watching them. He walked towards him and Shastlan followed.

"What is this place?"

"I do not truly know," Lomar admitted. "It's a world beyond ours, connecting places and events."

From somewhere ahead Kaplyn heard a short, sharp cry.

"I don't think that you should look," Lomar cautioned.

Kaplyn frowned and Lomar shrugged. Using their minds they travelled through the dark swirling mists. As they approached they heard whimpers of pain and, then, from the darkness, the imp appeared, its small eyes shut tight in agony as it repeatedly stabbed itself with the point of a small dagger. They watched the scene in stunned silence.

"Stop" Kaplyn commanded in indignation. The imp ceased harming itself and its eyes flared open. The thin slits focused with some difficulty on Kaplyn who put up a hand. "Enough, let there be no more."

"Continue!" Vastra's voice echoed through the mists. "It betrayed me!"

The imp looked at Kaplyn, the blade inches from its bloody chest.

"No!" Kaplyn commanded, realising Vastra's voice was merely an echo of the other man's dreams.

"It is what will happen to me when I die!" Vastra raged. "My soul is already trapped in Hell."

Kaplyn understood and saw the truth of the words in the imp's eyes. "We are better than that."

Vastra's voice echoed into the distance as he slept on, and the demon faded, a puzzled look on its face.

Kaplyn turned to the other two shades. They, too, looked shocked.

"No man deserves Vastra's fate," Shastlan said.

Kaplyn nodded. "I wonder," he said more to himself than the other two. "If a demon can be summoned to our world, then can we go to theirs? Perhaps we could rescue Vastra's soul."

Lomar shook his head. "We could not travel there in our physical form, surely. The demons possess magic and that sustains them through the barrier between worlds. Perhaps if we opened a gateway to their world then we could, but that would require a crystal from the Tree of Life to keep the gateway open."

Kaplyn touched his scar. "I think I have a means to travel between the worlds here."

"There would be a grave risk," Lomar warned him.

Kaplyn shook his head. "Not if it was our spirits that travelled to the demon world and not our physical forms."

"No," Lomar shuddered. "I have travelled but short distances in the astral plane, and, even then, I found it difficult to find my body when I returned. What you are proposing is impossible."

"That is why you must remain here," Kaplyn answered. "The crystal will sustain me. I feel my own body like a beacon shining in the night."

Lomar shook his head. "You must not go. It is folly. You cannot hope to rescue Vastra's soul."

"I must try," Kaplyn replied. There was a terrible pain in his eyes. "Then he would be free to aid us."

Lomar hung his head as he realised that Kaplyn would not be swayed. Gradually his shade faded from sight.

Shastlan looked at Kaplyn. "You have made a brave decision. I will accompany you for I have a desire to see this world."

Kaplyn smiled, grateful to the other man. In the real world, opening a gate between the worlds was difficult. In the spirit world, it was so much easier as he could sense the other worlds. Opening his mind, he was shocked at how strong the lure of the dragon world was, but he ignored it. He felt the weaker presence of another world and opened a passage to that.

Immediately darkness and cold greeted them. Kaplyn felt for the scar on his chest but it had gone. However, there was a faint silver luminance where it usually was as though in the spirit world, it was the crystal that was the ghost.

Together, they stepped through the opening that snapped shut behind them. Large boulders littered the ground and, in the distance, tall mountains soared high above the plains. The only source of light was the rocks themselves, which seemed to give off a green glow. A terrible stench of decay filled the air.

It was Shastlan who broke the silence. "This place frightens me above all others. This is the very heart of every nightmare I have experienced — both living and dead. Even still, I feel drawn to this place like a moth to the flame. This is where I belong," his eyes looked blank as he spoke and Kaplyn understood the other man's fears.

"No! You should return," Kaplyn suggested. "I will manage on my own."

The vacant eyes looked at Kaplyn and a shallow smile played across dead lips. "I think that I am bound to this course, and besides, do you know where to go?"

Kaplyn shook his head.

"It is my destiny to guide you then. I feel the source of evil as though my own guilt is drawing me to it. I could not return now, even if I wanted to."

With that, they arose and started walking. Their every step was agony.

"Why is it so painful?" Kaplyn gasped.

Shastlan forced back a smile. "Have you not realised?" he replied grimacing. "This is Hell."

Back in the cave, Lomar awoke to find that the others were gathered about the fire and had arranged Kaplyn as close to the heat as possible. Lars looked worried. "What is going on, Lomar?"

Lomar looked at Kaplyn's body, the flesh looked pale and the breathing shallow.

"He has left us for a while," he answered simply.

"My dream was true then?" Vastra asked.

Lomar nodded.

Vastra's eyes widened. "This is *folly* — what does he think he will achieve?"

"He intends to rescue your soul," Lomar replied.

Lars looked angry. "What is going on?" he demanded.

"Kaplyn's spirit has departed his body. He goes to the demon world to free Vastra's soul," Lomar said.

Vastra closed his eyes and groaned aloud. "Then we are truly lost," he predicted bleakly. It was at this point that Tumarl noticed Kaplyn's feet were bleeding.

Cresting a small rise Kaplyn saw a gully below their present position, running towards a tall imposing mountain, at the base of which they could see a cavern.

"There," said Shastlan pointing, "is the source of the evil, and that is where I at least must go."

Kaplyn looked into the darkness. The cavern entrance was practically invisible against the green glow of the rocks. "I have seen this place in my dreams," he stated with some awe. Boulders were strewn across the ground between them and the cave, but that was the only cover. The thought that he somehow knew this place terrified him though, and he had to summon all of his resolve to continue.

With mounting reluctance, Kaplyn took a few steps forward. They were the hardest of his life, and he hoped he would never have to experience such a feeling of utter hopelessness ever again.

As they drew nearer the cavern, Kaplyn saw movement. A huge beast lolled into the open only a few hundred feet in front of them. Its eyes were fixed intently on them. Kaplyn wanted to flee but his legs failed to comply.

The beast had two heads which looked very much like that of a large dog, but there the similarity ended. Its body was long, broad at the neck and tapering to a wide flat tail. Thick muscles made its hind legs look too large, whilst its forearms looked too short but ended in vicious looking talons.

Shastlan was ignoring the creature, heading towards the cave. When he realised Kaplyn was not following, he turned and beckoned. "It's all right," he proclaimed. "He guards the entrance to the underworld from the living, not the dead."

"Am I not living then?" Kaplyn asked.

"Not to me or the demon," Shastlan answered softly. "We see only your shaol." With that Shastlan continued towards the cave. Concentrating on putting one foot before the other, Kaplyn wished that the nightmare would end.

In pain they entered the cavern. The tunnel ran straight and flat for some way, and the walls were worn smooth as though water had once rushed through the opening. He had thought that the tunnel would be completely dark, but the same eerie green glow as outside enabled him to see some way ahead.

With a sense of mounting dread they continued.

Lars looked at the others, "We must do something," he said, his voice shaking with emotion.

"There is *nothing* we can do," Vastra said. "It is his choice and it must be his decision to return."

"Will *we* be safe in here?" Lomar asked Vastra.

The old man's face looked gaunt and haggard and dark circles ringed his eyes. "If the demons capture Kaplyn, they will try to find out where he has come from and, no doubt, they will trace the power of the crystal back to its source; then we would be in real danger. However, there is an even bigger problem … if the demons find Kaplyn's body, they could open a permanent gateway to this world, right here."

Lomar looked horrified. "He could be doing exactly what they want him to do," he said in a hushed whisper.

Vastra nodded; his look was enough to convey his fears.

As they continued down the tunnel, the image of the crystal in Kaplyn's chest faded until eventually there was barely anything to see other than a discoloration of the skin. The further they went, the wearier they felt, but still they continued.

Then a dull thump reverberated through the cavern floor, causing both men to halt. Kaplyn placed a hand on the rock and felt a tremor run through its cold surface. They couldn't explain what had happened, so cautiously they continued.

Soon they encountered other spirits, hiding in the shadows, crying pitifully. Kaplyn searched for Vastra but did not recognise any of the faces.

"Of all the souls here, mine is the only one deserving of this fate," Shastlan stated.

Kaplyn glanced at the other man, "The blame is not yours. You were under the dragons' spell."

Shastlan hung his head and continued to walk. Kaplyn wished that he could help but did not know what to say. Then the shades became more numerous, and their cries filled the tunnel which abruptly opened into a huge cavern. Kaplyn searched as many faces as he could, trying to locate Vastra's soul, but the task was impossible.

At that moment a shrill scream rang through the cavern and Kaplyn saw the first signs of demons. Dark shapes flickered across the cavern roof, tormenting souls wherever they went, and a great cry of fear followed the shapes. Kaplyn felt a searing pain across his back and turned to see a shape disappear into the shadows, carrying a long whip, randomly inflicting pain.

A closer scream caused Kaplyn to jump, and his eyes were drawn to a soul being roasted on a spit. The pain was real and, judging by the cries, the shade felt every lick of the flames. By its side, a demon feasted.

Kaplyn dragged his eyes away. The hall was immense, disappearing far into the distance. Thousands of ghosts milled around. They became part of the mass and were soon lost amongst the cries of woe and misery.

Imps materialised, gleefully spreading plague and other ills. Kaplyn saw souls suddenly spouting red spots, which immediately grew into blisters. Horrified, he watched as the disease spread and limbs turned gangrenous and rotted. The soul seemed to die a very real and painful death, but only moments later recovered, their eyes filled with pain and fear as new torments were thrust upon them.

Kaplyn seemed to be immune, and his crystal's glow returned faintly to his chest as though protecting him. He tried to keep hidden and, in this at least, seemed to be successful. Shastlan kept by his side and perhaps Kaplyn's magic extended to protect him.

"We are trapped here," Shastlan pronounced.

"No!" Kaplyn reassured him. "I can open a gateway back; do not fear. We will escape. Remember that."

There was no sign of Vastra and Kaplyn began to realise the enormity of their task. Occasionally a demon appeared carrying a whip or some other weapon and inflicted a real pain, which even Kaplyn's charm could not prevent. At these times they retreated with the other spirits, trying to hide amongst their vast numbers. They could not rest. Weariness dogged their every step, but somehow they kept on going. It was worse than any nightmare. Kaplyn feared they would meet someone he knew and that might very well tip the balance of his sanity.

"This is hopeless," he declared finally. "We'll never find Vastra's soul. We had better return. The risks are too great and, for all I know, my body might be dying at this very moment.

"I'll open a gateway, but not here. Not where the demons can see us." Kaplyn continued. They moved towards the distant entrance. Although they were technically ghosts, they felt the presence of the other spirits and could not pass through them as they had expected. In effect, they were constrained to follow any general trends in the direction of the crowd, which impaired their progress.

Tostor, a demon lord, fed on the fear and torment as he flew. He was newly back and basked in the darkness, cleansing himself of the impurities of the other world.

Abruptly an imp appeared before him. Tostor was tempted to ignore it, but its thoughts penetrated his own. He paused, his attention now entirely riveted on the imp, and he could barely believe what it was telling him.

"Where? Show me!" he commanded.

The imp darted off with Tostor's dark form following. Souls scattered before them, trying to escape the demon's wrath, but two failed to flee as quickly as the others did.

Tostor immediately recognised the soul of the Priest of Ryoch he had captured in Drishnack. Kaplyn was the name that came to mind, and a feeling of euphoria swept over him. So, Kaplyn had died and his soul captured. This should be fun.

Kaplyn and Shastlan had nowhere to hide. The dark form of a giant bird appeared and, with it, silence fell about them like a blanket. The bird changed shape and in its place stood a man. Kaplyn immediately recognised him as a satisfied smile spread across the demon's lips.

"This is the second time that we have met, and I get the distinct impression that our destinies are intertwined, for a short while, at least."

Kaplyn wished for his sword. His fist clenched and unclenched in frustration.

"The last time we met, I confined you to the dungeons." The demon paced around Kaplyn like a cat watching its prey, waiting and daring it to move. "I don't know how you died but I shall enjoy tasting you," the demon hissed, drawing closer.

Back in the cave Lars watched over Kaplyn. Suddenly he called to the others and, when they came over, Kaplyn was thrashing wildly while Lars struggled to hold him still.

"What's wrong?" Tumarl asked in fear.

"Just hold his legs," Lars commanded.

Tumarl grabbed Kaplyn's legs and, together, they pinned him down. Almost immediately his body relaxed and so they let go. Automatically his hand went to where his sword should be, groping for the weapon.

"He seeks his sword. Perhaps if he touches it he will be reassured," Lomar suggested.

Vastra brought the weapon over and Lomar laid Kaplyn's hand on the hilt. Fervently Kaplyn gripped the weapon, his knuckles went white with the effort and his body convulsed once more.

The demon stopped, its eyes wide with fear.

Kaplyn looked down. A blue light was in his hand and it took several seconds before he realised what it was. It was the ghostly image of his sword and its light seemed to cause the demon considerable stress.

Tostor tried to attack, but Kaplyn moved his arm up to defend himself, and instantly the blue light flamed. The power of the weapon increased the closer the demon came, and Tostor screamed, shielding his eyes and falling back.

"Follow me," Kaplyn cried out to Shastlan.

He pressed the demon and it retreated farther, confused by the light that filled him with such dreadful pain. Only his pride prevented him from fleeing altogether. This was his domain and he was not about to let a soul get the better of him.

Kaplyn was frantic. He concentrated on his scar, using the power from his sword to focus his thoughts. The sword's blue light shot along his arm to his chest. When the two powers collided Kaplyn felt exhilarated, and swiftly he opened a gateway.

"Shastlan! Quickly, go through." Other demons surrounded them, but they dared not attack for fear of the light.

Tostor hissed, sensing that they were escaping. In frustration his shape changed from a man to that of a large bat-like creature. The imp scurried away, fearful for its very existence and, when the hateful light winked out, they were gone.

In unison, the demons shrieked, their anger rippling through the assembled souls, a tidal wave of pure hatred. At the sound a great cry of despair echoed through the cavern.

In a dark corner of the underworld one soul watched in detached silence. He was separated from the others since his fate was different to theirs; as yet his body had not died. Vastra's soul watched the writhing mass. For years he had been witness to the demons torturing the souls, aware that any day he too would join them in endless torment.

The lesser demons set to watch over him drank in his anguish, whispering nameless horrors to torment him. A single tear fell down his cheek. A tear — as real as any in the world.

Kaplyn awoke with a pain in his side. He was lying on solid rock that dug mercilessly into his flesh. Memories came flooding back and he sat upright, a scream issuing from his lips. The cry echoed through the cavern and the others jumped with fright.

Lars was stunned by Kaplyn's look of abject terror. His face was pale and drawn and deep, dark smudges ringed his eyes. Great sobs racked his body as he tried to breathe. Seeing his friends eased his pain, but he had endured something that no one should ever experience, and he knew the horror of the demon world would haunt him for the rest of his life.

I have failed, he thought. The risk was too great, but it was his failure that made it worse. He was at the lowest ebb of his life, and, no matter how hard he tried, he could not banish the images of people being tortured.

His eyes searched those of his friends for reassurance, but he could not meet Vastra's gaze. He understood his fears now, and knew he had been his last hope.

Strangely, it was Shastlan's spirit that helped Kaplyn through those first few moments. He remembered the feeling of release Shastlan had experienced when he had died. The memory of the bright white light came back to Kaplyn, and he knew that even though evil existed, there also existed good. Kaplyn used that thought as an anchor to bolster his failing courage.

"It must end," he said at length, gasping in pain. He could see that the others didn't understand. "The demons must be destroyed." Kaplyn was looking at Vastra. "I am sorry," he said. "I tried. It was too much."

Vastra nodded, a tear coursed down his cheek at the same moment that his spirit shed a tear in the dark caverns of the underworld. "It is no more than I deserve. It's my fault that many have been sent to that dreadful place and many more are still to go."

"We are not beaten yet." Kaplyn hissed "By all that I hold dear, I will do all in my power to destroy them."

It was Lars who brought them back to the present. "Are we safe? Will the demons be able to follow Kaplyn here?"

"I think not," Vastra replied, "although I cannot be certain. The iron in the mountain will confuse them, but perhaps we would be safer moving on."

"Do you feel strong enough to leave?" Tumarl asked of Kaplyn, who nodded. He felt exhausted, but he also knew they had to leave.

Lomar was the only one to remain silent. He kept his thoughts concealed behind a veil of silence.

Chapter 12

Anguish

They left the relative safety of the cavern, venturing forth into an uncertain future. Kaplyn walked with his back bowed as though carrying the weight of the world's ills. If he had seen his image in a mirror, he would have been more concerned still. He looked half starved, pale from days of inactivity.

At that moment Kaplyn's courage nearly failed. More than ever before, he feared the demons and automatically his hand sought his sword's hilt. Almost immediately a bleak despair swept over him. He kept seeing the faces of souls, damned to an eternity of torment. In silence he trudged along, falling farther behind as a black depression overtook him.

Oblivious to Kaplyn's mood, Lomar looked up at the distant mountains which seemed so very bleak and inhospitable. They would have difficulty crossing those unobserved and he realised then the enormity of their task.

Thaneck was by Lomar's side and he saw the direction of his gaze. "The Chantell Mountains," the dwarf sighed.

Lomar realised he was being spoken to and freed his mind from his troubled thoughts. "Sorry Thaneck, I was thinking. What did you say?"

"There is a beauty about these mountains that I had not thought possible," Thaneck said.

Lomar looked once more at the towering pinnacles. Their peaks were lost in low clouds so he could only guess at their full size. Judging by their shape they were tall indeed and Lomar's earlier concern was replaced with awe as he tried to realise their height. "They are massive," he admitted, almost to himself.

"Long ago Boland, a dwarf chieftain, scaled the summit of BanKennet, the tallest in the range. We cannot see it yet; it is still a long way off. That was where he met the lord of the dristal, and so great was his achievement that the great bird spoke to him, the first time a dristal had ever spoken.

"The tales say that Boland bowed to the lord and the great bird promised that his race would serve the dwarves, acting as their steeds. Since that time, dristal have always served us loyally; however, there are only a few of the birds in Kaldor and their numbers, like the dwarves, are diminishing."

Thaneck's voice dropped to a whisper and Lomar had to strain to hear his final words. "I'm afraid of what we will find if we get to Thandor," Thaneck confided. "Many dwarves have trodden this path, seeking the fate of our people, and yet none have returned."

"It's a considerable distance and there are many perils between Kaldor and your homeland," Lomar said, trying to lighten the dwarf's mood. "Anything might have happened."

Thaneck shook his head sadly. "The land must be a dangerous place indeed if a dwarf is kept from his homeland. No, in my heart, I fear something evil has happened. Even at this distance the mountains seem oppressive and my feet, which should feel light and eager to reach our goal, now feel weary."

Both fell silent, each nursing their own thoughts. Lomar's apprehension increased as he looked into the distance, wondering what evil lurked there.

After several days, the group entered a narrow ravine between two tall, dark mountains wreathed in thick grey cloud that threatened snow. A turgid river, swollen with the thawed snows of the mountain peaks, ran swiftly through the pass. The water was thick with mud which concealed its true depth.

The path they were following wound its way alongside the river, but high above it. The drop from the path to the river was often vertical rock, making the journey all the more perilous. While walking along a narrow part of the path, Kaplyn's despair reached a pinnacle. His head was bowed and his gaze was fixed upon Lars' heels as the group slogged on.

The noise of rushing water filled his mind and, in its constant roar, he felt he could hear the wails of the spirits imprisoned in hell. The trees at this point were sparse and only a few managed to cling stubbornly to life on the steep slope. He was only distantly aware of the gorge's steep sides and how far below the river was.

Abruptly the group stopped and, wearily, Kaplyn came to a halt, realising as he did so that the others were discussing something about the path. With a great effort he looked up. An old suspension bridge dangled as if by magic between the sides of the ravine. In places planks were missing and some looked dangerously thin.

Tentatively Lars stepped onto the bridge that creaked and groaned beneath his weight. With care he started to cross, occasionally stepping over broken planks. Knowing his fear of heights, Kaplyn marvelled at his fortitude.

Lars finally made it to the far side where he stood for a moment to regain his breath, grinning back at the others. Kaplyn found himself walking towards the bridge. No one objected to his crossing next and the others simply let him pass.

Shastlan stirred and Kaplyn felt his sudden fear as he sensed Kaplyn's innermost thoughts. Kaplyn closed his mind to the voice that by now seemed so much a part of him.

At that moment Lomar looked shocked. Perhaps he realised his friend's intent, but it was too late for Kaplyn was already on the bridge and had started across. Lomar looked about wildly, but the bridge was too rickety to support more than one person at a time.

All at once Shastlan's voice fell silent and Kaplyn felt truly alone. He arrived at the centre of the bridge, which swayed gently beneath his feet as he paused, facing the river.

Far below the waters boiled like a seething, liquid mud. A tree trunk, caught in the fierce flow, thumped against the granite walls of the bank and then was swiftly carried into the river's centre, only to be smashed against the opposite side a few moments later. Kaplyn's legs suddenly felt weak with fear. The tree was an unnecessary reminder of the force of the river. He would be dead before he hit the surface he thought. The banks were narrow at this point, and the rock face protruded at several points before plunging sharply downwards.

The board beneath Kaplyn suddenly sagged and the wet wood creaked ominously. He felt thankful in a way, for he realised that he could never throw himself in. With a loud crack the wood splintered and he fell.

At the last moment he instinctively spread his arms, catching the wooden planks either side. The strain on his arms was unbearable, and he cried out, awaking a primordial feeling that has accompanied man since the start of time — the will to survive.

Memories came flooding back — no longer the dark depressing memories of the recent past, but happier memories of family and friends. He thought of Catriona and her image sprang to the fore. Tears cascaded down his cheeks as he cried out for help. He was weak from lack of food; without realising it, he had been starving himself. Desperately he clung on.

The roar from the river drowned the shouts of concern from his friends. On the opposite bank, Lars stepped onto the bridge. His action prevented the others from doing anything, as it would not support three. The ropes strained under the additional weight. The wooden planks were now steeper than with just one man on and Lars had to grip the rope rails to prevent himself from slipping.

Kaplyn was crying out in fear when the big man came within reach. Leaning back to brace himself, Lars reached under Kaplyn's arms before backing up, one step at a time. As Kaplyn struggled free, he finally managed to get his feet under himself. Free of his burden, Lars straightened and together they carefully made their way across.

Once on the other side, Kaplyn collapsed into a heap. The tears that he had bottled up for so long flowed freely and he sobbed uncontrollably. The others crossed one at a time without further event. Silently they waited for Kaplyn to recover.

Then Vastra knelt by Kaplyn's side. "The blame is not yours," he said. A tear slid down his old face. "I am to blame for what has happened, but I need you to be strong to help me. I promise I will do all I can to undo the evil I have created. I promise that with every fibre of my being."

Lomar, too, knelt by Kaplyn, placing a hand on his shoulder. He smiled at his friend, seeking to lighten his mood. "Evil will not prevail," he said simply.

Kaplyn felt Shastlan's presence and realised then why he had lost contact with his shaol. Shastlan had recognised Kaplyn's despair and had no defence to it. He had no option but to close off his own mind.

Kaplyn smiled at the others. He hoped they had not realised what he had intended, but, deep down, knew it had probably been all too obvious.

"Lars, I know now why you don't like heights," he said weakly.

Lars smiled back warmly. "Perhaps I'm cured. Flying a dristal probably helped."

By his side Tumarl looked as though he was about to say something, but chose to remain silent. Kaplyn wondered whether he had glimpsed his own inner turmoil, and his own death wish. Then the moment was lost and he fixed his gaze on the distant horizon.

A sudden flurry of snow forced his eyes half shut and he suggested that they continue. They were glad to leave the bridge to the mercy of the elements.

All that day the snow continued.

The path became steeper, taking them away from the river. All too soon the path was snow covered and the surrounding trees looked like an army of white skeletons.

Then the snow turned into a blizzard and, abruptly, they could no longer differentiate land from sky; both merged together in a single gray haze. Their senses, too, seemed to betray them. With the lack of a horizon, it was difficult to tell if they were going up or down, and only the exertion assured them they were still climbing. A fierce wind blew and the snow stung their eyes, forcing them to shut them for brief periods of rest.

As night fell they huddled together behind a large protruding rock, using its lee for protection. Vastra refused to use his magic to light a fire in such an exposed place and, with such a strong wind, they had little option but to remain cold. Eventually Kaplyn cursed and then pronounced they were better off walking. Rising, they continued with Thaneck guiding them.

Kaplyn found himself mesmerised by individual flakes as they gusted down towards him one moment and then rose abruptly the next. It was a terrible, hard slog and they simply bent their backs and climbed, putting one weary foot in front of the other. The night seemed to take an eternity to pass and, just as they were beginning to despair, the wind ceased and, as if upon command, the darkness lifted to welcome a weak, watery dawn.

In the renewed light they could see the top of the present slope and finally they reached the summit where a flat expanse greeted them. In the distance tall peaks arose upon the horizon and, seeing these, Tumarl groaned.

"Don't worry," Thaneck assured him. "This is as high as we go. Over there," he indicated the tallest peak, "is BanKennet — the highest mountain in the entire world." Unlike the other peaks, this was steep and craggy in the extreme. Its sides looked nearly vertical and the onlookers were impressed indeed that anyone had managed to climb it.

Exhausted after their hard night's toil, they rested behind a snowdrift. Sitting on their packs they ate a few paltry scraps before lying down to sleep, trying to ignore the fact that their food supply was dangerously low. Before them, a golden sun rose and the clouds withdrew to the horizon, giving the world a spectacular sunrise as though the very heavens had been set ablaze. With the rising of the sun, the snow took on a light blue hue and its unexpected warmth helped lull the weary travellers to sleep.

They slept until mid-day, and, as soon as they awoke, they decided to set off. Their journey was across relatively flat ground and, after their climb, they enjoyed the brief respite. Walking at a swift pace helped to dispel the cold and, for the first time in days, they actually felt warm and their steps lighter.

However, as the snow became deeper, the going became more difficult. Nonetheless their distant goal gradually drew closer and by mid afternoon they were standing on a steep incline on the furthest side of the plateau. With renewed hope they started the descent.

Chapter 13

Ambush

The small group descended the steep mountainside, taking care. Despite their care small rocks, hidden by a thin covering of snow, occasionally gave way beneath their feet, causing them to slide down the incline. Soon, to their relief, it became less steep and, after only a short while longer, the snow became patchy being replaced by rock and tufts of a hardy grass.

Thaneck caught up with Kaplyn and walked beside him. "We have been in the kingdom of Thandor for some time now," he declared softly. "I cannot be certain, but, in earlier days, there would have been dristal patrols. With the skies this clear, we should have been spotted by now." His eyes went to the heavens and his brow furrowed.

Thaneck's obvious fears troubled Kaplyn. "Can you advise us of a less travelled route to take us there?" Kaplyn asked.

The dwarf frowned. "I've deliberately kept us east of Thandor. The city is not easy to find and I feared that we might miss it in a blizzard. All we have to do now is stay at roughly this height and travel west. We should then cross one of the many dwarf roads. Whether we find one less travelled is up to chance."

"How much further is it?"

"Perhaps half a day — perhaps longer. I'm not too sure."

Kaplyn felt Shastlan's presence and used the shaol to search the vicinity for signs of life. As far as he could tell, they were alone.

Gradually a mixture of fog and cloud grew about them and the air became damp, but at least that hid them from view.

"How far are we from Trosgarth?" Tumarl asked from behind Kaplyn. It was the foremost question on everyone's mind.

"Below the mountains there is a large plain which was once part of Chalynth. Trosgarth's border is about twenty miles beyond that," Lomar answered

"If I'm not mistaken, it's getting colder the closer we get," Lars said.

Kaplyn nodded. "It's almost as though the cold is coming from there." An image sprang to mind of the demon world and involuntarily he shuddered. It was a memory he would prefer to forget, but that seemed impossible.

By Kaplyn's side Thaneck looked dispirited; his beard, soaked by the dampness in the air, looked particularly bedraggled. His eyes looked haunted and his tone lacked conviction. "We should reach Thandor today," he said. The others knew that he was uncertain, but tactfully they remained silent.

For most of the day they walked with Thaneck taking the lead. Gradually, weariness forced them to slacken their pace and, by late afternoon, they realised that they were not going to reach their goal that day. Reluctantly, as darkness grew about them, they decided to halt.

Desperately they huddled together for warmth. It was Kaplyn who finally decided they had to have a fire. They gathered what wood they could find and Vastra, using his powers, ignited the small pile. Eagerly they crowded around the flames, trying to conceal the glow with their bodies. Soon steam arose from their arms and legs.

Kaplyn, looking at the hopelessness on their faces and realizing that he had to do something to raise their morale, decided a hot meal would revive them. Taking up his bow, he told the others he would search for game. No one objected and so he slipped into the night.

Using Shastlan as his guide, he looked for signs of life, but was forced to travel farther from the camp than he felt comfortable with. White tendrils of mist drifted before his eyes, stirred by the mountain air. It was eerie being alone and he started to regret leaving the others.

All at once he felt a warning from Shastlan. Crouching down he listened, but could hear nothing. He felt vulnerable in the open and afraid. Without waiting, he hurriedly retraced his steps back to the others.

He was alarmed by their carelessness. Their fire burned brightly and their voices carried easily on the still air. Entering the camp, he gestured to them to be silent; his look of concern was a sufficient warning that something was amiss. Lars moved to scatter the fire, but Kaplyn stopped him — he had an idea.

He gestured to the others to rise, and hurriedly he started to lay blankets on their packs, trying to make it look as though the camp was occupied. The others copied what he was doing and, when they had finished, they retreated into the darkness. Kaplyn glanced back. In the poor light and with the fog, it looked as though several figures lay about the fire.

They continued climbing back the way they had come for a short distance and then they lay among the rocks to watch. Kaplyn and Lomar had their bows at the ready while Thaneck aimed his crossbow towards the campsite. Kaplyn wanted to see who it was that he had sensed. At least for the moment, he was satisfied they could go back into the darkness if there were too many enemies approaching.

Moments dragged slowly by. Kaplyn again used Shastlan to sense the surrounding area and was rewarded by the presence of several life forms, but, as yet, he could not be certain who or what they were. Even knowing that somebody was out there, it was still a shock when a lone dark shape crawled into the feeble light surrounding the campsite.

Several other shapes followed and, together, they crawled towards the fire and their packs. They were careless, and Kaplyn saw an irregular glint from a weapon and the occasional clink as something metallic came in contact with a rock. He counted four figures and sensed two more concealed amongst the rocks.

He waited until the nearest shapes were close to the fire before taking careful aim, releasing a shaft. The barb buried itself into the earth scant inches from the lead figure. Instantly the shape froze.

In a low voice Kaplyn challenged the intruders. "Do not move. We have more weapons aimed at you. At this distance we will not miss." His threat was taken seriously for the figures remained motionless.

"One of you, stand up and make yourself known," Kaplyn ordered.

The lead figure stood.

"Dwarves," Tumarl muttered.

The dwarf squinted into the darkness, trying to see who spoke and from where. "Be you man, devil or krell?" he growled.

"Fortunately for you we are men," Kaplyn responded.

The dwarf dropped his axe and raised his hands in a gesture of submission. "You have my pardon then. We mistook this for the camp of our enemies. If you are friends, then show yourselves and let us be away from this dreary place, else real foes stumble upon us." He motioned for the other three dwarves with him to arise and they did so, although they kept their axes by their sides.

Kaplyn gestured to the others in his own group to remain hidden and then stood up, making his way down towards the dwarves.

"Do dwarves fear to journey in their own kingdom that they have to travel at night?" Kaplyn asked. He saw anger flash across the dwarf's face; his question had obviously struck a tender chord.

"We go where we wish," the dwarf replied gruffly. "But only a fool takes unnecessary risks in these difficult times," he added.

Kaplyn realised that the dwarf was referring to their campfire, and it was his turn to be angry but he refrained from a retort.

"Are you alone?" the dwarf asked.

Kaplyn came alongside the dwarf and looked him in the eyes, but did not like what he saw. His clothes were threadbare and his beard looked like it had not been combed for months. Kaplyn risked a glance at the other dwarves and saw that they were similarly dishevelled.

"No. And neither are you," Kaplyn replied matter of factly. The dwarf's eyes narrowed and, before he could reply, Kaplyn continued. "Since we are not enemies, then there is no need for your colleagues to hide amongst the rocks."

The dwarf hesitated as though considering his options. With a broad smile he gestured and, in the darkness behind him, Kaplyn saw others arising. He was correct and there were only two more, both armed with cross bows.

When the dwarves were together, Kaplyn summoned his companions. The dwarves tensed when Thaneck came into view. Thaneck tried to hide his surprise at the rough appearance of his fellows but he didn't fool Kaplyn. For the sake of good manners, Thaneck bowed low in front of the lead dwarf.

"I have travelled far to learn what has become of our brothers and our homeland, Thandor," he said. "I am Thaneck and I bring greetings and messages from my Sovereign Lord, Elador."

As though remembering his manners, the dwarf leader bowed in turn. "My name is Haffa. You are welcome to our homeland, but we must hurry and return to the safety of our stronghold where you can sample our hospitality to the full."

His offer sounded genuine. Lars was clearly remembering the welcome that they had received from the southern dwarves and his eyes fairly shone at the prospect of good food and beer.

Kaplyn began to wonder whether his earlier mistrust was justified. Times were difficult for everyone, he realised, and perhaps the dwarves offer of hospitality was sincere now that they knew they weren't a threat.

"Is it far?" Kaplyn asked. "We have travelled a long way and are weary."

Haffa shook his head. "It's not far, and then you can rest."

Two dwarves ranged ahead. The group followed and, true to Haffa's word, they soon caught up with one of the scouts, sitting on a rock. Haffa approached and placed his hand on the rock surface, muttering something under his breath. Silently, a section of the wall swung inwards revealing a dark tunnel. Swiftly the dwarves entered. Kaplyn and the others followed and the rock shut ominously behind them with a dry click.

The group was left in complete darkness and Kaplyn suddenly feared a trap.

"Vastra," he hissed.

A faint light appeared above Vastra's head, illuminating a long dark tunnel. Haffa and the other dwarves were uncovering glow rocks like the ones within Kaldor, Thaneck's home. Seeing this, Vastra extinguished his own light. The reaction of the dwarves to Vastra's light was one of fear and they muttered darkly amongst themselves.

Several dwarves appeared from the tunnel's depth. Haffa met them and, together, they conversed in a low whisper. The dwarves kept looking at Kaplyn and the others.

Eventually Haffa turned to Kaplyn. "No doubt you will want to refresh yourselves before you meet our King. I will take you to suitable quarters where you can rest." He issued orders, disbanding his patrol and then gestured for the company to follow.

The tunnel was dark and dingy; a far cry from the spacious tunnels in Kaldor, and Kaplyn glanced at Thaneck to judge his reaction. The dwarf was looking about in disbelief, clearly not understanding whether this could indeed be the fabled Thandor. For long moments he looked as if a storm raged behind his furrowed brow.

Soon they came to a timber door blocking their way. Kaplyn could feel unseen eyes watching them from arrow slits cut into the stone either side of the doorway. When the gate swung inwards, the timbers groaned in protest. They passed a few more dwarves, standing guard. These were well armed but again they looked dishevelled. Kaplyn kept thinking back to Kaldor and the ornate carvings in the rock face and the abundance of plants and especially the clean air. Here the air tasted foul and darkness seemed to ooze from the walls, making the glow globes weak and ineffectual.

Eventually they came to a larger tunnel where more dwarves stopped to stare. Kaplyn had assumed that Haffa's group were dirty and their clothes threadbare because they had been out on a long and difficult patrol, but now he was not sure, for all the dwarves looked similarly unkempt.

They passed through several large doorways, each guarded by a dwarf who eyed the group with deep mistrust. When the last door in the series was shut behind them, Kaplyn's spirits fell. He felt like a fly helplessly entwined in a sticky silk web. He tried conversing with the escort but received dark looks and little else. Gradually the tunnels opened into a more spacious underground city. Still it lacked the grandeur Kaplyn expected. Large posts shored up overhanging rocks and the city looked half completed; there were cracks in most buildings where stone blocks had hastily been laid with little care to the fit.

Finally, their escort halted in front of an especially tall and forbidding looking building. "Enter and rest for a while," Haffa stated. "I shall return shortly with food."

Dispirited they entered, preferring the dingy interior to the stares of passing dwarves. Inside was more depressing than out. It was a derelict building and in a bad state of repair. The wooden panels around the walls and the few items of furniture were rotten and a thin covering of dust made the room smell musty.

Vastra went over to a fireplace set into one of the walls. A pile of wood and some coal had been left in the grate and, using magic, he lit this. The others crowded around, grateful at least for the warmth, the cheery blaze lifted their spirits, albeit marginally.

At that moment Haffa returned carrying loaves, some fruit and a dark cheese which smelled awful and looked nearly as bad. Behind him came a second dwarf, burdened with a pitcher of water. He was shorter than Haffa, but just as shabby. The new dwarf eyed the group with distrust and kept glancing nervously at Haffa as though eager to leave.

The group picked at the meagre rations, but not even Lars could face the cheese. Haffa and his companion remained, watching them eat as though it was the last food in the city. He hardly spoke at all, which surprised Kaplyn for surely news of Kaldor must be of interest.

As they ate, smoke filled the room, evidence that the chimney was blocked or perhaps, judging by the rest of the city, had never been completed. Nonetheless, the fire warmed their cold limbs and they decided to suffer the inconvenience of the smoke rather than letting the fire go out.

Eventually Haffa and his companion took their leave.

"Thaneck," Kaplyn spoke softly, arousing the dwarf from his stupor. "What has happened here?"

The dwarf shook his head. "Ah, my people," he said sadly, his voice thick with emotion. "All my life I have heard about the greatness of Thandor. Our parents used to tell us of its fabulous wealth. And now I have seen it, I know that we have lived a fool's dream. These dwarves could not save themselves, let alone help us."

"Is this then truly Thandor, do you think?" Lomar asked.

The dwarf's eyes shone with unshed tears. "I pray that it is not. Surely our dreams are not as hollow as the lives of these poor dwarves."

"Perhaps this is merely an extension to the city and the work is not yet complete," Lars suggested.

Thaneck shook his head, absently stroking his beard. "No. My people would never build such as this."

"Come," Lomar interrupted. "We are all tired. I suggest we sleep. The morrow might bring explanations that will appear all too evident when our minds are fresh."

With heavy hearts, they settled down, spreading their few blankets on the cold stone floor.

As he lay awake, looking at the cracks in the ceiling, recent events kept churning over in Kaplyn's mind. He could not believe that this was all that remained of the once seemingly steadfast race.

Other much more terrible memories plagued him; the destruction of Shastlan's world by the dragons and his visit to the demon world were still very fresh in his mind. He hated sleep; his dreams were tormented with the sights of hell. Instead, he turned his thoughts toward the Kalanth. It was the first time that he had ever prayed to the Old Ones, although he found little solace in the act. Gradually, sleep stole over him, but he awoke often and, more than once, he cried for the souls of the damned.

Chapter 14

A Strange Meeting

Lars was the first to wake. The big man stretched, feeling greatly refreshed. Instantly, his eyes alighted on a strange dwarf sitting by the doorway, curiously watching the big man. This dwarf was unlike the others. Where the others lacked vitality, this dwarf oozed it; his hair and beard were a light grey with ginger tingeing his whiskers at the corners of his mouth. His clothing was clean and colourful, much more reminiscent of the dwarves from Kaldor.

The dwarf stirred as if realising that Lars had woken.

"Goodness me, but your group is a strange assortment," he said, almost as though he had been speaking for some while. His voice sounded older than his appearance, and Lars decided that he liked it; it was clear like the tinkling of a mountain stream.

"That one — the albino," he said, indicating Lomar lying near the window. "Some say he's a demon." The dwarf smiled broadly at this as if remembering an old joke. He tutted softly, "I have heard of the Alvalah, but never thought that I would meet one. It's such an honour, if you don't mind me saying.

"And you, too, are different," a puzzled look crossed the old dwarf's features. "I have never seen or read about your like before. You carry an axe, but your size? Gracious me — how tall are you?"

Before Lars could reply the old dwarf raised a hand, silencing him. "No. You are not a dwarf, that much I can see." The eyes glittered mischievously and Lars found himself laughing heartily. It felt good; for too long he had known only fear. The others stirred and awoke.

"Who are you?" Kaplyn asked.

"Thackery," came back the reply. "A dwarf who remembers better times."

"Please tell us, what has become of my people," Thaneck asked.

"You want to know about Thandor and why it is as it is now?" Thaneck nodded. "It is a long tale ..."

"I know some of the story already — of Talwyn and the bane of our people. But, as to what happened to Thandor after our race was sundered, I admit I know nothing," Thaneck replied.

Suddenly the old dwarf stiffened as though alerted by a distant noise. "I must go," he announced. "I shall speak with you later, but in the meantime — beware my people."

He left through a doorway to an adjoining room. Within heartbeats of his disappearance, Haffa, accompanied by six other dwarves, came into the room.

"I trust you are rested?" Haffa asked. His voice by comparison to Thackery was a monotone.

"Yes, thank you," Kaplyn replied.

"Then you will accompany me." Without further ado Haffa turned and made towards the door.

"Where are we going?" Kaplyn called after him.

Haffa turned and a look of anger flashed across his face. Haughtily, he eyed the group. His confidence seemed to have grown within the security of his city.

"You are to be escorted to our sovereign. He will answer your questions."

"Very well," Kaplyn replied. Tumarl gave Kaplyn a warning glance.

Outside, the streets were busy although few even bothered to look at them. All along their route were signs of decay, and many buildings looked vacant.

Abruptly they turned a corner, entering a particularly wide street dominated at the end by a large, imposing building with a decorative façade supported by tall columns. Unlike the other buildings, this seemed to demand their attention. It was with some trepidation that they approached, climbing the few steps to its entrance.

Even though this building was near to completion, Kaplyn was still under the impression that the builders had abruptly downed tools and stopped work. He had an uneasy feeling that they were walking into danger. To make matters worse, Shastlan was repeatedly warning him, but about what he was uncertain. They entered the building and were immediately swallowed by darkness.

Inside, it was both dark and dank. A long hall, sparsely decorated and reeking of decay, stretched before them. Kaplyn glanced uncertainly at the others and saw disgust etched on their faces.

"This can't be the palace," Vastra said. Haffa glanced back, giving him an icy look, clearly angered that he dared to speak.

By Kaplyn's side, Thaneck looked about the room with a look of sadness.

Haffa stopped in front of a tall door which swung silently inwards, opened by two dwarves dressed in chain mail and carrying heavy axes.

They entered a long room with alcoves set at regular intervals. In each one stood an armoured dwarf. It was dark and eerie and an unnatural silence surrounded them.

Kaplyn peered into the gloom, trying to see the sentries as they passed by but darkness defeated him. His earlier depression threatened and he fought hard to deny it. Absently his hand snaked towards his scar. The future seemed so very bleak. Trosgarth was growing in power while the peoples opposing it diminished. Gone completely were the Eldric, and nothing remained of them other than a few crumbling relics. Now, to find the dwarves divided and no sign of their famous dristal, was too much to bear.

Before them sat a bent, wizened figure upon a tall regal throne. Skeletal fingers clutched the armrests, and thin wrists disappeared from view beneath the sleeves of an ornate robe. The hood of his robe was pulled low over the figure's head and, for a moment, Kaplyn was certain that he saw a glint from eyes.

"Welcome to our home," a thin reedy voice proclaimed. Kaplyn was uncertain from where the voice had originated, and he peered more closely at the figure on the throne. In his mind, Shastlan was still frantically warning Kaplyn of danger.

"What is the purpose of your visit?" the voice intoned.

"Sire, I am Thaneck from Kaldor. For many years now my people have sought news of our ancestral home and many dwarves have risked the perils of the road to learn of its fate, but none have ever returned."

"Your news saddens me," the King stated. "None of your brethren have ever reached us; otherwise, you would have been reassured that all is well."

Kaplyn's skin crawled. The more he heard the voice, the more he disliked it; something was very much amiss.

"But let us not dwell on melancholy. You have travelled far to come to my halls. Let each tell his tale and introduce himself. I have heard that one amongst you is a sorcerer. Let him speak first ..."

"Sadly I believe you have been misinformed," Kaplyn interrupted. "There is no sorcerer amongst us. I am Kaplyn and my companion here is Vastra. We are both from Allund. Tumarl," he continued, indicating the ex-farmer, "is a Thracian. Lomar is an Alvalan and Lars is from Gorlanth, a land across the ocean."

When Kaplyn told the King that there was not a sorcerer amongst them, he seemed to relax.

"Why are men from such different nations travelling together?" the King asked.

"There was a great battle at CarCamel, the Thracian capital," Kaplyn replied. "We fear greatly that Trosgarth has risen and seeks war. We need the legendary aid of the dwarves, calling upon them as our ancestors once did, to stand with us against the might of our enemy."

"Trosgarth is no more," the King stated. "It is no longer a threat and your fears are groundless. I do not doubt that you fought in a battle, but, as you have said, the land is a dangerous place; there are many *minor* barons who would seize power."

Kaplyn was angered by the King's response and he frowned darkly. It was true that there was no conclusive proof that Trosgarth's power had risen, but only a fool would dismiss the threat outright.

The figure on the throne sat back, sinking deeper into the darkness. "You must remain with us for a while and enjoy our hospitality. Tomorrow we hold our games. Join us there."

The King gestured that the audience was at an end. Out of courtesy, they bowed. Then Haffa led them from the throne room.

As they walked through the streets back to their lodgings, Shastlan was still trying to warn Kaplyn, but as to what he was uncertain. Whatever happened now, though, he was determined they should leave as soon as possible.

Chapter 15

Escape

Once they were back in their own room, they felt better. Haffa entered with them but the escort remained outside.

"I shall have food brought to you." Haffa offered and then departed taking the escort with him.

"This is an evil place," Lars stated. "There's no aid here; we should leave."

The others agreed, but it was Tumarl who voiced Kaplyn's concern. "I doubt that they will let us leave. Surely we are not the first to reach Thandor."

Lars nodded. "There is a madness amongst these dwarves which frightens me, and that King smelt of decay."

"What has become of my people," Thaneck wailed, turning to the wall to hide his grief.

"So you plan to leave us and snub our King's hospitality," a familiar voice announced from behind them. They turned to find Thackery standing in the doorway, leading to the adjoining room. The old dwarf was smiling warmly. "You have at least heeded my warning not to trust my people. That is good."

Kaplyn was shocked that the dwarf had managed to get so close without their knowing and was surprised that Shastlan had not warned him. He realised though that Shastlan was warning him and had been doing so for some time.

Tumarl had drawn his sword and was advancing towards the old dwarf. "Stop," Kaplyn said. Tumarl halted, his eyes fixed on the dwarf as though daring him to move.

"Yes, you had better hear me out, young man," the dwarf admonished, wagging a finger in his direction. "It's unwise to be rash, but that has always been the downfall of youth."

He walked into the room and stood before Kaplyn. "You must not go to the games," he announced cheerfully. "If you do, it will be your death." The old dwarf frowned uncertainly as if realising there was a flaw in his argument. "On the other hand, if you do not go that, too, could spell disaster." With that he sat down in the middle of the floor and started to mutter under his breath as though in heated debate.

The others looked on bemused. It was Vastra who finally interrupted the old dwarf. "Can you tell us of our danger so that we might be better prepared?"

The cloud on the old dwarf's face lifted. "Of course," he replied at once. "A trap laid bare is — now how did that old saying go?"

Lars' eyes rolled upward. The others, too, looked on as though their patience was wearing thin.

Then finally Thackery said, "The games are held regularly and everyone is forced to attend. They are not games though. At first they were. Dwarves who had been disgraced were sent there as punishment — public humiliation and all that. Oh, it used to be such fun, nothing serious — just a way of shaming those who had done wrong such as cropping off a beard, foolish and menial tasks..."

Kaplyn gave Thackery a dark look, annoyed that he was rambling. Thackery, seeing his look, coughed and continued. "Soon it became worse, with fights to the death. Initially these were rare, reserved for fights between murderers for example. However, the game's frequency increased until anyone who dared to speak openly against the authorities was persecuted. Now," he paused momentarily and looked sadly at the ground, "it's anyone who does not show obedience to the King."

Thaneck shook his head in disbelief, his eyes blazing with fury. "That's impossible. No dwarf would accept that."

"You no longer see dwarves," Thackery stated with conviction. He waved an arm encompassing the city. "These are but thralls of evil. You spoke earlier of the jewel, Talwyn, and the sundering of our people..." The others nodded.

"Talwyn was not lost as you said, but found. I will remind you of the events leading to this. Nester had fled the city with the jewel, and the King, Nynvanar, had set off with an army in pursuit. It was thought that Nester fled into KinKassack, which was not yet evil, but, even still, something happened to him and he was never seen again.

"The King's army was waylaid by an army of krell and was close to defeat. Nynvanar was slain by a death knight who took Hanet's axe. Your people, Thaneck, fled the battlefield and made their escape, taking the King's dragon armour with them and leaving a large part of the army to its fate.

"Oh, I do not blame your people," the old dwarf continued, seeing Thaneck's look of anger. "The battle was lost. But, before the krell attacked, they tormented us, holding up Nester's head on a spike and showing us Talwyn. They must have waylaid Nester and captured the jewel." The old dwarf looked grim. The memory was obviously painful and his eyes lifted to look at Kaplyn. "That was a mistake, probably deliberate though, methinks. The jewel burned into our hearts like a fire. It had already caused a great deal of grief and the sight of it, in enemy hands, infuriated my people. We fell upon the krell like a tidal wave. Our axes clove their necks like tinder and so fierce was the onslaught that the nearest krell turned and fled, screaming that Hanet himself had returned. In their haste to flee, they trampled their brothers, causing a rout.

"The enemy, which only moments before had stood before us gloating, disintegrated. Even the death knights fell before us and Straum, their leader, fled, taking Hanet's axe with him. We were victorious and stood amongst the dead with leaden arms, drenched with krell blood. Carrying Talwyn, we returned to our home in triumph."

"You were there, at the battle?" Lars asked.

The old dwarf nodded and Kaplyn realised how ancient he must be. Thackery continued. "For several years, Thandor returned to normal and, then, one day things started to change for the worse. The games were introduced, but not in the present arena for then we still lived in our ancient hall."

"Then this is *not* Thandor?" Kaplyn asked.

"No, it isn't," Thackery replied. "Many years ago we were forced to leave the ancient part of the city. These newer tunnels were built in haste. We left because of strange sightings and deeds, nothing more than rumours — at first. Some said that demons had come amongst us, collecting souls, and fear spread rapidly through the city."

"At this time the games were held more regularly. Talwyn was positioned high above the arena. The King swore that everyone would be able to see it, so that never again would dwarf fight against dwarf. As the years went by the games became more evil, and the will of our people seemed to falter. It was then rumour started that the city was haunted."

"Namlwyn declared the city cursed. He bid us leave and seal it off, which we did. We built a new city here, not far from the old one, but, as you see, it was never finished."

"How is it that you appear to be more normal than the others?" Kaplyn asked.

The old dwarf looked up, "Over the years I have managed to avoid the games. There are others, but our numbers are few and, if discovered, we will die in the arena. Fortunately few try to find us now. Their will seems to have been sapped almost completely."

"How does that explain the difference?" Lomar asked, somewhat confused.

"Talwyn hangs in the arena for all to see and is guarded day and night. Somehow it affects our people and causes the malady you see. Its influence is subtle. Few perceived the effects until it was too late, and those that did have since been hunted down and killed, all save a few. Now our people believe it is they who are cursed and not the city as was originally thought. In despair, they flounder in a sea of self-pity rather than face the truth. Over the years cruel dwarves such as Haffa have taken over and tyranny has replaced our ancient order."

Kaplyn considered the dwarf's words. "We must not attend the games then," he declared.

"They will either force you to go — or kill you," Thackery replied flatly. "After the games you will be denounced as spies or some other nonsense and then you will be disposed of."

Kaplyn frowned darkly, "Then we must make our escape tonight."

Thackery shook his head. "You will need my help, and for that there is a price."

Lomar glanced uncertainly at Kaplyn. "And what do you want from us?" Kaplyn asked.

"I know of several tunnels, leading to the old citadel," the old dwarf continued, ignoring Kaplyn's question. "One such tunnel is close to the great arena. I could show you this passage and lead you to the old city. From there, we could escape."

"And what do you expect in return?" Kaplyn repeated.

The dwarf smiled broadly. "Why, to destroy Talwyn, that is all!"

They looked at the dwarf in amazement.

"You said that it was guarded," Lomar said.

"I didn't say it would be easy," Thackery pouted. "Besides, you have no option. You cannot escape any other way."

"I shall help you," Thaneck stated with apparent conviction. "I could not leave, knowing the plight of my kin."

Kaplyn was immediately reminded of the demon world and the souls doomed to eternal damnation; he shuddered.

"We should go," Tumarl said. "There is little that we can do. From Thackery's description, Talwyn sounds like a kara-stone and they cannot be destroyed."

Vastra shook his head. "It *might* be possible to destroy it."

In silence they considered what they should do. It was Kaplyn who spoke first. "We cannot leave the dwarves like this. If we remove Talwyn, then at least the dwarves might, in time, return to normal.

"Thackery, describe where Talwyn is kept," Kaplyn said.

"It's above the King's royal box, on the farthest side of the arena and perhaps twenty feet above the ground. There are always guards close by at any one time; two are on duty in the alcove."

Kaplyn sensed that there was more. "Go on," he urged.

"Ah," said the dwarf and sighed deeply, "That is the problem. They also guard the King."

Kaplyn's skin crawled with an unbidden memory of the King. "Why is this a problem?" he asked cautiously, sensing that he wasn't going to like the answer.

"Oh, didn't I say? Our ruler is possessed." Thackery grinned weakly. The group were stunned, "Of course I could be wrong," he admitted, slightly miffed.

"A demon!" Kaplyn said incredulously.

Thackery attempted a smile, but failed.

Vastra looked at Kaplyn, comprehension dawning. "I should have guessed!"

At that moment Kaplyn realised why Shastlan had been warning him.

"There has to be some other way out of here," Lars commented hopefully.

Tumarl nodded. "Like out of the front door, in broad daylight!"

Kaplyn raised a hand for silence. His brow was knotted in concentration. He looked at Vastra, "We would need your help," he said. He knew that he was asking a great deal; if Vastra was killed, then his soul would be permanently damned.

Vastra frowned. "I will help, but it will take time to destroy Talwyn. It sounds very powerful."

"Would the dwarves be restored to normal if it was destroyed?" Kaplyn asked.

Vastra nodded, "I think so, but that also would take time."

"It's worth the risk," Kaplyn stated. "Too much has gone wrong. Perhaps aiding the dwarves will end our run of bad luck."

By Kaplyn's side, Thackery grinned broadly and thanked them all profusely.

The evening wore slowly on and the group occupied themselves as best they could. Thackery took the opportunity to describe the arena in more detail. There were several entrances, so getting in wasn't going to be a problem. From the arena, they could climb up to the royal box to steal Talwyn, and attempt its destruction once they had made their escape. The difficulty was how to gain access to the jewel in full view of the guards. Vastra said that he could deal with them, but would not elaborate. Kaplyn wondered how long they would be able to keep the jewel, remembering the dwarfs' history and their passion for it. He was also uncertain where they could escape to once they had it.

All too soon Thackery announced that it was time to go and the endless wait now seemed but a brief passage of time. They shoved their meagre belongings into packs which they carried on their backs. They had little food and what the dwarves had supplied, was rank.

Thackery was standing by a window and he turned to speak to them. "One of Haffa's men is watching this house from across the street," he informed them. "We can leave through the back room. There are tunnels connecting several of these houses, and these will help to get us beyond the guards watching over you. Now follow me," he said, leaving through a door to an adjoining room.

With heavy hearts, they filed out. The next room was completely bare, and Thackery went to its centre where he bent to examine the floor before triggering a mechanism set flush with the stone. Immediately a section of rock gave way, revealing a tunnel beyond.

The darkness looked menacing. Thackery descended first and Kaplyn followed. One by one, the others followed. Vastra conjured a light as Thackery closed the entrance. The old dwarf jumped with fright as a flame appeared above Vastra's head and Kaplyn had to explain that Vastra was a sorcerer. Tutting and mumbling into his beard, the old dwarf led the way. The ceiling was low and, with the exception of the dwarves, they had to crouch as they walked. Fortunately it was only a short distance until they came to another doorway, which Thackery triggered. They entered a derelict house also showing signs of decay.

From this building, Thackery led them out onto a deserted street, taking care to avoid areas where dwarves might be abroad. Occasionally, they had to take cover within dark recesses and Kaplyn helped by listening to Shastlan. The shoddy workmanship of the Thandor dwarves helped them now, for there were plenty of places to hide.

Soon the arena loomed out of the darkness and Thackery indicated this building was their destination. They crept silently towards a small door where they huddled together in the shadows waiting for Thackery to pick the lock.

Within moments, the door was open and they slipped through, closing it behind them. A short tunnel led to the arena. Kaplyn and Thackery crept forward to see what lay ahead. They paused before the exit, using the shadow to conceal them. The arena was vast, circular and surrounded by a tall spectator's gallery, along which burning torches were set at regular intervals. These burned with a blue flame, a clear indication that a demon was present. Kaplyn realised then why the palace had been in darkness, for torches might otherwise have alerted them to the fact that the King was possessed.

A baleful green glow caught Kaplyn's eye and he searched for its source. He found Talwyn, set within the arena wall, some distance off the ground. Below the stone was the alcove Thackery had described and, within that, movement caught his eye. Keeping his gaze fixed on the alcove, he thought he could make out at least two figures, but the shadows obscured much.

Slipping back down the tunnel, he described the arena to the others. The main problem facing them now was disposing of the sentries. Vastra accompanied Kaplyn back down the tunnel where he watched the alcove for a few moments before coming to a decision. Crouching, he chanted, drawing runes in the dust at his feet. Kaplyn crept to his side to watch, keeping an eye on the alcove.

Dark smoke curled lazily from the two brands burning either side of the alcove, seeming to coalesce into sinister shapes, hovering above each torch. The smoke drifted towards the guards, unfurling into thin tendrils of fog. As they inhaled the smoke they realised their danger and, too late, they sought to raise the alarm. By Kaplyn's side, Vastra's voice trailed into silence as both guards collapsed in a heap.

Kaplyn caught his breath, fearful that others might have heard the rattle of accoutrements. Moments passed, but nothing happened. Kaplyn gestured to the others to follow and, together, they stole towards the alcove. Lars went to the wall and stood with his back to it, cupping his hands in front of him. Kaplyn was hoisted onto his shoulders and reached up to grab the lip of the balcony. Using his feet to propel himself up the wall, he gained access to the alcove. Lars then helped Tumarl to climb up and, between Kaplyn and Tumarl, using one of the long curtains, they helped Lars up.

Lars positioned himself by the door at the back of the alcove where he stood, holding his axe in both hands. Tumarl and Kaplyn checked the bodies of the guards for signs of life. They were both dead. They then went back to the opening overlooking the arena to see if they could reach Talwyn.

Tumarl swayed, then soundlessly fell to the floor. Kaplyn grabbed him. Tumarl's eyes rolled back and he twitched in Kaplyn's grasp. Kaplyn realised that Talwyn was protecting itself, but for some reason the stone's power did not affect him, possibly due to his scar. Lars was going to come over to help but Kaplyn waved him back in case the jewel affected him.

With Tumarl forgotten, Kaplyn climbed onto the balcony to examine Talwyn and its setting more closely. The jewel was the size of his fist and perfectly formed. Light danced from its many faceted surfaces and for a moment he was held spellbound by its beauty. He understood, then, why the dwarves had fought over it.

Using his knife he cut a square piece of cloth from a curtain hanging from the balcony. With his dagger he pried the stone from the surrounding mortar, letting it fall into the cloth, careful not to let it touch him. He remembered all too clearly what had happened when he had touched kara-stones before and did not want a repeat now. He wrapped the stone carefully placing the bundle in his pouch. With the evil light extinguished, Tumarl awoke and, shaking his head, he looked up uncertainly at Kaplyn who smiled back reassuringly.

Suddenly Vastra called up. "We must flee!" With his shout all thoughts of caution were banished. Kaplyn, Tumarl and Lars jumped down to the arena floor as Thackery set off, leading the way. They had barely cleared half the distance to the opposite side of the arena when Kaplyn sensed a great evil behind them.

"Go on!" he shouted to Thackery who had paused as if sensing the threat. Kaplyn removed the package from his pouch and handed it to Lomar. "Take this and help Vastra to destroy it." Lomar left, hastening to catch up with the others.

Vastra and Tumarl stopped alongside Kaplyn and, briefly, he acknowledged their help. Kaplyn's glowing blade crooned as it came clear of the sheath.

On the balcony, he could see the figure of the King. His robes flapped eerily about him as he jumped to the arena floor. Immediately, a fearful scream rent the air, freezing the very marrow in their bones. Before, the King's face had been concealed by shadow, but, now, they could see it in the half-light of the torches. To all intents, he was dead; lank hair hung in tatters from a balding, mottled head and the flesh was lifeless and grey. The eyes were dark, unfathomable pits. Strangely, other eyes stared fixedly at them as though they did not belong to the body. Kaplyn realised that it was the demon's eyes they were seeing and, in an eerie parody, these seemed to move in advance of the head turning.

"You should have waited," the creature snarled. "Tomorrow your deaths would have been swift." He carried an axe in his withered hands and, with a suddenness that nearly caught them unawares, he pointed this at the three men. Strange guttural sounds emanated from his dead throat, making the hairs on their necks arise.

Vastra reacted swiftly, countering the spell, tracing a rune in the air about them and chanting words of power. For a moment the two faced each other, their voices rising and falling as each sought dominance. Abruptly, with a cry of rage, the demon-king leapt towards them with an astonishing speed for such a wizened frame.

Vastra shouted a command, bringing the demon to an abrupt halt and, at the same time, Kaplyn leapt towards the apparition as it struggled against the spell. If the demon had been fully in their world, rather than just its spirit, it would have been stronger, but having possessed the body of another, it was bound by its frailties.

Kaplyn caught sight of the old King's face. He had been dead for some time, and the flesh had long since started to decay. In parts he could see the skull beneath. From within the dark orbs of the dead monarch, the demon's hate-filled eyes stared at Kaplyn. Before Kaplyn could strike, it broke free and Kaplyn's blade wailed in fury as it swept through the air, scant inches in front of the demon's face. Kaplyn was off balance and, sensing victory, the demon swung its axe in an arc, aiming at his head.

Tumarl, as yet unnoticed, came around Kaplyn's side and thrust his blade deep into the King's chest. An almighty scream shattered the still air as the iron bit deep. The demon dropped its axe. Realising it was mortally wounded, it reached out towards Tumarl, trying at least to claim his soul. Ghostly talons burst through the dead King's hands, snaking towards Tumarl's chest. Tumarl froze in horror, too afraid to let go of the sword.

Kaplyn twisted his body, swinging his blade in a wide arc to catch the dead King below the nape of the neck. The blade sliced through flesh, crooning as it dispatched the demon to hell. A fearful cry split the air as the demon was vanquished, forced to return without a soul.

Tumarl recovered as the body of the monarch collapsed lifeless at his feet. He gave Kaplyn a look of gratitude. Distracted as he was, Kaplyn failed to notice movement in the alcove above. Several dwarves had appeared and were even now jumping down to the arena. One dwarf noticed that Talwyn was gone and his cry of rage filled the air.

Kaplyn, Vastra and Tumarl raced after the others. Lars waited for them by an exit, to show them the way.

"Follow me!" he urged. He led them only a short way along a narrow street before swiftly darting into a dark, dismal building. The three men followed close upon his heels. Thackery had opened a concealed door at the back of the room where he waited for them. When he saw Kaplyn and the others he looked relieved and gestured frantically for them to enter.

As soon as they were through, Thackery followed and his hands sought a mechanism set within the stone wall. He grappled with this frantically and, all the while, the not too distant slap of feet on stone made them realise how close the pursuit was. Abruptly the door slid shut, barring the way to the furious dwarves whose howls of frustration were abruptly cut short.

Thackery grabbed Vastra's arm. "Can you seal it?" he urged.

Vastra nodded and traced a rune on the door, his finger leaving a faint silver glow on the rock. When he finished an audible snick sounded.

"Then again," Thackery intoned, looking back at the blank wall, "Is that wise?"

In the darkness, Tumarl growled in exasperation and even Lars looked perplexed.

Vastra conjured up a light that revealed a long tunnel whose walls shone like glass, casting the light back at them.

"Thackery, what is this place?" Kaplyn asked.

The old dwarf grimaced. "This passage was constructed secretly by the old King. I learned of its existence from a friend, one of the few who escaped the stone's evil spell. She was a good friend," the old dwarf reminisced, sighing deeply. "She was discovered only a few months ago and sent to the games; there was nothing that I could do."

"Where does it lead?" Vastra asked softly.

Thackery looked down the tunnel. "I'm fairly sure it leads to the old city."

A sharp blow to the outside rock caused several of the group to jump.

"They're trying to dig through the rock," Lomar announced.

Thaneck looked at the stone as another blow loudly echoed down the tunnel. "It will not take them long; they are dwarves after all. We had better get moving."

For several moments they followed the clear cut tunnel. Then its shape and size changed. It became rougher and the ceiling became much lower as if whoever had made it had cared little for appearances.

"This is krell made!" Thaneck hissed.

"Can you be sure?" Kaplyn asked.

Thaneck nodded. "No dwarf would dig a tunnel this crude." Behind the group, the ringing of metal on stone could still be heard, although muffled by the intervening rock. The sharp blows sounded ominously like a giant heartbeat.

Kaplyn sighed. "Come! We should not dally." And with that he plunged down the tunnel, using his link with Shastlan to guide him.

The announcement that the tunnel was krell made worried Kaplyn, and the cries from the angry dwarves pursuing them only served to fuel his fear. He felt they were trapped and it was only a matter of time before pursuit would begin in earnest.

Chapter 16

Thandor Revealed

The passageway seemed to go on forever. Kaplyn wondered where it would lead and was not convinced that Thackery could be entirely trusted. Shastlan's presence seemed quite strong and that was a bonus for, at times, the link with his shaol was faint.

Shortly the sounds of the dwarves digging stopped. They halted and Thaneck pressed an ear to the rock. Much to their relief, he declared that the dwarves were still digging. At least they hadn't yet broken through.

However, to Kaplyn's distress, his sword's glow was not fading. Abruptly Shastlan sent a shrill warning, causing Kaplyn to jump in shock. Turning to the others, he put a finger to his lips and indicated to Vastra to extinguish his light. In darkness Kaplyn and Lomar bent their bows. By Kaplyn's side, Thaneck took his heavy crossbow from his back; cocking it, he fitted a bolt. Once armed, they crept forward.

A crude image formed in Kaplyn's mind of three or four beings some distance ahead, but, as yet, he didn't know who or what they were. Gradually he became aware of a dim light and he went forward silently to investigate. In the distance he saw four figures and Kaplyn immediately pressed himself against the rock. This close, there was no mistaking that the figures were krell.

Behind him Vastra made a gesture and the darkness surrounding them grew deeper. Kaplyn signalled to Lomar and Thaneck and, together, they took up positions in the centre of the tunnel, taking aim. "Now," Kaplyn whispered and, as one, three shafts flew silently towards their mark. Unfortunately, as a result of the gloom, one missile struck a protruding rock and clattered noisily from this as it bounced along the tunnel, instantly alerting their foe. Two shafts struck home and two krell dropped to the ground.

Kaplyn and Lomar had each nocked another arrow before the figures had fallen. Their bows sang as the two remaining krell froze for an instant,

565

uncertain as to what had happened. Seconds later they, too, lay in an untidy heap.

The group ran forward and, eerily, the darkness surrounding them followed.They swiftly confirmed that the krell were dead. Kaplyn grimaced; one krell stared sightlessly back. Its large round eyes seemed too large for its face, and its ivory fangs glistened in the faint light. The bulky armour seemed ridiculous on its wiry frame, and yet Kaplyn knew their strength, having fought them at the siege of CarCamel.

Alone, Kaplyn crept forward to find out what the sentries were guarding. In front of him the tunnel opened into an immense cavern. Kaplyn's position was high up on a cliff face, and a narrow stair led down to the cavern floor far below. Kaplyn stood in awe as he took in the scene. He was overlooking what he assumed must be the ancient city of Thandor.

Tall stone buildings, each looking like a palace, dominated the city's heart and, surrounding these, immense rock carvings on the cavern walls were a silent testament to the city's grandeur. One of the cavern's sides had been decorated in a vast mural. Quartz and amethyst deposits had been excavated and transformed into a pictorial history of the dwarven race.

Kaldor had been magnificent, but this was grander by far. In places, glow globes illuminated the old city. These would never be extinguished as long as there was sufficient dampness in the surrounding rock. Judging by their number and position, Kaplyn guessed many had been destroyed, probably by krell, but hundreds more still worked. By the light of these marvellous rocks, plants, moss and lichen, planted long ago, grew in profusion where, centuries past, large parks had been established.

As the others came forward, Kaplyn saw Thaneck's look of wonder and understood how he felt. Here was a city to be proud of.

In the gloom they could see small shapes between the buildings and Thaneck's expression instantly soured — krell. There was an army below and campfires burned in the streets. They retreated back down the tunnel, leaving Tumarl to stand watch in case a relief guard approached.

Thaneck, pressing his ear to the rock, listened to the progress of the dwarves pursuing them. His expression was sufficient to warn them; the digging had stopped. Kaplyn was furious with Thackery for bringing them this way. The dwarves would never give Talwyn up, even though it was evil. He considered their options, which seemed few. They could not just leave the jewel in the tunnel. They owed the dwarves that much, nor could they destroy it, not here at least. Vastra had said that it would take time to do so.

There was no time to delay. "Collect their armour and cloaks," Kaplyn said.

Hurriedly they stripped the bodies, and Kaplyn, Lars, Tumarl and Lomar wrapped themselves in cloaks, whilst Thackery, Thaneck and Vastra donned whatever armour would fit. The helms were the most useful since they hid their faces.

Once they were dressed, Vastra added a final touch. Tracing a rune in the air, he spoke swiftly, altering their appearance. Close up the disguise was poor, but, from a distance, they would pass as krell.

"That's the best I can manage," Vastra proclaimed with a critical look. When they looked at each other, they grinned broadly. Lars was the worst; he looked like a mountain krell, large and hulking with a huge broken nose and dark shaggy eyebrows.

Steeling themselves, they left the tunnel and started down the flight of steps. They did not know what time the next guard was due, which meant that their danger was currently greatest. Fortune was with them and they reached the cavern floor unchallenged.

Once down the stairs, they kept to the shadows, picking their way through the city's outskirts. At first they saw only a few krell and they walked past these as though they had every right to be there. Gradually, the number of krell they encountered grew, but their disguise held, for the moment at least.

Beneath the cloak Kaplyn was sweating freely. Nervously, he kept glancing behind, seeking the tunnel entrance high in the cavern wall for signs of pursuit by the dwarves. He had almost believed that the dwarves would not come when a distant shout caused his heart to leap. Looking around he saw several shapes carrying torches, standing framed against the tunnel entrance. A low murmur started all around Kaplyn, quickly escalating into angry shouts. More figures appeared at the tunnel's entrance as a great roar rent the air.

"Dwarves!" shouted krell. "To arms!" called others. Great horns brayed into the night, taking up the alarm, resounding around the cavern until it seemed as though the very walls shook. Kaplyn looked at the others. "This way," he urged and he led them into a nearby two-storey building with a flat roof. They entered just as krell rushed by their hiding place. None noticed them, they were too intent on the dwarves.

The dwarves were clearly disorientated. In wonder, they stared at what had once been their home and when they realised that krell inhabited their ancient city, a great cry went up. By now, there was a veritable army in the tunnel for many dwarves had armed themselves upon hearing that Talwyn was stolen.

Like floodwater they burst down the steep stair, hurling aside the few krell that opposed them. Both sides were caught by surprise, but the momentum of the dwarves propelled them deep into the ancient city.

Kaplyn and the others were effectively trapped. To flee the battle would betray them. In frustration, they ascended to one of the upper rooms. Graffiti covered the walls, and the ceiling had been partially demolished.

Together, Kaplyn and Vastra looked out of a window; from their vantage point, they could see where the fighting was thickest. Unfortunately the direction of the dwarves attack was heading straight towards them. For the moment at least, the dwarves were hard pressed; they were fighting as individuals with little thought of tactics.

"At this rate, the dwarves will be slaughtered," Lars declared, coming to Kaplyn's side.

"Talwyn is still affecting them," Vastra said. "They must feel its presence."

Kaplyn turned to Vastra, "We must destroy it now!" Vastra was shocked by the terrible look in Kaplyn's eyes. Any objections he would have offered died instantly on his lips. Reluctantly he took the wrapped jewel from Lomar before placing it in the corner of the room.

"Once I start its destruction, the krell will most likely be aware of us and then the rest of you will have to defend us." Without waiting, Vastra knelt by the stone and started to draw runes of power in the dust around it. Either it was a trick of Kaplyn's imagination or not, but a green glow was clearly visible through the cloth.

"Hurry," hissed Thaneck who had remained by the window. As if sensing a threat to their stone, the dwarves were pushing harder in their direction, oblivious to the growing threat of a large group of krell on their flank. Lomar and Lars stood by the stairs in case anyone tried to enter. Thackery took Thaneck's crossbow and joined them.

Vastra's progress was slow. The runes had to be precise otherwise the spell would be useless. With each letter, a fresh bead of sweat seemed to materialise on his brow and in response the light from within the bundle grew in intensity until abruptly the cloth burst into flames. Vastra ignored this as he completed the last rune.

He started chanting, his voice rising in pitch until he was nearly shouting. Whether attracted by the spell or by the magic of the stone, none could tell, but a single krell appeared at the bottom of the stairs. It stood there for a moment surveying the dark interior and the growing light above. Only at the last moment did it realise that there were three shapes standing on the stair, barely visible against the bright light. Lomar let fly his shaft and the krell fell lifeless, its cry of alarm instantly curtailed.

A shout sounded outside and several more krell charged into the building only to be cut down by more missiles. Kaplyn joined the group at the top of the stairs, leaving Tumarl and Thaneck guarding the only window to the floor above.

More krell entered and, within moments, a fierce battle raged. The krell were hindered by the narrowness of the stair and the bodies of their own dead. Kaplyn's blade shone brightly and sang as it killed. Lars' axe clove the krell's armour easily, whilst behind them Thackery and Lomar continued to shoot their weapons.

Several krell tried to gain access by the window but were cut down by Tumarl. Behind the fighting men, flashes of light illuminated the interior of the room as powerful forces clashed in a fearful battle of magic. Eerie noises emanated from Talwyn, threatening to distract the fighters on both sides, and Kaplyn and the others had to refrain from turning around to see what was happening.

Outside, the dwarves were facing their own problems; krell were now pressing them fiercely from both flanks. The dwarves were strung out and, all at once, a strong krell force charged the dwarf line snapping it in two at its weakest point. Still influenced by Talwyn, the dwarves did not even realise what had happened as stubbornly they fought with the single purpose of trying to reach the building from which bright flashing lights were emanating.

Within the room, Vastra chanted as swiftly as he dared while hastily drawing runes in the dark air. Silvery letters appeared briefly for an instant only to be extinguished into blackness scant heartbeats later. Vastra's arms flayed about his head quicker and quicker as he tried to cast spell followed by counterspell. And then he realised he was losing the battle. *He* could not die. The terror of what would happen to his soul if he did die, drained the colour from his face. Sweat soaked his brow and he suddenly found it hard to concentrate; abruptly his vision dimmed and, in panic, he started to stutter. The evil stone immediately countered his spell, and Vastra felt an immense pressure threaten to engulf him. Fearfully, he staggered back whilst trying to counter the growing force before him.

Behind him, the battle at the window was going badly. Tumarl failed to counter a blow from a krell swinging a hammer; it smashed his arm and he fell to the floor, crying out in agony. The krell screamed its success, leaping from the sill, intending to attack Vastra. Swinging his axe, Thaneck stepped in its way. The krell's scream of rage changed to one of pain and it was this cry that was Vastra's downfall. He mispronounced his spell; instantly the light within the orb grew in power and a high pitched keening filled the air.

On the stair Kaplyn sensed the change in the battle of magic and, even before Tumarl's arm was broken, was leaping up the stairs, two at a time. He entered the room just as Thaneck dispatched the krell, and he saw Vastra as he stepped back from the orb, his arms by his side and his spell forgotten. Kaplyn felt the awesome build up of power within the stone and knew that all would be lost unless he acted.

His only weapon was his sword and he did not know any other way of defeating the orb. With all his might he brought the blade down on the stone hoping to shatter it. The blade clove the rock like butter and, at that instant, the forces gathering within the orb burst outwards, their force channelled along Kaplyn's sword, hitting him like a sledgehammer.

The magic smashed into Kaplyn's body and, from the centre of his chest, a blinding, white, flash erupted, instantly quenching the green light. With the collision of the two magics, Kaplyn was flung backwards and slammed hard into the stone wall. An explosion followed and all about the room was suddenly flying stone and debris.

The instant after the explosion, everything was silent. Kaplyn tried hard to breathe. His whole body ached and, in pain, he wiped dust and dirt from his face. His sword was gone and, realising he was still in danger, he tried to get up to find it, but his legs gave way beneath him. Fortunately there was no enemy left alive in the room. The explosion had been directed away from Kaplyn and the blast had taken out the front of the building, killing those krell trying to get through the window. A section of the roof had collapsed and debris below the hole was piled high. Tumarl was fortunate to have missed the worst of the blast and lay stunned in the corner of the room. Vastra had also been bowled over by the blast and lay unmoving on the floor. Thaneck had fared the worst and was buried beneath a pile of rubble.

Lars and the others ran up the stairs to help. With the explosion, the krell trying to get through the door had fallen back, and even the fiercest now gave the building a wide berth. Lars lifted Kaplyn who collapsed into his arms. Kaplyn stared up at Lars with a puzzled expression, not understanding why the other man's lips were moving but there was no sound. Then all at once an angry buzzing started in his head, and he realised he was temporarily deafened. Struggling, he rose to his feet where he swayed, looking about the room for his sword. He saw it; the blade protruding from the floor where the orb had been. With Lars' help, he staggered across to the weapon. His legs felt leaden but, worst of all, his chest ached terribly. The scar burned fiercely and he realised that the magic contained within it had saved his life.

The buzzing in his ears changed suddenly to a whooshing noise and he felt momentarily faint and bright lights danced in front of his eyes. Abruptly he could hear once more, and the din of battle between the dwarves and krell suddenly sounded very loud.

Taking the hilt of his sword he withdrew it from the floor. Looking about at the others, he found that most were in a state of shock, but, apart from Tumarl's broken arm, none were injured. Lars scrambled on a mound of debris to dig Thaneck out. When the dwarf emerged he swore profusely while coughing and spluttering to clear his throat of dust. Behind him Vastra had arisen and was staring at the others groggily.

Lomar attended to Tumarl's arm. The skin was a ghastly blue-black colour and the ex-farmer grimaced and then yelped as Lomar reset the bone. Lars caught him as he fell to the floor and, together, he and Lomar bound his arm to his chest.

Kaplyn peered out of the gaping hole in the building, taking care not to be seen from below. The dwarves had managed to rally and the two halves of their separated forces had joined. He also noted that they were no longer fighting toward them, perhaps due to the orb's destruction. They were also starting to fight as a cohesive force; this was their home after all and the krell were the invaders.

Kaplyn watched the fighting for a moment longer. Suddenly from out of the darkness, a tall shape appeared, flaying dwarves from its path.

"A demon!" Kaplyn said. "The krell must have a necromancer. Lomar, give me your bow." The albino handed it over along with a quiver of arrows. "Vastra, follow me," he commanded. Without waiting for a response he scrambled up the stone debris and up through the hole in the roof where he lay down, offering Vastra his hand.

Vastra's eyes rolled in resignation; his body ached and he was feeling his age. Scrambling up the pile of stones, he took Kaplyn's hand and was hoisted up to the roof. As quickly as they could, they crossed the rooftops towards the heart of battle. Kaplyn led the way, stopping occasionally to allow Vastra to sense the power emanating from the enemy sorcerer.

As they approached the outskirts of the battle, Kaplyn dropped onto his stomach and crawled towards the building's eaves. Cautiously, he peered over the edge of the roof. A few hundred yards down the street, a number of krell stood guard around a solitary figure. They were too far away to see clearly and so he decided to continue across a few more rooftops. When Kaplyn next looked, he saw a tall dark-haired man, standing among the krell. The man's attention was upon the demon which had scattered the nearest dwarves and was killing a small, isolated group cowering in a doorway.

When Vastra joined him, Kaplyn indicated to the man below. "Can I shoot him?" he whispered.

"No," Vastra replied softly. "He will be protected by spells. I will cast a counter spell; shoot when I tell you to."

Kaplyn arose, taking aim. By his side Vastra drew a rune in the air and whispered a spell.

"Now!" he said. Kaplyn released the shaft that flew towards its mark with Vastra's spell preceding it. The arrow penetrated deep into the sorcerer's magic field. At that moment, the sorcerer turned as he sensed, too late, the attack. At the same instant, the demon paused in its slaughter.

Kaplyn's arrow hit the sorcerer in his side, spilling him to the ground. His krell guard ducked instinctively and their eyes turned towards Kaplyn's position, but they had forgotten the demon. Now that it was no longer in the sorcerer's power, it turned on them, seeking retribution for being used against its will.

Within seconds the krell lay dead and the stricken magi lay on the ground, whimpering in fear. Vastra and Kaplyn could only watch as, in mounting terror, the wounded man desperately sought to bring the demon under his power, his thin voice piercing the air as he tried to cast a spell. Unperturbed, the demon reached down and its sharp talons tore into the wounded man's chest, killing him and claiming his soul in one blow. For long seconds, the sorcerer screamed, long after he should have been dead. Then silence, and abruptly the demon vanished.

In the streets the dwarves rallied as more of their kin poured from the tunnel to join the fray. Like a torrent, they descended on the krell, their voices keening death chants as they slew. The krell, sensing defeat, started to break ranks, fleeing the carnage.

Thackery watched the scene from the gap in the building's front. He turned, just as Kaplyn and Vastra came back, descending through the hole in the roof.

"We must leave," Thackery stated. "If we do not go, then we run the risk of being captured by my people. They bear us malice for the Talwyn's theft and it will be some time before they forget."

The others readily agreed and once more they took to the rooftops, trying to avoid fleeing krell and the pursuing vengeful dwarves. All too soon, they were forced to return to street level and, running as fast as they could given their combined injuries, they continued along half-illuminated tunnels. They encountered several krell, but these fled before them in blind panic.

Thackery led them towards a wide tunnel at the end of which large oak doors barred their path. Thackery entered a room recessed in the stone. It was filled with cogs, gears and chains. From distant memories, he recalled how to operate the mechanism and pulling on levers he caused the oak doors to open, creaking and groaning n protest. Weak sunlight filtered through the widening gap and, even though it was diffuse, the small company shielded their eyes. As soon as it was wide enough, they ran through the exit while behind them the battle raged unabated.

Euphoria swept over them; they had escaped. Overhead, thick clouds filled the sky as far as they could see and a bitterly cold wind blew in greeting. Before them, a well-worn road, deep rutted with constant use, aimed towards tall, steep-sided mountains that dominated the distant horizon. They trudged along the road, constantly looking back in fear of pursuit from either krell or dwarves. What little of the day remained swiftly passed into dusk.

After a while, the path became one of many mountain trails and they followed one heading roughly north. As night fell, they were too weary to continue and they searched for a shelter as large flakes of snow started to fall. They found a large rock and took shelter on its lee side, huddling together for warmth.

"What do we do now?" Lars asked, shivering. They had been unable to restock their provisions and they had little food.

Kaplyn sighed. "There may also be fleeing krell coming this way and the dwarves will eventually send out patrols so we need to leave as soon as the snow stops."

There was a silence for a moment until Thackery spoke. He looked serious. "Tomorrow, I'm afraid that I will be leaving you. I intend climbing BanKennet to find the lord of the dristal; if that's still possible."

The others looked on in stunned silence. It was a strange decision fraught with danger.

"Why? It's such a perilous journey," Kaplyn stated softly.

"You have helped my people enormously and I am saddened that we cannot express our thanks. Perhaps when my people calm down and reflect on their folly, then you will be remembered for the good you have achieved." The old dwarf looked down as he stroked his long beard. "In the meantime, however, they might fall into despair. We need a feat worthy of the dwarves to redeem ourselves. If I succeed, then I intend to return — accompanied by a dristal, as Boland did so many years ago."

By his side Thaneck grinned broadly. "It is a worthy task," he concurred. "And, if the others do not object, I would be honoured if you would let me join you. Surely two hardy dwarves can climb BanKennet."

Thackery smiled at Thaneck and extended his hand. Thaneck grasped it firmly, "We will make our people proud," he declared triumphantly.

Kaplyn knew they would miss them. "You will need supplies for your task," he suggested. "Let us at least walk together for one more day. Tomorrow I will scout ahead and find game."

Thackery thanked Kaplyn and the group fell silent as they tried to sleep. They covered themselves with the few blankets they had, but the ground seemed to sap the warmth from their bodies, making sleep almost impossible. By morning the snow had lessened and they continued their journey. Kaplyn took his bow, ranging ahead of the group who were forced to walk at a slow pace due to Vastra's age and Tumarl's arm.

By mid afternoon Kaplyn returned, carrying a deer across his shoulders, toiling beneath its weight. Lars took the carcass and Kaplyn led them into a small wood. With relief Lars lay the deer down and Thaneck and Thackery set about butchering it whilst Kaplyn and Vastra built a fire. That night they ate heartily. The venison tasted good and a full stomach, combined with the flame's warmth, cheered them. When the meal was finished, they cut the remaining meat into strips, smoking these overnight.

In the morning the dwarves shouldered their packs. "We must take our leave now," said Thackery. "Once again, I thank you on behalf of my people. When Talwyn's influence has diminished, they will be grateful. I am sure that you would be welcome to visit us then, hopefully in better circumstances."

They accompanied them to the edge of the wood where they made their farewells. Thaneck turned lastly to Lars. "One day I would very much like to meet your people. Perhaps when things are normal, we can help you return to your homeland."

The offer was well meant and Lars felt a deep gratitude. For a while they watched the pair until they were just faint specks against the white background. Snow was falling once more and, with a heavy heart, Kaplyn turned to the others. "I'm going north, to Trosgarth. If you wish to accompany me, then now is the time to decide."

"Why go there?" Lars asked.

Kaplyn looked grim. "I need to recover the crystal from the tree of life," he said dourly.

For a moment, the others glanced at each other uncertainly and then, one by one, they agreed to accompany Kaplyn, as snow danced around them in swirling patterns. Their packs were full of meat and their hearts were less weary than the night before. With a grim determination, they set their faces into the icy wind which seemed to blow all the fiercer, as though challenging their resolve.

Chapter 17

The Plain of Chalynth

For two days they walked, following narrow mountain paths. To their relief they saw little signs of life apart from the occasional hare or bird. On the morning of the second day since leaving the dwarves, they climbed to the summit of one of the last foothills. Before them a vast open plain stretched into the distance where sky and land met in a grey uncertain haze.

At one time the plain must have been picturesque with small copses dotting the landscape and herds of animals grazing. Now it looked barren and forlorn. The trees had long since shed their leaves and, in the prolonged winter, no new foliage had grown for some time. Animals avoided the open expanse that seemed both eerie and dangerous.

"This infernal wind seems to be coming from the very heart of Trosgarth," Lomar said, shivering as he hugged his chest. They were already wearing every item of clothing they had, and still the wind seemed to cut through.

"Let's hope it is only the wind we have to contend with," Tumarl replied brusquely. Every step jarred his arm, causing him fresh pain.

Walking on the flat ground was a relief after the ups and downs of the foothills. After a while each member of the group had the uneasy feeling that they were being watched. No one said anything for fear of being considered paranoid. Eventually, however, Lomar could contain himself no longer. He walked alongside Kaplyn and in a low voice said, "I do not like this. I think we are being watched."

"I have had the same feeling and yet cannot see anyone," Kaplyn replied. In his mind he questioned Shastlan, but the link with his shaol seemed more distant than usual. A feeling of despair stole over him as he examined the open ground about them. There was little cover for them to hide in and Trosgarth was still some distance away. "We have no option but to continue," he declared finally.

"Let's stop for a while," Lomar urged. "I'll look into a kara-stone and see if sorcery will reveal anything." Lomar withdrew his stone, laying it on the ground whilst the others looked on curiously. For several heartbeats he stared into the pale orb.

Gradually a feeling of terror stole over Kaplyn and, abruptly, he sensed Shastlan's warning, but as yet was unsure of the threat. He glanced around. By their furtive glances the others, too, seemed to sense something. Kaplyn shivered. Upon the exposed plain the wind seemed colder and, to make matters worse, the light was failing. Overhead the clouds were thickening and it looked like it might snow.

"There are some hollows in the ground to our right," Kaplyn said. "Let's go there. It's getting late and they will conceal us and may offer some shelter from this cursed wind!"

Lomar scooped up his stone, looking puzzled. "The stone revealed nothing," he said as they made their way towards the hollows. Within moments they were huddled together at the bottom of one of these whilst Kaplyn peered over its lip. The wind chill seemed slightly less, but his feeling of unease grew. "Can you use sorcery to find out what our danger is, Vastra?" Kaplyn whispered.

The old man looked weary. "I dare not. The enemy would then know we are here. I will risk a spell of concealment though. That requires little energy and its casting is difficult to detect."

Kaplyn nodded.

As Vastra drew the necessary runes, night finally closed in about them although it seemed too early and the dark felt unnatural. Indeed, so dark was it that none of the group could see the other. Kaplyn drew his blade; immediately a faint blue radiance filled the hollow and Kaplyn saw the fear reflected in the eyes of the others.

Kaplyn suddenly hissed, his eyes wide with fear. "Something approaches." A feeling induced by Shastlan told him the direction and he felt several shapes, albeit some way off. As if to confirm his fears, his blade glowed more brightly as though welcoming a foe in challenge.

In Kaplyn's mind's eye, a grey shape appeared against a dark background. Concentrating, he was rewarded by the silhouette of a lone rider, some distance ahead of several others. Terror seemed to follow the rider and Kaplyn involuntarily pressed himself closer to the spongy turf. He found himself holding his breath, closing his eyes shut as though by excluding his other senses he could increase his second sight. He tried to relax and breathe steadily. The picture seemed to clarify slightly, and in so doing he sensed the figure stop as though searching the way ahead.

Immediately he cut the link and turned to Lomar. The albino's face was tinged with blue from the sword's eerie light. Kaplyn grabbed the other man's arm. "They can see our shaols," he gasped.

Lomar understood, "Then I must free my spirit and lead them away."

"The risk is too great; give me a moment," Kaplyn said. Using his link with Shastlan, he probed the surrounding darkness. There was no mistaking that the creatures were heading their way. The riders remained indistinct and difficult to see although the horses came sharply into focus. It was almost as if he was looking at a person's shaol rather than seeing the person. And then realisation dawned; the riders were not alive. The horror nearly made him forget to cut the link with Shastlan.

"You *will* have to try to lead them away," Kaplyn said. "We have no choice. I think they are ghosts, not men."

Lomar frowned. "Is that possible?" Without waiting for a reply, he lay down, closing his eyes, concentrating upon his inner-self.

Glancing over the lip of the hollow, Kaplyn sensed more riders and counted twenty. Suddenly a faint light flickered away to Kaplyn's left and he felt the riders pause. The glow became more distinct and Kaplyn recognised Lomar's shaol as it started to move away.

In unison the riders turned towards Lomar's spirit and started to canter after him. The albino's shaol increased its speed, fleeing before them. After a moment longer Kaplyn could not see the faint silvery spectre, nor could he sense the riders. For the moment at least they were safe, but for how long he was not certain.

Kaplyn glanced down at the albino. With the biting wind and the light from Kaplyn's blade, his pallor was a ghastly blue.

"Hold on," he muttered softly. He prayed for daylight which would help to hide their shaols. In the darkness they would shine out like beacons. The dawn, however, was a long way off.

Around the hollow, the dead sought the living in a deadly game of cat and mouse. Kaplyn and the others huddled as low as they could next to Lomar's body, which looked more like a corpse with every passing moment. Their fate hung by a narrow thread, already stretched to the breaking point.

Part 2

Chapter 1

Foreboding

Prince Fiad paced the anteroom, his temper wearing dangerously thin. A Crown Prince of Bhutan was not used to being kept waiting, especially by a Thracian clerk. Others sat in the room, each looking equally frustrated. The clerk in question sat by a dark, wooden table polished to a high sheen, signing a stack of papers. He looked nervous amongst such eminent company, clearly sensing their frustration. He cast Fiad a sideways glance, but turned away when the prince scowled angrily back. The clerk looked down at the paper in front of him as though absorbed in its contents.

Fiad continued to pace around the room like a trapped animal. He looked about at the other commanders, assembled from nearby kingdoms. Previously he had only met Tharn Harlester of West Meath. Sitting by Harlester's side was Thorlar, a dwarf chieftain from Tubarl, a small kingdom deep in the heart of the Charlot Mountains. Fiad had never met a dwarf before; that privilege was usually reserved for the merchant castes, eager to trade for minerals. He liked the dwarf, perhaps because he was such a dependable figure, reminiscent of the mountains from which he hailed. His eyes, partially hidden beneath thick shaggy eyebrows, were a deep blue which seemed to make his gaze all the more piercing.

Like most dwarves, he wore his hair and beard in long braids. That morning he favoured a thick leather jerkin, trimmed with fur and wore stout boots that looked well used. His axe was missing as the Thracians allowed no one to bear arms in the presence of their monarch, Queen Catriona, and certainly not since the assassination of their king.

Thorlar and Harlester were in conversation and, although their voices were low, Fiad sensed their impatience. Harlester dressed in bright silks and his attitude was cavalier, but Fiad knew better. He was a good friend, a fine swordsman and very brave.

He was a good looking man whose company was often sought by ladies of various courts. He enjoyed life to the fullest and nothing seemed to dampen his spirit, not even when challenged by various husbands. His off-hand manner had more than once threatened his career. Now it was almost his trademark and he seemed immensely pleased when he heard what others thought of his carefree attitude.

Fiad envied Harlester; Fiad was much more impatient, but perhaps that could be attributed to his youth. He was full of bravado and eager to prove his worth on the field of battle.

Fiad glanced at the other commanders and his eyes were immediately drawn to King Palastor. Suppressing a shudder, his first impression was of fear. He, like many others, could not help but liken the albino to a demon. Palastor was unnaturally thin, and his flesh and hair were purest white. It was his eyes that made Fiad shudder though; they were scarlet and seemed to bore into Fiad's soul. Like Harlester, Palastor favoured bright coloured clothing and, sitting side by side, the two men were difficult on the eyes.

Turning away, he went to a window, contemplating the vast army camped outside the city walls. He commanded thirty thousand troops while Harlester had twenty thousand infantry and fifteen thousand cavalry. Thorlar had led eight thousand dwarves from the Charlot Mountains, each bearing chain mail and axe. With close to thirty thousand troops from Thrace and twenty thousand from Allund and three thousand from Gilfillan, they had a mighty army. More troops were arriving from the outlying countries every day. Fiad's confidence was high and he could not understand why they waited; surely the best option now was to carry the battle to the enemy.

At that moment Tharn Ballan entered from the interconnecting door to the throne room.

"Queen Catriona will see the commanders now," he stated to the clerk before returning inside the room. The clerk looked grateful as he rose and held open the door, letting the others file past. Fiad went first and looked in interest upon the long throne room. On the wall a large portrait of King Sharroch who had been assassinated at the start of the recent conflict, stared accusingly down upon them.

Queen Catriona sat at one end of the table, tall and graceful, with a beautiful complexion and wide gentle eyes, although presently she looked troubled. Behind her, standing amongst the shadows, stood another figure and it took Fiad a few moments to recognise Astalus, the court wizard. He was a young man, dressed in a long brown robe tied at the waist with a silken cord. Fiad was surprised to see him for he had only recently returned from a trip to find an ancient Eldric city. He had heard that the wizard had virtually locked himself in his tower these last three nights. Beneath his arm Astalus clutched a thick leather book and, by his expression, he was loath to be parted from it. For a moment Fiad was shocked by Astalus' paleness.

The eyes, too, looked strangely haunted. Shuddering, he turned his attention away from the mage and back to the others. Patiently he waited for them to be seated and, as soon as silence descended, he addressed the Thracian queen.

"The army is ready to march," he declared abruptly, pacing across the room and halting before the portrait of her father. "We should confront Trosgarth now, before they have a chance to rebuild their army. We *must* take advantage of their recent defeat."

Catriona looked briefly annoyed that Fiad had chosen to stand beneath the portrait of her father. Was it a deliberate ploy to remind her courtiers that a woman now ruled?

"It would be foolhardy to march on Trosgarth," she said. "An attack would have been viable with Kaplyn leading us. With the dragons' aid there had been a real chance of our winning a war. But Kaplyn has gone, and we do not know where."

Fiad felt a twinge of jealousy at the mention of Kaplyn's name and did not like the feeling. "Have you looked from the walls upon our army? Never since the Krell Wars has such an army been assembled. We do not need a dragon to win this war."

"In the Krell Wars, we had the Eldric and their sorcerers," Catriona reminded him.

Fiad suppressed his anger. "And now we must face the fact that they, too, have gone. If we lack their power, then the enemy is similarly handicapped. You said yourself that the army besieging CarCamel was led by only one sorcerer. I believe that we can deal with such a threat by might of arms alone, and that does not even include the dwarves of Thandor, for they will surely aid us, as they have before."

Catriona did not look convinced. "That might not be true. Thorlar of Tubarl has informed me that his people have not heard from Thandor for many generations, and his envoys have failed to return."

For a moment there was silence before Catriona continued. "It is not my advice that we march," she urged the assembled men. The Prophecy is not yet fulfilled and we do not have a king to lead us. I would caution that we wait, learn more of the enemy's disposition and increase our strength."

Fiad was frustrated by not getting his own way, and the mention of the Prophecy angered him. His own people acknowledged him to be the King mentioned in those cryptic lines and, by a roundabout way, his birth could be explained by earth, fire and water. He decided to change tactics.

"What of Astalus then?" he asked, gesturing towards the silent figure. "What of his quest? I have been told that he returned three days ago and yet we have not been briefed about his findings."

Many eyes turned towards the wizard who took two paces forward, although he remained partially concealed by the shadows as if they followed him. Catriona was watching Astalus with foreboding in her eyes.

"I have returned from Namthrall with Haft Commander Tallin. Using magic, I summoned the city from the ruins, so that before us a mighty fortress rose. I entered the city, leaving Tallin and his command outside. In my absence, a large force of krell attacked them and all but Tallin were wiped out. The two of us were lucky to escape with our lives."

He fell silent for a moment and removed the book from beneath his arm. "But our journey was not in vain. I have returned with an Eldric volume which I believe to be the single most significant book of our time. It contains Eldric spells, the power of which we have only been able to imagine before."

An excited murmur went up from the assembled men. As it died down Astalus continued. His voice was quiet and yet he held everyone's attention.

"I have found one spell in particular which is of great consequence," he stated solemnly, pausing for effect. "With it — I can summon dragons. Not *one,* but as *many* as *I* desire."

The noise within the room was deafening as the commanders all tried to speak at once. Fiad held up a hand, and gradually silence fell. Glancing at Catriona, Fiad caught her looking at Astalus with irritation, and he guessed that she had not wanted him to reveal that particular piece of information.

"This is news *indeed.* Can you cast the spell?" Fiad asked.

Astalus nodded. "I've spent the past three nights in study. As you are no doubt aware, we Akrane lack the power of the Narlassar, but I have discovered to some extent the source of their power. I, at least, can now use their spells and, as a consequence, I have seen the dragon's world. It is a land of tall mountains and deep lakes. A dragon, a brown, came to my bidding. It was eager to help us for they hate demons with a passion."

Again the voices of the assembled men rose in heated debate, but Fiad insisted on silence. Turning to Catriona, he was surprised by how pale she seemed.

"The army is ready," he declared firmly. Several shouts of "Aye" from the assembled men confirmed their support. "With the dragons' aid, we will be invincible."

"Is it the will of everyone present that the army should march?" Catriona asked. She knew that the merchants would support a *yes* vote; they were horrified by the size of the army and were already counting the cost of feeding it.

Each of the assembled commanders supported the motion. By the conclusion of the meeting it was decided to send the army under Fiad's command north. In total, ninety thousand men would go, leaving only a few thousand to guard the city. Fiad and Harlester each promised an additional ten thousand troops to defend the city once they had been mustered.

At that moment the clouds parted and, for a few moments, warm sunshine flooded into the large hall. Within the room the commanders blinked uncertainly at each other, being unused to the bright light after so many months of darkness. Suddenly they felt as though an immense weight had been lifted from their overburdened shoulders, and all around the table smiles broke out. Only Catriona remained grim. Fiad looked at the queen and knew that he had won, but at what cost?

For several weeks the city was in mayhem. Vast quantities of supplies were required for the expedition and they had to await reinforcements. Few realised how much administration was required for such an endeavour. By the end of the first week, a task force was assembled in the main courtyard, led by Tharn Orrin. Their aim was to secure Pantril, the most northerly of Thrace's towns. The bulk of the army would rendezvous with them there one week later. The task force would forage the land and stockpile food to resupply the army as it passed through. They would then form the rear-guard.

Many of CarCamel's citizens turned out to watch the task force leave and the crowd cheered heartily while the troops looked uncertainly back. Too many remembered the recent conflict and, unlike Prince Fiad, few dreamt of being heroes.

As the troops left the city, merchants' caravans entered from the surrounding kingdoms. It was a time for profit as wooden wagons rattled through the cobbled streets to replenish the city's stocks, depleted by the recent conflict.

The preparations for the main army reached a climax the day before they were scheduled to leave. A lull before the oncoming storm settled over the city, and many took this time to bid a final farewell to loved ones. The troops from distant cities hosted noisy parties, eager to show that they were unafraid. The younger troops looked up to the veterans while they turned inward to look for courage. Many were thankful for the cold, grateful for its excuse to hide their fear.

Chapter 2

Departure

Nate breathed in the cool night air, absently registering the smell of wood-smoke, horses and men, as he surveyed the scene before him, marvelling at what he saw. His haft and the bulk of the Allund army, were camped on a small hill in front of CarCamel, and, before him as far as his eye could see, were a myriad of campfires disappearing into the distance like tiny fireflies. The walls of CarCamel rose before them and, atop these, Nate could see small watch fires burning brightly on the battlements.

Before the war, Nate had been a farmer and never in his life had he dreamed of seeing so many men assembled in one place. Some said there were over one hundred thousand troops. His haft had left the city only two days earlier, making room in the barracks for other troops who would defend the city once the army was gone. With the absence of a roof and four walls, the chill of the night penetrated his old bones. A tent was poor comfort, he thought, shivering, pulling his woollen cloak tighter about his shoulders. An itch started under his breastplate and he tried to ignore it, feeling frustrated that an itch always started some place you could not reach.

Nate turned his attention back to the camp. It was hard to believe that, at each fire, there were several unseen bodies. Nate looked up at the dark sky. No stars were visible and he cursed the cold. He imagined stars twinkling brightly on a warm summer evening, comparing them with the army's campfires.

Imagine, the stars could be like these camp fires with the spirits of our dead ancestors huddled around them, he thought. Perhaps that is where the King in the Prophecy is right now, looking down on the army and deciding when to come to our aid. He could almost hear the braying of trumpets as a host of dead soldiers flowed from the night sky to swell their ranks as they marched on Trosgarth. However, the thought of death quickly brought his thoughts back to reality. Thad's death, and that of the other good men he knew, was still fresh in his mind.

"Damn this itch," he muttered sullenly, knowing he would remember Thad for the rest of his life, which might not be too long with the battle imminent. Suddenly he could stand it no longer.

"Why do we have to wear this ridiculous armour?" he announced to no one in particular as he flung his cloak to one side. In irritation he tried to hook a finger under the breastplate to itch the stubborn spot.

Sarin laughed, enjoying watching the older man's struggle. Nate glared sullenly back as though daring him to laugh again.

"Take it off if you want," Harlam offered. "We are not moving out until dawn. You need to relax while you can. Once we start there will be precious little rest, so take advantage now."

Nate was glad of the sudden conversation. His thoughts had been turning gloomy and he found himself wanting to talk. The itch had miraculously gone and for that mercy, at least, he thanked the Kalanth. Swiftly he pulled his cloak about himself. "It's these coarse shirts," he complained. "Why can't we wear something less irritating? I bet the officers don't have to wear this rubbish."

Harlam shrugged and drew closer to the fire. "You should be glad that you have such a fine garment to wear and, if I were an officer, I would be wearing the same. It's thick and warm, and absorbs sweat better than any other material."

Nate sneered, shaking his head. "If I was an officer, I would have a silk shirt and be glad of the comfort."

By his side Sarin stirred, a sure sign that he was about to speak. "Where are we going tomorrow?" he asked, somewhat timidly.

"Tomorrow?" Harlam questioned, "We'll probably not get very far, not with all the wagons. It will take us about a week to reach the Thracian border. From there...? I am not sure what lies directly north. We might have to cross KinKassack. That's an evil place by all accounts. And there is also Thandor, the ancient dwarven kingdom. Tomorrow will be but a stroll, probably no more than ten miles."

Sarin nodded. As a soldier, he had learnt not to ask too many questions.

"I was told an army of dwarves joined us yesterday. I think that they are camped over there somewhere," Nate said, turning away from the city and pointing. "We should try to find them. I'd like to meet a dwarf. By all accounts they have a rare brew that will raise our spirits, if you take my meaning."

Sarin's eyes widened at the prospect of meeting the dwarves, and even Harlam looked as though he was willing to investigate. "Come," he announced, smiling broadly. "There's little sleep in me this night. Let's go and explore, and see what we can find."

Eagerly they arose.

Nate grinned wickedly. "It wouldn't be the mention of dwarf ale that's prompted your sudden interest, is it?"

Harlam returned the grin, patting his comrade on the shoulder. "It will help us sleep."

"And then some," Sarin added eagerly. The other two men laughed at this.

"Watch where you are putting your feet, you big oaf," the voice cursed from the darkness.

Nate felt the earth move and leapt back fearfully. With the contrast of light from the campfires and the surrounding darkness, it was very difficult to see. He realised that he must have trodden on someone and, by the sounds of their irate voice, they objected to the rough treatment.

"S...sorry," he stuttered as Harlam and Sarin collided with his back.

A large figure rose in front of him.

"I didn't see you there," Nate continued.

"Well then — what have we here?" the voice continued "You're not Bhutan by your accent."

"Certainly not," growled Harlam. "We're Allunds and proud of it!"

"Then I must assume that Allunds cannot see in the dark," continued the voice, although somewhat mollified. "Come, join me by our fire. I've never seen an Allund before." The shape lumbered towards one of the nearby campfires. As he entered the firelight he ordered the reclining figures to make room for guests.

"Look lively and smarten yourselves up," he ordered. "We've company. Garrick, get some wine for our guests." One of the figures rose and went to collect a jug while the large man sat down by the roaring flames. Harlam and the others joined them, arranging themselves in the spaces amongst the other men.

The introductions were quickly made. Nate and the others couldn't possibly take in all the names in one go. The large man, the haft commander as it turned out, was called Jorrant. At that moment Garrick returned with a jug of wine which he set down in front of the group before sitting down himself. He was a tall, lanky individual with a thin face and short-cropped hair.

"You will have to watch your purse with Garrick around; he's as crooked as a nine snath coin. He was told, *either join the army or go to prison for a year*. Unwisely, he chose the army."

Garrick grinned broadly, revealing several missing teeth and many more blackened stumps.

In the light of the fire they could see Jorrant more clearly. He was a big man and well muscled, with a short crop of dark hair. A deep scar ran diagonally across his forehead, cheek and lips, adding to his fierce countenance.

Nate looked around. All the Bhutans were dressed similarly, wearing bright red cloaks. They had no armour and instead wore metal-studded leather jerkins that looked comfortable and warm. Rather than breeches the Bhutans wore a short skirt, braided with leather thongs, and thick socks which came up to their knees. Each man carried a broadsword and a small axe.

At first the Allunds found the Bhutan accents difficult to follow, and Nate had to ask Jorrant to repeat himself several times when he spoke.

"You were in the battle, were you?" Jorrant asked more slowly, as if the Allunds were simple. The other Bhutans grinned.

Harlam nodded.

"They say there was a dragon," Jorrant said eagerly. "My men and me laid odds on whether there is such a thing. Did you see it?"

"I saw it," Sarin interrupted. "I was standing on the inner wall, about fifty yards from the main gate with a demon doing its best to kill us all. As tall as a house, it was, and I was frightened, I can tell you. We'd heard tales of how a demon can take your soul to hell."

Jorrant snorted derisively but the other Bhutans were listening in awe. Sarin ignored the big man and continued his tale.

"Suddenly there was a loud crack, like the snap of a whip, a giant whip at that. A sudden gust of wind caught us and I thought that another demon had materialised, and then suddenly a dark form streaked by us. It was so close I could have reached out and touched it!"

The Bhutans stared at Sarin with a mixture of fear and wonder. They had heard about the dragon and how it had saved the city, but the tales had been second hand. Even Jorrant was silent, drinking in every word.

Sarin closed his eyes to picture the dragon more clearly, remembering his first impressions. His voice betrayed the awe he had felt. Perhaps if a more seasoned warrior had told the tale, then the listeners would have been sceptical; it was his youth that convinced them.

"It was huge," he continued, "and its speed! At first I could not think what it was that had flashed by. It was as if my heart had stopped beating and time stood still. Then the dragon was through the gate, rising into the sky on outstretched wings that seemed gossamer thin, like the finest silk, and yet so strong. It was a red dragon. The neck was long and tapered to its head. The tail was also long, thick at the body and very fine at the tip.

"When I first saw it," Sarin continued, looking at each wide-eyed listener in turn, its body was stretched taut as an arrow; I assumed that was for speed. Kaplyn, he is an Allund and our King for that matter, sat astride the dragon just where the neck joined the body. He killed the demon with his sword which they say was Eldric made. I saw it and it glowed blue, as bright as the stars.

"The whole incident lasted for only a few heartbeats," Sarin said. "And yet I will remember it forever. I saw the dragon, later — high in the sky. It was coiled in mid-flight, its wings folded back as it started to turn for another attack. I remember thinking, *how did a rider stay on such a fearful creature?* Then it was gone from view. Shortly after that, the enemy was in retreat, their will to fight broken." Sarin's voice faded until the only sounds were the crackle of the fire and other distant voices in low conversation.

"Is it true that demons can take a man's soul?" one of the Bhutan soldiers asked.

By Sarin's side, Jorrant frowned darkly. Soldiers going into battle needed a high morale. "It'll have to get past me to get you, Callor, so you don't need to worry," he interrupted. All turned to look at the haft commander. In the dancing firelight his craggy face looked more krell than human and the long scar made him look fearful.

"If a demon comes near me, it will taste Bhutan steel. Stab them here," he indicated a point just below his throat, "and it sends them back to hell — pronto." No one doubted that he could do it, either; many present had seen him fight.

"Watch out," a Bhutan soldier by Garrick's side whispered to Nate. "When he is in this mood, he will tell you how he got his scar."

As if prompted by the words, Jorrant pointed to the scar, "Did I tell you how I got this?"

Nate and the other Allunds shook their heads; Garrick winked at Nate.

"I was on patrol in the Chanteal Mountains," he turned to Nate confidentially. "You know the routine — we were looking for krell to ease the minds of fat merchants. We'd been out for some time and were climbing a particularly steep mountain with a small stream on our right …"

"Left," interrupted Garrick, coughing gently. Jorrant turned on the older soldier, his eyes narrowing dangerously.

"As I said, the river was on the right," he continued to glare at Garrick who shrugged in resignation.

"A stone suddenly clattered down from above. We froze, instantly alert."

"Nothing of the sort," whispered Garrick to Nate. "His horse threw him and he ended up sitting on his rump."

Jorrant ignored the jibe. "I ordered the troops to dismount, and it was lucky that I did, for just then a hail of arrows landed amongst us. We knew it was krell from that instant; nobody makes arrows as badly as they do." This was untrue; krell arrows were as deadly as any other.

"We sought shelter as best we could and waited for them to run out of arrows. Within seconds though, an unholy cry went up and hundreds of krell attacked, seeming to come from the very rocks themselves."

Nate looked at Garrick for confirmation. Garrick nodded grimly; he was tense as though reliving the memory.

"A large krell, wielding a massive axe, strode towards us, and I marked him for myself," Jorrant stated bluntly. His eyes narrowed to thin slits. "I blocked his first blow but the shock shattered my blade. The axe followed through and I threw myself back, but not before it did this," he indicated the scar. "Damn nearly took my head off and I was blinded by my own blood. Instinct told me to roll and keep rolling. I heard his axe striking the rocks near me and I feared that I was finished. Garrick came to my aid, but this krell was strong. He simply swept Garrick to one side like a rag doll. The delay was enough though, even if it did cost Garrick his teeth — and his looks." The others grinned at Garrick who flashed the few remaining teeth back at them in a sheepish grin.

"I picked up a rock, slamming it into the krell's knee for all I was worth. That brought him up sharp, I can tell you. Broke his knee and felled him like an ox. With these I finished him...," he held up his hands for all to see, "...broke his neck."

"The rest, seeing their leader down, gave up and fled. They could have finished us if they had continued their attack," Garrick said in the hushed silence. "We were easily outnumbered — but, without their leader, they lost the will to fight."

"I didn't know that there were krell in Bhutan," Harlam said in surprise.

"There have been krell in Bhutan ever since the Krell Wars. Nobody knows how many live there, and it was with some reluctance that our people sent an army north at all; while we swan around up here our homes are at risk."

The Allund soldiers remained silent. Allund had managed to escape the ravages of the krell hordes. Perhaps the Priests of Ryoch had something to do with that but nobody knew for sure, and, now that the priests had turned traitors, perhaps krell were more active in Allund. Nate glanced at Harlam who returned his troubled look; both had wives and children at home and they had thought them safe.

Approaching hoof-beats stirred the group. Suddenly the Bhutans were on their feet with Jorrant saluting smartly. A rider materialised from the darkness, dressed as the other Bhutans, in a rich red cloak pinned at his throat by a large brooch of obvious wealth. A regal figure looked down on the soldiers and smiled warmly.

"Prince Fiad," acknowledged Jorrant. "It's an honour sir."

"The honour's mine," replied Fiad, dismounting. "But what's this? Are we entertaining Allunds or is it the other way round?"

Nate and the others had also risen to their feet and they looked in awe on the Bhutan prince. None of them had seen Fiad before let alone met him.

Seeing their uncertainty, Fiad bade them sit and then squatted down himself before anyone could object. "Have you been telling them tales of the famous scar Jorrant?" Fiad asked. Jorrant nodded and the prince smiled. "No mean feat from what I heard."

Jorrant grinned, broadening the famous scar. In the quiet the fire popped sending a flaming ember flying from its ferocious heart. The ember burned brightly as it flew, but away from the heat it swiftly faded.

"Is there any wine?" Fiad asked, flashing a grin. The others looked on blankly and Garrick held up his half empty pitcher. Fiad shook his head and, rising, went to his horse where he unhooked a large flagon.

The others looked at each other nonplussed as the prince went around the group filling their mugs with the rich red liquid.

By morning no one could remember the idle chatter of the previous night, but the prince left them with fire in their hearts. His brief stay gave them confidence and suddenly it felt right to go into the wilderness to face the enemy. They were strong, stronger than any army ever assembled.

When Harlam, Nate and Sarin left the group to return to their camp, their heads had been spinning and not just from the wine. As the sun rose, trumpets blared to greet the dawn. In the light of day, the weary Allunders passed by other small groups in the scarlet robes of Bhutan; then these changed to the silver livery of West Meath. They had travelled farther than they had thought, but had not managed to find the dwarves. Still they had spoken with a prince! Everywhere there was an excited clamour as troops of all nations breakfasted and welcomed the dawn.

Suddenly a fanfare sounded from the high walls and towers of CarCamel, and the partly repaired city gates opened as a host of riders issued forth. At the head rode Queen Catriona and, behind her, came the cavalry and then infantry. Their orange cloaks seemed suddenly brighter as the sun broke through the mass of clouds. Warm, gentle light surrounded the Thracians and a great cheer went up from the assembled throng. For a moment Catriona was bathed in light and everyone felt heartened. Then, as suddenly as it had started, the light failed as dark clouds closed ranks. From the north a chill wind sprang up, forcing the assembled men to pull their cloaks tighter.

Trosgarth was calling.

Chapter 3

Betrayal

Ariome stood on the top of her high tower, peering between the battlements, watching the colourful spectacle below. A feeling of glee rose from within her and she smiled, her eyes glittering with malice.

"Fools that you think you can challenge the might of Trosgarth," she whispered. "Catriona, if you think the loss of your father and brother were hard to bear, then wait until you see your subjects enslaved. For you will — that *I* promise. Drachar will want you alive to make his victory all the sweeter." She hissed the last word through clenched teeth. A breeze sprang up blowing her long dark hair behind her.

That night one of the city guard, an old soldier with many years of good service, felt something unseen and yet fearful pass overhead. A thrill of fear ran down his spine, and he pressed himself hard against the reassuring stones of the city wall, his eyes searching the darkness. He could see nothing and slowly his fear subsided. Even still he was sweating hard and his breathing was laboured.

He shook his head. "Calm down, you old fool. You're jumping at shadows."

"Fothar, is that you making that din?" came a familiar voice from the guard tower several yards away. For a moment he considered telling the guard commander of his fear, but then reconsidered.

"It's nothing," he replied. "I tripped. It's a dark night out here."

"Well, keep an eye out and stop daydreaming," the voice retorted full of sarcasm.

Fothar grinned, half at his own fears and half at the guard commander. He was an old friend and he found comfort in his voice. As he continued with his watch, his eyes constantly searched the heavens.

Ariome watched the flat roof from a doorway at the top of the steep stairway as she sheltered from the biting cold wind. She held the hood of her cloak tightly about her chin so that only her eyes were visible. All at once she heard the beating of wings, and then a dark form coalesced from the night as it hovered above the roof.

Immediately fear assailed her in nauseating waves, but she was prepared for it. With a murmur, she drew a rune, banishing her fear. A long lizard-like creature rested on the roof. Its small, beady eyes stared towards her hiding place and a pale tongue flickered over rows of small sharp teeth. The creature's wings were tucked tightly behind its long neck as it awaited its passenger.

Ariome stepped forth, her cloak falling back to reveal sombre clothes of thick wool. Her message was too important to leave to a carrier pigeon, and besides there was nothing left for her here. She wanted to be in Trosgarth, especially for her master's triumph. Then her reward would be great. There would be a need for monarchs to rule over the defeated enemies and she wanted to be in the right place when they were chosen. Mounting, she urged her steed into the sky. It lurched towards the heavens and Ariome was thrown back in her seat.

Within the city, several citizens felt the creature's passage, and they made warding gestures against evil as they hurried home.

It took the army four days to reach the northern boundaries of Thrace and the town of Pantril. Tharn Orrin's advance party were relieved to finally see the main army coming towards them, and many cheered as the ranks of soldiers filed into town.

Fiad, Queen Catriona and the other commanders held a briefing in the old town hall. At one time it had been a grand building; oak panels adorned the walls and a large fireplace, now unlit, dominated the main reception room. Poor light, cast by a few feeble lamps, obscured much of the splendour and draughts caused dancing shadows as the commanders inspected a large map spread across what was once a dining table.

"Our progress is too slow," Fiad said impatiently, evidently in a poor mood.

"Patience," Harlester urged the younger man. "What would you have us do — leave the supplies and wagons behind?"

Fiad's look suggested that was precisely what he intended.

Catriona shook her head. "Impossible. That's exactly what the enemy wants us to do. They would attack our supplies and then cut off our heads into the bargain."

Fiad's temper was rising. "Trosgarth and Aldrace might not even have an army. We must strike swiftly before they have time to reorganise."

Harlester interrupted, trying to bring order back to the meeting. "Trosgarth has had a long time to prepare for this war. It is unlikely they would commit all their forces so early on."

Fiad chose not to argue. Instead he glanced at Thorlar, hoping that the dwarf would support him. His people carried their belongings and were not burdened by wagons. However, Thorlar refused to meet his look.

"Then what do you propose?" Fiad asked sullenly.

Harlester shook his head. "We must travel with the supplies. On this matter, there is no option."

"And where do we go next?" Fiad asked.

Thorlar pointed to the map. "The plain here is what is left of Chalynth. That country was practically destroyed in the Krell Wars. It's quite close to Thandor and from there we will be able to enlist the aid of my dwarven brothers."

Catriona studied the map where Thorlar was pointing. It was old and very worn. A large area was simply marked as Trosgarth and another Aldrace. Between their present position and the point where Thorlar was indicating lay KinKassack and north of that a mountain range. They could not avoid the forest.

"Where is Astalus?" Catriona asked in mounting frustration. "He should be here." Turning to a sentry, she commanded him to find the wizard and bring him to the meeting. For a moment there was silence as everyone studied the map.

Catriona could not help but think that they were making a mistake, remembering the lines of the Prophecy that a king should lead them. But there was not a king amongst them. For all his posturing, Fiad was a prince, at least while his father lived. True the King was old, but he might live for many years yet. Harlester was a tharn. Thorlar was a Chieftain, but not a king, and she was a queen. She looked at Palastor; the albino was intently studying the map. Even he was not a true king. If any deserved that title it was Lomar, but he had gone with Kaplyn. The memory of Kaplyn caused her pain and, for a moment, she wished that she had known his intention to leave, for then she might have been able to stop him.

"Our forefathers fought Trosgarth at DrummondCal," Thorlar the dwarf was continuing. He was indicating a point some way into Chalynth, close to the border with Trosgarth. "It seems to me to be as good a place as any. Perhaps some luck from the last victory lingers."

Harlester looked quizzical. "We will need to go through KinKassack. Even in West Meath we have heard of this evil place. Can we not go around that at least?"

Catriona shook her head sadly. "To the west of KinKassack the mountains are nearly sheer. To go east would take us too close to Aldrace. For the moment at least all we can do is journey towards the forest and, once there, either burn or cut a way through."

Harlester's eyes narrowed. "We're taking a huge gamble," he announced. "The forest behind us cuts off any retreat."

Fiad nodded. "We have little option. Do not forget though that we have Astalus with his spell to summon dragons."

At that moment Astalus entered still carrying his precious book. The wizard had pulled his cowl over his head and made no move to remove it.

"We are discussing how we will get through KinKassack," Fiad said.

"I believe that we will find a way through," Astalus stated confidently.

"Have you spoken with the dragons since the last time?" Catriona asked.

Astalus shook his head. "There's no need. They will come when I summon them."

"We should summon them now," Harlester said. "I mean, surely it would be wise to have them here with us now, to protect us."

"No!" Astalus exclaimed. "We should keep the dragons as a surprise."

Fiad agreed. "We need to end this war once and for all. That was the mistake the Eldric made, not finishing the task when they were able. I still believe that the bulk of the enemy army was destroyed at CarCamel. Now we need to draw out what remains and crush them forever." He slammed a hand down on the table, the slap reverberating around the room. "If they knew we had dragons, they would hide in Trosgarth and then the war would never be won."

Tharn Orrin had been quiet during the discourse, but now spoke. His voice seemed prophetic in the small room. "Fiad is right. How many more generations must suffer fear, not knowing when Trosgarth will spill forth once more like some vile cancer? The dragons might not even be necessary. With this army we could march into the very gates of hell and order Drachar's shade to come forth."

Harlester grinned. "And who would sit in judgement?"

"I," snapped Orrin, "And every man, woman and child who has lost a loved one." Orrin's eyebrows bristled and his eyes smouldered with rage. Harlester found that he could not meet the older man's gaze and was forced to lower his eyes.

"I meant no offence," he declared.

"So be it," Fiad declared. "When the time comes, Astalus, you will find us a way to cross KinKassack. I do not care how you do it. Burn the accursed place if necessary, but find a way. With your permission?" Fiad said, turning to Queen Catriona. She nodded, although her eyes reflected her uncertainty. "The main body will leave in the morning." Fiad continued. "With luck we will meet up with the dwarves of Thandor before we reach Chalynth. If not, Trosgarth will have to settle with fighting us alone.".

With that, the meeting closed and, one by one, the commanders left, filing past Queen Catriona. As Fiad left the flame from the fire reflected momentarily in his eyes. For an instant he looked like his soul burned with eagerness for the coming slaughter.

"Nate! Nate!" came the voice from the darkness, "Wake up you lazy farmer."

Nate rolled over. At first he thought his eyes were still firmly shut, then realised he was indeed awake. "It's still night," he complained bitterly. He could just about make out Harlam's dark form leaning over him.

"Never mind that," Harlam replied. "We're leaving. Get the others up. We are going to sort out Drachar himself and no mistake."

Nate's stomach knotted at the mention of the enemy's name and he realised then just what their journey really meant. They were marching into the unknown to face an enemy that nearly destroyed them barely a few weeks ago, and that was when they had the protection of CarCamel. He hoped that someone in command knew what they were doing. He prayed for it in fact.

Chapter 4

Dark Thoughts

Ariome cursed; her legs were stiff with cold and she could no longer feel her fingers. Even with spells of warming, the cold penetrated to her bones. She had been forced to land earlier and was frustrated by the delay. When she had dismounted, she had let the creature go in search of food and rest in whatever manner it required. It had been gone for most of the day and returned only shortly before nightfall. Its breath had reeked of rotting flesh and briefly she wondered what it ate before deciding it was better not knowing. Hurriedly she mounted.

Freezing cold, she now regretted the manner of her transportation. That it was some form of dragon was evident, although it was clearly not a real dragon; she had witnessed a real one at the battle of CarCamel and this creature was much smaller and its hide sleek and leathery rather than scaled. It was a powerful creature, nonetheless, and it could probably carry a full-grown man into battle. She then realised its true purpose. The dwarves had helped defeat Drachar, riding dristal. In his wisdom he had somehow conjured up this creature to give his army steeds on which to ride, steeds that flew.

All at once she shouted into the night, angry and frustrated by the cold, long journey. She tried to make the creature fly lower, but it ignored her. Its snout pointed stubbornly north and she realised then that she had no control over it which made her blood boil. But it was a beast and there was nothing she could do. Uncomfortable as she was, she tried to calm herself, muttering all the while under her breath.

Much later, from out of the darkness, tall towers materialised and her steed aimed towards these. Morloch, she realised, and an apprehensive shudder coursed through her slim frame as her steed descended. She had never visited the capital before, and the name carried fear with it. She was surprised to see lights about the city and realised her error. People still inhabited it. It was only demons which shunned the light and, of course, krell. But krell were merely pawns in this game, not real creatures with feelings.

With barely a bump, the creature alighted on a rooftop. She saw several figures awaiting her arrival and a tall figure approached. A soldier, possibly an officer by his bearing, held out his hand to help her dismount. His robes were dark and made him difficult to see; dawn was still several hours away.

Ariome noted with satisfaction that his eyes blazed with anger when she rejected his hand as she slipped off the creature's back. His anger was replaced by a smile as her legs gave way beneath her. She fell to the stone floor and fury welled up inside her as the officer turned on his heel and walked away. A few paces on, he turned and waited for her, obviously expecting her to follow.

The blood flowed back into her legs, causing her considerable pain for a few moments. Angrily she bit her lip and tried to stand. Awkwardly she followed the escort. Two more soldiers fell in behind them and, without a word, the small group descended a flight of stairs. Ariome fixed her eyes on the back of her escort and concentrated on the dark form, hating it and wishing the confident man would trip.

Suddenly she bumped into him as he abruptly stopped to open a door, concealed by the darkness. In the confined space he stood to one side, holding the door open, waiting for Ariome to enter. She looked into the darkness but could see little. Not wanting to betray her fear, she haughtily passed the officer and entered. A faint light caught her attention and, gratefully, she went towards it. The door shut ominously behind her.

She found another door slightly ajar and opened it. Before her was a temple in the front of which was a large statue of a man. The effigy caught her attention and she realised she was looking at the likeness of Drachar. The statue's eyes held her spellbound and, for the moment, all she wanted to do was withdraw from its presence. She felt unworthy under the powerful gaze.

Her attention was suddenly diverted towards another figure within the room. A soldier stood before the statue, wearing ceremonial dress. His tunic was a bright red and his trousers were grey with a blue stripe down the side. The silver cross hilt on his sword and buttons reflected the firelight. He was a young man and very handsome Ariome noticed.

As her eyes became used to the light, Ariome detected others within the room. She suddenly wondered if the escort had brought her to the wrong place, or whether the officer was playing a trick on her. She was unsure what to do and decided it would be better to wait and watch.

At the farthest end of the room, she recognised a Priest of Ryoch and the familiar sight relieved her. The priest turned to face the soldier who stood motionless, as though unable or unwilling to move.

She glanced at the others around the room. Figures, armed with long spears and dressed in dark hooded robes, stood rigidly to attention. Each wore an ornate dagger that caught her eye. The scabbards alone must have been worth a fortune.

Ariome realised then that the priest was holding a similar dagger in both hands and he was offering this to the soldier. A ceremony, Ariome realised. The soldier moved, taking the dagger, in turn holding it reverently in two hands, in homage to the statue.

"Drachar, hear my words," the soldier said. His voice was strong and clear and made Ariome jump. "I wish to serve you. Lord, I pledge my allegiance. I will obey your every command. Accept *me* into your service, great Lord."

"And how far are you prepared to go in the service of your lord?" the priest said. By comparison to the soldier, his voice was weak and the words came out with a hiss.

The soldier seemed confused. Obviously the ceremony was unrehearsed. "I am loyal," he said finally after a few moments pause while he thought. "I am already a haft commander and I will be a Tharn within the year. I offer all that to Drachar if he will allow me to join the ranks of the elite." The soldier looked towards the hooded figures that remained motionless, oblivious to the scene before them.

Ariome licked her dry lips. She found herself trembling and tried to will her legs to be still. Something about the scene frightened her; perhaps it was the dark look on the statue's face? Whatever it was, there was a strong aura about the room, something akin to the fear that had accompanied her during the night's journey.

She realised that the priest had not replied. She frowned, sensing the soldier's bewilderment. What was he expected to offer to gain entry into the ranks of the elite? She wondered herself. He seemed eager enough, strong and intelligent. What more was required?

Then it was said. The soldier, obviously eager not to be rejected, blurted out before them. "I offer Drachar my life! I would willingly die for Drachar."

The priest smiled eagerly and nodded. The soldier looked back upon the priest, uncomprehending.

"So be it!" the priest declared.

The soldier waited, uncertainly. The priest became impatient, "You have made the offer. Prove yourself to Drachar."

The soldier suddenly looked around at the other figures as though they would come to his aid. Ariome saw his face briefly. He was so young, she realised. His eyes were filled with fear.

"Your life — give it to Drachar," the priest snapped impatiently.

His arms shaking, the young man took the dagger from its scabbard and placed it to his chest, gripping the shaft with both hands. His eyes locked on the statue as though seeking a reprieve.

"Drachar commands it!" the priest ordered.

Ariome was holding her breath. There was a noise, which she didn't comprehend. Then the soldier crumpled to the floor. A crimson stain spread from beneath the body. The noise she realised was the grating of the blade against the boy's ribs.

The shock of the scene was numbing. She fought for breath, which suddenly came in large gulps. Her eyes fastened upon the figure on the floor, her pulse racing. One of the hooded figures approached the priest and handed him a dark robe. The priest took it and stepped towards the body.

For a moment Ariome thought that the priest was going to cover it. Instead he unfolded the cloak reverently and placed it seemingly on the air above the corpse. To Ariome's shock, the cloak held in place as the priest released it. In mounting horror she saw the cloak take form and then realisation dawned as ethereal hands adjusted the robe, placing the hood over an invisible head. Ariome thought she saw ghostly eyes before the hood covered what should have been a face.

The priest unbuckled the belt and sword from the corpse and withdrew the dagger from the wound. He wiped the blade on the soldier's tunic and placed it in its sheath. He threaded this onto the belt and handed it to the figure, bowing in homage.

"You have earned the right to wear the dagger of the knights of Drachar," he said. Unseen hands took the belt and fastened it about its waist. The figure turned towards the other dead knights who started towards the newcomer. They met as though rejoining with a long lost friend, clapping each other on the back.

Soon all had departed save the priest who looked towards Ariome. She wanted to hide, but her ambitious half recognised that she belonged here. She had witnessed power used before, but nothing could compare with what she had seen that night. To make a man willingly take his own life, and then to resurrect his *soul*. With mounting confidence she stepped forward to meet her destiny.

Chapter 5

KinKassack

The march was long and weary. Nate and the others felt like pack animals. They had to carry too much equipment and looked with envy on the mounted troops. However, the cavalry, in turn, looked on the infantry with similar envy, riding for long stretches was uncomfortable and they longed to stretch their legs.

Another halt was called and the ranks came to a stop. Grateful for the brief respite, many threw themselves on the ground. Heavy packs overbalanced them and they lay at awkward angles, too exhausted to move.

"How much farther?" Nate gasped.

Sarin was too tired to answer the older man. His eyes were closed and he was greedily drinking in the cold air as though it was his last.

Harlam refused to sit. He knew that would be a mistake when they were forced to resume the march. "A long way yet," he replied. His eyes were fixed on the distance. The land was still gentle with only slight undulations, and yet he could not see the horizon. The grey dismal clouds blended with the equally grey land so that he could not tell which was which. He half-fancied that he could see mountains, but realised that they were merely clouds.

Looking along the line of troops, he saw that it was starting to move again. A wagon had lost a wheel and was being pushed out of the way for repair. Troops passing the wagon were being burdened with its contents and they groaned under the extra weight.

Nate followed Harlam's gaze. Aloud, he thanked the Kalanth that they were too far away to be burdened themselves. Sweat dripped down his face and stung his eyes, and the cold wind dried it, making him shiver. He looked uncomfortable, hot from the march and yet at the same time cold from their brief respite.

With a weary groan he tried to get up, but his pack made the task difficult. Finally he stumbled to his feet and cast Harlam an angry look for not helping. He helped Sarin, who groaned twice as loud as Nate had, to rise.

"Are we expected to fight once this hellish march is over?" Sarin asked in disbelief.

Nate watched Harlam nod. "You will get used to it."

Sarin looked unconvinced.

The shaking of Nate's legs only served to convince him that they would never reach the battle. He though about dropping out of the line and decided that it was not too bad an idea. At least then he might have a chance.

Harlester and Fiad rode along the length of the long column, encouraging the struggling troops, calling to those they knew by name. The march was gruelling, but there was no alternative. Pantril had been a disappointment and Tharn Orrin's men had found little food. The weather had ruined the few crops that had survived the invading krell. It was unlikely that they would find more food farther north. Now they were relying on carrying sufficient provisions to last them through the campaign. So far the terrain was relatively easy going and yet already two wagons had broken axles.

Fiad shook his head. He had initially thought wars were won and lost on the battlefield. Suddenly he realised this one could be lost before they even got there.

Nate and the others lay on the ground in disordered ranks. The army had finally stopped for the night. Many were too tired to even bother taking off their packs and these men had simply lain down, using their bulky burdens as supports.

Harlam was walking amongst his own haft, encouraging them to remove the packs and start a fire, knowing that a good hot meal would invigorate them. The difficulty was in convincing them. Sarin was already asleep and looked as though no amount of bullying would rouse him. Harlam decided to leave him.

Darkness descended and, all about the camp, weary soldiers lit fires and tried to nurse aching limbs back to some semblance of normality. Sarin finally awoke to find the others huddled around roaring flames, their cloaks pulled tightly about them. Wearily he arose and went to join them, taking his blanket with him. Harlam noted how pale he looked.

"It's too cold to sleep," Sarin complained bitterly as he seated himself as close to the fire as he could.

Nate smiled. "You seemed to be sleeping well enough to me!"

Sarin scowled back.

"Come, eat. You will feel better," Harlam said, offering a charred stick with some meat on it. Sarin ate hungrily, looking miserable all the while although some colour returned to his cheeks.

The night air was suddenly filled with screams and shouts off in the distance. The group jumped fearfully. "Grab your weapons!" Harlam ordered.

All across the army similar orders were given. Bone weary soldiers looked to their weapons, unsure of what was going on. Confusion reigned in the darkness. Then, all at once, the screams abruptly ceased. Men stood with weapons drawn, facing the direction from which they thought the sounds had come.

Fiad and the other commanders on duty were also alerted to the cries, and all at once the command tent was a hive of activity. Fiad paced the interior, taking his frustration out on a young haft commander whilst Harlester and Thorlar looked at the map, stretched out across a collapsible table. At the back of the tent Gant, a Thracian wizard, was trying to cast a spell over hot coals.

"Send out a patrol. I need to know what is happening," Fiad ordered.

The haft commander looked somewhat confused. "Sire, there's a patrol out already."

"Then send another," Fiad ordered. "Make it a haft and you lead it. Sweep the camp's perimeter and report back when you know what's going on."

The haft commander saluted and hurriedly left.

Harlester went over to stand by Gant to see what he had achieved. The old man was staring deeply into a brazier filed with hot coals. The orange glow from the fire upon his face highlighted his deep wrinkles. "There's a spell of concealment about us and I can't see anything beyond the camp's perimeter."

Fiad suddenly felt helpless. "I need to know what's going on. Fetch Astalus," he commanded, turning to a sentry by the entrance.

Gant traced a rune before sprinkling herbs on the coals. Immediately a sweet aroma filled the room. The dark scene within the flames shimmered briefly, then returned to darkness. Once more Gant sprinkled herbs on the fire and, this time, something formed within the darkness and the trio strained to see what it was.

Gant leaned closer, trying to decipher the difficult image. Fiad and Harlester looked on, not quite sure what was occurring. By the table Thorlar continued to inspect the map. It was dark within the tent and the two lamps cast only a feeble light.

For what seemed ages Gant stared into the coals. The heat warmed his face pleasantly, but dried his eyes so that he was forced to blink often. Just as he was about to give up, the image seemed to coalesce into a single form. Both Fiad and Harlester saw the change and they too moved closer.

The shape was small at first, and then it grew larger as if coming towards them. Gant was immediately on the defence. The image was not what he was expecting. Abruptly his hand was tracing a rune of protection and he hastily spoke words of power. All at once a long skeletal arm took shape within the image. The very horror of it stunned the onlookers. Swiftly they threw themselves away from the brazier. Gant's voice rose in panic as he completed his spell.

Immediately the two magics collided and exploded with a tremendous force. Fragments of hot coal and dust exploded from within the heat of the fire, erupting outwards into the tent, throwing everyone backwards. Gant bore the brunt of the blast, but, since he was the focus for the counter spell, most of it was diverted away from him.

Gant, Fiad and Harlester tumbled to the ground. Each was burned, although not seriously. Thorlar and the soldiers by the tent's entrance were the first to recover and they rushed to the aid of their stricken comrades. The noise of the blast caused panic outside the tent, and confusion spread through the army like ripples on a pond.

Within the tent Fiad raised himself on one arm and started to cough up the dust that was still settling around them. A Thracian soldier helped him to his feet and then stood staring at the blackened prince. Fiad looked around and saw that both Gant and Harlester were also recovering.

"What the Kalanth was that?" Fiad asked.

Gant frowned. "Someone within the enemy camp must have felt my spell and sent a counter one," he coughed harshly and his face reddened. When he recovered he looked at Fiad; his face was also blackened, which in other circumstances would have been funny. No one laughed. It had been too close a call for comfort.

"My counter spell was barely in time," Gant conceded. "I don't know what would have happened otherwise. There might be some good that will come from this — whoever was at the other end of this spell would also have been affected by the blast. Let's hope they were less fortunate than we were."

Fiad glanced at the brazier. The two lanterns had been extinguished and soldiers were relighting these. In the renewed light the prince realised how fortunate they were. The brazier was twisted badly, but none of the shards had broken off. Its shape had channelled a large part of the blast upwards so now there was a gaping hole in the tent roof. Fiad could see the clouds above, dark and brooding in the night sky.

"It seems we will have to wait for news of the patrol after all," he announced grimly.

"We could send out yet another patrol," Thorlar suggested.

Fiad shook his head. "We've already committed a large force; any more and we will merely add to the confusion. Send word to the officers to stand down the troops but to double the perimeter guard. We will wait until morning to find out more."

The night passed slowly. Gradually reports that all was silent filtered into the command centre. Fiad waited but received no news from the haft that he had sent out to investigate the camp's perimeter. Astalus came to the tent, but could offer no more of an explanation than Gant. He studied a brazier of hot coals, having assured Fiad that he had protected it with spells, but nothing showed.

Looking over his shoulder, Gant frowned. It seemed as though Astalus committed little effort to the spells of seeing. Astalus left, claiming fatigue, and since there was nothing else to do, Gant also retired. After a while Fiad also turned in for the remainder of the night, but slept poorly.

In the early hours, cooks started to prepare a hot breakfast. Their noise carried across the camp upon the still air and the smell revived flagging spirits.

At first light Fiad ordered two more haft to investigate the night's events. Both the original patrol and the haft sent to find them were missing.

The news, when it came, was grim. About half a mile from the camp, the dawn patrol came across the signs of a battle. The original patrol had been ambushed. The following haft had pursued a force of enemy krell only to be ambushed by an even larger force. From the tracks it looked as if several hundred krell had been involved.

Fiad was furious. He arranged for one thousand cavalry to be readied immediately; with the order that the remainder of the army continue on its original route as soon as soon as possible.

With Fiad in the lead, the cavalry left. The army watched it go with a mixture of fear and anger. As soon as possible, they too were ordered to move out. A detail was left behind with the unenviable task of burying the dead. These men watched the others leave with a mixture of feelings. On the one hand, they would not have to suffer the slow progress of the army, but on the other, they were being left alone in the wild.

It was mid-day when Fiad realised that the enemy patrol he was following was heading towards KinKassack. They pushed the horses harder to catch up before the enemy reached the forest. To his frustration KinKassack appeared all too soon and it became clear that the enemy had already escaped.

Fiad gave orders to a messenger to find the rest of the army and to bring it to their current position. The rider rode off, glad to leave the forest behind.

Fiad was frustrated by the turn of events and he simply stared at the forbidding wall of trees. However, even he knew better than to set off in pursuit. The trees were close ranked and darkness gathered beneath their great boughs in murky pools of night. Many of his men glanced fearfully at the forest whose reputation for evil preceded it.

In the late evening a dust cloud marked the arrival of the army's main body. As the sun sank men started to file past Fiad, all eyes turned fearfully towards the trees.

Fiad gave orders for the commanders to meet and for the army to prepare a camp for the night. As the commanders gathered, Catriona voiced their concerns. "We are mad to continue our advance. The enemy know we are here."

Fiad shook his head, "The enemy was a small force only and they were lucky to escape. If it was not for the trees, we would have caught them."

"How many do you think there were?" Harlester asked.

"We didn't catch sight of them," Fiad admitted. "They had too good a start. From their tracks I would say that there were no more than three or four hundred, perhaps a remnant of the army that fought at CarCamel."

"And a necromancer as well," Gant interrupted. The mention of sorcery caused Fiad to look about for Astalus, but the mage was nowhere to be seen. He issued orders for the wizard to be found.

Catriona grimaced. "We need to be more cautious. I still believe the enemy are stronger than we think."

Fiad looked bleakly on the dark line of trees which stretched as far as the eye could see in either direction. "We need to find a way through," he declared bitterly, indicating the trees.

At that moment Astalus appeared, carrying his book beneath his arm. His hood was pulled up over his head, which was not unusual, for it was bitterly cold.

Fiad was more annoyed than usual and his anger was directed at Astalus. "You must find us a way through," he commanded forcefully. "In the meantime I will send scouts out to either flank, but, if we cannot find a path, then we are relying on you."

Astalus merely nodded.

"And what about tonight? The enemy might attack again," Catriona said. She did not like Fiad's mood and was not sure why he directed his anger at Astalus.

"Tonight," Fiad replied, "we will be better prepared. I have given orders for beacons to be lit at points around the army. There will be no patrols after dark and I want the guard doubled."

Catriona nodded, although she looked far from convinced. The others, too, glanced nervously towards the forest. It had a reputation for evil and they seemed to feel its presence as though it were alive. As the commanders left, more than one felt they were being watched.

Some time later, after most of the preparations for the night's camp were completed, those assigned to rest went wearily to their beds while those on guard stared into the night, keeping a firm grip on their weapons. The night passed uneventfully and, at first light, Fiad sent riders off along the tree line to look for paths through the trees.

Once more Fiad and the other commanders joined Astalus and Gant at the edge of the forest. A detachment stood within the edge of the trees in case of attack. These men glanced nervously back at their leaders as though urging them to hurry their business.

Gant was clearly perplexed and his frustration showed. "Prince Fiad, I have tried setting light to the trees but to no avail. Nothing in this forest seems capable of burning. Either the wood is damp or it is beyond mortal means to damage it. Look," he said indicating a particularly large tree, "I used a spell to ignite that one, hoping the flames would spread to the rest. Nothing! Not even a scorch mark. And that was my most powerful spell. Something protects this forest, something sinister, by the feel of it."

"What is your opinion, Astalus?" Fiad asked.

"Gant has tried magic and failed. I do not think that our power will help us to pass through."

"That's not what you told us earlier," Fiad fumed.

"Do not fear, a way will be found," Astalus answered cryptically.

"We will have to wait for the outriders," Fiad conceded. He was frustrated by the wizards and felt let down by their lack of help. "There must be paths through the wood. Otherwise how did the krell raiders get through?" Turning to Astalus he tried once more. "Both of you remain here and try again. There *has to be* something you can do."

Later that day, just as the sun was starting to set, the riders returned. The news was bad and there had been no signs of a passageway in either direction.

Fiad was beside himself with rage. He was convinced that he had the means to destroy the enemy and yet everything seemed set against them. In the growing darkness he ordered the troops to gather as much tinder as they could and build bonfires within the forest perimeter. As night came they set light to these and returned to the camp to await the morning. The fires lasted most of the night and, when at last the sun arose, Fiad, accompanied by an escort, went into the forest to see the effect for himself. The earth was scorched black in several places and yet there was very little damage to the trees.

"Send out riders once more," he commanded bitterly. "Find me a way through this accursed forest."

Once more riders set off in either direction, and this time scarcely an hour had passed before the riders sent off west returned excitedly. "Sire," said one. "There is a broad passage barely two miles away. We even went part way into the forest. It seems to extend to its very heart. How it was missed yesterday we cannot say."

Fiad was relieved, but was also angry that the path had been overlooked. "Recall the other riders. Get them to follow as quickly as they can. I want the army ready to move immediately."

Few had slept that night and they were ready to move quicker than hoped for. The Bhutan cavalry led with the infantry sandwiched between them and with the West Meath cavalry bringing up the rear. The long line of men was soon marching towards the path reported by the riders.

All too soon they came to the clearing. It was wide enough to accommodate four or five men marching abreast and this only served to fuel Fiad's frustration that it had not been found earlier. He considered summoning the riders of the day before to question them about their lack of observation, but decided against it. Spurring his mount on, he passed beneath the large leafy arch and the army followed behind.

It took half the morning for all the men to pass through the arch into the darkness beyond. Once they had gone, a silence settled over the area, almost as if the army had never been. It was an unnatural silence, the silence preceding a storm.

Chapter 6

Voyage into the Dark

Their greatest fear now was that of ambush. Either side of the path was overhung with thick vegetation, making it difficult to see more than a few yards beyond. The men's fear was palpable.

"I've never seen such tall trees before," Nate declared in awe. Sarin was likewise staring up at the thick canopy with a look that suggested he expected a large spider to drop on him at any moment.

"Watch the trees either side of the path," Harlam cautioned. He was nervous of so many dark places. The air was too still and there was unnatural stillness. Besides the noise of the army's passage, nothing else could be heard. There were no birds singing and even the rustling of branches seemed muffled as though they dared to offend the quiet.

Suddenly a deep sonorous groaning broke the silence. It was louder by far than the army's progress and, all along the line, the troops halted in fear.

"What's that?" Sarin asked, his eyes wide. The others did not reply. No one knew what was causing the terrible din.

Somewhere ahead, Fiad and Harlester urged the men on, although neither of them understood the source of the noise or what it might pertain. Both knew it was important to keep the men moving.

Slowly the line responded, and Nate and the others marched onwards, bug eyed and staring into the dark depths of the ancient forest as though expecting an attack at any moment.

All around the line, the groaning continued.

"It is the wind in the trees," Nate declared. The explanation was plausible, although there was no motion of the thick trunks to indicate that this was the case.

The farther they travelled into the forest, the darker it became and the louder the groaning seemed. After a while longer the forest floor became carpeted in twigs and branches, and occasionally a fallen tree blocked the path. As a result the going became more difficult and stops became more frequent.

Fiad and the commanders rode behind the Bhutan cavalry and even Thorlar was riding a mountain pony. Dwarves seldom rode but, on this occasion, he had made an exception. As if to deliberately frustrate Thorlar, the column ground to yet another halt. "We must press on," he said anxiously, more to himself than anyone else.

Fiad overheard the remark, thinking it was addressed at him. "We can only go so fast," the prince declared, glancing at Catriona. She seemed pale; the forest was clearly unsettling her. "There are trees blocking the path and these have to be cleared to allow the wagons free passage."

Thorlar had jumped nervously when Fiad spoke. He had not realised the prince was so close, having been preoccupied with his own fears. "We must be out of this accursed forest before nightfall," he stated bluntly. "There is evil about. I can sense it."

Dwarves were more used to dark, confined spaces than men and so for them to show fear was a bad omen. Fiad shook his head, sensing that the army was coming apart on him.

"Night will make little difference," Fiad replied. "It's already so dark we can hardly see. Light torches; that will help morale." The command was passed back and all along the line torches were issued and lit.

"It has probably been ages since anyone has set eyes on this forest," Fiad stated in awe.

Thorlar looked around fearfully, not comforted by Fiad's interest in the forest. Even though his people were used to dark places, this experience was totally alien to the dwarf and he nervously tugged at his beard. The caves of his home were dark, but there at least there was solid rock all about you. This was terrifying. There could be thousands of enemy concealed all about them and they would never know. The shadows that had initially leapt back when the torch had been lit now mysteriously seemed to draw in once more.

Abruptly the column started to move and the clink of weapons sounded from ahead. However, they had only gone a short way before they stopped once again. With mounting frustration, Fiad decided to ride ahead to find out what was happening. Troops parted to let him through.

A Bhutan haft commander met the prince at the head of the column. Fiad recognised the officer, Galamere, he remembered. He was a good man, reliable and with many years of experience. He saluted the prince. "There's a deep chasm ahead, sire. It was probably an old river at one time, but it's dry now and has been for several years by the looks of it."

The prince cursed inwardly. Together the two men went to the chasm to inspect it. Galamere's troops had lit several torches and, in the gloom, Fiad could see the problem. The banks were quite steep. It would be difficult for the infantry and cavalry to cross and impossible for the wagons. There was no option; they would have to build a bridge.

"It's not wide," Fiad said. "Cut down some trees and bridge the gap."

"We've already started to do that, Your Highness," Galamere answered. "However, the wood is proving difficult and blunts even the sharpest axe. It will take a while."

Fiad growled darkly. "Do the best you can," he urged. "Use as many men as you require." He turned his mount to rejoin the other commanders. His frustrations grew as he made his way back through the densely packed troops who were crowding together out of fear. The darkness around them seemed impenetrable now, and even the torches did not illuminate very far into the thick forest. A feeling of expectancy was growing around the army. Fiad could sense it.

All at once a hoarse shout sounded some distance away and a ripple of fear spread through the ranks. The creaking of the trees seemed to grow louder and the ominous groaning grew in pitch. Fiad pushed his way through the troops and arrived at the command centre.

Harlester and Astalus were in conversation. Fiad, as usual, checked that Astalus was carrying his book and, with relief, he saw it tucked under the wizard's arm. He realised then that for the first time in many days Astalus' hood was thrown back, revealing his youthful face, etched with lines of worry. He appeared to be concentrating hard and beads of sweat dotted his forehead. Fiad frowned; it was warm in the forest, but not enough to make a man perspire. He hoped that it was not a sign of fever. The last thing he needed was for a plague to strike down the army.

"What was the shout about?" Fiad asked.

"One of the men claims that he saw something in the wood to our left," Harlester answered. Thorlar joined the group. His axe was in his hands and the light of battle was in his eyes. Fiad realised with mounting panic that they were too bunched.

"Spread the troops out," he commanded urgently to the others. He waved his arm emphatically, "Get the rear troops to fall back! We need room."

Astalus seemed to be having difficulty breathing when suddenly his eyes widened. By his side Gant looked alarmed.

"Something comes," he said.

Many voices were suddenly raised in loud shouts, and the press of bodies surged towards the prince as the fear that had threatened to grip the army suddenly erupted.

"Light, we need light!" Fiad declared.

Gant drew a rune in the air and shouted words into the darkness. A blinding light erupted around the prince and the surrounding troops. All along the line the other wizards performed similar spells and suddenly the darkness was thrown back. With the light the troops became less fearful and some order returned, although they were far better targets now than they had been earlier. Shouts sounded and with it came cries of terror.

"Get me news of what's happening," Fiad demanded. A runner turned away, heading down the column towards the source of the noise.

The sounds of fighting continued and then, almost as abruptly as it started, it faded.

Messengers trickled in to report. Something had attacked the army, but whatever it was had gone as quickly as it had arrived. It turned out that there had been three separate incidents. Whatever had attacked was large and fearsome; twenty-six men were dead and many more wounded.

Later Fiad discovered the men had nearly been ripped in two. Surprisingly, no one could describe clearly the creatures that had attacked.

"It was as if the darkness had suddenly become alive," one of the soldiers reported. "A large figure burst through the tree line and charged straight at us, hurling bodies into the trees. Some archers managed to loose arrows, but they appeared to sail harmlessly through it.

"Just as I thought I was next, a light erupted. One of the wizards must have cast a spell and when I looked, the creature was gone. There were no signs of its passage and no one saw it go. It just vanished!"

Others had similar tales. The attack had been sudden and well timed. The troop's morale was already at low ebb, and now many glanced fearfully back, wondering whether the way they had come offered greater safety. The news Fiad did not share with the other commanders was that several hest at the rear of the column had simply disappeared. He assumed that they had run off, back along the way they had come, but deep down was not sure.

At that point King Palastor rode forward, threading his way through the press of bodies. He carried in his hand a kara-stone, shining whitely in the contrasting gloom.

Behind Fiad, Astalus shielded his eyes from the bright stone and turned away. No one noticed his unusual behaviour.

"Prince Fiad," Palastor stated urgently. "Kara-stones are helping in the defence. They seem able to cast back the darkness."

"How many do you have?" Fiad asked.

"Every fifth Alvalan carries one," the albino replied.

"Then please be so good as to distribute these men along the column," Fiad commanded.

Harlan rode off and, within a short while, some of his people threaded their way through the assembled men. Between the Alvalah and the wizards, a clean white light illuminated the troops.

For as long as they could, the wizards and Alvalah kept up the light, although it was weary work. Whether the light helped or not nobody knew, but no more attacks occurred.

Just then, the bridge was finally completed. They started forward when suddenly a wolf was heard in the distance. Many other wolves took up the fearful howling until a dreadful hubbub seemed to surround the army.

"Werewolves!" Sarin declared.

"Nonsense," Harlam answered. "It's just wolves." He was uncertain himself, but did not want the others to panic. He gripped the hilt of his sword tightly, keeping his eyes on the wood. Nate cast him a worried look, but remained silent, for which Harlam was grateful. His haft had been some distance from the earlier attacks by the unknown beasts, and they did not know as yet what had happened. They had heard screams from some way back, and news had filtered forward that the army had been cut in two and half at least destroyed. Harlam was sensible enough to know that was not true for there had been too few shouts, but he wished he knew what was occurring.

Now the howling, combined with the ominous groaning from the trees, threatened to shatter the little resolve that remained. For most of the day the army marched through the dread forest and, all the while, the wolves followed. Just when the men could take no more, the horrendous wailing came to an abrupt stop. To their amazement silence reigned and even the creaking of the trees ceased. The men strained their ears, trying to catch the faintest noise, but all was deathly still.

At this time the wizard's light and that of the Alvalah failed. Many of these men were too fatigued to continue and had to be carried either on horseback or on stretchers by weary troops. Fortunately, the forest seemed to have become lighter and less fearful. The air, too, seemed fresher and many now realised how oppressive the air had been earlier on.

Thorlar muttered to Fiad, "I feel uneasy going on, especially knowing that this forest lies behind us. What happens if we have to retreat? We will effectively be cut off, for I will not pass through this accursed place again."

"We will be victorious," Fiad assured the dwarf. "With the dragons' aid we cannot fail. When we've destroyed Trosgarth, we will not need to come back this way and will either go over the mountains or through Aldrace."

"We could ask the dragons to destroy KinKassack," Catriona said. Fiad had almost forgotten her presence and he credited her brave, indeed, to pass through that dreadful place.

"Even these trees will not withstand dragon fire," she continued with some certainty.

Thorlar grinned, though it was almost maniacal. "I would willingly witness that," he answered.

The trees thinned noticeably and they became lighter shades and straighter, much less gnarled than in the darker parts of the forest. The morale of the troops rose perceptibly, although all dreaded the thought of ever returning. The difference soon became extreme; where the forest had been dark and dreadful, this was bright and cheerful. Even the exhausted wizards and Alvalans seemed to brighten and find new strength.

At this point King Palastor came forward. The albino was shaking visibly. "Never again will I endure that forest," he declared.

Fiad was pleased to see him. "Your men and their kara-stones were a great help. You have my thanks."

Palastor forced a smile and tried to still his shaking nerves. He looked about at the forest as though realising the change. A sense of wonder came over him. "This is more like my home in KinAnar."

Catriona looked on the forest with awe; the transition to beauty was abrupt. The wood they now found themselves in was golden, and a faint, delicate mist hugged the ground giving it a fairy appearance.

"Surely this is a holy place," Thorlar said. Fiad could not dispute it and, for the first time in many weeks, he felt as though a weight had lifted from his shoulders.

He glanced across at Astalus who rode with his hood up once more. He looked asleep and his shoulders sagged as though he suffered beneath the beautiful trees. Fiad considered asking him if anything was wrong but then remembered that most of the wizards were tired from their recent exertions.

Where there had been few signs of life in the evil forest, here life was abundant. All around them birds sang and squirrels scampered from branch to branch, leaving them swaying in their wake.

Occasionally, they came across a dark and twisted tree. These stood out like a cancer, reminding them of the dreadful forest behind. Palastor looked at these dark shapes, shaking his head sadly. "Eventually all this beauty will fade if we cannot stop the ill from spreading, and then the whole forest will become evil."

They made good progress and, shortly an excited ripple passed through the ranks. The lead troops had emerged from the trees where they found themselves standing on the edge of the golden forest overlooking a vast plain. On their left, tall mountains dominated the skyline.

When the dwarves emerged from the trees they shook their heads and pulled their beards upon seeing the site of their ancestral home. Their desire to visit Thandor was strong, and many petitioned Thorlar to forsake the army and lead them there. The dwarf chieftain was in a quandary, and it was with some relief that Fiad commanded they make camp for the night; at least his decision could wait until morning.

Fiad fixed his gaze on the northern horizon. They still had a long march, but the enemy was nearer now. He gave thanks to the Kalanth for their deliverance through KinKassack. Finally he would have his chance to destroy Trosgarth and he intended to take it.

The army continued to pour from the forest and men were directed to either flank. The setting sun left a fiery red glow beneath the clouds. To the troops it looked as though the very flames of hell had ruptured, consuming all within its path.

Later that night Fiad was woken by a messenger requesting his presence. Sleepily he rose, following his guide to another tent close by. Inside, a single lamp illuminated the interior and Catriona crouched over a recumbent figure, a look of worry on her face. Fiad came to her side and realised that it was Astalus on the bed. The mage was asleep, although his brow was covered with beads of sweat. Behind them Gant entered and the old wizard came alongside the other two.

"He's ill," Catriona declared, her voice betraying her fear.

Gant leant over to examine the younger man, checking his pulse and looking into his eyes. The older man shook his head uncertainly. "I do not know what ails him," he declared at length, sitting back on his haunches. Just then he noticed the book that Astalus usually carried. Gant picked this up; a dark frown creased his brow.

"What is it?" Fiad asked, sensing the other man's confusion.

"Is this the book that Astalus returned with from the Eldric City?" the old man asked uncertainly.

Catriona and Fiad looked at it. "Yes," Fiad answered.

Gant's frown deepened. "It cannot be."

"Why?" Catriona asked.

"It is a gardening book," Gant declared.

"You are mistaken," Fiad said, snatching away the book as though he could read the Eldric writing.

"Have you not seen it before?" Catriona questioned.

"No!" Gant replied. "Astalus kept it to himself, refusing to let anyone else see it."

Fiad looked stunned. "Are you certain?"

Gant took back the book and leafed through its pages. "This is an Eldric gardening book," he confirmed, handing it back.

"Perhaps he has hidden the other book." Fiad looked at Catriona in despair. If they couldn't summon dragons, then they were in real trouble.

"That's the book he's been walking around with every time I've seen him," Catriona replied. Her face was pale; she, too, clearly recognised the severity of their predicament.

Gant was tracing a rune over Astalus' forehead. His look of concern deepened as he summoned words of power. He bent over the unconscious man and examined his eyes.

"He's possessed!" he hissed, recoiling as though burnt.

Both Catriona and Fiad pulled back. "How can that be?" Fiad asked.

Gant shook his head. He was tracing runes of protection about the group. "I do not know, but I can only assume that somehow the forest is rendering him unconscious. Perhaps the demon has partially retreated in the presence of a greater power; something that once lived here. A Kalanth, perhaps."

"An Old One?" Catriona asked.

Gant nodded. "We must carry him back into the forest a short way. That might drive the demon farther away so that Astalus can reawaken. The Alvalah might also be able to help. Their kara-stones are very powerful."

Catriona arose and left the tent. Gant heard her issuing orders presumably to a soldier outside. Fiad remained where he was, unmoving. His face was pale and he looked ill.

Shortly two sentries entered followed by an Alvalan. Together the sentries lifted the unconscious man and carried him back under the trees. As they went Astalus murmured in his sleep and started to twist and turn as though trying to break free. Gant judged the moment when the unconscious mage seemed to be most distressed and then ordered the men to set him down.

The Alvalan that accompanied them was a young man that Catriona had not seen before. Gant explained their fears and the albino's eyes widened.

"What can I do?" he asked. He was a brave man. If Catriona had been given the option, she would have been miles away by now.

"If there's a demon possessing him, then it should be weakened by the forest's presence. I also hope that your kara-stone contains power that might further weaken the demon's hold."

The Alvalan nodded, although he looked far from confident. He withdrew his kara-stone from his pouch and waited while Gant chanted spells of protection. Gant would have preferred a fire to focus his spells, but did not want to delay. Once the spell was complete, he warned Catriona and Fiad to leave but both refused.

The Alvalan approached the body, placing the kara-stone on his brow. He, too, chanted and immediately a white fire issued from the stone. The fire passed through the Alvalan's hand and he cried out and nearly let go of the stone with shock, but nonetheless managed to continue the chant. The fire burned brighter and Astalus writhed. Then, all at once, a guttural scream tore from his lips and his eyes sprang open.

"Leave me alone!" he commanded in a deep voice, full of menace. Spittle ran down his chin. The eyes became wider; the pupils were cat-like slits. Gant realised he was looking into a demon's eyes.

"Go!" Gant commanded, tracing a rune. Astalus screamed, arching his back. "The demon's trying to kill him. Hold his arms and legs," Gant commanded of the sentries. The two men looked terrified but rushed to comply. Beneath their grip Astalus bucked, trying to break free. Abruptly darkness engulfed the kara stone's flame and the Alvalan screamed that his hand was burning.

"Hold on!" Gant cried out. "Don't let go." He chanted words of power, drawing runes in the cold night air. The light from the kara-stone broke free of the orb and spun around in a frenzy. Gant screamed a spell, binding it.

It spun in tighter circles, gradually fading until it eventually winked out of existence, leaving darkness. Apart from Gant's laboured breathing, a silence remained and the onlookers simply continued to stare at the spot where the light had been.

"How's your hand?" Catriona asked of the albino. The Alvalan examined it and found that it was unblemished and not burned as he had imagined.

"We should have waited for dawn," Gant said, reproaching himself for his mistake.

"Is Astalus all right?" Catriona asked, moving to the wizard's side.

Gant felt for a pulse. He traced a rune over his head and smiled in satisfaction as he sat back. "He sleeps."

Catriona sighed with relief. "Let's take him back to camp and see how he is in the morning." She half expected an argument from Fiad and was relieved when he remained silent.

In the morning Astalus awoke. He sat up and found Catriona sitting by his side, asleep. Gently he shook her arm. She stiffened and awoke.

"How are you?" she asked, rubbing her eyes.

Astalus smiled. "OK, I think."

Catriona smiled back and at that moment Fiad entered. "Is he well?"

Catriona nodded. Fiad sat down next to the mage. "Have you asked him anything yet?"

"No."

Astalus frowned. "What's happened? Where am I?"

"How much do you remember?" Fiad asked.

"Namthrall is my last memory, sitting in the library, reading."

Fiad brought him up to date, starting with their departure from CarCamel. He concluded the tale, telling the stunned wizard of his possession.

"What happened to Tallin and his command in Namthrall?" Astalus asked. His voice already betrayed his fear that the news was bad.

"Tallin's command was destroyed. You returned with Tallin although he was badly injured. He was left in CarCamel where he should make a complete recovery, but that will take time."

"And we have passed through KinKassack?" Astalus asked uncertainly as though he did not believe that part of the tale.

"Yes," Fiad answered. He paused before continuing. "While you were possessed, you said that you could summon dragons. Was that true?"

"I found a book that mentioned the dragon world. It contained a spell to summon a dragon. I could use my powers to try to jog my memory."

Fiad was excited. "Do it," he commanded.

Astalus nodded. He looked weary and clearly wanted to rest.

Fiad and Catriona left, giving Astalus time to himself. "He needs rest," Catriona admonished Fiad once they were out of hearing range.

Fiad shook his head. "The army will wait here for one day. Tomorrow we will continue."

"And what if Astalus cannot remember the spell?"

Fiad span around. "We have no choice. The men will not go back into the forest so we cannot return that way. We are vulnerable here with the forest at our back. We have no choice but to go on."

"We do not have the strength to defeat Trosgarth, not if Astalus cannot summon dragons," Catriona pleaded.

"We *do* have the strength," Fiad continued with certainty. "Now, you must excuse me. I have to speak with Thorlar before his dwarves decide to leave us, which *cannot* be allowed to happen."

Catriona watched him go. For a moment she considered returning to Astalus to tell him of her fears, but she decided against it. With a heavy heart, she returned to her own tent.

That night was very cold and few managed to sleep. By morning the army was ready to leave and the long line of wagons awaited the command.

Astalus reported to Fiad; he looked tired. "I cannot remember the spell," he said, looking dejected.

Fiad nodded as though he expected as much.

"What now?" Astalus asked.

"We will continue. Perhaps tomorrow you will remember it."

Astalus shook his head. "I used every spell I know. If I cannot remember it now then I never will."

"Nonetheless we will continue," Fiad insisted.

Astalus looked shocked. He considered arguing but the look on Fiad's face convinced him that was pointless. With a heavy heart, he left the tent.

As the army set off, an air of uncertainty descended over the marching troops. The commanders, too, were perplexed. When they had been told that Astalus could not summon a dragon, an uproar had followed. No one was happy with the prospect of continuing without their aid, but they were also afraid of returning the way they had come. The only good news was that Thorlar had persuaded the dwarves not to leave, but many of his kin looked towards the mountains with longing in their eyes.

For three days they marched. On the third day snow fell, carpeting the land and muffling the sounds of the marching troops. On that evening, as they made camp, a rumour spread that they were one day's march from the old battlefield of DrummondCal. To the west the mountains seemed closer; they dominated the skyline, their snow capped peaks tall and majestic.

On the morning of the fourth day, it remained thickly clouded so that not even the faintest chink of light could penetrate. As the army awoke, men looked at one another in bewilderment. Never before had anyone seen the morning so dark.

Jorrant looked up. So low were the clouds that he felt he could almost reach up and touch them. To make matters worse, his scar ached which was a usual forewarning of impending battle. His thoughts went suddenly to the Allunds he had met earlier. He could not remember their names and, for some reason, that seemed important.

Too much had happened in the last few days. KinKassack. He tried to dispel all thoughts of the forest; it was a dark and terrible memory. This was nearly as bad as the forest; he could barely see a hand in front of his face. And the cold. He doubted that he would be able to hold his sword, his fingers were so numb.

He remembered again the battle with the krell long ago and, absently, he fingered the scar, reflecting on the strength of the krell that had so very nearly ended his life.

What if...? he thought. *What if they were defeated?* He doubted that he could face KinKassack again.

He jumped. In the distance a drum thumped and, as he listened, the beat continued and each sound carried clearly over the distance. The beat seemed to match pace with his heart, and he looked around seeing familiar faces looking to him for guidance. He looked down at his numb fingers.

Boom. Boom, continued the drum.

Thud. Thud, replied his heart.

Suddenly he knew fear. A fear carried on the cold wind of his own doubts. This was no game. It never had been. Before, home had always been close, but now it was so very distant. This was for real; there would be no mercy. Death lay before them and fear behind them.

Jorrant swallowed dryly as their own trumpets sounded in challenge; loud and clear in the quiet of the still morning air they brayed. Jorrant thought about his wife and children and a tear coursed down his cheek.

Chapter 7

A Meeting of Souls

"They've gone," Kaplyn announced. He knew without any doubt that whatever had threatened had departed. "They've gone," he repeated looking hopefully towards Vastra for confirmation. The wizard returned his look but there was doubt reflected in his eyes.

Lomar lay by Vastra's side as if asleep, his face ashen and his breathing barely perceptible.

"Quickly! We must revive him," Lars spoke. His voice was hoarse. The big man shook the albino by the shoulder, calling his name gently at first and then more urgently.

"His spirit is too far away," Vastra said.

Kaplyn knew he had to act swiftly. "I'll find him. I'll release my soul on the astral plane." Lying down he closed his eyes and relaxed as best he could in the circumstances. Immediately sleep beckoned, but he fought against it. The link to releasing his spirit lay with Shastlan and his guardian's presence was there; it always was.

Opening his eyes, he looked around, finding that he was looking down on his own body. For an instant he was startled by his own appearance; he looked gaunt and terribly tired. Vastra sat by the rim of the hollow, looking into the distance. Kaplyn followed his gaze and felt a terrible fear. Whatever had been stalking them was in that direction and that was where he would find Lomar's shaol.

Willing himself onwards, the ground passed beneath him, gradually increasing in speed. He could feel an evil presence ahead. The riders were moving away, clearly having lost interest in the small group. They had been summoned elsewhere for there was greater game waiting for them now.

Abruptly Shastlan's ghostly spectre joined Kaplyn.

"Lomar is that way," he said, pointing.

Kaplyn corrected his course and, after only a short while, was rewarded by the sight of a shimmering light. Slowing, he came alongside the spectre of his friend. Lomar's spirit was standing as though in a trance. His eyes were closed and he swayed as though to an unheard tune. Kaplyn tried to lay a hand on the albino's shoulder, but failed. It was merely a gesture for, even though they were spirits, the action made Kaplyn feel somehow closer.

"Lomar," he called. The albino flinched. Again Kaplyn called his name. The frequency of the albino's swaying changed, gradually slowing. Lomar looked towards Kaplyn as though seeing him through dead eyes.

"Where?" he said, as his eyes focused on Kaplyn. He saw Shastlan by Kaplyn's side and gradually comprehension dawned.

"We must return," Shastlan prompted. "You are both a long way from your bodies and for both of you, the link is tenuous."

Shastlan spoke truthfully; the ground around Kaplyn was starting to change, becoming foggy and less distinct. He realised that his body craved sleep; already his brain was slipping deeper into dreams and, once that happened, the link with his body might fade completely and then he would die.

"Come!" he said to Lomar. "You have saved us. Whatever stalked us has gone."

Shastlan guided them back. Even to Kaplyn the final few yards seemed vague as though he was dreaming. Then, abruptly, he knew no more.

With a start, Kaplyn awoke. Lars was shaking him and calling his name. Relief flooded across the big man's face as Kaplyn's eyes flickered open. Kaplyn smiled back at his friend.

"Riders are coming," Vastra announced flatly. Kaplyn sat up. To his relief Lomar was awake, although he looked bewildered as though awakening from a nightmare. The thump of hooves on the hard ground echoed about the hollow, confusing his senses. Together they peered over the hollow's rim. Kaplyn knew it was dawn, and yet it was terribly dark and clouds almost completely blocked out the light.

In front of them the silhouette of riders formed against the dismal sky. Kaplyn blinked, trying to recognise the shapes. His sword was part way drawn before the riders drew rein and a voice challenged them.

"Who is there?"

Kaplyn and the others arose. "Kaplyn," he answered, "from Allund."

"Are there others with you?" came the puzzled reply.

"There are five of us," Kaplyn replied.

"One of you approach and be recognised."

Kaplyn walked forward. He relaxed visibly when he recognised the livery of Bhutan. "You are Fiad's troops."

The men held spears at the ready but they, too, seemed relieved that Kaplyn did not appear to be a threat.

"What are you doing so far from CarCamel?" Kaplyn asked. The men remained silent although they looked uncertainly at each other.

"The army, is it here?" Kaplyn asked in disbelief. When he did not receive a reply, he continued with some urgency. "You must take us there at once."

The lead rider nodded. "You will have to ride double; we don't have spare mounts."

Swiftly Kaplyn and the others mounted. The riders, thirty in total, turned and rode back the way they had come. Kaplyn fought his fatigue, but found himself nodding nonetheless. All too soon his rider drew rein and Kaplyn awoke with a start, feeling weak and groggy. He was momentarily at a loss as to where he was, and it took a few moments for his memory to return.

It was still dark and, all around the riders, men milled about, taking down tents and packing stores ready for the days march. Kaplyn looked behind and was relieved to see Lars and the others. He recognised the men of the army in their immediate vicinity by their livery; silver cloaks and tall helms marked them as from West Meath. As they went by, men curiously looked up and their pale complexions and gaunt appearance shocked Kaplyn. Evidently they had suffered during their march.

Then ahead he saw Fiad and some of the other commanders. He recognised the albino King, Palastor, and he glanced towards Lomar to see how he reacted with the other man's presence. Lomar did not seem to mind and he smiled at his countryman who smiled back. Kaplyn frowned when he realised that there was a dwarf amongst them.

At that moment the riders stopped and dismounted. Their passengers also dismounted and were escorted towards the group of commanders. With a mixture of feelings, Kaplyn caught sight of Catriona and his heart leapt, but then he was dismayed she was so far from the sanctuary of CarCamel. Astalus stood by her side and he felt gladdened to see familiar faces once more.

Fiad's attention was riveted on Kaplyn. Once recognition dawned, a look of disbelief crossed his face as though he had not expected to see him again. Kaplyn felt like a beggar by comparison to the other man. Fiad wore a scarlet cloak, trimmed with fur and embroidered around the edge with gold thread. His boots had recently been cleaned and, even in the dull light, they gleamed.

"We have important news," Kaplyn announced once within earshot. "It's imperative you hear us before the army moves out."

Catriona turned at the sound of his voice. She smiled when she realised who it was. "Kaplyn. Are you well?"

Kaplyn nodded.

Fiad saw her look and frowned. "What's your news?"

"It is for the commanders' ears only," Kaplyn stated.

Fiad turned, ordering his men away. Once they were sufficiently distant, Kaplyn continued to speak, albeit softly. "The dwarves of Thandor cannot aid us."

Fiad's expression remained neutral, much to Kaplyn's surprise. He had assumed that the army wouldn't have ventured this far without the expectation of aid from the dwarves. Stories of the last war and the part played by the dwarves and their dristal, was legendary.

"What has happened?" Thorlar asked. His voice carried more than a hint of menace.

"Where are you from?" Kaplyn asked.

"I am from Tubarl in the Southern Kingdoms," the dwarf growled angrily. "And who are you to talk ill of my people?"

"This is Kaplyn," Catriona interrupted. "He is acknowledged as the Allund monarch by their army."

Thorlar seemed mollified by Kaplyn's title although a dangerous light shone in his eyes.

Kaplyn briefly explained their journey to Thandor and the dwarves' plight. Thorlar looked crestfallen but, to give him credit, he refrained from interrupting. When Kaplyn told him that he had killed the possessed dwarven King and destroyed Talwyn, Thorlar looked more hopeful.

"Thaneck thought that your people would recover now that Talwyn is destroyed. He set off with another dwarf, Thackery, to find the lord of the dristal."

If Thorlar had doubted Kaplyn's tale up until that moment, he doubted him no more; only a dwarf would consider scaling the heights of BanKennet to find the lord of the dristal. "You have my thanks," the dwarf said. His eyes shone with unshed tears. "After this war is over, I will lead my brothers to Thandor to see what aid we can offer."

The other commanders were perplexed by Kaplyn's news. "There is more," he said. He waited for their attention before continuing. "Upon the plain of Chalynth, we encountered a dreadful evil. Dead riders stalked us last night. We were saved by Lomar and this morning the riders rode off. I fear they might still be close."

The others looked sceptical and so Kaplyn turned to Astalus. "I have spoken truthfully before," he reminded the wizard. "The riders were dead, of that I am certain. What is more, they hunted us by our shaol. If that was so, then they must be aware of the army."

"Nothing you have said has any bearing on our plan," Fiad said after a moment's pause. "We have a strong army which has endured much.

Through bravery and determination, we stand here ready to defeat the enemy."

Kaplyn couldn't believe his ears. "The only reason that Trosgarth was defeated in the Krell Wars was because of the Eldric and their sorcery. We do not have a tenth of their power, and, if my guess is correct, then Trosgarth has a new and very deadly weapon in these dead riders. In my opinion, it is also no coincidence that Thandor has been reduced to the state that it is now."

"Be that as it may," Fiad replied icily, "by might of arms we will defeat Trosgarth, once and for all." His voice shook with anger.

"You will be able to help," Catriona interrupted. "I believed, like you do, that to march was folly, but with your aid we can win this war. Summon a dragon and help us!"

Kaplyn shook his head. "I have seen their world. I now know the dragons' intent. They want to find a new people to subjugate and then *destroy*. We *cannot* rely on them; at least not in numbers, for then we would never be rid of them." He could tell by their looks that they were not convinced. "Why do you think that the Eldric never summoned dragons? Surely they had the power to do so."

"We should return to CarCamel before it's too late," Catriona said.

Fiad shook his head. At that moment a drum sounded in the distance, a deep sonorous beat that carried with it a hidden menace. The sound was repeated moments later and a silence descended over the army as men stopped what they were doing to listen.

Astalus called for the materials for a fire to be brought forward. Two men left and returned moments later, carrying branches and sticks between them, which they lay in a pile on the ground. With a wave of his arm the wizard ignited the wood and started to chant a spell of seeing. Almost immediately, a look of dismay came over his face. The others huddled around to see what had alarmed him.

There was little reason for the enemy to hide their full power now; a dark tide of men and krell spilled across the plain of Chalynth. Accompanying them came an utter darkness. Their hope that Trosgarth's might had been crushed at CarCamel was instantly banished for the size of the army was formidable. Endless ranks of dark, swarthy krell led the army while behind them came ranks of soldiers from Trosgarth judging by their livery.

"How far away are they?" Fiad asked.

"Six miles, perhaps less," Astalus concluded. He was bone weary from his recent possession and his strength was already drained. He chanted and moved the image to the east.

A long dark column snaked across the land and, when they looked closer, they saw men of Aldrace marching behind priests of Ryoch.

Fiad was horrified. "What about to the south?"

Astalus started to chant. The scene within the fire slowly changed and they recognised KinKassack. The front ranks of trees seemed to be crawling with dark shapes. Astalus spoke further words of power and they saw krell emerging from the tree line.

"And west," Kaplyn asked. Again the scene changed, but the foothills of the mountains remained bare. "So that is why there was a krell army in Thandor," he exclaimed. Fortunately that army had been defeated and in that direction at least there was an escape route, but a perilous one.

Fiad was stunned by the magnitude of the enemy forces arrayed before them. For the first time he realised the enormity of his decision to bring the army away from the sanctuary of CarCamel. "The army to the north is our greatest threat. They are the closest, unless I am mistaken," he said. Even to his own ears, his voice shook.

Astalus nodded, "The army to the east is at least half a day's march away."

"And it took us three days to reach our present position from KinKassack," Fiad said.

"Could we outrun their army and head west?" Harlester asked hopefully.

Fiad shook his head, "We could if we left the wagons and unburdened the troops, but we would be without essential supplies. The mountains are too harsh to cross without warm clothes and food. Our only hope is in summoning the dragons," Fiad said flatly. His eyes went to Kaplyn, "And you say that hope is false, Kaplyn."

Kaplyn nodded. It was the only thing he was sure of.

Fiad didn't say anything. He didn't have to. He had led the army on a fool's errand. They were trapped.

"Perhaps I could summon one dragon," Kaplyn suggested. "At CarCamel I controlled one, or at least I thought I did."

Vastra stepped forward. "I can summon a demon. If I am successful, it will fight on our side."

"My sorcerers have learnt a great deal since the battle at CarCamel," Astalus stated. "We are not completely defenceless and there are the Alvalah and their kara-stones."

Fiad called the officers together and issued orders for the preparation of their defences. They had, at the most, half the morning to prepare. The sorcerers left to prepare their own defence and soon only a few people remained.

Lastly Fiad turned to Kaplyn and his small group. "Get them armour and weapons befitting their ranks," he instructed of a retainer. "Kaplyn is about my size. Give him my spare armour."

Kaplyn thanked him.

The camp was suddenly a hive of activity. The cold was forgotten as troops prepared defences. Earthen ramparts were dug and, on the side of these, sharp staves were set to slow the enemy advance and channel them into killing zones, covered by archers. All along the army's front, large bonfires were built. It was hoped that the light from these would hinder the krell and serve as a warning if a demon was summoned.

The wizards went about the battlefield, laying spells in ambush. Counter spells were also laid and Astalus and the others spent some time preparing one final spell, so intricate it required all the sorcerers to complete it.

Kaplyn saw Astalus later. He managed a weak smile when he saw Kaplyn in his new armour. It fitted him well. However, instead of a crimson cloak that Fiad wore, Kaplyn wore Allund blue.

Lars, Tumarl and Lomar had also been given armour and weapons. Lars carried his Eldric axe; Lomar had a long bow, a quiver of arrows and his sword that he had brought with him from Gilfillan. Tumarl had a broadsword since he had lost his own in Thandor. His arm was in a sling which would severely hinder him in the coming fight.

Together they went in search of Vastra and found him back at the armoury. He had declined armour, saying that his frame was too slight to bear such a heavy burden. He did, however, take a broadsword, which he tested, swinging the blade in an arc, feeling its weight and balance. They watched Vastra practising before he realised that he was being observed. When he did, he seemed embarrassed. Nevertheless, he motioned to Kaplyn that he would speak with him, and the two men walked together a short distance from the others.

"It may come in handy," Vastra said, hefting the heavy sword. His wrists looked too frail for such a weapon. He lowered his eyes to the ground as he walked. "I would have things changed if I could," he stated softly. "I'm truly sorry for what has happened."

Kaplyn shrugged, "You were duped as were we. If it hadn't been you, then it would have been somebody else."

Vastra smiled weakly, "I wanted to be the greatest sorcerer ever, and yet I was merely a pawn...."

"I am afraid to die," Vastra continued after a moment's pause.

Kaplyn could say nothing to comfort him, knowing his soul was already forfeit. "Many are afraid to die, and there will be many souls claimed by demons this day."

Vastra grimaced at the reminder of his fate. "We can still win," he stated boldly. "We have courage on our side, and right."

Kaplyn returned the smile. "I hope so. My biggest fear is the enemy opening a gateway to the demon world."

"That, too, is my fear. I have been thinking of nothing else for some time."

"What happened to the other crystal, do you think?"

Vastra looked to the distant horizon and his voice sounded like a portent of doom. "We will know. Soon," was all that he said.

All morning the drum continued. Fiad sent out a mounted patrol to silence it, but they failed to find it. Astalus suggested that the sound was made by sorcery. Its beat sapped the men's morale, making them believe that the enemy was closer than perhaps they were. And then, all at once, a dozen riders raced into the army's line and headed towards the command position. The scouts bore bad news. The enemy was at hand.

The commanders took up their positions at the centre of the defence, on a small rise overlooking the battlefield. In front of them, the infantries of West Meath and Thrace formed the centre. On the right flank were the dwarves and on the left the Alvalah. To the rear, the Allund infantry were held in reserve. The cavalry were placed on the right flank with instructions to break the first wave and then to return.

All at once, the waiting was over as a seething mass of krell appeared. With a deafening howl, the enemy leapt forwards. The allied cavalry swept around the army's flank to intercept them. The initial clash was fearful and men watched in horror as horses and riders went down. However, the cavalry attack was well timed and, although some men fell, many broke through, their lances taking a deadly toll.

Immediately confusion reigned amongst the enemy ranks as krell looked to their broken flank. In fear some turned to flee, making the cavalry's task easier. Once the enemy line was truly broken, the cavalry disengaged, returning to the safety of their own lines. Nobody cheered. This was but an initial clash, nothing more than a skirmish.

Almost immediately, a second enemy wave materialised from the gloom, halting the retreating krell who swiftly swelled their ranks. From the allied line, a hail of arrows brought them to a halt and the front rank seemed to melt into the ground as arrows punched through armour. The archers' task seemed futile; when one rank fell, another replaced it, continuing to march towards the waiting shield wall. The defenders gripped their spears more tightly, looking to companions for support.

Suddenly the krell were at the defence's perimeter. The staves held, forcing them to bunch together. Wizards summoned their power; fire swept the enemy ranks burning the lead krell who screamed in agony as their own side carried them forward in the charge. It seemed that a wall of flame was advancing on the allied lines. More magical traps were triggered, and bright fires consumed large portions of the assaulting forces, illuminating the massed enemy ranks still advancing behind.

For a moment the enemy's charge stalled and, in one place, actually went in the wrong direction, impaling hundreds of krell on stakes. The defenders continued to loose volley after volley into the teeming mass. The krell were close enough to see their faces, contorted into hideous snarls, clearly eager to be set loose upon their foe. Axes and spears were lobbed from the enemy ranks, and the first defending troops went down as missiles struck home.

Suddenly, all along the enemy line, trumpets sounded. For a moment the attack faltered as snarling krell looked with hatred at their enemy. Fangs glistened white and spears and swords were raised high. Then the line retreated to be swallowed by the darkness.

Other enemy troops must have positioned themselves close to the allied lines, and it was their turn to suffer as arrows rained down. The magical fires that still burned now served to aid the enemy and the allied ranks became an easy target. Archers returned fire, but were blinded by the blazes.

"Douse the fires!" Fiad commanded. The wizards in the group worked feverishly to kill the flames that, only moments before, they had laboured so hard to feed.

As the lights dimmed, Kaplyn and the other commanders saw the initial stages of the conflict. The battle had lasted only moments and yet a mound of dead krell lay before them. Runners passed messages to the commanders who waited fearfully to receive them.

Fiad's relief was evident when he was informed that their losses in the initial stages were light. "Astalus!" he called. "Locate their command centre and see if you can attack it in any way."

Astalus bowed and went away to prepare.

Kaplyn looked at the dying fires to their front. "What next, do you think?" he asked.

Fiad looked at Kaplyn. "My guess is that they will try to use magic of some sort, perhaps even a demon. Our wizards will have to prove their worth."

Kaplyn eased his own weapon from its scabbard. The blade shone brightly. "This at least will sting any demons careless enough to come close."

Fiad looked at the magical blade. "I wish we had a thousand more like it." At the moment their lines held, but thousands more enemies were arriving at every passing moment.

Jorrant looked out into the growing darkness. Silence had settled over the battlefield. Then the awful drumming started afresh, making him want to scream out for it to stop. The first assault had unnerved him. Never before had he seen such reckless disregard for life. What vile power could drive so many krell to their deaths?

Fortunately there had been no losses in his haft. Garrick stood grinning in front of him, for once, the grin was reassuring and Jorrant found himself grinning back.

Abruptly Jorrant realised how heavy the toll had been on their store of weapons, and a few men from other hafts were running forward to recover spears and arrows. They were recklessly endangering their lives and orders were being issued, summoning them back. They had a good supply of weapons and, for once, Jorrant blessed the wagons that only days before he had cursed. Barking commands, he sent a couple of men scurrying back to replenish their stores.

His troops were coping well, they stood in a line with shields interlocked and spears at the ready. Silently he thanked the wizards for the fires. However, he knew they would not risk going forward again to set more traps; that would be too risky.

To his front, wounded krell tried to crawl towards their lines and, to his horror, none of the enemy tried to help them. Jorrant cursed them, cursing the krell, first and foremost, and then their commanders. They could not be allowed to win. His thoughts returned to his wife and children. There had to be a future for them. He loosened his sword in its scabbard and gripped his spear more fiercely.

Astalus looked at the enemy camp through a spell of seeing. With little difficulty he found their command centre by watching messengers hurrying to and fro. The enemy didn't seem to care that they were being observed and, after only a few moments, he realised they were constructing a very complex spell.

Tentatively he sent a spell against their defences, but could find no weak points and could only watch in trepidation as the spell grew in power. A small crystal was placed on a pedestal and five men formed a circle about it.

Their words couldn't be heard through his spell, but he could see their lips moving.

Abruptly a dark rent appeared in the air behind them, slowly widening until a large jagged tear appeared.

Astalus' heart hammered in his chest. He was leaning too close to the fire and was forced to withdraw marginally, feeling the heat from the hot coals subside. This must be the crystal from the Tree of Life that Kaplyn and the others had recovered. Their greatest fear was coming to pass and the enemy was opening a gateway to the demon world.

Gradually the scene within the flames dimmed. He sought to prevent the image from fading but could not. The enemy was aware of his scrying and was constructing spells of concealment.

Abruptly he felt the enemy probe his own defences and hastily drew additional runes of protection. Once satisfied he withdrew from the fire. The others looked at him for news but he could not meet their looks. With fear in his heart he went to inform Fiad.

Fiad was confronted by several problems all at once. A large force of krell was massing in front of the dwarves and clearly an attack was imminent. To complicate matters, in the centre opposite his own command, men from Trosgarth were assembling. Behind these, enemy cavalry were massing, their riders wearing dark cloaks with hoods concealing their faces.

Kaplyn's premonition about death knights came to mind and involuntarily Fiad shuddered. A breathless runner arrived with news that a strong detachment of the Priests of Ryoch were assembling on their left flank. They were clearly about to face a full assault. He needed Astalus and he gave an order to have him found.

Before the runner had left, Astalus appeared. His face was ashen. "Sire, they are creating a gateway to the demon world. We could be facing hundreds of demons at any moment."

Many drums started to beat a monotonous rhythm and their terrible booming made it difficult to think. Fiad's brow knotted in concentration, he tried to stare into the gloom to see what was happening but all he saw was darkness.

"Prince Fiad," Harlester said. "The enemy is moving."

Suddenly a chilling howl went up along their front. News came in that grakyn were supporting the priests of Ryoch. At the same time, a report came in that several, as yet unidentified winged creatures were also attacking. A fearful dread accompanied these creatures, and many of the men were throwing down their weapons in despair.

Fiad was grateful that the Alvalah were holding, their kara-stones inflicting a heavy toll upon the enemy. However, the priests were formidable and, being able to communicate across the battlefield, they swiftly took advantage of any weaknesses.

Another runner arrived and it took him a few moments for his breathing to recover sufficiently to allow him to speak. The news of the right flank was better. The dwarves were holding, but only barely. The krell were numerous and their sheer number could decide the dwarves' fate. The main problem was their centre which was crumbling and, if it gave way, they were lost. Putting on his helm, Fiad pointed to the centre of the line.

"We are losing ground," he said. "I will lead the reserve troops to strengthen the centre. Harlester, you take the cavalry. Sweep around the right flank and support the dwarves."

Without further ado, Fiad rode to the reserves, leaving Kaplyn and his companions alone with Catriona and her personal guard. She looked terribly afraid. It was clear that the enemy was far stronger than Fiad had anticipated.

By Kaplyn's side Vastra looked ashen. "I can feel the gate being opened to hell," he announced.

"Can you help to delay them?" Kaplyn asked urgently.

Vastra nodded. "The hour of my redemption is at hand."

"Lomar, can you use your kara-stone to help Vastra?" Kaplyn asked.

Lomar nodded and withdrew his kara-stone, laying it on the ground.

"Lars, Tumarl," Kaplyn said. "Stay here. Protect Vastra and Lomar."

"Where are you going?" Lars asked.

"It's time to summon a dragon. We have no choice."

Kaplyn walked away, knowing that, if he lost control over the dragon, he would have to fight it, and he did not want his friends there if that happened. He glanced back towards Catriona and her guard. The Queen turned to watch him go and, raising a hand, bid him farewell.

Chapter 8

Battle is Joined

As he walked away, Kaplyn glanced over his shoulder at the figures silhouetted against a bleak sky. A dreadful feeling came over him that he might not see them again. He tried to concentrate, thinking back to the last time he had summoned a dragon, suddenly afraid he might fail. Judging he was sufficiently far away, he stopped and raised his sword, as he did once before on the roof during the battle of CarCamel. Then, burning runes had danced along the blade but now it remained dull.

Placing a hand on his chest beneath his armour he felt his scar, trying to focus his thoughts through that. Behind him the din of battle escalated causing him to look nervously about in case the enemy had already breached their defence. The line stood solid; war cries and the clash of steel filled the air.

His fear of failure prompted memories of family and friends. In his mind's eye, he saw his father, mother and brothers, knowing that he had failed them as well. He could see their faces as clearly as though they stood before him.

No! his mind screamed. Abruptly the burden of his guilt overwhelmed him, and his sword arm sank under the weight of the brightly burning blade. "No, I cannot," he moaned. The ghosts started to fade as if his inability was their release.

"No!" Kaplyn cried, trying to stop them and then he was alone. All about him the air grew steadily colder and then his blade burned brighter as a blue flame leapt along its length. As if in response, the watch fires turned blue and he knew that somewhere a demon was being summoned. Kaplyn's heart nearly ceased. If he couldn't summon a dragon, they were doomed.

Fiad rode at the head of the Allund reserves. Already he had encountered soldiers fleeing the front line; many were simply too fearful to stop. The prince tried to halt them.

635

"Stop!" Fiad cried. He didn't understand why they fled; there was nowhere to go. The army was their salvation and their sanctuary.

One Bhutan soldier, upon seeing his prince, paused in his flight, a look of shame upon his face. "Majesty," he panted, wide-eyed with fear. "The battle is lost. The enemy is too strong. A new evil confronts us."

"Explain yourself," the prince ordered, signalling the troops to halt.

"We cannot stop them! I saw one enemy rider pierced with three arrows, and yet he rode on — not even scratched. I saw another with a pike through his chest; he merely plucked it out as though it was nothing more than a splinter. We cannot kill them, Your Majesty."

Fiad looked up; the line was crumbling before his eyes. With determination, he set his helm. "Stand fast!" he bellowed at the troops, who were backing away whilst others threw down their arms and fled. "Turn and fight!" he screamed.

The soldier, seeing his prince's attention elsewhere, ducked and joined the others running away.

Behind Fiad the Allunders watched him go and an angry muttering started.

"Forward!" Fiad ordered.

At that moment the centre of the defence finally broke and a dark tide of enemy troops spilled through the breach. At their front rode knights dressed in long robes, with hoods concealing their faces. A gust of frigid air blew aside their leader's cloak and Fiad could only stare in horror. He could see the enemy troops following behind as though there was nothing in the saddle.

Jorrant raised his spear and threw it with all his might. The priest warrior simply side-stepped and the missile sailed harmlessly by. Jorrant shouted a curse and looked about for another weapon. Suddenly a great fear rolled across the defending troops and many fell to the ground, covering their heads. At that moment the phalanx of priests hurled spears with deadly accuracy. Jorrant saw Galamere go down and he cried out in anger. His fury was short lived as overhead a dark shape loomed over him, and his fear escalated beyond endurance. Jorrant instinctively flung himself to the ground. A long arrow took Garrick in the throat and he fell backwards, spewing forth his lifeblood.

Jorrant remembered then the krell chieftain who had nearly killed him so many years ago. A fierce rage burned through his body, causing the scar on his face to burn red. His fear fled in the face of his rage. Rising, he picked up a spear and flung it skywards towards the dark shadow of despair. A terrible wail filled the air and a heavy object fell from the sky, crushing men and krell from both sides. Only then did Jorrant see the Priest of Ryoch, standing a few yards from his exposed flank, his spear levelled at his chest and a gleam of anticipation in his eyes.

Vastra drew a rune of summoning in the air and, immediately, the imp appeared, its evil face split in a grimace as its tongue darted over rows of razor sharp teeth.

Vastra spoke words of command and the imp shook its head as though terrified by what was being asked. It mewled pitifully and clawed at the air, flinching backwards in fear. Vastra's voice rose in power, his spell carrying clearly above the battle's din.

Lars gripped his axe and stared at the magician with mounting terror as Vastra's spell reached its climax. He did not understand the words, but Vastra's tone and the imp's reaction suggested that something terrible was about to happen. The big man prayed to his gods to help them, but felt no comfort. This was surely the end, he thought as the uproar of battle escalated to fever pitch.

The cold was intense and his arms felt numb as he gripped his Eldric axe. He glanced at Tumarl. He was holding his sword and watching the advancing enemy as though longing to join the fray. A wild light was in his eyes and, for a moment, Lars thought that he was going to leave them, but he glanced towards the big man and remained where he was.

At that moment the imp vanished and the group stared at the point where it had been in fear. If Vastra failed, then a demon would appear and they would be forced to fight for their lives and their souls.

Kaplyn's thoughts turned to his friends and his earlier fear of failure turned to anger. Strength returned and, with renewed conviction, he lifted the blade to the heavens. Eagerly he sought Shastlan's presence.

Immediately, words formed within his mind, mysteriously reflected in a fiery silver script along the length of his sword. He recognised the writing and, in a rush, he shouted them out to the heavens. All at once the world became unfocused and he realised why; his world was superimposed on another. This was a world so very different from his.

He was looking into a green valley with an azure lake snaking along its length. Mounting giddiness nearly made him fall and he turned his eyes towards the heavens. Against a perfect, blue sky a small shape circled, gliding on thermal currents. The shape spiralled lazily towards him; long gossamer wings caught the frigid air, slowing its descent. A long sinuous neck supported a small head from which beady eyes fastened with intelligent guile on the diminutive figure.

Somehow Kaplyn knew that this was the same dragon he had summoned during the battle of CarCamel. How he knew, he could not be certain. The dragon approached and with it came waves of nauseating fear. Strengthening his resolve the fear passed and then the dragon was standing before him, folding its great wings behind it. In his mind he heard words of greeting, eager, well meant and yet so very unpleasant.

Kaplyn sensed the dragon was deliberately stalling, possibly hoping to trap him between the worlds whilst it summoned more of its kind. Abruptly he felt the magic in the other world aligning itself with him. Astalus had cautioned that, if he remained too long between the worlds, he could become trapped, creating a permanent gateway.

Pointing his sword at the dragon, he commanded it to come forth into his own world. The dragon stared lazily back, blinking slowly, stubbornly remaining where it was. Shastlan was warning Kaplyn and, turning his attention to the sky, he saw movement in the distance.

With deliberate intent, he backed away from the dragon. It was hard work retreating from the other world. "I shall close the gate!" he shouted.

Real fear was reflected in the dragon's eyes. They were selfish creatures he realised; slowly the dragon crawled towards him on its belly.

"Come!" Kaplyn demanded. "Hurry!"

The image of the dragon world changed as he stepped back until abruptly it winked out of existence. A scream of frustration from the dragon world was replaced by the din of battle. The dragon scented the air, looking at Kaplyn with anticipation in its eyes.

The dragon smiled. *Command me,* Kaplyn heard its thoughts echo in his mind.

It was the most heroic thing Nate had ever witnessed as Fiad rode alone towards the breach. The reserves were simply too afraid to continue. Light enshrouded Fiad encapsulating him in glory as though an Eldric Lord of old had stepped upon the land.

Brightly shone his helm and spear. If the gods ever favoured a man, at that moment, it was Fiad. Stillness hung in the air and a silence descended so that even the enemy halted.

The leader of the death knights forced his way to the front. Low he bowed in mock salute and, with a cry of terror that pierced the night, he charged, lowering his spear. Seemingly unafraid, Fiad accepted the challenge, setting his spurs to his mount's flank; in turn lowering his spear. Fiad's aim was true and his spear took his opponent in the chest. The blow should have been fatal, but the spear passed through the death knight as though meeting nothing more than air.

In turn the death knight's spear splintered on Fiad's shield. Bright sparks flew from the metal and Fiad grunted in pain. His war horse kicked out at the enemy's mount, causing it to rear, momentarily distracting the death knight who fought for control. Fiad threw his spear, which passed through his opponent's cloak, tearing it, but inflicting no harm.

Fiad stilled his fear and drew his sword. His mount turned, lashing out at the death knight's mount. The knight drew his sabre and attacked. Fiad parried with his shield and lashed out with his own sword. The death knight caught the blow on his shield and sought to open Fiad's defence, but the young prince was strong and his heart resolute.

Fiad's mount once more lashed out at the death knight's, causing it to rear back, screaming in pain. The turning mount presented the death knight's back to Fiad. With a scream of rage, he plunged his blade through his opponent's heart. A great cry rent the air and the death knight's cloak and helm crumpled to the ground.

A cheer went up from the Allund troops. Fiad had shown them the death knight's *were* vulnerable; iron through the heart *would* kill them. More death knights appeared, filling the breach left by their lord. Their numbers made even the stoutest defender's heart quail. The Allunders hardened their resolve, forming a shield wall with spears held at the ready as a mighty cry went up, and the enemy rode forward, spears held in anticipation of the slaughter to follow.

At that pivotal moment, when all seemed lost, a mighty dragon fell from the sky, spewing forth flame and venom. As one, horses and death knights perished. Screams replaced the earlier cries of impending victory as the dragon and its solitary rider flew along the enemy, engulfing them in flames before rising to disappear amongst the low clouds.

Heartened, the Allund troops rushed to fill the breach and, for the moment, the line held. Fiad rode at the vanguard and glory followed him. He seemed to burn with an intensity that none could withstand and, where he went, krell and men fell before him.

Nate drew back his spear and, with an almighty roar, hurled it at the dark shape only yards ahead. The priest did not see the spear, so swiftly did it fly; he was too intent upon his victim who stood transfixed, waiting for death. The priest did not heed his shaol's warning. When he did, it was too late. He tried to turn, forgetting his victim at the last. The spear caught him squarely in the chest, toppling him backwards, a crimson stain spreading across his ochre robes. Lifeless, he hit the earth with a thud.

The priest's intended victim stirred as if awakening from a dream. He shook his head, turning to face his saviour. Jorrant recognised Nate, although he could not remember his name.

For a moment there was a lull in the battle as Fiad and his reserve forced the priests back. The Allunders knew to keep their distance and hurled spears or loosed arrows into the enemy ranks, killing them by the sheer number of projectiles. The priests gave ground, the confusion too much even for their shaol.

Nate turned to Jorrant and both smiled. Jorrant shook his head, unable to believe his luck. "Thanks," was all he could manage. His eyes fell on Garrick and he closed them in grief.

Then the screams of the dying reminded them that the battle was not yet won. Together they recovered spears from the fallen and set off at a loping run to catch up with their comrades.

Still the priests withdrew with Allund battle cries ringing in their ears. Side by side, men of Allund fought with those of Bhutan and, at their head, rode Fiad and a shining halo of light followed the prince as he slew the enemy.

Harlester's cavalry swept around the enemy's flank, charging clusters of men and krell as they tried to reform. All at once Harlester found himself free of the fighting, overlooking the battle on a small hillock. A large formation of krell were massing in preparation for an assault. The krell were intent upon the dwarves and, as yet, the cavalry was unsighted.

Thrusting his spear in the enemy's direction, Harlester bellowed out orders. All along their line, troop commanders relayed his orders and riders formed into ranks, setting their lances at the ready and loosening their swords in their scabbards.

With a roar, Harlester spurred his mount forward and, with a great cry, his troops followed. Too late the krell heard the thunder of hooves and, even as the riders hit the mass of bodies, some were still uncertain what the trembling meant.

A great cry accompanied the initial clash. Lances ripped through armour killing krell in the hundreds. In close combat, the men of West Meath drew their heavy sabres, setting about their enemy in earnest.

So swift was the assault that many of the krell became disorganised. Some turned to flee, but there was nowhere to go for suddenly before them were the dwarves. Thorlar urged them forward, brandishing his axe. With a great cry he swept his axe high over his head, leaping towards the confused ranks. At that moment, many krell were looking over their shoulders, having heard the cries of their fellows behind. The dwarves attack came at just the right moment.

The krell wavered and then crumbled, many dropping their weapons and fleeing, but unable to escape in the press of bodies.

For the moment at least the army's right flank was saved.

All across the battlefield grakyn harried the allies, striking from height before returning to the safety of the skies. Defending sorcerers cast spells, destroying some, but many more appeared.

The threat from the enemy's dragon/demon hybrid was at the moment the army's greatest danger. The fear that followed these creatures was enough to cause even the stoutest defender's courage to fail. Unlike real dragons, however, these creatures lacked the protection of scales; arrows and spears could penetrate their hides and kill them if the defenders had the courage to face them.

From dragon-back Kaplyn saw this threat. His dragon had also seen these creatures and Kaplyn felt its anger at the abomination that the enemy had created. The great serpent tucked in its wings and went into a dive, sweeping low over the enemy dragon hybrid. A great wall of flame engulfed the lesser creatures, incinerating their wings and tumbling them from the sky.

Time after time, the dragon rose above the enemy in search of fresh prey, and it took delight in killing these counterfeit dragons. Grakyn massed in their defence and tried to counter the threat from the dragon, but it was too powerful. The greatest danger was to Kaplyn as missiles flashed past him or bolts of fire from the grakyn exploded close by.

As they flew, Kaplyn searched the enemy ranks for signs of the demon gate, but his control was tenuous. The dragon's attention was on the dragon-hybrids, hampering his search for the gate. No matter how hard he tried to make it do his bidding, the massive creature stubbornly sought its own prey, ignoring Kaplyn's threats. On the ground, the defence held but fresh enemy forces were arriving at every moment, and Kaplyn knew that armies were also marching from the south and east. They had to finish this fight, and soon.

Vastra peered into Lomar's kara-stone and watched the enemy magi as they strove to open a gateway. He knew that their preparations were nearly complete and he had to act swiftly. The first part of his spell was cast and the imp was gone. Quietly at first, he started to chant as he cast runes of power.

The hairs on the nape of Lars' neck rose and cold shivers ran down his spine. He felt raw power grow in the air around them and he looked about at the others in fear. Everyone was standing stock still, staring at the magician with fear in their eyes. Once again Lars prayed to his gods for he knew enough about demons to be truly afraid.

In the darkest recess of hell, a being stirred. Never before had anyone dared to summon it, and now it felt its name being called across the great void. Its anger escalated and its roar shook the ground as it was forced to awaken. Heavy limbs flexed, cracking the rocks that had grown about it during its long sleep. With a scream of rage, it stood. More rocks splintered sending a hail of shards flying in all directions. It stood within a dark cavern protecting it from the weak light in the demon world and looked about, searching for the person who dared to summon it.

Gradually strength returned and it fought against the summons, casting spells of its own, but the power of the summoning increased until it knew that it could no longer resist. Howling with rage it allowed itself to be drawn through the void, promising that it would make its summoner pay for disturbing its rest. And then it was gone.

Within the enemy camp a group of necromancers and acolytes stood in a circle about a small crystal set on a wooden dais. Their leader, a tall individual with a thin, pockmarked face, was drawing runes upon the air. His long arms looked almost comical as they moved faster and faster to the rhythm of the spell.

A glow surrounded the crystal and, as the moments passed, its brightness grew until it hurt their eyes. Then, a loud click sounded and the rent in the sky suddenly glowed green. For a moment it wavered, but then held. The gateway to the demon world was open.

All at once, a demon materialised to one side of the group. It screamed at the diffuse light that burned its eyes. The lead necromancer paused, realising this demon had not come through the gateway. Knowing that it was not under his control, he frantically waved his arms, casting spells of protection. The acolytes also realised the demon was a threat and, in fear, turned to escape.

An icy wind blew from the rent in the air. The huge demon tried to cross into the void, but a powerful force forbade it. It screamed, lashing out at the fleeing figures, ripping bodies in two. A group of sorcerers defied its advances as they erected spells of protection. The demon briefly fought the spells, but they were too powerful. It turned instead upon the soldiers by the sorcerers' side, tearing them apart with each sweep of its huge limbs. All about the demon, panic spread, rippling outwards towards the front line troops who looked fearfully over their shoulders.

Above, the crystal the gateway held. Cold from a dead world seeped through the opening, threatening the very existence of life in this world. Behind the void, dark figures massed, eager to be freed to kill and maim. The gateway held and, as one, the demons leapt forward, screams of pleasure on their lips. Behind them a darker shadow waited, knowing that the moment of its victory was at hand.

Vastra tapped hidden reserves of power as he summoned more and more magic, channelling it through his body to the demon.

"Fight!" he commanded. His eyes blazed as his powers increased. *He was immortal; the greatest sorcerer ever.*

His demon stepped forward, blocking the gateway. From within the void, a scream of frustration escalated into a cry of hatred. A swift, dark shape shot forth to attack the monster demon. Fast though it was, the strength of the defending demon was superior; it struck, cutting the lesser demon in two. Its maimed corpse fell to the earth, its blood tainting the ground.

The big demon screamed, venting its rage. With each kill, its own power grew and this had to be matched by its summoner, merely to keep it under control.

In the distance Vastra called on yet more power, drawing runes and strengthening his hold on his demon. He could feel its resistance, but as yet he was in control.

Within the gateway the demons recognised the power opposing them and knew they could not pass. Still, in frustration at the nearness of the battle, demon after demon tried to gain the world beyond. While the battle raged around the gate, Vastra fought with all his might, knowing he could not afford to fail.

The battle hung in the balance, requiring only one mistake by either side to change the tide. The gateway to the demon world was effectively blocked whilst, in the sky, Kaplyn and his dragon repeatedly attacked the enemy lines, killing dragon-hybrids, death knights and priests. The ranks of defending troops held and ranks of krell marched to the slaughter. Sorcerers fought against wizards and flashes of light filled the sky.

On a small rise Ariome watched the battle, looking in awe at the dragon and its rider. It rose high and, folding its wings, dove to the ground for yet another kill. Its speed was awesome and arrows and magic seemed to splash harmlessly against its side. She tried to make out the rider, knowing that it was Kaplyn, but the dragon flew too fast to see him clearly. He, too, must be protected against magic, she realised, as yet another bolt of flame engulfed the pair. The dragon emerged unscathed and its breath destroyed several grakyn. She watched in detachment as their bodies fell from the sky.

She was in her element. "How do I destroy a dragon?" she muttered. Ideas flashed through her mind, but none seemed sufficient. She could not afford to be directly involved, for then the dragon would attack her. She witnessed another terrifying assault; behind the dragon a great swathe of burning bodies scarred the battlefield. Already the dragon was rising high into the sky, seeking its next target. At the zenith it stopped, pausing in mid flight before swooping down.

Ariome felt a pain in her leg and, looking down, she saw a zelph. She hated these insects that fed on the blood of others but, before she swatted it, an idea occurred. A broad smile spread across her face. *So simple*. She trapped the fly in her hand and lifted it from her leg. The dragon was already climbing and pausing in its flight. Her smile turned to a laugh. By her side the officers turned to look at her in obvious confusion.

A mixture of emotions swirled around the young Trosgarth commander's mind as he viewed the spectacle before him. How could such a pitiful army hold him at bay? To add to his frustration, a voice was screaming in his mind to do something, or suffer the consequences.

"Enough!" he bellowed and for a moment the voice fell silent. His confidence was high. Agreed, he had committed most of his forces, but he felt supreme. The demon gate was open; he knew there was a problem. At that moment a runner came to report that a mighty demon forbade the gate to those beyond. The enemy must have a necromancer of their own. Shouting commands, he urged his own sorcerers to locate him. The power required to summon such a demon would be enormous and they should be able to find him with ease. Almost immediately, he felt better and a smile touched his lips.

By his side his necromancers worked fearfully, searching the battlefield with spells of seeing. Flashes of magic used by both sides hampered their progress but these swiftly faded allowing them to continue their search.

Whoever was defying them was careful. However, given time, they could find him, but time was one luxury they did not have. When the commander was given an update of their failure, he was furious. Immediately he ordered grakyn and dragon-hybrids into the air. "Search!" he ordered. "Search the perimeter and attack enemy groups to their rear. Find the necromancer and kill him!"

Across the battle lines, dark shapes lifted into an equally dark sky. Lightning flared in the heavens as if the war was not confined to the earth alone, and the bright light illuminated the seething mass of bodies locked in deadly conflict. Thunder crashed drowning even the noise of war, but, when it faded, the dreadful sound of death marching through the ranks continued unabated.

Lars looked up as something out of the corner of his eye caught his attention. He signalled to Tumarl and Lomar, wishing as he did so that they had chosen a less exposed spot. The roar of battle soared above the fading thunder and Lars craned his neck as he searched the heavens.

Abruptly his worst fears were confirmed; a grakyn appeared, hovering in the sky. Magical bolts of flame flashed from its outstretched arms and Lars cried out a warning as he flung himself to one side. A wall of flame engulfed him, singeing his hair and beard, and then the world seemed to tip upside down as an explosion followed, hurling Lars aside.

For terrible moments Lars was unable to rise. Stunned, he half registered that Vastra was unharmed, standing over Lomar's kara-stone as he continued to cast spells. By Vastra's side, Gant appeared, defending Vastra, hurling magical bolts at the grakyn, but more grakyn gathered overhead. One landed and, at that moment, an arrow struck Gant in the chest. The old wizard fell slowly to the ground, clutching the shaft with both hands, a look of disbelief on his face.

Trying to stand, Lars shook his head to clear the ringing in his ears. A grakyn had seen Vastra and was coming up behind him, its sword raised to strike. Vastra, too engrossed in keeping the demon under control, failed to see it. By his side Lomar lay on the ground, either stunned or killed by the blast.

Scrambling to his feet, Lars grabbed his axe already knowing he was too late. Then something arose from the debris between Vastra and the grakyn. The grakyn screamed in agony as Tumarl, with a primeval scream of rage, thrust a knife into its belly. Both fell to the earth with Tumarl entangled beneath the grakyn.

Two more grakyn landed and, splitting up, they attacked both Vastra and Tumarl who was still struggling to push the corpse of the last grakyn off him. Shouting a battle cry, Lars leapt after them, trying to save his friends. Tumarl managed to stagger to his knees, clumsily raising his sword. Lars' cry at least stopped one grakyn which turned to face him whilst the other attacked Tumarl.

Lars swung his axe but the grakyn stepped back and the axe swung harmlessly by, throwing the big man off balance. Throwing himself bodily at the grakyn, Lars butted the creature with his helmet's edge. A loud crack rewarded him as he fell into the creature. It took vital moments to untangle himself and his heart was beating wildly as he clambered to his knees.

A terrible cry sounded from behind him, freezing his blood. He turned in time to witness Tumarl kneeling before the second grakyn, clutching his head in his hands. Blood oozed between his fingers and a terrible look of pain was etched on his face. Lars sensed rather than knew that Vastra was exposed to attack. In desperation he hurled his axe at the grakyn standing over Tumarl, knowing he was leaving himself defenceless.

The weapon tumbled in flight, slamming into the grakyn's back. The creature arched, throwing its arms wide but somehow remained standing, clutching its sword. For an instance it staggered and then, with a terrible slowness as though mocking Lars' failure, it aimed a blow at Vastra's head. Lars cried out, rising to his feet, but it was too late; Vastra was already toppling to the ground. By his side the first grakyn he had stunned arose, its sword in hand and a look of victory in its eye.

A horrifying scream of triumph came from the battlefield as the large demon was released from its thrall. With massive sweeps of its arm, it turned on those around it, careless of whom it killed. It wanted vengeance and cared little for who should pay. Behind it, demons leapt through the portal. Creatures of many shapes and sizes, some on two legs, others on four, leapt as one onto the soil of a New World.

All across the battlefield, fires burned blue, heralding their arrival as they fanned out from the gateway.

Lars watched Vastra crumple to the ground. By his side the grakyn brought up its sword, intending to gut Lars. Frantically, he stepped back, knowing it was too late.

Suddenly Lomar's bow sang and a black-feathered shaft appeared as if by magic in the chest of the grakyn. A frown replaced the creature's earlier smile as it slowly toppled backwards.

Lars ran to Vastra's side, but it was clear he was dead. Vastra's fate had finally caught him up and his soul was forever trapped in the demon world.

Using his bow for support, Lomar staggered over to Lars.

"Tumarl?" he asked.

Together they went over to the ex-farmer. He, too, was dead and Lars felt a great sorrow at his passing. Cries focussed their attention on Gant; he was wounded and it looked mortal. Lomar took up his kara-stone and sat by the old wizard, using the stones to take away the old man's pain.

"The battle, have the demons broken through?" Lomar asked.

Lars could not find any words to reply. Everything was going horribly wrong.

Kaplyn heard the terrible shriek and searched desperately for its source. Finally the dragon responded to his command; turning, he urged it to seek the demon gate. Sensing the demons, the dragon flew eagerly to the gateway. Without pausing, the serpent swooped down to attack, engulfing several demons at once in flame. Those within the gate paused staring hatefully up at the dragon as it arose, waiting to attack.

The dragon's wings snapped against the cold air as it rose high into the sky. Then its movements abruptly felt sluggish and Kaplyn wondered if it was tiring. Below, dark shapes darted from the gate and Kaplyn urged the serpent to attack. Suddenly the lizard twisted in mid air and sent a blast of hot breath along its own flanks, nearly unseating Kaplyn whose heart lurched at the thought of the long drop below. His immediate fear was that he was betrayed and the dragon was trying to unseat him. Then he felt its pain. All along the dragon's body needles of fire shot through the immense creature. It bucked and turned and flew as fast as it could, heading away from the battle as it sought to escape its pain.

No matter what Kaplyn did, it flew in a straight line, heading away from the battle. Already the din of conflict had faded far behind as the ground passed swiftly beneath them. Again the dragon bucked before rising high into the sky. Fearfully, Kaplyn glanced down at the distant ground while the dragon's flight became even more erratic. Then it was gliding and the ground started to rush to greet them.

Ahead, Kaplyn saw the outline of a forest and realised it was KinKassack. With a bone wrenching shock, the dragon landed, throwing Kaplyn from his seat. Instinctively, he rolled, jarring himself badly in his armour before coming to rest.

For a moment he was stunned, but he urged himself to rise. His whole body ached. Before him were the golden trees of the forest and he remembered then Astalus' warning that another army was marching from the forest. They must be between himself and the battle he concluded turning around, but there was no sign of them.

His immediate concern now was for the dragon. The large creature had not stirred since landing and so Kaplyn went back to investigate. It lay unmoving, its eyes closed and its sides moving albeit faintly. Gently he lifted one of its scales, but immediately dropped it, taking a large step backwards. An image flashed through his mind of a writhing mass. Uncertain of what he had seen, he went back. This time he realised they were zelph, but they were far from normal. These were much larger, almost the size of Kaplyn's hand. As he watched, the zelph aged and died before his eyes. More insects were born and these rapidly grew to full size, feeding hungrily. Somehow he guessed that their metabolism had been accelerated, and their size was probably due to the richness of the dragon's blood.

Whatever was happening, the dragon was beyond pain and its fate was sealed. The thought struck him that once the dragon was dead, the zelph would look elsewhere for food and Kaplyn was a very convenient source. He ran, not really thinking where to go, gripping his enchanted sword. The blade glowed only faintly, suggesting that, for the moment at least, he was safe. He considered summoning another dragon, but was afraid that by now there might be too many of them waiting for him to open a gateway. He also felt that each time he called a dragon, it increased the risk of his being stuck between the worlds.

The thought reminded him of the gateway to the demons' world, and he realised that Vastra must have failed. He hoped that he and the others were all right, knowing that the demons were now unchecked.

The tide of war had once more turned and the moment of Fiad's glory was at hand. The Old Ones seemed to favour him and no enemy could stand against him. Advancing at the head of the Allund army, the enemy centre gave way.

On the left flank the fight was still in doubt and the priests of Ryoch had recovered from their earlier losses. However, seeing the centre collapse and not wanting to be caught in a trap, the Priests of Ryoch grudgingly gave ground.

On the right flank, Harlester and the dwarves advanced unchecked. A fierce light shone in Thorlar's eyes as he led the dwarves. Their axes sang and the necks of krell parted like young saplings before them. The only hindrance was the sheer number of krell.

All about Fiad a light shone brightly and, in that moment, many thought he was indeed the King described by the Prophecy. "Fiad!" the men chanted, as they advanced, slaying as they went.

Then the sky darkened and Fiad's light was dimmed. Demons howled into the night, racing to the fight. Men fell, screaming, hearts and souls ripped from their bodies. The cry of "demon" replaced the earlier chant and men stopped, too afraid to go on. Almost as one they started to back away as word spread like wildfire, sending forth ripples of panic that swiftly grew into an avalanche.

The demons advanced, killing in a frenzy and pausing only to taste human flesh. Running, crawling and leaping across the battlefield, they screamed their rage, freezing the blood of their enemies.

Even Fiad's heart quailed and, for a fleeting moment, he, too, considered flight, but he would not. Shouting his battle cry, he urged his mount towards a demon whose cat-like eyes fastened eagerly upon the prince. Rows of sharp teeth flashed in the uncertain gloom as it roared its challenge.

Fiad's horse reared in terror, spilling the prince from his saddle before bolting. Swiftly he clambered to his feet, his sword held before him and his eyes fastened on the approaching demon.

Its movements mesmerised the prince; then it darted toward him and, instinctively, he lashed out with his sword. His blow was ill timed but even still the demon veered away. Momentarily, relief flooded through Fiad as he spun to face the demon, but then pain lanced through his arm. Looking down, thin rivulets of blood appeared as if by magic, running down his wrist. The thought that demons carried disease sprang to mind and he realised he might already be mortally wounded.

His eyes darted quickly back to the demon, the pain in his arm momentarily forgotten. Hissing, the demon crouched defensively, as it awaited the prince's attack, clearly in no rush to end the encounter. Its talons gleamed white, reflecting the light from the many fires. Its eyes narrowed and wrinkles creased its face as it snarled.

Behind the demon, men of Trosgarth advanced, leaving the prince to his fate. Before them the allied lines crumbled as demons pressed the allies back. None could stand, nor was it easy to retreat; too many men were clustered together for that.

The demon leapt and, as it did so, its tail lashed to one side, unexpectedly changing the direction of its attack. Wrong footed, Fiad fell backwards as talons raked his breastplate. He hit the ground and rolled quickly, feeling pain where his breastplate now dug into his ribs. Swiftly he gained his feet, spinning around as he searched for his enemy. Several feet away, the demon sat eyeing the prince balefully. Realisation dawned that it was playing with him, enjoying his fear.

Fiad felt weak. As he feared, he had been poisoned and it was slowly sapping his strength. He lowered the blade slightly trying to conserve the muscles to the last. All hope of escape failed as another demon approached, crouching behind the first as though content to watch.

Turning his attention to the first demon, he saw its tail twitch, a sign he now realised signalled it was about to attack. He twisted to face it, pointing his sword to his left. The demon switched its attack to his right at the last moment. There was no chance for the prince to counter the attack; the demon was too fast. However, the ground to his right was slick with blood and for a brief instant the demon slipped and had to correct its balance. The few moments were all he required. He reversed the blade, bringing it around in a backward stroke.

The blade bit deeply into the demon's flesh and Fiad guided it into the creature's heart. A howl of anguish and pain came from deep within the demon's throat, ending in a bloody gurgle as it died.

That was the last of Fiad's reserve and he could barely move. He fell to his knees and a passing krell thrust its spear at his unprotected back, killing him instantly.

The watching demon screamed, leaping at the krell and breaking its back with one massive blow. The demon raged as it searched for Fiad's soul but it was too late. In disgust, the demon howled before setting off, searching for fresh prey.

And so Fiad died.

On the battlefield darkness closed in, extinguishing his brief light and a cold wind blew. Across the length of the battle, men fled in panic.

Chapter 9

The End of all Things

Astalus, and the few sorcerers with him, watched the flood of retreating soldiers turn to a rout. Now was the time to cast the final spell. Astalus recited the spell that he and the others had prepared and, almost immediately, a blinding flash illuminated the sky. Demons and krell fell to the ground in terror and pain. It was as if the sun had momentarily burst through the clouds.

The troops continued to flee, eager to put as much distance as possible between them and their enemy. His spell would last for a while; then it would fail and the chase would start in earnest. Men amongst the enemy paused, too afraid to press the attack without their allies. Turning, Astalus went to his horse, mounted and waited for his queen to do likewise. Together they fled the field, soon catching up with the first foot soldiers who looked about in terror, clearly expecting the demon horde to fall on them at any moment.

The rapid turn of events had horrified Catriona. In disbelief she had watched Kaplyn's dragon flee the battle. When the demons broke through, she knew the day was lost. But where could they hope to escape to now? Instinctively they were heading towards the mountains but, even if they reached them, the narrow mountain passes would hinder them. By her side, Astalus looked grim. They had gained some time, but how much? Looking about her, Catriona saw the look of resignation on the soldiers' faces. One or two called to the Kalanth for help. Many more glanced back at the light, their eyes reflecting their fear that it should fail.

And so the army retreated and few dared to ask where. They were merely putting distance between themselves and the forces of hell.

In the distance Kaplyn saw the intense flash on the horizon and knew immediately what it meant. Astalus had told him of the final spell should the demons breach their lines.

At that moment a dark cloud arose from the body of the dragon as, in their hundreds, zelph arose, forming a dark mass against the suddenly bright sky. Kaplyn turned in panic and started to run. He knew that the flies were searching for a meal and his immediate concern was that he was it.

His armour weighed him down as he fled. Glancing over his shoulder only part of the cloud followed him. The rest dispersed in other directions, searching for food.

Sweat poured down his face and cramp threatened his legs but he dared not stop. Another backward glance made him gasp; a large swarm was closing the distance. So intent was he on the swarm that he failed to see a large root sticking up in his path. The air was knocked from his lungs as he tumbled to the ground. Winded, he rolled, trying to force himself on.

The swarm was almost upon him and desperately he scrambled away on all fours. Insects landed on him and he brushed them away as others landed. Then he realised they were falling on him rather than landing. They were too long from their last meal and their increased metabolism couldn't support them. They died as they landed, ageing before his eyes. In the distance he saw other clouds similarly dissipating.

Kaplyn's leg hurt; he must have twisted it in his panicked flight. Slowly he arose. Much to his relief the light on the horizon still held. The enemy sorcerers would be trying desperately to break the spell, and he wondered fearfully how long it would take them. His thoughts went to Vastra. What had happened? *Catriona*. Despair washed over him. They were beaten. That was inevitable. He gripped his sword, deciding that he would wait there for the enemy to come to him. Then he would make them pay dearly for his life.

In the silence he felt Shastlan's presence. His shaol, he realised, had been trying to warn him for some while. Quickly he turned around, looking for danger, but the only thing he saw was an endless line of trees. He calmed himself after checking the sky for signs of grakyn and then realised that Shastlan was not warning him, but was trying to guide him. Kaplyn arose and, with weary steps, followed Shastlan's direction, entering KinKassack.

The forest was not what he expected and the beautiful golds and reds reminded him of Lomar's homeland. Small animals were abundant and they frolicked amongst the trees, oblivious to the encroaching evil. The sounds of birds chirruping high in the branches helped to lighten his mood as he walked deeper into the heart of the golden wood. Where Shastlan was leading him, he did not know but walking was preferable to waiting....

The army continued to retreat. Every so often men glanced over their shoulders, looking back into the silver light, praying that it would not fail. Amongst the press of men, Nate and Jorrant trudged together, side by side.

Jorrant still felt that he did not deserve to be there, so close had death seemed. He surveyed the army about him. Nothing would stop them now and he wondered where they were going. *Let the commanders worry about that,* he thought. *After all, that was what they were paid for.*

By his side Nate stumbled. He righted himself and cast Jorrant a weary smile to reassure him that he was all right. The big man smiled back. Both had lost friends and no doubt they would lose more before too long.

Then their worst fear was realised.

Abruptly the light failed.

Fearfully men looked at one another and then a wail of terror escalated along the long line. The cavalry rode to the rear trying to find suitable ground for a quick ambush. Men looked to the cavalry for salvation on the one hand and pity on the other as they quickened their pace. Very soon the wounded started to fall behind and, at points, the line of troops was stretched perilously thin. All unessential items were dropped and a trail of debris littered the army's path.

With a roar of triumph, the demons set off in pursuit, swiftly outdistancing the krell who seemed only too keen to follow behind. Men of Trosgarth formed long lines and followed in their wake, glad to have the demons before them and not behind.

From the demon gate, a great darkness appeared. The men in the vicinity dropped to their knees in homage, and Priests of Ryoch cried out in joy, raising their arms in prayer. Few dared to look within the dark and, those that did, saw a terrible sight that would remain with them for the rest of their lives. Riding upon a scaled demon, Drachar had returned. His pennant blew in the breeze and souls, held in thrall, followed, carrying banners and proclaiming his arrival with brazen trumpets.

The Prophecy had finally come to pass. Drachar strode amongst the living with vengeance in his heart.

Even between the densely packed trees, Kaplyn saw the light fail and with it went his last hope. At first he could not believe it, thinking his eyes deceived him. Screaming into the night, he fell to his knees. *Why?* he sobbed between breaths. Why bring them this far only to fail? Gripping the earth in his hands, he gazed into the distance as though willing the light to return. But it did not.

Gradually calm returned. Only then did he become aware of a strange sensation. one akin to the feeling he had in Kaldor when he had found a kara-stone. He realised there must be another nearby. With growing urgency he arose, looking around. Squirrels scattered overhead and branches swayed wildly with their passing as Kaplyn searched. Beneath a large tree he knew he had to dig and, using his dagger, he hacked at the soft ground. His progress was too slow so he took off one of his greaves to scoop out the soft earth.

Very shortly he struck something solid and with, mounting urgency, scraped away the soil, revealing a large kara-stone. He thought back to the moment when he had touched Lomar's kara-stone. He had a fleeting memory that he could not explain; for a moment he had seen the world through the eyes of a Kalanth. He did not know how it had happened but suspected that a kara- stone was what was left of a Kalanth.

Reverently he laid his hands on the stone and, immediately, a strange feeling swept over him. His vision swam and abruptly he was looking down upon the world as though from a great height. The scene was ancient. He recognised a figure walking across the land, stooping occasionally to tend a plant or a tree. It was a Kalanth, one of the Old Ones.

Where were they now? Surely gods could not be destroyed. The Kalanth tended the world, nurturing growing things like a gardener, banishing disease so that health shone from the fauna like a beacon. Occasionally Kaplyn saw others, both male and female and, together, they created lakes, rivers and mountains. Forests, unlike any Kaplyn had ever seen before, grew to maturity in a blink of the eye and their beauty enthralled him.

"What is the good of this?" his mind wailed. This does not help. He clutched the crystal fiercely as though he could wring the truth from it. As he watched, he became aware that the gods were placing a small part of their power into everything that they were creating and, as aeons passed, more and more power was lost to them. Gradually they were fading, becoming insubstantial before Kaplyn's very eyes.

The gods could not die, he kept thinking. Then he realised, they were stretched so thinly over the centuries that eventually only a memory remained, perhaps in the howl of the wind or the stirring of the oceans. A thought occurred to him. He had opened a gateway to the dragon world; why not then open a gateway to the past?

He concentrated hard, seeking his link to Shastlan and his vision swam as he looked, simultaneously, on his own world and one of long ago. Birds, long since dead, sang merrily in the golden dawn of time. The air seemed fresher and the sun gently warming.

He called to the Old One, but his voice was lost in the vast emptiness of time and nothing happened. He could not give up! His friends were depending upon him; he had to succeed. Gripping the jewel more tightly he concentrated harder. Why did the Old One not hear? Perhaps only a small essence of the god existed in that time. To succeed he had to open gateways to many different pasts, all at one time. If that was possible?

The crystal scar on his chest burnt fiercely as he opened more and more gateways, relying on the crystal's power to hold these while he opened others. Concentrating hard on the kara-stone, he tried to imagine the Kalanth in the images in each time. Soon he stood transfixed like a spider in an intricate web of his own weaving. He felt confused as to who or what he was, and his mind wandered down each strand in time, turning and twisting until he felt as though he no longer belonged in any world. His thoughts were scattered and he could no longer focus his concentration on any one thing.

Faintly he heard his name being called as though across a great distance. Dizziness swept through him and, abruptly, he felt as though he was falling. Again he heard his name. It sounded closer and he tried to concentrate, realising as he did so that it was not his own name that was being called but that of someone else. At least now his mind was focused and, with a jolt, he found he was standing in his own world once more.

A giant, nearly as tall as the trees, looked down at him. Light radiated from him and, for a long while, the two simply stared at each other and then the Old One smiled. His smile was like warm sunshine and Kaplyn felt himself smiling back. This was the Kalanth he had seen in his visions, but seeing him in his own world left him in awe.

The Kalanth looked around and a frown creased his brow. Slowly he dipped his hand into the soil. Kaplyn almost felt as though he understood. The god was breathing life into the earth, correcting the taint that was spreading through KinKassack. A loamy smell pervaded the forest and a lightness touched the leaves, dispelling the gloom and lifting Kaplyn's spirits.

Suddenly he remembered the battle and a memory of demons sprang to his mind. The god looked about urgently as though reading Kaplyn's thoughts.

With a sweep of his giant arm he picked up Kaplyn and, carrying him, turned towards the distant battlefield. Kaplyn looked about in alarm. He tried to speak to the Kalanth but he shook his head; either speech was not required or he did not understand.

As he travelled, the Kalanth seemed to flow across the land as though it was the land that moved rather than him. Darkness descended the farther they went and then, in the distance, Kaplyn suddenly saw a long line of krell. He realised that this was the army that Astalus had seen coming from KinKassack. As yet they were unaware of the Kalanth. Kaplyn became afraid. They would have to pass the krell to get to his own troops, and there was no way around. He tried to communicate with the Old One, but the Kalanth ignored him.

As they drew closer, some krell turned and, realising their danger, threw down their weapons and fled. The panic spread and others joined their brethren in flight, many colliding in their haste. But the bulk of the enemy army stood their ground.

The Kalanth stopped and Kaplyn felt a great sorrow coming from the demi-god. Some of the braver krell threw spears at them, but the range was too great and their fear made their aim poor. Spell casters were summoning power and commanders were issuing orders.

Ignoring them, the Kalanth knelt, placing Kaplyn by his side. With a huge show of strength, he plunged his hand deep into the earth and Kaplyn felt the ground tremor. The krell shouted in confusion and then fear. Kaplyn watched in horror as they seemed to melt into the ground. It was almost as though the earth was reclaiming them. Gradually the screams subsided as their numbers dwindled, and soon weapons were all that remained, littering the ground for as far as the eye could see. The enemy army had been vast, but it had gone in a matter of moments.

The Kalanth stood, picking up Kaplyn. Again Kaplyn felt his sorrow, whether because he had killed the krell or for what they had become he could not say. His mind was abruptly brought back to the present; they were moving and the ground rolled swiftly beneath them.

Far away Kaplyn espied another dark shape against the horizon. His heart lurched as he realised it was the allied army in retreat. Many of the men were wounded and fear was etched on their faces. Some saw the Kalanth and threw themselves to the ground, calling upon the gods to protect them. Others shielded their eyes as though they were unable to look. A great wail went up as the men realised they were trapped with the demons coming behind and a new threat coming from their front.

In the distance growls and screams announced the demon horde. A dark tide was streaming after the allies and, amongst them, rode Drachar, a dark shape against the vast rush of his demon hordes.

Chapter 10

The Kalanth

The enemy was snapping at the heels of the retreating army. The fastest mounted krell and demons were already overtaking the fleeing cavalry who, only moments before, had bravely formed the rearguard. Soldiers crouched low over their mounts, urging them to greater speed.

At the army's front, men stopped, forming a logjam, while men at the rear screamed at them to continue as the dark tide continued to close the intervening distance. Fear assailed Catriona as she forced her way forward, and she looked desperately in the direction many of the troops were pointing.

On the horizon a bright light appeared, seeming to float across the ground at great speed. The shape was hazy and indistinct but, within the aura, a body could be seen. From a distance, the armour looked like Fiad's but why would he be coming from their rear and what was carrying him?

As the light came closer, her heart lifted as though her fears were banished. Glancing around, she saw others smiling as they too felt their fears cast out. A low, excited murmur started, gradually escalating until many were shouting out aloud, questioning what they saw.

Troops parted and the light passed between them. Men gawped in awe and then someone shouted "Fiad!" Others, too, shouted until the chant of "Fiad!" reached a crescendo across the army.

Lars and Lomar stood within the ranks of milling soldiers and they, too, watched the shimmering halo of light. They had joined the retreat when it became apparent the battle was lost and, like the others, they had become alarmed when the army had halted. Lars was the first to see the ghostly shape and he, at least, recognised Kaplyn. Together the pair watched helplessly as the image passed them by.

"It was Kaplyn," Lars announced as the cry of Fiad went up from the surrounding men.

"Yes," replied Lomar. "And a Kalanth."

Lars looked at the other man in stunned silence. "Then we are saved?"

Lomar smiled. "We will see. Drachar still lives and that battle remains to be fought."

Lars looked after the retreating beacon of light and his thoughts went out to his friend. "Be safe," he whispered. "Be safe."

Harlester urged his mount to greater speed. A large number of cavalry had been cut down in the last attack, and he knew that he could not afford to turn the troops for another assault until the distance between them and the pursuing demons was greater. His mount blew hard as it galloped across the uneven ground. Behind him he could hear the howl of the demon horde, and, too late, Harlester realised they could not outrun the demons. They were closing too swiftly.

Suddenly a bright light passed between his racing riders. Harlester felt a sudden surge of joy and wanted to shout aloud. A figure was within the light, and Harlester found himself involuntarily slowing his horse and turning to face the direction the light was travelling, even though it meant facing the demons. By his side, other riders followed his example. No one questioned their actions, they felt inexorably drawn to the light and the figure within.

"Fiad!" Harlester heard somebody shout. Excitedly others took up the name until all the mounted men, including Harlester, were calling out his name. The light paused before the vanguard of the demons whose exultation at closing with a fleeing enemy was replaced with cries of terror.

The demons ground to a halt and an uneasy silence fell. The Kalanth stood between the armies, the demons to his front and the allied army behind. Heartened, the fleeing soldiers in the allied army stopped and joined the cavalry to watch.

Then the demons parted and a dark cloud came to the front. Sorcerers accompanied the cloud and, as though upon an unseen command, they started to hurl spells at the Kalanth. The demi-god stood his ground, unaffected by the bolts of energy. Kaplyn, too, was protected and he realised that the god was made of the very magic the enemy sought to use against them and as such was impervious.

The enemy's spells failed. The dark cloud concealing Drachar moved ahead of his army, coming towards the Kalanth. Power burned ferociously from within the darkness and, in quick succession, bolt after bolt of flame lashed out. The energy never reached the demi-god, instead seeming to splash against an invisible barrier a scant arm's length before him. Kaplyn survived, somehow protected by the Kalanth, although each blast threatened to rupture his eardrums.

Looking up at his protector, Kaplyn blinked in confusion. It looked as though the Kalanth was growing as Drachar expended his might. He glanced back at the cloud and the darkness seemed less substantial. After a moment longer, he could see movement within it and realised the darkness was retreating as Drachar consumed his power.

Regardless of his plight, Drachar advanced, leaving his army in his wake in stunned silence. Gradually the darkness surrounding Drachar drew back and, as though linked to his loss of power, in the heavens the clouds parted and a shaft of light stabbed down, spearing the gloom. Demons wailed, falling to the ground, and krell covered their eyes, screaming in torment. Only the men of Trosgarth were unaffected, but, seeing their allies disabled, they hurled aside their weapons and sought to escape.

Drachar, seemingly oblivious to the plight of his army, continued his assault. All at once the darkness concealing him failed and at that moment so, too, did his power. The ghost that had once been Drachar stood exposed for all to see, and yet his arms still flayed as though still casting spells; gradually he started to fade. Ghost once more, he was bound to his eternal fate. Moments later he was banished to the wind. A howl filled the air as demons suffered his loss and krell cried out in fear.

In wonder Kaplyn looked on at the spot where Drachar had been. He was vanquished utterly.

Only then did the Kalanth move as though awaking from a long sleep. He knelt, lowering Kaplyn to the ground. Plunging an arm into the earth, he destroyed the demons and krell in the same manner as before, leaving an army of bewildered men staring at the ground where only moments before their allies had stood. Arising and carrying Kaplyn, the Kalanth moved on, ignoring the men who stared on in disbelief. The Kalanth paused twice more to destroy more demons, krell and death knights. Then ahead, Kaplyn could see the battlefield. A shimmering rent marked the demon gate and around it stood a sizeable force of men and krell while demons threw themselves at the gate in their haste to escape.

Ariome waited by the demon gate. She had avoided Vastra's demon as it had rampaged through both armies, but only just. The demon had nearly cost her her life and it was only quick thinking on her part, to dive behind a Priest of Ryoch, that had saved her. The blood from the priest had soaked her clothes and she still felt the dampness. The defeat of the dragon was her supreme accomplishment; that would never be equalled and would guarantee her a rich reward.

The zelph had been a masterstroke. She had taken no chances and had enchanted a number of the flies, sending them to various points in the battlefield. One or more must have successfully penetrated the dragon's scales and it had been exquisite watching the dragon fleeing the battlefield.

The dragon's defeat had released the demons and, with glee, she had watched them pursue the defeated army. Demons of assorted shapes and sizes, many malformed, streamed from the darkness of the gateway. Their cries of eager anticipation even now seemed to hang upon the air. The alliance was beaten; there was no need for her to follow. Let the demons finish the task she had started.

She looked about her. A small rearguard remained, comprising several thousand men of Trosgarth whose banners fluttered lazily in the breeze. Many of the troops looked pleased that they did not have to chase after the enemy, and they stood in idle gossip, joking amongst each other as men do after having faced terrible danger and survived.

Immediately between her and the soldiers were the necromancers and their acolytes. Many rested around the dais they had worked so hard to protect. They, too, joked and laughed, grinning at one and another. Their fate would have been terrible if they had failed — now they expected a big reward. Ariome turned away disgusted; they were pawns, nothing more.

Several moments later, when she was thinking that the alliance must be utterly destroyed, a cold dread filled her heart. Sensing the change, the necromancers hurried to their braziers to cast spells of seeing. Abruptly demons emerged from the gloom, fleeing in terror.

Ariome tried to halt one, but the task was impossible. Escape was their only intent. With single mindedness, they threw themselves at the gateway. Many fought at the entrance that swiftly became too congested to allow them all through.

"What's happening?" Ariome demanded, turning to one of the necromancers.

"I do not know, but I no longer sense Drachar's presence," the man said looking back blankly.

The enormity of his words struck Ariome dumb. At that moment a silvery glow materialised on the horizon, approaching the gate at speed. With it came true fear and, for the first time in her life, Ariome was uncertain. Within the aura was the figure of a man. *Kaplyn!* she mouthed with shock.

Still some distance from the gateway, the being stopped , beneath her feet, she felt the earth tremor. Then all around her, krell and demons melted into the earth. It was a terrible sight. They seemed to shrink as the ground claimed them. They screamed in fear but, as their legs melted, they were simply held like wasps in treacle. Ariome drew a rune of power about herself in defence and, by her side, the necromancers did the same, calling on the powers of darkness to aid them.

"Fight it," Ariome commanded. The necromancers looked at her in horror.

More from fear than anything else, Ariome summoned power and hurled it at Kaplyn. She did not see the result. The necromancers tripped over each other in their haste to escape. Ariome simply melted into the ground until all that remained was the small kara-stone she had been so proud to possess.

To give them credit, the men of Trosgarth held their ground but, when the necromancers fled, that was too much for them. Many threw down their weapons and, all along their front, others followed suit until all were fleeing. Very soon, all that remained before the gateway to the demon world was a bright glowing form and the small insignificant shape of a man.

Alone, the Kalanth set Kaplyn down. Before them, on a dais, was a small crystal. It was the very one Vastra had taken from the Tree of Life so long ago. It burned now with a baleful green light, and Kaplyn pulled aside his shirt to see that his scar burned with the same colour as though in sympathy with its twin.

The Kalanth approached the dais and reached out to take the crystal, but Kaplyn rushed between it and the Kalanth. The demi-god looked down at Kaplyn with sorrow in his eyes. Kaplyn wanted so very much to speak with the Kalanth to tell him of his intent but, by his look, the Kalanth already knew.

"Thank you," Kaplyn said simply. The demi-god smiled, raising a hand in farewell.

Turning, Kaplyn looked into the gateway. A cold wind gusted and a green glow emanated from its dark depths. In his hand, Kaplyn's Eldric sword blazed brightly as he stood on the threshold between the worlds. His courage nearly left him but he hardened his resolve. He had seen the souls suffering beyond the portal and knew he had to attempt to free them. Knowing that they suffered, he could not live with himself without trying to help.

With a final backward glance, Kaplyn crossed the threshold into the demon world and, immediately, his world was plunged into night. Behind him he felt the gate snap shut as the Kalanth removed the crystal from the Tree of Life. Kaplyn's way back to his own world was irrevocably closed.

No one was there to witness Kaplyn's bravery as he stepped through the gateway to the demon world. When he vanished, the Kalanth removed the crystal from the Tree of Life from the dais. The rent in the air snapped shut with an audible snick. For a moment the Kalanth watched the empty air where it had been with a look of sorrow on his face. Then he took the crystal from the Tree of Life and buried it deep within the earth before passing a hand over the ground where it was hidden.

Without Kaplyn to sustain him, the Kalanth was fragmenting. Slowly he faded from view as he was banished back to the centuries. Desperately his eyes searched the land as though yearning to remain to complete his work. He sang a song of healing and, as he disappeared, only a faint whisper remained on the wind.

Except for the wounded and dying, the battlefield was deserted. Occasionally one of the wounded would cry out in pain, oblivious to the events that had transpired. In the distance a bird suddenly sang a merry tune, and a warm wind sprang from the south to replace the chill north wind which had held sway for so long. The rumble of thunder faded into the distance as a final flash of lightning marked the storm's passage. Even the clouds looked less threatening and bright patches appeared, heralding the start of a new day.

Some time later the first alliance soldiers returned. Harlester looked at the battlefield, his eyes haunted and tears threatening. *So many have died. And why?* He turned as Thorlar and Catriona joined him and, together, the three commanders surveyed the field.

"What happened, do you think?" Catriona asked. She sounded bewildered and her eyes conveyed the same look of horror as Harlester's.

Harlester shook his head and tears streamed down his cheek. He could not even begin to explain how the enemy was defeated.

"Was it Fiad?" Thorlar asked in disbelief.

"Today I would believe anything," Harlester replied.

The trio surveyed the field silently, and then Thorlar broke the silence.

"Do we follow the enemy?" he asked.

Harlester shook his head. "No! We have lost too much. Besides I don't think that the men would obey us."

Thorlar nodded, stroking his long beard. His eyes were distant and filled with unshed tears. "If this is victory, it leaves a sour taste."

For several moments they stood in silence, each lost in his or her own thoughts as they watched more troops arriving to search for wounded.

"Come!" Harlester announced at last. "There is work to do. Let us find our wounded and bury our dead."

None noticed the small silver shoot that had appeared where the gateway to the demon world had been. Already the shoot was strong and if anyone had remained there long enough they would have been amazed by its rate of growth. Then again, the gardener who had planted it was an exceptional being.

Chapter 11

A Return and Unwelcome Journey

A numbing cold assailed Kaplyn as he looked about at the bleak landscape. A cold moon looked down on a deserted world. Much to Kaplyn's surprise, shades of grey were everywhere. He had become accustomed to a green glow with everything associated with demons. He breathed in — the air was thin and tasted foul.

Sharp needles of pain lanced through his legs as though the very ground objected to his presence, and he then realised demons must experience similar pain in his world. Steeling himself, he started walking, each step an agony.

The world was different in some way than the one he remembered from the last time; the bleakness seemed much more pronounced. He could not see Shastlan but he felt his presence. Vaguely he recognised the landscape and then came Shastlan's warning. Instinctively he dropped to all fours, crawling forward to a large boulder silhouetted on a small rise.

A large plain stretched before him and he knew what lay below from his previous visit. In the middle of the plain he could see a dark mountain rising steeply into a sombre sky. He remembered the approximate location of the tunnel entrance, but the memory gave him little comfort for a fearful beast guarded it.

Taking a deep breath, he tried to calm himself. Apart from a few folds in the ground, there was little cover between him and the cave. Stooping, he ran swiftly towards the cave. He felt Shastlan assuring him that, as yet, there was no danger. Even though he could not see him, he was grateful for Shastlan's presence.

The pain of being in the demon world was intense and he was frequently forced to rest. All too soon, what little cover there was petered out and he could go no further without being seen. The tunnel, just a stone's cast away, felt as remote as the moon. He considered drawing his blade knowing full well that its light would alert the hell-hound.

Shastlan was trying to tell him something and he concentrated hard. He was being told to wait. Lying flat he felt Shastlan leave. A few moments later, away to the right, he heard rocks falling and the sudden din made him jump.

A dark shape came out from the tunnel and he recognised the two-headed dog he had encountered previously, although this time it seemed different. It was older and great folds of skin flapped awkwardly as it ran. Even so, it was a fearsome creature and Kaplyn watched it from the relative safety of his boulder as it raced away from the entrance.

Kaplyn took the creature's departure as his cue. It took only moments to cross the open ground, but to Kaplyn it felt like a lifetime. In the tunnel he still didn't feel safe so, drawing his sword, he continued into the darkness, using the glow from his blade to see.

He broke into a run. Soon the tunnel changed direction, hopefully hiding the light of his sword from the hound. He gasped in the thin air. The slope helped to propel him on and suddenly, from behind came a fearful baying. The hound was warning the demons that someone had entered.

Running through the tunnel was tiring and, all at once, he burst into the large cavern he remembered from his previous visit. A dreadful fear assailed him and he skidded to a halt, having hoped to enter more discreetly. Immediately dark shapes retreated from the glow of his blade, howling in agony; the pain from the sword's light seeming tenfold worse in their domain. Many demons simply scattered and hid.

All about Kaplyn he felt the souls of the damned, but could not see them. Their wails mixed with those of the demons and memories of their torment came back to haunt him. Spinning around, he saw in his mind's eye their anguish. Disease and sickness would even, at that moment, be striking them down, and souls would be dying in terrible agony, only moments later to be resurrected so their torture could start afresh. It was too much and he screamed, tears coursing down his cheeks.

The war would be meaningless unless the souls could be saved. A memory came unbidden of Shastlan's death and the intense white light that had appeared at the moment of his demise. He remembered the sense of calm and joy that had accompanied the light.

By now the demons' curiosity was overcoming their fear. The braver ones were inching forward, shielding their eyes and trying to see what it was that threatened. Some cast spells against the intruder but to no effect as Kaplyn's scar protected him.

All at once Kaplyn became aware of the demons edging towards him. All around him, souls continued to shriek, gibbering into the night, screaming in terror and pain, adding to his fear. Then, to his relief, Shastlan returned.

He concentrated on Shastlan's memory of death, conjuring images of his last moments by the small stream and the arrival of the dragons. Suddenly his memory came sharply in to focus.

Shastlan remembered his sword and a desire for vengeance swept through his very being. Crying out his battle cry, he threw himself at the dragon with a fury borne of desperation. It was futile. He felt like a mouse turning on an owl. His sword felt heavy and his arm leaden. The futility nearly made him smile; dragon scales were impervious to swords.

He didn't even make two strides. A blast of dragon fire engulfed him in a searing wall of flame.

Kaplyn smelt his own flesh cooking before the agony erupted. He cried out in pain and then it was over.

All about him a blinding white light fountained. Kaplyn held out his sword, for the third time speaking the words of power reflected upon his blade. The intensity of the light increased and abruptly a rent appeared in the air before him. Demons shrieked, hiding their eyes and turning their backs to the light. Some of the nearer demons were consumed, their bodies vanishing in an instant.

Kaplyn shielded his own eyes with splayed fingers, peeking into the magnificent blaze. He tried to see within it but failed.

He knew then what he must do.

Dropping the point of his sword, he stepped into the light, immediately feeling dizzy, akin to the times he had stepped partially into the dragon world. Taking a step forward, he felt himself cocooned in the light's warm embrace. He took another step, then another and stopped, waiting. If he remained too long, his scar would trap him between the worlds forever, but he also knew he must bear this fate if the souls were to escape. A tear trickled down his cheek as he remained where he was, holding open a gateway between the demon world and the source of the light.

Abruptly something ice-cold passed through his body and Kaplyn sucked in his breath. The experience was brief and yet not unpleasant. It was a soul, escaping the demon world and then others followed. Their number grew until there was a continuous stream passing through him and he felt he would expire with the shock. It took a long time and yet still they came.

Eventually the feelings slowed until only one or two passed through him at a time.

In the silence that followed, Kaplyn felt Shastlan by his side and his shaol informed him that another spirit was with him. An image of Vastra formed within Kaplyn's mind, no longer bent with age but youthful, like he was at their first meeting. Vastra did not smile and looked instead at Kaplyn with great sorrow.

Kaplyn managed a smile, not knowing whether the spirit could see him or not. "It's worth it," he said into the light. "I had seen their torment," he said referring to the damned souls. "I couldn't live with that."

Kaplyn was surprised to hear Vastra's voice, or at least thought he did. "I'm sorry," he said. "I am so truly sorry."

"Don't be," Kaplyn replied. "We have defeated the enemy and saved the souls of thousands."

Vastra shook his head, tears flowed freely down his ghostly cheeks. "It's too much to bear. I am the cause of this."

Unshed tears stung Kaplyn's eyes and nose. "We all were. Now go. Take Shastlan with you. You were both used. You must understand that."

For many moments the spirits lingered but the attraction to the light was too great. Kaplyn felt them depart and his tears flowed freely now. Openly he wept whilst behind him the remaining demons wailed as they cringed behind rocks, hiding from the terrible radiance. Gradually, their cries faded until Kaplyn could only hear faint whispers. He tried to move but, as he expected, he was trapped. He had delayed too long between the worlds.

Kaplyn slept, he needed to. Dreams merged with reality to produce a confusing mass of endless shifting patterns. Something substantial within the melee caught his attention, and the confusing images stopped, giving way to the bright light once more. Shapes coalesced and he found himself intently watching these, half-expectant. He could barely distinguish the figures for the brightness. One shape stood forward and, with mounting joy, he recognised his father, the King. The old monarch smiled warmly, causing Kaplyn's heart to contract with the pain.

Father! his dream echoed; the King laid a hand on his son's shoulder and Kaplyn found himself recognising other shapes as they approached. His mother, his brothers and sisters formed a semi-circle around him.

"He sleeps," he heard his father say.

"I love you my son," his mother said. The hurt on her face stung Kaplyn's heart. As though sensing his thoughts she smiled tentatively.

"Does he hear us?" Haster, his elder brother, asked.

His father nodded. "I think so," he said softly.

Kaplyn wanted so much to awaken, and yet something prevented him. He relaxed, sighing softly. His family saw his sigh, and he could tell by their looks that they took it as a reply. His mother smiled more warmly. Kaplyn looked at her and was reminded of her beauty.

Gradually the figures faded, but the light remained. Another shape approached and, as it came closer, the light increased. In Kaplyn's dream he shaded his eyes and tried to turn away. The figure looked sadly at Kaplyn and, for a brief moment, he thought that he recognised the man. He remembered then the blind seer from the Eldric tower at Tanel.

"Sleep," the figure urged gently. "I will aid you. It would be best if you forget for you have seen too much horror. If you did not, you would be forever haunted with evil images, which no sane man could endure."

Kaplyn felt warmth creep over him and felt incredibly tired. Something compelled him to listen to the voice; he knew that what was being said was important, as sleep stole over him.

"You will have reward enough in your lifetime," he heard as he finally slept a deep undreaming sleep.

Chapter 12

Amongst Friends

"He's waking," he heard. The tiredness wore off and Kaplyn opened his eyes. He saw Queen Catriona looking down upon him. Excitement was reflected in her eyes and a broad smile lit up her face. She was beautiful beyond comprehension and, for many moments, he simply stared into her eyes. Another figure appeared by her side and Kaplyn recognised Lars. The big man grinned broadly reminding Kaplyn of a small boy receiving a well-deserved treat.

Kaplyn was lying on a comfortable bed. He felt sore all over and his back ached. Slowly he raised himself onto an elbow. He was within a tent and, just across from him, a small table had been set with a bowl of fruit and a pitcher of wine. The tent flap was open, and warm, gentle sunlight streamed through. It was the first sunlight that Kaplyn had seen for such a long time.

He felt weak and hungry, although in a way he also felt very contented.

"I'm hungry," he announced.

Lars beamed back at him, "I should hope so. You've slept for nearly a day. We thought we had lost you."

The big man handed Kaplyn the bowl of fruit. "Astalus says that you are to eat only a little. Tonight you can eat more."

"Where is Lomar?" Kaplyn asked, afraid to ask the question.

"He is tending the wounded," Catriona replied.

"And the others?" Kaplyn asked. He saw pain reflected in their eyes.

"Both Vastra and Tumarl are dead — Fiad also." Lars answered softly.

Kaplyn closed his eyes and fought against the tears. "I remember nothing after the dragon fled the battle," he said at last. His voice was husky and a tear slid down his cheek. He tried to think back and was angered by the blank that his memory had become. However, he could still remember his dragon flight and the battle. After that — nothing. He did not know it, but his memory of his previous visit to the demon world was also gone.

Lars shook his head. "You were found near the gate to the demon world."

Kaplyn sat bolt upright. "The demons!"

Catriona placed a hand on his shoulder. "It's all right," she said. "They have been defeated."

"How?" Kaplyn asked.

"We do not know for certain," Lars answered, grinning broadly. "A mysterious shape appeared from the south. Astalus thinks that it was a Kalanth, possible from KinKassack. He was carrying a figure with him. Many thought it was Fiad."

Kaplyn saw the doubt reflected within his friend's eyes. "But you believe differently?" he questioned.

Lars nodded. "Fiad was wearing a red cloak. The figure was wearing a blue one. Was it you?" Lars continued after a moment's pause.

Kaplyn smiled. "I don't think so, I cannot remember."

"Astalus found the dragon's body, some way from the battle field," Catriona interrupted.

"You must have crashed and been thrown clear of the body," Lars explained. "At least that's what Astalus thinks. He said insects had killed it, although that's hard to believe. Mind you we saw its body. Harlester brought it back to camp. His men have stripped its scales to make armour. You know, like in the dwarf tales."

Kaplyn smiled, then frowned. "What happened in the battle? We were losing."

Lars nodded. "Aye, we were beaten. There's no doubt about that. The Kalanth saved us and, faced with his power, the demons, krell and death knights simply vanished. The men of Trosgarth remained and many have been taken prisoner. They seem like a decent bunch, as afraid of their commanders as they were of us. If you ask me, they are relieved that the war is over."

"I want to go outside," Kaplyn said.

Both of his friends objected.

"I feel as though if I have been in darkness too long," he told them. "The best cure now is sunlight."

Catriona nodded, although Lars looked concerned. Kaplyn arose from his bed, smiling broadly to reassure them. Although he felt tired, he otherwise felt well; indeed, he had not felt this well for some time. Outside, he revelled in the sun's warmth.

Astalus and Lomar were tending the wounded. Both men came over as soon as they realised that Kaplyn was up, smiling as they approached.

"Thank the Kalanth. When we found you, we thought that you were dead," Astalus declared seriously. "It was Lomar who insisted that you were alive, and he and Lars carried you here between them. Catriona has been tending you ever since; she has hardly left your side."

Kaplyn glanced at the Queen who smiled shyly at him. His heart leapt for joy and he smiled back. Astalus was still talking, telling him about the dragon. "I could not believe the dragon was dead," he was saying. "It must have taken a clever spell to defeat it, I can tell you. By far, though, the biggest surprise was your scar though," Astalus continued.

Kaplyn looked puzzled.

"Oh — you had not realised?" Astalus said.

Kaplyn unbuttoned his shirt and looked down at his chest. There was no sign of his scar.

"I'm as puzzled as you," Astalus admitted. "Then again — it *was* a day of miracles."

Kaplyn did not care. He felt too much at ease to worry about unexplained mysteries. There was one more, however, that needed explaining. Tumarl and Vastra. He was greatly saddened to hear about their deaths and his voice choked as he asked about their fate.

Lars described their deaths. "Vastra died bravely, especially given that he knew the fate that awaited him. And Tumarl; he died a hero, trying to save Vastra."

Of all the deaths, Kaplyn found Tumarl's the hardest to bear. The ex-farmer had wanted to die for so long and Kaplyn had hoped that he would be spared.

The thought of Vastra's soul, forever lost to the demon world, was also a terrible thought, and he wondered for a moment about all the other souls taken by the demons. The others, too, spoke about the demons and the souls taken captive to hell. Kaplyn shook his head. "You know — I think that somehow they escaped," he said.

"I hope so," Lomar said and the others agreed.

"Well, on to less morbid thoughts," Astalus declared. "Tomorrow we return to CarCamel. It will be good to experience a warm bed and real food once more."

"And there's talk amongst the Allunds of returning to Dundalk to claim your throne. Tharn Orrin is adamant that he will see you crowned," Astalus continued.

"Orrin's alive? That is good news," Kaplyn said. The thought of returning to Allund pleased him. He had not considered going home and, to return as its monarch, was almost too much to bear. But, somehow, he felt that his father would approve.

"Home," he said in disbelief.

He saw Lars' expression and understood his grief. "You must come with me, Lars. And you, too, Lomar. You are both more than welcome. You all are," he said speaking to them all, especially Catriona whom he hoped to see a great deal more of in the future. "I think I'll introduce a new type of reign, where the king spends all of his time hunting and drinking."

The group laughed. "When you are well, you can ride with a guard of honour to Allund, but for now you need to rest and eat," Astalus insisted. "So, by your leave, we will let you get both."

Kaplyn was soon alone. He sat outside his tent watching the others working, enjoying the warmth of the sun on his body. A breeze gently blew, and Kaplyn listened to the soft rustling of leaves, and of banners and canvas flapping. He remembered that someone had once told him that, if you concentrated, you could hear the voices of the Kalanth within the wind. Closing his eyes, he lost himself to their gentle tones.

Thus ends the Prophecy of the Kings

ENJOYED THIS BOOK?
THEN PURCHASE A COPY FROM
ONLINE BOOKSELLERS

The three volumes are:

Book 1 - Legacy of the Eldric
Book 2 - Dragon Rider
Book 3 - Shadow of the Demon

Visit http://prophecyofthekings.com/

Contact the author at Legacyoftheeldric@blueyonder.co.uk